PUSHCART PRIZE XLVI

2022
PUSHCART PRIZE XLVI
BEST OF THE
SMALL PRESSES

EDITED BY BILL HENDERSON
WITH THE PUSHCART PRIZE EDITORS

Note: nominations for this series are invited from any small, independent, literary book press or magazine in the world, print or online. Up to six nominations—tear sheets or copies, selected from work published, or about to be published, in the calendar year—are accepted by our December 1 deadline each year. Write to Pushcart Fellowships, P.O. Box 380, Wainscott, N.Y. 11975 for more information or consult our website www.pushcartprize.com.

Acknowledgments
Selections for The Pushcart Prize are reprinted with the permission of authors and presses cited. Copyright reverts to authors and presses immediately after publication.

Distributed by W. W. Norton & Co.
500 Fifth Ave., New York, N.Y. 10110

Library of Congress Card Number: 76-58675
ISBN (hardcover): 978-09600977-4-6
ISBN (paperback): 978-09600977-5-3
ISSN: 0149-7863

For Neltje

INTRODUCTION

Years ago, borrowing from a Ray Carver story, I described the Pushcart Prize as "a small good thing." It still is. But the small good thing has gradually evolved into an international prize drawing nominations from small presses around the globe and comparisons to other major accolades.

All of this is heartening and a bit scary. The Pushcart is first of all just a sample. No anthology—not even one of this heft—could possibly include more than a hint of the grandeur that has been featured in our little magazines and presses in recent decades. Forty-six years ago, the Pushcart was limited to American presses. Now all this has changed, with nominations from just about everywhere.

Why the rush to small presses? Because commercial book publishers and magazines are mired in a commercial muddle, because writers no longer need them, because most writers prefer not to be somebody's bottom line item.

Not so long ago dozens of independent literary publishers flourished. Over time they were incorporated into conglomerates, becoming mere imprints. And now the Big Five, finding it impossible to make enough money on their own, have collapsed like leaning trees into each other. Soon the Big Five will become the Big Three until eventually we have the Big One—all about big noise, big money, big control. The same for the commercial magazines. Chasing ad revenues, they follow what is hot if they want to keep their advertisers. "Lifestyle" is the obnoxious word and styles change with light speed. Authors become mere content providers for the present moment.

Alarming? Yes. But in 1976 Robie Macauley, in his New York Times Book Review consideration of the very first Pushcart Prize, wasn't particularly worried about all this commercial consolidation. "The small presses will save our literary culture," said Robie presciently.

9

And my goodness was he ever right. Never before, in the estimate of this rather seasoned observer, has our literary world been in better shape. So many of the stories, poems, essays and memoirs nominated this year have been gloriously good. Because finally we writers have found we don't need the approval of the bean counters to create what is beautiful, disturbing and true. We are locked out of the money apparatus and have emerged free.

The Pushcart Prize is the result of that freedom.

Why is all this important? I quote from Amanda Gorman at President Biden's Inaugural ceremony "to me words matter," Gorman said. "What I wanted to do is kind of reclaim poetry as that site in which we can repurify and resanctify—not only the Capitol Building that we saw violated, but the power of words and to invest that into the highest office in the land."

On the same subject, Poets & Writers Magazine quotes Charles Johnson about how demanding the work of the writer is because of the power words hold: "The reason it's worth it is because you're giving a gift to readers," Johnson said. "You're giving your best thought, your best feeling, your best technique. And it's not about fame, it's not about fortune, it's about giving with generosity. Because this is how we repay the richness we have received from the literature we have absorbed from the time we were young, which changed our perception and revolutionized the way we see something, so we can never see it in the old way again."

❖   ❖   ❖

With your indulgence I quote myself—in May 2021 the American Academy of Arts and Letters presented Pushcart with its Distinguished Service to the Arts award. Here is a portion of my acceptance.

"My thanks to the Academy for this surprising and welcome award. It means so very much for Pushcart Press and for the thousands of small press editors, writers and readers around the country, and indeed around the world.

"Over the decades the Pushcart Prize has drawn so much love, often from the very commercial establishment that we question. We all agree that our publishing culture is awash in a commercial frenzy—that if your literary vision doesn't promise a cash payout you might as well toss it in your desk drawer.

"I think it is fair to say that most of the poems, essays, memoirs and short stories in the 46 annual editions of the Pushcart Prize, and the dozens of overlooked manuscripts in our Editors' Book Award series, would never have been written if commercial publishers still held a lock on our hearts and minds.

"Well now we have broken that lock. This is a true, quiet revolution. Let's keep it!

"Again, my thanks to the Academy for all you have done since 1898 to keep our visions bright and clear."

❊   ❊   ❊

On the following pages you'll find listed the many Contributing Editors that made this small good thing happen. Also, my thanks to Guest Editors—Ellen Bass, Robert Pinsky, and Mary Ruefle (Poetry), and Meng Jin, Aamina Ahmad, and Molly Antopol (Prose). As always, our thanks to our noble distributor, W.W. Norton & Company, employee owned and independent since 1923. For decades Norton has supported this project with dedication

Thanks also to the donors to our Pushcart Prize Fellowships Endowment. We don't ask for and don't receive government money or grants, nor do we charge reading fees. Somehow because of our benevolent donors, listed later, we stay afloat. Perhaps you would like to join them?

And finally, an appreciation to Philip Schultz of Writers Studio, Cedering Fox of Word Theatre, Mary Kornblum, our arts director, and to Ruth Wittman, who heads our office in Berkeley, California. Ruth keeps meticulous records on thousands of nominations every year and keeps us sane.

Also, as I say every year, blessings on you Dedicated Reader.

Love and wonder,

Bill

THE PEOPLE WHO HELPED

FOUNDING EDITORS—Anaïs Nin (1903–1977), Buckminster Fuller (1895–1983), Charles Newman (1938–2006), Daniel Halpern, Gordon Lish, Harry Smith (1936–2012), Hugh Fox (1932–2011), Ishmael Reed, Joyce Carol Oates, Len Fulton (1934–2011), Leonard Randolph (1926–1993), Leslie Fiedler (1917–2003), Nona Balakian (1918–1991), Paul Bowles (1910–1999), Paul Engle (1908–1991), Ralph Ellison (1913–1994), Reynolds Price (1933–2011), Rhoda Schwartz (1931–2013), Richard Morris (1936–2003), Ted Wilentz (1915–2001), Tom Montag, William Phillips (1907–2002). Poetry editor: H. L. Van Brunt

CONTRIBUTING EDITORS FOR THIS EDITION—Steve Adams, Dan Albergotti, John Allman, Tony Ardizzone, David Baker, Mary Jo Bang, Kim Barnes, Graham Barnhart, Eli Barrett, Rick Bass, Claire Bateman, Bruce Beasley, Karen Bender, Pinckney Benedict, Bruce Bennett, Marie-Helene Bertino, Linda Bierds, Sven Birkerts, Marianne Boruch, Michael Bowden, Fleda Brown, Rosellen Brown, Ayse Papatya Bucak, Christopher Buckley, E. S. Bumas, Elena K. Byrne, Kathy Callaway, Richard Cecil, Jung Hae Chae, Ethan Chatagnier, Samuel Cheney, Kim Chinquee, Jane Ciabattari, Christopher Citro, Suzanne Cleary, Bruce Cohen, Michael Collier, Lydia Conklin, Lisa Couturier, Paul Crenshaw, Claire Davis, Jack Driscoll, John Drury, Karl Elder, Angie Estes, Nausheen Eusuf, Kathy Fagan, Ed Falco, Beth Ann Fennelly, Gary Fincke, Maribeth Fischer, April L. Ford, Robert Long Foreman, Chris Forhan, Ben Fountain, Alice Friman, John Fulton, Frank X. Gaspar, Allen Gee, Christine Gelineau, David Gessner, Nancy Geyer, Gary Gildner, Karl Taro Greenfeld, Becky Hagenston, J. N. Harrington, Jeffrey Harrison, Timothy Hedges, Daniel Henry, DeWitt Henry, David Hernandez, Edward Hirsch, Jane Hirshfield, Andrea

Hollander, Chloe Honum, Rebecca Gayle Howell, Maria Hummel, Allegra Hyde, Mark Irwin, David Jauss, Ha Jin, Leslie Johnson, Bret Anthony Johnston, Jeff P. Jones, Ilya Kaminsky, Michael Kardos, David Kirby, John Kistner, Ron Koertge, Mary Kuryla, Peter LaBerge, Fred Leebron, Sandra Leong, Shara Lessley, Jennifer Lunden, Margaret Luongo, Clarence Major, Hugh Martin, Matt Mason, Dan Masterson, Lou Mathews, Alice Mattison, Tracy Mayor, Robert McBrearty, Nancy McCabe, Jo McDougall, Erin McGraw, Elizabeth McKenzie, Edward McPherson, David Meischen, Douglas W. Milliken, Nancy Mitchell, Jim Moore, Joan Murray, David Naimon, Aimee Nezhukumatathil, Nick Norwood, D. Nurkse, Colleen O'Brien, Joyce Carol Oates, Dzvinia Orlowsky, Tom Paine, Alan Michael Parker, Molly Peacock, Dustin Pearson, Dominica Phetteplace, Catherine Pierce, Leslie Pietrzyk, Robert Pinsky, Mark Jude Poirier, Dan Pope, Andrew Porter, C. E. Poverman, Kevin Prufer, Lia Purpura, Anne Ray, Nancy Richard, Stacey Richter, Laura Rodley, Jessica Roeder, Dana Roeser, Jay Rogoff, Mary Ruefle, Maxine Scates, Grace Schulman, Philip Schultz, Lloyd Schwartz, Maureen Seaton, Poppy Sebag-Montefiore, Asako Serizawa, Ben Shattuck, Annie Sheppard, Suzanne Farrell Smith, Justin St. Germain, David St. John, Maura Stanton, Maureen Stanton, Melissa Stein, Jody Stewart, Ron Stottlemyer, Ben Stroud, Brian Swann, Mary Szybist, Nancy Takacs, Ron Tanner, Katherine Taylor, Elaine Terranova, Susan Terris, Joni Tevis, Jean Thompson, Melanie Rae Thon, William Trowbridge, Lee Upton, G. C. Waldrep, BJ Ward, Michael Waters, LaToya Watkins, Marc Watkins, Charles Harper Webb, William Wenthe, Philip White, Diane Williams, Kirby Williams, Eric Wilson, Sandi Wisenberg, Mark Wisniewski, David Wojahn, Pui Ying Wong, Shelley Wong, Carolyne Wright, Robert Wrigley, Christina Zawadiwsky

PAST POETRY EDITORS—H.L. Van Brunt, Naomi Lazard, Lynne Spaulding, Herb Leibowitz, Jon Galassi, Grace Schulman, Carolyn Forché, Gerald Stern, Stanley Plumly, William Stafford, Philip Levine, David Wojahn, Jorie Graham, Robert Hass, Philip Booth, Jay Meek, Sandra McPherson, Laura Jensen, William Heyen, Elizabeth Spires, Marvin Bell, Carolyn Kizer, Christopher Buckley, Chase Twichell, Richard Jackson, Susan Mitchell, Lynn Emanuel, David St. John, Carol Muske, Dennis Schmitz, William Matthews, Patricia Strachan, Heather McHugh, Molly Bendall, Marilyn Chin, Kimiko Hahn, Michael Dennis Browne, Billy Collins, Joan Murray, Sherod Santos, Judith Kitchen,

Pattiann Rogers, Carl Phillips, Martha Collins, Carol Frost, Jane Hirsh-field, Dorianne Laux, David Baker, Linda Gregerson, Eleanor Wilner, Linda Bierds, Ray Gonzalez, Philip Schultz, Phillis Levin, Tom Lux, Wesley McNair, Rosanna Warren, Julie Sheehan, Tom Sleigh, Laura Ka-sischke, Michael Waters, Bob Hicok, Maxine Kumin, Patricia Smith, Arthur Sze, Claudia Rankine, Eduardo C. Corral, Kim Addonizio, Da-vid Bottoms, Stephen Dunn, Sally Wen Mao, Robert Wrigley, Dorothea Lasky, Kevin Prufer, Chloe Honum, Rebecca Hazelton, Christopher Kempf, Keith Ratzlaff, Jane Mead, Victoria Chang, Michael Collier, Steven Corey, Kaveh Akbar.

ESSAYS EDITOR EMERITUS—Anthony Brandt

SPECIAL EVENTS EDITORS—Cedering Fox, Philip Schultz

ROVING EDITOR—Lily Frances Henderson

EUROPEAN EDITORS—Liz and Kirby Williams

EDITORIAL ASSISTANTS—Violet Ward, Mara Plekss

CEO—Alex Henderson

CFO—Ashley Williams

ART DIRECTOR—Mary Kornblum

MANAGING EDITOR—Ruth Wittman

GUEST PROSE EDITORS—Meng Jin, Aamina Ahmad, Molly Antopol

GUEST POETRY EDITORS—Ellen Bass, Robert Pinsky, Mary Ruefle

ASSOCIATE PUBLISHER—Genie Chipps

EDITOR AND PUBLISHER—Bill Henderson

CONTENTS

PUSHCART
PRIZE XLVI

SUFFERING IN MOTION

fiction by McKENNA MARSDEN

from NEW ENGLAND REVIEW

IDENTIFICATION

Hannah has read it's a myth that sharks will die if they stop moving forward but chooses to believe in it anyway. If it was allowed, Hannah's driver's license would say: *Clark, Hannah—Height: 5'5", Hair: Blond, Eyes: Blue—A Shark.*

HANNAH IS FASTER THAN YOU

This morning, every morning, Hannah wakes up at 5:50 to run. Through four municipalities, from the unsightly traffic of Medford, Massachusetts, along the Mystic River into north Cambridge, onto the bike path through Arlington to Lexington. Not up to usual pace today. No clear reason, except maybe an odd pain in the sole of the right foot. Hannah starts to feel something like resentment or anxiety, which brings up anxiety about talking to Mom later today, which settles into a general high, weird pall over the day's run. Nothing for it but to keep running. Running works all these things out.

Around mile seven a man passes from behind, and the feeling hardens into hatred and points right at him. Hardly anyone passes Hannah anymore, but those who do are always men. Hannah hates his basketball shorts and his crew socks pulled all the way up, hates his earbuds and the phone he holds in his hand. Hannah wants to stop him and say, *I just wanted you to know that you've done nothing to deserve your body and I'm actually faster than you.* Hannah watches his shoes bobbing slowly away on the pavement ahead and wants to say, *You piece of shit asshole motherfucker.* Still running, Hannah wants to push him to the ground and spew abuse too vile for words onto his face, to vomit black acid from deep in the gut at him, acid to burn the skin.

What Hannah does instead is fuck up the day's recovery run and kick up to a 5K pace, pounding foot to pavement until the man gets closer, closer, closer. The men who pass Hannah can almost always be caught and Hannah sails past this one, hoping this anonymous idiot learns a lesson in humility, and that this doesn't hurt too much tomorrow.

It's only several miles later, still running too fast, that Hannah notices the tendons of the right foot again: a light tension under the skin that winches a little tighter with each footfall.

WE ARE EXPERIENCING CONNECTION ISSUES

The image of Hannah's mother in the Skype window is bright and over-exposed. Between the broken overhead light and the tiny north-facing window the screen emits most of the light in Hannah's room. Hannah sits patiently as the picture jerks and freezes and fragments. This is what you get for using the WiFi from the Dunkin' Donuts next door.

Hannah's mother says from the screen, "—package arrive in time?"

"Yes," Hannah says. The box was left on the porch yesterday, a day early for Hannah's twenty-sixth birthday: six pairs of running socks and a fluorescent vest with blinking lights all over it. "Thank you. I'll definitely use those."

"I just worry about you out there running at night. Cars aren't looking for you."

"I know. I'm careful. And now I'll be super visible." Hannah smiles. That vest is going to stay in its box forever. The socks are useful—Hannah works at a running gear store and could theoretically buy socks at an employee discount any time, but in reality just uses the same ones for days in a row. That's all beside the point right now, though. "I actually, um, I actually wanted to talk to you about something."

"To—what? You cut out."

"To talk to you about something. To tell you something." When Hannah's mother appears to be present and listening Hannah says, "So I wanted to tell you that I'm non-binary."

"What?"

"Non-binary."

After a long pause Hannah says, "It means I don't identify with either—"

"I know what it means. I've heard of it." Hannah's mother remains frozen with a furrowed brow and it's unclear if the issue is emotional or technological. Eventually she says, "You know that women can be anything they want to be, right? You don't need to have a label for yourself. It's okay to just be different."

"I know, it's not that I feel like women can't be—how I am. I just don't feel like I'm a woman." Hannah feels strange even saying the words: *I'm a woman.* Not upset exactly, but like they're completely irrelevant to the fact of Hannah's existence. Hannah's not sure how to explain this to another person.

Hannah's mother starts to say something and the computer chirps and freezes. She moves without sound for a second, then fades out as Skype traces dots across the screen and makes radar ping sounds: *We are experiencing connection issues.*

When Hannah's mother comes back she's saying, "—just worry about your safety."

Hannah tries to think of what could have led up to this sentence and says, "Sorry, you cut out for a second—I already wear a reflective orange jacket when I run every day. I look like a safety cone."

"No. No, not from cars, from people."

PERFORMANCE ENHANCEMENT

Hannah's girlfriend, Eddie, comes over with a backpack full of stuff for the weekend and her electric violin so she can practice tomorrow morning. When they started dating almost a year ago they incorporated each other into their practice/training routines almost immediately, a key factor in the success of the relationship. Eddie slaps her hands on Hannah's neck in the doorway. "Feel how cold my hands are!"

Hannah says, "Eh," even though Eddie's hands really are freezing. This is a game they have.

"It's colder than a witch's teat!"

They trudge up the two flights of stairs to Hannah's room and Eddie sheds the backpack and rummages in it. "Wait wait wait." She takes out a book-shaped package wrapped in Christmas paper. "Happy birthday!" Hannah unwraps it: *Edge: A History of Performance Enhancing Drugs in Athletics.* Hannah laughs.

"We had that conversation about testosterone a couple weeks ago and then literally the next day I saw this at a bookstore," Eddie says. "I flipped through to see if it was any good and read like fifty pages. It's actually really interesting."

"Maybe I'll decide I want to take hormones after all," Hannah says, looking at the table of contents. Because that was the conversation they'd had: Eddie asked if Hannah was interested in taking testosterone, and Hannah had not understood what she meant and said of course not, that was cheating.

"I don't think those are the right reasons to make a decision like that."

Hannah puts the book down to slide closer to Eddie and kiss her. "I like my body how it is."

Eddie kisses back. "I like your body too."

After a minute of making out Eddie stops and says, "But I would also be fine with it if you wanted to change it."

Hannah laughs and turns away for a second. "Eddie, like—you don't need to be supportive *all* the time."

FEET

It is thirty-four degrees and raining. Hannah goes for a twenty-mile run. It's Hannah's day off work and therefore long run day and therefore sacred. They run out to the suburbs where rich people build horse farms and nature preserves. There are no horses outside today. They've all gone wherever they go to get out of the rain. Hannah runs. Foot, foot, foot, foot, foot, foot. Moving forward at a pace impossibly slow.

Hannah mentally tries out pronouns, in rhythm with the footsteps. They, them, they, them, they, them. Hannah uses it in a sentence: *Hannah is doing their long run today. They are running the Boston Marathon in two months. The rain is making them wet and cold.* It's awkward, but there's something appealing about it. The suggestion of containing multitudes.

As Hannah is feeling this idea out in the bones and tendons of their feet, by the condos and sports fields of east Arlington, the pain under the sole of the right foot comes back. It seems worse than yesterday. These are fresh shoes, it's the same surface Hannah runs on every day. Nine miles from home with numb toes and ice water running into their eye sockets, there's nothing Hannah can do about it but keep running. It will probably go away on its own.

Another runner in wet fluorescents approaches from the opposite direction, blurry in the rain. Hannah has not seen another person for miles. They labor towards each other. He's in the category that may or may not be faster than Hannah. When they are close enough, he smiles and gives a casual salute.

"Nice weather," he calls.

"Gotta love New England."

"Have a nice run."

"You too."

They pass by each other. Hannah continues smiling for a couple hundred yards. Hannah can sometimes forget in the moment that they don't actually hate their competitors, that they don't know the personalities or motivations or gender identities of the male-looking people who can pass them. It's easy to forget that other runners are people, usually nice ones. It's easy for Hannah to forget while running that they, Hannah, are a person. A person with a worsening pain in their foot.

At home Hannah trudges up both flights of stairs to their bedroom and sits on the bed, clammy. They start the process of looking at the bottom of their foot. Hannah has extremely tight hamstrings and it takes some rocking and leveraging, but Hannah is patient. Eventually they can see it: something in the arch of Hannah's foot, stretched from ball to heel like a guitar string under the skin.

MEDICAL ADVICE

No one wants running gear in February, so the staff at Atalanta Sports Supply hang around the register and chat or play with their phones in the backroom. Brandon, who's also running Boston, puts different technical caps on Pierre the Mannequin and takes opinions on which ones suit him best. Lindsay, whose tricky IT band keeps her from running races longer than 10Ks, changes over the sign counting down the weeks to the marathon.

"Eight weeks," she says, and waggles her eyebrows. "Are you ready?"

"No," Brandon says. "Oh God no. I'm still like three weeks behind on my training plan from when I got bronchitis. I'm completely fucked. Hannah's going to have to find me and rescue me when I'm puking in the bushes at mile, like, twelve."

Lindsay puts on a mock-snotty voice. "Um, actually, Brandon, Hannah's starting at the very front of the pack with the women's elites. She's going to be crossing the finish line on TV by then."

"Sorry. I guess you'll be puking alone," Hannah says. They never know what to say when anyone brings up that they are the best runner on staff. This is a good opportunity to bring up what they do want to talk about, though. "But for real, my training's not going that great either. I've got this weird foot thing. Like this sharp, tight pain across the bottom of my right foot. I've never had anything like it and it's throwing me off." Lindsay is studying to be a physical therapist and resents her coworkers pumping her for free advice. She'll only ever give it if they don't sound like they're asking for it.

Lindsay doesn't look up. "You should probably go see a doctor about it then."

Hannah looks to Brandon, who makes a someone's-in-a-bad-mood face.

DULY NOTED

Eddie sits at the kitchen table while Hannah boils water for coffee in a saucepan. Hannah lives in a four-bedroom apartment with three graduate students named Dave, David, and Joe. No one knows when the apartment was last fully vacated or who brought in most of the furnishings. There are two electric kettles that don't work, three microwaves, a towering stack of paper bags that no one ever recycles, and a dull tacky film on every surface. Hannah spoons instant coffee into mismatched mugs. Eddie says, "Have you told anyone at work?"

"No. I think I'm going to wait until after the marathon. I don't think anyone would even remember if I said anything now. But I still want to invite Brandon to our after-race thing and then he'd find out before everyone else. Ugh. I hate this."

"That's fine. It's okay to start with the people you're most comfortable with."

"But then it becomes a thing," Hannah says. "And he'll be like, 'when are you telling people, Hannah?' I hate it when some people know and some people don't. I feel like I'm being dishonest."

Dave, the roommate Hannah is friendliest with, shuffles into the kitchen in his sweatpants and looks in the fridge. He says, "Me, I'm one of the people who doesn't know."

Eddie laughs. "What do you even think we're talking about?"

"Whatever it is, I don't know it."

This is exactly the kind of situation Hannah doesn't like. Not telling Dave now would feel like keeping a secret from him, so Hannah says, "Fine: I'm non-binary."

Dave finds the jar of homemade kombucha he was looking for and stands up. "Like for gender?"

"Yeah."

"Okay. Cool." He looks between Hannah and Eddie, seems like he's about to say more, but then instead starts shuffling back out of the kitchen. He taps his head. "Duly noted."

GREEN AND PURPLE

It comes back a little worse every day. It starts earlier with each run and then it hurts when Hannah isn't running, a dull tightness that comes and goes. Hannah understands pain. Hannah's legs and feet are in pain almost constantly; it's normal and unconcerning for things like bending over and going down stairs to hurt. There are different kinds of pain, though. There's the rich deep-muscle pain of getting stronger and the superficial pain of blisters and bruised toenails that can just be ignored, and there's this: a pain that slides in and grows and destroys with its own will. This is an evil pain. It's accomplishing nothing. It's not getting better.

Hannah gets up at 5:50 and starts a tempo workout. Twenty-minute intervals at the maximum pace at which the lungs and heart can process oxygen. Hannah feels like their lungs are literally burning, like a steam engine, but at the beginning of the second interval the foot starts to tighten. Ten minutes in, the force of slamming it into the ground again and again is bringing tears to Hannah's eyes, and at fifteen minutes the pain is so sharp it makes Hannah trip and stumble. They stop. They put their hands on their hips and stand there on the path, looking into someone's backyard in the dark, breathing hard, getting cold in their flimsy windbreaker. They remember the twenty-minute timer still going on their watch and turn it off. They are six miles from home. They clench their teeth and bounce on their toes and start back, each step like a steel cable cutting into flesh and bone.

When they get home Hannah lies on their bed and groans. It's still dark. They see the notification light blinking on their phone and flop across the bed to look at it. There's a text from last night from Hannah's mom:

Hi Sweetie. I was thinking about our conversation the other day and I just wanted to say it makes me so sad to think of you being unhappy. You are such a unique, independent person and I hate to think of you getting caught up in all the fads going around these days. No one gets to tell you you aren't a real woman. Love to you and give my love to Eddie—Mom

Hannah puts their face down on the bed and goes limp. They breathe into the blankets. They shouldn't be reading this right now because they shouldn't even be home; they should be somewhere out in Lexington, moving. Hannah's phone slides out of their limp hand and clatters loudly on the wood floor.

They slide off the bed and scoot over to look at it. The screen lights up in bands of green and purple, the surface cracked into irregular panes. They put the phone back down on the floor. They reach down for their foot and feel it, gently, exploring the hard things under the skin.

PRIMARY CARE

Hannah meets Eddie as she's finishing her shift at the neighborhood hipster café. Eddie looks the same as always—with her edgy haircut and sleeve tattoos and septum piercing—but seeing her through the window Hannah feels acutely aware of their coolness differential. Hannah usually walks around in their least favorite running tights and an oversize U Mass Boston sweatshirt and gives themself a quarterly buzz cut with Dave's beard trimmer. But when Eddie sees them she waves goofily and does an awkward little run out the door and gets her arm stuck in her coat. She says, "Sorry that was so confusing to coordinate. It's weird to be reminded how dependent we are on our phones."

"I had to pick up all these paper bus schedules," Hannah says. "I didn't even know they printed those anymore."

Hannah has no idea who their primary care provider is supposed to be and made an appointment at a random clinic in East Cambridge that could fit them in quickly. They take a bus to a train to a station and then another bus. They walk into the waiting room and look around stupidly for a minute before Eddie points out the check-in desk. They provide their name and ID and date of birth. They go sit with Eddie in the green vinyl chairs of the waiting room. There's a tube TV bolted up in the corner playing Dr. Phil with closed captions.

"This one's about a guy who got catfished and refuses to believe she isn't real," Eddie says. "I think we as a society invented online dating just to torture ourselves."

"It's like social media where everyone does it but everyone hates it."

"If only I'd known when I was wasting all that time on OKCupid that really I just needed to be getting into minor traffic accidents."

30

"Thanks, horrible SUV man!" Hannah says, because that is how they met: a man in an SUV clipped Eddie on her bike, and Hannah stopped (mid-run) to make sure she was okay.

After a while Hannah says, "Thank you for coming. You really didn't have to."

"Pssh," Eddie says. "Doctors are scary."

Eddie dislikes doctors, she's told Hannah before now, because when she was thirteen she was hospitalized with a ruptured ovarian cyst that several doctors insisted was just gas pain. Hannah isn't actually that bothered by doctors—the only reason they don't go is that nothing is ever wrong with them—but Eddie insisted on coming along as moral support.

Eventually a guy in scrubs comes out and says Hannah's name. Hannah jumps up, ready to perform. He takes them through some hallways with mysterious and unattractive metal equipment parked along the sides. They see glimpses of other people in exam rooms, bored, waiting to explain the problems with their bodies. The man in scrubs weighs and measures Hannah, takes their temperature and blood pressure and pulse, looks at the readout on the machine, and takes their pulse again. He leaves. Hannah sits. They have no phone and didn't think to bring a book. There's no TV in here. They look around the room at the cabinets and the sharps disposal box. They try to figure out Portuguese words from a trilingual poster about preventing the spread of the flu.

The doctor comes in. He's a guy in his mid-fifties with a hawk face. He looks at Hannah's information on the computer, then at Hannah, then back at the computer. He says, "Runner?"

"Yes?"

He nods. "They thought your resting heart rate was too low to be right. That explains it."

Hannah feels irrational pride at the slowness of their heart.

The doctor says, "So what's the trouble?"

Hannah explains about the guitar string. The doctor has them take off their shoe and examines the foot with his warm fingers, like it was a thing not connected with Hannah. He says, "And how much do you run?"

"About a hundred miles a week." When his eyebrows go up they add, "Not all the time. Right now I'm getting ready for the Boston Marathon. Usually I'm doing, like . . . sixty to eighty? It depends."

The doctor leans back in his chair. Hannah doesn't like the look on his face, smug and authoritative. "What you've got is plantar fasciitis.

31

Inflammation of the fascia—the tendons—in your foot. It's rare to see it in female athletes but in your case I'd say running a hundred miles a week could do it."

"Plantar fasciitis?" Plantar fasciitis was something that freshman boys on their high school cross-country team got from running in bad shoes. Now that they think of it they have only ever heard of men getting it. Hannah should not be getting men's athletic injuries without getting men's times, they think, and then remind themself about the difference between sex and gender, and then still feel like it's unfair. What they say is, "I've been running this volume for years. Why would I get that now?"

The doctor says, "Sometimes the body reaches a breaking point. It could be the cumulative years of running, it could just be getting older. It's definitely a spasm of the plantar fascia. You can see it right there, it's clearly visible on the bottom of your foot."

"I know. I told you it was."

The doctor rolls back to his computer and clicks around, printing something out. "You'll need to keep off the foot. Completely. Try to avoid walking or standing for too long. Definitely no running."

Hannah is too angry to be disappointed. "For how long?"

"It should start clearing up in two to four weeks. With rest."

The race is in six weeks. Hannah does not have two to four weeks. Saying anything about that would probably just make the doctor even less agreeable, so they say, "I work in retail. I have to be on my feet all day. Isn't there physical therapy or something I can do for this?"

"A physical therapist would tell you the same thing. You'll need to talk to your manager about getting duties that let you sit down. There's really nothing you can do to make tendons heal faster. I know it's not the answer you want, but rest is the only thing for it."

He gives Hannah a print-out: *What is Plantar Fasciitis?* It's all Hannah can do not to ball it up and stuff it in his mouth.

HELPING THING

At home that night, when Hannah has been mostly silent all evening, Eddie says, "What an absolute asshole that doctor was."

"Yeah."

"Do you want me to Google it and see if I can find more information?"

"No," Hannah says. "Please don't."

After another few minutes Eddie says, "Do you want to hear what I've been working on?"

"Yeah. Yeah, play me what you've been working on."

Eddie takes out her violin and plugs it into the tiny amp she keeps in her backpack and turns the volume on low. She starts a dreamy synthesizer and drumbeat going on her phone and sits up straight on the bed, cocks the violin. She starts making something, sweet and scratchy and hypnotic. Hannah listens. They weren't particularly interested in music before meeting Eddie and it's taken practice to pay attention to long instrumental pieces like the ones she makes. Hannah has gotten better at it. The trick was realizing there wasn't a trick and there wasn't anything Hannah was supposed to be doing. It was another way of just existing, sinking into a thing. It wasn't so different from running.

Eddie stops. "Something like that. I don't know how to end it yet. I could just stop abruptly but that's what I always do. I want to branch out." She makes branching fingers.

"That was great. I really liked that." And then, "I wish I was able to say more about it."

"You don't have to say anything. You just kind of listen." Eddie puts the violin down and rubs her forehead. "Tell me what to do that will help."

"You don't have to help," Hannah says. "It's not a helping thing."

FRIENDS

Hannah wakes up at 5:50 and looks out the window to see what the weather is like. They remember that it doesn't matter what the weather is like, since they're not running. They lie in bed and stare at the ceiling. They reach for their phone before remembering they don't have one. They lie there, wide awake. They try to think of all the state capitals. They try to remember every object in their childhood room. They flex their toes under the blankets. It hurts. They try to think of reasons to move.

At work Hannah stands at the staff computer and looks at reviews of running shoes. They try to stand on the other foot. The music is insistent and annoying and their coworkers' laughter abrasively loud. Hannah reads the same sentence about heel drop six times. It takes them a few seconds to register that Brandon is talking to them.

"Hey," he says, "sorry, I was just wondering, since you did Boston last year—what are you doing about your stuff? The whole thing where you put it in the little bags and drop it off and pick it up seems . . . complicated."

Hannah responds automatically. "My girlfriend's meeting me with it at the finish. It's way easier if you can just give it to someone and not have to deal with the weird bag system."

"Your friends are coming to see you race?" He laughs. "You've got better friends than me."

"*Girl*friend. I've only got the one."

"Ah, yeah. Okay." Brandon's face goes through some different stages of processing the information and conveying that he's cool. Hannah now realizes they've never had a conversation with Brandon that wasn't about running. They talk to Brandon every day. They'd been planning on inviting him over to an after-race party. His marathon time is 2:35, ten minutes faster than Hannah's, even though he's not as good a runner. Hannah tries to remember that Brandon has done nothing wrong. That they like Brandon. He says, "Well, I don't have one of those either. I guess I'll just have to deal with the weird bags."

"It's not that bad. I did it last year," Hannah says. They think about saying something else, something like, *My girlfriend's name is Eddie which is short for Edith and she makes weird electronic music. And also I'm from Freedom, New Hampshire, and all my best friends as a kid were dogs, and I've never known how I'm supposed to be or act or what gender is and so I decided I'm non-binary, what do you think about that?* But Brandon sees a customer come in and goes to the door, so Hannah looks back down at the computer and the sentence about heel drop.

STATIONARY

Hannah wakes up at 5:50. They trudge through a shift at work, in a thin, nervous exhaustion. They don't think to ask if Eddie's free to hang out until after the shift is over. By the time they get home and send an e-mail and Eddie can see it and respond it will be too late. They go home and get into bed and lie awake until 2:00. They wake up the next morning at 5:50.

They go to the YMCA down the street and get a day pass. Hannah has only ever gone there to use the treadmills as a last resort during major snow events. It's an old brick building that might have always been a YMCA, since it has the feel of a nineteenth-century boarding house. Hannah gets confused on some dirty vinyl stairways before finding the

34

main cardio room. Almost no one is there before seven on a Friday. There's a continuous squeak and rattle from the old machines. The faulty boilers fill the room with a foot-smelling fug. Hannah gets on a stationary bike and pedals. They have told themself that they're just doing this so they can sleep. It will also keep up their aerobic capacity so they can pick up their marathon training again without too much loss, and then they think about the marathon, and then try not to. They once read a book about Buddhism that said the key to happiness was non-attachment. Don't mind the outcome. Don't mind the suffering. Biking uses muscles just different enough from running to feel frustratingly difficult, and Hannah stares at the wall ahead of them and tries to feel non-attached about it. After what feels like an eternity spinning in place on flimsy metal, Hannah looks down at the display of the machine. They have been pedaling for four minutes. They try to non-attach harder.

GRAY PILLS AND GREEN POWDER

Hannah spends too much money on day passes at the Y but doesn't want to commit to buying a membership. This is temporary. They spend five days waking up at six, pedaling their feet around and around on the stationary bike, waiting, avoiding conversation at work, lying awake. They dream of digital numbers that don't move. They dream of opening the skin of their foot and feeling inside, a damp-basement feeling, and finding scraps of rusty metal; rotted ropes and cloth; spiny, tentacled insects.

There are no evening runs after work. Hannah gets home and sits on the bed and picks up the book Eddie gave them, about performance-enhancing drugs. They start reading a story about Andreas, formerly Heidi, Krieger, an East German shot-putter from the nineties. Sixteen-year-old Heidi was sent to a prison-like training facility, was given gray pills and green powders, lost her period and grew a moustache, won Olympic medals, retired, then got surgery and became Andreas. Andreas says he'd always questioned his gender identity but felt the drugs he'd been given as a teenager forced his decision about it: "I wish I'd been able to decide for myself which sex I wanted to be."

Hannah flips to other stories about East Germans. They follow a similar pattern. Teenagers taken from their homes into athletic compounds, physically and mentally warped into sport machines. Their bodies made into whatever shape would perform best. When they reached the ends of their athletic careers they were turned out into the world, spines and knees and shoulders held together with surgery and steroid shots, stripped of educations and interests and genders. Hannah puts the book down.

Hannah sits on their bed having weird feelings about bodies, about their body, about what it is and what it's good for. They try to think of something to do. They end up watching YouTube videos of dogs on their laptop until too late, then lying sleepless in their bed for a long time after that.

SLOTH

After a week Hannah can't take it anymore. They come home from work and suit up and go out to run. Just a few miles, to see how it feels.

The freedom of movement makes Hannah feel they could float off the ground. They push it a little faster than they should just for the feeling of moving through space. *See*, Hannah thinks, *the doctor was stupid. I'm fine.* After a mile or so the pain starts. It starts low and Hannah tries to ignore it. *Well, yeah, it's a little crunchy. It's not anything to stop running for.* It gets worse. Hannah stops. They see a glass bottle on the sidewalk, look to see if anyone's around, then pick it up and hurl it into the gutter. It makes a satisfying, musical smash. They turn around and go home, at a jog and then a walk.

David and Dave are sitting in the living room drinking beer and watching *Planet Earth*. Hannah joins them, still in their running clothes.

"Is your foot better?" Dave says.

"No."

He goes to the fridge to get another beer.

While he's up David says, "So Dave said you're non-binary?"

"Oh. Yeah. Sorry, I keep forgetting I only told him."

"No, no it's cool. I just want to get it right."

"I appreciate that."

Dave comes back and gives the beer to Hannah. The three of them sit on the couch and direct their attention to the TV. Halfway through the first beer Hannah's saying, "I just—why can't I be a sloth? Look at them. They just hang out in trees and grow algae on them and *exist*. I wish I knew how to be a sloth."

Dave and David exchange a look. Dave says, "Were you drinking before you got here?"

"No."

"Have you eaten anything today?"

Hannah considers this. "No."

36

"Hannah . . ."

"It's my foot!" Hannah says. "I don't get hungry when I'm not running. I don't know how to feed myself. I don't know how to sleep. I don't know what I'm supposed to be doing. I'm just—I don't know how to be a sloth."

MESSAGES

Hannah gets an e-mail from Eddie while they're at work:

Hey, I've still got late shifts every night like a loser but wanted to check in. Between your mom being weird and your phone and the foot it's been one shitty thing after another for you the last few weeks. Happy birthday:/ I was just thinking about it and just wanted to say that I know you'll get through this. Even if you have to stop running for a while, I just know you're going to, like, take up tai chi for recovery and then become the world's greatest tai chi person because you are awesome. And it's not because you're an amazing runner, it's because you dedicate yourself to being amazing.

They also get an e-mail from their mom:

Oh Sweetie, I'm so sorry to hear about your foot. You've always been so careful about injuries but they can happen to anyone. I know you'll take the doctor's orders just as seriously as you take your running and you'll get through this. Maybe it's good for you to take a break! This could be a good time to do some thinking and learning to be happy with yourself.

They close their e-mail. They feel both these messages have some kind of subtext. None of this helps.

DOING NOTHING DOES NOTHING

Hannah searches for a physical therapy office. It has been a week and a half since they went to the doctor and nothing appears to have changed. They refuse to believe the problem is really this bad. There has to be some stretch or exercise or something that will clear it up and get things back to normal, that will allow Hannah to think again. They look at the rates. They're pretty sure their insurance won't cover this without a referral. Eddie would tell them to go back to the doctor and try again for the referral. They have already lost so much time. Eddie doesn't need to know about this.

They arrive for their appointment two days later, at 7 AM. There's no TV in the waiting area here, just a view of the therapy studio and the people in it. Hannah tries not to stare at them. There is a young man on a stationary bicycle holding a piece of doweling over his head like he's being crucified. A middle-aged woman in deep concentration taking tiny steps sideways with a band around her feet. A girl shrugging up her shoulder and then swinging her arm precisely forward and backward and sideways, marching-drill style. Hannah looks down at their foot. They try to feel the inside of it. They can't tell if it's hurting right now or not.

A young woman greets Hannah and brings them through the studio to an exam room. There are anatomy charts on the walls and a plant that might be fake. The PT has Hannah sit and Hannah shows her their foot. The PT runs her fingers along both sides of the tendon and twists. She flexes Hannah's toes back and curls them forward. She rotates the ankle and pulls it to either side. The pain is precise and immense. The PT lets go and stands back, frowning, and looks back up to Hannah's face.

"I'd say your doctor was right about plantar fasciitis. What did he tell you to do about it?"

"Nothing. Just rest for two to four weeks. It's been two weeks now though."

The PT sighs. "I don't know why PCPs keep saying that. Doing nothing never does anything for tendon inflammation. What's happening is that all the muscles around the tendon have clenched down. You have to get them moving and stretching in the right ways for them to let go. If you don't move them they'll just stay that way."

Hannah nods. This feels truer to what Hannah knows about their body. That it does not like to be static. That it is a machine of many moving parts, whirring and locking together in ways that are not always apparent but do always meet their own mechanical logic.

The PT says, "I don't know where he got two to four weeks from. It's hard to say what a realistic recovery timeline would be. Just on first look, I'd say at least a few months."

"Okay," Hannah says. They nod some more. "Okay. Okay." There is nothing to say. They pick up the ruthless machine of their body and bring it into the therapy room to start the adjustments—minute movements of incredible difficulty, suffering over spans of inches.

INDULGENCE

When Hannah gets out of the therapy office what they want to do is get trashed, but it's 8 AM and they're broke, so instead they go to the fancy doughnut place next door, get four doughnuts, and sit down in the shop to methodically eat them.

The guy who was behind them in line, in his fifties with a newsie cap, observes Hannah for a few seconds and says, "Are you going to eat those all yourself?"

Hannah just looks at him.

He chuckles. "Big appetite for such a little lady."

And Hannah says, "Go fuck yourself."

OH NO

At some point in the last two weeks, unknown to Hannah, winter has started easing up. March promises nothing in Boston, but there's a possibility of days like today, sunny and mild. There are customers waiting outside when Hannah unlocks the store and there are customers all morning. Hannah does shoe fittings, measuring the length and width and arch of people's feet, crouching with their tight hamstrings and shit foot to watch the roll of the customers' ankles as they walk up and down the store in socks. Hannah smiles and laughs and chats and recommends. All of these people coming in and out of the store are able to run.

There's a traffic jam of staff in the backroom trying to find things. Brandon is digging through a stack of technical shirts and saying, "I've been getting these calf spasms lately though. I never used to get them and now it's like—it's every night when I'm about to fall asleep, which is annoying but whatever, but then I'll also get them during runs and it completely throws me."

Lindsay says, "It's probably just all the mileage you've been adding. Are you doing dynamic stretching? You find something to stand on—like this—and . . ." Lindsay steps onto a footstool to demonstrate something. Hannah keeps their eyes on the shoeboxes they're piling into their arms. Brandon, apparently, is worthy of free medical advice. Maybe that's what the extra nine minutes he has on Hannah's marathon time are good for.

Brandon sees Hannah and says, "Hey, can I ask you a question about how the corrals work when you have a second? Because it makes no sense to me."

"Yeah," Hannah says. And then, "Actually—actually I'm not running the marathon."

It falls out of their mouth and they realize it's true. No amount of wanting can change the reality of what their body can and can't do.

Brandon looks confused, so Hannah says, "That thing with my foot ended up being plantar fasciitis. It's impossible to run on it and it might take months to get better."

Everyone erupts in sounds of sympathy. Brandon looks genuinely upset and says, "Oh no. Oh no. Oh no, that's awful." Lindsay steps morosely off the footstool. Hannah's irritation vanishes. Everyone was rooting for them. Everyone wanted Hannah to succeed, to achieve this pointless, brutal thing for them all.

EXTRA-COMMITTED

Hannah sends Eddie an e-mail that doesn't mention the physical therapist but does say they've decided they can't run the marathon. Eddie comes over that night with a case of Narragansett and a jalapeno-pineapple pizza, which Hannah likes and Eddie doesn't. None of the roommates seem to be home, so they settle in on the living room couch.

Eddie says, "I'm sorry. This completely sucks. And you totally get to be bummed out about it, but—it will be okay. I bet you'll be able to run a different marathon by fall. You don't even like Boston much, right?"

"Yeah. Boston's actually kind of a shitty marathon," Hannah says. "There are bigger problems to have."

Eddie says, "Your mom was weird again, too?"

"Oh, God. I don't even know. She might have been like, 'learn to be happy with yourself and stop being confusing,' or she might have just been trying to be nice. I don't know. I never know what people mean."

Eddie sighs. "I told *my* parents and they didn't bat an eye. They just said that was very nice and when were we both getting real jobs."

"I don't want a real job. I like my job. I just wanted things to stay the way they were."

"Talking to my parents also got me thinking about what I call you now. In relation to me. If it isn't girlfriend."

"Oh, yeah. I guess I hadn't really thought about that." Hannah shrugs. "Personfriend? Booface?"

"People usually say 'partner.'"

Hannah blinks a few times. Hannah thinks of "partner" as a thing people said before they could say "husband" or "wife." They say, "Uh, yeah. That works too."

"It kind of sounds more serious."

"I—yeah. That's fine though."

40

"That was my first thought too, when I was thinking about it. 'Partner' like 'domestic partner,' like someone you live with."

"Yeah," Hannah says, and laughs. "That was the only reason I got confused there."

"I mean, is there any reason we shouldn't—both our leases finish in June . . ."

"Oh."

"Are you not—?"

"No, no I just wasn't expecting—I'm just surprised."

"Do you not want to?"

"I—we've only been dating for a year."

"That's a pretty long time," Eddie says. "You don't want to."

"No, no I just—we haven't talked about this."

"So we're talking about it now. You don't want to. That's fine." Eddie finishes her beer, sets the empty can on the table, and goes to the refrigerator to get another, without looking at Hannah.

When she comes back Hannah says, "It's not that I don't want to. I just get this feeling like—for a while now, like you've been acting kind of extra-committed? To sort of show how okay with the gender thing you are? And you really don't have to. I know you're okay with it. I don't feel any different about anything, I don't feel, you know, insecure or anything."

"I'm acting more committed because I want to be more committed," Eddie snaps. "I've been thinking about this for a long fucking time actually. I only started with the partner bullshit because I was afraid to bring it up. Which was because I was afraid you'd react exactly like you're reacting. But fine. You know, I think I'm actually just going to go home." She sets her unopened beer on the coffee table and stands up again.

"What the fuck, Eddie?" Hannah says, following her to the door. "I didn't say no. I just wanted to think about it a little."

"Fine. Think about it." And she leaves.

FORUMS

Hannah makes good progress on the case of Narragansett alone. Late that night they look at running forums to read about plantar fasciitis. They've hardly ever looked at running forums up to now. Forums are mostly just echo chambers of bragging and bad advice. They find they were right not to want to consult them about this before.

The disembodied voices of the forums all agree that plantar fasciitis never really goes away. They were all given recovery timelines by doctors and PTs and all those timelines were bullshit. It can sometimes be made manageable. It sometimes can't. There's no way to know. Either way, even if you stop running, your tendons will never forgive you for the ways you've used them. It will follow you to your grave.

THREE MILES IS NOTHING

Hannah has the next day off work. They wake up at 5:50. They lie there. They ought to feel hung over but don't. Just miserable. They want to cry but can't make themself. This is one of the things that always made Hannah feel un-female: the inability to cry.

They lie there a long time. They pick up their laptop from where it's sitting next to the bed and turn it on. It takes a long time to boot up. Hannah's had it since college. It's only a matter of time until it too breaks and sets Hannah fully adrift in the world. They wait patiently. When it's functional, they check their e-mail to see if Eddie wrote. She hasn't, which makes sense since it's 6:20 in the morning. Hannah composes an e-mail quickly saying they're sorry and they do want to move in together. They're not sure they really do. They hadn't considered that Eddie might go anywhere, that anything between them might change, that Eddie might start wanting more from them. They think about what it would be like for Eddie to be there all the time, the expectations and over-closeness. They think of Eddie lugging her violin around and her cold hands and her laugh and then of all those things being gone. Either way there will be suffering. Events to this point have already put suffering in motion.

They look up local races. They find a small 5K happening later that morning in Somerville and get dressed in running clothes and leave the house to go. It starts raining, or maybe sleeting. They stand at the bus stop shivering and grinding their teeth. Three miles is the blink of an eye to Hannah. Three miles is nothing. Three miles can't possibly hurt their foot more than it's hurt, and they need to feel like they exist.

The race is at a little park on the Mystic. It was a small race to begin with and it seems like most of the runners have bailed because of the weather. There is a white tent on the grass, with a bib pick-up table and flats of Vitamin Water and bananas. There are some parents and some teenagers. There are people who look like they've never run a 5K before and people who look like they do these for fun sometimes and three guys who are clearly competitive, doing warm-up sprints. Hannah gets registered and does some strides on the grass. Their foot feels fine. The competitive guys stop what they're doing for a minute to watch. *Yes, motherfuckers*, Hannah thinks, *notice me*, even though they are not a guy and not a 5K specialist, even though they will almost certainly not win this race, even though the tendons of their foot might come to furious life at any point. Hannah lines up at the starting line, choosing to believe for now that they are limitless.

Nominated by Maura Stanton

EVERY POEM IS MY MOST ASIAN POEM

by CHEN CHEN

from HOBART

Including the poems I have yet to write.
For example, the one about the two
gray pubes, discovered during last Tuesday's

trim. Or, the one about the fourth
hedgehog of the post-apocalypse. Or, the long,
tragic one about how the frenemy of your frenemy

is your frenemy. The short one that seems
to be about love, but is about
SUNY Geneseo. The one about my best friend who always

mistakes everyone for Anne Carson,
tentatively titled, "Why Canada Cannot Stop
Weeping." Of course,

there's the one that begins, *Exquisitely
inquisitive, I wander with my well-moisturized elbows.*
& ends, *To aubergine or not to aubergine, that is*

never the question. This great poem I will
never write, for I am too busy staring
at my graying or correcting my best friend. & in the end,

I only know the beginning & the end. Everything else
is a superlative question—a supervoid
I have come to view as my innermost joy.

Nominated by Hobart

REMEMBERING THE ALCHEMISTS

by RICHARD HOFFMAN

from CONSEQUENCE

> *The children are always ours, every single one of them, all over the globe; and I am beginning to suspect that whoever is incapable of recognizing this may be incapable of morality.*
>
> —*James Baldwin*

In the paper there was a photo of police on their hands and knees, crawling in the high grass beside a playground named for a little boy killed there by gunshot a few years earlier. They were looking for a more recent shell-casing, however, still unfound two days after the shot that struck a ten-year-old girl whose aunt had brought her there to climb and swing.

In the photo, the faces of the officers seemed desperate, as if they needed to find the shell-casing to save the little girl, who was then in critical condition at Children's Hospital. Their features suggested they might bring the casing to the hospital where a doctor would remove the pellets from the child's body, tamp them back into the casing, poke it back into the barrel of the shotgun, put it back into the hand of the young man full of rage who had pulled the trigger and stop him so that the aunt could stand behind her niece on the swing, giving her a push at intervals, her hand on the small of the child's back, careful not to push her too high.

In fact, by the time the photo was published the child was already gone; the doctors only waiting for her family to sign the papers to remove her from life support.

❧   ❧   ❧

I've been trying to recall the first time I heard the word bullet. I have a snapshot of myself at age three or four aiming a toy pistol at the camera (probably my father was taking the picture.) "Pow! Pow! Pow!" I would have said, not having mastered, yet, the *a capella* imitations of gunfire that accompanied our make-believe combat. We didn't yet have a television to watch the cowboys shoot at the Indians, the soldiers shoot at one another, the cops shoot at the bank robbers, so we didn't know yet how a gun really sounded. When we did finally get a TV, I was especially proud of learning to make the sound of a bullet when it ricochets off a rock you're hiding behind: you make a good gunshot sound, lots of spit behind your front teeth, and then you add a little whistle at the end.

I used to take the foil wrappers from my mother's cigarette packages and roll them into what I meant to be silver bullets for my six-shooter because The Lone Ranger used only silver bullets in his Colt .45 so he could stop the bad guys without killing them. Like the virtuous masked man, I didn't want to kill anybody. I only wanted to be a hero, mysterious, on a white horse.

Bullet is a strange word. I used to picture a little bull in the dark, at the beginning of a long tunnel, stomping head down in its stall, waiting to charge into daylight and gore its victim—man, woman, beast, child. But no, the dictionary says it was once spelled "bollet," a small round boll or ball, especially a cannon-ball.

When I was eight or maybe nine years old, I had two silver six-shooters, cap-pistols that shot red paper rolls of caps, that I kept in the holsters of a toy gun belt embossed with cow horns, horses, lariats, and other Western icons. I tied them to my thighs at the bottom because that's what gunfighters did so they could draw quickly. We used to have competitions in my neighborhood to see who was the fastest draw. I learned to twirl my guns before slipping them back in their holsters, sometimes pretending first to blow the smoke from their barrels.

Life imitates art. It follows that bad art begets bad lives. It's a safe bet that without the continual refreshment of our fatal ballistic romance, our obsession with guns would have long passed away, a relic of pioneer days, like the Conestoga wagon or buckskin britches. But the gun has been front and center in American film and television since we have had film and television. It's product placement hiding in plain sight. And it ensures bad art because it serves storytellers as the most common and simplistic deus ex machina of all: *Bang! You're dead.* Even worse: *Bang! Justice!*

A friend of mine, a poet and psychologist, wrote an essay about men and sexual violence for *The Good Men Project*, an online journal that claims some three million visitors a month and whose tagline is *The conversation no one else is having*. Midway through his essay, an ad appeared for the chance to win a free pistol, the latest US Army certified Sig Sauer, "The Military's First New Handgun in the Last 1/3 of a Century Delivers Reliability, Force and Spot On Accuracy Right Out of the Box."

When I alerted my friend, he couldn't see it. I don't mean that he couldn't see grounds for my dismay, I mean that he couldn't see the ad itself. It seems that an advertising algorithm had determined that I was a likely target (and yes, I intend the irony of that term.) Now, if the pitch had been for a fountain pen or even a hair-growing gel, I'd understand it as the latest in savvy marketing, but I have never owned a gun since I twirled that cap pistol, have no desire to own one, and otherwise prefer paperclips to ammo clips, literary magazines to 30-round magazines, and ploughshares to swords across the board.

So what does it mean that I am nonetheless a mark for a gun monger? Is it simple spillover, a supersaturation of advertising? Was the algorithm looking for sites that contain the word "men" or that have a male readership? But my friend did not receive the same ad. He inquired about it with the editors. They told him they had little control over the ads on their site, that they were selected by a third party with whom they had contracted.

What does it mean that one would never, ever, find an ad like that in a "women's magazine?" Well, for one thing, it points to the relationship between masculinity as we now understand it and destruction. It suggests that real men can be identified by their power to reorder the world by means of lethal violence. In this version of masculinity, not every man needs to actually inflict violence or bodily harm to be considered suitably masculine (which also means, in this discourse, heterosexual) but there has to be at least some signaling that he is willing to do so. Or maybe it's enough simply to not object to this weird definition of manhood. Maybe it's enough to keep your mouth shut.

But let's truly have it, the conversation no one else is having: Is it normal that every day more than a million Americans pack their lunches and heigh-ho heigh-ho go off to work manufacturing increasingly efficient instruments that have no other purpose but the killing of other human beings? Well, yes, it is, has become, normal. The question is whether or not it is acceptable. And so far the answer seems to be yes.

Somehow a combination of economic pressure, rhetorical dishonesty, and a corporate culture similar across industries has managed to hide the fact that America's paychecks are stained with blood, to hide it even from the people who assemble its killing machines. The companies make "integrated systems, products, and solutions," offer young people the opportunity to "make your future with us" or even claim to be "making the world a safer place." For most, the work is straightforward, assembly-line work, and the tedium is relieved by creating a social nexus that includes holiday parties, athletic teams, fund-drives for local charities, T-shirts, and ballcaps with the company logo. Most days there's a card to sign for somebody's birthday or engagement or baby shower: Congratulations!

In the early 1970s, with the exuberance and promise of the antiwar movement and counter-culture turning to disillusion, the poet Charles Simic asked the question I am circling here:

Poem Without A Title

I say to the lead
Why did you let yourself
Be cast into a bullet?
Have you forgotten the alchemists?
Have you given up hope
In turning into gold?

Nobody answers.
Lead. Bullet. With names
Such as these
The sleep is deep and long.

Recently the President of the United States vetoed bipartisan legislation forbidding the sale of arms to Saudi Arabia, which as I write this is conducting a genocidal war against the people of Yemen, largely with American arms manufactured by Raytheon, General Dynamics, General Electric, Boeing, Lockheed Martin, and other companies central to our economy. He followed this by appointing Raytheon's chief lobbyist Director of Defense, who was swiftly confirmed by congress. Nothing new in that, of course; indeed, this is business-as-usual, following most recently the examples of Dick Cheney and Donald Rumsfeld.

I know, I know—big news: the president is corrupt, the congress is craven—but are we willing to admit that killing people is America's business model? I know that putting it so bluntly will seem unfair to many, but consider that if you combine defense contractors and manufacturers of other weapons and munitions we are talking about a ninety-billion-dollar sector of our economy. What does it mean to be the foremost arms dealer in the world? The health of our American economy presently depends upon the murder of other human beings. How did we get here? When did we make this deal with the devil? How long have we been addicted to this poison?

The answer involves a mysterious figure known to few: Zachariah Basileos Zaharoff, sometimes referred to as "Zed Zed" after his scrawled "ZZ" signature. Born in 1849 in what is now Turkey, he was employed, at age 12, by the local fire brigade in Istanbul—as an arsonist. As a teen he became a procurer for the local brothel, a role he expanded to trafficking young girls and blackmailing the men to whom he sold them. The son of a merchant, Zaharoff learned not only how to buy cheap and sell dear, he also found ways to elude regulation of his enterprises by keeping all his accounts secret, a modus operandi he maintained for his entire life. Summoned to court in London for "export irregularities," he sought protection in Greece where, it seems, his career as a salesman of weaponry began with his exclusive contract to sell the first-ever truly automatic, deadly rapid-fire machine gun, the Maxim, and the first (not very reliable) submarine. Zaharoff made several trips to the US to contract with industrialists to provide them with "factory girls" from Ireland, and on one trip married a wealthy Philadelphia heiress, providing him an infusion of capital and, by the way, making him a bigamist since he was already married to an Englishwoman. As he consolidated his wealth, he found that his ability to exploit international tensions was more lucrative than any other enterprise, and he devised what has come to be known as "le systeme Zaharoff": sell to the Greeks, then sell to the Turks, then sell to their enemies' enemies, sell to the Russians, create and monger fear for profit, stoke conflicts, provoke war, and furnish weapons to both sides.

And the profits were astonishing. Soon Zaharoff was consorting with kings and prime ministers, financing arms manufacturing and development, advising militaries on three continents and generally amassing a great fortune. His model's similarities to a straightforward protection racket clearly derive from his boyhood job as an arsonist in Istanbul.

As his clientele engaged in the butchery of the First World War, his power increased with his ability to tip the scales in the direction of one or another of the combatants. With the fortune Zaharoff amassed, he was able not only to buy immunity from several prosecutions, but even to endow a Chair named in his honor at Oxford, and later to have himself knighted. His conversion to respectability was ensured when he founded British Petroleum. Shortly before his death in 1936, he removed from his safe the relatively few records he had kept of his dealings and burned them. It would take a whole book, one written by a more talented investigator than I, to peel apart the many plies of exploitation, manipulation, greed, sycophancy, blackmail, deception, secrecy, and ulteriority that comprise the crooked route that ZedZed took to become Sir Basil Zaharoff. I can only say that the course of that journey has become a model, creating markets, setting standards, creating norms, and generally poisoning the ethical understandings of our era. The deadly plume of oil purling from his BP's disastrous rig in the Gulf of Mexico offers a ready metaphor for this toxic history.

I was born in the middle of the twentieth century, in the immediate aftermath of the bloodiest war in human history, with eighty million people slain, and the development of the most nightmarish weapons the world has ever known, weapons with the capacity to make every apocalyptic vision the imagination ever concocted a practical reality. I am therefore not like human beings who were born in earlier centuries. The impulse to forget this basic fact is strong: who doesn't wish to see himself in the stable frame of ancestors and descendants? I locate myself that way most of the time. It takes a great deal of denial, though, a variety of mental maneuvers and artful refusals of the truth, to go on ignoring the precarity the previous century has created, and the terror, both existential and metaphysical, in which it has steeped me.

By now the epoxy of innocence has been laid on so thick, the propaganda of 1950s and early 1960s pop music and TV is so entrenched, and the sentimentalizing of childhood so pervasive that it might seem to some that I exaggerate when I describe those years as terror, but dread shadowed childhood then. The cold war wasn't cold for me as a child; it was aflame with a horror actively conjured for me by my teachers, envisioned again and again as a mushroom cloud, a terror refreshed by photos of weapons tests, warnings about godless communism's sole wish to see us all dead, and school- and community-wide air raid drills. I used to lie in my bed at night shaking, near tears, praying the rosary for "world peace," for the Russians to come to their senses and not incinerate us. I dreamt the entire conflagration many times when I was eleven or twelve years old, and the Cuban missile crisis of 1962, when I was thirteen, made me sick with fear. For years afterward I often woke from a nightmare in which I saw the burning tail of a missile across the sky's canopy reach its apogee and begin its horrifying descent.

In that dream I always tried to ascertain the missile's trajectory, praying that it would land on someone else.

The best people I know are trying, steadfastly, not to succumb to nihilism. With great difficulty they hold fast to an ethical system that poses restraints, that shapes their behavior, that values sacrifice. The great mass of people, by contrast, appear to have defined virtue as obedience to a set of conventions. I used to believe that very nearly everyone possessed at least a modicum of empathy; now most days I feel foolish and wonder where the hell I ever got that notion. I used to believe one could appeal to conscience, or at least to law. But conscience arises from axioms upended entirely in a might-makes-right world. And law, it has become increasingly clear, exists not to ensure fairness but first and foremost to legitimize and protect hierarchic power.

"Have you given up hope/In turning into gold?" Yes. Evidently, many of us have. We continue to set new records for opioid deaths and suicides. In our shame and despair we have developed an ingenious and largely unconscious disruptive faculty that breaks connections wherever we find them, wherever such connections sneak through the colossal megacomplex of money and noise we call American culture to challenge our delusions.

In a very real way, we are all warriors for the empire; no matter what we think we are doing, no matter what we make. We are inside the largest militarist society the world has ever known, and we are at war always. Trillions of dollars of pensions—teachers', firefighters', nurses' pensions—are tied up in the arms trade. Major universities have hired lobbyists to procure millions in defense contracts. Security is always the stated aim, or technological progress, but the end result is the creation of new markets for weapons. Statecraft involves knowing how to conduct wars that do not spiral out of control, that do not roil the market, that only kill populations with little political power. Appreciation of others, respect for other ways to be human, becomes first a Sunday-school lesson, then something to sneer at, and finally something to rally against to prove we belong with the winners. We live with and export a baseline level of stress the world has seldom known before, and most of it has been normalized by convention. We dare not let down our guard.

The argument is put forth that people need jobs: What people? What jobs? We need teachers; we need builders, farmers, doctors, nurses, plumbers, electricians, firefighters, carpenters, grocers, engineers; we need people to make shoes, boats, pianos, clothing, novels, furniture, music; people to care for the sick and the elderly, to bless us and bury us and repair what's broken.

My next-door neighbor, among the nicest guys I've ever met, is retired from his job as a machinist at General Electric. His house is surrounded by ceramic squirrels and bunnies, gnomes, a birdbath. We talk about the birds, the robin who built a nest in my bicycle helmet, the cardinal with whom he is sure he has a personal relationship (every morning he shells a peanut and leaves it for him.) We talk about our grandkids. His come by on weekends and I hear him chasing them around the yard, "I'm gonna get you! Run! I'm gonna get you!" He catches them and tickles them. He worked at GE for 30 years. I don't know what he was making all those years. Neither does he.

What discourages us from making the connection between a child shot dead in Afghanistan, Syria, or Yemen, and a child shot dead in Newtown, Connecticut, or in Parkland, Florida, or on a playground swing in Boston? Politicians and even gun-control activists seem to believe that the best we can do is modify the technology, the means of killing students and shoppers and concert-goers; they want to reduce the number of bullets—"rounds"—in the magazines of weapons, as if the problem were only that too many people were being killed too fast. The resistance to the carnage largely focuses on the N.R.A., and rightly so; however, the N.R.A. is merely a trade organization like any other, doing all it can to protect its industry. At political debates, or gatherings after the latest episode of crazed killing, people dependably cheer the line, "These are weapons of war and do not belong in our neighborhoods!" What keeps us then from asking whose neighborhood they do belong in? Sometimes people say that the AR 15, manufactured exclusively by Colt, is a weapon developed for the "battlefield." As if there were such a thing anymore, as if there were separate militarized areas free of everyone but soldiers who lined up on either side of the field and advanced on a signal like Hussars or Napoleonic infantry. According to creditable sources, civilians account for somewhere between 75 and 90 percent of deaths in conflict, and more than two thirds of them are children.

The tower will come down, one way or another, the tower of piled weaponry, but before it does, the wars will all have come home; their poisoned waters are already flooding our shores.

❖   ❖   ❖

The ten-year-old girl shot in the park was named Trina. The park was named for nine-year-old Jermaine, shot there eight years earlier. Of the twenty-seven people gunned down at Sandy Hook Elementary School, twenty were children. Their names have been published along with their photos. Online there is a video taken just moments before the missile struck and roasted the children inside the Yemeni school bus; the boys are laughing and throwing a crumpled ball of paper around; and there is a photo of their schoolmates, later, standing by their coffins.

And then there is also, or was, Christopher, eight-years-old, his father standing behind him, hands on his shoulders, proud, as he fired an Uzi at an event held by a Massachusetts Sportsman's Club: "It's all legal & fun—No permits or licenses required!" according to the ad for the event. The fun was to have been shooting at pumpkins, watching their soft flesh splatter, but the Uzi recoiled, jumped in the boy's hands, and in a fraction of a second a bullet entered below his chin and tore through his head.

What maniacal dream unites us? I think back to my cap guns and BB rifle, my heroic silver bullets bringing justice with their delusional righteousness.

Or what about that other neighbor of mine, whose son killed his brother accidentally with a gun his father had not secured? Dear god, that man, whose pain I can barely fathom, whose guilt is forever in his eyes, whom I wish to understand even as I try not to recoil from him: my fellow father, my tragic contemporary, what is his life since then, his post-life life?

❖   ❖   ❖

Our discourse is poisoned by all that we do not allow ourselves to see about the ways the world has changed, about how it has come under the domination of "le systeme Zaharoff." We are militarist to the max: our rhetoric, our entertainment, our athletic events, our cars, our aesthetics, our very conception of ourselves is congruent with warfare's axioms. More than that, all of nature herself has been compromised by our weapons, our radioactive seawater, our spent uranium, our carcinogenic defoliants. You cannot make modern weapons without mining—

54

iron, bauxite, uranium, lithium—and the required forging of alloys to make death's gleaming toys is a demonic process that surpasses most other industries in poisoning the ecosystem. The resulting cascade of extinctions, could we see it, would look like those films of the glaciers crumbling into the sea. What's more, like arms manufacturing itself, the mining and metals industry is propped up by vast subsidies and a corrupt jiggering of debts, along with bribes, kickbacks, and global systemic corruption.

What will it take to extricate ourselves from this unholy covenant? If we start right now, how many generations? How long before a child on a swing in Boston, a child in a classroom in Connecticut, a child on a school bus in Yemen, a child in a hospital in Syria, is safe from the bowling team at Raytheon, the softball team at Colt, the company picnic committee at Northrop Grumman?

What is the future with the present so precarious? We are layers away from any possible clarity, layers of lies from the truth. And so, it could be that this is truly who we are, that it really is our intractable human nature to see strangers as always threatening, as potential aggressors who must be discouraged by our own greater capacity for violence, and to destroy ourselves sorting people into victors and victims. In my lifetime I can find no evidence to the contrary. And yet I cannot allow myself to believe it. I suppose that is the definition of faith—not hope, faith: I have to believe, have often to work to make myself believe, that compromised as we are, we are not cursed, and that although "the sleep is deep and long," we can wake.

Nominated by DeWitt Henry, D. Nurkse

REALITY TV

fiction by MICHAEL KARDOS

from THE CINCINNATI REVIEW

I was feeling nostalgic the other day while talking to my wife about the malls of New Jersey. I was surprised she didn't remember the Wood-bridge Mall, the one with the tigers. She'd grown up in Wilmington, Delaware, but that wasn't so far away.

"The TV show?" I said as a memory jog. Nothing. So I told her how the Woodbridge Mall had been sprawling and adequate, not fancy like the Menlo Park Mall two miles down Route 1 with its posh anchor stores and food court full of healthy choices. For the holidays, the Menlo Park Mall went all out: enormous tree in the atrium, tens of thousands of lights, fake snow, the works. A carousel was brought in special for the season. Track laid all the way from Nordstrom to Lord & Taylor for a train driven by an elf. *Toot toot* went the little engine.

The Woodbridge Mall couldn't compete with that level of family-friendly extravagance, so they went in another direction. They found twelve volunteers, chosen for their neediness and grit, and gave them all an hour together in the mall. For those sixty minutes, every item was free, theirs for the taking. They had only to carry the items they wanted to one of the exits. For these twelve people, this was a game changer. Maybe a life changer. This year there would be gifts for their families, gifts for themselves, thank-you gifts, gifts of apology, gifts that spoke of every shade of human connection. Gifts to hock later for cash, if cash was their primary concern. No one would judge. For sixty minutes, everything was theirs. It would be the merriest of Christmases. The happiest of New Years.

"Except," I reminded Carly, "for the jewelry in the department stores. That was off-limits."

"Too expensive?" she asked.

"I think that was the official reason. Probably it was more about making good TV." I remembered the contestants frantically dragging luggage and kitchen appliances and furniture and designer suits and dresses. Way more visually compelling than jewelry in the pockets.

"I guess that makes sense," my wife said.

Also during that hour, twelve half-starved Bengal tigers were set loose in the mall.

Obviously, this proposition wasn't for everyone. But the twelve contestants were willing and ready to shop, to appear on TV, and, they hoped, to avoid the tigers. They had signed the release forms and were determined by the show's team of physicians to be in acceptable physical condition.

"Seriously? None of this is ringing a bell?" I asked my wife. There weren't even many shows like it back then.

"So, people really got eaten on live TV?" she asked.

"It was taped, not live," I told her. "And it was all tastefully edited. They knew where to draw the line, editing-wise."

"But people got eaten?"

"Honey, these were hungry tigers in a mall." I remembered being a kid, my family together on the sofa, bowl of popcorn, rushing through homework during the commercial breaks. At first the tigers had trouble running on the hard floor. Their claws, designed for the grassy plain, had nothing to grip. Their legs would tangle and slide out from under them. This was played for comedy: the editors added a cartoony *whoop-whoop-SPLAT* sound effect. Soon, though, the animals got the hang of it. They'd crouch and creep, sniff their new territory. They'd pace and snarl. Dozens of mounted cameras throughout the mall gave the editors plenty to work with. The show's host drove a golf cart fitted with steel bars. He rode around and narrated in an excited whisper while a cameraman beside him shot footage. He'd spot a tiger and whisper something like "I'll tell you what, that tiger looks like he wants more than a bologna sandwich." Or: "I think Anita from Sayreville has her sights on the GE microwave oven with the rotating dish and automatic pizza setting."

The show, *Malled*, ended after just nine episodes. During the taping of the last episode, all the contestants banded together and murdered a tiger. Then they kidnapped the host and tied his cameraman to a metal bench to show they weren't fucking around. They looked right into one of the mounted cameras and said, "This is bullshit. Look what poverty and desperation have done to us." They demanded passports and plane tickets and money wired to an overseas account. They demanded safe passage. The tigers ate the cameraman. The cops moved in and shot three contestants.

The audience hated it. It's a game show, they complained. The contestants knew what they were getting into. They had no business getting political.

And I know. It seems like a long time ago, back when children gathered in person for school. Back when the government ran the national parks. Back when radiation levels east of the Mississippi allowed entry. Back when there were shopping malls. Back when there were tigers. Back when Christmas was celebrated on December 25. Back when you could find a microwave oven. Before the Ten-Thousand-Year Flood and the Accident and the invention of the quickbullet. Before the Freedom Rampage. Before Crowdscatter. Before universal bar codes. Before anyone had ever heard of the NX250 virus. Back when airplanes. Back when passports.

But it wasn't so long ago. I still remembered the one couple they had on the show, how they raced for the exit together, clutching each other, each one also holding a floor lamp, the cords dangling behind. Telling this to my wife, I touched my monitor and she touched hers, and it was almost as if there were no Great Quarantine and she and I were in a room together—truly, the same space. Almost as if we were holding hands.

Nominated by The Cincinnati Review

REVENGE

by B.H. FAIRCHILD

from SMARTISH PACE

One day my father said, *Get in the goddamned car,*
and so I did, and he drove us about five miles
out of town, where he parked on an empty shoulder,
shut the Ford's engine off, and then turned to me
and said, *You have a weak personality.* I said,
What the hell does that mean? And he said, *You know,*
when you speak, the way you talk, laughing and using
all that fancy-assed, flowery language, you do not
impress other men, serious men, for whom life
is a serious business. I said, after a long silence,
weighing my fate for what I was about to say,
I don't give a flying fuck about impressing
other men. I can tell you, though, that I care
about impressing Patricia Lea Gillespie,
if that's the sort of thing you're worried about.
You read poetry, he said. *Yes, I do. I even*
memorize it. His eyes widened. *Why would you do*
a thing like that? So that I can recite it, I said.
Here's one that I recited to Patricia Lea
quite late just the other night. And so I began.
His car at that time was a two-tone rusted-out
Ford Falcon with a sluggish, nervous ignition, so
when he quickly reached for the key and turned it,
wrenched it furiously, swinging that small tragedy
of a car back onto Highway 83 and headed for home,
I began, as I say, not just for the moment
but for all time and for all young men caught

59

in the rush of passion and sudden confusion
when the heart cannot speak but the man—oh yes,
the man—absolutely must, *she's so beautiful,*
the moon in platinum waves rippling down
her raven-black hair, and I rolled down my window
of that piece-of-shit car and I sang it out, far out
beyond the stalks of uncut wheat, beyond the corn
and soybeans, oh ever beyond the soybeans, and even
the beef cattle standing mute behind barbed-wire
in a boredom so gigantic, so heavy it should
put God to shame, beyond Bryan's Corner where I once
saw Kerouac and Ginsberg and William Burroughs
stopping for a cheeseburger and fries on their way
to south Texas and future literary fame and
an almost endless supply of what native Texans
called Marihoona. My poem, I swore, spoken loudly
and very well as my father stomped the gas pedal
with each burning syllable, would never end,
even after we hit the gravel in the driveway
at home and I finally leaped out and took a bow
for Dylan Thomas, and all of Kansas rose up
in the dry fields and applauded the art of poetry
and Patricia Lea Gillespie later that night
gave herself to a boy who loved to read poetry,
a language so sweetly powerful and burdened
with the mysteries of the human heart that it became
my language:

> *In my craft or sullen art,*
> *Exercised in the still night*
> *When only the moon rages*
> *And lovers lie abed*
> *With all their griefs in their arms, . . .*

And I remember the grim, tight mask of his face
inflamed now by the porch light as he lurched
for the front door and I sang to Kansas poems
I so loved that they became a kind of revenge.

Nominated by Ed Falco, Edward Hirsch, Charles Harper Webb, Smartish Pace.

LET'S PLAY DEAD

fiction by SENAA AHMAD

from THE PARIS REVIEW

There was a man, let's call him Henry VIII. There was his wife, let's call her Anne B. Let's give them a castle and make it nice. Let's give her many boy babies but make them dead. Let's give him a fussy way of being. Let's make her smart and sneaky, because it's such a mean thing to do.

Let's make it so she can't escape.

Let's seal the bottle, and shake it, and shake until our hands fall off.

It takes two swings to cut off her head. Everyone does their best to pretend that the first one didn't happen. In the awkward silence afterward, the swordsman says something about mercy or justice, a strangely fervent soliloquy in French that might have made Anne herself emotional, but it's a touch long-winded, and no one's paying him any attention. And she's dead, so it's especially beside the point.

The ministers dither in the courtyard, chancing last looks, murmuring, *Exquisite mouth, just exquisite.* She is so beautiful, they agree, even beheaded.

Henry will return to the body later, when everyone is gone and what's left of her has been moved to the chapel. He will stand on the threshold, halfway between one momentous decision and the next. He will kneel on the dais beside her severed head and lay one ornately rubied hand along her frigid cheekbone. Maybe he will stay five minutes. Maybe he will stay thirty-five. Maybe he will cry softly, but it doesn't matter, because there isn't a nosy patron around to commission an oil painting

61

for the textbooks, and it doesn't matter because she's dead, she's still very, very dead.

He will leave as furtively as he came, wiping his hand on his smock. Anne's headless body and bodiless head will be left to their own devices, her blood blackening, thickening on the ground, the gristle of her neck tougher with every minute. The clock ticks. Night falls.

It is her head that speaks first. It says, "Is he gone?"

Her body spasms, maybe a shrug, or maybe just a reflex.

Her head opens its eyes and looks this way, that way. It says, "It's over? It really worked?"

We don't need to stick around while her body crawls its way to her head and fits itself back together. Every excruciating inch of the stone floor is a personal coup, and every inch lasts the whole span of human history. It is slow. It is clumsy. The head falls off a couple of times. The body is floppy with atrophy. There is a lot of blood. She probably, definitely cries. It does not befit a queen.

He is reading the Saturday paper, still in his shirtsleeves, when she breezes in the next morning. The horizon of the paper lowers to the bridge of his nose. He is a man who wears his tension in the way of a beautifully tuned piano, and in this moment he vibrates at a bewildered middle octave.

"Anne," he says, at an absolute loss.

"Henry," she says, the picture of politeness.

She sits at the table. Not a hair out of place, not a leaky vein in sight. She butters her toast in four deft strokes. A servant steps out from the shadows to fill her teacup to the brim. It's all very serene, domestic. If it takes her a few tries to put her toast back on the plate, or if he dabs his napkin with a little extra violence, well, who can say. She slurps her tea, which they both know he hates. He hoists his newspaper back up. Like this, they go on.

Of course she knows what comes next. Let's not fib.

She is seized from her bed some weeks later, in a state of drowsy dishabille, the wardens bristling with royal braid. This night will have the consistency of a dream. The palace swims in sound and darkness. The youngest one, the boy or man who grips her arm with one rubbery fist and studiously avoids her gaze, reminds her of the sons she has lost in the womb. She wants to tell him, *Don't worry, the thing you're afraid of, the girl, the job, the rising cost of real estate in London, it will all work out someday—you'll see, it all comes to pass,* but he is leading her to her death, so it seems a bit impolite.

The cooks are baking down in the kitchen. The yeasty comfort of this aroma, which reminds her of the seam of volcanic heat that escapes when she cracks a fresh loaf, of a day opening beneath her, is too much. She shuts her nostrils. Her silk nightgown flaps at her ankles. When she can, she reaches out and touches the walls, the radiators, the edges of doorframes. Reminding herself that she is here, now, she is alive, that this dream is all too real. She can't falter yet. There's work to do.

A gibbet stands in the courtyard beneath a lonesome moon. They thread the noose around her neck with genteel care, snugly, even though the youngest one quakes every time his skin makes contact with hers. Up in the turret window, she sees Henry watching at a distance, as he does best. A coward in his big-boy breeches.

It is a quick death. The noose is tight. The drop is long. No one's trying to be cruel here. One person cries out but is quickly silenced. The wardens double-check, triple-check to make sure she's properly dead this time. From the courtyard to the turret, they flash a thumbs-up to Henry. He lets the curtain fall. This time, he does not visit her tenderly. It is done.

The wardens will return to their card games, all except the youngest one, who will mourn her without meaning to. He will simmer with sorrow for hours until, without warning to himself or others, he punches a wall so hard he fractures most of the knuckles in his right hand, leaving a fist-size whorl of buckled plaster as a signature.

And when she wakes up, hours later, on a slab of wintry marble in the royal morgue, it's with a broken neck and very little air in her lungs. She adjusts her neck the way she might correct a crooked hat—difficult without a proper mirror, but she manages. She tightens the belt on her flimsy nightgown and slips through the haunted halls, pausing only when she reaches the king's chambers. She doesn't knock. She doesn't crow or look for consolation, although the pang is there, and it feels unstoppable. Instead, with great effort, she continues on to her apartments, where she goes right back to bed. She is wiped and the throb in her neck is telling her to conserve strength. But most of all, it is such a trivial insult to him, so small, so vicious, to fall asleep as soundly as she does this night.

For a time, it is quiet. Henry waits. He consults his advisers, who are just as baffled. He tries to get his head around the situation, but at least he has the good grace to do it far from her.

You will want to hear that Anne takes solace in these precarious days, so let's say that's true: she takes that trip she always meant to, an ethereal island resort where every day the indigo waters whisper *Get out, get out while you still can* and the jacarandas whistle a jaunty tune of existential dread. She cashes in her many retirement portfolios, she doesn't so much throw parties as fling them, handfuls of bacchanalia into those feverishly starlit nights.

Or: she digs her heels deep into the Turkish carpets of her palatial apartments and doesn't budge. In the bruised hours between dusk and midnight, she feels a joy so grandiose that it fills the empty canals and sidewalks within her. She takes to promenades around the gardens, drinking in the virtuous geraniums in their neat rows and the slightly ferocious hedge maze with its blooming thistles and uncertain corners. She grows sentimental about centipedes and spiders and wasps and belladonna and ragwort and nettles and every other hardscrabble weed, every pernicious pest. *I'm still here*, she says to the wasps, the centipedes, the belladonna, the ragwort. *I'm still here.*

The joy of the narrow escape is that it unfurls into hours, hidden doors that lead to secret passages of days, even if those days are numbered, even if she knows it. None of it is hers and it's all she's got. She loses herself, like a woman in a myth, unstuck in borrowed time, unraveling with possibility.

And yes, maybe she feels a few inches of gratitude for the armistice he has granted her. And yes, of course, the waiting days smother her, the twinned knowing and not-knowing what happens after, imagining Henry at every turn, cartoony with rage or puzzlement, but what is she to do?

After that, he drowns her himself. And who could blame him? If you want a job done right, you'd better know the end of this sentence. He comes upon her in the bath. He wraps his hands around her bare shoulders and thrusts her beneath the bathwater. Soap bubbles and air

64

bubbles bloom in multitude. An artery in his skull skitters wildly. The water fights. The walls steam with tension.

She tries to thrash away from him, of course. She tries to defend herself, of course. But he's six foot two, built like a linebacker, and she is not. There is nothing more complicated here. He is not the first man to do this, or the wealthiest, or the angriest. He certainly isn't the last. As they say, it's a tale as old as time.

Eventually the water stills. Her body floats. He sits on the brim of the tub, head bowed, the cuffs of his doublet dripping, his fingers pruning a gentle shade of violet. Up close, murder is a messy business, decidedly unroyal, too much flesh and screaming. He sits in wait—for how long, who knows. When the surface moves again and she sits up, feral-eyed and vomiting bathwater, he sighs.

"What do we do with you?" he says, not so much a question as a regret. And she has no answer, of course she has no answer.

It is he who helps her out of the tub, although she resists. He hands her the bathrobe, courteously studying the mosaic of the floor while she covers up. He helps her back to her rooms.

You will want her to scream at him, perhaps. To shove her house key through the soft wetness of his eye, to land a solid, bone-cracking punch to his solar plexus, or at the very least to kick him in his royalest of parts, but she has just survived death. She is alive. Today, that will have to be enough.

Anne's ladies never stray far. Where are they going to go? They hold their tongues. They massage their fists back into impassive hands. They, too, have intimate knowledge of the place between a rock and an even harder rock.

Sometimes they will perform small acts of metonymy. A pamphlet folded into a paper airplane is a clandestine invitation to the city. They will fetch her those darling meringue pastries if she is doleful, and so when they say, *We will bring you the French cookies*, it means *We are rooting for you to find a way.*

Or: an elegantly embroidered handkerchief means *I bayoneted this cloth 9,042 times and imagined it was the flesh of your enemies.* A pair of white gloves means *We will help you bury the bodies. We will not ask questions. We know you did what had to be done.*

65

If they tune up her automobile restlessly, it's to say, *Are you listening? We have a plan.*

A book of poems with no poems inside is this: *You are not defined by the tragedy of it. There is always one more page.*

They will nod with such enthusiasm that they black out, which means *Do you know how much we hate this?*

Sometimes they will weep in private, because there is too much to be said and nowhere to say it. Because they know that leaving is the most dangerous thing she can do. Because all they want is the impossible and is that really so much? Because this is one of the very few ways they can uncork their anger, and it is such a fine vintage, the very best. Because their fury is the scaffolding upon which their waiting lives are begotten, and it is so fathomless and pure, it clenches up their jaws and grinds their teeth into their gums. In this particular case, their tears mean *We will be your remembrance. We will salt the earth with the blood of our eyes so nothing can ever grow again.*

Henry is learning.

He gets crafty. He invents the portable long-barreled firearm. Then he invents the firing squad. Then he invents acute ballistic trauma. Then he sends his wardens to find her.

But while he's busy doing all that, she's been busy, too, inventing: cardiopulmonary resuscitation. The telephone. The 911 call. First-response teams. Modern-day surgery. Organ transplants. Crash carts. Gurneys. Subsidized medicine. She improvises like it's the only thing she knows how to do.

It is ugly, obviously. There is quite a lot of blood and gore and spattered internal organs. But she lives. Still, she lives.

Lest you think it's all maudlin garden strolls and gallows touched by moonlight, let's admit that Anne and Henry still have their moments. Like the time a scullery maid starts a stovetop fire and trips the palace-wide alarm. All around the castle, the sprinkler systems kick in, first in the kitchens, then in the great hall, and then everywhere, misting porous manuscripts, Brylcreemed foreign dignitaries, the throne room, everyone on their toilets, Henry's collection of vintage cameras, and Anne in her finest silk pajamas, snoring over her watercolors. Still very much not dead.

She escapes to the nearest balcony. And as she wrings her ruined shirt and her hair in futility, a window creaks open and who should climb through but Henry, his arms filled with soaking scrolls almost as tall as himself. He sees her sodden in her nightclothes and begins to guffaw.

She says, "That's not very kingly," feeling hurt, and more vulnerable than she wants to be, and probably a little foolish.

He says, "Well, you don't look especially queenly," and drops the scrolls in a heap. She despairs at her reflection in the window.

"The gossip magazines are going to love this look," she says.

"Easy fix," he says. "Here." He sweeps up to the balcony's edge, blotting her from view of the courtyard. So close that she's immediately on high alert. She steps back. Every muscle clamped.

"You need more width," she says, with all the calm she can summon.

He begins to windmill his arms like a complete fool. He doesn't say a word, just churns his arms up and down with intense concentration. And to her own surprise, she starts to laugh. She can't help it. He does his best deadpan, smile uncracked, but it's there in the twitch of his eyebrows, the twinkle in his eye.

"What's your plan here?" she says.

"Trickery," he says, not missing a step. "Misdirection. Excellent upper-arm strength."

You may be thinking that this would be an opportune time to push him off the balcony, make it look like an accident, and maybe you wouldn't be wrong. But he's still the size of a world-class heavyweight boxer, and she is still most decidedly not. And yes, she's eager to please, and yes, even now, he can find ways to disarm her utterly. And yes, this moment, precious as it is, has a kind of power on its own, a force, and the ache of laughter in her abdomen will sustain her a few days longer. Do you really want to take that away from her?

It's easy to say that it becomes a game for him, and a game for her. In Anne's case, if it's a game, the game is Monopoly, her game piece is a pewter chicken *décapité*, the banker is a scoundrel and a cheat, the properties disintegrate every time she lands on them, and the dice are made of fire. What game is this to him? If he's winning, does it even matter?

But for her, how's this for an alternative: on a spectral day in autumn, a cockroach tumbles across Anne's writing desk like a very squirmy, very small shooting star. It is swift, intrepid. In its wayward progress, it hemorrhages anxiety.

Its clumsy, heroic journey plucks the tenderest meat inside her. Is it any surprise that she sees something in the cockroach that hums on the same frequency as she does? She builds tranquil highways with her hands, one at a time, and is rewarded when the roach travels safely through. Her triumph is no small thing.

She hopes it is a girl cockroach, that the baseboards and the cracks in the wall are seething with her unhatched eggs, that beneath the floors the concrete is bulging with her magnificent cockroach babies. She hopes they are abundant and hungry. That every day, each year, the cockroaches and their cockroach babies encroach in an ever-expanding circle from their nest. That when civilization crumbles into the ground, and textbooks get chucked en masse into the sea, and all of this is done and gone—and it will be done, it will be gone, she's got to believe that the universe has a long memory and a short temper and that this, this is nothing—they will still be here, in the walls, under the floors, teeming, multiplying, ravenous, devouring, surviving.

He has his body servant stuff handkerchiefs down her throat. What you might call a reverse magic trick. Silk handkerchiefs, floral handkerchiefs, designer ones, handkerchiefs dipped in eau de cologne, ones that carry the perfume of another woman, while Henry lurks in the doorway, exultant.

It is such an absurd way to die that she begins to laugh, and once she starts laughing, it's too late, she can't stop. She even helps the servant stuff them down her throat. It is not pleasurable, by any means, but it bewilders him and leaves Henry stunned.

"Um, should I keep going?" the body servant is asking Henry, the last thing she remembers before she dies.

Sometimes he is fuzzy on the details. Sometimes he will forget and call her by the names of his other wives and she will have to correct him. He might leave her alone if she were somebody else, it's true. But she is unwilling to be forgotten.

"I'm Anne," she says impatiently. "*Anne.* Remember? Not Jane or Other Anne or Catherine. You haven't killed those ones yet."

❖   ❖   ❖

He lines up everyone she has known, her mother and father, her dead brothers, her childhood friends, her nursemaid, her tutors, her grandmother, her priests, the snooty cousin she almost married, all the kids in high school who made fun of her. One by one, they tell her every mean thing they have ever thought about her.

"You're such a needy person," her grandmother says. "I often dread the sound of your approach."

"You're much less attractive than you think," says her snooty cousin.

"We always thought your jokes were kind of repetitive," her dead brothers confess.

"You probably shouldn't have started the English Reformation," one of the priests says.

"I didn't want another daughter," her mother admits.

"You *still* smell like farts," says one of the kids from school.

"I always thought you had so much potential," says a childhood friend. "I wish I could take more pride in having known you."

It goes on like this for hours. In the center, Anne, lovely Anne, poor Anne, with her hands over her face, bawling, full-on ugly-crying. Shoulders shuddering, snot-nosed, basically a mess. At some point, probably during her father's seven-minute monologue about everything they could've spent their fortune on if she hadn't been born, she will faint with grief and maybe dehydration, and the court physicians will not be able to revive her. Everyone goes home: her mother, father, dead brothers, and so on. She passes later in the evening, with little fanfare, most likely of a broken heart.

There is a version of her story where she doesn't die again and again and again.

There is a version of her story where she shivs him in his sleep.

There is a version where she is born in the future, and when she meets Henry at one of those rickety self-serious parties at Oxford, his discount-aristocracy vibes, prickly disposition, and fixation with his own poetry are clanging alarm bells. She walks away and never looks back.

There is a version where she gives birth to a daughter. In this version of the story, Anne still dies in the most ignoble and depressing of fashions: a sword, a Frenchman, a chopping block, gawking ministers, a wordless husband. It is her daughter who will avenge her mother—with the throne she takes by force, the wars she wages, the playwrights she patronizes, the papacies she outwits, the rebellions she crushes, the cults she accidentally spawns, the people she forgives, through all the many men she meets and never marries.

She wakes up one morning and the whole castle is closed for renovations. The imperial estates are empty and eerie. Set painters are giving the outer walls a fresh coat. A few crew members crawl on their hands and knees in the chapel, swabbing delicate graining details into the marble flagstones so they don't look like plastic. In the state room, a prop maker wheels away a vase, completely oblivious to her presence. He replaces it a few minutes later with an almost identical, slightly more era-appropriate vase.

When she passes Henry in the hallway, he's just as perplexed as she is.

But later that day, on instinct, he swipes a can of paint from the art department. He composes a sprawling landscape. A canyon, right in front of Anne's apartments. He's not the best artist, but what he lacks in talent, he makes up for in cruelty. When she steps out of her room, she plunges right in, all the way to the bottom of the canyon, where she breaks her leg.

She tries to call for help. Of course she does. She yells until her voice is hoarse. Her leg is an unsteady line of fire beneath her. For days after, she can still hear the sound of the bone breaking.

And this time, yes, it's bad. She's hungry, thirsty, in tremendous pain. She is depleted from the ache of the last death, a grief she didn't know was still possible. She's worn down by his anger, his relentless need. There's a limit to what she can endure, maybe, and it doesn't seem so far away. She can't do this forever. Did you think she could do this forever?

Still, she looks for a way out. She tries to set the bone herself, with little success. She prays to her god for an answer. It would be better if she knew how to die, if she had the grace of a dead girl. But she is not a woman washed ashore at the start of a film, or arranged artfully in a back alley for the cameras to find. No, she's disorderly, desperate. There is skin beneath her fingernails, and throw-up on her T-shirt.

And do we want her to die? Do we want this to be the end? Isn't it better if she finds a miracle, a mystery machine swooping out of the sky to save her?

Think about it: Do you want her to be just another dead girl? Do you really, truly want her to die?

She does not die this time. One of the production assistants drops a permanent marker down the canyon by accident and Anne scrawls an amateurish ladder to freedom. Or, no, as everyone's packing up to leave, a decorator spies the velvet flag she's manufactured out of her French hood. He doesn't seem to understand who she is, but she bribes him to haul her out with two fat pearls.

Either way, it's definitely a miracle. Most unexpected. We'll leave it up to you.

On another day, she rolls over and looks at him.

"What?" he says.

"It doesn't have to be this hard, right?" she says. "We don't have to live like this."

He doesn't respond right away. He takes so long, she thinks he is considering the enormity of her question, that perhaps it has left him winded. She thinks maybe this is the moment he will realize how pointless it is, how hard she's trying, how much time he's wasted, how defeated they both are. Maybe he will say, *Huh, why didn't I ever think of that.*

But he doesn't answer, no surprise. He doesn't have anything to say. Maybe it's too obvious for words. Maybe he doesn't think she deserves a response. When he looks at her, she has the sense of a man who is making up his mind one way or another. A man who stares at a dead end and sees his opportunity.

Maybe you will want to look away for this part.

She will be taken to a laboratory, which, in the style of laboratories of the time and perhaps every laboratory in every time, feels a bit like the underbelly of a dungeon. Here she will be injected with a poison that liquefies her insides in a matter of hours. One of her captors will spill the poison on himself and this will derail the proceedings. They will perform an autopsy to confirm that she is dead. With a delicacy that is surgical, or at least very thorough, they will crack every bone in her body. They will take out her internal organs, still gooey and falling apart, and feed them to any nearby dogs, who may need a fair amount of persuading. She will wake several times, but never for long. There will be quite a lot of screaming, most likely, but you don't want to hear about that.

They will set her corpse on fire, and put the scorched bone fragments and teeth and shreds of flesh into a box. They will ship the box somewhere very far away, perhaps the remote island from earlier on. They will wrap the box in weights and cast it into the ocean. They will train a shark to develop a palate for mysterious boxes wrapped in weights so it can devour her remains. They will send a nuke from outer space to the precise coordinates of the shark. The bomb will vaporize the island, too, and everyone who lives there, a few thousand tidy deaths, but it's probably worth it.

They dispatch a courier to Henry immediately. The courier tells him, "She's dead," and Henry sags against the wall in relief. He spends the day in devout prayer. He waits a week or two for the obvious to happen. But no, she doesn't return.

He asks for extravagant bouquets to be delivered to her apartments, a mix tape of her favorites: English roses, bloody chrysanthemums, black tulips. He summons an architect to begin the blueprints for her memorial. He spends a whole day telephoning her parents and loved ones to break the news, with each call recalibrating his gravity, sorrow, and air of quiet suffering, depending on how much they care.

He will come to his bedroom later that night, a little weary, and there she will be, just like that. No explanation. She will be curled up in his favorite armchair like the slyest of cats, fast asleep, looking content. Fully intact, organs back in her body, insides unliquefied, most definitely *not* in a box, or a shark, or an ocean, or heaven, or hell.

Do you want to know how she did it?

Here's how she did it: her ancestors were microorganisms, and a few years later here she is. The secret is this: her great-grandparents were monkeys and now she can do long division. The only trick is to know better. Didn't anyone teach you to know better?

Here's how she did it: she was always rooting for the cockroach. No one mourns the cockroaches, the dust mites, the bacteria, the weeds, the worms. The chickens that endure their own beheadings. But she remembers. She remembers the things that survive and those that don't, and there are so many that don't, so very many.

Here's how she did it: she knows there's no difference between the entrance and the exit. It's not so difficult to turn around and walk right back in. Is it?

Here's how she did it: no one wants to see her die. Did you know it's that easy, to stay alive?

When you die, you should tell all the dead girls.

Nominated by Ayse Papatya Bucak

TO AUTUMN

by CARL PHILLIPS

from COPPER NICKEL

>   Whatever it is that, some nights,
> can rescue cricket song from
> becoming just more of the usual
>   white noise—tonight, it's working.
> The hours toss with the apparent
> weightlessness of leaves when each
>   leaf seems, for once, its own dream,
> not part of the larger, more general
> dream of leaves being limited to tossing
>   with either diminishment
> or renewal, when why should those
> be the only choices? What about joy,
>   and despair? What about
> ambition?
>
>   ❋
>
>   If wild, I was once
> more gentle. There's a version of
>   autumn where the stars' reflections
> on the river tonight look, at one moment,
> like freight thrown overboard;
>   at the next, like signal-lights cast up
> through water by a city submerged
> where the river's deepest. There's
>   another version. Holiness has
> no limits, there, only two requirements:
> to be hidden; to adore what's hidden.

Nominated by David Baker, Jane Hirshfield, Joyce Carol Oates, Michael Waters, Copper Nickel

BIOLOGY

fiction by KEVIN WILSON

from THE SOUTHERN REVIEW

Last night, someone from my hometown posted on Facebook to say that our eighth grade biology teacher, Mr. Reynolds, had died. There was a link to the local funeral home's memorial page, where I stared at a picture of Mr. Reynolds as I remembered him twenty-five years previous, his thick, black-rimmed glasses and buzz cut, his hair so blond it looked white. He had gray eyes. His face was always red, not like a rash but like a tint to his skin.

My boyfriend asked me why I was crying, though he didn't look up from his book. I was someone who cried a lot, over the slightest things, but what was strange was that I didn't realize that I had been crying. And once I noticed it, I thought more about Mr. Reynolds. His first name was Franklin, and there was a time when I would call him by that name. And I cried and I cried, and finally Bobby said, "Oh, God, what's wrong? What is going on, Patrick?" and he held me, and I put down the tablet, and I didn't say a word because I didn't know what to say. Because nothing I said would have made sense to him. It wouldn't have made sense to anyone else in the world. The only person who would have understood was dead.

In eighth grade, like every single grade leading up to that year, I was unpopular. I was too fat for sports and I had all these weird habits, little tics, that, even though everyone in our town had grown used to them, kept me from getting close to anyone. I cried sometimes if people smiled at me too long. I grunted a lot when I was reading to myself. I was an island, but not far enough away from this huge body of land that was the rest of my town, so I could easily feel the separation.

Since I was about eight or nine, I'd been updating and revising this card game I'd invented called Death Cards. It was this big stack of index cards, and most of the cards had interesting life events like graduating high school or winning an astronaut scholarship or having sex for the first time. But there were also death cards that featured people dying in horrific, graphic ways. Nobody would play the game with me, so I just played against myself. By eighth grade, there were more than four hundred cards in the game. I couldn't stop playing, finding my way to whatever kind of life I could have before I died violently.

And, whatever, but it was clear to most kids that I was effeminate, too sensitive, which suggested something was deficient in my makeup.

And Mr. Reynolds was famously weird. He lived with his mother. He'd been in Vietnam, which wasn't weird, really, but there was a long-standing story that one time a car in the school parking lot had back-fired and Mr. Reynolds had immediately sprawled on the floor, his face radiating panic, and the principal had to come convince him to get back up and keep teaching. My cousin, who was eight years older than me, said he'd been in the class when it happened, but he was such a fucking liar, so who knew. Mr. Reynolds was very shy and quiet, and students often talked over him when he was teaching. He drove this tiny little foreign car, and the driver's side door was a completely different color than the rest of the car, and he'd duct-taped the rear bumper, but sometimes it would loosen and drag across the asphalt parking lot. Every day he wore short-sleeved shirts, weird plaid, and olive green chinos, and ugly brown loafers. He was freakishly tall, which seemed to embarrass him, and he didn't take advantage of it in order to make himself seem imposing. He just looked stretched out like a cartoon character.

But I liked listening to him, the way he talked about this kind of bird where the babies fight each other to the death in order to be the one who gets the food from the mother. One time he brought in this weird slug and told us about how its mouth was like sandpaper and it could tear out the eyes of a baby bird, or something like that He talked about egg wars, where different bird species tried to fuck each other over. Maybe eighth grade was the bird year, or maybe Mr. Reynolds just really loved birds, but he seemed embarrassed by the sections that talked about human biology, our own weird bodies, and so he focused on animals, the natural world, the horrific shit that all living things did just to keep themselves alive.

I made straight As in his class, sometimes even drew pictures of dead animals to support my short-essay answers. And he would mark each one with a very detailed drawing of a thumbs-up symbol. "Good job," he'd whisper to me as he passed by my desk, handing back tests. He would stoop down and gently place the test right in front of me, and I'd feel dizzy a little. His class preceded the pep rallies or assemblies that happened every Thursday afternoon, and he said that, if I wanted, I could stay in his classroom, that I had his permission to skip the pep rally. I thought maybe he'd heard about the fact that in seventh grade someone tripped me, or probably I just tripped on my own, and I fell down the bleachers and fractured my wrist. But I was happy for the respite.

He'd pull out weird taxidermy from the cabinets in his classroom, rodents and reptiles that looked so shabby that I wanted to set them on fire. I asked if he made them, and he said he'd bought them out of a catalog. "I had high hopes for myself when I started teaching," he told me, his voice so soft and deep at the same time. He never had stubble, the smoothest face I'd ever seen. "I knew I wasn't an academic," he continued, "and I wouldn't be a scientist or anything like that. I barely passed college. But I thought I'd be a good teacher."

"You are a good teacher," I told him.

"I don't think I am," he said.

"You're my favorite teacher," I said.

He just smiled and then showed me some bones that he said he thought were a raccoon's.

There were these girls in my class, badasses, and they played basketball and dipped and wore these huge earrings that looked painful as shit. And they burned Mr. Reynolds alive if he gave them an opening. They talked about his car, how ugly it was, how slow it was. They said sometimes they saw it parked out in front of their houses and they figured he was spying on them, trying to see them naked. They said he looked like a giraffe.

"C'mon now," he'd say, getting flustered.

If I'd had a gun, if I knew how to get a gun, I would have murdered everyone in the classroom.

I guess he'd been a pretty great basketball player in high school, had led the team to a state championship, but the girls asserted that he couldn't keep up with them. They talked about this all the time, how they'd wear his ass out on the court. And he'd shake his head and talk about how sharp an eagle's talons were, the violence they could do to a human body.

Pretty soon, I started eating my lunch in Mr. Reynolds's classroom. I'd sit at my desk, and he'd sit at his, and we'd eat in silence, me chewing on some rubbery ham sandwich. He always brought a thermos of soup and a package of peanut butter crackers. Afterward, he'd drop an Alka-Seltzer into a cup and drink that because he said his stomach wasn't great. I asked him about his car, and he chuckled. "The kids hate that car, don't they?" he said.

"Why don't you get a new one?" I said.

"They cost a lot of money," he said. "And I like that car. It's a kind of science project, I guess, just seeing how long I can keep it running."

I kind of understood him, and then he said, "This might help you, Patrick. If people think you are strange, different, they can be cruel. They look for instability, an opening. My car, it's not me, is it? It's just this piece of metal that I drive to work every day. But people can look at it and laugh, and they think it hurts me, but it doesn't Because it's not me. If you give people something easy, they'll take it. And some-times, that's all they need."

I thought about how there were so many other things about Mr. Reyn-olds that the kids made fun of, but I still knew what he meant. I reached into my backpack and pulled out my huge bricks of index cards.

"Now what is this?" he asked, curious.

"Death Cards," I told him.

"Is this maybe your thing?" he asked, a little smile on his face.

"I think it could be," I said.

I showed him how it worked. There were four stacks: Childhood, Young Adult, Adulthood, Old Age. For each stack, there were life events, with death cards mixed in. The object was to draw four cards from each stack without getting a death card. If you got a death card during Young Adult, then you looked at the life events up to that point and that was the sum total of your life.

"What happens if you make it all the way through the game without getting a death card?" he asked. I couldn't believe he was taking it seri-ously. I was shaking a little.

"You still die, but you die in your sleep," I told him. "Peacefully."

He seemed to like this possibility. And so we played. Mr. Reynolds won a spelling bee, and escaped from a kidnapper, and rescued a puppy, and got a dirt bike for Christmas, an amazing childhood. He made it all the way to his second card of Adulthood before a business rival poisoned him. This seemed to please him. "This is a good game," he said.

"I play it all the time," I told him.

He reached into his desk and pulled out a blank index card. He drew a sketch of a man, a cartoony version of himself, standing in front of a chalkboard. He wrote "Become a junior high science teacher" at the top, and then he slipped it into the middle of the Adulthood deck.

"I hope I never get that one," he said.

"Maybe that's like your own secret death card," I said, and this made him smile and turn a brighter shade of red.

In the section on evolution, things got a little weird. Our town wasn't that far away from where the Scopes Trial had been, which always embarrassed me. Mr. Reynolds outlined the details of evolution, how it worked. Kima Walker, one of the most beautiful girls in the school, said, softly, kind of sad, "I know that I did not come from some monkey," and I waited for Mr. Reynolds to destroy her. My parents both worked factory jobs, my mom had dropped out of high school and my dad never went to college. But they were smart people. They told me about evolution when I was so little, and they told it to me with such happiness. I think they liked the idea that you could be something but turn into something else. Around that same time, I asked them about the Bible, and my mom just shrugged. "Just stories," she said.

"Do you think we evolved from monkeys?" Jeff Jeffcoat asked Mr. Reynolds, who seemed to think about it.

"Well," he said softly, "evolution takes place over thousands of years, these slow incremental changes. For us to evolve from monkeys, the world would have to be much older than we suspect that it is. So I'm not sure that evolution is fully proven. There are certainly verifiable instances of it, but I think it requires more analysis, maybe more than we can do in the lifespan of human beings."

I felt like someone had punched me in the stomach. Kima Walker looked so happy. The whole class seemed to take Mr. Reynolds and place him in a better part of their consciousness. The rest of class that day went so smoothly. I barely listened. I took out an index card and drew a picture of a gorilla stabbing a human being with a huge spear. I wrote "Mishap at the Zoo" at the top.

My disappointment with Mr. Reynolds, and the other students' truce with him, ended a week later when Marigold Timmins, who played power forward on the girls' basketball team, told Mr. Reynolds, after she'd made a D on a quiz, that she could destroy him in a game of one-on-one. Mr. Reynolds had been writing some notes on the chalkboard, and I watched his body stiffen, his hand just hovering there.

"You think you could beat me?" he asked, and it looked like he was talking to the chalkboard, about to fight it.

"I could," she said.

Mr. Reynolds turned around. "How much do you wanna bet?" and the class went, "ooooohhhhh," and Marigold said, "Twenty dollars."

"Let me see the twenty dollars," he said, and Marigold said, "Let me see if you have twenty dollars," and the class went, "ooooohhhhh" again. Mr. Reynolds reached into his wallet, fucking Velcro, and slammed a twenty on his desk. Marigold reached into her purse and counted out ten ones and a five. "That's all I have," she said, and Mr. Reynolds said that was just fine.

"Patrick," he said, and I got scared. "You hold the money," and so I got up and waddled around the room to get the money.

"Let's go," Mr. Reynolds said, and he walked into the hallway. It took a few seconds, some giggling, but soon we all followed him, down the hall, out of the main building, and into the gym.

The gym teacher, Coach Billings, seemed perturbed to have us in there. His class was playing badminton on one half of the gym.

"Franklin?" he asked Mr. Reynolds. "You doing a science project in here or something?"

"Jimmy, I need to use that half of the court for a demonstration. It's all about"—he paused, trying to think of something—"physics and whatnot."

Mr. Reynolds went to get a basketball, and Marigold was stretching.

"Can't have those shoes on the court, Franklin," Coach Billings said apologetically, and Mr. Reynolds just kicked off his loafers, peeled off his socks, and walked onto the court. "We'll play to five," he said, "one point per basket. Make it, take it."

I know for a fact, one-hundred-percent, that I was the only person in that gym who wanted Mr. Reynolds to win. Marigold's boyfriend had called me a queer one day when he saw that I had a handkerchief that had little roses embroidered on it.

Marigold took the ball from Mr. Reynolds and started dribbling to her right, looking to blow past Mr. Reynolds, but he stayed with her, and when she went for a lay-up, he swatted it away so easily that the whole class seemed to groan at the same time. In his bare feet, toes as long as fingers, he ran down the bouncing ball and immediately put up a weird set shot that came from his hip, and he buried it easily. "One-zero," he said, and Marigold looked puffy and angry.

Mr. Reynolds scored three points as easily as possible, even hitting a skyhook over Marigold's ineffective defense. When he got the ball back, Marigold dug in, scuffed her sneakers on the squeaky floor, and Mr. Reynolds faked a shot. In that second, he dribbled past her, wide open, and he leapt into the air. It looked like he was going to dunk it, but he just didn't quite have the height, and so he bounced it off the backboard at the last second and the shot fell through.

The class hooted and hollered, and Marigold was crying. Mr. Reynolds came over to me, and I handed him the money, and he put it all in his wallet. I could not believe that he was taking Marigold's money; I thought that would be illegal. Mr. Reynolds calmly put on his socks and loafers, and we all marched back into our classroom and sat in silence until the bell rang a few minutes later.

"That was amazing," I told him, the last one out the door.

"I've not been that scared in a long time," he said, huffing a little, his teeth chattering.

I thought about what kind of life card that would be, but it seemed too complicated, too much text to write to explain it.

We were playing Death Cards in his classroom one day during lunch, and I made it all the way through the game without drawing a death card. Mr. Reynolds had fallen into a pool and drowned as a child, but he seemed happy to watch me accumulate experiences on my way to a quiet death.

When I was done, I shuffled the cards again, but Mr. Reynolds said, "Not a bad life."

"I didn't have sex though," I said. There were sex cards interspersed through the decks, though the pictures I drew were just fancy hearts.

"It isn't necessary for a good life," he said. I felt like we were friends, and I wondered if Mr. Reynolds had any other friends. I knew that I didn't.

"Have you ever had sex?" I asked, and he blushed, but he didn't seem angry with me.

"Yeah," he said finally. "In Vietnam. It was awful."

"It was?" I asked, and he nodded.

"It was a kind of, like, a payment situation," he said. "All the guys did it and they really wouldn't leave me alone until I did it too. I hated it so much."

"But never again?" I asked, feeling so sad.

"Nope," he said. "Never came up again. Never went looking for it again. Never felt like I needed it."

"And you feel like you've had a good life without it?" I asked. I needed to know what my life could be like.

"I haven't had a good life," he said, looking right at me, his eyes kind of watery. "But it wasn't because of sex. It's like your card game, Patrick. You just pick cards and you can't really control it."

"But you only get to play the game once," I said.

"Yeah," he said, "that's true."

"Maybe that's why we like this game," I offered.

"Maybe," he replied.

"Do you believe in heaven?" I asked.

"It doesn't seem scientifically possible," he said. "I don't even know if I'd want there to be one. Whoever made earth, made heaven, too, right? So who's to say that heaven would be any better?" He seemed to not even register that I was there, that I had a body and was right next to him. He seemed like he was staring into some black hole.

I reached over and touched his hand. "You're a great teacher, Franklin," I said.

He smiled. "Thanks, Patrick."

The next part of the story, I don't even want to tell it. It's not the important thing, but it's necessary. Latisha Gordon, who was the star player on the girls' basketball team, a point guard who could score in waves, was impossible to shake off when she played defense, could dribble like a playground legend, challenged Mr. Reynolds to another game of one-on-one for twenty bucks. And Mr. Reynolds said no. Latisha wasn't even in our class; she had study hall that period and just came in because she was friends with Marigold. I imagine that they had been planning this for weeks and weeks.

Finally Mr. Reynolds said OK, and I gathered up the money, and we all marched into the gym. And Latisha scored two quick baskets, but then Mr. Reynolds came back with two of his own, and then he went for a lay-up and came down weird and his ankle just snapped.

He didn't even make a noise in reaction. We heard that snapping sound, like a tree branch breaking off, and then it was just silence. And then we all saw Mr. Reynolds's ankle, turned the absolute wrong way, and he was holding his leg with both hands, kind of elevating it. And then kids started screaming, so loud, so sustained, and one boy threw up in the bleachers, this soupy vomit running down and dripping to the wooden floor under the bleachers.

Latisha didn't even look at Mr. Reynolds, just jogged out of the gym, afraid of getting into trouble. I wanted to run to Mr. Reynolds, to hold him, but I was paralyzed. Mr. Reynolds had drawn a death card, such a bad one, at just the wrong time. The money was in my hands, getting sweaty and warm, and I ripped it up into tiny little pieces, and I threw it down, and a few pieces fluttered around and got stuck in the vomit.

Coach Billings finally went over to Mr. Reynolds, and then an ambulance came, and they carried him out of the gym, and the principal was standing there, looking so confused and so angry, and Marigold was trying to explain what had happened. The bell rang for the next class, and I still didn't move. I just sat in the bleachers, and I stayed there the rest of the day, and I was so invisible in that school that no one even noticed. I just sat in the bleachers and cried.

That night, back at home, I drew about forty new death cards, just awful, awful scenarios. I surprised even myself. I didn't put them into the decks. I just made it a single deck, all on its own, and I turned them over one after the other, nothing but death, nothing but humiliation. I did that all night, didn't even sleep, and when I went to school the next morning, Mr. Reynolds wasn't there, and this old lady was our substitute. When we asked about Mr. Reynolds, she said he was on medical leave and would be gone for the rest of the year.

"Was he fired?" Marigold asked, and she seemed sheepish, a little guilty.

"Heavens no," the woman said. "He'll be back next year."

❊   ❊   ❊

I found Mr. Reynolds's address in the phone book, and on Saturday, I rode my bike the nearly six miles to his house, my body covered in sweat even though it was still cold out, the last bit of winter. My thighs hurt so bad and my stomach was cramping. The bike was something I'd outgrown and then shown so little interest in that my parents never bought me a new one. But I made it to Mr. Reynolds's house, his car parked in the driveway, and there was no going back now.

His mom answered the door, ancient but surprisingly sturdy, really tall, even though she was hunched over from age. She had been a teacher at the same middle school, English, but that was way before my time. My mom didn't even remember her.

"Yes?" she asked, a little afraid of this fat kid with long eyelashes. I wondered if anyone besides the two of them had been in the house in years.

"Is Mr. Reynolds here?" I asked. I reached into my backpack and showed her a box of Russell Stover chocolates that I'd bought with my allowance. "I have a get-well present for him."

"Oh, how sweet," she said. She turned around and walked back to her recliner and picked up this big book, which I remember was a biography of Sammy Davis Jr., and simply said, "He's in his room at the end of the hall."

The house smelled clean, like lemon, and everything was in its proper place. I had imagined mold and cat piss and mounted deer heads everywhere. But this was an ordinary house, a little nicer, actually, than the house I shared with my parents and younger sister. I knocked on the door, and Mr. Reynolds said, "Mom?"

"It's Patrick," I said. There was a long pause, and then he finally said, "OK, come in."

He was sitting up in his bed, a mystery novel on his lap. There was a big desk in the room that had all these science books neatly arranged on it, lots of notes. He had a framed, signed poster of Kareem Abdul-Jabbar on his wall, and some Audubon prints that were really beautiful and looked expensive. On the nightstand was a plate with peanut butter crackers and a glass of tomato juice.

"Patrick," he said. "What are you doing here?" He seemed embarrassed to see me. He was wearing old-fashioned pajamas and a knit cap for the cold.

"I brought you this," I said, handing him the chocolates.

"Oh, that's really nice of you," he said. He looked at me for a second and then back at the chocolates. "Would you like to eat some?" he asked, and I nodded. He ripped off the plastic film and we each ate about four chocolates, chewing the nougat in silence.

"Are you OK?" I asked.

"I will be in a while," he said. "No permanent damage, surprisingly enough. The doctor says the bone will actually be stronger at the break than it was before once it heals." I tried to look at his legs, but they were under the blankets.

"And you're not in trouble?" I asked, and he blushed.

"The principal says that I can't play basketball against my students for money." He paused, thinking about things. "I can't play basketball with them even not for money," he then said. "And I'm on a kind of probationary period. But no, not really. It's hard to get fired, I think."

"That's good," I told him. "I miss you in class."

"Well, I miss you, too," he said, and then I just started weeping. I don't even know why, but the sight of him there, broken, so accepting of his sad life, it made me want to die.

"Patrick," he said, reaching out for me. He touched my face, which made me feel better.

"I don't know what to do," I said, hiccuping, "I'm a freak. I hate my life."

"You are not a freak," he said.

"I'm gay, I think," I told him, the first time I'd told anyone, "but I don't even know if I'm gay, really. How would I know? There are only about three other boys in the school who are gay, and I don't even know if they know that they are gay. And I'm just stuck here."

"If you're gay," Mr. Reynolds said, "it is not a bad thing. OK, Patrick? It's not."

And then I looked up at him, still crying. "Are you gay?" I asked.

He looked pained but seemed to consider the question. "I don't think so," he finally said. "At one point I might have been, but I kind of missed that window. I don't think I'm anything, Patrick."

"Could I kiss you?" I asked, fumbling for something, trying to figure my way into my own life.

"No," he said. "You do not want your first kiss to be with me. It will be something you think about every single time you kiss another person."

"Please, Franklin?" I asked. Was this the reason that I'd even come here? I had no idea. I didn't know exactly what I was doing or saying.

"Life does not always have to be bad, Patrick, but maybe right now it has to be for you. But get out of here, go to college, a college in a big city or with a lot of students, and then maybe you can figure this out. Maybe you can find happiness."

"But maybe I never will," I said. "Maybe this is it."

"Maybe," he admitted, "but just try, OK? Just try."

I sniffled, trying to gain some composure. "OK," I told him, and he smiled.

"Do you want another chocolate?" he asked me, but I said that I thought my stomach was hurting. He put the chocolates away and regarded me with tenderness.

"Did you bring your Death Cards?" he asked, and I nodded because I never went anywhere without them. I reached into my backpack and produced the stacks, held together with rubber bands.

"Could we try something?" he asked me. He took the first stack of cards, and he went through them, removing every single death card from the deck. He took the next stack and did the same, and I took a stack and removed the death cards. I finished removing all the cards from the last stack, and we stared at them, spread out over the quilt on his bed. There were so many ways to die, I realized, so many ways that things would just stop and never start again.

Then Mr. Reynolds drew a card, and he held it up for me, and it made me smile. He had won a baby beauty pageant. And then I drew. And then he did. And we did that all afternoon, without the possibility of death, an entire life, and then a life stacked on top of that, and then another life stacked on top of that, until there was nothing but life, always happening, never stopping. And I held his hand at one point, and I thanked him again, and he just nodded.

I never saw him again after that. I moved to the high school the next year, and I nearly killed myself, but I held on to the part of me that I wanted to keep. And I made it out of that place, which wasn't even a bad place really, or no worse than any other place for someone like me. And I got to somewhere good. I didn't evolve, nothing like that. I just held on to myself and found a place where I could keep living. And eventually I stopped thinking so much about Mr. Reynolds because thinking about him meant thinking about that time in my life. And he just sat there, in this tiny little part of my heart. And he never changed either.

And now he was dead. And there was no way that I could explain it to my boyfriend. He would not know how those cards worked, the sensation of drawing them, each time wondering what awful thing might appear, and how much of a relief it was, even if it was ordinary, that you were still here, still in this world.

Nominated by Andrew Porter, Joni Tevis

LEAVE NO TRACE

fiction by DANIEL OROZCO

from ZOETROPE: ALL STORY

1.

When he was six years old, Little Rutger's mother was killed by an exceptionally rare and virulent spinal cancer, and his father, a benign and devoted alcoholic who embraced the memory of her ghastly suffering to the exclusion of everything and everyone else until he himself died a half decade later, took his only child aside the day after they had buried her, and told him this:

"Everything goes, little buddy. Your mother is gone. I'll be gone someday, and you'll be gone, too. Life is a slog, one cold, dark, slippery, uphill slog. There'll be a crack of light or two to see your way. That's called hope. And a handhold here and a toehold there. That's mercy. But the light, that'll wink out and you'll be in the dark again. And the holds, they'll crumble and down you go. So crush hope. Let hope die. And mercy? Well, don't quit your day job! And what about love? I loved your mother. You loved her, too. We watched her suffer and die, and—*boom*! She's feeding the worms now and we're alone. Love is pain, little buddy. So harden your heart. Take that precious, meaty-beaty little muscle of yours and turn it into a fist of stone.

"Everything goes. When I go, the only mark I'll leave is in here—" Little Rutger's father touched his son's head, surmising the traces of his mark inside with gentle fingertips. "And when you go, that's all she wrote. No memory of me left at all. *Boom!*

"So keep your head down. Sit in the back row and don't raise your hand. Play dumb. Avoid the spotlight. Don't make a fuss. Bring a book

87

and just wait in line. Don't answer the door. Don't order the special. Don't travel. Don't ask her out. Don't color outside the lines. Expect nothing. Don't reach, don't strive, don't *try*, just be!

"Be invisible. Be smoke. Be a ghost. Leave. No. Trace."

And so Little Rutger didn't. Or at least, he didn't mean to.

2.

Rutger is eleven years old, sent to Uncle Willy and Aunt Midge—already in their late sixties and active retirees: early risers, weekly players of tennis and four-handed bridge, intrepid solvers of thousand-piece jigsaw puzzles, hardy day-hikers and trusty community volunteers and avid gardeners of tomatoes and beets and kale. They are always *doing* things—shoulders to wheels, noses to grindstones, and all that. "What do you like to do?" they ask the boy. He shrugs and says, "Everything." And he does do everything—he gets a paper route, babysits for several families in their church, plays junior-league soccer, picks up litter from playgrounds and highway medians with his Boy Scout troop. He takes on household and gardening tasks as Uncle Willy's eyes and Aunt Midge's joints incrementally deteriorate. They teach him how to ride a bike, fly a kite, tread water, bake bread, fold hospital corners, rewire a lamp. He learns to sew on a button, use a compass, measure twice and cut once, read a night sky, bone a chicken, even play bridge, sometimes sitting in as an emergency fourth. He is adequate at everything he does. The papers are mostly delivered on time, and the ball usually moved downfield. The babysat children are safe though bored, the buttons sewn on secure but crooked, the merit badges earned if just barely. He always loses at bridge, yet sometimes respectably so. He approaches every new and untried thing dubiously, as if it were primed with explosives. Only bread-making alters this affect, the steps of a recipe imbuing him with a semblance of confidence. Bewildered by this nephew out of the blue, Uncle Willy and Aunt Midge are—though well-intentioned and devoted—intensely awkward caretakers. They pat him on the back, or tousle his hair, and tell him that he's a good boy. "You're a good boy, Rutger!"

Aside from these clumsy tendernesses, nothing is amiss in the home of Uncle Willy and Aunt Midge, bought decades ago in a now-upscale peninsula community with a robust tax base and well-funded schools teeming with solicitous teachers and counselors perpetually after Rutger about his passion. "What is your *passion*, Rutger? What are you interested in?" He shrugs and says, "Nothing," which is not entirely true, but the investment in his success—from Mrs. Heinz and Mr. Cockrell and all the others—torments him until he finds respite with Mr. Rosa, who teaches geometry and algebra/trig and is serenely indifferent to his students' passions. While Rutger enjoys the methodical process of solving for x or proving the congruence of angles a and b, his x is often wrong and the logic of his proofs easily unraveled. Mr. Rosa gives him Cs and Ds, and by the end of his first year of high school, Rutger to his great relief is officially pegged an Underachiever and off the hook investment-and-success-wise. He avoids the locker-room bullies and the cafeteria cliques by allying with the theater students and, now identified and dismissed as a Theater Fag, is mostly left alone. He works in the fly loft, climbing ladders and traversing catwalks, belaying and tying off ropes that move light rigs up and down and swing sceneries in and out. For three years, he watches on the stage below a girl named Nina, willing her to look up. She is Ado Annie in *Oklahoma!* and Emily in *Our Town*. She is Nurse Kelly in *Harvey* and Lotus Blossom in *The Teahouse of the August Moon*.

After high school, Uncle Willy asks, "What now, Rutger?" The boy shrugs, so Uncle Willy arranges a job at the airport, where he had worked as a ramp supervisor. Rutger waves jetliners into their parking spots and chocks their wheels. He steers telescoping skyways onto fuselage doors and tows baggage trailers and drives refueling trucks and catering trucks and pallet loaders. Uncle Willy stumbles and breaks a hip on one of his vigorous walks in the foothills. He soon dies, and Aunt Midge thereafter becomes fretful and frail, and Rutger cares for her until she dies, too, and Rutger's cousins Janie and Jeannie turn up to evict him from what they presume is now their house until a lawyer appears with an ironclad will leaving the entirety of the modest estate not to the errant and ungrateful daughters but to the nephew. Rutger signs documents, unpacks his recently packed duffel bag, sits on the sofa, looks around. Porcelain tchotchkes on the mantel over the gas fireplace. An oakwood dining table that seats ten. An antique hutch filled with hundred-year-old china and silverware and embroidered linens. Matching Barcaloungers. Rutger takes in, apprehends, understands. His tchotchkes now, and his Barcaloungers. His house.

He spins LPs on the RCA Victor record player he inherited, while working on a jigsaw puzzle at the dining table, or reclining in one Barcalounger, or the other. Uncle Willy's is not unpleasantly gamy, redolent of wet lumber and musty tobacco; Aunt Midge's is more aromatic, herbal/floral with an astringent undertone, like medicinal tea. Listening to Glen Campbell, or Bobbie Gentry or America or Chicago, Rutger opens his eyes, swings himself upright, switches chairs, and inhales again. He sniffs through the bedding and blankets in the closet, stands in the kitchen's tiny larder with the door closed, settles into the Chevy Impala in the garage with the windows rolled up, sticks his head into dresser drawers that hold her gloves and scarves and wraps, his blue paisley kerchiefs and watch caps and distended leather wallet. Nothing. Uncle Willy and Aunt Midge are gone.

He is fit, though he could lose a few pounds. Every workday, he walks two miles, rain or shine, from his home to the train station and back. He brings a book and pretends to read intently so he can listen undisturbed to the other train passengers. It is always the same book, and no one ever notices, and all of what he overhears is mundane and uneventful and extraordinarily ordinary, which is always a great relief. At home, he listens to the radio, to *Dr. Laura* and *Piano Jazz* and Click and Clack, and to a show that plays old serials—Burns and Allen and *The Great McGinty* and *Chandu the Magician.* He listens to a man who broadcasts from an undisclosed location so the government won't find him. He listens to the recorded lectures of a sixties guru who says that "the phenomenon moon-in-the-water is likened to human experience," and though Rutger has no idea what this means, he writes it down and magnets it to the refrigerator door. He bakes bread. He bakes a lot of bread—baguettes and ciabattas and challahs, loaves and rounds and sticks. He eats what he can and freezes the rest, but he can't eat it fast enough, so he slips frozen loaves into the garbage the night before collection day. Also written down and magneted to the refrigerator door: *If wishes were horses the poor would ride. The cat turned chicken and ran like a dog. The nail that sticks up gets hammered down. Life is a brief spark between one abyss and the next. Twenty dwarves took turns doing handstands on the carpet.*

Rutger is a team player, and he works hard though he does not work smart, but give him a thing to do, everyone on his crew agrees, and it'll get done, and in this way he ensures himself a job for life. Except for Erica, whose boyfriend works over in Concourse A, the crew gathers for lunch at a remote table at the edge of a food court and listens to young Dante talk about O. J. and Columbine and 9/11 and Enron and Katrina. They know about these things, of course, but the boy recognizes how something that happens all the way over there has an effect on you here and now. They nod and murmur, "Ain't that right," and Rutger listens and nods and sees young Dante on the rise in the world and, for the boy's sake, hopes that his father was wrong about hope. Young Dante's plan is to work for two years to save money for college, but his girlfriend gets pregnant, and so he stays and he becomes ramp supervisor, and two wives and three children later he is old Dante collapsing from a stroke while looking for his car in the airport lot. Rutger is the only one left from the original crew. They come and they go. Everything goes.

On the Internet, he finds Nina McGovern from high school. She is Nina Siracusa and then Nina Quade and then Dr. Quade working in conflict zones around the world and coming home without a scratch, and then she is dead by her own hand, and Rutger mourns, attempting to drink a pint of vodka one weekend but getting sick and pouring the rest of it out, and though they never exchanged a word, he still thinks of her as the One That Got Away, and he knows this isn't true, not by a long shot, but what's the harm? On the Internet, he finds pornography and masturbates to climax, and though the physical release is pleasurable, he still feels guilty using the memory of a now-dead woman to ejaculate, so he stops masturbating but continues to watch. He knows that the participants are paid actors, coworkers, maybe even friends, doing their jobs, touching each other in the myriad ways that porn actors do, with an intimacy born not just of practiced routine but of fellowship and trust and perhaps love, and the images of them engender in Rutger nothing arousing anymore, yet instead a serenity that feels like slipping into—but not under—a warm bath. On Sundays, he attends the service at the Unitarian church. He can wear whatever he wants, and the Bible is not *the* Truth but a Truth, and as a gas-powered flame in a bronze cup flickers to represent the light of reason and the warmth of community, Rev. Joanie and the congregation chat with each other and sing and pray. And then there is quiet meditation, and everybody holds hands, and this is the part Rutger looks forward to—silence and somebody's hand in each of his. There is coffee and Bundt cake afterward, which Rutger doesn't stay for, which is cool with Rev. Joanie. Everything is cool at the Unitarian church. Returning home, in good weather, he sits outside his basement door on concrete steps leading up to a backyard rank with listing weeds as tall as a man. He sits naked to the waist and leans back on his elbows with his eyes closed, taking the sun, cranberry red on his lids and oven warm on his skin. He asks a question out loud, always in the simple future tense with himself as the subject. It is always a different question, sometimes passionately inarticulate and

91

heartfelt, but more often than not addressing some very precise and practical everyday problem. He hears thundering silence in response. It is always the same answer.

The night before collection day, Rutger drags his neighbor's garbage bin out to the curb. Mrs. Tessier stands just inside her front door to direct him in his task and gives him a dollar because she is not a Charity Case. He cannot bring himself to spend Mrs. Tessier's dollars, which he keeps—nearly five hundred of them—in rubber-banded rolls in a shoebox on a shelf in a closet. One such night, she doesn't come to the door to direct him or to give him his dollar, and returning from work the next evening, he rings her bell and hears only the flap and squawk of her parrot, Mr. Chips, and two evenings after that, he finds a dumpster in front of her house and a moving van and two small-faced men— these are Mrs. Tessier's sons—and this is how Rutger learns that Mrs. Tessier is dead. The dumpster is brim-filled, and among the array of items on the sidewalk being loaded into the van is a square wire cage with a bird in it. This is Mr. Chips, a small, yellow-breasted, green parrot with pink-tipped wings and a grayish-blue head. The bird screams. It weaves and high-steps along the length of its perch, toward Rutger and back. One of the sons laughs. "Hey, he recca-nizes you!" Rutger has never set foot inside Mrs. Tessier's home but soon apprehends that Mr. Chips knows his voice, has heard him outside speaking to the old woman once a week for the past ten years, trying and failing to refuse her dollar. "Nono!" the bird sings. "Nono! Nono!" And Rutger, flustered and rattled by this joyous display—all for him!—walks away without offering his condolences to Mrs. Tessier's sons.

Invitations to weddings and birthdays, to retirement send-offs and pub crawls and holiday gatherings, are unheeded. Exploratory emails from long-lost relations and bygone acquaintances are trashed, phone messages deleted, knocks—of opportunity and otherwise-ignored. Days pass unseized. And yet there is a man named Chava, a barista in a coffee shop in Concourse B, who during several weeks of Rutger's early tenure on the night crew engages him in what can only be construed as flirtation, and which one evening culminates in what can only be described as a make-out session in a secluded corner of a desolate boarding terminal—ninety seconds of groping and kissing that leave Rutger's lips and chin rasped and raw, and Rutger himself at first all buzzy and ashiver with wonderment, then simply embarrassed, and finally nostalgic, looking back upon and observing this rapturous interlude from a great and rueful distance, bemused at how funny people can be. He is not an unhappy man, but he isn't an especially happy one either, and the few times he tries to introspect upon exactly what he is in this world—while alone in the backyard casting his questions into the Void, or alone in bed awaiting sleep—the impulse is always waylaid by the world itself. At night, the whir of crickets is soon blitzed by the rattling of his refrigerator, on and then off, and then the engines of a distant jetliner, whose recedence in turn leaves only the incipient patter of rain, its steady increase lulling him until he drifts off, at last. And mornings, on the concrete steps, a glint of sunlight reveals beneath the sill of a basement window the untidy web of a black widow spider, which he captures in a jelly jar with grass and twigs, and for several days observes, implacably still, before letting it go. Any present moment for Rutger reveals no trail of associations to the past, opens no door to the speculative future. Yesterday's gone! Tomorrow's not here yet! Gazing idly out a window, he tracks the steady course of clouds across a sky, watches the light diffuse through them and flare around their edges, the atmosphere shred and ravel, and it reminds him of nothing. No insight or epiphany arises. Clouds are just clouds, and that's enough.

On Saturdays from nine to noon, Rutger sits at the breakfast nook with the window open. He drinks coffee and listens to somebody somewhere practicing piano—scales and arpeggios, up and down, up and down, then the same three minutes of music, over and over, stopping and starting, correcting and starting again, again and again, never finishing, always approaching without ever arriving. His coffee mug reads *Cranky Bitch.* The cupboard is filled with such mugs, gifted between uncle and aunt: *Grumpy Bastard, Good Morning Gorgeous, My Husband Is Hotter Than My Coffee, Your Personalized Message Here.* He can go for days without hearing the sound of his own voice. A stray cat slips beneath the back fence and stays for a month, then disappears before Rutger can come up with a name. His one, enduring regret, which he rubs at like the scar of a wound, is not asking Mrs. Tessier's sons how much they might want for the bird, not offering to pay any amount.

One early morning, Rutger boards the train, sits by his usual window. He is forty-nine years old. He faces rearward, preferring to watch the landscape come up alongside and pull away rather than rush at him. He sees mostly his own reflection in the glass, against the predawn darkness, and then the concrete walls of tunnel abutments rise and the train dives underground for six minutes, and in that time the day breaks open. The sky goes black to purple, and a wash of amber surges along the horizon, and the shapes of the city emerge from shadow. A band of sunlight shutter-flashes in the upper reaches of the window. The announcement for the airport station rattles over the intercom. The train slows. Passengers move toward the doors. Most are travelers with flights to catch, lugging bags. Some are airport employees like him, heading to work, and he nods as they exit. But today, he doesn't follow. He catches the eye of a stranger or two, yet no one recognizes his distress, for he feels suddenly very heavy, earth's gravity pressing him down, yet also lightheaded and floaty. A sharp pain tears into the meat of his shoulder. These are the only symptoms of a cardiomyopathy present within him since birth, undiagnosed and dormant, until now. The train empties. The doors whoosh and close. He is terrified, but also somehow giddy and elated. *What now, Rutger? he* thinks, as he takes his last breath and slumps toward the window, tapping his skull on the glass and squinting into the dazzle of full-on daylight, and—

3.

We remember almost nothing.

Memory is the junk drawer in your kitchen with Everything in it, and you're looking for the flashlight batteries but instead come across those needle-nose pliers you needed last week, a lone glove, fourteen dollars in Monopoly money, credit card receipts for things you don't remember buying (a bucket of fried chicken, a pedicure, a tank of gas in a town called Sparkle), a collar with tags for a long-dead dog (Prince), a bottle opener shaped like a spread-eagle man with a corkscrew penis that you swear isn't yours, a ring of keys that you have no idea what they're for, what locks or doors they may open, and . . . What were you looking for again? Memory is a jigsaw puzzle with eighty-six billion pieces, and the picture on the box keeps changing. Imagine the Book of Your Life, the nuance and texture of your every experience transcribed in its infinity of pages. Now imagine the Book obliterated, gone forever except for its table of contents and index, and these in no particular order and with all the page numbers missing. That is memory.

You remember a name that means nothing to you, embedded in a fissure of your brain like a small, hard seed in your teeth that your tongue goes to again and again. It is Teutonic, strange, its syllabic sequence a nonsensical chant—*rutger*-voss *rutger*voss *rutg*ervoss. No one you know recognizes it. Did you invent it? Did you read it somewhere? It is an enigma until a neural pathway lights up, and you decide that you must have gone to high school with him. High school, that repository of dead

94

names, assimilates this one, and the seed is dislodged, and the mystery solved.

Nina Quade, on the other hand, née Siracusa née McGovern, didn't remember the name at all. But what it would have pointed to—the boy in high school up in the flies, crushing on her—remained vivid and sweet in her recollection as long as she lived. Back home in the States, bored and unsettled between assignments in Darfur or Kurdistan or the West Bank, she would conjure the Crayola smell of stage makeup and its loamy taste in the corners of her mouth, and the itchy costumes she wore, and most of her lines, still. She'd sing medleys from *Oklahoma!* or *Mame* while on heli-transports or in surgery. She'd summon the steadfast gaze of a Secret Admirer, who saw in her what no one else did, though back then Rutger's gaze had not been endearing but just plain creepy. She had even urged one of her boyfriends to teach That Little Creeper a lesson, because Nina McGovern in high school had been a fatuous little tart, and Nina Quade in her desolate moments would dress the girl she once was in the more durable raiments of her adult self— brooding and cynical and willfully remote, with a boy in the flies as her Savior in the Wings, so to speak.

The children Rutger babysat have grown up, and none is worse for his care so long ago, and they remember him, if at all, in the most benign way, via some oblique and trifling detail—the yeasty smell of baked bread, the shave-and-a-haircut toot of a car's horn, the errant Chinese Checkers marble or Parcheesi pawn peeking from under the sofa.

A man sits on a sofa, his relatively new girlfriend tucked into him and sipping at a goblet of rosé. They face a picture window with a view of nothing much—a featureless brick wall across a narrow street, a tangle of denuded tree branchlets, a strip of sky. The man's name is Phillip, and he is forty-four years old, and he likes this girlfriend, whose name is Maya, and he is hopeful as they approach the Six-Month Cutoff that she won't dump him. "What are you thinking right now?" she asks dreamily. The lowering light of an autumn dusk steeps his living room in cozy darkness, and for some reason he's never been able to understand, the twilight hour observed from indoors always brings to mind the face of a babysitter he had when he was five or six, a boy named Rutger, grinning wide as he observes something other than Phillip. And while the image incites no particular emotion in him, no fear or dread or joy or whatever, the sheer weirdo irrelevance of it—like a clown nose among papal portraits, or a smiley face in Picasso's *Guernica*—inevitably gives him pause, and for five or so seconds he's locked into a thousand-yard stare, and the girlfriend elbows him gently, and he turns to her and lies: "I'm thinking of you."

Two of Rutger's other former charges, brother and sister, are doing their own babysitting now, one in a seedy but picturesque old lumber town along the Columbia River floodplain, the other in the arid, sun-blasted exurbs of sprawly Phoenix. She provides daycare for five multi-parented grandkids that drive her crazy. He is raising two sullen boys that a wayward daughter dropped off a year ago. Both are committed to a duty prompted by blood and guilt and also love, but they are peril-ously pooped, too, worn down to their respective frazzles and prone to lurid yet harmless daydreams of liberation—ditching the berserkers at some remote TravelCenter of America, say, or drowning them one by one in the kiddie pool. But after the horde has been picked up by their parents for the evening, after the boys have been sent off to school for the day, and sitting alone at last in a bay window or at a kitchen table with two or so fingers of bourbon, brother and sister are often troubled by the same recurring premonition: that something terrible will hap-pen to their beloved grandchildren.

When he was nine years old, Douglas Amador rode the train home one evening with his dozing mother, intently observing a man reading a book at the window seat across the aisle. By his wristwatch, he timed this man reading the same page for the entire trip, forty-four minutes, from Civic Center to their stop. It was his first wristwatch, a gift for his birthday, and he timed everything: "We're six minutes late!" "It took her eleven minutes to bring us menus!" "You peed for thirty-two sec-onds!" Years later, he deduced that pretending to read a book signals *Leave me alone, I'm not here, Go away*, and to this day, when alone in public, Douglas Amador pretends to read, too, though turning a page once in a while. A woman named June Moon—who would fly home to St. Louis for family weddings and anniversaries and birthdays, for christenings and memorials and every goddamn holiday—sat in the airport food court during one late-evening stopover, picking at her chicken pad thai and pretending to read while watching a half-dozen men around a table scattered with trays and napkin wads and cups. They were ground crew workers, and they all wore black boots and navy-blue pants and sweaters and nylon parkas whose pockets were stuffed with caps and gloves. Their parkas rustled as they shifted in their seats, and the radios clipped to their orange vests crackled low as they spoke, one of them in particular as the others listened and nodded and some-times broke into subdued laughter, and they were all Black except for one. June Moon's frequent visits home were prompted by fear and guilt more than by any true devotion to family, because family-wise the Moons were all unreformed racist louts, and her memory of those gathered and tranquil uniformed men—that one white face among them—somehow offered a trifling hope and solace as she humped to St. Louis and back again for thirty or so years, until every last Moon was finally feted or wedded or dead in the ground, and she never had to fly ever again.

If life is a journey, then memory is the map, the terrain of your experience, infinitely searchable, though scan-and-zoom is capricious and unreliable. Click on *Paris*. Zoom in, expecting to find That Tucked-Away Bookstore and That Romantic Chambres d'Hôte and Bruno's Liquid Eyes, but instead find That Shit-heel and That Fight and the Flight Home Alone. Click on *Home* and find Why Are You So Stupid and Clanking Radiators and Overly Warm Rooms and Uncle Handsy. Wrong home! Click on *Other Home*—with Good Brad, and his big Slobbery Labs, and the unbroken prairie shivery with switchgrass and clover, and all that sky!—and the traces of several very good years emerge and materialize, but you still feel stupid, and you fucked it up anyway, with Uncle Handsy tap-tap-tapping at some psychic back window.

Gilbert LaRocca was once sent by a girl he adored to beat up a boy she disliked. He had come up from behind as this boy was unlocking his bicycle, punched him twice in the back of the neck, clean-and-pressed him overhead—Gilbert was hale and fit, an all-state wrestler two years in a row—and tossed him into a dumpster. Gilbert picked up the bicycle and tossed that in, too. And slammed the bin lid shut. And stole the bicycle lock. He never got caught, and the girl he adored soon broke up with him. He joined the Air Force, married, divorced, remarried, and settled in Fort Lauderdale, where he runs a small air-charter service shuttling tourists and corporate types to the Bahamas and the Caymans. Business is booming, and he rarely flies solo anymore, but when he does, on the occasional return leg, lofting and thumping along the currents high above the clear water and sun-scalloped straits, ensconced within the propellers' chain-saw chatter, he remembers. To say that the memory of this beatdown haunts him would be an exaggeration, but forty years gone it still comes to him unbidden. His nape prickles, and his heart quickens, and a bilious liquid rises and settles in his throat. (The body remembers, too!) And this is the lesson of Repression: struggle to forget an awful thing, and it pounces, sharp as a razor blade, making a ruin of a glittering view.

Decades after Rutger's death, a woman sits bored at a dinner party. Her hosts have gotten hold of a slab of wild salmon, endangered and pricey these days, and are grilling and sharing it with a dozen of their dearest friends. Her name is Elizabeth, and she goes by Lizzie, but when she was twelve years old everyone called her Lizard. Back then, she was exceptionally miserable, even for a twelve-year-old girl, and after a horrid argument with her mother and father, they left for eleven o'clock mass without her, and she lay on the lawn in her backyard, trying to stare into the sun until she went blind, because that would fucking show everybody, but instead only squinting sidelong at the periphery of its light, until she heard beyond the fence the click of a latch and the scrape of a door and then nothing for several minutes. She crept stealthy and spy-like to a crack between planks and saw the man next door with no shirt on, reclining on the concrete steps with his eyes closed. (Her stupid mother called this "taking the sun.") She knew nothing about this neighbor, had never noticed any activity in his backyard, all overgrown and jungly, and now here he was, quiet and unassuming and probably polite if you ever ran into him, and you know what they say about men like that, and she imagined him beckoning to her, and she imagined going to him, inside his house, never to be seen again until they dug up her bones in his basement, and that would fucking show everybody, too. She lay spread-eagle and immobile under a bush in the dirt and watched him, still and at rest, until he opened his eyes and convulsed as if he'd been pierced and cried out—a question, choked and urgent and anguished—and then went still again, and Lizard thrilled at her witness to this secret and certainly shameful thing, until she realized that evening over dinner with her stupid mother and father that she had no one to tell about it, so she never thought of it again, until now, and Lizzie is enthralled all over. She doesn't remember the question—though she's certain she heard it, she knows she did—but it doesn't matter, because she does remember how it affected her. And as the feeling returns, as she shudders and squeezes her napkin tightly in her lap—*am I coming?*—the clod her hosts seated beside her asks if she's all right, and she looks at him a moment—*no words, no words*—and then pulls it together and smiles and tells him to shut up and finish his fish, and he laughs. And Lizzie—decades from now she will go by Lizard again—decides that she doesn't particularly like these friends of hers, and probably never has.

Memory is nostalgia, perfect in honeyed light, clichéd and contrived but no less potent for being so—the lowing of a lonesome foghorn, the smell of the sea, or of your father's aftershave, the mineral tang of impending rain or the shush of its eventual fall, the rise of baking bread, the scrape of a stubbled cheek, the rustle of a tulle wedding dress, the opening notes of this symphony or that. Memory is the catch in your throat as the car radio plays "Stairway to Heaven" or "Sweet Caroline" or "Black Water" or "[Your Song Here]." Memory is Williams's red wheelbarrow and white chickens and sweet, cold plums; Hemingway's swift, cold rivers; Dickinson's fly's stumbling buzz. Memory is Proust's tea-dipped madeleine—a whiff or tone or texture that crowbars open seams to lost worlds.

In Yuegang'ao—once nine discrete prefectures and two special administrative regions on China's Pearl River Delta, now combined by bridge and rail and administrative edict into a megacity of a billion residents—an old woman recalls, on a visit to the United States as a child, watching through the window of a jetliner as a man with Day-Glo orange traffic wands did a little dance while guiding the pilots from taxiway to ramp. By the time she raised her phone, he'd disappeared, and the lack of physical record would render the moment somehow sharper and brighter for her, like a relic restored and pristine, and until her death at ninety-three, the memory would often arise and manifest as she skipped nimbly from taxicab to curb, or shuffled from room to room in her apartment: a hitch in her step, one-two one-two, then a crossover and a hop.

In a coffee bar in the Miraflores borough of La Paz, Bolivia, a man tells of his dissolute life in the United States. He is fifty-seven and looks it but claims to be younger. He has recently returned home to care for his mother, and his friends think maybe he isn't quite the Boss he makes himself out to be. All toothy and vulpine, he regales them with a bawdy chronicle of seduction and subterfuge. "I was a shit!" he brags. "*Was*, Chava?" one of them says, and they all laugh. Rutger is not among the stories. To some people, you're gone gone gone.

Memory fades. In the late-nineteenth century, a psychologist named Gustav Spiller did the math and calculated that the average thirty-five-year-old with approximately thirteen thousand days of total lived experience remembers only twelve *hours* of it. Walking home one winter evening, Rutger slipped on an icy patch and performed the classic pratfall, horizontally airborne and then flat on his ass. Six people witnessed it. Four laughed, two were horrified, none came to his aid, and none recollect it now. Myriad strangers have glanced at his face, and thousands have looked into it and engaged for moments or minutes—clerks and tellers and panhandlers, toll takers and food servers and Jehovah's Witnesses, airline passengers and flight crews, train commuters, three plumbers, two lawyers, one mugger, one cop, a roofing contractor, a tree trimmer, a mortician. Five doctors, three dentists, two pastors. Of the fifteen hundred cumulative members of his Unitarian church over the course of his sketchy attendance, about a dozen recall only this: a quiet man with nice hands, warm and firm, smooth hands, dry and steady hands. Every summer in high school, a boy named Tommy Seymour worked for his father's roofing company and hated it—backbreaking, tedious labor under a hammering sun, his fellow roofers bullies and thugs one and all, and his father an Ahab, every job his White Whale. Yet Tommy Seymour the old man reminisces with fondness on one particular house, and the six-packs of beer the owner would leave for them in the afternoon shade. Courtney Betts wasted much of her reckless youth rebounding from one disastrous relationship to the next, and today, in the fortieth year of a placid and colorless marriage, while she can no longer distinguish one lout from another, she can think back on a dazzling spring day as she sat in a vast downtown plaza at high noon, bawling over a text message she'd just received, and a stranger handed her a folded handkerchief, leaning in and assuring her, "It's clean," and vanishing before she could look up and thank him. (She still has it, tucked away somewhere, its blue paisley now sun-faded and soft.) Everything goes, on and on.

Birds remember. A species of nutcracker can find the precise locations of its winter seed stashes, up to five thousand of them over a fifteen-square-mile area. Mockingbirds can recognize a human face. Crows can distinguish a voice. They hold grudges, too. In ornithology labs, assistants returning after summer vacations are shunned at first by the parrots, like miffed spouses; those who visit after years away are regaled as prodigals with dancing and shrieking. The pitch and cadence of speech, a song drifting from an open window, a crinkly cereal bag, a new tennis ball—any of these can evoke emotional states from the past. After Mrs. Tessier died, Mr. Chips was taken in by the younger of her sons, Ronny. (The older one, Randy, wanted nothing to do with the bird.) Ronny set its cage in his living room just as his mother had set it in hers, but after a month, his wife made him move it to the basement, where Mr. Chips screeched at all hours and took to panicky flight inside the bars. When it snapped a tiny chunk out of their little girl's finger, the bird had to go. The veterinarian recommended a family with two other parrots, but Argo and Buster were siblings and didn't warm to Mr. Chips, who'd grown aggressive and querulous, and was soon placed in a sanctuary, housed and fed and unsuitable for adoption for its remaining twenty-two years, hunkered down on a low perch, diligently chewing its feathers out, never vocalizing except for the rare instance on an early evening when it would rise up and cast around and scream, "Nono! Nono!" over and over, which was presumed by those who heard it to be a manifestation of some past trauma, an inchoate flashback to neglect or abuse, when in fact the very opposite was true.

Serena Harrow was twenty-one years old, returning to London after an extended vacation in the States, her gift to herself for graduating from university, and lugging a huge rolling suitcase that she and her father had nicknamed Mum because it was just about the height and girth of her mum. Following the others toward the train doors, she looked idly about and saw him, in a seat facing her, preparing to stand but not doing so, and in seconds she took in a round, cleanshaven face with light-brown eyes and thin eyebrows that arched upward as if startled, tufts of dark curly hair peeking from under a navy watch cap (a silver strand or two lit up from the sunlight falling through the window), a palm-size expanse of forehead with an incipient pimple on the left temple, a Roman nose that skewed a few millimeters to the right, beige-to-olive skin tone with scant freckling high on the cheekbones, a narrow philtrum descending into a sharp median notch of the upper lip, the lips thin and dry and flaked and slightly parted in an awkward smile, and so on, on and on—dozens of traits of his physiognomy, for Serena Harrow was back then an as-yet-undiagnosed Super Recognizer, and among the one percent of the population who can remember everyone they've ever seen, retrieving and assembling the features of a particular face from among the many millions of others stowed in the fathomless hidey-holes of their inferior temporal cortexes. Serena Harrow is fifty-five years old now, and her mum is gone, the namesake suitcase filled with junk and stowed in an attic, and she commutes by bullet train from Grantham to Westminster (her nose in a book), where she works for the Metropolitan Police, perusing photos from Interpol and IDMS databases, then scanning CCTV footage for matches. And if Rutger Voss were to appear on the screen before her—ducking into a chemist's shop, say, or running for the closing doors of a tram—she would press a button and freeze him and angle forward, press it again and rock him back and forth, frame by frame, and . . . *Boom!* She's twenty-one again, disembarking a train in the States, glancing over her shoulder as his head tips toward the glass. And although he is a stranger to her—they all are—the instant of recognition never fails to elicit a wistful flutter of affection, like the memory of a cherished friend. *Ah yes. I remember you.* She leans back in her chair and smiles. *I'll always remember you.*

Nominated by Robert Wrigley, Zoetrope: All Story

THE HOLY SPIRIT
OF THE MOON

by RED HAWK

from SLIPSTREAM

In the months before they went to the Moon
the Apollo 11 astronauts trained
in a remote desert in the west, home
to several Indian tribes. One day, it is reported,
an old Native elder came to them and asked

what they were doing there. He was told,
We are preparing to explore the Moon.
Visibly surprised, he thought long and hard,
then he said, *My people believe Holy Spirits
live on the Moon. Will you take*

an important message to them? Smiling,
the astronauts agreed. The old man
spoke in his native language, which
the astronauts could not understand.
He had them repeat it over and over until

they had it word for word. When they asked
what it meant, he said it was a secret
only the Holy Spirits could know.
The astronauts searched for weeks until
they found someone to translate for them.

The message said: *Don't believe a single word*
these people are telling you.
They have come to steal your land.
It is not reported whether the astronauts
delivered the message.

Nominated by Slipstream

HOUSEKEEPING

fiction by KARIN LIN-GREENBERG

from THE SOUTHERN REVIEW

Franco Tyrone's suicide at The Corvid Motel was the biggest thing that had ever happened in Galaville. Franco had been in town to film an episode of his television show, *Finding the Heart of America*. The day after he killed himself, he was supposed to talk to the LaBella brothers, who baked made-from-scratch fruit pies in an old pizza oven, and then he was supposed to interview Dizzy Garrity about tapping maple trees for syrup, and then he was scheduled to meet with me at Galaville Orchards and film me talking about how I make our famous cider doughnuts. I should say the doughnuts were not actually famous, but a sign in our front window declared FAMOUS CIDER DO-NUTS, so Franco was supposed to call them famous and maybe, once they were on TV, they would become famous, and people from the city driving upstate to admire the fall foliage would stop and buy dozens. Like the doughnuts, I was supposed to be on television, and, like the doughnuts, I thought I would get a little famous. Franco always made it seem as if the people he talked to on *Finding the Heart of America* mattered, and the places they came from mattered too. I'd hoped being on television might make me someone interesting, might make it so I wasn't only thought of as just the smart, uptight girl, the nerd destined to be valedictorian of Galaville High.

But, of course, there was no interview with Franco. My sister worked as a maid at The Corvid, and when she went to clean Franco's room at noon, she knocked and then shouted out "Housekeeping!" three times and entered the room when there was no answer, and she discovered him hanging. She was interviewed by the Albany news stations and then, because Franco was famous, she was interviewed by the national news shows. Everyone wanted to talk to the girl who'd discovered Franco's body. "It was terrible," she repeated in every interview. "It was the worst thing I ever saw. And I'm just so sorry for his family and friends." When the reporter from Albany with the crooked tie and slicked down hair asked Tess if she had any suspicions about why Franco killed himself, she tilted her head and said, "How can anyone know that?"

Because Tess was beautiful, she became a meme, screenshots from the news interviews of her outside the motel appearing all over the Internet. In these screenshots, Tess was standing below the wooden THE CORVID MOTEL sign with the silhouette of a crow, her hair blowing in the breeze. Her image was superimposed with phrases like "When Life Gives You Lemons, Make Sure Your Hair Is On Point" or "Stay Sexy Through Tragedy!" She became known as the "Hot Crier" online. A few weeks after Franco's suicide, the Internet spent more time talking about my sister's cheekbones and lush cascade of dark curls blowing in the wind than they did about what had driven Franco to kill himself. His story was sad and tragic, of course, but not fully unexpected. He'd had a few good years, a few famous years, people said, but fame and money don't solve anyone's problems. He had a history with severe depression, starting in the days when he was a PhD student. When he turned fifty, he took an extended leave from his university teaching job, and to keep busy, he traveled the country by car and started a blog about under-the-radar places and people in America. Then the blog blew up and then the Travel Network came calling and he became a star and officially quit his job teaching American History to college students. But I guess what haunts you always haunts you, and some people are just too haunted to push aside what gnaws at their minds. So there wasn't much more to say about Franco after the initial shock and sadness, but Tess, well, she seemed like someone fascinating whose story was continuing on, a young woman with model good looks wasting her life away in upstate New York, working as a motel maid and caring for her sixteen-year-old sister.

Tess was my legal guardian. My parents were alive but out of the picture, as they were unsuited for the responsibility of parenthood and could not resist the lure of opioids. That's all I'll say about them. Their story is generic enough to be a cliché, and I prefer not to dwell in the details. When she turned eighteen—six years ago—Tess became my legal guardian, and since graduating from high school she'd been working at The Corvid Motel, which provided enough of an income for us to live very modestly. I contributed to our family of two by working at Galaville Orchards after school and on weekends and in the summers. I worked in the orchard store in the fall and winter, hawking apple-flavored comestibles and country-kitsch items (potholders, candles, aprons, Christmas tree ornaments) meant to evoke a Norman Rockwell America that never actually existed. In the spring and summer, I worked in the orchards, picking fruit and directing the customers who came for pick-your-own to suitable aisles of trees or bushes. It was, of course, not a privileged upbringing, but it worked for us until our lives got turned upside down.

I suppose I shouldn't have been terribly surprised when the producers of *Great Catch!* came calling a few weeks after Franco's suicide, asking Tess if she wanted to be a contestant. By then, everyone in America with an Internet connection and any interest in popular culture knew who she was. The producers told her she'd be a fan favorite with her sad backstory, and if she went far enough on the show without actually winning, there was a good chance she could be the lead on the next season of *Great Lady Catch!*, where twenty men competed to become "the one." You know *Great Catch!* and *Great Lady Catch!*, I'm sure. On *Great Catch!*, twenty women vie for the heart of one man, and each week several are eliminated in what the show calls "the quest for love." The show culminates in a proposal. Never mind that out of the twenty-seven final couples the show has produced over the years, only four have made it to the altar.

Shortly before Tess found Franco's body she'd broken up with Ricky, her boyfriend of four years, so she was single and free to be a contestant. (Although, according to the gossip sites, plenty of contestants have come on the show while dating someone else; the lure of television and the possible fame it could bring was too much for some people to turn down.) I always pretended to be annoyed by Ricky, but he wasn't a bad guy. He was an auto mechanic, and he kept our car running. He could fix the things that broke around our house, capture and bring outdoors spiders neither Tess nor I wanted to touch, clean the gutters. He liked watching videos of idiot animals online. When he was at our house he'd always call out to me, even if I was in a different room, say stuff like, "Look at this raccoon falling off a roof!" and hold up his phone to me, and we'd cackle about the dumb raccoon together. Tess didn't find animal videos amusing. "What percent of the Internet do you think is taken up by animal videos?" she asked one day, and Ricky said, "Not enough of it."

"You're leaving me to go to California to film a show?" I asked after Tess got off the phone with the producers of *Great Catch!* I'd listened to the entire conversation—her side of it—and was able to piece together what was being asked of her.

"Elaine will look in on you," she said. "It'll only be for three weeks."

Elaine was our neighbor. She was sixty-two years old, was an accountant for the State of New York, owned three malodorous ferrets, and had a fondness for polyester clothing for both work and play.

"The issue here isn't my care and maintenance. I'm self-sufficient," I said. "I'm like a cactus. Here, but not needy."

"This is an opportunity, Benny," Tess said. "This fell into my lap, and if I say no, then what? I don't want to work at The Corvid forever. It's maybe a way out. For both of us." In fact, Tess hadn't been back to The Corvid since she found Franco. The manager of the motel had generously given her a week off with pay, but then Tess couldn't make herself return after that week was over. She said she just couldn't slide a key card into a lock, couldn't push down the door handle and open a door, not knowing what was waiting for her inside. By the time the producers of *Great Catch!* called, Tess hadn't worked in almost a month.

"I don't want Elaine looking in on me. Can you ask Ricky to do it?"

"I haven't really talked to him since we broke up. And I think it'd be weird if he took care of you. People might think it was improper. A teenage girl and a twenty-five-year-old guy shouldn't be hanging out alone. People talk in this town."

I sighed, loudly and dramatically, in case it wasn't clear yet to Tess that I was appalled about what she was going to do. "Funny that you care about impropriety while being willing to go on television to stick your tongue down some dude's throat," I said.

"Stop, Benny," she said.

"Stop what?" I said, as innocently as I could.

"Just stop your Bennyness. The judgmental stuff. Just please stop."

Of course Tess went to L.A. to film *Great Catch!* I told her that Hudson Plum—the supposedly great catch starring on this season of the show—was a goober, but she didn't care. I knew there were more damning pejoratives than *goober*, but Hudson was so banal that he did not warrant a more severe descriptor. Hudson was rejected by Samantha "Sammi" Jensen, the star of last season's *Great Lady Catch!*, after he brought her home to visit his family, and the audience felt sympathy for

Hudson's heartbreak even though the family visit made it clear he was a spoiled trust fund kid. After college, he'd embarked on a career as a rapper named H-Plummy. A *white* rapper. A white rapper who grew up in a mansion in Connecticut. There were some kids like him at my high school, white boys who didn't believe they had any culture of their own so they liked to appropriate the cultures of other peoples, whose backgrounds were filled with much more struggle and strife than theirs. Hudson's sob story—because everyone has to have one on these shows— was that no one took him seriously as a rapper because he was rich and hadn't had much hardship in his life. Based on the snippets of his rapping shown on *Great Lady Catch!*, I knew the issue was really one of utter lack of talent, not the fact that he was rich and white and privileged. He was no Eminem. He wasn't even Macklemore.

So Tess went away to try to win H-Plummy's heart, and I kept going to school and working at Galaville Orchards. Elaine stopped by every evening to make sure I was still, in fact, alive. Sometimes she brought food, dense, cheesy casseroles, but I threw them away because I found a ferret hair in the first casserole she brought over. It was quiet at home without Tess, who was always there after I returned from school or work. I wondered for the first time whether Tess had taken the job at The Corvid because it worked with my school schedule. Now, of course, I didn't need anyone home with me after school, but when I was younger, even though I was capable of making my own after-school snack, I liked having Tess home, cutting up an apple for me, slathering each slice with peanut butter, handing me my apple slices on a plate and asking how my day went.

I got to talk to Tess on the phone every few days. The contestants weren't allowed to have their own cell phones, but the few young mothers (who would inevitably be kept around for a few weeks so H-Plummy wouldn't seem completely cold-hearted for cutting the mothers immediately, but what twenty-eight-year-old man wants a ready-made family and the baggage of another man's child?) were allowed to call home and speak to their children, and because Tess was my legal guardian, we got to talk, too. But she couldn't say very much because there would always be a handler in the room with her, so mostly she asked questions about my day and was elusive with answering my questions about what she was up to.

"Is he as much of a goober as I think he is?" I asked the first time we got to talk.

"We haven't talked much one-on-one," she said. "But he seems nice."

"The crossing guard is nice. One of Elaine's ferrets is nice. Nice isn't worth much."

"All right, Benny," Tess said. "I'm calling just to check and make sure you're OK."

"I'm OK," I said. "I'm fine. It's pretty great having the run of the house. How many girls do you have to share a bathroom with?"

"All right," she said again. "That's all I needed to know. I just need to know that you're OK. And you have the number to call in case you need me, right?"

"I'm fine," I said. "You just go and fall in love with H-Plummy, and then we'll have his rich family buy us things. That's the plan, right?"

"I'm glad you're doing OK," said Tess. "I'll call again when I can." And then she was gone, even though I hadn't said good-bye yet.

I waited by the home phone each night to see if Tess would call, and I kept checking my cell to see if I'd missed a message, but she didn't call for three nights, and I wondered if she was having a great time and had forgotten about me. Even though Hudson was a loser of epic proportions, the other girls were probably fun, and Tess could be having the time of her life without me. Tess didn't have many friends in Galaville. She was smart in high school, and she hung out with the other smart girls. And these girls were long gone. Everyone knew Galaville was a dead-end town, and if you had more than two brain cells, you got out. If you didn't want to go too far, there were some colleges near Albany, and if you wanted to get out and never look back, you kept driving until New York state was far behind you in the rearview mirror. The people—besides Ricky—that Tess spent the most time with in the last few years were the other maids from The Corvid, but most of them were older, complained incessantly about sore backs and cracked skin on their hands, or they were from other countries and barely spoke English. Sometimes there were some younger girls who worked at the motel for a few months, but it was hard work, and if other opportunities came up, these girls would jump on them. I thought about Tess living in a mansion in L.A. with all the other contestants, and I thought how this might be her idea of heaven. She could talk to these other girls about things I didn't care about—makeup and hair products and women's magazines—and it would be like a three-week slumber party. It didn't even matter if she liked Hudson or not—it was just an escape from life at The Corvid and life at home with me.

When Tess finally called again, her voice sounded pinched, embarrassed. "I need a favor," she said.

"Do you need me to send you something?" I asked. She'd packed nearly the entire contents of her closet before she left for California. She'd also packed eight cocktail dresses for the champagne ceremonies, during which each contestant who was being asked to stay was offered a glass of champagne. (There were theories online about how the contestants the star liked the most were offered the bubbliest flutes of champagne, but I was unsure if there was validity to those theories.) We, of course, did not have money for cocktail dresses, but Ricky's older sister had done the pageant circuit for a few years when she was in high school, and there were dresses left in a closet at their parents' home, and she'd said Tess could have them. I knew Tess contacted Ricky's sister directly, so she wouldn't have to go through Ricky because she didn't want to tell him she was going to be a contestant on *Great Catch!* The dresses were all a little short for Tess since she was taller than Ricky's sister, but they'd have to do. They were also about fifteen years out-of-date, but maybe they were so out-of-date they were coming back into fashion.

"I need you to write me something," Tess said. "A poem."

I know I said Tess was smart, but she was more a science and math person, and I was more of a reading and writing person. Put our brains together, and we'd be a genius. I was smart enough to get As in math and science classes, but I was never going to break a mathematical code. And Tess could write her five-paragraph essays and identify literary terms, but ask her to do something creative like write a poem, and she'd have trouble.

"Why do you need a poem?" I said.

"Well, sort of a poem. It's more like a rap."

"You need *me* to write you a rap?"

"Hudson and I have been getting along. We had a one-on-one date. And he wrote me a rap, and the producers were thinking I could write one for him for our next one-on-one. They have one written, but I thought you could do a lot better."

"Can I hear it?" I said. "The one they wrote for you?"

"Oh, I don't know," she said.

"If you rap it for me, I'll write you a rap."

"I'll *read* it to you. I'm not rapping it for you."

"But they're going to make you rap, aren't they? There's no way they'll let you just read a poem as if you're reciting Emily Dickinson."

"I'll read it to you. Take it or leave it."

"Take it."

I heard Tess sigh, then I heard the sound of unfolding paper. "OK," she said. "Here it is:

Yo, Hudson Plum
I ain't dumb
Heard you like like me
And I like like you too
Got all the feels over you
My champagne flute flows over
I'm luckier than a four-leaf clover
I'm luck luck luck-eeeee
'Cause I love this love between you and me
Yo, Hudson, when you gonna
Get down on one knee?"

"I might vomit," I said. "Suddenly I'm feeling extremely queasy."

"I *know*," she said. "And I know you can do better."

"That's not really a compliment."

"Look," Tess said, her voice low. "This will help me advance. It'll give me a story line, make me a front-runner. Could you write me something that's not totally embarrassing?"

"I can write you a sonnet," I said. "Let me know if you'd prefer Shakespearean or Petrarchan. How you choose to deliver it is up to you, but I would highly suggest not rapping. All anyone is saying about you online right now is that you're beautiful. You don't want to become a joke once the episode airs."

"I know," said Tess. "Of course I know that." She sighed then said, "I miss you, Benny."

I waited a few seconds without answering, and then Tess said, "Benny? You there? Hello?"

"I'm here," I said. "Of course I'm here. Where else would I go?"

The next day, Ricky came into the orchard store during his lunch hour. He had grease all over his gray jumpsuit, black streaks on his face. He took off his baseball cap, as if he were entering a church. I hadn't seen him in over two months, since he and Tess broke up. He looked tired and older, and the skin on his forehead where the baseball cap had covered it was a few shades lighter than the rest of his face.

"I'm here for doughnuts," he said, before I even said hello. "A dozen."

"We only have three left," I said. "There was a big group on a school field trip that passed through earlier. They bought the rest."

"I'll take the three then," said Ricky. "I was going to get a dozen for the guys at the shop."

"Did you screw up? If you screwed up, you can't cut up the doughnuts into quarters and make people share them."

"Why would you say that, Benny?" He rubbed his hand across his forehead and left another dark streak. "Why would you assume I screwed up?"

"It's just that people don't usually go around buying doughnuts to give away unless they screwed up. If you can wait awhile, I can make more. It'll take a few minutes for the oil to get hot enough."

"I've gotta get back. I'll just take the three."

"Will you get in trouble if you're a little late? Would you get fired?"

"I'm kind of in charge nowadays."

"You are?"

"Tess didn't tell you?"

I shook my head.

"Mike had a stroke, so I've been in charge for a few months."

"Is Mike going to be OK?" Mike owned Rooney's Tires and Repairs, had worked there most of his life. He'd inherited the shop from his father. He wasn't that old, maybe fifty, not old enough to stop working.

"He's doing rehab now. Physical therapy. But I don't know. I'm trying not to think too far into the future."

"Do you make the guys call you Boss Man?" I said.

"I make them call me Sir. And they have to bow when I walk in the room."

He smiled, seemed to relax a little, and felt more like the Ricky I used to know. "Hey, so, have you heard from Tess? I heard from my sister she's out in California." He said it casually, as if he didn't really care whether I'd heard from her or not, but then I realized the whole reason he came into the shop was so he could ask about Tess. The doughnuts were just an excuse.

"Yeah, she calls every few days."

"So is she head over heels in love with H-Plummy yet?" He said it like a joke, but I could tell all of it bothered him.

"He wrote her a rap. That's all I know," I said. Ricky looked sad, so I added, "I don't think she really likes him."

"Right," he said. He put his hat back on his head, adjusted it so the brim was straight. "So the doughnuts? I'll take those three."

I packed them up for him in a white paper bag and handed him his change.

"See you around, Benny," he said, and he left, and I wondered when I'd see him next. He'd been such a part of our lives for four years, and now we never saw each other. The only time I'd ever see him now was if we accidentally ran into each other.

All afternoon, I made more doughnuts, even though Mrs. Crenshaw, who ran the orchard store, told me to slow down, said we weren't going to sell them all before closing. If there were doughnuts left at the end of the day, I was allowed to take them home, but usually there were only one or two left over, and I'd eat them on my walk back to the house. But I wanted there to be a lot of extras that day because I wanted to go to the repair shop with a dozen doughnuts. They'd give me an excuse to hang out with Ricky.

After work, I walked to Rooney's Tires and Repairs with a large paper sack filled with fresh doughnuts. The warm grease from the doughnuts seeped through the paper, and I wished I'd taken a stack of napkins with me too. My phone rang as I was walking, and I had to stop, sit on a big rock by the side of the road, and set the greasy bag on the ground.

"Do you have the rap written? Or the poem or whatever you want to call it?" said Tess.

"You only asked me to write it three days ago. I have homework to do. And I'm working every afternoon this week," I said. "I'm not some poem-on-demand service."

Tess sighed. "Since we talked, there's been another champagne ceremony. The producers said I have to present him with a rap before the next one. And that's in two days. If I don't share a rap with him, I might not make it to the overnight dates."

"Are you going to have sex with him during the overnight date?" I asked.

"That's none of your business, Benny," she said.

"Even if you don't, the show will insinuate that you did," I said. They always showed the contestants the next morning in bed, the sheets rumpled, their hair askew.

114

"I know what I signed up for," Tess said.

"It's just that if you have sex with him, and you're only really interested in all of this for money and opportunities, you're kind of prostituting yourself."

Tess was silent for a few moments, then said, "I told you, I know what I'm getting into. And I know that all of this can make things better for us."

"If I write you a poem, does that make me an accessory to prostitution?"

"Don't be this way, Benny."

"Guess who came to the orchard shop today?"

"I don't know. Who? Someone famous?"

"The only famous person who ever came to Galaville offed himself."

"I know you're mad that I'm away, but don't act like this. I'll stop calling if you do. I'll just call Elaine and ask her if you're doing OK."

And that was the threat that made me change my tune. I didn't want Tess to stop calling. "I'm doing OK," I said. "I'm cooking real things for dinner, not just microwaving stuff. I made chicken piccata last night. I found the recipe online."

"That's good," said Tess. "That's really good. So who was it?"

"Who was what?"

"Who came into the store?" she said.

"Oh, just Mr. Gallagher. He bought some apple butter." I didn't want to talk about Ricky right then, so I made up the lie about Mr. Gallagher coming to the store. I thought it might upset Tess to know Ricky was asking about her, and it might upset her more to know I was on my way to see him with a sack of doughnuts. Mr. Gallagher taught ninth and tenth grade English, and both Tess and I had been in his class. We'd both loved him for his enthusiastic readings of poetry, even though the other kids made fun of him behind his back. "Do I dare to eat a peach?" other kids belted in the cafeteria, holding up fruit they'd pulled out of their brown paper lunch bags, then snorting with laughter at their imitations of Mr. Gallagher, but both Tess and I thought it was nice that Mr. Gallagher cared so much about poetry that when he read it, his eyes closed and he had all the words memorized, like a favorite song.

"He was a good teacher," said Tess. "You know he e-mailed me a couple of times in the past few years, encouraging me to apply to college?"

I hadn't known that. "Did you?" I asked.

Tess laughed. "Of course not," she said. "How?"

There was so much packed into that one-word question, so much about how it would ever be possible for Tess to afford college, go to college, and so much unsaid about how my presence, my always-present presence, stood in the way of Tess's moving forward.

"I'll get you that poem by tomorrow, OK?" I said. I wanted to give Tess something, though I knew even a mediocre poem would signal to Hudson that Tess had fallen for him so much that she was moved to write verse. But I wanted to write her a poem that would stun both Mr. Gallagher and H-Plummy with its depth and insight into the human condition. I wanted Tess to win the show and be happy and never have to work again, and I wanted her to lose and come home. I wanted a lot of things, most of them in opposition to each other.

When I got to Rooney's, there were no customers in the waiting area and only Bo was at one of the computers, logging something from a stack of receipts.

"Benny! Long time no see," he said. He had cinnamon sugar in his goatee, and the empty bag of doughnuts was next to him. Some afternoons, Tess and I would visit Ricky in the shop, so everyone there knew us. I hadn't been to the shop since Ricky and Tess broke up, so that's why I didn't know about Mike's stroke.

"Is Ricky here?" I asked.

"Back office," said Bo, pointing backward with his thumb. "Go ahead."

I made my way through the door with the EMPLOYEES ONLY sign on it, and walked down the hallway leading to the office. Ricky was watching something on the computer, completely absorbed. Behind him there was a calendar with a photograph of a piglet on it It hadn't been there the last time I'd been back there. When I got closer, I saw that it was from the Humane Society, the kind of gift you get for donating money, and I wondered if Ricky gave money to them. I got all the way to the doorway without Ricky noticing me, and then when he did, he quickly minimized his browser, and I wondered if he was watching porn. Was that what the men who worked at Rooney's did when it wasn't busy?

"Hey, hey, Benny!" he said, sounding nervous and guilty.

"Are you watching porn?" I asked, as I made my way around to the back of the desk. "Did Tess break up with you because you're addicted to porn?"

Ricky looked at me as if I were insane, and clicked on his browser so it filled the entire screen. He was watching a clip from *Finding the Heart of America* on YouTube. His eyes looked teary, and I felt bad for accusing him of watching porn. "I brought you doughnuts. A dozen, like you wanted before." I held them up in front of his face.

"Everyone's gone home already," he said. "Except for Bo, and he ate the three I bought earlier."

"You can leave them out for the morning, even though they'll be a little stale." I didn't care if they got stale, though; the doughnuts were just my way of saying "I miss you, I wish you still came around the house, I want to watch videos of raccoons with you, I know it's weird if we hang out now, but I wish we could."

I put the bag on top of a metal filing cabinet. I knew there would be a grease spot left on the cabinet, but there was nothing I could do about it.

"You ever watch this show?" Ricky asked, clicking Play on the video and then muting the volume. I pulled up a folding chair next to him, and we watched Franco Tyrone in the home kitchen of an old woman in West Virginia. Franco and the woman poked wooden spoons into a big pot of some sort of brown meat boiling on the stove.

"Yeah," I said. I'd been a fan of Franco's since the show started, and when I'd learned Franco was coming to Galaville, I'd rewatched a lot of episodes, studied them, watched the way he was with people, the way he could make even the humblest place or person seem like something special and worth filming.

We were quiet for a little while and watched the silent action on the screen, an episode I hadn't seen before, where Franco and the old woman chopped an onion and then a carrot and tilted the chopping board so the onion and carrot went into the pot with the boiling meat. And then I saw the title of the episode, and said, "Oh," and pointed to the screen. "A Raccoon in Every Pot."

"I know," said Ricky, and then he started to weep, and I looked around for tissues and couldn't find any, so I just sat there and did nothing and kept my eyes on the screen, where Franco was now dancing in the kitchen with the old woman, lifting one arm and spinning her, and she was delighted and had her eyes closed, and I thought about Mr. Gallagher reading us "The Love Song of J. Alfred Prufrock" and how there were so few moments in life when you're so happy, so satisfied that you want to close your eyes and smile. Ricky tried to make a joke of it, said, "Not the kind of raccoon video we usually watch, huh?" and I shook my head.

"Are you sad they're eating a raccoon? Is that what's going on?" I said, even though I knew his sadness was about something bigger.

"Did Tess tell you I was addicted to porn?" he said. "Is that why she said we broke up? Because that's not true at all."

I shook my head. "You just looked so guilty when I stepped into the office. Like I caught you doing something you shouldn't be doing."

"I should have been working on the books, but I can't stop watching *Finding the Heart of America*. I don't know why. Like it's going to give me any answers about anything."

"About Franco?"

First Ricky shook his head, then he nodded, said, "Maybe. I mean, how can you care so much about people, act like everyone is important, act like everyone's story is a good one, and then do this? Doesn't this mean he thought his own story was worthless? Do you know he has a daughter? She's twelve."

"I didn't know that," I said. It was awful, this left-behind daughter. Ricky kept crying, and I got up and went to the bathroom down the hall, came back with a stack of rough brown paper towels, handed a few to Ricky, and put the rest under the bag of doughnuts. He wiped his eyes and face with the paper towels, crumpled them, and dropped them into a wastebasket. He sniffled hard, as if he was trying to suck all his sadness back into his skull.

"Why'd you break up?" I asked.

"Tess never told you?"

"I guess there are a lot of things she doesn't tell me."

"I asked her to marry me."

I was stunned. If I were a cartoon character, my eyeballs would have popped out of my head. Why had Tess kept this information from me? Why would she consider a proposal grounds for a breakup? If Mr. Gallagher were here, he'd say the fact that Tess was filming *Great Catch!* with the hope of being proposed to shortly after turning down Ricky's proposal was an example of irony. "She broke up with you because you proposed?"

Ricky shrugged. "She said she wanted something more than Galaville, and wanted to know if I'd ever leave. I told her I have a good job here, my family's here. My life is here, you know? And, look," he said, pointing to the screen, "just because someone leaves home, travels, sees the world, it doesn't mean they end up happy."

I nodded. I always thought I would be the one who'd get out, and I'd always imagined Tess would be here, ready to welcome me home anytime I wished. I had pictured myself older, coming home to visit, and Tess cutting up an apple for me, spreading peanut butter on every slice, asking me to tell her about my exciting life. Tess was an inextricable part of my conception of Galaville, and maybe it was that way for Ricky too. Sure, she'd come back for a while, try to make things work, but Galaville would feel different, small and stifling. I knew how these things went, how the people cast on reality shows started dreaming big, started wanting different lives from the ones they'd lived.

"I just can't stop thinking about how she was the one to find him," Ricky said, gesturing to the screen. "That kind of thing can ruin a person, haunt them, you know? Do you think that's why she had to get away?"

"Maybe," I said. And maybe finding Franco had been the catalyst for Tess's departure, had given her the opportunity to leave, but Tess's turning down Ricky's proposal meant she'd never wanted to stay here forever.

"I just wish he'd never done it. For a lot of reasons," Ricky said, and I nodded.

"Hey!" shouted Bo from the end of the hall. "I'm closing up!"

"Thanks, man," said Ricky. "We're heading out soon."

On the computer, another clip of Franco played. He was in Maine now, sitting at a picnic table near the ocean wearing dark sunglasses and eating a lobster roll, his gray curls blowing wildly in the breeze coming in from the water. Franco was sitting across from a younger man, who wore a barn coat and pointed out toward the ocean as he, too, ate a lobster roll. Then the screen went black and in the next scene Franco and the man in the barn coat were in a lighthouse. The man showed Franco the switch that turned on the beacon that beamed from top. Then they climbed the spiral stairs and went out onto the catwalk outside the lighthouse. The volume on the computer was still off, and we listened to Bo up front shutting down and locking up while Franco talked to the man in the barn coat. Ricky got up and took the sack of doughnuts off the filing cabinet, unfolded the bag, tilted it toward me, and I took one. On the screen, Franco stood on the catwalk, one hand shading his face from the sun, the other pointing at the horizon line, where water met sky. We sat silently in the back office as Bo shouted good-bye, ate the doughnuts, and watched Franco explore the big, wide world.

Nominated by The Southern Review

THE LOSS OF HEAVEN

fiction by DANTIEL W. MONIZ

from THE PARIS REVIEW

He weighed 210 pounds buck-ass naked; 217 in his leather jacket and boots, which he wore that crisp March evening to the bar along with a gold stud pin in his lapel. It was shaped like a spade, a gift from his wife when they were young, once she'd discovered how much he liked expensive-looking things. He wasn't handsome but his light skin, wavy hair, the polished gleam of his fingernails, and the bills pressed tightly in his wallet almost made him so. As he entered the Albatross he stopped just in the doorway, imagining his body filling the width of the frame, giving the occupants time to look and wonder who he was. The jukebox played the Temptations and threw colored light onto his face, and a couple of women at a nearby table glanced up from their pastel martinis, one sucking the cherry from her drink. Satisfied, he walked in. Hilda swept a dishtowel along the bar top, looking bored, smiling out from under her bangs at a trio of men at the counter, a pretty laugh spilling from deep within her chest. He chose a stool in the middle, with an unobstructed view of her.

"Hey there, Fred. Jim and Coke?" she asked, the start to their ritual. Her low, drawling voice pulled something tight inside his stomach.

"You know it, kid," he said. He slid his jacket off and draped it on the back of his chair as she filled a rocks glass with three large cubes of ice, so big they could sit in a drink a while before melting. In the few months since he'd met her, Fred often imagined tracing one down the contours of Hilda's spine, recording an exact ratio of body heat and melting points.

"No lime," Hilda sang, placing his drink in front of him on a square of white napkin she'd sprinkled with salt. "Start a tab?"

120

"I'll pay as I go," Fred told her, as he always did, and placed a five on the bar. Hilda disappeared the bill into her apron in one discreet, fluid motion. She never brought him change.

The Albatross hosted a quiet crowd on Tuesday evenings, a mix of suits, day laborers, and truckers with three-day scruff. The bar's aesthetic lingered somewhere between a dive and a lounge, sporting wood details and burgundy upholstery along with burger specials and streetwise games of pool on red felt in the back. Older gentlemen sat at tables in dim corners sipping rye whiskey, talking with other men about matters only other men would understand; some kept their hands high on the thighs of women who were not their wives—girls, really—who did not yet keep house and so still had inexact ideas about how the world worked and all of the ways in which they could be disappointed. The girls possessed a malleability, a willingness to be impressed, their cheeks, soft and new, flushing at even the most trivial compliments. These were sweet, bygone qualities the men wished to bottle and harbor for themselves.

Fred took a swig from his drink and watched the young bartender over the rim of his glass. He liked the healthy way her hips moved under her black uniform skirt; the deep brown of her skin; the way she talked to other men, her oiled hair sweeping forward as she leaned over the bar to take their orders, a grin under every word. He liked that she knew what a two-dollar-a-drink tip was worth, and that his glass was never empty. Hilda smiled every time she made him a new one, as if they shared a secret—as if she *knew* him—and sometimes her fingers would linger over his, creating heft and heat.

"Still good, Fred?" she'd ask from time to time, letting him watch her. Making sure he never lost sight of his importance. He was good. Fred lifted his glass to her, the bite of bourbon still glowing in his throat. "To beautiful friendships," he said, and when Hilda laughed, even that seemed just for him.

Fred spent thirty dollars at the bar before heading home. He kept the radio off, preferring just the sound of his tires crunching gravel on the road, the shake of the V6 under his seat. He'd bought the '85 Buick Regal brand-new—metallic blue with a racing stripe—as a present to himself after he'd turned fifty-two. When he'd driven it into the yard six years ago, his wife had laughed to see it, asking if this was the Band-Aid for his midlife event. "What's next," she'd hawed, "a mistress?" Fred had been offended. He wasn't old, not yet, and he deserved nice things. Now, he caught his reflection in the rearview mirror.

"You're still the man," Fred told himself, and watched his eyes to see if he believed it.

Gloria was on the porch in her nightgown when he pulled up, a cigarette dangling between her elegant fingers. Fred cut the engine and sat for a moment, flexing his fists around the steering wheel, trying to calm himself. It wouldn't do to start a fight. He got out of the car and hauled himself up the porch steps, leaning against the railing next to her. He studied her profile, the tufts of newly grown-out hair like shredded brown cotton, the petite ears and dished forehead, her angled jaw. The small triangle of skin beginning to loosen beneath her chin. The sheer nightgown slipped from one burnished shoulder and piled on the floorboards around her crossed ankles; it swallowed her. She looked like a child dressed in her mother's clothes, and in that moment, he loved her terribly.

The porch light glowed orange and flickered with dazed moths as Gloria let him watch her. She brought the cigarette to her mouth and took a long smooth drag. Fred imagined the smoke swirling down into the cage of her chest, every bone illuminated, turning what was left of her lungs the color of stone. She finally turned to face him, her eyes wet and penetrating in their dark hollows, and he remembered when he used to call her his little bit of Glory. He didn't know when he'd stopped.

"How was today?" he asked.

"Fine as can be expected," Gloria said, flicking ash.

"And the doctor? What did he say?"

"Fred." She dropped his name like an anchor. "It's fine."

He started to speak, then changed his mind. He wanted to shake her, grip hard into those bird-boned shoulders until he felt them snap, but only a monster would treat a dying person like that. Instead he held out his hand. "Let's go inside."

She smiled at him, but didn't move.

"I'm sitting with the night," she said, and looked over the yard toward the low edge of the horizon, still crimson from the parting sun. Fred's shoulders sagged under the weight of sudden gravities: that she preferred her cigarettes and her own company to him. That she had even started smoking the damn things again in the first place, and now wasn't troubling to hide it.

When, two months ago, her oncologist had hustled them into his office with his grim face and rattled off his list of bloated, ugly words—recurrence, metastasis, inoperable—Gloria had taken it, dry-eyed, her head bobbing as if she too were a doctor, comfortable with the impersonal language of death. He recommended immediate and aggressive treatment and Fred had coughed into his hand. "What are our chances here?" he'd asked, and ignored how Gloria's head whipped when he said it. "We're not worried about the cost." He wouldn't let this white man or anyone else think they were poor. The doctor cleared his throat, said, "Studies suggest that patients in this stage, with targeted therapies prescribed in conjunction with homeopathic remedies, and rigorous adherence to the plan—" and Gloria stood up and left.

Fred found her ten minutes later posted up at the car with her purse on the hood, pretending to pick dirt from her fingernails. As he unlocked the door, he'd given her a questioning look and she'd just shaken her head. Fred reflected that only *she* could look annoyed after hearing a scary verdict like that. Only she could be so rankled. The first time they'd gotten this news last winter, she'd climbed back into the car and bawled the entire drive home and he'd had to carry her into the house. Fred waited for this delayed reaction, but she didn't cry. Gloria said, looking out the window at the street going past, "None of that had anything to do with me. All that was, was two men talking in a room."

The reaction did come later that night as they ate dinner—smothered pork chops and mashed potatoes and peas—but not the one he had expected.

"I'm not doing the chemo. I'm done."

"Baby, you're in shock," he'd told her, because he certainly was.

It had been hard on her—the chemo, the radiation, each feeling more like additional sickness than any kind of treatment. They'd cut Gloria open and removed a lobe of lung, and now a long pillowy scar curved under her right breast, raised several centimeters from the surrounding skin. She said it was her last-minute souvenir, like *Haha, what'd you bring me back from Cancerland?* Forgetting the scar, the loss of her hair, the sores in her mouth, and the dizzy nausea and fear of it all, they'd beaten the cancer back. And just as they were celebrating, finally crawling toward something like normal—this. It felt like the worst betrayal, but Fred knew if they did it once, they could do it again. He repeated that, financially, they were good, just in case she felt guilty over how much killing the cancer cost. Fred was a provider—always had been, always would be—a retired car-hauler who had worked since the age of thirteen. Above all else, he was a man, and he took care of his own. No one could say any different.

Gloria set down her cutlery and rubbed the place between her eyes, and when she spoke again, she looked tired and patient, like some kind of martyr; he remembered feeling irked by it. "Fred, you're not hearing me. I said I'm done. If it's my time, it's my time."

He hadn't believed her then, but shortly after that night, he began to smell smoke on Gloria's clothes. At first she spun the usual line, it was others smoking near her, but then he'd found a half-full pack on the floorboard of her backseat. She'd been in the living room reading when he confronted her, glasses sliding down her nose. He flung the pack at her and it hit her in the chest.

"I guess you've made up your mind," he growled.

"To live the way I want to live?"

"You mean die the way you want to die!" and she'd said, "What's the difference?"

She was punishing him, he knew, and Fred's stomach seized at the thought of all the things Gloria didn't say, that she kept at bay with such inconsequentialities as "fine" in answer to his nearly every question. Fred was certain that she somehow saw everything about him. That this cancer, as it ate at her body, had imparted in her a kind of godly knowing in exchange for what it took. When Gloria looked at him, Fred could feel his wrongdoings bathed in light: his dalliances with other women, that he had denied Gloria children because he hadn't wanted to be encumbered by their need. She knew, too, about the mad money tucked away in a secret compartment in his wallet; about the disgust he'd felt upon first finding out about the tumor, at the weakness of her body; his resentment at swapping roles, when she was nine years younger and supposed to take care of him. And the worst possibility—that Gloria could taste his absolute terror at being left alone, the bitter tinge of his shame dissolving on her tongue. She knew he would be a coward without her, and he believed a part of her enjoyed the thought.

Fred went inside alone, trailing through the three-bedroom, split-model house that they owned outright and which she often said was too large for just the two of them. She thought he'd bought it because he'd wanted a family, but he liked the acre of land it sat on and the idea that he could own it. Over the years, he'd let Gloria fill the rooms with art and plants and rare books, since she couldn't fill them with children. In their bedroom, he removed his boots and leather jacket. He left his oxford and undershirt on a growing pile of clothes Gloria had yet to wash, then stepped out of his pants and double-checked that the ten crisp bills in the hidden pocket of his wallet—all hundreds—were still there. He took the bills out and ran his fingers along their creased edges, measured their weight on his palm. When he was younger and his older sisters in dating range, he'd listen to their mother caution her daughters any time they went out with a new boy, giving them money to hide in their socks. He'd never seen either of his parents so free with cash, but when it was his turn to court, his father merely said, "Don't get them pregnant." Fred never got the lecture or the mad money, and felt left out. What if he needed to escape?

Holding the money gave Fred a sort of chill, a pulse of irrational pleasure at the thought of getting into his Buick and driving away. Maybe he'd leave the swampy stench of Florida and go back home to the Tennessee foothills to live in the house his father had built. Maybe Hilda would be with him, riding shotgun, her luxurious, heavy hair whipping in the breeze. He pictured her red-lipped smile, her hand on his arm—and wasn't that the most coveted thing? A pretty woman content to be near you?

Standing in only his underwear and socks, he put the bills away and searched through Gloria's side table, as he did whenever his own fantasies made him paranoid. He found nothing—no secret money, no getaway plan, just an unopened pack of Virginia Slims. Her little sticks of spite. He would've liked to trash them, but it wouldn't matter. There was always another pack. Fred closed the drawer, then walked to the bathroom to remove the rest of his clothes. Naked, he stood upon his scale and closed his eyes. When he opened them, he found he still weighed the same, even with all of his transgressions nestled snugly inside him.

Over the next few days, Fred had restless dreams: Gloria hanging blood-spattered sheets to dry in the yard; Gloria standing before him against an empty sky; Gloria, gone, and the goneness blotting out the world. One night he woke suddenly, startled and lost, and flung out a hand to feel her beside him, her slight frame set sideways, precise as a blade. He tugged her closer and pressed himself against her, wishing he could push her inside of his body and make them one again. Gloria responded, pressing back, and they fumbled from their nightclothes. Bare, her bones bumping at him, the reality of her smacked into the room; she seemed proud of this ugliness, of what she was becoming. She latched her lips to his and Fred felt he could taste the sickness in her mouth.

Repulsion shuddered through him, somehow spurring him on, and he entered her, overcome by the expanse of his love and disgust. He bucked beneath her, filling his fingers with the memory of her prior flesh. He moaned, "Glory, Glory, Glory," but the past didn't come. There was only this new wife, skeletal and knowing, grinning down at him in the dark with what seemed like contempt.

Gloria's panting turned to wheezing and she slid off him, coughing viciously, her body crumpled on the sheets. When she finally stopped and sat up, wiping her mouth with the back of her hand, Fred asked, "Any blood?" She didn't answer, but riffled through her side table for her cigarettes. His lip curled without his consent. "You're really begging for that grave."

Gloria made a sound, though whether a laugh or a cough, he couldn't tell. She dressed slowly, with her back to him, her spine pronounced in even that sparse light, but when she walked to his side of the bed, her expression was muzzy. Fred wanted to turn on the lamp and recognize her, his Glory, but her eyes kept him fixed.

"You know, the closer I get to it, the clearer I see," she said, and left to blow blue smoke at the moon. Fred lay there, awake through the night, wondering why she didn't seem afraid and if she still loved him, but he was too afraid himself to ask.

He started closing the Albatross down on Tuesdays, staying later to spend time in Hilda's validating company, to bask in the beer-and-vanilla scent radiating from her skin. He liked to consider that he was personally responsible for keeping her lights on, for putting food on her table. That he, in some ways, was responsible for the girl herself—Hilda's dependable goodness a reflection of his own.

Returning home from the barber on a Friday in mid-April, Fred heard the telephone ringing on the other side of the door while he dug for his keys. Two times. Three. He scowled as he stuck his key into the lock and hurried inside, tripping over his feet, cursing as he scuffed his recently polished shoe. He could sense Gloria moving at the back of the house and wondered why she didn't pick it up. He answered, breathless, on the fifth ring.

"Mr. Moore." The usually clipped voice of Gloria's oncologist sighed through the line. He sounded relieved. "I was hoping to reach you." A band of muscle in Fred's chest tightened.

"How can I help you, doctor?"

126

"Your wife was in today for a checkup, and I'm afraid she threatened to find another physician. As you know, I was highly against the decision to forgo radiation." He went on about his professional concerns, his responsibilities to the Hippocratic oath, his reputation. He told Fred that Gloria's treatment was a matter of limited time. Maybe only months. "I know I don't get a say, but I was hoping *you* might still convince her. Mr. Moore?"

"Yes, I'm here," Fred said, eyes sliding again down the hallway to their bedroom. "I'm sorry, doctor, I—can I call you back?"

He hung up and stood for a moment with his hand on the receiver, hoping, if he waited long enough, it would ring again and the verdict would be different. When it didn't, he trudged back to their bedroom. Gloria was folding clothes neatly into her overnight bag, a cheerful pink suede thing that didn't match the energy in the room.

"That was Dr. Howard, wasn't it? Shithead. You know he has me listed as 'noncompliant' in my files?" She tucked a couple of dresses into the bag. They were so small, like doll's clothes, and he wondered at how she could even be real. "I'm getting rid of him. I need a doctor who's on my side."

"How can anyone be on the side of something so crazy?" Fred said. She didn't need to punish him. Didn't the sinner always punish himself? He felt a stinging warmth gather at the corner of his eyes, and he hated her for it.

"Fred, you don't know how it was for me the first time."

"I was there! I was right beside—"

"You. Don't. *Know.*" Gloria came around to him and put her hands in his, but his fingers remained limp. "Do you want me like that? Dead alive?"

He just wanted her, full stop, but he wouldn't say it, couldn't give her the pleasure of seeing him break. He gestured to the bag.

"You're leaving." He felt cheated. There had been no sign; he'd looked for it. He wanted to ask her where her money was hidden.

"Just going to visit my ma and sister for a few days," she said. "While I still can. While they can recognize me." She had a flight tomorrow afternoon.

Fred had a strong desire to knock the bag from the bed. To scatter the clothes, to burn them, to chain her to the bedposts, and Gloria saw.

"You want me to stay, just say it."

Fred saw himself sinking to his knees, as he'd done all those years ago when he proposed. He could wrap his arms around her, rest his face against her hip. He could give her what she wanted, whisper *Don't go* into that stark, hollow place. But his pride, his fear, kept him from it. He cleared his throat. Stepped back from her. He asked if she needed a ride.

Without her hair, Gloria's feelings sat plainly on her face. She stared into Fred's eyes until he had to turn away. She brushed a few spare hairs from his forehead that the barber had missed and thanked him for his offer. She continued to pack. Fred smiled to stay standing. "When you get back, let's drive to St. Pete. Spend a weekend on the Gulf. How'd that be?"

"I'd like that," Gloria said, but there was no pleasure in the words.

It was busy at the Albatross the next evening, a noise and bustle Fred wasn't used to and wasn't sure he liked. After he'd dropped Gloria at JAX for her 2 PM flight, he'd driven around the city, aimless and sorry, until he ended up in the parking lot of the bar, blinking at the squat little building nestled against the sun as if he didn't understand how he'd come to be there, and then understanding all too perfectly that he had nowhere else to go. Shamefaced, he sat in the car with the windows down until, at 4 PM, he'd seen Hilda stroll in; then he waited half an hour more. Fred entered the bar nervously, his fingers beating at his thighs through his pockets. Paused in the doorway, he thought he might leave but then Hilda saw him. "Look at you! Gracing us with your presence on a Saturday!" she'd called, and he'd felt immediately reassured. He was wanted here; *she* wanted him, and Fred regained his swagger. He withdrew his hands and grinned, feeling like the man he knew he was. "Jim and Coke?"

"You got it, kid." The jacket came off and Hilda brought him his drink, and for the first hour or so, everything felt the same. But now he was sitting shoulder to shoulder with a group of rowdy, younger-looking patrons, all swarming the bar for attention, and every other sip, someone jostled him, making him spill his drink. The Top 40 blasted from the jukebox—unfamiliar simpering over synthetic beats—and he watched people gyrating throughout the bar, as if any open space were a dance floor.

"It's like a dirty club in here," he'd scowled when Hilda finally appeared in front of him. His ice was a pile of chips in his near-empty glass. He didn't like this Hilda, skin glowing with sweat, hopped up from the rush and all the young bodies, and too busy to see after him.

128

"Saturdays," she said by way of explanation and—sloppily, Fred thought—fixed him another drink.

The big man sitting to Fred's right paid his tab and left, but before he could be grateful for the extra space, another body took his place. Fred, irritated and more lonesome than when he'd arrived, told himself he'd finish this drink quickly and then be out the door. He'd make sure to keep to Tuesdays from this point on, and he smiled to himself, already imagining how he'd jokingly berate Hilda for the poor quality of her service tonight, get her feeling just a little bad and eager to make up.

The new man tapped Fred's shoulder and Fred saw he wasn't a man at all, probably just old enough to be in the bar. He wore a white cap over a tapered cut, a green sweatshirt with a couple of holes in the collar, and a pair of black Dickies slung low on his hips like every other youngblood in the place. "Got the time?" the boy asked.

First, Fred pulled his comb from his shirt pocket and raked it back through his hair. Then he hitched up his sleeve to glance at his watch. It was gold-faced with large numbers, on an imitation leather strap. Most people thought it was a Rolex, but he'd never spend that kind of money to tell the time.

"Quarter to nine."

"Thanks," the boy said, then offered his hand. "Antonio. Well, friends call me Tony."

"Fred. Pleasure." He made sure to squeeze Tony's hand good and hard, and a look crossed the boy's face.

"My pops always said you could measure a man's integrity by his grip." Fred puffed himself up. "Your pops wasn't lying."

"Busy in here, right?" Tony said, turning to frown at Hilda, who still hadn't come for his order. Fred looked at her, too; she was down at the other end of the bar, laughing with one of the fry cooks as he handed her a basket of greasy onion rings. Her hand lingered on his arm.

"Downright shameful service," he said nastily, then to the boy, "What do you drink?"

"I don't know. Beer, I guess. A Bud?" and when Fred laughed, Tony asked, "What, that's too green?"

"Might be. What do you do, youngblood?"

Tony was enrolled in trade school to be a mechanic, which he knew was fruitful work. He said barely any of the kids his age even knew how to change a tire. Fred agreed that this was true and Tony asked, "What about you, sir?"

"Commercial car-hauler, thirty-five years." He didn't bother to mention he was retired.

Tony's eyebrows disappeared into the rim of his cap. "Wow, I can't believe it."

"What?" Fred said, ready to be affronted.

"My pops used to do that work. Those double-decker rigs?" When Fred nodded, he added, "That's real honest work. Skilled work."

The boy's respect warmed Fred like the bourbon. He could tell this one had been raised right; if he'd been a father, his son would have come out just the same. He decided he'd stay a little while longer. Fred signaled to Hilda with a piercing whistle that cut through the din of the room. She looked over her shoulder at him, her mouth parted prettily. The fry cook slunk back into the kitchen, where he belonged. "A drink for my friend. Two of these, on me," Fred said, raising his glass.

Hilda brought them both Jim and Cokes, her nose scrunched up like she had something to be mad about. "Get you anything else?"

Fred didn't look at her. He thumbed condensation from the side of his glass and wiped the finger along the edge of the bar. Then he threw a twenty down, letting his money speak for him.

They both ordered the burger special—fried onions, Muenster, garlic mayo—and as they ate and kept drinking, Tony asked a lot of questions. *Whereabouts are you from? How much did it cost for a car like that? A watch like that? A house like that?* The drunker Fred got, the looser his tongue. He told Tony he came from nothing. Not a dime to his family name. "And now I got that nice car. These nice clothes. I own land!" He slammed his glass down on the bar, the drink sloshing up the sides. "Most people don't understand upward mobility. Always got their hands out, asking for something. Not me! I take care of mine!" Several people glanced over, concerned or annoyed or amused.

Tony watched him, too, his eyes careful and bright. "Bet your missus is a knockout," he said and Fred's stomach lurched, thinking of Gloria, gone. He put his head in his hands and agreed that she was. Hilda came by with her dishrag, cutting her eyes, wiping around Fred's mess, and Tony angled closer to his ear. "Prettier than her, right?"

Fred snapped up to consider Hilda. If he put them together at the same age, Gloria would take the girl two to one. But Hilda had been good to him, barring tonight; they were friends! He wanted to show Tony that he still had a way. That he was still the man. He grabbed Hilda's wrist, pulling her toward him just as she was walking away.

"Don't run off," he slurred, trying to hold her eye. "Stay and meet my new friend."

Hilda laughed and tried to pull her arm from his grasp, but Fred gripped it tight. Her second laugh came out mechanical and strained. "Fred, you're hurting me."

"Just stay still a minute," he barked. Why didn't anyone ever stay?

"Fred. Let me go." The words plunked down, heavy between them. Fred studied her face and considered that she wasn't so pretty; it was just youth that made her special. He'd had a million just like her. Feeling superior in this conviction, he opened his hand and let her go, his expression snarled. The boy next to him looked on and heat flooded Fred's ears.

Fred watched Hilda scurry back to the end of the bar where the slinky fry cook again waited, posted up against the counter. She said something to him, rubbing her wrist, and the guy's dumb face swiveled in Fred's direction, his jaw tight. Fred downed the rest of his watery drink. "Yeah," he muttered to himself, "come try it, buddy." He stood abruptly and wrenched his jacket on.

"You won't stay for one more?" Tony knocked his own empty glass against the counter and Fred sneered. He'd played right into the boy's trap; he was just another nobody with his hand held out, and Fred had nothing to prove, not to him or anybody. He said to the boy, "Haven't I done enough for you?"

Fred strode from the bar, his anger a molten coil in his chest. The parking lot was quiet and dim. In this light, the building looked shoddy, unworthy of his business. He spat on the ground and vowed that he'd never come back. Fred reached the Buick and as he searched for his key in the dark, fighting through his inebriation and embarrassment, an arm looped around his neck; he dropped the key ring and his mind went blank. The arm flexed, and by the time Fred began to struggle, it had found a solid hold.

"You're hurting me," he gasped, surprised that it was true, but the grip continued to tighten across his windpipe until he felt his breath sucking distantly into his lungs like the pull of a stopped drain, slow and then slower. His vision grayed at the edges but sound sharpened— crickets whirring in the nearby grass, the highway's white noise. The steady puff of the man's breath. Fred grabbed at the arm, managing to turn his head and catch a glimpse of Tony's face furrowed in grim concentration before it—and everything else—faded into black.

He woke on the asphalt alone, his body twisted halfway underneath someone else's car. Where the Buick had been, there was only litter, an oil stain dark and spreading. His wallet lay splayed beside his cheek. Fred struggled up from the ground, his throat throbbing. He snatched up the wallet and searched through it, muttering, "No, no," as if the incantation would make this act undone. His license was there, all his credit cards, but the cash in the main pocket was missing. Fred closed his eyes before opening the secret compartment. *It's still here*, he hoped, but of course it wasn't. The mad money, his wedding ring, the Buick, gone. Tony had left the watch, not fooled after all. Thick with shame, Fred hobbled back inside.

"Call the police!" he shouted, and the bar quieted, all eyes turned to him. "I've been robbed!" Then, commotion. Several men went out to the parking lot, as if Tony might still be there; another led Fred to a stool at the bar, and the patrons cleared the way for him. A woman with a beehive updo and rhinestones affixed to her long, painted nails offered him her glass of water. "Haven't even sipped it," she said. Hilda, who had been pulling a beer, slammed the tap closed and whirled out from behind the counter, disappearing into the kitchen.

Fred slumped onto the seat, wincing as he massaged his neck. In the mirror over the bar he saw the skin there already bruising, purple rising steadily under red. The other patrons issued automatic condolences and indignation on his behalf. "Damn shame," the men mumbled, hands in their pockets, fingering their own wallets. Fred accepted their shallow comfort, feeling the slick bar top beneath his hand, and also Tony's strong arm pressing hard into his Adam's apple; the way Tony might have slid his ring from his finger, gentle as a lover. He wondered if the boy had let him down easy, or if he'd dropped him quick, all 210 pounds, like a worthless bag of potatoes.

The police showed up just after closing time, both of them white and jacked with blue eyes and short-cropped hair, walking in as if they owned all the hours in the world. Fred buried his resentment and explained what happened. Hilda wiped the same stretch of bar for five minutes, listening. The cops were writing it down and so was Hilda's boss, trying to look official, his yellow legal pad headed: Incidents. Fred felt slighted, and tired, and important. He told them, "He could've killed me," and paused to see what reaction this stirred in Hilda, but with her hair swung over her face like a partition, he couldn't tell.

The officers spoke with a few of the other patrons who'd stayed behind. Asked if anyone had seen where the man went. "No," one man said, pleased to be questioned, "but I saw him leave. The way they were talking, I figured they were friends."

"Friends?" Fred croaked, his eyes bulging in disbelief. "It's a crime to be nice?" Everyone started talking over one another, wanting their opinions heard, and the officers beckoned Fred away from the bar, into a more intimate corner, to ask their questions. He turned toward Hilda, opening his face to her, giving her an opportunity to return to him all that he'd paid for. "You'll wait, won't you?"

Hilda turned her back, organizing receipts at the register. "Uh, sure, Fred. I guess I could stick around for a little while," she said, but a few minutes later, he saw her slip out from behind the bar, apron folded in a neat square hugged to her chest. The fry cook's arm was draped around her waist, comfortable there, and she left without even once looking back. Fred couldn't help it, a raw little sob bumped up his throat, and the officers shifted their eyes. He kept answering their questions—yes, no, yes, I don't know—his tongue leaden in his mouth. The cops said they'd call as soon as they had something. "Oh, we'll probably find the car soon enough, stripped and burned in some abandoned lot," one of them said, a little too brightly, "but I wouldn't count on the boy. Cases like these are usually open-shut." They finished their report and offered Fred a ride home, and when they put him in the back and shut the door, he understood he looked like nothing more than a criminal.

Fred grabbed the spare key under the fake rock near the steps and let himself inside. A dense silence lay over the house, the click of the front door, his footfalls, all sound disappearing smoothly into it, as if there were nothing physical to his being. What he wouldn't give to have the phone ring right now, shattering that awful, accusing quiet, so complete, implying to him something eternal and dreadful from which he could no longer hide. Would that the doctor might call with better news, or the officers, even Tony—who could have still been a good boy gone wayward, who might have looked up his name in the phone book and wanted to check that he'd left him alive. Fred wished so hard he thought he heard a ring, and he ran to the phone, jerking it from the cradle and slamming it to his ear. "Gloria!" he shouted, hurting his throat, but only the dial tone answered.

Fred felt all the tears he hadn't cried with Gloria the day before rocket up inside of him like soda in a shaken bottle, and for a few merciful minutes, he let himself weep, needfully and gasping. When he was empty, this noise, too, vanished quickly. Fred wiped the snot from his nose with the tail of his shirt, then unpinned the gold spade from his lapel and held it in one hand as he stripped. The oil-stained jacket, his boots, his pants. He left his clothes in a pile in the front hall, and wandered into each dark room of the house, rolling the pin on his palm, the fact of his nakedness following along the corridor. In the bedroom, the closet gaped, absent of Gloria's blouses, her favorite pair of shoes, a purer darkness leaching from within. Fred went to close it, and when he crossed the mirror, he would not look.

Nominated by Ayse Papatya Bucak

THE BEST-EVER DOOM METAL BAND

fiction by LARA MARKSTEIN

from SANTA MONICA REVIEW

The best-ever doom metal band out of Oakland played for an aging audience lounging in lawn chairs that had sunk into the Savannah sludge so that their occupants appeared drunk, perched at odd angles between the RVs and the oaks.

"At least no one complains about the noise level," Cleo said between songs.

Like their listeners, who'd lost the last batteries for their hearing aids, Aubrey didn't catch Cleo's joke. She was high on whatever she'd mixed in the back of the truck and plucked at her strings with a singular focus, as though with the right notes she could cleave the steaming field in two so they wouldn't have to clean the mud later from their pedals and chords.

Cleo whispered into the microphone and kicked the drum machine when it petered out, which happened more frequently since they'd hit the south. The weather had been grim; endless overcast skies and flash thunderstorms. They'd stacked their solar panels uselessly beside the spare tire and jack. Cleo didn't actually mind the warped sound. She imagined their songs lumbering up like some half-formed beast from the swamp.

The last chord reverberated through the camp to a scattering of applause. Their audience was already packing away their coolers and canopies.

"Fucking Floridians," Cleo said. "Can't even spare a beer." She almost missed Sam, the fool, who'd gone to every one of their shows, greeting her afterwards with liquor and a towel, as though she really were someone. A pity his greatest dream was to sleep beside her, growing old. "How many days till Austin again?" They'd booked The Moody Theater, a career-defining coup that could launch them onto the international stage. On a Monday, sure, but for a fee that was financing this whole ridiculous escapade.

"They're refugees," Aubrey said. "Give them a break." But even she curled her lips at the grubby cables that had to be wound into plastic crates. This was not what they were used to. Cleo and Aubrey (and Skeet in the day) played second-tier indie venues, with roofs, the bodies beneath them swaying like a small, sweaty wave. But here they were, because it turned out that crossing Savannah's new network of bridges from isle to isle cost a month's rent.

Cleo slapped at a mosquito. The bugs had rallied in the evening air.

"Hey, kids!" She called to a pair of skinny Spanish-speaking children. "You want a meal?" When they nodded, she chucked them a couple of cloths. "Clean this shit up." Cleo explained how to loop the wires with a flick of wrist and made them practice before her till they got it right.

Aubrey handed Cleo a bong. "We haven't got food."

Cleo inhaled. "There's squirrels fucking everywhere."

Aubrey grabbed her revolver from the cab, where her phone was ringing still. Her parents were always calling, wasting their lives worrying about their precious child.

"They're probably diseased," Aubrey said, swinging a bleeding carcass at Cleo. She was a crack shot, even blazed. Her boots made sucking sounds in the mud.

"So? Cook it good and no one will know." Cleo had fixed far worse for her family when money was short. She skinned the creature quickly and threw it in one of their pots with the last of their distilled water and some roots Aubrey had found. By the time the kids had finished, the stew didn't smell bad.

Cleo and Aubrey watched the children eat greedily as the thunder rolled by. Flashes of dry lightning tore through the camp, then the rain churned the grass to mud. The kids did not move and their shirts stuck soaked to their skin. You couldn't swim in the rivers here, what with the alligators and snakes and the waste overflowing from outlying hog farms. The Floridians lifted their faces to the downpour as though there were grace to the cool sting. An old couple washed each other beneath the rain, all humility vanished. Naked as wrinkle-assed cherubim except for baseball caps.

"Shoot me if I get that old. Christ," Cleo said.

"Rege Satanas," Aubrey agreed and passed Cleo a powder from a dirty plastic bag that had been reused too many times and leaked. They'd had a death pact as teenagers, the three of them, back when things were just starting to go bad; when the oceans reared up on stilts to trample the lowlands and the storms thrashed whatever had not drowned. They wouldn't grow old and ugly, worrying about some bullshit future for their bullshit kids (they wouldn't have kids. Cleo's siblings had produced plenty, all in those same damn rooms they'd grown up in, and still not enough in the broke-ass fridge). They'd flame out, bright and beautiful.

Although they couldn't agree on the exact means. Aubrey thought they should kick it in some wild, drug-induced orgy. Hedonistic till the end. Skeet said they should stick to the classics: knives, arrows, guns. Cleo wanted something that would etch their names in the soon-to-be-forgotten history books. A rocket blasted into outer space, from which they could explore the vast stretches of the inhospitable universe until finally, one by one, they perished, their eyes wide.

"Alright then, scram," Cleo said when the kids had finished licking the pot clean. "This isn't fucking Disneyland."

* * *

Cunticle was on tour. Ravaging storm surges and a thresh of fires could not quash the band as they stampeded across the country, bearing beats and distortion pedals and the sorrow of a generation that had lost the Earth upon which it had been born. From the swirling Atlantic over the thick-jungled Appalachians to the Great Plains that had once produced endless golden horizons of corn to the pink pancake crusted deserts and a bleached and barren sea. The music would play on.

But it was not easy these days to arrange such a trek, and Cleo and Aubrey waited in a long line of cars at a state border checkpoint, their windows wide, feet hanging over the glass. Police, armed with machine guns, stopped every car.

"You got rid of everything, right?" Cleo asked.

Aubrey pulled out her earphones. "Yeah. I mean mostly . . ."

"Fuck, Aubrey . . ."

"Hey, you're the reason we don't have the paperwork." Aubrey had been in charge of procuring the first set of visas to take them to the East Coast. Cleo was supposed to shepherd them home. For some states—the shit states—a simple online form and money transfer sufficed. For others you needed letters of invitation, proof of onward transportation, sufficient bank balance . . . the list went on. Cleo was bored while sifting through the ever-changing regulations, and finally she'd forgotten the stack of documents beneath her bed. Organization had been Skeet's job. She planned their expeditions as though they were military operations with backup generators and batteries. Without that extra crap, Cleo and Aubrey had more space for booze, which by now they'd mostly drunk.

"Shit, do we really have to see Skeet when we're back in town?"

"Don't get your panties in a twist. It's weeks away still. You going to call Dionne's kids?"

"Christ. At this rate we'll never make the Chicago gig." Cleo reached over and honked the horn so that Aubrey leapt. Several officers swiveled and walked towards the truck.

"Fuck, Cleo. Fuck. Everyone's trying to get across this border." Chicago was one of the cities that hadn't been affected as badly by climate change. The Great Lakes had tempered the hike in temperature, and the locals welcomed the heat. The ones who hadn't been priced out of the state, that is.

"I'm sorry," Cleo batted her eyes at the officer. "I must have nodded off a moment and my arm slipped." She was nowhere near the horn. Cleo was used to getting what she wanted, being beautiful. Men and women and goddamn animals tried to please her. She strolled through the Deep East of Oakland like she was charmed.

The officer asked to see their papers. "They must be somewhere. We're a band, you see. On tour. Maybe you've heard of us?" Unlikely. Theirs had been a slow-burning success in a genre that had never penetrated mainstream music tastes. Cleo made a show of searching through their trash. "Maybe you'll come see us play tonight?" She flashed him a ten-thousand-watt smile. Their solar only supported two-fifty at a pinch.

So they didn't see Chicago. There were too many people there. They'd just booked the show because they were on their way to Austin anyway.

❁   ❁   ❁

They drove through Indiana, Missouri; through denuded fields of cotton that had crept North year after year. The spindling branches scraped the sky clear. In St. Louis and Kansas City, they played gigs at the houses of friends. "Making hay out of a shitstack," Aubrey said, cheerfully, as they unloaded again. The shows were small, ten bodies jammed on counters and windowsills; no chance to make a buck. But they drank and ate and crashed on couches for free. These were musicians, after all, they'd met on tour once before. Acquaintances of classmates whose numbers they'd long since lost.

"What happened to Skeet?" Ciara asked. She'd been the drummer for an epic doom band called Vicious Rite. "She okay?" People assumed there'd been some accident. A disease.

Cleo said brightly, "Skeet quit. Good riddance. She was a control freak. Everything had to be done on schedule. The nut job tried to time-table our goddamn shits!" Skeet was the daughter of an accountant and UC Berkeley math professor—she liked order. Aubrey was the daughter of a doctor and lawyer; she rearranged the refrigerator so no one could find the eggs. But Aubrey had liked the Jacksons. They'd let the girls convert the basement into a studio and never mentioned the missing alcohol.

"Then she'd be furious when practice ran long. Though she was the one who wanted to go over every note a hundred times."

Aubrey said, "Skeet reckoned that's how you got famous: doing things perfectly." The fool.

❖   ❖   ❖

Aubrey had been perfect once. She'd been a perfect five-eight, one-twenty pounds, straight As. She not only played the guitar, but also the piano, and could dance en pointe. It had been Aubrey everyone'd ex-pected to quit. Aubrey, who held herself aloof from every argument, as though she did not need to dirty her knuckles in the melee, because she was going far. Far, far away from that basement on Euclid Avenue. Cleo had known she was going places, too, and she was ready to punch out your teeth to prove it.

Aubrey did leave for a while. She enrolled at Harvard University, where her parents had met as freshmen in a dramatic production that had seemed surreal before the world outside their windows seemed stranger still. She'd taken classes in cognitive science and chemistry and planned a career in research psychiatry. Then the schools closed, and then the universities.

"Fuck Harvard," Aubrey said, back on Euclid again. "I hated it there."

But it had taught her a few things: how to make drugs out of com-mon weeds and chemicals, which became important as air transit van-ished and shipping routes were routinely disrupted by fragile economic alliances. She'd become a veritable master in the dark arts of finding a high.

*　*　*

In most towns, Cleo and Aubrey knew no one. So they continued driving along endless straight roads that stank of animal rot. Storms drowned the possums, maimed the deers; coyotes and snakes and skunks, which had multiplied, burned. A plague of carcasses that bred disease lined up like a welcoming committee. At night, they pulled into whatever field they found and made camp; this the type of foolish decision Aubrey's parents feared. The highways weren't safe in the dark. Newspapers ran stories on truck hijackings and violent robberies. Cleo figured the interstates were safer than home, where her sister Dionne had taught Aubrey how to shoot. After she'd returned from Harvard, Aubrey bought herself a gun and appeared on Cleo's crumbling doorstep to aim at fence posts without the neighbors calling the police. As if someone like Aubrey, who lived in a fancy apartment with running water still, would need to kill anyone.

Aubrey worried less about bandits and more about the wildlife. She was convinced that as towns collapsed and whole populations packed out, the animals had gone rogue.

"Don't wander off to pee," she warned Cleo. "Those turkeys are organizing."

"Let me know when their union presents a bill of demands," Cleo said. But it was true that she felt their marbled eyes surrounding her as she pulled her pants about her ankles. Their rubbery necks lengthened, their dinosaur beaks clacked open and closed.

"Just try me, fuckers!" Aubrey yelled. She ripped off her underwear and pissed in a circle around the truck, convinced her feral scent would scare the birds. The turkeys were unimpressed. So Aubrey shot the bastards, one by one, until she ran out of bullets and passed out half-naked in the back, leaving Cleo to fix the carcasses. They ate turkey for breakfast, lunch, dinner, snacks. Then the meat went bad and they threw it out to sicken the vultures that lined the roads.

*　*　*

"Whatever happened to Bong-Ripper?" Aubrey asked when they finally passed the outskirts of Tulsa.

"Overdose," Cleo said. They eyed each other: Cleo was driving with her knees so she could roll a joint while Aubrey practiced chemistry in the passenger seat. Then Aubrey snorted and they both laughed so hard Cleo had to swerve to keep from smashing a speed sign.

140

"Of course," Aubrey sighed. Five years earlier there'd been a spate of suicides in the doom metal community. Cunticle wasn't the only group that'd made a death pact. Bong-Ripper and Acid Bath and Espiritus Cock all had their own contracts.

No one would have known if Acid Bath hadn't fulfilled their end of the bargain in such style. The musicians booked an expensive hotel, loaded up on caviar and champagne, then dissolved their bodies in acid in a massive jetted tub. In the video they streamed of the night online, just a necklace, looped around the empties, remained. The necklace, rumored to be made from the skull of a man called Death, was a giant fuck you. For years, black metal had claimed the title of the darkest, deadliest crowd. Acid Bath proved that at the end of the world, when the lights really went out and all turned to gloom, there was nothing like doom. Everyone agreed Acid Bath's suicide was as Metal as it got. An example to follow.

And follow they had: Bong Ripper to overdose, Candle Congregation in an inferno of fireworks, the Electric Blood Forks in an impressively gory DIY situation that fueled gossip for months (what motor had they attached to their kitchen utensils? Did they sharpen the tines first?). Suicide fell out of fashion after that. Cleo said that the pinnacle had been reached; there wasn't a decent death left. Aubrey thought there weren't many bands that remained.

Cleo must have known that, too, because she began to claim that they were the best this side of the Mississippi—and the theater they'd pitched in Austin, which was far larger than any venue they'd played before, hadn't disagreed. It only took a massacre and an interstate travel ban for Cunticle to receive the recognition they deserved.

Aubrey rolled up the window against the smell of dead things.

✲　✲　✲

They slipped into Texas with a quick hand job behind the booth, courtesy of Cleo. Aubrey played their first record in the truck and smoked a jay so she wouldn't have to hear the border control agent moan. The throbbing base of her guitar wound about the songs, chaining Cleo's rising vocals to the asphalt and beneath that the dirt, the shale that formed the very crust of the earth. A geologic reckoning.

"You think we should play 'We Will All Burn'?" Aubrey hadn't noticed Cleo reappear, and she scooted across to the driver's seat.

"We don't have an encore." The engine, which had needed servicing the past thousand miles, roared over the rest of the track.

141

From the highway, Texas was all scrub; dry grass that would burst into flame like some biblical smoke-sign of their destiny. Only when their truck overheated and they pulled aside to the stench of scorched oil, there was no divine missive, just a stretch of empty clay. In the distance, a stand of elms promised a trace of shade, but Cleo insisted they practice while they wait. They shared a joint instead, their thighs sticking to the seats, and dreamed of air conditioning.

Austin itself was barren of vegetation. Ordnances forbade the very greenways that had once been the hallmark of the city after fires tore through a canyon, trapping thousands. Now, only the weeds in the pavement were allowed to sprout.

At the Moody Theater, the facilities manager watched the two unload. "You ain't got staff?" Their truck took up just a small corner of the space marked out for buses. Still, he did not offer to help.

For hours they tinkered with levels with the sound technician, the bass growing powerful, the drum machine heavy, Cleo's vocals shattering. When Cleo was finally satisfied, they lay back, exhausted on the vinyl floors. "Don't you have to set up for the opener?"

"Saint Boofus?" The engineer eagerly accepted Aubrey's joint. "No one told you they bailed?"

"They couldn't find a backup?" Aubrey asked and Cleo said, "More profits for us then."

"Sure." The engineer blew smoke circles in the air.

"We could play a longer set . . ." Aubrey said, but Cleo shook her head. The new tracks were raw still, untried.

"Re-lax," the engineer's words catapulted off the high, high walls and Cleo and Aubrey stared at the empty seats, imagining.

Above the crowns of their heads, smoke hung like halos.

❖   ❖   ❖

Cleo and Aubrey would remember the moment they walked on stage at The Moody Theater their whole lives. They would recall the soft squeal of their sneakers on the resin. They would feel the heat of the stage lights like a brand on their newly-laundered skin. They would never forget how the blood seemed to clatter through their veins like coins, a jangling sobriety Cleo would hold responsible for subsequent mistakes. This was the moment they had been waiting for their whole lives. Ready, world? Cunticle had arrived.

Then they plugged in their instruments and the guitars screamed and they faced the men and women who would spread their name across ocean and sky.

All thirty of them.

Thirty was not a bad crowd—about the audience they pulled in San Francisco. But in the three-level theater that seated over two thousand, those bodies seemed pitiful.

Then Skeet's drums began; loud and slow and strong and Aubrey struck her first chord. Cleo didn't have time to worry about the meager turnout, she leaned into the microphone, waited, the drone of the riffs lurching forward, a rumbling of heavy tectonic plates. She closed her eyes and felt the pressure build.

She sang, her voice crystalline. Then she plucked gently at her guitar.

The crowd was rapt.

Cunticle built a skeleton out of bare drums, conjured movement from these bones in the bass, which trudged through the darkness of these last twenty years, and brought a monster to life with lyrics that floated, fragile, above a rhythm 'n blues guitar.

They were good and they knew it. The best-ever doom metal band not just out of Oakland but the West Coast, the world. In any other universe, where metal wasn't a joke, they'd have been famous by now. Concert halls like the Moody Theater would hardly have been able to contain their fans. Which was why, when they'd run through every song, Cleo picked at her individual strings, her fingers flying, seeking to remember notes they'd only recently laid down.

Aubrey came in three bars late, but she caught Cleo's shift, picking up the melody, which she anchored with a pounding bass. A psychedelic landscape of distortion and doom that should have seized the audience by the lungs.

But the music wasn't coming together right. Their parts appeared disjointed, confused, and Cleo felt the audience's attention shift.

When they ended with a long reverb, no one called for an encore.

✿   ✿   ✿

At the loading dock, the facilities manager passed Cleo a bottle of moonshine. "Y'all were good," he said.

Cleo stowed the last of their cables in a cracked plastic bin. The bottle clinked against her teeth. "The theater was empty."

143

"Not much to dance to." Hope, that's what sold. Some synth-strewn, auto-tuned pop. "Still. It's nice to hear a band from another state."

"How you still working?"

Cleo meant it as a joke, but the asshole said, "I ain't. I come here cos it's something to do and I probably would have killed myself otherwise."

What was she supposed to do with that? Nothing, her sister Dionne would have said. But Cleo polished off the bottle, spilling liquor down her bra.

In the alley, they fucked. Cleo could see every one of the man's pores. When he came, the pounds he could not yet afford shivering, his body crushed her against the big brick wall. Dirt tattooed her scraped back. In the end, Cleo was like Dionne: just another bleeding cunt.

She didn't think the day could be more disappointing.

Then the earth shook, shattering the windows and toppling a street light that dented the roof of their truck.

"Fracking," the asshole said, zipping up his pants. "Careful of the sinkholes on your drive."

Cleo crawled out from behind the trash, where she'd hid. She could have used a sinkhole. She'd have leapt into its gaping mouth. In her dream that night, she'd only be saved from hurtling down, down, into the planet's molten core by the cables she's twisted together. Tight, like a noose.

✿   ✿   ✿

Across the panhandle and over the high sandstone plains of New Mexico, they climbed, heading home. It was a long drive of dust flatlands, of hardy juniper and rock and grass—and the dark silhouettes of derricks, rising like wraiths, beneath slabs of heavy cloud. The metal pinions spun and the rod dipped, bowing towards the earth as though in prayer.

Oil, oil everywhere, and they were running low on gas. Cleo drove fast to catch a warm breeze because they couldn't afford to run the AC. Plus, the noise of the engine drowned out Aubrey's phone; her parents calling again. ("A hundred dead, dear. Please, just text that you're alright.") At that speed, they leapt over rocks, barely weaving around potholes.

"Craters," Cleo said. Erosion had formed great cavities in the road. Where there were roads. Concrete had cracked and washed away in flash floods, the desert turning to dark rivers that would carve out new canyons within the century. And the rest of the world wanted them to drive compact electric cars, sourced from sustainable materials, that would not further defile the environment? Had they seen how vast this country was? How savage still? Only a diesel-starved truck could survive its ravages.

* * *

Aubrey studied the desert through the windshield. Mesas rose up in the distance like long abandoned skyscrapers, and the pink earth shimmered in the heat, transforming into tin foil lakes.

That final day at Harvard, she'd taken a motorboat to the airport, which had been hitched onto a plateau of fill, then moved because its flood gates broke every storm, then hoisted high again.

The Boston of her parents' past was such a sturdy place: they'd walked on centuries-old streets, lived in buildings with basements that only flooded after rare hurricanes. Over the years, the hurricanes blew in more frequently, and the storm surges swelled. Eventually, the T had washed out so often, the trains stopped running. Eventually, certain neighborhoods never drained.

But it had seemed so beautiful to Aubrey, that wet city of hers, which existed in no one else's memories. In the library stacks, she'd felt herself marooned. Like some ancient explorer aboard a vessel built of books. She navigated by the skylights.

When, after two years, she climbed onto that boat on the Charles, taking a final look at the Elliott clock tower before speeding off past Boston University and what was left of Fenway park to one of the last commercial planes that would ever fly, she had felt as though something had been stolen from her. Her parents felt this way, too. Their dreams had drowned.

Aubrey closed her eyes and clutched the steering wheel of their truck in this dry, dry land, and pretended she were still sailing through the city she had loved.

* * *

"The problem with Skeet," Cleo shouted over the wind that buffeted the car, "Was that she thought she was so good."

Ever since they'd crossed the Arizona border, great gales had swept south. In the desert, small tornadoes of dust disturbed the horizon, then disappeared.

"Just because she came up with our name, she thought she was in charge."

145

The band had been called many things over the years. They'd gone by Bloodsob first—Cleo's pick. For a concert poster, she'd stenciled a dark red stream issuing from a girl's blank face. It was a striking image, but Aubrey had been pleased they'd rebranded by the Year of the Suicides. She'd imagined choking on thickened gore. A few years later, when they still weren't famous, Cleo calculated this was the name's fault. So: Acid Boof was next. But then Acid Bath went and killed themselves elaborately and the name became a joke. Men in the audience volunteered to off them with their dicks. Skeet punched a particular prick. "You fucking cunt!" he'd said. "This cunt's good for more than fucking," Skeet said. And Cunticle was born.

"There's hardly any drums in our tracks, you know? But she acted like she was some freaking genius. Like it takes talent to whack out a d-beat." They'd only let Skeet into the band because she'd had a basement. "I'd been wanting to kick in those drums of hers forever."

The boot that broke the camel's back. All because Skeet had called a melody on one of their newest songs leaden. "It's a goddamn dirge," she'd said.

"We're a doom metal band?" Cleo had reminded her. Admittedly, largely because they'd figured that doom would finally rise to its rightful prominence with the world's destruction. They hadn't reckoned on folks staring down the barrel of humanity's eclipse and wanting something fun.

Skeet claimed the bass and drums already had that Valley-of-Death vibe. The melody had to be delicate. Haunting. In a rage, Cleo had rammed a foot through a snare.

Cleo had called Skeet an amateur. The glowing reviews of their first album had hardly mentioned her after all. Cunticle wasn't yet mature, but Cleo's mournful voice promised great things. They were a band to watch. Their second EP had received even more praise, particularly Cleo's melodies, which were "exquisite tapestries." But a tapestry that relied on old formulas. "A solid band, if they want to enter cultural memory, they'll need originality."

"We don't have a problem with Skeet," Aubrey said. "We don't have Skeet."

✿   ✿   ✿

But who they didn't have made for a long list. Such as Sam, who had believed in every one of Cleo's dreams.

Aubrey had claimed he wasn't good enough for her. "You just lie together on the couch." Weren't they supposed to see what was left of this world? Where were the stage lights and the jet planes to new continents?

"He wants to ruin your boobs with babies," she'd said in disgust. Would Cleo really coo over some kid crawling? Was Cleo prepared to praise some finger painting of a house that would be underwater one day? They'd both seen what had happened to Dionne. Talented as fuck. Could have been something. Instead she'd bred and bred until she lost her looks and when she might have left, she'd gone and gotten strangled by that man she'd loved. "He's selling you a bunch of bad checks."

Cleo hadn't been sure. So Aubrey had kissed Sam one night, jamming her tongue down his malt-liquor throat. He'd reeled back, shocked, and Aubrey had flopped on the bed. "I don't know why you're upset. It's not like Cleo doesn't fuck anything that moves when we're on tour."

This wasn't entirely true. Cleo only fucked when she was too high, too lonely, too unknown still.

※　※　※

What was left of Cunticle pulled into Oakland at night, the highway following the dark stretch of Bay. Since the embargo, container ships no longer anchored offshore. The smugglers used smaller vessels and operated without lights.

"Where are you going?" Aubrey had flicked her indicator to exit into the flood zones of the east.

"We're not staying with my parents," Aubrey said. After the cleaning lady had discovered her drug paraphernalia beneath the bed, Aubrey's parents had taken to spying on their daughter. Never mind that her chemical concoctions kept the band alive. No matter where in this God-given country they found themselves, there was someone willing to buy. If she'd had any ambition, Aubrey could have grown rich on the spoils.

"Fuck," Cleo slammed her palm against the busted glovebox so that it popped open. Cleo had never let her friends visit the East. At first, Aubrey had thought she was ashamed of the poverty of her place, with its rusted burglar bars and wood-paneled windows, the walls blossoming in brilliant white curtains of mold. Then she'd figured from the gunshot holes in the particleboard that Cleo was concerned over their safety. Ha! When Aubrey finally appeared uninvited, she'd realized Cleo was embarrassed of them.

"West Oakland then," Cleo said. Aubrey swerved back onto the highway.

Skeet's parents had lost the house on Euclid Avenue to the third set of hill fires that had torn through Tilden, thanks to overburdened power lines. Only the charred concrete foundations of their home remained. If years before they hadn't lost their jobs, like others they could have built again. As it was, Skeet moved them south, into a Victorian that would have been beautiful if it weren't for the stripped wood and the stench of mildew and the many bodies splitting apart the once stately rooms. She let a studio herself four streets down, and over shared meals, they told each other how lucky they were to be alive.

"You ready?" Aubrey had parked with two wheels on the sidewalk, and Cleo felt a little skew, too. But she kicked open the car door and hauled herself onto the curb. Kids lounging on the street watched them grab their guitars and bash shut the doors, which they didn't bother to lock so their shit could be stolen without smashing a window first.

* * *

"You survived." Skeet handed them each a straight fist of gin in dusty mugs she did not wash.

"Barely," Aubrey added, leaning against the loud fridge. "Hurricanes, earthquakes, checkpoints—I know. I'll call my mom tomorrow."

"Good . . . gigs?"

Cleo did not delight in Skeet's jealousy exactly. All the same, she was pleased by her friend's pretense of indifference. "We played alright," she said before Aubrey could complain about audience numbers and missed shows. "But look what you've done with this place!"

"Mom's design." Skeet drained her mug and poured out more gin. "I hardly cook with the lines for groceries." It didn't seem she ate much either. Skeet had shorn her hair short, and the cut called attention to the bones around her neck, the hollow sockets of her eyes.

They clambered onto her bed. "It may not be what we pictured as kids, but I'm luckier than most." There were so many homeless: under corrugated lean-tos, stuffed inside abandoned pipes. Most everyone had fled from the Valley after the ground cracked beneath their feet and sunk. What farms remained trucked in workers, who tied bandannas over their noses as though this would save them from lung disease and the fever in the dust. In Oakland, new cities mushroomed overnight. As the winds changed, stolen tents and ripped tarps flapped through the air like spores.

"I'm working in the shanties now, studying nights to be a lawyer. Your mom seemed to think it was a decent idea." Skeet nodded at Aubrey.

"What?" Aubrey froze.

"I figured she could help?"

"You talked behind my back!" Aubrey whipped her palm around to slap Skeet's cheek, her glass never wavering.

Across the room, the refrigerator thrummed.

Skeet wiped a drop of blood from her lip with her thumb. "Grow the fuck up."

Cleo emptied the bottle in her glass. "Are we really going over this argument again?"

"You both shut your eyes to reality even when your noses are shoved in its shit."

"What does it matter what we do when we're all going to die? Aubrey, you got pot?" Aubrey pulled out her stash.

"You can't pretend you'll be famous one day. You know you won't fly anywhere. We're not fifteen. This is our fuck-up to fix."

"And what exactly have you fixed?" Aubrey asked, licking the wrapper of her neat roll. The blood vessels in Skeet's thick jaw pulsed. "No, I'm curious." Aubrey coughed and passed the joint across. "Saint Skeet, please, tell us mere mortals how you're turning back the fucking tides."

They stared at their grubby feet on the bedsheet, silently, waiting for their heads to fill with fog. Small marijuana clouds floated above them, providing not a lick of rain, incapable of anything, even shade.

❖   ❖   ❖

Aubrey asked after Skeet's parents. "They holding up okay?"

Skeet massaged her puffed pink cheek. "The smoke from the fires's killing them, but that's the same for all of us. I'll tell them you say hi."

"You playing tomorrow?"

Skeet glanced at Cleo. "I wouldn't know the songs."

The joint hung from Aubrey's lips as she fetched her bass. "We'll practice."

"I got to work," Skeet said, the implication being that they didn't (well, Aubrey didn't).

Cleo tore herself from the bed to gather her guitar. "It's one night. For old time's sake. The world will still be ruining itself when we're done. Give me a toke."

As Cleo puffed, Skeet pulled her drum sticks from beneath the bed, along with a metal bucket and books she arranged in a practiced curve.

Then she removed the shade from the lamp with a flick of her nail that made the brass ring. Cleo had smoked enough that she heard the cymbal in its ding.

Then Aubrey strummed and Skeet began the beat. Without the amps, it took Cleo a few bars to catch the track; the first song they'd written that had made it onto their EP. There was the bluesy bass, the tom-tom slap; Cleo shoved the joint between Skeet's teeth and sang about a tiger's lost love, her voice tiptoeing over the drone.

The next song was off their past album. Fewer drums this time: each one a punch to the gut. The riff was slow and jazz-inflected, the lead guitar a flash of psychedelic inspiration. Cleo's voice teased through the registers, weaving the synths with the darkness of the beat. Now they were playing. Cleo could feel the music in the pricking of her fingertips as they slid over the frets.

Then Aubrey began a song they'd only just composed. Cleo tried to catch her eye, but Aubrey was focused on her finger work. Skeet took a moment, two, then she began tapping at her make-believe set. Lightly at first, the sound against that country twang foreboding, then harder, and harder still, the drums a terrible pummeling, and it was Cleo's turn to join. She opened her mouth; her voice soared.

This was what they'd been missing, of course. This was why they'd never finished the track. And Cleo knew that with the hammer of Skeet's sticks, the song was devastating. The best they'd written perhaps; the ethereal notes like whispers that seemed to escape from some hot, messy core. Cleo gripped her guitar, the lyrics boiling in her throat, and keened until the music stopped and she couldn't breathe.

They stared at each other, panting and covered in sweat, afraid to move. As if the slightest twitch would undo all they'd created the past four minutes twenty-two.

A neighbor banged on the floor.

"Fuck," Aubrey said, disappointed and Skeet packed away her makeshift kit. Then they all three climbed onto the thin bed, laying top and tail, knees jamming into kidneys, toes grazing ears. Cleo turned to face the wall. She did not want to catch Aubrey staring at her with those big eyes, saying, See? She refused to believe that Skeet was responsible for anything.

Skeet was wrong. The band wasn't some childish waste of time. Cleo wasn't pretending the world wasn't screwed. The world had been ruining itself far longer than Skeet realized.

Poor and black, Cleo's family had been murdered by police, gangs, bad luck, for centuries. Now that everyone else was suddenly at risk they thought she should get involved. They were fools. Cleo had seen what fighting back did; it ground you down till you were dust before your time.

Cleo had promised herself she would not let the world crush her like that. Like she was nothing and no one and could be trampled over carelessly. Life was short and she would die, but many years before Cunticle had sworn their death pact, she had vowed that her departure would be magnificent. She would create the finest band that had ever played on this ill-fated Earth, and she would sing until the amps cut out and the flashlights broke and the oceans had swallowed the deserts whole.

❄   ❄   ❄

By the time Cleo woke, Aubrey had already scrounged through every cupboard. "Nothing?" Cleo's stomach coiled in a hard knot. They hadn't eaten since Nevada.

So they picked their way through ash-coated streets, which stank of shit and smoke and the brackish flood waters that had been trapped in potholes and sunk fill.

Aubrey handed over too much of their weed for a couple of overbaked tamales. Still, they quickly licked the last crumbs from the corn husks so their food wouldn't taste of chalk now the wind had turned. In the haze, their eyes burned.

"Would we have her again?" Aubrey asked when they stopped for a breather on their way back. The smog triggered her asthma, and she crouched low, hoping to duck beneath the yellow haze, her forehead almost touching her once-ballerina toes. Neither had respirators.

"She better beg if she wants in." Skeet should have been grateful for the chance to play in their band. She should have bent over backwards trying to please them. After all, the night before, she'd plunged into the songs as if the notes were fresh water she could choke on. Only, Skeet rehearsed her martyrdom. Lay her graying head across her creaking, too-small bed, like some half-charred sacrificial bird.

"That's not Skeet's style."

They could barely see ten paces ahead through the fumes and took twice as long returning to the apartment, Aubrey coughing the whole time. When they reached the truck, she collapsed on the curb. "Do your folks believe you'll make it?" she asked.

"It doesn't matter what they think," Cleo said, fierce. "They'll fucking believe when we own penthouses and vacation in Greenland."

Aubrey wrote their band name into the film of ash on the bumper. Only Skeet's parents had ever thought they'd succeed. It had been rich then when the Jacksons' bad luck had forced Skeet to abandon their dream. Not that Aubrey had noticed; Skeet had withdrawn in increments. She couldn't practice as she searched for apartments. Then she couldn't tour, because her parents needed cash. By the time Cleo realized Skeet no longer gave a shit about Cuticle, she only ever spoke of getting involved. But this hellscape needed a whole lot more than a good vacuum and some TLC.

"I should visit my parents," Aubrey said.

"Yeah. Me, too," Cleo lay back against the hot pavement, where her sister might have walked, listening to the country breathe.

* * *

They waited for Skeet over an hour, then Cleo slammed the trunk shut. Already, they'd missed their chance for a tech check; if they didn't leave now, they wouldn't make their slot. Still, they stared down the street, hoping for some sign.

But there were just kids playing soccer blindly through the smog, a scavenger in full face mask digging in the trash, a sky so brilliant they'd never see the likes again.

Cleo tapped the vehicle twice, then climbed inside. When the engine revved, Aubrey followed, feeling a fool. She'd really thought they'd perform together again, the three of them. In a small corner of her mind she'd imagined that this would change everything. Their music, fame; the world itself would transform; the storms weakening, temperature dropping, and the gash in the ozone would stitch itself up.

Cleo clanked the truck off the curb and drove, not looking in the rear view once. At San Pablo, she gunned the motor, as though she could shoot their way out of the disappointment of this town. Then Cleo screeched to a stop. Aubrey's head slammed back.

"The fuck . . ."

Skeet stood in the crosswalk.

"Get in!" Cleo yelled, though they were already too late to stop.

"The Camanche fire hit the Oakland hills," Skeet said. "You haven't smelled the smoke?" But there was always a fire somewhere. You couldn't keep track of every inferno. A car horn blared as the vehicle tried to pass. "I need your truck. We have to evacuate the refugees."

"Hasn't everything there burned to a crisp ten times now?" Cleo said. "The homeless took what was left."

"Their fault then." Cleo shrugged. "You have a gig. Live for once. Christ."

"It's an emergency." Skeet ripped open the cab door and grabbed Cleo's arm, yanking her from the seat. Cleo clutched the wheel and the truck lurched sideways. Aubrey jerked the parking break up just as the vehicle rolled onto the median. Neither Skeet nor Cleo noticed. The two tore at each other with knuckles and nails.

"Back the fuck off." The gun in Aubrey's hand did not waver.

Skeet stared at her. Whether from the fires or frustration, her eyes were wet. "Please?" And Aubrey was reminded of how when they were young, for soundproofing, they'd nailed blankets to the basement walls. She or Cleo, she couldn't remember who, hammered four neat holes through a quilt sewn by Skeet's gran. Skeet had cried. Sat on the floor of that dark room, inconsolable. They hadn't known what to do, but they'd waited with her for what seemed like hours, until her tears had dried.

"It's just one night. For old time's sake. You can ignore the world tomorrow, too."

They'd known each other so, so long; they still chafed at the ways they'd changed.

✲　✲　✲

Cunticle had its biggest audience at the San Francisco show: a hundred cheering fans. Cleo leaned into the microphone and whispered, "San Francisco?" as though her mouth were filled with rocks. She was high on Aubrey's homemade painkillers. The crowd roared. "San Francisco, are you ready to die?" Then the drum machine began; a seismic bass that shook the bones like splinters from their spines.

On the street, their truck waited empty for them.

"Maybe we should go somewhere new," Cleo said when they loaded their instruments later. She stumbled into the cab. Aubrey turned the key and headed south, away from the Oakland hills.

"We might be the best doom metal band on the planet," Cleo said.

"The only doom metal band," Aubrey added. "Hail, Satan!"

Aubrey pulled off the road to pee when they hit the crumbling coastline. Cliffs had pitched over, spilling out to form new promontories that washed away in the storms. With gun in hand, she squatted over the slick boulders, only a faint stench of smoke against the brine of the sea.

Aubrey aimed at the vehicle, which must have been two hundred feet away. More. She pulled the trigger. Once, twice, three, times, four; she blasted each and every tire, except the spare. She could not say why. Not even the turkeys stirred.

Cleo, head leaning out the open window, as if detached, did not notice the car sinking violently. She stared up at the night. Her world was spinning so fast she could almost believe she was on that spaceship she'd dreamt about, that would shoot them through the unexplored galaxies. No chord could tie her to this earth.

Only, the universe wasn't so strange in the end. If you closed your eyes, you could hear the stars pounding out the bass they'd been searching for since Skeet left: a drumbeat of little sledgehammers puncturing the pail of the burnt early morning sky. All that sweetness, running out.

Nominated by Santa Monica Review

FALSE TEETH

by TOM SLEIGH

from THE THREEPENNY REVIEW

in memoriam for my aunt, Pauline Thyfault

After the viewing, they took her new false teeth,
inhumanly gleaming, out of her mouth, then slid
her body in the oven and turned up the flame.
They offered them to me as "a keepsake,
a remembrance," but I turned them down:
all I wanted to see, all I wanted
to remember was the old wrecked Acropolis
of her shattered grin. She, whose soul had been
tight-jawed, gap-toothed, a cavity-drilled
dissenter, possessed in her new dentures
the permanent reminder of how all those years
she'd hidden her shamed smile. It was as if
the porcelain grins of the ones she called
the bosses, and hated with the purity
of a blowtorch cutting steel, had become her grin
mocking her from the water glass she soaked
them in at night, their perfect alignment
and corrected overbite become my little
nightmare, gnashing, tearing, hyperbolic
in their appetite, as if they embodied
hunger stripped of any satisfaction,
the anti-food of hunger hungering
to eat and eat never stopping, chewing
the void between each tooth to the least

nano of a nothing. Once, when I went
to see her and she still recalled her name,
I saw her staring at those teeth, saying
something like gobble gobble gobble but might
have been her mumbling nonsense syllables
while those teeth faced her down, square and perfect,
no jaw or skull to detract from their exactness,
knowing nothing of all her years driving Jersey's
back country roads checking in on what she
called God's beloved crazies though she didn't
believe in God, nor did she see them as crazy—
the social services lady who went house
to house and got Millie out of her locked room,
took Charlie to a matinee where he pissed himself
and she had to clean him up in the Men's
while the teenage ushers looked the other way.
Once she drove me to an abandoned house where
a dentist had his surgery, the chair still there,
kapok on the floor, even the little pedal
he pumped with his foot to drive the drill,
windows broken, stained posters of dancing
gleaming teeth as a hand without an arm
brushes that smile to little sparkles
leaping from too-pink gums. Just why or what
we did fades into my looking into
her mouth, at the wildly spaced voids between
each tooth as she talked to another lady;
but if you think I'm going to tell you
what I saw, play the little boy smitten
with the flawed, go back and read again:
I said nothing about her smile being
anything but a cause of shame, nothing
about a husband, a child, a female lover,
though she lived with a woman named Joy
who brought her anything but, haranguing her
in old age to change and change again
her paltry will. Instead, her dream of overcoming
the rich for the kingdom of the poor
all those years she hid her teeth behind her hand

vanished in one instant of these new damned teeth
that make everything taste like metal, as straight
and even as these pretty boy newscasters
shoving their perfect mugs into your face.

Nominated by Lloyd Schwartz, The Threepenny Review

MONARCH

by CAROL MUSKE-DUKES

from KENYON REVIEW

Whether they find the milkweed
By sight or smell, they drift by us
& care nothing for our witness.
Or the ridiculous name, honoring
An Orange king. So little time to
Be alive: to survive is to propagate.
As if imitating, unaware, the noble
Distinction the title confers—resistance
Of all human longing. Let the pretender
Viceroy mimic these fire wings, black
veins, this natural toxicity. A true
Monarch cares only for the brief reign
of perpetuity, unshadowed days as
Sun King. Mindless talk of the soul,
Of transformation, reveal only how
All politics derive from common illusion.
A winging sceptre named for hopeless
Desire: to be ruled by air, by indifference.
Yet in belief of the ragged premise of miracles.
The monarch cannot see you. Somewhere a
Royal body is drawn to the flowers earth offers
At last. So few left & each one dying in its majesty.

Nominated by The Kenyon Review

OUR VICES

fiction by DOMINICA PHETTEPLACE

from WIGLEAF

We re-enacted the Revolutionary War and the Civil War, too. The Underground Railroad and the Japanese internment camps. I was a Red Coat and then a Gray. I didn't get to be Harriet Tubman but I did get to be Noguchi, who interned himself voluntarily but then spent seven miserable months at Poston as both a prisoner and an outcast.

Ms. Spence had not always wanted to be a high-school history teacher. Once she had wanted to be actress. She had gone to Stanford in the nineties and told us about it whenever we were between reenactments.

We fought over who got to throw the first brick at Stonewall. I had to be Joe Biden three times, once during the Anita Hill hearings, once during Obama's inauguration and once during the Iowa caucuses.

And then suddenly we were caught up to the present. We had re-enacted every single moment in American history and we still had a month left of school.

"I've nothing left to teach you," said Ms. Spence. "You've learned it all."

It was just what I wanted to hear but still it didn't feel quite right.

"Can we do the Spanish American War again?" I asked. "I want to be Hemingway."

"That's the Spanish Civil War and no," she said, "History can only happen once."

Ashley Jacobs raised her hand and didn't even wait to be called on. "What about parallel universes?" She didn't know it, but she was my nemesis. That made all of her ideas bad ones, even the ones I agreed with.

"What about them?" asked Ms. Spence.

"Didn't you say there were an infinite amount?" Ashley continued as if she were giving a TED talk. She reasoned that the infinite parallel universes operated much in the same way that the infinite monkeys on the infinite typewriters did.

"What has this got to do with Shakespeare?"

"If there are truly an infinite amount of monkeys, then they aren't just typing out the complete works of Shakespeare. They are typing out every thing that could ever possibly happen. That means there's a monkey typing out the exact words I'm saying." The whole class oohed at her rhetoric, which had an obvious flaw.

I raised my hand impatiently. Ms. Spence called on me.

"Those monkeys aren't real. They're a rhetorical device meant to illustrate the vast incomprehensibility of infinity." The class looked disappointed.

"Of course, the infinite monkeys aren't real. But parallel universes are . . ."

"Just because quantum theory allows for them doesn't mean they exist."

Ashley ignored my interruption. ". . . and because there are an infinite amount of parallel universes, that means anything we could make up is actually happening in one of them. All fiction is alternate history," she concluded, and the class clapped, everyone but me.

"You can't just ignore the continuum hypothesis. There are different types of infinities." Ashley was intentionally conflating the countable with the uncountable. It made me so mad.

"This isn't math class," said Ms. Spence, wistfully. She told us that things would have turned out differently for her had she been able to do higher mathematics. She would have enjoyed her time at Stanford more. She could have been a STEM major.

Despite democracy being the best-worst system, we put Ashley's alternate history reenactments to a vote. It passed, so we proceeded.

I'm not sure how, but fan fiction began to creep into our re-enactments. Blame it on the perniciousness of pop-culture. We fought the Civil War again, but this time the Union was led by Hermione Granger. The Confederacy was commanded by a Hitler-Voldermort hybrid we started calling Hitlermort to save time.

I continued to participate, even though it was stupid. Thor won the Iowa Caucuses, with the remaining Avengers in a nine-way tie for second and this time Joe Biden, aka me, came in eleventh place.

I told the class I didn't want to be Joe Biden anymore.

"And no more Dick Cheney or Dan Quayle either. Al Gore maybe, no George HW Bush."

Ms. Spence was intrigued by my stand. "If you can name the rest of them, you'll get an automatic A and be excused from re-enactments."

"Mondale . . . Rockefeller . . . Ford . . . Agnew . . . Johnson . . ." And then I was out.

Our teacher sighed a disappointed sigh. She had taught us everything and I had forgotten most of it. The class was not unmoved by my plight. Ashley stood up and recited the rest of the vice presidents. And we, as a class, were able to work out a compromise. We would each take turns being Joe Biden until we didn't need him anymore. And then we would discard him altogether.

Nominated by Wigleaf

MY FIRST BLOOD

by REBECCA CADENHEAD

from THE HARVARD ADVOCATE

"Don't worry," Carolina says. "It'll be quick. It won't even feel it." I believe her. I agree to help.

I'm watching a cat drink out of a bowl of blood.

Apparently, cats love the taste of blood. Maybe this should be obvious. Cats are predators; they're technically not even domesticated. A cat digs into a freshly killed rodent because it likes it, not just because it has to.

Still, as I see the fur around the cat's mouth stain red, I realize I haven't thought about this before. *Why didn't I know that?*

I'm learning a lot of things today.

A few minutes ago, I was taught how to slaughter a lamb, which is the source of the blood. The lamb's carcass, still fresh on the table, is leaking bodily fluids out of both ends onto the concrete floor. Blood is still dripping out of its neck into a bowl, where the cat waits to lap it up. It's red, poppy-red, so bright it seems fake.

I'm starting to feel like I'm hallucinating.

I'm playing at butcher as a sort of cultural experience. This is not without some irony. By the time my grandfather was my age, he had killed countless chickens; when you grow up as a sharecropper, it's an essential skill. He showed me how to do it once, miming instead of using a live bird. You grab the chicken by the neck and twist sharply, until you snap the vertebrae. Today, he goes to Walmart to buy Vienna sausages, and his granddaughter has to travel over five thousand miles to see something he would've considered standard. Progress, I guess.

I'm doing a backpacking expedition in Chilean Patagonia with an outdoor education program. My group mostly consists of the kind of

American and European teens who are disaffected enough to disappear into the woods for over a month, but wealthy enough to do it on another continent. For the majority of us, this is part of a gap year or semester off. The exception is the lone Chilean student, who needs to take this trip to qualify as a tour guide in Torres del Paine.

Patagonia has a special appeal for the outdoor-minded. The climate has always been too harsh for large-scale agriculture or development—it's mountainous, infertile, and as cold as Alaska. Ongoing assaults of earthquakes, wind, and ice have carved out an army of looming, jagged peaks. Many of the ranchers who lived here are gone, lured away by jobs in tourism and homes in larger cities. Pumas have eaten the horses and cows they left behind. In their stead, the Chilean government created a system of national parks covering nearly ten million acres of land.

Currently, I'm not in school because my body has decided that I need a break. By senior year, the pressure cooker of my high school had shredded my nerves along with any desire to do academic work. The thought of enduring college had become almost unbearable. Upon graduation, sensing that I might be fragile enough to crack like an egg, my parents let me take some time off.

I'm similar to many in this group in that I might be a failure. Most of us are the children of middle and upper-class professionals whose trajectories we have deferred from, sometimes to their sharp disappointment. We each internalize this differently. Only I and a quiet Canadian girl, whose rugby career was abruptly cut short by an injury, seem to have the acute sense that our lives have fallen out of alignment. The rest, to varying degrees, have co-opted this and transformed it into a point of pride. The absence of education, of jobs, of plans, is a sign of moral fortitude. They can turn their lives into a series of adventures instead—of which this is one.

There is a universe where I probably *would* view it that way, assuming a few of my essential characteristics were changed. I immediately notice that I'm the only black person in this group. I'm also one of only a few girls. On our first night, we sleep in tents segregated by gender: one for the girls, three for the boys. Perhaps if I were different, I would have the freedom some of these boys seem to possess; they walk like where they step doesn't matter. I, meanwhile, have been raised to ward against the danger of mistakes.

In my head, I call them American Boys, though they're not all American. Still, they embody something particular about our national character. It's not just their whiteness, their maleness, or their physical strength, though those certainly are factors. It might be how unburdened they are.

I sense that these are people who, unlike me, are not persistently aware of their vulnerabilities. I'm unsure if this feeling of mortality is more attributable to my background or my anxiety. They're probably related.

Our trip is thirty days long, starting and ending at the program's base, which is also a fully-functioning farm. In the intervening period, we live out of our packs, bushwhacking and kayaking around the Pacific coast. Upon our return, the farm's butcher, Sebastian, asks us to help kill the lamb. It's for a traditional Patagonian-style barbecue, meant to celebrate the completion of our trip. Like most of the kids in this group, I've eaten plenty of meat, but I've never really seen anything die before. Truthfully, the anticipation of what I'm about to see makes me a little nervous.

"Don't worry," one of our instructors, Carolina, a slight Chilean woman, says. "It'll be quick. It won't even feel it."

I believe her. I agree to help.

*　*　*

When you're an American, you can make the inconvenient invisible.

It's almost implied by what we call ourselves: "Americans", as if there aren't 34 other countries in the Americas. Our dominance takes the form of ignoring other people's existence. Felipe and Carolina, our Chilean instructors, take great pains to point this out. They call us "U.S.A.-ans". This moniker never really catches on in our group.

The American food system benefits greatly from our ignorance. We don't know the basic facts of where our food comes from, probably because a separation between us and the things we eat is important for maintaining our sense of ourselves as moral people. Contained animal feeding operations and fields tended by migrant workers are not pleasant to envision. Fortunately, we aren't reminded of these things at the grocery store.

Our power shields us from the truth. It starts at the beginning—in America, farming means ownership. From our nation's inception, a number of those whom we've labeled "farmers" have rarely done much planting or harvesting; that's left to the people whose labor they've bought. Thomas Jefferson, foundational in our country's mythmaking, called himself a farmer. He also had over 600 slaves.

164

My family used to be the kind of people who were owned by other people. Until very recently, we were not Americans, even though we were brought here almost four hundred years ago. To this day, "American" is probably the last identifier my granddad would use to describe himself. He's a Christian, a black man, even a veteran. He is not, in his mind, an American.

Granddad was born a sharecropper, which is to say, a slave. Sharecropping was an arrangement in which wealthy white landowners "rented" plots of land to poor, often black, families. They paid back their debt by cultivating the land, giving almost everything they produced to their landlords. Often, when their output was tallied, families would mysteriously wind up with more debt than they'd had the previous year. If sharecroppers tried to complain, or worst of all, unionize, they would be hung from trees. In this way, an ostensibly temporary arrangement could last for generations.

While the rest of the country started to eat prebutchered meat from industrial slaughterhouses, Granddad's family got what their landlord, Mr. Beasly, didn't steal. Sometimes, this was one chicken for over a dozen mouths. To this day, whenever my grandfather eats meat, he gives thanks for what he calls "the blessing of the flesh." He thanks the animal for giving up its life force because he understands its value. Even as he lives through an era of artificial abundance, he still believes meat is a luxury.

The ceremony of eating meat, as in a celebratory Patagonian barbecue, is rooted in scarcity. I suspect that the significance of such an event is lost on people who have always lived like they'd never be hungry.

✳   ✳   ✳

I realize quickly that lambs know when they're going to die.

We stand in front of their pen and pick one out, and then two boys from the group go retrieve the animal. They are the only ones strong enough to carry it, since lambs, as it turns out, are *not* small. When they enter, the lambs panic, backing away until they've coalesced into a formless blob of wool and jittery knees in a corner. They bleat in terror as the boys approach, each one fighting to recede into the mass. Eventually, the boys get too close and the bubble bursts like a spider's egg sack, lambs scattering across the pen.

I watch from outside the pen and think about dodo birds. When they lived on Earth, they didn't fear us. They had no predators, so when approached by humans, they didn't flee, and that was the beginning of their end. If the lambs are afraid, I reason, they know what's coming.

The selected lamb fights back, bucking when the boys try to lay hands on it. It isn't enough. Eventually, the boys catch it, grabbing its legs so that it can't run. It writhes for a few moments, trying to break free, and then abruptly goes still.

They carry it into a shed near the pen—a minislaughterhouse. The smell is suffering: sweat and urine and the metallic tang of blood. In the center of the shed, there is a table on which the lamb is tied down. It quivers, but otherwise does not move. Sebastian places a bowl on the ground, just beneath its head.

Sebastian draws the knife—a surprisingly short, blunt blade—and the lamb flails wildly, or as much as it can while tied down. It knows, just as well as I know, what the knife means. It manages one bleat before Sebastian's hands clamps its mouth shut. Its eyes are wide, rolling around in terror. He cradles the lamb's head and quickly slices its neck open. Blood pours out into the waiting bowl.

The cat arrives. It has been lingering in the corner, flicking its tail in anticipation.

At this point, two of the girls in the group, who were previously watching, leave the room. One of them looks like she's going to be sick; the other's lips are pressed so tightly together that they're colorless. The first one, I recall, has recently been complaining about how much she missed Chick-fil-A.

I don't want to be in the shed. The stench of the lamb, I am convinced, will linger on me forever. I want to take a shower so that it won't stain my skin. I briefly contemplate leaving, but then I glance up at the American Boys. Two of them are smirking. I stay, but it's getting harder to breathe.

*　*　*

Here is the great irony of Patagonian tourism: the same forces that preserve this place will eventually destroy it.

Patagonia is extremely popular among the world's wealthy, a fact that is immediately obvious. In thirty days in the backcountry, we encounter one human settlement: a half-finished geodesic dome on the far side of a fjord. It's likely owned by the richest man in Chile, Julio Ponce Lerou, a former son-in-law of Pinochet, who has bought large swaths of land in the area.

Maybe he's building the house to escape people who hate him. His wealth comes from a mining industry that is infamous for destroying ecosystems and poisoning water, causing some public ire. The only way to reach the house is by a two-hour long boat ride, combined with a six-hour long hike—or a helicopter.

Interestingly, you can't find the location of the house on a map, at least not a physical one. It sits in a fiord formed by a branch of the Southern Ice Field, which is rapidly receding. The last time it was surveyed, around World War II, it was still covered by a glacier.

Patagonia's crowning asset—its ice—is disappearing. Its glaciers are melting remarkably fast, partially because there's a hole in the ozone right above it. Its visitors, who come here to admire it, are often the kind of people whose carbon-emitting trips and over-consumptive lifestyles kill a planet. But maybe this doesn't mean much to them.

One of the particularly cruel aspects of climate change is its fundamental inequity. The parts of the world that are warming the fastest, or are most vulnerable to natural disasters or droughts, are disproportionately in the Global South. These regions also produce vastly fewer emissions than the Global North. So, the drivers of climate change will never experience the worst of its effects.

We have come to Patagonia to see its beauty before it's all gone. Our presence is also part of the reason why that beauty is vanishing. We're like thieves, stealing pieces of this place until there's nothing left.

Our instructors, Felipe and Carolina, seem painfully aware of this. Their salaries require them to spend most of the year in the field. So, unlike us, they are not voyeurs in this place—it's their home. Probably as a result, they seem to have internalized the cost of their lifestyle. If climate change is the result of our collective consumption, then each of us is responsible. In light of this, Felipe and Carolina don't buy new things, don't eat meat, and rarely travel. They want to live without impact.

I think they might be on a mission to change us, too. While we're here, they announce on the first day, we will Leave No Trace. We will act like we want to erase our existence. Unfortunately, we are never very good at this; throughout the trip, we trample endangered plant species, accidentally spill soap into sensitive freshwater environments, and secretly dump our food waste onto the forest floor.

Maybe Leave No Trace requires more significant unlearning than Felipe and Carolina imagined. American thought isn't predicated on such ideas of limitation and restraint. As a culture, we rarely challenge the notion that Americans should take what they want.

In the mid-twentieth century, amidst genuine environmentalism, corporations that produced disposable packaging began to fund antilittering campaigns. Instead of questioning the underlying logic of making things you can only use once, they encourage us to "properly" dispose of our waste so that it doesn't dirty our community parks. In many places, Earth Day is now synonymous with cleanups—as if the carbon emissions of a plastic bottle are offset when you put it in a trashcan. In reality, our waste is just put somewhere else, usually shipped to developing countries or piled together in undesirable neighborhoods.

In America, conservation is when you make a mess and then force someone else to clean it up.

❊　❊　❊

I'm wondering why the lamb isn't dead yet.

It's been minutes and it's still staring at me, or at least it feels that way. I'm so unnerved that I involuntarily step back out of its sight. Its stomach is still rising and falling, ever so slightly. The blood fills the bowl and then overflows, spilling out and into a drain in the floor.

I can't move. In my mind I chant, *This is natural this is natural this is natural*, and hope that the repetition makes it true. *This is how my ancestors lived.*

That fact seems to be mocking me at this moment. My mother always wanted to send me back to Arkansas. She thinks I'm too sheltered. "You don't know how lucky you are," she sometimes mutters. "When your *grandparents* were your age . . ."

There's a part of me that understands that this needs to be done, that this has always been done. In many ways, this is probably the most ethical way to eat meat. But another part of me wants to leave. Something about this feels out of context, its meaning distorted. We aren't slaughtering this animal because we need to; we're doing it because we want to see what it looks like. Still, my feet remain planted.

I notice that even without thinking, I have been holding myself extremely still. My spine is so straight that it has begun to hurt. It reminds me of a bear encounter I once had, when I was alone in the woods and my screams would have been swallowed by vegetation. I remember thinking that the bear was so large that my head could fit comfortably in its mouth. I was still then too, trying desperately to make myself invisible, convinced that if I moved the bear would realize that I was something it could devour. We stared at each other for what was probably a second, but felt like hours. Then it lumbered back into the forest, and I ran as fast as I could to the nearest road.

So, perhaps I remain out of fear. The departure of the other girls meant that the group is now overwhelmingly male. Looking at the expressions of the American Boys around me, which range between impassive and smirking, I have the sudden conviction that to register any discomfort would be dangerous. If the word "empathy" literally means to be "in feeling" with another, then expressing what I feel would be an admission of identification with the lamb, a marker of myself as potential prey. I don't want to be eaten. I stay where I am.

All of this, I think, is meant to be a lesson on the cost of things. But I am unsure of what this means for us, who will never really have to pay for anything. It strikes me that there aren't very many consequences for someone like me. I look again at the American Boys, who only seem to register this as a performance. There are even fewer consequences for people like them.

A milky film forms over the lamb's eyes, and I know that it is finally dead. I exhale slowly, releasing the air in my throat. I'm glad it's not looking at me anymore. Its gaze seemed like an accusation.

❖ ❖ ❖

In September 1973, the United States government, under the front of the Chilean military, overthrew the country's democratically-elected president, Salvador Allende. They replaced him with Augusto Pinochet, a rightwing dictator who killed thousands and tortured ten times more, but fortunately was not a socialist. Most Americans are unaware of this, probably because the U.S. government covered it up for over twenty years.

A decade earlier, Granddad was entangled in another of America's interventions to liberate people of color from self-governance, this time in Vietnam. It was the military or sharecropping, and he picked the former. Death in a jungle, or death in a cotton field. He calls this a choice.

Currently, Granddad's body is slowly decaying. He uses a walker and his hands tremble involuntarily every time he raises them, the result of rheumatoid arthritis. He has a number of health problems tied to Agent Orange exposure in Vietnam that the V.A. will not recognize, because when the majority of the sufferers are old, poor or foreign, it's not a priority.

Granddad was one of the oldest of 18 children, and so his absence didn't mean much for the family's harvest. But when his younger brother, Lionel, tried to leave for high school, he was met by Mr. Beasly, their landlord. Mr. Beasly pointed a gun in Lionel's face and told him that it was the fields or a bullet. He chose the fields.

Lionel is one among a faction of my relatives who are highly invested in my academic success, and who I probably disappointed by taking a gap year. Truth be told, we don't know each other very well. I suspect that I am more of a symbol than a person to him. A few months ago, on a trip back to Arkansas, he ran into Mr. Beasly's daughter. Apparently, she and her husband are now unemployed and on the verge of bankruptcy. They might lose their house—her father's house. He recounts this with something like glee. "I wanted to tell her," he says, grinning, "You're broke, and I got a niece going to *Harvard!*"

My other grandfather, the son of industrious Scots, also went to Harvard. He is an excellent American Boy. One of his professors there was Louis Fieser, the inventor of Vietnam's other predominant chemical: Napalm. Napalm was developed in Harvard labs specifically for killing. It was originally intended to set Japan on fire, though it's most famous for burning whole swathes of jungle in Southeast Asia, including the people inside it. Fieser later remarked, "I have no right to judge the morality of Napalm just because I created it."

"You know, he was the nicest guy," my American grandfather says, contemplative. "You'd never know he'd made a thing like that."

One grandfather had to drop Napalm out of planes, the other got to chat with its creator. Some kinds of people are always at the mercy of the decisions of others. When Lionel looks at me, he sees someone with the power to make those choices. He sees an American.

✢ ✢ ✢

Sebastian cuts along the skin of the lamb's underbelly, just deep enough to puncture the layer of wool, and forces his fist in between its pelt and its stomach, separating the two. This, he explains, is how the animal is skinned. He looks at me, smiles, and steps back, inviting me to continue his work.

The eyes of the others are on me. I step forward and hesitate for a moment, but then I remember my audience. I shove my hands inside the gap Sebastian has already made, slowly pulling the two layers apart. It is unsettlingly warm. One of the American Boys hoots. The message is clear: *you've passed a test.* When I pull my hands out, they are sticky.

Eventually, when the lamb is sufficiently skinned, Sebastian cuts it open and pulls its organs out, discarding them on the floor. "We don't waste here," he says. As if cued, the cat abandons the blood to nibble on the gallbladder.

Sebastian strings up the carcass so that the fluids can drain and we leave the shed. The fresh air is startling. "I'm glad that he was so respectful with the animal," one of the boys says to me as we walk up the grassy hill towards the farmhouse. I pretend I haven't heard. I don't say what I'm thinking: *the lamb didn't give a shit if we respected it when we killed it.*

Later, the lamb is served for dinner. It is a great success. Everyone eats it, including the girls who left the shed. Including me. The only exceptions are Felipe and Carolina, who are both vegans. As I chew on the meat, I contemplate my weakness. *Fucking conformist,* I hiss. *You'd do anything to blend in.*

But I was just trying to survive, I whimper.

Maybe that's not quite true, though. Survival is different from the path of least resistance. I make a mental tally of the major actions of my life; did I do them because I had to, or because I wanted to? *I wanted to,* I realize. The thought is unpleasant. I'm in Patagonia because I want to be. I'm going to Harvard because I want to. I have been *taking and taking and taking* my whole life, mostly just because I can.

I wipe my greasy fingers on a paper napkin and stare out the window of the dining room to the glaciers in the distance. The sun has just begun to dip behind the horizon, turning the sky a pale pink. I'm trying to memorize this view, because I know I probably won't see it again. In a few days, I will fly two hours to Santiago, and then eleven hours back home to New York. These flights will help kill this place. I wonder, if I do return, whether the ice will still be here. It seems unlikely.

Over our meal, we talk about a lot of things that don't matter. One girl misses the fried chicken place in the Denver airport. Another of the boys discusses his next adventure: scubadiving and spearfishing in the Seychelles. I wonder if they know how they sound.

❊   ❊   ❊

A few months later, I'm on a train from New York to New Orleans to visit part of my family. The train ride is 36 hours, criss-crossing sections of the country that I have no real relationship with but, I suppose, could be considered an ancestral homeland. In spring, the Southeast becomes dense and green with vegetation. After Virginia, the landscape is almost indistinguishable, creating the odd sensation of a divorce between time and motion; the hours pass, and we don't seem to be going anywhere.

I could've taken a plane with my parents, but instead I'm in the coach class of an Amtrak. This, I told them, is part of an effort to live more sustainably. In reality, it's less altruistic than that. I'm attempting to cure myself of the feeling that I might be a bad person. I now walk most places, and if I can't then I take the train. I've been much more careful with the things I buy. Soon, I'll stop eating meat.

I still remember the lamb. It mostly appears in my dreams, which have become increasingly vivid. Often, they're about the various ways I might die; drowned in a flood, eaten by a puma, cut open by a butcher. Guilt, I've found, pairs poorly with anxiety.

Nominated by The Harvard Advocate

FATHER'S BELT

by KURT LUCHS

from REED

I don't like holding his pants up.
He's gone to fat since his discharge
from the Marines, and frankly
it's a chore. Nor do I care
for being hung in the closet,
left in the dark between two dress shirts
that haven't a clue
as to the horrors and pleasures that life holds.
The worst thing that ever happened to them
was a ketchup stain on the cuff,
easily removed by the most inept of dry cleaners,
his dry cleaner. No, what I like
is when he takes me off, and not to put away.
I like when his rage comes bubbling up,
never far from the surface,
set off by whatever you little bastards
have done today, it doesn't really matter what,
does it? Then his hands are strong again,
I feel his love through me
as he folds me in half and makes me
snap against myself with a loud crack.
That's to make you afraid.
It hardly seems necessary
yet I assure you, it's an essential part
of the ceremony, it's foreplay.

The smell of fear is an aphrodisiac.
Then all at once I'm whistling
through the air, my flesh meets yours
in a mad rush, and there is joy in heaven,
my ecstasy cannot be contained.
The red welts come quickly, purple bruises
will follow, and sometimes if his passion
is fierce enough there's a bit of blood
from my buckle end, the sweetest release.
He says he loves you, he does it all for love.
I don't mind. I know it's me he really loves.
I love him too.
And I love you, all seven of you,
each receiving my affections differently
because love is unending, there's always more.
Do you realize, aside from him
you're the only ones I ever get to touch?

Nominated by Reed

THE REAL THING

fiction by OLIVIA CLARE

from McSWEENEY'S

Level Two was peach, and Cora held one, undimpled, in both hands. Had held it for seven minutes, squeezing. She'd been at Level Two for three weeks. The peaches were getting softer, and she was not improving.

"You know what I'm going to say," Abbey called from the back of the room. "You're not trying. You're not trying at all."

Now Abbey walked to the front of the room and spoke to her nine other students, in rows of brightly colored chairs. "Remarks for Cora? Comments?" No one said anything; Abbey tilted her head and let the silence breathe. Then she said: "We're all agreed."

Cora had been on the class waitlist for two years. Her agent had had to ask a special favor to get her in. What would Cora owe him now? "Just please book a job," her agent said.

She squeezed that smooth little peach moon, that fucking fuzzy rock, but the skin showed no wrinkle. The moon would not give way. Next week she'd be demoted to Level One with a fleshy plum, or a firmer virgin plum, depending.

"What should she do now?" Linda asked Abbey. Linda was a talented older student. She'd had a whole stage career, a Drama Desk Award nomination, a lifetime ago. She fluffed out her red hair, parted like frizzy wings on either side of her head.

"She should practice at home," said Abbey, looking at Cora. "She should be practicing for hours."

If you made any dents, you could take the fruit with you. You could eat it. Abbey took the peach from Cora's hand and squeezed until the skin slid away from the flesh like thin peels of satin curtain.

"Was anyone timing me?" Abbey asked the students.

"Seconds," someone named Mark said. He'd just booked a soap opera. Abbey was a saint to him.

"When you can afford the one-on-one work," Abbey said to Cora, "that's when we'll really get somewhere." Abbey had been teaching the class for five years, but she'd told the class it felt like so much longer. It's amazing, time racing, she said, students getting bolder and younger. She was only forty-two, she liked to remind the class, younger than some of her students. She was tall with very dyed blond hair, and her own headshot was at least eight years old. Last week, a group from a former class—a few already somewhat successful in film—had surprised everyone in the middle of scene work. Lights were turned out, and there was Noelle Fox carrying a cake with trembling candles, and Lawrence Horn shouting, "Happy fifth anniversary!"

Cora received the discounted monthly per month—it was still twice as much as her rent. This was Acting Anger for the Screen, and Abbey had made herself known because of it. The Lander School had a class for each emotion: Acting Sadness for the Screen, Acting Envy for the Screen, Acting Doubt for the Screen, Acting Cheer for the Screen. They called it "cheer," not "happiness" or "satisfaction." They called it "doubt," not "uncertainty" or "insecurity" or "agnosticism" or "loneliness." Cora thought they should call things what they were. In the Anger class, Abbey famously began with fruit. Unripe apricots, soft watermelons, hard watermelons. Cantaloupes were the most advanced level. You had to squeeze one until you bruised it, using your fingertips or palms, not your nails, *not your nails!*, or better, until the whole fruit opened and collapsed heartily upon your hand, until its innards made themselves sparkling and known. This was the great revelation, the culmination of your work. You could not thrash the fruit on the furniture. You could not thrash it against a wall or an object. It must only be you. There is, after all, only that.

Cora had no anger. She'd been told this. And even though it should have been easy for her to bruise a peach with a simple squeeze, out of anger or not, the peach would remain unblemished in her hand. She could never act angry, because she had not found the experience from her life to draw from, and she believed that. You must believe it to accept it, to change it. She was twenty-seven.

✿   ✿   ✿

176

Her apartment in LA was in a house that had been split into five low-ceilinged one-bedroom units. No central air conditioning, and the hot water ran out in ten minutes. Her neighbor below, an aspiring model, said cold water was better for your skin, anyway, and she liked being woken up by another neighbor's vocal warm-ups at 5 a.m., because that meant she'd get up early. That neighbor was a very positive person. And she was healthy, from California originally. She even kept up with dental checkups. In one corner of Cora's bedroom, the wallpaper was shedding in long strips. There'd been an infestation of silverfish in the closet, so she kept everything folded and wadded in stacked suitcases. And Philip would not spend the night—he didn't feel clean there, he said. He'd told her that after their third date. Tonight he was taking her out, his treat, because he'd just wrapped the second in a series of four laundry detergent commercials he'd booked, and he wanted to celebrate. Also, he had a callback for a sci-fi horror film in Toronto. Also, he'd just paid off his Visa.

In the Spotless detergent commercial, Philip had a fake family, a wife who worked a long week and a daughter who played in the marching band. He played a stay-at-home husband—he had loads of laundry to do, and after trying many other detergents, he trusted only Spotless. The next commercial in the series would feature Philip and the family's border collie, and Philip was particularly nervous about that. "Animals and children," he said at dinner. "Everyone says they're difficult."

"You've never even worked with a kid," Cora said. They'd ordered decent champagne, and she had ordered a glass of merlot on the side. This was celebration. This was cheer, wasn't it? This was how they were happy. "Isn't your 'daughter' nineteen playing twelve?"

"I did a production of *The Music Man* in Minneapolis," he said. "So many kids. That was no joke."

"I was in that when I was nine," said Cora. "Back in Texas." She'd done community theater growing up outside of Houston, left for Los Angeles when she was eighteen. Everyone in LA wondered where her accent was, and she always said she didn't have one, which was half-true.

Philip said, "The director told me I read like a dad on camera. I think I'd be a terrible dad. The director thinks I *am* a dad, you know. I had to tell him that."

"I can't even picture it," said Cora. Would that hurt him? Please him? She'd already told him about that day's class and Abbey. About her humiliation. She had texted him from the Lander School parking lot. Now

177

she looked at his face—she'd hurt him a little. It was, as always, hard to tell. "Sorry. I've had a rough day."

"Didn't you tell me your stepdad kind of hated you?" he said. He often said this when he was trying to help her with her anger.

"I already used that for sadness," she said. "All of it."

"Every single thing?"

"I've been through them all."

This had begun as a trend and had never gone away. Reality TV had become so popular that people didn't want actors anymore, not in the old sense. More and more, casting directors looked for the real thing. If you were going to act something, then it had to be drawn from your life. It had to come from you, be you. This was what the Lander School taught. But it was beyond Method acting. If you used a memory for one emotion, you could not use it for another. She'd sat down with a Lander coach at the very beginning, and together they'd cataloged all of her significant childhood and early-adult events. They'd used her social media posts and medical records as a guide, and her own memory provided what it could. For homework, she wrote out a seven-thousand-word personal narrative. Her stepfather, her mother, her cat Lee-Lee. Her stepfather brought flowers home after fights. Once, her cat was injured and would let only Cora touch her. These were generic things, the coach warned her. Could she get more specific? The flowers were grocery store tulips. The cat's wound was large and bloody, near the tail. Each episode went on an index card—a summary of what had happened on the front, the appropriate emotion on the back. When they were done, Cora had a tall stack of cards to bring home with her. She could find so much in her for sadness. In the end, that was most of it, sadness and only a little joy. Jealousy. Insecurity. Wanting.

Philip would tell you that the business wasn't like this even five years ago, but he understood it, he said. Of course he did. He'd had many things happen to him in his life; there was so much he had inside of him! He would tell her this often.

"You should come to the set next week," Philip said. "I'll introduce you."

"I have class," Cora said. "And work." She and Philip worked for a caterer several nights a week—this was how they'd met—but Philip had been calling in sick. He needed to get up very early, and his face puffed, he said, if he stayed up too late. He blamed nothing on cigarettes or alcohol, only late nights. She'd finished all of her champagne and all of her wine and had ordered more sushi than Philip. She told everyone that her agent had told her to gain some weight, but that wasn't true. Her face was puckered and tired—she had her mother's face but had nothing like her mother's life.

Level One was plum. She'd managed to bruise one in class in those first days, but now she'd failed Level Two and would have to prove herself again. She practiced with a very ripe plum at home and had managed a small dent, a shadow, a ripple, but that was all. She was trying, "studying." In class, Abbey began with a short craft lecture and then asked Linda to step to the front. From the folding table of assorted fruit, Abbey took up a soft miniature watermelon. Linda walked to the center of the room, took the fruit as though it were already a trophy, stood still, paused, held a breath, then stood some more, transfixed. She was drawing from her well. She had two ex-husbands and an estranged daughter, and there it all was. There the coursing heat came. After two minutes of squeezing, the rind broke, the watermelon came apart in her hands. Abbey began the applause. Linda came out of her trance and smiled. She fluffed her wings of hair and looked to be herself again, but who could know?

"Someone will clean that up," Abbey said. That was the job of the lowest-performing student of the day, to clean up the fruit pieces on the floor, the mush.

"That was rough," said Linda, shaking her whole body, back in this world as best as she could be. "I barely remember it."

This was what Abbey said: That when you'd found the anger, when you were in it, you couldn't describe it afterward. It all existed on some other plane.

Now there would be Cora and her plum, a beautiful new one. She walked to the front and Abbey handed over the plum—the only plum; it was meant for Cora—and Cora waited. Nine students in their chairs with their notebooks stared. Cora thought of her stepfather, the stiff tulips from Kroger, but these were meant to be drawn from only for sadness; this was cheating, and she couldn't let herself. Nothing came from the well. She thought she might pull from the periphery of some memory, a moment waiting on the side.

No, nothing. Nothing came at all.

But there was her hair. She had that, something to help her generate, get her started. She knew how to do it. She took some hair from the back of her neck and twirled its ends around her finger and pulled.

She let go, and with the same hand, she made small, punctuated slaps at her cheek. The plum skin rippled, wanting to give way.

"Stop! Stop it!" Abbey called. She put a hand to her forehead and rubbed dramatically. "This is not how—No, no. That's not how we do this. You don't go to a different object and transfer the energy. It comes from *you*. And, goddamn it, you know this."

It was a trick Cora had used before, and it wasn't, as Abbey said, "Lander." One of the students smirked, and Linda just nodded.

"If there's nothing there, then play the nothing." Abbey snatched the plum from Cora and threw it into the trash. "I swear to god."

"I'm sorry," said Cora.

"Don't apologize to me," said Abbey. "Don't ever."

Cora had an audition the next day. It was for one scene in a show about forensics, and she was being questioned about a murder. She was to cry, she was to show hatred and curdling anger. Her agent was nervous for her; she sensed it on the phone. This, they both knew, was a stretch. In the waiting room outside the casting office, she sat with other young women who looked like her—just-below-average height, in their twenties or thirties, dark hair—who read their sides with moving lips, checked their phones, checked their eyelashes with a compact mirror. Philip texted Cora a photo from the detergent commercial set, his makeup-ed face filling the frame.

How could she prepare for anger? She tried to remember the face of a bully from middle school who was now a successful dermatologist. Lauren. She could try to be angry with Lauren. But Lauren had been a sad child at the root of it. How was it fair to be angry at her?

In the casting room, Cora made small talk with the casting director, who, looking at Cora's headshot and résumé, asked about the Lander School, how she liked it. "It lives up to its reputation" was what Cora always said. Then it was time. She read with the assistant, who delivered her lines in a monotone and sipped coffee from a mug that said LAGUNA BEACH in large script. When it came time for tears, Cora had them at the ready. When it came time for anger, she did not pull at her hair. She sat quietly. She waited to pull from something inside her. She waited for the inevitable piling up of all things to pile upon her and spill out. She tried again with Lauren the bully's face, but she could not remember it. Cora could remember only that she'd always felt sorry for her, and she felt no anger in that sympathy.

The assistant read Cora's cue again. "Are you going to tell us what you know?"

"You fucking wish, you fucking piece of shit" was Cora's next line. It was a bad line. A cliché line.

Nothing came. There was the sadness, the glowing, round wound of it, and that was all.

She drove to class, a mercifully short trip on the 45. Her tires were low. Her windshield was cracked. She had no money for these things, and she'd never ask anyone. For her birthday her mother had given her a beaded clutch, soft and designer, but it still sat in its velvet drawstring bag in a suitcase.

Abbey had asked her to arrive early that day. She had something waiting for Cora: a peeled hardboiled egg. It was the first time they'd had an egg in the classroom, Abbey said, and she'd boiled it herself, in her own renovated kitchen, in her own pot, on her own stove! Cora held the egg and pressed, and squeezed, and broke through until the bits spilled to the floor. Abbey said, "Well." Abbey said, "Thank god," and Cora told her, smirking, then smiling fully: "But that was sadness."

She told Philip about it at dinner, that she'd finally squeezed something, but the celebration dinner was for Philip again. He'd booked a speaking role in the movie that would shoot in Toronto. He had five lines, including "What should we do with it, boss?" and "No way."

"You wouldn't believe everything going on," he said. "I have to renew my passport. Store my car somewhere. And they keep changing the script on me." He was giddy. He was undone. "I'm unspeakably busy." She'd never heard him use the word unspeakably before, but she'd already witnessed him pick up words and idioms from those around him who were more successful. Oh, he was on the brink of happiness.

"Store your car?" said Cora. "It's three days."

"Street cleaning. They'll tow."

They were eating sushi again, with martinis this time, because Philip had already had champagne on his own. She didn't like martinis, but she drank them, and she didn't like sucking on the olives, but she did that too.

"Could I keep it at your place?" he said. "Your parking spot?"

"What about my car?"

"Park it on the street. You can move your car for street cleaning. I'll be working."

She could imagine anger unfolding within her like wings—she thought of Linda's red wings of hair. They'd have to spread, feel themselves out, keep dry, but they might be there.

"Give me your keys and I'll move it for you," she said.

"On your street? No, thanks."

"Fine. Keep it on yours. I'll come over and move it for you."

"Sounds great, love."

This is what he'd been after all along, and she'd give him a ride to the airport, too, and would help him pack. He picked up a tongue-colored piece of fish and flung it into his mouth. No, she wasn't even angry. Why not? She wished she could murder that plum.

For the next day's audition, she was to wear no makeup, and she was to use no product in her hair. There was no script, and the call was all the way out in Burbank. But she *had* put on makeup, natural makeup, had gelled back her flyaways and wavy wisps. The casting office was in a house with palms in the front and a cloudy green pool in the back. She signed in on the sheet in the living room and sat with five other women.

In twenty minutes, the assistant called Cora's name and led her to a study set up as a casting office.

"You're wearing makeup," the director said. He was the only one in the room, seated behind a cheap card table. He looked Cora's age, maybe younger. A worn leather jacket and a pretentious smile. Cora wanted to know where he'd gotten the money for a film, even just one day of shooting. Incredible. She didn't ask. The assistant took her spot behind the camera. "How old is this headshot?" The director held it in his hand. Cora had brought one, but he had everything already. That's how some of them were.

"A year."

"Really."

The assistant was already filming. "Give me a slate?" she said. And the money to employ her—where had it come from?

"Cora Ann Quinn," Cora said slowly into the camera.

"Now talk to me," the director said, leaning toward her. "Just talk. What did you eat for breakfast?"

"I didn't eat breakfast," said Cora. "I usually don't."

"Diet?"

"Money. Saves me a few dollars a day. Maybe a hundred dollars a month."

"Do you like this house?" the director said. He didn't look around. He looked at her. "It isn't mine. Don't worry."

"It's supposed to be nice, but it isn't. No one's looking after it." That's all Cora wanted to say, but this was an audition, and he wanted her to keep talking. "No one's looking after it," she repeated. "Look at the corners, that's where you can tell. Everything collects there. The walls are dusty, the outdoor plants are dying, and the indoor plants are fake. I could hear the busted pool motor from the living room. Maybe no one lives here. Upkeep is expensive."

"Say that again?" The director put a fist under his chin, concentrating. "Turn to the side."

"Upkeep is expensive."

"Now your right side."

Cora turned again. "No one lives here."

"Okay." He sat back. "Thanks very much."

Her agent called that afternoon to tell her she'd booked the job, and Cora could tell from his voice that he himself couldn't quite believe it. She'd booked only one role with him before, and that scene had been edited out of the true-crime show.

"They don't want you wearing any makeup to the set," he said. "And let your hair air-dry. It's a three-day shoot. It doesn't pay much, but it's something, at least." He sighed.

She texted Philip, who congratulated her, but he was busy packing, getting his shoes shined, buying a proper suitcase. She texted her mother, who wrote back "So proud!!!!!!" and then an image of a rose from the garden. Her mother was spending the day outside in the Texan green, wearing her gardening gloves, probably sipping tea, and suddenly that life seemed much more pleasant, healthier, than all of this desiring.

Cora *was* happy, briefly, but it was a sunken happiness, fleeting and painful. She celebrated by driving to a boutique coffee shop and purchasing a large, extravagant latte. She even chatted with the barista, found herself sharing the news, and the barista took time to scrawl "Yay" in the foam.

The script, which her agent emailed to her, was skeletal. It was a quarter of the length of a proper feature, and much of the dialogue was substituted with ellipses. "Yes, this is everything," he'd written. There wasn't much to memorize. She spent part of the weekend washing her hair and arranging it in various ways before letting it air-dry. She drove Philip to the airport at 4 a.m., and he slept most of the way. She emailed Abbey, composing and re-composing the lines in her head before she sent them. She tried hard to sound casual: "Afraid I won't be in class until Friday. I've booked a film. Thanks."

Her call time on Monday was 6 a.m., and they were filming in the Burbank house from the audition. She washed her hair and combed it in a side part, she wore no makeup, she washed her face in cold water and used a moisturizer her mother had given her, one she saved for special occasions. "Thank you," she said to the air, not knowing to what exactly, as she parked on the street. She checked in with the AD, a young woman in a zippered fleece vest—there was to be no hair or makeup, no wardrobe, and minimal lighting was being set up now. The film wasn't SAG, and there was no craft services, just a bowl of fruit, a box of donuts, a thermos of coffee. Cora took a plum and devoured it.

She waited in a bedroom with a peeling vanity and a broken ceiling fan. The young director came in with the AD.

"How're you feeling?" he said.

"Nervous," said Cora.

"Good. The scene we're about to do isn't in the script." He was wearing the same brown leather jacket, and now, looking closer, she was sure he was younger than she was. She pictured him out with his film school friends, drunkenly yelling into the night. She pictured him having sex with a stranger. She pictured him asking his father for money.

"You're going to listen to my directions through this earpiece," he said. "I want you to just walk through the house. Like a normal person. Not like an actor. Please. Please don't be an actor."

The AD approached her and hooked something into her ear.

"When I say so," said the director, this terribly young (she thought), wealthy, fearless-for-now soul, "I want you to leave the room. And then just walk. Just walk and react."

"React to what?"

"There will be surprises. When I say so, you'll come out this door. A camera will be there."

He moved her hair from one side to the other, ruffled it a bit, then left the room with the AD. Cora went to the closed door and waited. She tried to anticipate: *surprises*. Could they hurt her on camera and get away with it? But that wouldn't make sense. The script, even in its skeletal form, was a lesbian love story. She was playing the part of a younger sister, and she had one scripted scene, a funeral scene. When were they filming *that* scene? And what was this scene? After ten long minutes, she heard the director shout from a distant room: "Stand by." Then "Rolling," then "Action."

Cora stepped out into the dark. A cameraman was there with the Steadicam strapped to his chest.

"Walk to your left," the director said in her ear. The hallway felt dusky, though it was morning. The windows had been hung with blackout curtains, and there was a light that followed Cora, though she didn't know where it came from.

"You're nervous," he said. "Be nervous."

And she was. She put her hands in front of her, feeling her way.

"Good, good," the director said in her ear. "You can talk, by the way."

"Shit," she said.

In her ear: "Good."

"I can't see anything."

"Now stop," he said. "Move to your right."

She was entering the room she'd auditioned in.

A light was on. The desk wasn't there, and the room was no longer an office. Potted plastic plants hung from the ceiling, ferns and ficus covered the floor. The windows had been boarded up. A deep buzzing sound played from a speaker hidden in the room. The camera was just behind her. "Steady," the director said. "Steady."

Someone in a cartoonish bunny mask leaped out from behind a potted lemon tree.

"Fucking dammit!" Cora shouted. "What is this?"

"Good," said the director. "Very good. Now follow them."

A red light came on in the hall. Cora followed the masked person. They were much taller, with bunny ears from the mask peeking over the top of their head. The buzzing followed her through more hidden speakers.

"Now leave them," the director said in her ear. "Go into the bedroom. The one you were just in."

She went back into the room, walked to the center, and turned, scanning. She held her arms crossed over her chest, as if in protection. The closet door opened and an unmasked man appeared.

"Run."

She ran. She could hear the man running after her. She could hear the cameraman running after her.

"You're terrified."

She was. Everything in her, she was. She thought about nothing else except getting away.

She was in the dining room, which looked out onto the pool. She hid, without being told to, beneath the table, clinging to its ornate base.

"Great! That's great."

The man came into the room, burbling and tripping over the shag carpet. Maybe he was drunk. She realized she knew nothing.

185

"Now," said the director. "Stand up."

Cora didn't move.

"I said stand."

This time, she stood. The man watched her and stayed where he was.

"You're incensed," said the director. "This man has wronged you. You want to tell him off. Now do it! Now say something to him."

"No," said Cora.

"Say something."

She did want to say something. What? She didn't know, couldn't think of it. She brought her hands to her face, she squeezed her cheeks. She slapped them: swift, painless slaps.

"That's good! I like that too."

Cora slapped her right cheek, harder now. The man stared at her. Said nothing. His face was smooth and indifferent. She took her hair up and twisted it. She pulled and felt a clump dislodge from her scalp.

"God, that's good," the director said. "That's so damn good."

"Fuck you," said Cora. The man stood still before her, now with a sour face.

"God, it's perfect," said the director.

She pulled at herself. She let handfuls of hair fall to the floor. "Fuck you."

Her agent called that evening to say her other scenes were delayed, but that the director was pleased, and she wouldn't be working again that week. She didn't mind that; she'd planned to take herself out to dinner that night, but instead she went to bed and fell asleep early. She showered the next morning, washed her hair, and didn't eat. She was different now. She would go to class, having booked a job, having just spent time on a set. She must look slightly altered to those around her, just as other Lander students looked to her when they'd booked something. But she wondered if they, like her, didn't feel nearly as joyous as they thought they would.

She arrived early, and Abbey was there in the large main office, signing some papers.

"I thought you weren't coming in," Abbey said.

"We filmed yesterday," said Cora. "And we'll do more next week."

"Great," said Abbey. She scanned the papers in front of her. She looked put-together and unworried. Cora couldn't imagine.

"I was angry," said Cora.

"Were you?" said Abbey. "So the class has worked for you then."

"He liked it when I tore at my hair. When I hit myself. I didn't know what to say to him. He liked it."

Abbey stood now and took off her glasses and put them on the desk. Now she gave Cora her attention, something Cora felt she had from her so rarely. "The director?"

"Yes," said Cora. "I didn't know what to say, but it was working. What if I have to do that again?"

Cora readied herself—Abbey would rail against him, she thought, say his methods were utterly wrong.

"Well. If he liked it, he liked it," said Abbey. "That's what counts. He knows best."

"Does he?"

Cora wanted to describe him to Abbey, to tell her he looked fresh out of film school, not *Lander*. This wasn't Lander.

"Do what he says," said Abbey. "In my class, you work our way. On set, do what he says. And, you know," Abbey tapped a pen to her teeth. "People who book jobs pay an increased rate for classes."

"Seriously?"

"Depending on the job, but yes," said Abbey. "It's a Lander rule. Talk to Sheila. She'll bill you."

"But it's low budget. I hardly talk. It's tiny."

"It doesn't matter," said Abbey. "You still pay more. Think of it this way: Would you have gotten that job without me?"

Abbey went back to her papers. Cora walked to the classroom and stopped at the door. Linda was already there, warming up her voice. "Red leather, yellow leather. Silly Sally swiftly shooed seven silly sheep." Linda recited the words quickly, a soprano practicing her scales, running up and down the octaves, as though she was excited for something that hadn't even begun yet. A new job, a bit part on a soap or crime show, her Lander Method at work, and a line on a résumé to show for it. On the table beside Linda were watermelons, peaches, and plums. A bruised cantaloupe sat next to a peeled and shining egg.

Nominated by Colleen O'Brien, Lee Lipton, McSweeney's

THE CREATURES OF THE WORLD HAVE NOT BEEN CHASTENED

by LIA PURPURA

from EMERGENCE MAGAZINE

Because this, too, is a way to begin, I'll begin at the end. We're all in some way beginning at the end now, aren't we?

10/26/19: I found a deer, dead in the patch of urban woods where I walk every day. The cream of his belly rose up like a moon. He was hurt at the rump, but I couldn't see how. None of the brush around him was broken. The simplest explanation felt right: he chose precisely this spot to lie down in peace.

By the next day, the maggots had come, a wave of them creek-lapping the banks of the body, eddying in shadows, lacquered in sunlight. I got down very close and yes, I *heard* them—soft shushes like carp mouthing along a pond's surface.

In two more days, they'd pared the body back to hide, moving up the bone-cliffs and into the hollows, a tide floating parts of the wet world back to deep.

The maggots started from the hurt, open end—all hungers seek a way in through our wounds—and then advanced across the body. Standing back, the method's clear: it's not each on their own grabbing and loot-ing, but a collective force working according to plan. (Some collectives are so much more easily loved; the murmuration of swifts en route to the Amazon, which spend weeks every fall here in Baltimore, recon-vening at dusk above the Bookbindery's old chimney. They circle in a darkening cloud until the last one arrives and then funnel in like smoke sucked back to a fire below, spark to ash, ash to wood, every element made whole and restored to its silence as evening comes on.)

It was the dark cave of the chest the maggots found next. They left the legs, mostly tendon and bone, too much work for too little harvest—*wisdom* we call it, to spend our energy efficiently. And the balancing of incoming and outgoing forces, all the cascades and contingencies ordered? Those are *decisions*. Nothing here is predator-or-prey. This is die-and-be-changed. Maggots are gleaners who find their way to fruited corners. They take nothing down. Beckoned, they come. Their feasting is perfectly fit to our need, clears a space for our living—or as humans inflect it, their work is performed on our behalf.

Maggots keep at it in all conditions—frost-sifted, heat-swelled. Somehow in this week's pounding rain, they hold on and are not overcome by streams of mud and shifting ground.

After a few more days, they've moved so far into the chest I can't see them, except for a swatch at the edge, wrinkling with movement like a shirttail untucked. Consider all they've worked through in just over a week: coils of intestines, liver, stomach, all the small hiddens, tough heart, heavy lungs. Every bit of muscle and flesh. The ribs are as clean as the staves of a barrel, a ship's rigging, stripped beams. Such neatness! They moved every bit of indigestible hair and laid it aside, like a shadow cast or a blanket turned down at the foot of a bed.

Because I know the ways of my kind, how we cut the tethers and stopper the cycles, I was afraid the plume of rot released would call forth the human need to tidy, and soon a truck would come to cart the body away. Though a day later now the scent is more focused, sharp in the cold air, a sting not a muck, not so moist and mud-lofted.

Why do I go?

To be with the *rightness*—my word for the work of restoration. Persistence in its various forms, the efforts of those who plant and tend, reclaim against odds (others, themselves), keep on with the heliotropics. The rightness has heft. It rides like a loose pelt over a bear. It's how a poem lands in the body first. A commotion issuing from the edges, it sidesteps the notion of central command. It's from exactly that place, two years ago now, this came—as sharp and clear as ice cracking, bright, bracing:

The creatures of this world have not been chastened,
are not subject to chastening
and are still blessable.

189

A voice that was not a voice spoke these words. No need to lay in my stability creds or preempt with *"this might sound woo-woo but . . ."* I have my practices. I know how to listen. I have been waiting for the moment of exposure, for these words to find themselves a context, to speak from a ground I might recognize and into an occasion presented: body of deer, work of maggots.

And what does the occasion bear along, in its meaning?

First, rest your attention on *creatures*—they have not trespassed. A creature is wholly unlike those who withhold themselves from the designation.

To feel *chastened* is to accept a quietude, the aftermath of having been warned but not having heeded, a space for reflection, since only after rumination can restoration begin.

And *"still" blessable*? Able to receive, even now, enduringly. And from who-knows-where—it's the receptivity that matters. And being sought.

Blessing wants to land somewhere, to locate a body and go to work.

To sidle up then to creaturely ways? If I had to say so (and I'm working alone here), there is a chance for this still.

Forgive me for parsing the vision so badly. I have no elders to help me along, to whom I might bring this for illuminating, and who can design a more beautiful reading. Or fill in the creation part of the story, say the names, teach the practices of homage and reciprocity; and balance out all this end-driven angst. I work, as so many of us do, in exile from our deepest origins. Our tethers cut and practices stopgapped. Stories lost. Community frayed and DIY. My delivery is clumsy. I'm always in some state of jittery. But of this I am certain—the maggots: a current; bearing away. The deer: becoming dispersed; and more. What passes between them is a most ardent rightness.

And there are so many stories of rightness. That of the pin oak; told in four parts each year for decades, or, in the far slower tongue of Bristlecone pine, over the course of thousands of years. Story of peepers singing the teachings into their young as evening purples, then blackens down. Of crows, gathering in grief, their wailing and rending breaking into your peace. Turtles who made this world—or snakes, coyotes, buffalo, who come to speak it into being along the volcanic ridges at dawn, on moors and in canyons and mesas, for those who have been trained to hear. And here, today, right under my feet, the story told in hoofprints and mud. I squat down and hover a hand, fit my fingers to the teardrop declivities. It hardly takes much imagination, but it's good to start small and work up: there was a body where now is my body.

190

Then: where mine is, there will be others.

Once you get that move down, consider more, with variations. Not the hard-and-fasts—the leanings. Bents and veerings. Sheer things. Wanings. All that is *counter, original, spare, strange*. The not squared but queered, the in-from-the-side and too often sidelined. A feel for the bodies of the used and weathered. An eye for filmy, silver-rashed mirrors. Singed wooden spoons. Quilts pieced from jeans worn for fieldwork and slaughter (that fieldwork and slaughter shadow each fiber). A sheen expressive of time passing and passed, the spotted and tarnished and oiled by hand use. Spaces that gather up mold, rime, and moss. Sunken, lopsided, softened, dried places. Slowed and quieted. The useful still. The scattering of burns on the sleeve of a coat that now bears a field of satin-stitched scars. The quieted, slowed, and useful still. I'm not suggesting an aesthetics of depletion ("from hunger" as my grandmother would say, pitiful, wanting) or an eros of the compensatory (settling for the insufficient), but that each moment of the cycle has always been with us, is here now, and each in its way keeps on giving—the fat green summer breasts of milkweed, their late fall silk offerings blown from their silvery cloven-hoofed hearts, up against the sadness of forced blooms in winter, those sugary oversweet paperwhites made to perform before their time, solo in their decorative pots.

❀   ❀   ❀

AND RIGHT HERE, the rupture came.

After letting these words sit and rest awhile, the world-moment, the era, everything changed. (I had just laid aside a critique of those I called the Bad Boys of Realism, zealous bearers of apocalyptic news on climate, who on behalf of the innocents and as a public service force us to face up to the Dire, correct the childish need to persist in acts of creation—i.e., hope. After a few passes I lost interest in extending their arguments or engaging with, as Adrienne Rich said of the patriarchy at large, "a self-generating energy for destruction.")

At the moment, everyone I know is sewing.

Masks of course. And at one of the churches in my neighborhood, reusable bags from old T-shirts for the food pantry to fill with groceries (last week came a load of extra-larges, each with "Hines Ward is a Douche Bag" printed on them, which we reversed before packing). (The work of restoration can be weird as shit.) Now, almost three months in, skies have cleared over Beijing. Someone spotted an alligator in the

191

harbor here in Baltimore. Without constant mowing (university ground crew all furloughed) the muddy low field near the deer spot is drawing red-winged blackbirds—who by lending their presence designate the land "marsh," along with the cattails and milkweed / fountain grass that has sprung up. Last summer I meant to get my 1940s-era Singer repaired. My grandmother, a tailor, taught me how to sew on it (the "new one," with an electric, not foot-operated pedal). I've made three quilts in my life, way "Before COVID-19": one for a man who didn't care, another for a woman who did very much, and one for myself. I offer no big metaphors here; the facts themselves extend in all directions. So many of us have been accumulating good scraps for years, bags and boxes full, with some belief that they'd come in handy. No plan, just belief. Last week I found the little kerchiefs my mother made for me and my sister—mine has bright yellow flowers on a blue-purple background, and I loved it so much as a kid, I could hardly bring myself to wear it. My sister's is red with small yellow and blue flowers. I washed and ironed them both and now use them as masks.

One response to loss is the remaking of things.

In Memory
Margaret Purpura 1966–2019
Maddalena Purpura 1934–2020

Nominated by Nancy K. Geyer

CRIME AGAINST GRIEF: MYTH OF AN AGE

by XIAO XIAO

from MANOA: A PACIFIC JOURNAL

At that time, the family of Wang Fugui
were preparing for a wedding ceremony. For a year and a half
they tightened their belts and lived off bits of rice and vegetables
they saved from the crevices between their, teeth,
they calculated that the happy day
would fall on the ninth day of the ninth month in 1976
a most auspicious wedding date

they had all lived like paupers
but double happiness was just around the corner,
counting relatives and neighbors
they would need at least six tables for the guests

Wang Fugui's parents brought out meat coupons, food coupons
    and oil coupons
long stashed away and saved in the bottom of boxes,
bitter poverty stored up for almost half a lifetime,
then with teeth clenched they went to town to purchase
Old White Dry, pork, tofu, noodles,
the dishes and burning liquor essential in those days at wedding
    dinners

when all was ready and they were urging the bride to get into the
    sedan chair
the Supreme Leader suddenly died

the nation went into mourning and all entertainment was
    suspended

this was a time without fridges and freezers
the wedding dinner was sitting out spoiling
and wouldn't wait for anyone
so in spite of everything, the Wang family had to finish the business
two days later, the public security cadre came
and arrested the shameless father and his son

charged with what crime?
impertinent celebration
taking pleasure in the death of The Great Leader
the highly educated political commissar came up with new terms

and so, father and son were paraded in front of the public
written on the big boards hanging on ropes around their necks:
crimes against grief

Translation from Chinese by Front Steward, Ming Di

Nominated by Manoa: A Pacific Journal

WHAT I'LL MISS

by DENNIS HELD

from TERRAIN

What has become clear to me is that when it comes to our end times, everything becomes dear.

It's hard not to think about the things I'll miss. I don't imagine myself sitting on a cloud with my angel wings on and feet dangling, moping about everything I'm missing. No, it's more of a series of sharply observed moments, bittersweet, but mostly sweet. Things I might not have noticed before the diagnosis. Together, they represent the small gifts that make up a lifetime. My lifetime.

Like gathering wild fruit—foraging. Driving around the Palouse Prairie, watching for overgrown homesteads and abandoned orchards, grapes unpicked along fence lines, hardscrabble raspberries climbing the rock piles back home in Harvey Metztger's field: all of it free! Huckleberries on Mt. Spokane; morel mushrooms along the river; tiny yellow plums, no bigger than my thumb; and the best pear *ever*, outside of Asotin, Washington, looking for an apple tree I thought I had seen. The best finds can come aslant: arrowheads reveal themselves in the flat glint of flint faces, struck 4,000 years before by human hands. In the night, pennies will reveal themselves as they will not during the day, reflecting the streetlight glare from the parking lot.

Maybe I should have eaten more Chicken in a Biskit; should have used the air conditioner in the car more often; should have had more shrimp, and more bacon; gone back once more to the ocean; kept and loved one more dog.

The languid, heady, Southern smell of honey locust blossoms in the spring: I'll miss that. Gardening, turning the soil. Tomatoes and peas, sunflowers. And beets: who knew I'd learn to love beets late in my life?

Until recently, I did not know that they make chocolate pound cake—now I'm going to miss that; that it's really simple to spray WD-40 into a car lock, and it will work better; that there are two different spellings of "discreet" and "discrete." I did not know what it would feel like to have a definite end.

Sometimes, especially when I'm on the phone, the elephant re-enters the room. The other person says, man, I'm having a hell of a time with my hip lately, and—oh jeez, yeah, that's right. Umm. I mean, you're like going to, well, you know, and here I am bitching about a sore hip. I'm sorry man, I just wasn't thinking and. . . . No. Stop. Thanks, but it's okay.

How to be graceful, in times like these, might be worth some attention, on my end. What has become clear to me is that when it comes to our end times, everything becomes dear. Becomes worthy of note. And what we encounter as individuals turns out to be contained within something that is much larger, much more like a plasma, or a gel, that simply encompasses and encapsulates it all. All the hard parts, the pointy bits, the tragedy and the melancholy, sit comfortably alongside the ecstasy and the joy at the miracle of simple human existence. Everything gets absorbed. That's it: in the end, it's all the same material. Fluid. Welcoming, even. I don't know if that's idiotic or profound. For now, it's enough.

I'll miss all water, really, every creek and rill: the Spokane River, Devil's Lake in central Wisconsin, Lake Michigan east of my home, the channel called Porte de Morte: Door of the Dead. Freshwater lakes that never warm up. Lightning bugs. Camping at Terry Andre State Park. Those dunes.

Along the Snake River, Buffalo Eddy petroglyphs, 8,000 years old and counting. Pecked deep into the burnished rock, other-worldly visions.

Cooking for others. And how I'm going to miss basketball: sneaky step-backs, up-and-under layups, left-handed hook shots. I'm 61, and until recently, when I make a shot, my friend Andy says, *"There's the Old Coyote!"* But since my surgery, no more.

I get to wear my slippers any time I want now—even to the grocery store. I can eat chocolate ice cream with impunity, and a bigger spoon. Less oatmeal. More Fudgesicles.

Small tricks I can do with my hands: skipping stones a dozen times, twirling a baton. Learned that in third grade, on the playground practicing those over-and-under-the-finger rolls. Catching a Frisbee behind my back, between my legs, on top of my head. Card-into-hat flipping and Toss the Pen in the Tall Cup.

Music? Hard to get started. Doc Watson, Merle Watson, and the Frosty Mom Band. *"Alberta, let your hair hang low. I'll give you more gold than your apron can hold, if you'll only let your hair hang low."* Ooof. Guy Clark and his dad's Randall knife. Emmy Lou Harris, Graham Parsons. Annie Lennox. John Hiatt. Any list I make excludes too much.

Knowledge. Just finding things out, going deep, pushing off with both feet: local history, who lived where, and geology—every lump of pegmatite, each batholith. Fossils slay me. Colossal geological floods. The Channeled Scablands of Eastern Washington! Digging up old bottles from farm dumps.

Driving along a Wyoming dirt road and finding a slab of mother-of-pearl fossilized clam shells in perfect replication, upside-down, from the ocean floor and heaved up to the roadside. Actual dinosaur bones pulled from an eroding hillside south of the Badlands near Scenic, South Dakota.

Having to juggle together the recognition of one's imminent mortality with thoughts of doing the laundry and shopping for bananas can get things a little mixed up, in your head and in your heart. Can complicate things. One has to set certain thoughts, certain truths, even, aside, to get on with the business of everyday life. And that, in itself, can be a kind of a blessing, too. A balm. To enter back into the dailiness of life, out of the rounds of grim waiting rooms and stark facts and cold comforts. Of six different doctors' appointments in four days. Of walnut-sized "ports" surgically implanted under the skin and two-drug cocktails and a gamma "knife" we all know is not really a knife. Out of the medical world. Back into the world.

I'll miss being useful. Not feeling useful, but *being* useful. Set the table, fold the metal chairs at the end of a meeting, do the dishes, the laundry, the floors, on hands and knees. Doing a good job of it.

Ponds, for sure, with turtles. Mucky ponds too, the whole rank and file—mostly rank—with liberty and cattails for all. Half my childhood was spent in the company of crayfish, caught in streambeds and quarries and ponds, Knowing how to get them to scoot backwards into your hat, your net, how to grab them right behind the pincers and render them helpless, how to wave them at girls walking by on the beach while making fake dinosaur roaring sounds.

Huge, rolling Midwestern thunderstorms that blast stick lightning to the ground and pour down rain: gully-washers, branch-breakers,

197

flooders of fields. Ice storms that form on tree branches and bring everything down. Big hail. Gale-force winds. Stories told across the table while the latest storm is still flashing all around, of the time lightning came through the kitchen window, busting it out, and traveled around the room in the wires inside the walls, popping off the wall plates on the way by, and running out onto the porch where it blew the gutters off. Nobody hurt, though. Sheesh.

I love oiling a pair of good leather boots. Where you get the neatsfoot oil down into all the little cracks and creases, and it cleans everything up, and makes it all supple again.

What do I have? I have Stage 4 cancer, the worst kind. As a friend reminded me, there is no Stage 5. I have malignant melanoma, a kind of cancer almost always associated with the skin, although it can enter the body through the skin and settle in anywhere. In my case, that was the gall bladder. It took my doctors a long time to track the whole thing down, because the tests came back negative for gall bladder cancer, but positive for melanoma. How rare is that? My surgeon says that he's found 12 other cases in the entire medical literature. I have asked every medical professional I've met to give me as much information as possible, as soon as possible, so I can make the best decisions. So far, I have been afforded that courtesy, every time.

I believe in the power of warm bubble baths, especially for men: lavendar-scented, epsom-salted, candles flickering in the dark, soft music in the background. . . . No general ever stepped out of a bubble bath and declared war.

I won't have to buy Christmas stamps. It's okay if I'm starting to go deaf. And I won't have to get a colonoscopy.

Yes to sandbars, to caramel sauce, and ice-cream sandwiches. Yes to tadpoles in classrooms, tadpoles with legs and a tail, tadpoles all the way to frogs. And then, let go, into the swamp.

Dragonflies. Moose.

Vellum-covered books, a warm stocking cap, heavy-duty long johns.

The Pacific Ocean and everything in it. Kelp bulbs and fronds that look like cheerful waving aliens. Sea urchins. Tidal pools. Haystack Rocks. The Aquarium at Monterey Bay, the Shedd Aquarium in Chicago, the Newport Aquarium on the Oregon Coast, any damned aquarium anywhere. The first time I saw a starfish at 25 years old: fiery orange as a kid's drawing of the sun. Curious seals bobbing toward me in the Pacific surf, sea lions illustrating the word "bask" at Florence, Oregon. Whales off Yaquina Head. Even the slow-going freighters that crawl the horizon are parcel and part, are connected to the Kon-Tiki and the Makah tribal whalers and every human outward seagoing endeavor: Go! Go find out!

Rattlesnakes? The first was in the Klickitat Canyon in southcentral Washington, a timber rattler, curled up against the trunk of a big blue sagebrush off to the side of the trail. The first clacking, clattering sound, the first dry, hollow shatter of it got into my body and I was reduced to the truth. *You could die.*

I'm undergoing Gamma Knife radiation treatment, and then immunotherapy. The Gamma thing is not a blade, but a highly focused radiation tool that sits in a room by itself and weighs 64 tons and shoots gamma rays from 200 different points to focus a super-fine beam on a tumor, to shrink it. These tumors are in my brain, a total of seven of them, mostly small, except for one larger mass. This is the most advanced therapy of its kind, and it has a low rate of side effects. The doctors are confident of good results, and everything looks positive in that department.

Immunotherapy consists of a regimen of two different drugs, three weeks apart. The intent is to boost the immune system enough to fight the cancer. The infusion is a three-hour process where I bring a book along with me and they have me sit in a recliner. Sometimes, it's the best part of my week. Almost. The resulting side effects are much reduced from those experienced during chemo or general radiation. I am receiving two new drugs, one just released by the FDA, specifically meant to treat melanoma.

But there is no cure for Stage 4 cancer. It will kill me. None of my doctors has been able to offer me an "end date," even though I sometimes ask, "Can you give me a ballpark figure here? Weeks, months, a year?" It all depends on a matrix that has too many variables: I'm in good health, I'm relatively young, I have no other heart or lung conditions to complicate matters. The PET scan showed that I don't have cancer in my bones, where melanoma often runs to—that's a particularly good bit of news.

Just six months ago, back in May, I had no idea there was anything wrong. I was playing basketball once a week with some of the other old guys and getting up tricky shots with my left hand. But in June, while I was driving, I had a sudden feeling of pressure inside my chest, on the right side-not a heart thing, but something I'd never felt before. I drove to the ER, where they diagnosed a blocked bile duct (goes from the liver to the small intestine) and they put a stent in the duct, and removed some suspicious material. Thus began the first mystery: What was the "sludge" (their term) they found in the blocked duct? A biopsy took ten days to come back with a definite conclusion. The gall bladder material tested negative for most cancers, including gall bladder cancer, but positive for melanoma. Can't be. They had to rerun the tests, twice. Turns out, that's what it is.

So the oncologist hands me the keys to the hearse and says, "Drive slow."

I'll miss the loopy, heady feeling I get when I smoke pot. I like the fine disordering of the senses, the associative surprises that can arise when I'm high. I don't take edibles; they put me to sleep. And I don't vape that 90 percent concentrated stuff. Too high by half. Every once in a while, just put a little puff in a pipe. I have for 40 years.

My odd case got kicked upstairs from Dr. Puri to Dr. Mejia, who explained that my gall bladder, which was left in after the first surgery, would now have to come out. Also, there was a chance he'd have to re-sect, or remove, a piece of my liver where it was in contact with the gall bladder. That surgery, in mid-July, revealed that the cancer had been spread through the lymph nodes that were near my gall bladder to other parts of my body. Dr. Mejia removed the gall bladder and the lymph nodes, and recessed the liver, which tested negative for cancer. Once again, it took a long time—ten days—for the report to come in, confirming the diagnosis: melanoma of the gall bladder.

At the bank, there's an overeager teller—Ben—with a seven-dollar haircut, a tip-hustling voice and a steel-trap mind who always asks, "So Dennis, what ya got goin' on tonight? You going out?" He nods at my empty ring finger. So tonight I say, in the flat voice of a serial killer, "No, Ben, tonight I'm going to sit in my basement in a cocoon of self-loathing and despair and shake my fist at the sky while burning with contempt for humanity." He blinks twice, and says only, "Okay, here's your cash."

Late-night walks, end of August, the air buoyant, uplifting, the cool starting to slide in under the day's heat. And conversation. As much as anything, conversation. Simple back-and-forth. A laugh, now and again, at an unexpected turn of phrase. Easy repartee. Wit.

Junk shops, second-hand stores, thrift stores, The Thrifty Grandmothers store in Colfax, estate sales, farm auctions, all of it. Every last chipped glass and plate of it. When I was 12 years old, I went to a yard sale across the street and bought six pink Depression-era wine glasses for two dollars. I still have five. Just because I'm dying doesn't mean I have to quit shopping.

Found notes. I've kept these for 40 tears: *Yvonne, Call your mother before your visit to the psychic.* Ragtag snips of sentences, inmate mail, more than 200 letters. Also, I have a wooden box full of found pennies; the ones that are the worse for the wear are the best. The run-over, the beat up and bent. The farther away from money they come—the closer back to copper they go—the better.

On the Palouse Prairie in harvest time: grain trucks lined up like circus elephants in a cutover wheat field, each truck's tail grabbed by the trailer behind it.

Colleen comes to get me from the waiting room, wearing blue scrubs. She's handsy, patting my arm, my back, my knee once I'm seated on the examining table. She's very interested in what I do for a living, how everything has been going since the diagnosis, if I have friends to help me through. She's warm and genuine and takes more than a passing interest in me as a person and a patient. She is also not afraid to tear up. She introduces me to Jill, who will walk me all the way through the procedure and will, it turns out, be there for me when I begin to cry unexpectedly. Jill is a rock-solid nurse with 33 years on the job and 16 years doing this particular work. Yet she still lets her eyes fill up and has to take a tissue of her own after handing me one. Like Colleen, she has somehow found a way to stay compassionate, to keep her heart open to the truth of her patients' lives, short though they may be, and still offer all the strength and support she can muster. It's a rare combination— it's so much easier to guard the heart.

Kicking a pine cone down a trail, and having it roll a long way.

Should I store my summer shorts over winter? Is Christmas likely? How about rubber bands? Should I even bother saving them?

Dumb jokes. Bad puns. Word squirts. Why can't you run in a campground? Because you *ran*—past tents. I have 25 friends who are letters but I don't know Y. My mom had a bunch of set-pieces she could trot out: "The drunker I sit here, the longer I get. I've only had tee martoonies." I still love gags—especially sight gags. The Buster Keaton flying prat-fall. And *Mad Magazine* (RIP). Any kind of laughter. Carson. Keeton. Chaplin. Also Robert Benchley and Red Skelton and Gilbert and Sullivan. Danny Kaye, for sure. Definitely Danny Kaye. (Watch him dance with Liza Minelli on his 1960s TV show on YouTube. Smashing.) Smothers Brothers in red sweaters. George Carlin? A saint. Firesign Theatre? Geniuses.

In the neurosurgeon's office, the first thing I notice is the dog bed. Then Fiona the dog trots in and plops down. Meanwhile, the neurosurgeon is pointing to the view from the top of my brain down, working his way through the layers and cross-sections, and describing the seven tumors. He shows me a small cloudy area where some blood has spread into the brain. The doctor's affect is decidedly flat. It's not that I want a flamboyant neurosurgeon or something, but I'm just hoping for a reaction. The dog stirs, sighs. My neurosurgeon has a loose shock of white hair and a dandy, flowing mustache, a bit like Mark Twain. I trust him immediately. He thinks we'll have to do three treatments, just to be sure. Good idea, I say. Very good idea.

Three treatments. Two weeks apart. Whatever it takes. The dog snuggles into its bed. The doc has me sign a consent form. He looks at my handwriting, and finally, he laughs: "You have a worse signature than I do."

Some of the better wack-a-doodle books: *Poor Richard's Almanac. The Diary of Samuel Pepys.* Boswell's *Life of Samuel Johnson.* Lin Yutang, *With Love and Irony* and the *Analects of Confucius.* Lafcadio Hearn, all the way. e e cummings near the top of the list for sass, and sincerely mocking the worst of capitalism. Whitman because, well, Whitman: perhaps the original American. Gary Snyder. Marilynn Robinson. Wendell Berry. Kurt Vonnegut. Saul Bellow: all the fiction, and especially the essays, *It All Adds Up: From the Dim Past to the Uncertain Future.*

Unlimited bratwurst: no more cholesterol checks. Apple streusel goes on that list of what I'll miss. It's all about how you crumble the butter into the brown sugar-flour mixture. One pound butter, two cups flour, one cup brown sugar. Good fat. My friend Sean calls it "crack cake." Goes well with the weed. And everything else.

Job 7:7–10: Remember, O God, that my life is but a breath; my eyes will never see happiness again. The eye that now sees me will see me no longer; you will look for me, but I will be no more. As a cloud vanishes and is gone, so one who goes down to the grave does not return. He will never come to his house again; his place will know him no more.

So now it's slow and steady and we'll all try to get through this with some grace and decorum. One thing I know—wait, what was that thing? I'll keep you posted.

Nominated by Robert Wrigley

O DESPOT! MY DESPOT!

fiction by PATRICK DACEY

from ZOETROPE: ALL STORY

I listen from my room below, as my despot weeps in his above.

Such torture!

But what can I do for him? He does not respond well to leaving his comforts. Yet leave he must, or else be forced out, along with myself and the few loyal nationalists who remain in the Great House, who keep guard and order, though I suspect even these proud men and women will in short time dismiss their fidelity and make themselves subjects of documentaries, like so many before them, reclaiming their love of country in the face of our great despot's fall from grace.

In the morning, he will address the nation one last time, and it has been my job these past few months to prepare him for this address. This, he's been told, will be his best chance to revive his legacy, to prove that he is healthy and fit, and leaving of his own volition.

Oh, how did we get here, my despot? I ask in silence. Sometimes, I do feel that our minds are one and we can hear the other without speaking.

He would tell me that this is nonsense. But I perceive, in his cries and his hacking coughs and midnight howls, a man who blames only himself.

Wasn't it you, my despot, who once said, long ago, that we must be as vigilant as the earthworm, so that when we are cut we can regenerate still, and dig and furrow and provide for our land?

Yes, I grew up having misunderstood the true meaning of sacrifice, and I saw my parents give their lives away to ideas and thoughts and dreams.

It took time for me to realize what it meant to be grateful.

Many beatings and lectures. Many sprints and cold showers. I was poor and flabby. You, my despot, made me rich and lean.

* * *

Each night has been worse than the last.

My despot can't sleep.

"I won't sleep!" he cries.

What terrible nightmares he has when he closes his eyes.

"Pieces of me began to fall off, Dalton. First my ears, then my nose, lips, arms, and nails. All that was left were my eyes, so that I could see how terrifying I looked!"

I try to calm him by bringing him warm milk and singing a lullaby, but he won't repose; he drinks his milk and paces around the bedroom. I begin to doze, and he wakes me with a kick to the gut.

"More milk!" he demands.

I can safely report that my despot's health is just fine, but he doesn't look healthy. We have attempted to address this with makeup under the eyes, yet my despot fusses and pushes away the stylists.

"Let them see!" he shouts. "Let them see what it takes to run this country!"

"But your appearance, sir," I say.

"Yes? What about it? I am a man of peace, Dalton! Any man of peace looks like they've been kicked sixty ways to Sunday. Gandhi. Mandela. Jesus. So what if I'm beefy? Does that not mean I suffer?"

Oh, the level of hatred!

Cause of such anxiety, such debilitating depression. Truly, my despot suffers to know there are those who want to see his eye sockets filled with maggots.

"They call me so many names, Dalton. They say I'm weak, and my teeth are crooked, and my head is full of mashed potatoes."

"Such indecencies, sir."

"And blatantly inaccurate, Dalton. Feel my arms. No, not there—up higher."

"Hard as rocks, sir. Nothing short of impressive."

"And look here."

"Perfectly straight, sir. Not even an overbite."

"Shall I name every world leader in alphabetical order?"

"What would be the point, sir?"

We have tried desperately to restore my despot to good physical shape. He has been on a strict diet of root vegetables and fish, but he cannot go a day without peanut butter cups, and without peanut butter cups he's not very nice.

As usual, though, my despot never ceases to amaze. Just last week, spurred by ridicule, he called for me to put on my jogging suit and come to his room.

"We must get fit!" he cried. "You're the boy for the job, Dalton! I need to build my glutes. In my heyday, I had such glorious glutes!"

I noticed that my despot was wearing shorts that must have dated from the era of those glorious glutes. Now, however, his backside was rather large and dimply. The mustard-colored fabric barely disguised his dingle, the middle seam splitting his crab apples.

"Did you know that I was once a very good athlete, Dalton? I was considered one of the fastest men on earth."

"I think I knew that, sir."

"You think? Where's your sense of history? You watch, Dalton."

First, we performed knee bends, backbends, and light squats. Then I suggested we jog through the Great House.

"Do you know how many hallways there are, Dalton?"

"That I don't, sir."

"They are endless."

"Yes, sir."

My despot turned our amble into a trot, taunting me by galloping backward and squealing. Then he began to sprint, his glutes bouncing mightily. A moment later, he was doubled over.

"Oh, something terrible has happened," he said.

That night, I sat on a stool beside my despot as he soaked in the tub. The doctor had instructed him to spend fifteen minutes in warm water and fifteen minutes out, and to keep doing so until his crab apples unwound.

When the first fifteen minutes were up, my despot called for his robe, and I draped it over his shoulders. As he reached for his dingle, I reminded him of the doctor's orders.

"Let them unwind on their own, sir," I said.

"Yes. OK," he said.

He soaked and stood, soaked and stood.

"Can you play an instrument, Dalton?" he asked.

"I can blow on a harmonica fairly well, sir."

"I mean a real instrument, Dalton."

"No, sir. I don't have much of a knack for music."

"I haven't heard music in so long. I just remembered that. I wonder what happened?"

"Sir," I said, looking down. "They've unwound."

"So they have," he said, and tied his robe. "Much to look forward to, Dalton."

"Yes, sir."

He walked through the doors to his bedroom.

"Sleep well, sir," I said.

I held a moment, hoping he'd heard me.

If this document ever becomes an historical record, please don't think that I'm speaking badly about my despot's nature. For, even with his balls tied in a knot, the strength and certainty of his eyes equip him with immeasurable powers. He has a handsome face with a sharp chin, and by the evening, when the stubble has grown back, he takes on the appearance of a rugged gentleman, adept at shooting clay pigeons.

His very presence commands attention from the vilest divisions in our nation. He walks and points, and where his eyes go so do yours, and then back to his, as now he is looking at you, the way he does from the banners draped along the crumbling buildings in City Center (even half of his face covers a good deal of crumble), and then he is passing out of the once-quiet room, leaving it in a state of confusion, unrest, and quickening instability.

I have seen how people follow my despot, as though in a trance, up to the barricades, to the great fleet of armored cars, where he turns and waves, ushering them back into the wild.

You cannot disremember that glorious day, years ago, when we stood at attention and listened over the caws of crows, and the laughter and screaming, as his voice boomed through the loudspeakers bolted to the trees in the green square. You cannot disremember the next day either, and the sight of a man being dragged by his feet from the back of a chuck wagon through the same square, now smattered with bird poop.

Boy, how times have and have not changed!

My despot closes each address with the same righteous sincerity:

"What more can I give to you than my heart, my soul, my life?"

And we stand there silently, as though listening to a prayer.

But now, my despot seems to be increasingly unpopular with his people.

"What can I do?" he exclaimed once, after we had watched a slanderous comedy skit on television that showed a much smaller and chubbier man using a bridge made up of his own constituents to cross a gator-infested tributary. "They don't know the man I was before I was the man I am."

What words! I thought. What humility!

"Dalton, are you aware that I'm an orphan?"

"No, sir."

"Because I'm not! Still, I have great empathy for orphans. My parents never knew how to nurture me. But I miss them, Dalton. I miss summer. I miss the ocean. I miss the porch and seeing my trunks hang over the railing, dripping at the bottoms as they dried in the sun. I miss the smell of peaches! And, by God, I've never even liked peaches all that much. What a world my memory is! What a muscle my mind! How long must we suffer in its spontaneous revolution?"

"Sir, this is the raw stuff. This is what you need to share with the people."

"No, Dalton. Tell the people your private thoughts, and they'll ache from hope."

Oh, but he aches! He weeps for days past and days to come! He weeps sometimes without knowing why!

"Dalton!" he cries. "My poor eyes won't ever dry!"

"Sir, my hands are full of used tissues."

"Kids are dying."

"Yes, and grown men and women, too."

"Grown men and women and kids."

"Entire families, sir."

"So many tragedies, Dalton. How much empathy can one have?"

"It's a great feat to summon all that empathy, sir."

I have been serving the despot now for more than half of my short life, and there are still days when he seems to not know who I am and orders the guards to have me stripped of my clothes and searched in all the obvious places, and also some not-so-obvious places.

Yes, I was warned about the long nights he would spend weeping, his fickle stomach, the self-induced blackouts. One night, during the first week of my post, my despot began to feel nauseous after his supper of rockfish. I, too, had eaten the rockfish, and found it bland and pleasant, yet I dutifully followed my despot into the washroom, where my empathy for the noise (and smell) of his vomiting soon had us taking turns chucking into the rose-tinted latrine.

Once we were finished, we sat back against the wall and caught our breath.

"That was a doozy!" my despot finally exclaimed.

They were the first words he had ever spoken to me.

"Where are you from, Daniels?"

"Not far."

"And your folks? What did they do for a living?"

"My mother was an artist, sir."

"Is that right?"

"She never liked to stay in one place for too long."

"Do you miss her?"

"I do, sir. But not as much as I did before my days of self-reflection."

"Good boy. And your father? How did he fail you?"

"He was not a strong man, sir. He had a perfect body and big muscles and a square chin. But inside, sir, his heart was made of applesauce."

"Weakness, Delaney, is the bane of existence."

"Yes, sir."

"Please," my despot said, and reached out for me to help him to his feet.

Each morning, I read to my despot from his own memoirs as he soaks his heavy skin. When he is finished soaking, I shave his face. Depending on his mood, he might playfully grab at my nipple, almost causing my hand to slip. In one instance, he held my wrist and pulled it toward his neck—the razor pressing against his Adam's apple, a touch of blood—and then laughed me off as though I were a second-rate performer on audition.

After his soak and shave, I groom my despot as he gazes at his sensitive documents.

Once, upon noticing a fair bit of dirt and sock fuzz beneath his toenail, I guided his foot into my lap and gingerly inserted a pick to scrape the gunk out; and though my despot complained that the pick tickled, and threatened me with all manner of violence, he allowed me to continue. I then tended to the nail itself, which was due for its regular upkeep. As I clamped down on the hardened keratin and squeezed the clippers, a chip shot skyward and nicked my left eye.

My vision impaired, I wavered about and fell back against the tiled floor.

"Oh, a freak occurrence!" my despot lauded.

I moaned. I gritted my teeth. I put a hand to my eye and lowered it, and with my other eye saw the blood.

"I'm sorry for your pain, Dalton, but do you not love the freak occurrence? What else makes this great life worth living?"

"Yes, sir," I said.

I held my bloody eye and crossed my toes tightly. The pain was not so severe in light of my despot's excitement.

"I don't trust you to finish my nails, Dalton. But I cannot let you leave until I've finished my reading, and now that some pages have fallen onto the wet floor and into your blood, we must wait for fresh ones. You understand."

"Yes, sir. I am happy to wait."

I believe that the eye became infected during the subsequent hours, while my despot finished his reading, but what choice did I have?

After this morning's grooming, we drove in a caravan to my despot's hometown again.

We walked the main street, passing the church and library and penny-candy shop, and around the corner to his house, which is repainted twice daily to cover the heinous graffiti.

"Dalton, that is where I slept, there on the second floor. I looked out that window while my mother smacked my bottom, and I could see the penny-candy shop, and I thought how one day I would rule this sorry nation."

"Was it that window, sir? Or the north-facing window?"

"You're right, Dalton. It was the other room, wasn't it?"

"I believe so, sir."

"I dreamed so many dreams in this house, Dalton. Where did they all go?"

We went around to the backyard.

"I had many animals as a child—rabbits, goats, dogs—but none of them liked me very much. Nor did my mother."

Hanging from a large tree were two ropes tied to a wooden plank. My despot's eyes brightened.

"Oh, how I would swing, Dalton!"

He grasped one of the ropes.

"Will you give me a push?" he asked.

"Of course, sir."

He sat on the plank, and the tree branch began to give way. The detail heard the crack, and before his bottom hit the ground, they shoved my despot out of the way. One of the men took the blow from the fallen limb and was ushered to the hospital with a brutal head wound.

"My poor swing!" my despot cried. "My poor childhood!"

* * *

Now my despot has ordered us to leave him in peace so that he can prepare for tomorrow.

Three times I asked if he wanted warm milk to help him sleep, and three times he denied any affinity for milk—whatever the temperature, whatever the hour.

"Many great leaders have enjoyed a glass of warm milk before retiring their brilliant minds for a few hours," I reassured him, "including one or two popes."

The truth is, asking for a glass of warm milk makes him feel embarrassed.

So I brought the milk anyway, and he tipped the tray over onto my shirt front and slammed the door shut. I frowned at the stain, because I don't have many nice shirts, as there has been a crackdown on unnecessary spending since the war began, in order that we can keep building our military to show strength and unity.

But don't pity me. Pity Emilio, who has to milk the cow.

Oh, my despot, didn't we one night have such fun dancing in our underwear to happy music on satellite radio?

My despot is surprisingly nimble! Such impressive flexibility!

"Not many people know this, Dalton," he said, "but in my youth, I wanted to be a professional dancer."

I felt light, yet sure-footed and safe, as we floated across the room and he spun me like a young lover before snapping me back against his chest. The sharp whiskers on his face pressed against my neck like a dozen needle points.

"I'm being foolish tonight, Dalton," he said.

"There's no harm in being foolish on occasion, sir."

"But what's the occasion?"

"In my experience, sir, foolishness is most enjoyable when it comes about spontaneously."

My despot twirled me away and released my hand. He plucked a pair of damp towels from the pyramid of damp towels and tossed one to me.

"What you're saying, Dalton, is that I shouldn't feel guilty for wanting to dance while so many of my people are sick and dying?"

"Yes, sir. Even the sick and dying enjoy a dance now and again, if they're up for it, that is."

210

He pressed the towel against his forehead and sat on the sofa and crossed his legs.

"We are so wasteful, Dalton. That's one lesson the aliens can learn from us—and I don't mean the aliens down there," my despot said, pointing vaguely southward and frowning, "but up there, in the galaxies or whatever. We really know how to build some waste. Great big piles we crush into smaller piles. And someday, the smaller piles will be the bigger piles, and we'll have towers of waste that's been crushed and stacked and crushed and stacked until it finally topples over and we're gone. That's what's going to do it, you know. Long before we run out of water or burn to a crisp, we'll drown in our chicken buckets."

Shortly, his composure turned to one of dire constraint.

"Dalton," he said. "I've been sick and dying all my life."

In volume two of his yet-to-be published memoir, *My Life Philosophy*, my despot says of his life philosophy:

> The past is only a test, but we forget the purpose of the test, which is to prevent us from making mistakes in the future. Instead, we say, "We failed," and that's the end, and we study for the next test, which will require us to know new things, further pushing away the old things we never really knew, so that, in the end, we know nothing and are unable to do anything. In order to prevent the mistakes, we must study the information, yes, but then we must execute across untested ground, building a new past as we go, taking with us only those willing to sacrifice ever more investigation into what was once home. We have been tested long enough—there have been so many songs about this, and even those popular songs, the ones that still play in the drafty houses where carpenters hammer away at wood like children or sons of God, even those everlasting three-and-a-half-minute symphonies can't inspire us to move forward—and so, yes, no more teachers, and so on, or, to think of it another way, all the rounds are real and everything's at stake. At this point, you do not have time to think about how this came to be.

The first night the people attempted to overrun the Great House and were ultimately destroyed, my despot shouted from his study:

"But I'm a good person!"

"Yes, sir!" I came running, crying. "You are a good person, sir!"

"And well-mannered! Mom made me learn to wash the butter dish correctly. Do you know how filthy a butter dish gets, Dalton?"

"No, sir. We used a tub."

"Of course you did, Dalton. My apologies."

"It's nothing, sir."

"My legacy, Dalton. Think of the men they compare me to. Did you know that Hitler was impotent?"

"No, sir."

"He'd get off by hiring prostitutes to defecate on his chest."

"Such indecency, sir."

"Stalin wore boots to bed because he was embarrassed by his deformed left foot. If a woman laughed at him naked in his boots, he'd kick her in the crotch."

"Ouch, sir."

"Mussolini stabbed his lovers for fun."

"Double ouch, sir."

"Saddam starred in gay porn flicks, for crying out loud. He went by the name Omar Studdif. Did you know that, Dalton?"

"No, sir."

"Later, he married his cousin, and cheated on her with married women in order to humiliate their husbands."

"Not just indecent, sir. Torrid."

"Can you imagine? These are the men I will be pictured alongside in the annals!"

"But, sir. I will make a record of your virtues for the annals."

"You won't be wicked, Dalton?"

"No, sir. I, too, am a virtuous lover."

"What do you know about making love, Dalton?"

What did I know?

So little.

The one time I thought it was in, it wasn't.

"No. Better leave my annals to me alone, Dalton."

"As you wish, sir."

I just now had a very personal moment with my despot while attempting to deliver his third glass of warm milk. He'd left the door open, and I entered carefully with the tray so that I would not be down another shirt.

He had the curtains tied and the lights low and the fire going. He sat on the bed with his legs crossed and his belly settled like a net of fish on his knees. He stayed this way, looking off at a point on the wall.

"Can I ask you something, Dalton?"

"Yes, sir."

"Will you go to my desk there by the fireplace and open the second drawer and take out the folder and read the piece of paper inside?"

I started for the desk before he finished his instructions, and quickly fetched the paper, which was folded into squares like a middle-school note.

I read the first words: "I am living proof—"

"To yourself!" my despot shouted.

"Of course, sir," I said, and I can still remember those words exactly:

I am living proof that things
do, too, die
in the spring.

It was a poem!

Oh, my heart!

"Tell me in all honesty, Dalton. Is it very good?"

My mouth was dry. I couldn't speak.

"Please, Dalton."

"Perhaps," I started, and a sharp pain spread across my chest.

"Yes?" my despot said.

I thought of something sweet smelling—candy shops, split-pea-and-rose-petal soap scrub, cinnamon.

"Perhaps," I muttered, "you could omit the *do,* or the *too*?"

He thought about this, then put on his glasses, then removed them, then hid them beneath a pillow. He studied the poem for a while, and ordered me to hand him one of the freshly sharpened pencils in the drawer. (He trusts me with a sharp pencil.)

He made a mark on the poem and refolded it into squares and slipped it into his breast pocket.

I will never know what my despot had decided just then, or if he had crossed out another word entirely.

"Would you believe me, Dalton, if I told you that all of this is a dream? That, when you wake, you'll be on a boat, in a calm lake, surrounded by towering pine trees, and the air will be so clean that your lungs will burn with gratitude? Would you trade this life for that one?"

"I've never been on a boat, sir."

213

"Forget the boat."

"Forget the boat?"

"Yes. Just picture the lake."

"Lakes frighten me, sir. I don't like the squishy bottom."

"Forget the lake."

"OK, sir. Lake forgotten."

"Where are you, Dalton?"

"Now?"

"Yes, now!"

"In a boat on a lake, sir?"

"Good boy, Dalton. And can you fish?"

"No, sir."

"Then what will you eat?"

"Whatever's in the boat, sir."

"There is only a single sleeve of saltines, Dalton."

"I will eat those."

"And once they run out?"

"I don't know, sir."

"What will you drink?"

"The water from the lake?"

"No, Dalton, you fool! You'll get sick!"

"Then I'll boil the water, sir."

"Did you bring matches, Dalton? Pots, kindling? Did you not antici-pate the worst? Have I taught you nothing?"

"I don't know, sir."

"So, you'll admit then that this country does need me after all?"

"Yes, sir. There is no doubt."

"How can we possibly move forward with a nation full of unprepared dreamers?"

"We can't, sir. Unless, as you said earlier, this is all a dream."

"Sometimes I dream I am burying people alive, Dalton. Hundreds and thousands."

"Psychology tells us this has to do with burying some kind of pain from your past, sir."

"Yes, Dalton, and the bodies, too."

My despot rose and walked to the fire and took the poem from his breast pocket and tossed it in.

"Now, go and rest your head, Dalton. Tomorrow is an important day for our nation."

"Sir?" I said. "Your milk, sir?"

"By now, it has cooled, hasn't it?"

"Yes, sir."

"Oh, well."

It is just after two in the morning, and I must be awake in four hours to prepare my despot for his speech. As I lie here, though, I'm too afraid to sleep, and even more afraid that if I sleep, I will wake up.

I cannot help but think of my father and how he had been a loyal and faithful worker, taking only three sick days during his entire career at Balthazar Inc., and all three due to my being sick with a cold, which, he often reminded me, unfortunately became unbearable during an evening rather than a morning, forcing him to take one more day than was probably necessary, and thereby ensuring his defeat to Neville Dirkenroot, the senior VP, who had taken only two sick days, and both near the end, when he had forgotten where he worked and drove instead to a nearby Dunkin' Donuts and ordered turkey dumplings.

Ultimately, all my father's bitterness toward me, and toward the long-deceased Neville Dirkenroot and my mother and a host of hapless telemarketers, cashiers, and waiters, was for nothing. Just prior to his retirement with full pension, he was let go for wearing mismatched socks twice in the same week (noticed because of his great long legs, and how he often crossed them and dangled his foot while pondering). This, he understood. Years before, during one of the three talks that we ever had, he avowed the idea of acquiescence as a cure to the curse of terminal uniqueness. A willingness to conform and to receive bits and pieces of pleasure for your service to a larger structure that had existed long before you were ever known. Something was not right, he knew. And on the many nights when he refused to come to the table for dinner with my mother and me, remaining in his room, his head a blotch of darkness against the glow of the computer screen, I'd hear him tell her the same, over and over, "Something's not right," until she could finally convince him to take a bath. I'd eat and clean up alone, then peek through the cracked door to see her washing him and shaving his face.

My poor father.

I remember him with great remorse.

Finally, it is light out, and the sad day begins. Crowds have gathered around the Great House. I can see their maddened faces. I can feel their hatred and disgust. I can taste the blood as I bite down on my tongue.

But I can't hear any noise from above. No crying, no shouting, no pained moans. Fearing the worst, I dress in a frenzy and bolt up the stairs, only to find—to my ecstatic relief—my despot in the tub, shaving his own face, grooming his own nails.

"Are there no sensitive documents for me to read, Dalton?"

"No, sir."

"Oh, well."

I go to the closet to gather his clothes.

"Please, Dalton," he says. "I must learn to live without you."

He struggles into his pants and socks and stands there in the closet, with the button open at his waist and the socks stretched loose at his ankles.

"Oh, Dalton."

I fasten the button and secure the sock garters snug around his calves.

"Thank you, Dalton," he says.

We proceed down the many halls of the Great House, the window at the end of each blinding us with light, until finally we pass through the doors to the dying garden.

He pauses for a moment and looks out at the people in their sea of rage, and then he steps to the podium with his head high and eyes downcast. The crowd halts and heels, the formative training modules so ingrained in our psyches.

There is such great silence, and one ill-timed flatulence.

"My God . . . ," he says. "What life!"

We wait for more. We salivate like dogs.

But that is all.

He turns and walks through us, and we dutifully part and follow him out to the helicopter pad, where he lifts off and thwaps away to his encampment in the hills.

I am left to watch his people tear the Great House down.

I am left to watch it burn.

O despot! My despot!

From above, you must feel you have escaped such a fiery hell!

Nominated by Sandra Leong, Zoetrope: All Story

A SMALL NEEDFUL FACT

by ROSS GAY

from HEART POEMS (WORD PRESS)

Is that Eric Garner worked
for some time for the Parks and Rec.
Horticultural Department, which means,
perhaps, that with his very large hands,
perhaps, in all likelihood,
he put gently into the earth
some plants which, most likely,
some of them, in all likelihood,
continue to grow, continue
to do what such plants do, like house
and feed small and necessary creatures,
like being pleasant to touch and smell,
like converting sunlight
into food, like making it easier
for us to breathe.

Nominated by Ruth Wittman

TREZZO

fiction by SETH FRIED

from THE MISSOURI REVIEW

Mr. Hyde wrote *digestive system* on the board, and Ronny Trezzo's hand shot up. Hyde turned to face the class, then froze when he saw Ronny already had a question. The classroom was quiet except for the burble from the aquariums along the far wall and Ronny's impatient grunts as he pumped his hand in the air. Hyde leaned back into the chalkboard as if to brace himself. I'd been in classes with Ronny before and had never known him to be a curious student, but that year in Hyde's life science class he'd started sitting in the front row and asking questions.

If evolution was real, why did people have to invent shoes? How much food would you have to give an elephant to kill it? What would happen if you shot an atom bomb with a bow and arrow? At thirteen, Ronny was already five ten and thin but tough-looking, with a head of dark, matted curls. Hyde was half a foot shorter than Ronny and tended to answer his questions as if humoring a superior. Ronny's hand stayed raised, and Hyde let his shoulders slouch as he almost whispered, "Yes?"

Ronny cleared his throat and said he actually had two questions. First, he wanted to know how our bodies told the difference between pee and poop. Second, he was curious if the two ever got mixed up, pee coming out of a butt or poop coming out of a peehole.

The students who usually laughed at Ronny's questions looked at one another with their mouths hanging open, trying to read from each other's faces if they'd heard him right. Hyde's bald head turned a velvety shade of red while Ronny waited for an answer, a chewed-up Bic poised over the open notebook on his desk.

"That is enough," Hyde said, his voice husky with rage. "That is enough out of you."

"If you don't know," Ronny said, "just say so."

"Quiet!" Hyde shouted. "I don't want to hear another word."

He slammed the stick of chalk he was holding into the board's metal tray. The stick broke, and the top half fell to the floor, rolling under his desk.

The class was caught off guard by Hyde's overdue outburst. Everyone was silent as he banished Ronny from the front row and told him to keep his mouth shut for the rest of the year.

His new seat was next to mine, and when he dropped himself into it the legs gave a quick screech against the tile. Ronny cracked his knuckles and seemed to think the situation over before turning to me and whispering, "It's because I stumped him."

I had a healthy fear of Ronny, so I nodded. He could have told me he was the eighteenth president of the United States, and I would have nodded all the same.

In the fifth grade Ronny had picked up our lunch chaperone, Mr. Vestruvio, and placed him upside down in a garbage can. He narrowly escaped expulsion on account of his seemingly earnest belief both during and after the incident that he and Mr. Vestruvio had been "just clowning."

Before that, when Ronny was nine years old, he'd allegedly killed his next-door neighbor's horse, and the story had followed him ever since. Once while he was trading insults with Roger Mahalak in gym during a game of broomball, Mahalak shouted that Ronny was a sicko who'd used his alchie dad's rusted-out truck to knock the head off a horse. In response Ronny just stood there, using the handle of his broom to scratch his chin while we all stopped to look at him.

"So," he said after a while, "what've you ever done?"

There were plenty of reasons for me not to be excited to find myself sitting next to Ronny Trezzo, but on that day I was thinking mostly about Annie Miller, whom I'd practically been sitting next to before Ronny got moved to the empty seat between us.

Annie was a serious girl with brown hair who wore floor-length denim skirts and mature-looking blouses with lace collars and ruffled sleeves. She approached life science with an air of professional determination, taking relentless notes and prolonging the end of class by asking Hyde lawyerly questions about the homework. When called on, she answered in a tone that suggested a deep and long-standing knowledge of the subject matter, as if oxygen and carbon dioxide exchange was something she and her friends liked to discuss in their free time. I was an average student and came from what I'd heard adults refer to as a broken home. My mom was a single parent who worked hard but could get so far behind on bills that sometimes there was no electricity when I got home. For me, Annie wasn't just a crush. She was a glimpse into a world of dizzying stability, a place where there were beautiful girls with green eyes and all the right answers.

We never spoke. I knew without having to try that I couldn't flirt with her like your pretty-boy Eddie Vecklemans or your jockish Lucas Murnsens. That's why Ronny's idiotic questions had been a godsend. When he asked if alligators were bulletproof or why no one had ever invented a shower you could flush, the students around us typically joined in the resulting laughter, but to impress Annie I always shook my head as if I disapproved. The first time I did it, she nodded in agreement and mouthed, "Oh, my god." Over time we settled into looks of studious camaraderie that were the highlight of my day. But those fleeting interactions were gone forever, now that Ronny occupied the space between us, his body odor making the air smell suddenly like lunch meat and cut grass. I leaned forward to exchange a glance with Annie, hoping she might want to share a furtive laugh at our misfortune. Instead she stared straight ahead in steely annoyance. It seemed obvious she'd never look in my direction again.

Ronny noticed my pained expression as I watched Annie and mistook it for a reaction to Hyde's treatment of him.

"Right?" he said. "All I did was ask a fucking question."

Hyde looked sharply back at us, his forehead covered in the nervous sweat of the naturally conflict-avoidant. A tense moment passed before he continued his lecture. I could tell when Ronny started to fidget in his seat that more questions had occurred to him. When he finally went still, lulled into a state of grisly fascination by a detailed description of stomach acid, I noticed him staring down at the closed spiral-bound notebook on his desk. Its pages were curling up at the corners, and it had a distressed blue cover on which Ronny had scratched the word EXPERIMENTS.

In the hallway after class, I was surprised to hear his voice over my shoulder.

"Hey, Life Science," he said, as if it were my name.

He had followed me to my locker, and the sight of him approaching made me freeze in the act of retrieving my history book. It was only a few minutes till the next bell, but he was strolling casually with his notebook tucked under one arm, along with a copy of our school newspaper, *The Bronco Bulletin.*

"Did you hear that stuff today?" he said, leaning against the locker next to mine.

"In class?"

"No," he said, "in my spread-open butt."

I stared at him, my hand still on my history book.

"Of course in class."

"About digestion?"

"Exactly," he said, leaning toward me. "Stomachs, man."

I told him I had to get to class and held up my textbook as proof.

"Wait," he said. "You seem like a smart kid, and I could use some help."

"I'm not smart."

Ronny appraised me for a moment then reached into the back pocket of his jeans and pulled out a crisp twenty-dollar bill.

"Hear me out."

I followed Ronny out behind the gym while he explained that the money had come from his dad's wallet. According to Ronny, his father's alcohol tolerance used to be untouchable, but eight months ago he'd gotten into a bar fight with a man who'd tossed him through a window. His left arm and half his left leg ended up having to be amputated, and the loss of body mass as well as the three weeks in the hospital drying out meant he now came home swaying on his crutches, his wallet fat with the undrunk tens and twenties from his disability check.

"Is your dad okay?"

Ronny looked back at me and squinted. "I just told you how he is." He belched loudly enough for it to echo against the gym's cinder block, then took a seat on a picnic table that rested on a grassless patch of dirt between two dumpsters. I was five minutes late for history and risking a write-up for loitering, but the twenty-dollar bill in my pocket was all I could think about. At home our cupboards contained cans of olives and pumpkin-pie filling we'd gotten from the school's can drive. When they'd been collecting nonperishables in our homerooms, I'd brought in a dented can of green beans to avoid the embarrassment of not contributing. Later an elderly volunteer in a two-door LeBaron dropped a box of food at our house, and I was grimly amused to find that same dented can. With Ronny's twenty dollars I was already planning my trip to the grocery store after school.

Ronny rolled up the newspaper he'd been carrying and chucked it out into the parking lot.

"Sit down," he said. "I'll tell you about the experiment I want to do."

I sat next to him, and he started flipping through his notebook.

"How are you doing in Hyde's class?"

"All right, I guess."

"I'm getting a C+."

The way he put emphasis on the plus made it clear he was bragging. He looked up from his notes to make sure I understood.

"I'm no suck-up," he said. "Science is just interesting."

"Yeah," I said, caught off guard by so much sincerity coming from a boy who once had to be banned from the cafeteria for trying to fart on people's lunches. "It's pretty cool."

Ronny slapped my chest with the back of his hand.

"Right on," he said. "That stuff about stomach acid was killer, but Hyde doesn't have the stones for real science."

Ronny opened his right hand and showed me a folded square of paper the size of a nickel. He said he wanted me to eat it to determine the destructive powers of the human digestive system. Would I be able to see it when it came out? Would the text still be readable? Ronny needed to know. And if the results were interesting, there'd be another twenty in it for me.

We regarded each other for a moment in which I considered the money already in my pocket and that dented can of green beans.

"Why me?"

Earlier he'd said I seemed smart, but since intelligence clearly wasn't a prerequisite for what I was about to do, even he could see that a more honest explanation was needed.

"You're poor," Ronny said. "I figured you could use the money."

"How did you know?"

Ronny laughed and pinched the sleeve of my T-shirt as if admiring silk.

"I've got this same shirt."

After I got off the bus, I walked past the screened-in porch of our brick duplex and cut across the empty field of dead grass separating our house from the DeVeaux shopping center. At FoodTown, I headed for the frozen pizzas, where a three-for-one sale meant there was enough money left over for a box of Zebra Cakes and issue #365 of *The Amazing Spider-Man*.

At home, Mom was asleep on the couch with her department-store vest still on. Attached was the plastic name tag that said her name was Tina even though it was actually Pamela. During the day she worked at a jewelry counter, where her manager had explained that the tags were expensive and her real name didn't matter.

My brother Sam got to ride his bike home from high school, so he was already watching a rerun of *The Simpsons* in the other room. I snuck back to the kitchen to put the pizzas I'd bought in the freezer, then went to my room, where I stashed my other purchases under my bed.

Mom woke to the smell of a pizza baking in the oven and found me getting plates down for the three of us.

"What could smell that good?" she said, rubbing her right eye with the heel of her palm.

"A guy from church dropped off pizzas."

I'd rehearsed the lie in my head and was worried it might not be believable that the man from Blessed Sacrament who occasionally dropped off stale loaves of Wonder Bread had delivered us something appetizing.

Mom opened the freezer and frowned at the shrink-wrapped pepperoni pizzas stacked like bullion in a bank vault.

"Wow," she said eventually. "Score."

She let the freezer door fall shut and smiled. In a few hours she would have to leave for her job as an all-night clerk at the Best Western near the airport. She had taught herself to sleep without disturbing her makeup. When she smiled with showy surprise, her expression and dark lipstick reminded me of the night two years ago when Dad had made a sale and taken us all to the Putt-Putt out by the interstate. I remembered her laughing between a stone waterfall and a plaster giraffe.

"And you're cooking one up for us?" she said, peeking into the oven.

I said yes and showed her the plates in my hand. Her eyes glittered with mom-ish pride.

We cut the pizza into thirds and went out to the TV room to join Sam, who greeted the miracle of pizza with a "Heck, yeah." We ignored the TV in silence as we ate. Then Mom left for work, and Sam seemed confused when I didn't stay to fight him for control of the TV. Instead I went back to my room, where I read my comic in bed and ate a pair of Zebra Cakes, delighted by my own strange luck.

That afternoon Ronny had encouraged me not to chew the square of paper before I swallowed it. The corners were uncomfortable on the way down, and there had been an itch in my throat during dinner. Otherwise I felt fine. I still wasn't sure if I planned to look in the toilet for it, but the small effort of swallowing paper seemed like a fair trade for the sight of my mom pleasantly surprised.

I thought again of that night at the Putt-Putt and then of the last time I'd seen my father. I was in the passenger seat of his red Ford Taurus while he lectured me on the trials of adulthood.

"Once people know you're poor," he said, hitting the steering wheel for emphasis, "they never let you forget it. Doesn't matter how smart you are, how hard you work."

His car smelled like cigarettes, and in the back seat there were laundry baskets filled with crumpled clothes. Mom had insisted he spend some quality time with his sons, and in exchange he got to crash on our couch as he passed through town on his way to Fairbanks, Virginia, for a new job. He had taken Sam to lunch at the mall earlier that day and was driving me to Dairy Queen for ice cream. In Virginia he was taking a job selling aboveground pool sealant, an opportunity he said would help him send us money every month. The money never came, of course, and the satisfaction I now felt at having provided my family with frozen pizza made my father seem impossibly small to me.

A feeling of pride burbled up in me like a joke. I found myself laughing as I remembered Ronny's excitement over the piece of paper I'd eaten. He'd made sure I didn't unfold the square of paper or try to examine it before swallowing it. He wanted to be certain that I only read it, well, *after*. The ridiculousness of it set me off laughing even harder until I came up with an idea that made me go quiet and sit up in my bed.

The paper, I recalled suddenly, had been peach-colored, the exact same shade of stock on which *The Bronco Bulletin* always printed the school's lunch menu. All I had to do was pull out an issue of the *Bulletin* from the loose papers in my backpack and copy the menu verbatim in order to provide Ronny with what he was sure to think was some valuable data. And so that's what I did.

I waited a few days to hand Ronny the menu I'd copied. He looked down at the paper wide-eyed before telling me that I was "fucking disgusting." But there was admiration in his voice as he said it, and he asked me to follow him back to his locker, where he gave me another twenty-dollar bill and told me to meet him out at the picnic table after class.

When I found him outside, he was writing in his notebook, his free hand holding down the pages as they fluttered in the breeze. He told me to sit down, and I did.

"All right, Life Science. Thanks for showing up."

"My name's Jacob."

Ronny looked at me.

"Jacob Dixon."

"Okay," Ronny said, seeming to give this some thought. "I'm probably gonna keep calling you Life Science, because that's what I've been calling you in my head, and I feel like we'll lose momentum if I try to remember a whole new name."

He started to flip back through his notebook as if looking for something. "Do you know what momentum is?"

Before I could answer, he held up his index finger and read his own definition: "It's how big something is and how fast it's moving in a direction."

I sat there blinking.

"Fine, Jesus," he said, mistaking my silence for stubbornness. "Jacob Dixon it is."

He wrote my name in the notebook and flipped back a few pages to where he had taped the piece of paper with the school's lunch menu in my handwriting.

"Jacob, the results from our experiment were awesome." He tapped the page with his index finger. "But I got questions."

"Sure," I said.

He flipped to a blank page. "Did you shit blood?"

"No."

"Did it hurt coming out?"

"No."

He made a notation. "What did the paper smell like after?"

I pretended to give this some thought. "Like poop," I said. "You know, bad."

"But just like normal shit smell?"

"Yes."

"That's great," Ronny said before writing for what felt like a long time.

When he was finished, he asked if I wanted to make some more money. He explained that the digestive stuff was interesting, but Hyde's lectures on the circulatory system had gotten him into blood. Was it flammable? What did it smell like if you boiled it? Could you turn it into scabs yourself? He might have gone on listing questions forever, but I told him it wouldn't be a problem. I could get him some blood.

That night at FoodTown I bought some Karo syrup, a plastic vial of red food dye, and one can of beef broth. At home we'd eaten pizza all week, so I also bought a few boxes of macaroni and cheese, which I figured I could slip into our cupboards without anyone noticing. For Mom, I bought a chocolate bar with the word *Melodious* written on its wrapper in dark red calligraphy. I placed it on the end table near where she was sleeping on the couch. I'd planned to tell her I'd won it at school, but as soon as she woke from her nap she sat up and ate it without question. Only after she'd finished did she call out to me where I was heating water in the kitchen for macaroni.

"Jacob, I'm sorry. Was that candy bar yours?"

When I told her it wasn't, she shouted to Sam in the TV room, "Sam, sorry, honey!"

There was a pause before he gloomily answered, "Whatever."

One of my brother's many defects was that he preferred Daredevil to Spider-Man, so I bought him two issues that I planned to tell him someone had left on the bus. When I handed them to him in the TV room, he eyed me with suspicion. On the episode of *Cops* he was watching, a police officer with a buzz cut was pulling a man out from under an RV.

"Why don't you want them?" he said, like he thought they might be rigged with explosives.

"Because Daredevil sucks."

He grinned and snorted through his nose. He and Dad had always joked hard with each other, and I could tell he missed it.

"He could beat the shit out of Spider-Man," Sam said.

"If he did, it'd be the most interesting thing about him."

Sam laughed, and I surprised myself by casually slapping the door frame on my way out of the room, calling out behind me that there was mac and cheese in the kitchen. Sam was already looking through one of the comics and responded with a distracted "Nice." Mom had gone back to sleep next to her empty chocolate wrapper so only answered with a half-conscious "Hmmn."

I grabbed a bowl of macaroni in the kitchen and went back to my room to whip up Ronny some blood.

I delivered it the next morning, two liters of dark red syrup in an old soda bottle. In addition to the bodily smell, the beef broth gave the clown-nose red of the food dye an earthy brown tint. As I approached Ronny's locker, he was on his hands and knees holding his blue notebook in his mouth like a dog while he searched through the mound of loose papers and fast-food wrappers at the bottom of his locker. He stood up when he saw the blood, folding his notebook in half and tucking it into the front of his pants before taking the bottle from me. He shook it up, then screwed the cap off to take a sniff.

"Fuck," he said, recoiling from the smell and putting the cap back on. "Where'd you get this?"

I was about to make something up, but he raised his hand for me to stop.

"Better if I don't know. It's human, though, right?" He was already pressing two twenties into my hand.

"Yup," I said.

He put the bottle in his locker and stared down at it with his hands on his hips and his notebook still sticking out of the front of his pants.

"Mother of bicycling Christ," he said. "Remind me to stay on your good side."

Later that day he came into Hyde's class five minutes before the bell and moved his desk closer to mine. He showed me a list of experiments written out in his notebook. Beneath all of it he had written an estimate for what he felt was fair compensation: $180.

The seats around us were beginning to fill up, and Ronny was watching me closely. I circled the amount with my pen and nodded.

That was when I noticed Annie looking at us. Her smile suggested she was witnessing something particularly heartwarming. It occurred to me that the sight of me conferring with Ronny over his notebook had given her the impression that I was tutoring him. When she noticed me looking up, she wished me a good morning with a warmth I'd never heard in her voice before.

At this interruption, Ronny glared at her and placed a protective hand over his open notebook.

"Can't you see we're having a conversation, you goddamn Ritalin addict?"

Annie's expression narrowed into a scowl, and in a flash of bravery I whispered loud enough for her to hear that if he didn't apologize I wouldn't help him.

Ronny's nostrils flared in disgust, but when he saw I was serious he rolled his eyes and shrugged. "Fine, geez," he said. "I didn't realize she was your aunt."

He turned to Annie and said in a mock polite tone, "So sorry about that. I never learned how to act." He closed his notebook and half stood, muttering that we could talk later as he duck-walked his desk back to its usual place.

During Hyde's lecture I caught Annie staring at me again. She blushed and smiled before turning her attention back to the front of the class.

In that moment, my only wish was that I could jump back in time to the passenger seat of my father's rattling Ford Taurus and tell him that life could be so easy if you just took the chances it gave you. Meanwhile, Hyde was saying that just as the porcupine had its quills and the lion its strength, mankind had its superior brain to outwit predators and impose order on the world. In response, Ronny turned to me and rapped his knuckles on the cover of his blue notebook, as if Hyde had been talking about whatever madness was written inside.

The next day I told my mom I had to work on a group project and took the bus to Ronny's house after school. From his stop we crossed through yards littered with beer cans, dog dirt, laundry baskets, and the occasional mattress. We walked through a loose stand of pines, then wound up behind Ronny's house, a bungalow with white aluminum siding that was beginning to buckle. The grass looked ripped-up in places and too long in others. An old push mower was lying on a patch of bare dirt, and Ronny explained that he had mowed in anticipation of company.

Inside, Ronny's father was snoring on the sofa in front of the local news. There was an afghan over his one-and-a-half legs and a handle of Wild Turkey under his remaining arm. The sound of Ronny letting the screen door slap shut disturbed his sleep enough for him to mumble, "Fuck you," but wasn't enough to wake him. He only readjusted his grip on the Wild Turkey before starting to snore again. The way he was lying with his mouth open made it look like his run-in at the bar had happened earlier that afternoon. I was sad to realize how much he reminded

228

me of my mother, the way I always found her after school looking obliterated by the day.

"Come on," Ronny said, heading back to the kitchen. "We've got shit to do."

The first experiment of the afternoon involved Ronny's dog, Knife, who was in the habit of chewing the crotch out of Ronny's underwear. Ronny had me bring a pair of my own underwear to see if this behavior was specific to his crotch or a broader phenomenon. The experiment he designed involved soaking our underwear in separate bowls of water on the kitchen counter. He then prepared two dishes of dog food, one with a splash of my underwear water and another with a splash of his, before calling Knife into the room to see which he preferred.

There was the sound of Knife jumping to the floor in some unseen back room and the gentle tinkle of his collar as he wandered out to the kitchen, where he showed himself to be a black pit bull mix with wide-set eyes full of boredom. He scanned the kitchen floor for food, then trotted over and emptied both bowls in seconds, licking the floor around them for a bit before pulling an empty pizza box out of a nearby trash can and curling up on the floor to gnaw at it.

Ronny looked at me in amazement.

"He ate mine first!"

I gave a thumbs-up, even though I couldn't remember which dish had been which.

"Shit," Ronny said, writing in his notebook. "Think of the uses."

"Like what?"

Ronny laughed and drummed on my head with his pen as if he expected a hollow sound, but he had to think for a while before he could come up with an example.

"You could put it on dog medicine," he said finally, then invited me to follow him back to his room.

The wood-paneled hall was dark and empty except for a single bookcase with each of its shelves covered in decorative shot glasses. Above it was a framed poster of a topless woman in rawhide boots. She was wearing a Native American headdress but holding her arms out as if she were on a surfboard. I hadn't seen any evidence of Ronny's mom in the house, and the presence of this poster seemed like confirmation that she had little to do with the daily lives of the Trezzo men.

In Ronny's room there was a mattress on the floor and a card table with a folding chair. The floor was covered with library books, their spines all bearing call numbers and the name of the branch. They had titles like *A Student's Primer in Biology* and *Beginning Topics in Chemistry*. Ronny had bookmarked and dogeared them to the point where many of them couldn't close. There must have been forty of them.

"How many books does the library let you take out at a time?"

"They've got a window in the bathroom," Ronny said. "You just take whatever you want in there and chuck it outside."

He told me to take a seat at the card table and placed a bowl in front of me with a raw potato in it. He rattled around in a toolbox and then handed me a bottle of lighter fluid. He also gave me a pen and notepad, instructing me to drip the lighter fluid on the potato a little bit at a time and write down any observations.

After observing me to make sure I was dripping the lighter fluid correctly, he sat on his mattress with a plastic bin of cleaning supplies and an ashtray. He would pick up a bottle, read the list of ingredients on the back of it, and pour a little into the ashtray to light it with a match. He took notes whenever the liquid caught fire and conscientiously wiped out the ashtray with a rag between tests. This went on for about an hour before he checked my progress. In my notebook I'd observed that the potato had gotten darker as it got wet and that the lighter fluid was odorless.

He nodded.

"All right," he said, "time to take her outside."

In his backyard, Ronny put the potato in a bucket along with some of the cleaning supplies he'd tested. We stepped a few paces back and he started flicking lit matches at it. He kept missing, and the matches let out little tails of smoke in the grass.

"So," Ronny said, his tone suggesting it might take a while to ignite the potato, "do you know what you want to be when you grow up?"

He lit another match and threw it.

"I haven't really thought it over."

Ronny clucked his tongue as if my lack of ambition disappointed him.

"Are you gonna be a scientist?" I said.

Ronny lit yet another match and held it up between his thumb and forefinger, watching it burn down a little.

"Nope," he said. "I already am one."

He threw the match with a snap of his wrist, and it landed noiselessly in the bucket. There was a flash of light and a low boom, followed by Ronny telling me to look alive while he searched the sky for the potato. Thirty seconds later it landed with a thud on the roof of Ronny's house, and he had to climb up the TV antenna tower to retrieve it. He tapped the potato to make sure it wasn't too hot to touch, then picked it up and bit into it, spitting it out immediately.

"Tastes like chemicals," he shouted down to me. "And the explosion didn't cook it all the way."

He threw the rest of the potato over his shoulder and climbed back down to the yard to record the results in his notebook.

"What were you hoping for?"

He closed his notebook and looked up to where he'd abandoned the potato on the roof.

"Edible fireworks," he said.

I stared down at the bucket as I considered the concept.

"That's a fantastic idea," I said, meaning it.

Ronny smiled.

"Well let's not stand around tugging each other's nuts," he said.

Next we dug a small firepit, in which we spent some time trying to blow up a magnet that Ronny had gotten off his refrigerator. When that didn't work, he brought out a pepper shaker and had us take turns snorting the pepper, holding our eyes open with our fingers when we sneezed to see if we could make our eyes pop out. This didn't produce any significant results, so he went back inside, eventually bringing out a red party balloon and a six-pack of sodas. He placed the inflated balloon in the grass and had us chug the sodas. We waited a few minutes and then one at a time endeavored to pop the balloon by peeing on it. By the time I was ready to pee on the balloon a second time, we were both laughing so hard I could barely hit the thing. Ronny's backyard was wild with the sound of crickets, and peeing on a balloon felt like a kind of freedom.

Fun, I would realize later. We were having fun.

"The subject, a balloon," Ronny narrated through his laughter as he wrote, "withstood the force of six cans of soda peed on it with ordinary force."

After a few more experiments, I realized how late it was and told Ronny I'd have to call my mom to pick me up. But when I called from the phone in Ronny's kitchen, no one answered. Mom had assured me this was her night off, but either she'd fallen asleep or Sam had the volume on the television so high they couldn't hear the phone. I was starting to feel the typical, stranded panic of a latchkey kid when Ronny took the receiver from my hand and hung it up.

"Don't worry about it," he said. "I'll give you a ride."

231

Before I could ask him what he meant, he was standing over his father in the other room, rifling through the sleeping man's pockets for the keys to the Trezzo truck. Once he found them, he twirled them around his index finger and shoved them into his back jeans pocket.

"That reminds me," he said, pulling out his father's wallet. "I owe you some money."

Seeing Ronny going through his sleeping father's wallet made me understand exactly what it was I'd been doing over the past few days.

"That's okay," I said.

Ronny must have noticed me looking down at his father.

"The money's not his," he said, taking out a stack of bills. "It's from the government."

He took half the bills and put them in my hand. The rest he pocketed.

"And anyway, you'll be doing me a favor," he said. "He'll just drink it."

He threw the wallet back into his father's lap and gestured for me to follow him out the front door. He let me go out first, then held the screen door open and called back into the house.

"Knife! We're going to Arby's."

At the word Arby's, Knife shot out of the house and sprinted to the driveway, where he leaped into the back of the old red pickup and started to bark.

Ronny insisted that dinner was his treat as we pulled into the drive-through. The attendant was a boy only a few years older than us with a patchy mustache. He laughed when he saw two kids alone in the cab of the truck. Ronny handed him a twenty-dollar bill and told him to keep the change before accepting two giant root beers and the heavy white bag filled with a dozen roast-beef sandwiches. The attendant gave us a "Keep it real, dudes" and cackled when Ronny revved the engine and peeled out.

As he drove, Ronny kept fishing out roast-beef sandwiches and throwing them to Knife through the cab's back window. Knife caught them before they hit the truck bed and ate them, foil and all. I asked Ronny if I could unwrap them for him, but he shook his head as he handed me my root beer.

"He won't eat them without the foil. I've tried it."

He handed me one of the sandwiches and told me to eat up, then activated the cruise control and popped the lid off his root beer. Steering with his knees, he held the cup out the back window so Knife could lap up half of it.

"Do you have a dog?" he said, lowering his knees and putting his left hand back on the steering wheel.

I told him I didn't, and he took a long sip of the same root beer he'd offered to Knife.

"Oh, you should get one," he said. "They're wonderful."

We ate in happy silence, but as the country roads became more suburban, Ronny seemed to be unpleasantly reminded of other people. He straightened up behind the wheel and frowned at the passing houses that were suddenly all around us.

"There's this rumor at school," he said a little abruptly as we turned onto Elmer. "People say I drove this truck into a field and knocked the head off a horse."

I told him I'd heard it, and he took a bite of his sandwich, chewing slowly and looking down at his hand on the wheel.

"It's not true," he said.

"It isn't?"

"Not at all. It was a mule. Completely different species."

He balled up his empty sandwich wrapper and threw it on the floor of the cab.

"To be honest," he said, "I never felt great about it."

I told him that must have been a tough time, and he seemed to think this over, keeping his eyes on the road.

"I guess I was just a kid," he said. "Your parents are supposed to be the ones stopping you from doing that shit."

I knew how he felt. It'd been about a year since my mom had asked me what I'd done at school that day.

"That's why I like science," Ronny said. "It's the only rules you can't break. Hyde could drop dead tomorrow, and a horse would still be different from a mule."

We got quiet again, and after a while I told him it would have been great if we could have popped that balloon. Our laughter lasted until we reached my house. Ronny squealed to a stop when I noticed we'd almost passed it. He congratulated me on a good day's work, and I said I'd see him tomorrow.

"Bet your ass," he said.

As he pulled off down the street, Knife raised a leg and started peeing over the side of the truck bed. It was a powerful stream that reached all the way to the sidewalk. Ronny laid on the horn and raised a friendly middle finger out the driver's side window as he took a left onto Douglas Road and hit the gas, roaring out of sight.

When Ronny wasn't in class the next day I assumed he'd been pulled over or gotten into a wreck. I felt only somewhat guilty over my relief that I'd gotten out of the truck when I did. I told myself that whatever it was, he could handle it; I was distracted by a *pssst* from Annie, who seemed to view Ronny's absence as an opportunity to talk to me without being insulted. She was wearing a plaid dress and a rose-colored clip in her hair.

"Hey," she said, "when's your lunch?" She was smiling.

I told her fourth period, and she wrinkled her nose as if she didn't understand why I hadn't told her earlier.

"No way," she said. "Who do you sit with?"

I sat in a lonely corner of the cafeteria with a table of band kids who all spent their lunch playing Magic: The Gathering and ignoring me. I told Annie that I sat here and there, and she seemed to find that funny.

The bell had rung, and she leaned in, lowering her voice while Hyde told everyone what page to turn to in their books.

"Well," she said. "I sit by the windows. You should—"

Before she could finish, there was the sound of a man clearing his throat. Even Hyde was surprised to see Vice Principal Schlesinger standing in the door.

"Sorry, Ted, need to borrow a student."

Hyde waved that it was fine, and Schlesinger turned to the class.

"Jacob Dixon?"

Annie smiled and gave me a fake-scared look. I managed a casual shrug as I rose from my desk, knowing I was about to find out what trouble Ronny had gotten into.

Schlesinger told me to bring my things but was silent once I was out in the hall. He was a large man with orange-blond hair and a way of carrying himself that suggested he had once been an athlete. He led me to his office at the end of C hall. It was a cramped, windowless room with a heavy metal door that he let fall shut as he told me to take a seat in the vinyl chair across from his desk.

Schlesinger sat down and looked at me with his lips pursed in a way that said Ronny wasn't the only one in trouble. That was when I noticed the blue notebook on Schlesinger's desk with the word EXPERIMENTS gouged into the cover.

"At five AM this morning," Schlesinger said, "our janitorial staff found Ronald Trezzo breaking into the honors anatomy lab. Do you know anything about this?"

234

Later I would find out that Ronny had smashed the lab's window with a brick. He almost made off with a duffel bag he'd filled with jars of fetal pigs, but a janitor grabbed him just as he was climbing back out the window.

I told Schlesinger I didn't know anything about it, and he leaned back in his seat but kept his hands flat on his desk like it was a pulpit.

"Well, that may be," he said, "but he had this on him."

He tapped the cover of Ronny's notebook, which was when I recalled the pure, idiotic misunderstanding that had made Ronny write my name inside.

Schlesinger laid an open palm on the cover of the notebook.

"Son, I gotta tell ya, everything I read in here is beyond the pale. Absolutely beyond, I—"

He had to gather himself before adding, "You'll get a chance to tell your side of this. But first, *first*, you're telling me where you got that blood."

He picked up the receiver of his phone and waved it at me. "And I had better believe every word you tell me, or I'll get someone from the sheriff's office down here in a hot second."

I told him it was just corn syrup and food coloring, and he looked relieved as he took my statement on a yellow legal pad.

"The notebook says he paid you for it. How much?"

When I said forty dollars, his lips parted in disbelief.

"Forty dollars," he said. "For forty dollars you lied about having human blood and brought it to school? Was that worth it?"

Without thinking I answered yes, and for a second it looked like Schlesinger might shout, but he was able to restrain himself.

"So that's it, Jacob? That's what your integrity costs?" He sounded disappointed in me, like suddenly he'd known me my whole life.

"Imagine," he said, "what your mother will think when she gets here and I have to explain all this."

I figured he was confused. "She's at work," I said. It was a Wednesday morning, which meant she'd be at the jewelry counter. Her manager had once fired one of her coworkers for showing up in open-toed shoes twice in the same month. The idea that she could have left her shift to come to school was absurd.

"We already reached her," Schlesinger said. "She's on her way."

A pained look must have crossed my face because Schlesinger smiled. "Forty dollars isn't so much now, is it?"

"You shouldn't have called her there."

He might have yelled at me for talking back if I hadn't started to cry. I didn't cover my face but just stared at a place on the wall where Schlesinger had hung a photograph of himself in a beige vest holding up a fish that looked too small not to throw back.

"You might have thought of your mother when you came up with your brilliant plan to go around selling fake blood."

His voice was still angry but defensive, as if it were an unfair turn of events that I should appear helpless. But he'd misunderstood. I wasn't sad or scared. I wanted to kill him. Actually kill him. The only person I hated more than Schlesinger in that moment was myself. I had managed to land my family in a worse way than when I'd started and was forced to wonder if I was perhaps more like my father than I'd hoped.

I sat there with my eyes wet, while Schlesinger lectured me on the seriousness of the situation. "I hope we can get this cleared up without getting the law involved," he said. "I really do."

After a while there was nothing left for him to say, and I just stared at the floor while we waited for Principal Judmann to notify us when my mother arrived. Schlesinger seemed relieved when his phone finally rang. He listened to what was said and grunted into the receiver before gathering up Ronny's notebook and his own yellow legal pad.

"All right, Jacob," he said, putting down the phone. "It's time."

I wiped my face on the sleeve of my T-shirt and followed him out into the hall. Over an hour had gone by since I'd been pulled out of class. It was the middle of fourth period, which meant that Jessica Chandler, an eighth grader who volunteered in the main office, had heard about the notebook and was spreading the word. By then the stories had already begun to change. In the months to come I would hear that Ronny had paid me to wear diapers for a month, burn my privates with a match, and to drink his dog's urine.

As Schlesinger and I passed a homeroom, I heard someone whisper, "No way it's him." We walked by the cafeteria, and a whole table of people I didn't know saw me and laughed. Annie was sitting three tables back. One of her friends whispered something in her ear and pointed in my direction. Annie's eyes went wide, and she covered her mouth with her hand.

"Once people know you're poor," my father shouted from the far end of the hall, "they never let you forget it."

When we reached the main office, Schlesinger paused in front of the frosted glass door. He looked both ways to make sure he wouldn't be overheard, then put his hand on my shoulder.

236

"Look, Jacob," he said, "I've never heard your name before today, and that's a good thing."

He held up Ronny's notebook. "I won't put up with this sort of behavior in my school, and I was right to come down on you, but in general you don't seem like the type. Whereas Ronny's always been a problem. If you were to tell me and everyone in Principal Judmann's office that he bullied you into this, hell, I'd believe you."

He gave my shoulder a squeeze, and I understood what I was being asked to do. I just had to point to Ronny, and like that I'd be transformed from culprit to victim, a poor boy lured into revolting acts with threats and stolen money. As soon as a story was settled on, the sheriff's department could be called and Ronny would disappear once and for all into some vast institutional world where troubled boys were jumpsuited and caged and marked for life.

Schlesinger opened the door and led me inside. The usually bustling office was quiet, and there was no one behind the front desk. As we got closer to Principal Judmann's door, I could hear the grave murmur of adult voices. I thought about Annie's look of disgust and of Ronny flying down an empty country road in his father's truck, feeding his dog a root beer. Schlesinger was walking on one side of me with his hand still on my shoulder, but he didn't notice when I mouthed the word "No." I hadn't been bullied. Ronny, I would tell them, was the smartest person I knew. And I was proud of the work we'd done.

Nominated by Robert McBrearty

OLD WOMEN TALKING ABOUT DEATH

by JENNIFER L. KNOX

from AMERICAN POETRY REVIEW

When did I become one of them? I used to
roll my eyes at their gory stories: EMTs found
a neighbor at the bottom of her basement steps,
a head-to-toe hematoma. "'Use a cane,' I told her!"
[shrugs]. Grandma and the great-aunts itemized her
injuries. "Poor dear. How long till she was found?"
They told their stories picnicking atop our people
at the cemetery, atop all the men in our family who
died young. The rest disappeared [shrugs] so no stories
for them. These days when I call K, she tells me about
her friends who are dying or have died since we last spoke,
and I feel closer to her, an adult. Yesterday, J filled me in on
M's cancer. "It's baaaad," she whispered. I leaned forward.
M's doctors removed her necrotic uterus through her
abdomen in two jammy black hunks because her insides
had decayed into a sarcomatous tar pit—then her incision
dehisced. I cocked my head. She made a starburst
motion over her belly button. [Ah!] "I've heard that happens
with cancer," I said, grateful Z described the process
to me after her stepmother died. Now I even have a
name for that indignity. Thank God. I hate surprises.

Nominated by Christopher Citro

MIDNIGHT IS A BEAUTIFUL CURSE

by DORIANNE LAUX

from ADRIOT JOURNAL

Blue water in a pond goes black, spills
down the gutter like a vine, its mineral
smell, its splash of black pearls.

The moon is a silver spoon sunk
in the galaxy's cold soup. I don't know
where the light ends and I begin.

When I sleep I'm a vulture, my bald
red head slick in the belly of a deer,
my eyelashes lit with gore, my dark mouth

done with kissing. I unwind its power
with my beak, devour its unborn
into eternity, disappear its entrails

from a bed of acorns and pine needles.
When I wake I turn back into a scientist,
looking for the intersection

between my heart and my hunger.
If we understood the beauty of the world
we would curse it, let it eat us alive

if we let it, the hidden music inside us
measured out like a necklace
of bones, alleys we cultivate

in the quiet, the hidden life that grows
without light: mushrooms and mold,
spider plants and snake plants, dracaena, dra seen ah

the delicate, narrow, many-leaved fronds
of the maidenhead fern, turning
in the dark on its thin black stalk.

Nominated by Claire Davis, Jane Hirshfield

NIGHT COWS

by JENNIFER BOWEN HICKS

from THE SUN

—For E. and S.
With thanks to Todd Hido and Maggie Steber

The cows showed up just as the world began to end. They were there when I returned to Minnesota from Manhattan, where I'd gone to pick up my older son after his spring 2020 college semester had been canceled. As a single parent with full custody of two kids, I had little time to spare. The day I left, I slid a pork shoulder into the oven for the younger teenager, then loaded up on crackers and coffee so I could drive solo to retrieve the older boy. Because I was passing through Philadelphia, I also picked up his ex-girlfriend, my bonus child, who a few days later began exhibiting symptoms of the virus.

There are forty or so cows, seven calves, and no bulls. They're dairy cows, the type of black-and-white beauties you might see lounging on the green hillsides of Wisconsin or on winding back roads in Upstate New York, back when people traveled winding back roads. They wear white plastic ear tags stamped with four-digit numbers. Their barn, which is located in the corner of a university campus, has beds of hay in the back and a concrete trough at the front, but it looks less like a barn than a carport filled with cows, likely brought here by agriculture professors just in time for the campus to empty. Their pens are open, so the cows can get up and follow me and my dog, Toby, along the fence, as they sometimes do if there is not food in their trough and the day is long. Toby understands to be gentle with them when they amble over. The cows first seemed to view me as secondary—just the thing holding on to the dog—but they have since learned that I can pet them and the dog cannot. The cows and Toby do lick each other's tongues. I call this kissing, though to the animals it is probably something different. The cows' tongues are spiraling and salt-seeking, a secret muscle that moves like a dancer.

The prisons are locked down, and I can't go inside to work with my writing students, most of whom I've known for a decade. Not only do they no longer have classes; they cannot have visitors either: no moms, no daughters, no brothers, no beloveds. Through word of mouth I hear how my students are faring. Thankfully they are all still well, but the virus has brought a disruption to their routine, and for some it's brought terror. One man I've worked with, whom I consider a friend, wants his story to be part of the public record. He wants to tell the world what the pandemic is like for him, a caged man who lived through the Cambodian genocide. When the Khmer Rouge came, he says, "I was thirteen and at school. My family fled their home but couldn't find me. I was lost. But even in this moment, my dad risked his life to return home to unlatch the gate that kept our hogs penned in. He knew the pigs would die if they were locked in the cage and he wasn't there to feed them, to care for them. I wonder: With COVID coming into the prisons like the Khmer Rouge, will we be forgotten in our pens? Who will remember the prisoners in a time like this?"

I can send him a note about a class, but I am not allowed to send him a personal note. If I could, I would say, *We will memorialize you if you die. We will tell your loved ones how much we loved you, and we will tell them why. We are thinking of you daily.*

My son's ex-girlfriend is now quarantined in my basement with what we think is a mild case of COVID. In these early days, tests are for sports teams and the dying, so we cannot confirm. The uncertainty leaves room for doubt. Most of the time I am numb, and when I slide out of denial, I tell myself that we nearly bathed in hand sanitizer while smooshed together on the car ride. I tell myself that she's too young to develop serious symptoms. She is often upright and, to my relief, sassy enough to ask me to stop checking on her so often. I allow myself to believe that if this is how the virus hits the young, she and my sons will be all right. As for me, I make contingency plans in my head: How far could my boys stretch my pittance of life insurance? Would the one who knows how to cook feed the one who refuses to learn? But we are not at that point and likely won't get there.

A week ago, as I drove to Manhattan, my son's ex pinged my phone hourly to make sure I hadn't changed my mind about giving her a ride. It was eerie in her suddenly empty dorm, she said. Now I overhear her tell an instructor on a screen that she is too sick to sing—and, by the way, also quarantined with her ex and his mom.

The calves suck my coat sleeve and attempt to eat the cardigan tied around my waist. A few cows sniff my hand when I extend it, and I feel the warm breath from their nostrils. Several will lick as much of my arm as I'll allow. I allow it all. One, whether due to her personality or the texture of her tongue, leaves red, raw splotches on my skin that, depending on her vigor, can last an entire day.

Number 3214 is the one I look for. She's not the softest or the sleekest. She doesn't have the biggest eyes. On the bridge of her forehead, where most of the cows have black fur, she has a thick swirl of dirty white. She is bony, and her coat has lost its shine. But isn't it always the case that we can't help but love those who seem to love us? I make this bold claim because 3214—"Fourteen," for short—recognizes me, or so it seems. She moves to the front of the herd deliberately and looks right at me, as if trying to hold eye contact.

I should disclose that my divorce from my husband of twenty-four years became final during the third week of the stay-at-home order—the same week I quarantined a feverish bonus daughter in my basement, just seven days after I'd driven from Saint Paul to Philadelphia and then on to Manhattan to scoop up two college kids who were being sent home to shelter in place. My attorney's e-mail simply said: "You are officially divorced. Please see the attached filed documents for your records." I mention all of this because it's possible that if your divorce were finalized during a pandemic, even a necessary and humane divorce, and if you realized that for the first time in your adult life you were truly partnerless—this as couples you knew did puzzles together and took walks together and cooked lamb together and had sex and watched

243

movie marathons and fought together—then under these circumstances it's possible you might misread a cow's expression.

But I don't think I have.

Fourteen's dark eyes focus on mine, and she sticks her big head through the gate, shoving the other cows' heads out of the way. When she's arching her neck to maintain eye contact, the stretch causes her eyeballs to bulge and roll back so that three-quarters of the whites are exposed and only a sliver of cornea. This makes her appear scary and out of her mind, but she is neither. I let her sniff my hand. Then I pet her nose and forehead. The other cows give up, which allows her more room. Eventually she pushes her head all the way through the bars so that I can pat the side of her face. She leans heavily into my hand.

I say to her: "Hello, Fourteen. Hello, sweetie. Thanks for saying hi. You like my hand on your face? Yes, you do. Hello, hello."

Since the dying began and the loneliness washed in, people in Iceland have started hugging trees. The forestry service there is clearing a path so those who can't hug a human can embrace a tree. According to an Icelandic forest ranger, "When you hug [a tree], you feel it first in your toes and then up your legs and into your chest and then up into your head."

In the photos that accompany the article, one man hugging the tree looks *very* into it—a whole-body embrace of a large trunk. Another gentleman has his arms around the tree, but only his fingertips touch the bark. A woman weaves her body in and out of branches with joy. In a separate photo she kisses the tips of the buds like she means it.

Are many of us now experiencing some small semblance of what it feels like to live in a cage: The physical separation from loved ones and the world? The lack of touch? It's an unfair comparison. Still, the solitude causes (or reveals) a gaping feeling in my chest. Is this the way the body holds isolation? How impossible it is for a person to carry the totality of all that is not present.

My son and his ex are friendly now, two teenagers quarantined together. One of my students is newly in love and, I hear, in good spirits despite the lockdown. My neighbor across the street allows one visitor to her home. He wears a bandanna over his long hair, and when he leaves her house, he waves to me and shouts, "Hey, have a good one!"

The last two times I've visited the cows, Fourteen hasn't bothered to get up from the back of the pen. At first I thought she was gone, though I couldn't imagine where she'd go or why, and I felt a small twinge of panic. Then I saw her there, just chilling. She's over me, I guess. I find myself looking to develop a new attachment with another cow.

Comedian Ali Sultan says, "A fun activity for couples quarantined together is to go to the park and run in opposite directions."
"Ha ha," I say when I read this. "Hahahahahaha."

Photos by photographers who are sheltering in place keep showing up on my screens. "In this unnatural state of isolation," a *New York Times* article says, "photographers show us the things that bind." One image is of a woman standing behind a sheer curtain in a bedroom, looking out the window in the soft morning light. There's a bed behind her, and I can see wrinkled sheets, an embroidered pillowcase. I assume she is the photographer's partner, and I envy the connection between these two people, one of whom saw the other in that light by that window and captured her image. But when I read the text, I discover it is a self-portrait. The photographer, a war correspondent, is sheltering alone. She doesn't mind being alone, she says. She was raised by a single mother, a parasitologist who taught her to be grateful for small things.

Fourteen is hot and cold. One day she's into me; the next she can't be bothered, happily licking a board inside her trough. She attends to the board so vigorously, it rattles the metal. The other cows see and want some of that action, but she will not share.

One of my friends, who hears a lot about the cows, sends me piles of temporary tattoos so I can decorate myself with wildflowers. It's a lovely gift, but it's also possible that she wants to change the subject.

A calf, number Thirty-seven, stands back from the gate. She watches but does not move forward. Thirty-seven is special, though it's taken me some time to realize it. When I visit at night, and all the other cows are

245

asleep, and the Icelanders have stopped hugging their trees, and even the new moon and Venus are social distancing, she is the sole cow standing. She has the world to herself, whether she wants it that way or not. She stares straight at me, and I stare back.

I've found another photographer online whose images look the way the inside of my chest feels: Empty streets in fog. A house with just one light on. Wide-open skies under which nothing moves. Footprints in the snow heading toward a house. ("I'll meet you at the window," the photographer's caption says.) A single streetlight shining on a parked car. "Another lonely night in quarantine" is the caption on that one. I read the comments below it:

> *Damn. That light.*
> *Very silent.*
> *All of a sudden, I miss everyone.*

What will happen next? It feels like this planet is a car that has screeched to a halt, and we've been thrown forward by the sudden braking. By instinct we fling our arms out to stop other people from flying through the windshield, even while their arms are flinging out to stop us. And after the car has stopped, we all look around to see who is still here, who is injured and bleeding. My children are safe. The light outside has changed. Is someone missing from the car? *Is someone missing from the car?*

Some days I cry over everything. I cry over the parade of elementary-school teachers in their cars, wearing masks and honking to their students, who are standing on the street corners and also wearing masks. I cry for a friend who has lost family. I cry over the way my nowhome, healthy son dances while he eats cereal. Over the other son's sketch of a boy staring at a computer while the pandemic rages in his periphery. Over a gray painting of Saint Paul trains going nowhere in the snow. And for my students, people in cages who've lived disconnected, isolated lives for decades.

Someday the world will spin again. What will we do when the shock wears off and the debris is cleared? A friend who also teaches in prison

246

says that when she returns to class, she will sneak in flower seeds: a tiny act of rebellion. How many wild columbine seeds could she slip under her pinkie nail? How many lupine seeds would fit inside the cap of her pen? It would do nothing to free her students from their cages or loneliness, but it would whisper: *I have not forgotten you.*

For my part, I plan to pull the car over at every opportunity and say, "Want in?" I will throw the doors open to my people—both those I've long known are mine and those who still could be. I am realizing I will need a bigger car, maybe a whole damn camper, yet somehow I believe this can happen. And maybe, once everyone is inside, we will hug each other *and* some trees, because this is my dream, and, besides, we're not here long, and the cows would approve. I will say to the people inside my camper: *Hello, sweetie. Thanks for saying hi. You like my hand on your face? Yes, you do. Hello, hello.*

A few nights ago, in bed, I craved the weight of exactly one human hand on my lower back. It refused to materialize, so I got up and took Toby for a walk. It was late, and I walked and walked down the empty streets toward the cows. Thirty-seven was also awake, standing alone in the barn while the other cows slept. The sight of that insomniac calf brought me inexplicable comfort. I took her photo and sent it to a few friends, all of whom had seen pictures of this same cow before, standing oddly awake in the orange light. From the houses where they were sheltering, a few kind friends, still up and phone-addicted, responded immediately, as if they'd been waiting all week for another image of the strange, sleepless cow. On the walk home Toby rubbed his head against my thigh, and I snapped a photo of the moon.

Nominated by Daniel L. Henry, The Sun

IN A TIME OF PEACE

by ILYA KAMINSKY

from TERMINUS

Inhabitant of earth for forty something years
I once found myself in a peaceful country. I watch neighbors open

their phones to watch
a cop demanding a man's driver's license. When a man reaches
    for his wallet, the cop
shoots. Into the car window. Shoots.

It is a peaceful country.

We pocket our phones and go.
To the dentist,
to buy shampoo,
pick up the children from school,
get basil.

Ours is a country in which a boy shot by police lies on the pavement
for hours.

We see in his open mouth
the nakedness
of the whole nation.

We watch. Watch
others watch.

The body of a boy lies on the pavement exactly like the body
    of a boy.

It is a peaceful country.

And it clips our citizens' bodies
effortlessly, the way the President's wife trims her toenails.

All of us
still have to do the hard work of dentist appointments,
of remembering to make
a summer salad: basil, tomatoes, it is a joy, tomatoes, add
    a little salt.

This is a time of peace.

I do not hear gunshots,
but watch birds splash over the backyards of the suburbs.
    How bright is the sky
as the avenue spins on its axis.
How bright is the sky (forgive me) how bright.

Nominated by Jane Hirshfield, Michael Waters

RECOM/MEN

fiction by DEVON HALLIDAY

from PLOUGHSHARES

A good man can be hard to find—but here at RecomMEN, we've already found them for you! Our patented algorithm sources profiles from all the most popular dating apps and pairs them with 100 percent honest reviews from vetted community members who have actually met them in person. Tired of getting bait-and-switched? Tired of swiping through endless identical profiles? RecomMEN puts an end to all that by putting you in touch with the only people who can tell the truth about men: women!

"Within a week of making an account on RecomMEN, I had met the love of my life! I don't know who @LatteSlutl 1 is, but I owe her one. Her review of Nate was thorough, detailed, and totally gave me insight into who he was and what he was looking for. As soon as he walked into the Sushi Express (thx for the tip Latte!) I knew I'd made the right decision. We've been together two years now and I couldn't be happier. :)" –*Rachel from Ann Arbor, MI*

"Jamal is patient, sweet, understanding, and an amazing chef. And I never would have known all of that if not for RecomMEN. I wasn't planning to text him back after our first date, but I thought what the hell and checked to see if anyone had written about him on here. To my surprise, @belugakatie had written like a five-page essay on how great he was and how supportive he was about her startup and how after six years together they realized they just weren't compatible but how she really hoped he'd find happiness. I agreed to go on a second date and the rest is history!" –*Anita from New York, NY*

Showing posts 1–25 of 4,102, filtered for New York, NY, filtered for "kind", filtered for "understanding", sorted by most recent

Posted by @volleyballbabe 2 hours ago

Alec. 36

[Photograph: Profile shot of man in line at cash register, excavating wallet from left-side pocket, blurry.]

So first things first, Alec is actually better-looking than his pictures, which never happens. I tried to get a good shot while he was distracted but I'm not sure if you can see him! This was during our third date, and by then I'd basically decided it wasn't going anywhere but wanted to give it one last chance because he was really nice and normal compared with a lot of the guys you meet on Lobster. Knows a ton about classic film if you're into that **kind** of thing, had some cute ideas for dates. I feel like he'd be perfect for someone romantic and low-key with sort of nerdy interests. Not for me but he was super **understanding** when I said we should just be friends. Hope someone sees this and gives him a chance! (Ignore the bad profile pics)

0 hearts, 1 dibs

View Alec's profile on FindMe and Lobster!

Posted by @_lacreperie_ 5 hours ago

Rabih, 25

[Photograph: Selfie of man grinning with free arm around younger college-age woman, squint-smiling.]

Dated Rabih for 3 months but I'm moving to SF in June and it didn't make sense for us to do long distance. Shorter than it says on his profile but I'm short too, so I didn't mind. On our first date we talked for like 6 hours straight in a coffee shop that closed at 9 and then went to a diner next door and kept talking the rest of the night—I was going through a lot of family stuff at the time and he was really empathetic and **understanding** about it. Think he was **kind** of leaning toward long distance at the end there but I wanted a fresh start, which he said was fine. Not great in bed but very eager and will go down on you all hours of the night, which helps. If you don't mind the height thing, I recommend at least meeting up with him.

4 hearts, 0 dibs

View Rabih's profile on FindMe, Twist, TrueLike, and Lobster!

Posted by @girlnextfloor 10 hours ago

Martin, 29

[Photograph: Direct shot of man raising self-conscious eyebrows across the table, a wide slice of pizza balanced two-handed.]

Martin is actually a friend of mine; he's seen me through like six break-ups, but he's having no luck romantically and refuses to use the apps. I can vouch for him in all categories: he's brilliant, he's funny, good listener, **kind**, thoughtful, **understanding**, etc. Seriously, he's been there for me so many times and I just want him to find someone so I can be the shoulder to cry on for once haha. If you're interested just DM me @girlnextfloor because he literally never checks his Twist profile. PS if you meet him don't tell him I posted this he'd kill me *2 hearts, 0 dibs*

View Martin's profile on Twist!

Posted by @chelseaqueen123 10 hours ago

Luka, 31

[Photograph: Angled shot of man bending down to pet dog, blurry.]

cute funny **kind** to waiters vegan plays guitar. wanted sthg serious & was **understanding** about it when I just wanted sthg casual but then decided it wasn't working for him. decent in bed. if you end up going home with him could you check for my purple scarf on the floor bc I think I left it there but he says he can't find it

1 heart, 15 dibs

View Luka's profile on FindMe, Twist, and Meetsters!

Showing posts 1–25 of 112, filtered for New York, NY, filtered for "introvert", filtered for "relationship", sorted by most recent

Posted by @opheliet 6 days ago

Kevin, 25

[Photograph: Half-obscured shot of man lounging on couch holding a red plastic cup as bodies blur around him.]

Kevin & I met on FindMe and went on five or six dates but it didn't end up working out. He's very into the NY social scene so if you're good at staying out late and partying he's probably a lot of fun. I'm honestly more of an **introvert** and after a while I felt like I just wasn't being myself or that myself was someone he wouldn't really get along with or something. Anyway he's good-looking in person too and I brought him to a work party once and I think my coworkers will probably go for him if you don't. He can seem kind of shallow at first but we actually ended up talking a lot about his **relationship** with his sister and his mom's side of the family back in Indonesia and I feel like he could be a really good fit for someone who is more normal around big groups of people. This picture is from our fourth date.

3 hearts, 18 dibs

View Kevin's profile on FindMe and Twist!

Posted by @joXsunsetp 3 weeks ago

Adam, 30

[Photograph: Computer-lit profile of a man's face, jaw rigid with concentration.]

Adam is extremely intelligent, ruthlessly good at debate, well-traveled, nihilistic, and he has a certain kind of look which might not appeal to everyone but definitely appeals to me, lanky verging on emaciated. Maybe that all makes him sound like your typical overeducated asshole but he's also got this deeply sympathetic worldview that you catch glimpses of if you probe for long enough. I can't really explain it. Just listening to him talk I got new insights into the whole human experience— he's an anesthesiologist at a hospital in Queens and knows everything about bodies, and on our first date (which lasted for two days—drinks and then dinner and then drinks and then his place and then breakfast and then lunch and you get the idea) I remember this moment when we were sitting at the bar and he takes my hand and starts telling me about all the bones and nerves and muscles that make it up, telling me about each one by name and telling me the Latin root and the evolutionary history of each one and somehow it was like being seen for the first time, like I knew that when he looked at me he was really *seeing* me, all the hidden veined bloody parts of me there under the surface. He's like that. He's an **introvert** in the extreme and easy to talk to and hard to get close to and I think I fell in love with him somewhere in the middle of that first date, the second night as I was lying there looking at his skeletal body in my bed, just sort of marveling at it, the fact that there was this skeleton in my bed, but after a few dates he said basically that I seemed really nice and he didn't want to hurt me and he thinks he probably shouldn't be in a **relationship** right now because he's had a lot of depressive episodes lately and he's kind of experimenting with going off his medication and he knows it wouldn't work out et cetera. I know it seems strange that after all this I would RecomMen him but I feel like he's just absolutely brilliant and strange and wonderful and I hope he falls in love someday, though obviously it's not going to be with me.

0 hearts, 6 dibs

View Adam's profile on Lobster!

Showing posts 1–25 of 307, filtered for New York, NY, filtered for "fell in love with him", sorted by most recent

Posted by @beachbabe24643234 1 minute ago

Chase, 29

[Photograph: Man lifting weights.]

Chase is so strong and sexy **I fell in love with him** immediately when I saw him he's really good in bed text me at 2128731297 I will set you up with him!!

0 hearts, 0 dibs

View Chase's profile on FindMe, Twist, Meetsters, TrueLike, Lobster, BmeetsK, and Mixxr!

Posted by @beachbabe24643234 2 minutes ago

Chase, 29

[Photograph: Man lifting weights.]

Chase is so strong and sexy **I fell in love with him** immediately when I saw him he's really good in bed text me at 2128731297 I will set you up with him!!

0 hearts, 0 dibs

View Chase's profile on FindMe, Twist, Meetsters, TrueLike, Lobster, BmeetsK, and Mixxr!

Posted by @beachbabe24643234 3 minutes ago

Chase, 29

[Photograph: Man lifting weights.]

Chase is so strong and sexy **I fell in love with him** immediately when I

Showing posts 0 of 0, filtered for New York, NY, filtered for "good listener", filtered for "forgiving", filtered for "commitment", filtered for "doesn't mind tattoos", sorted by most recent

No posts found. Try widening your search! Trending search terms include:

funny | romantic | cute | good with kids | looking for something serious | nice | lives alone | dog

Showing posts 1–13 of 13, filtered for New York, NY, filtered for "forgiving", sorted by most recent

Posted by @tequilas0da 1 week ago

JD, 37

[Photograph: Angled shot of man leaning along bar to face some better-lit part of the room, which casts the left side of his face in purple light.]

so didn't end up working out between me & jd but wanted to post on here b/c he's like the one person i've met through truelike who's like a genuinely self-actualized independent functioning human instead of like the archetypal bewildered/resentful nice guy tm searching for his manic pixie dream girl which you end up noticing after three or four dates with them where if you're not as bubbly quirky fun as you might have seemed on the first date they get sort of confused & hurt & start asking what's wrong & why you seem distracted from their fascinating anecdotes abt their one-week backpacking trip through europe which like changed them as a person . . . anyway jd was just a normal not exceedingly attractive dude but i see all the time on here posts from these girls forgiving all sorts of flaws b/c the guy was so Nice & they feel so guilty it didn't work out & god for once can we not reward guys for exhibiting the bare minimum ability to hold a conversation when the

Showing posts 1 of 1, filtered for New York, NY, filtered for "will forgive all your flaws", sorted by most recent

Posted by @gemma_redem 3 years ago

Nick, 28

[Photograph: Underexposed profile of a man bending down to light a candle, his expression gentle, muted.]

Whoever ends up dating Nick should know that he is the best you will ever have. His company is a privilege, his body is a revelation, his love is a gift. We were together four years and he changed my life. He is deserving of the love of everyone reading this and all the happiness they can possibly bring to him. I know that sounds like an exaggeration but I'm finding it hard to speak in anything but clichés. Nick is steady. He will be there for you and listen to you and support you and care about you. He **will forgive all your flaws** and ask nothing from you but your whole honest self, which you have to be sure to open up to him without deflection, without artifice. Nick is the most intelligent person I've met, and the wisest, which is more important. He will challenge you to be a better, more authentic, more generous version of yourself, if you let him. He saved me from my worst tendencies and he probably would have stayed with me forever if I hadn't let my paranoia take over and ruin things for us. He's all the usual things that you're looking for too, he's sexy and he's funny and he's kind and all the rest, but what I really want you to understand if you end up dating him is that he's unique—his steady love for you and trust in you is unique. No one else you ever meet will love you with the same unflagging askless permanence that he does. I was too afraid to be fully completely one hundred percent honest and trust that he would love me if he saw all of me and so in the end he couldn't. Which is on me. But he made me the happiest I've ever been and even now I am happier because of who I became in his eyes. If you are with him you should never let him go. Apologize for the things that don't matter and be honest about the things that do and try to not take him for granted while still conversely taking for granted the fact that he loves you, which you will have to take for granted and sort of memorize as a fact about the world because the more you get to know him the harder it'll be to believe. If you need advice or if you have questions or if you find yourself headed down the wrong track with him where things seem to be getting worse and fights are getting longer and apologies are getting shorter and the relationship becomes something you talk about like it's concrete, The Relationship, like it needs to be fixed or saved, please DM me at @gemma_redem because I want him to be incredibly, inordinately happy and if he thinks you're the right person for him then you probably are. He will see through you; let him look.

81 hearts, 173 dibs

View Nick's profile on FindMe!

Showing posts 1–25 of 30, filtered for New York, NY, filtered for "love", filtered for "happy", filtered for "good to me", sorted by fewest dibs

Posted by @northangera 1 month ago

Charlie, age 25

[Photograph: Young man glancing up across expensive cutlery with uncertain half-smile.]

So, honestly, Charlie is an incredibly sweet guy and I was just not at all what he's looking for. He got attached very quickly, he's chivalrous and affectionate and (maybe a little clingy and) in the end I just felt I was exhausting myself trying to make him **happy**. Don't let that put you off, though, because I think what he wants is just someone to be good to (the way he tried to be **good to me**, whoops). He's a born romantic, which is great as far as romantic gestures go (bought me flowers on a random Tuesday) but also fair warning you might get the **I-love**-you a little sooner than you'd expect. Probably perfect for someone—I think most of us are.

0 hearts, 0 dibs

View Charlie's profile on FindMe, TrueLike, and Lobster!

Posted by @yourlocalbarista 4 months ago

Zach, 27

[Photograph: Close-up of man angling head to get ramen noodle in mouth, chopstick grip mostly correct.]

257

went on a date w/ Zach to a ramen place btwn our two apartments and ended up having a surprisingly good conversation about **love** and loneliness and nyc and dating apps ofc. he has a lot of opinions and strategies on how to game the system and it was all really interesting to listen to though by the end I was like pretty sure I didn't want a second date. he was cute but I got this weird vibe like in his world being cynical is superior to being **happy** and as a person who generally tries to be **happy** that did not seem **good to me** on like a base compatibility level. so I'm not sure why I'm recomMENding him except that the date itself was good and I don't know, if he texted me for a second date I would probably say yes.

2 hearts, 0 dibs

View Zach's profile on FindMe and Twist!

Posted by @blackbeltX 2 hours ago

Min, 31

[Photograph: Shirtless man striking exaggerated pose on corner of a messy bed.]

I love this dude. Did friends with benefits for like a year and a half, called it off because he's looking for something serious now supposedly. Amazing guy, you will never meet anyone with such a positive outlook on life, like his only two settings are **happy** and tired but optimistic. Total

Showing posts 1–25 of 810, filtered for New York, NY, filtered for "Nick", sorted by most dibs

Posted by @gemma_redem 3 years ago

Nick, 28

[Photograph: Underexposed profile of a man bending down to light a candle, his expression gentle, muted, limitless.]

Whoever ends up dating **Nick** should know that he is the best you will ever have. His company is a privilege, his body is a revelation, his love

Warning:

This link will direct you to a nonaffiliated site. While RecomMEN partners with various dating app websites, we cannot guarantee the safety or accuracy of profiles you view on these sites. Are you sure you want to continue?

Error 602

Profile not found.

Have an account on FindMe? Sign up to have access to the profiles of more than 40 million users around the world. With our basic plan you get 100 swipes per day, or upgrade to premium for unlimited swipes plus

Showing posts 1–25 of 810, filtered for New York, NY, filtered for "Nick", sorted by most dibs

Posted by @gemma_redem 3 years ago

Nick, 28

Showing posts 0 of 0, filtered for New York, NY, filtered for "won't break up with you in a train station in Baltimore after you just spent the week-end with his family", sorted by most dibs

No posts found. Try widening your search! Trending search terms include:

cute | tall | looking for something serious | romantic | funny | athletic | dog | lives alone | honest

Showing posts 0 of 0, filtered for New York, NY, filtered for "just like my ex but doesn't want to change me", sorted by most dibs

No posts found. Try widening your search! Trending search terms include:

Showing posts 1–25 of 189, filtered for New York, NY, filtered for "texts back", filtered for "something serious", sorted by most recent

Nominated by Ploughshares

YOUNG AMERICANS

by JABARI ASIM

from STOP AND FRISK: AMERICAN POEMS *(Bloomsday Literary)*

Dead children make mad noise
when they march, sounding their frustrated yawps
over the rooftops of Chicago. Neither wind nor monstrous
guns can stop their stomping.

    Dead children make mad noise
    when they march. The doomed, solemn-eyed youth
    of Chicago are putting boots on the ground,
    gathering in ghostly numbers
    to haunt us with their disappointment.
    It's hard to miss them swelling the Water Tower crowds
    at rush hour, clogging Cottage Grove inconveniently,
    taking up all the seats on the El.
    The Dan Ryan is stop and go
    from all the phantom overflow as they troop
    through the city's arteries.
    South Side, West Side, all around the town.

Battered and battle-hardened,
the spirits of collateral children rise up
armed with experience, the worst kind of knowing.
The spirits of collateral children drip blood
across the big-shouldered city, spattering
the landscape like poppies dotting Flanders Field,
looking for someone, anyone, to take up their quarrel.

They high-step in rhythm, according to a cadence
only they can hear:
Hup! Two! Three! Four! Through that hog butcher history,
Sandburg's singing niggers, Capone's cutthroats,
bullets falling like fat rain on a street in Bronzeville.

    The slaughtered innocents of Chicago,
    young Americans who loved and were loved,
    are braving the crossfire
    of hand-wringing and corruption,
    the photo-friendly choirs
    and drive-by eulogies, politicians'
    cue-card declarations of sorrow.

    The slaughtered innocents of Chicago
    ain't going nowhere gently.
    Circling the sad metropolis
    in loud, unearthly ranks,
    they raise their voices to the bloody sky,
    above the roar of the monstrous guns and the
    bullets, falling like fat rain.

Nominated by Bloomsday Literary

IMAGE

by LOUISE GLÜCK

from THE THREEPENNY REVIEW

Try to think, said the teacher,
of an image from your childhood.
Spoon, said one boy. Ah, said the teacher,
this is not an image. It is,
said the boy. See, I hold it in my hand
and on the convex side a room appears
but distorted, the middle taking longer to see
than the two ends. Yes, said the teacher, that is so.
But in the larger sense, it is not so: if you move your hand
even an inch, it is not so. You weren't there, said the boy.
You don't know how we set the table.
That is true, said the teacher. I know nothing
of your childhood. But if you add your mother
to the distorted furniture, you will have an image.
Will it be good, said the boy, a strong image?
Very strong, said the teacher.
Very strong and full of foreboding.

Nominated by David Hernandez, The Threepenny Review

BREATHING EXERCISE

fiction by RAVEN LEILANI

from THE YALE REVIEW

When she began to have trouble breathing, Myriam tried to wait it out. She monitored the daily pollen count, bought a Neti pot, and tried not to think about the gallerists who no longer returned her calls. After an opening of her new work which had only three attendees—a pair of Danish tourists and a woman who wanted to know if the toilets were free—she went to a party in Poughkeepsie and received a crushing pep talk from a sculptor whose assistants were always under the age of twenty-three. *You're still young*, he said, and all night people offered similar condolences for her career. Later the host of the party corralled everyone into a room with an old tube TV. When he turned it on, she could hear the crackle of the cathode. He adjusted the antennas and said he was going to show them a documentary. It was about competitive tickling; as they watched, a hush settled over the room. A man looked into the camera and described being bound and tickled. *They told me it was about endurance*, he said; *I was thirteen*. It made Myriam uneasy, and she excused herself and took the earliest Metro North into the city that she could find.

As soon as she got on the train, she put her head between her knees and tried to breathe. She called her mother, and they had a nice conversation until they came to the subject of her work. It had been eleven years since she'd left home, eight since she'd graduated from a mid-tier art school and made her name showing audiences how much abuse the human body could withstand. It isn't sustainable, her mother said, and, technically, she was right. As Myriam was getting off the train, the first email came. *Hack bitch*, it began, before segueing into a surprising deconstruction of one of her more recent shows—soft depictions of black women in ornate Victorian dress: horsehair crinoline, ivory boning, bantu knots. Subtler than her larger body of work, meaning it involved significantly less self-harm. *Why not just kill yourself,* the author wrote, after a long treatise about the Round Earth conspiracy.

At home, she tried to open up her airways with peppermint oil and steam. She took a Xanax and walked around in circles with her arms above her head. A man was playing trumpet across the street, and she opened the window and asked him to stop. Not for the first time, her apartment felt as if it was too small. It was 545 hyper-utilized square feet, a one-bedroom in Bed-Stuy that she could afford only because the closest subway station was five blocks away. She regretted going to the party, but invitations were not coming the way they had when she was twenty-five—when she fed yam and pig intestines through a cotton gin and could still be someone's age-inappropriate girlfriend, when she rigged a voting machine to a hose and stood in a glass tank as patrons cast their votes, when the confluence of an unimpeachable pelvic floor and a strong debut made her into a wanton, Brooklyn-dwelling monster; those were the days. Days when her mother called and asked why she would do these things to herself in public for white people.

Myriam didn't have a good answer, only that there was something pure about force, about a fervent belief in her own body, which could be technically boiled down to such clichéd maxims as Mind over Matter and No Pain, No Gain. She found a place in her mind that was dark and cool and still, and then she opened a show at the Domino Sugar Factory and let herself be repeatedly pushed down a flight of stairs. Now she was twenty-nine, and her career was not going as planned. *Myriam Says Relax,* a show in which she sat for two hours with a lye relaxer in her hair, had not been received well. After an hour, the sodium hydroxide had begun to eat through her scalp, and she was hospitalized. The reviews were embarrassing: articles on the vague hotepian undertones of the project, on the self-inflicted martyrdom for a problem as tired—as *nineties*—as western European beauty standards. And finally, the criticism which at first felt shallow but now worried her as she moved beyond an age where it was good enough just to shock and awe: that she was making a spectacle of black pain, feeding the machine she loathed.

She made attempts to remedy this, projects organized in secret with scrappy, progressive galleries unfazed or actively down for the legal repercussions of not letting white people into her shows, of charging

264

them double, of making them wear signs around their necks that said, *I am not welcome here.* She put on shows like *George Washington's Teeth*, in which she collected the teeth of white patrons and made bespoke silver grillz. But ultimately how she explained it to her mother was that she had somehow broken into an industry in which *she* was not particularly welcome, and she was just doing what she could to survive. She had made a Rube Goldberg machine—fifty dominoes, eighteen gumballs, seventy rubber bands, and one glass of warm salt water poised above a synthetic hymen to terminate in the utterance of the *n*-word. She branded herself with erasure poems she'd drawn from excerpts of *Huckleberry Finn.* White people came in giddy droves, excited to say the few words they were not allowed under the guise of discussing art.

A few days after the party, there was another message. She knew it was from the same person because of the email address, a generic dot org with no corresponding organization, but this time he signed his name. *Tragic Negress*, it began. *I read your interview with _____ and I had a few points.* She imagined he was normal, indistinct. To imagine him grotesque somehow felt less true, like a child's idea of evil, in which there is no dissonance between the heart and the face. It was just as likely that he was a competent and active community member, a new father, a guy on Lexapro with a dog waiting for him to come home. Of course Hitler's dog must have loved him too. The only thing she knew was that he was local, as he spoke obsessively about an exhibit he'd seen recently at Hauser & Wirth, in Chelsea. *Dear Richard*, she wrote, *You think you hate me but you are actually obsessed with me and that is the thing you hate*, and even this made her feel out of breath.

   She hoped she might feel better after going to the gym, but after two minutes on the treadmill, she had to stop. It took her aback that her body, which she had punished thoroughly for years, was now incapable of accommodating such a small request. She started the treadmill again, but it was too much. She had the sensation that there was something hard and insoluble in her throat, like a diamond or some amalgamation of the microplastics in New York's water supply. Her trainer took her aside and asked if she was all right. He was a jarhead from Staten Island who didn't believe in excuses, and sometimes he pinched the fat that still remained around her stomach and made her keep going until she cried. But now he put his hand on her shoulder and told her to breathe, and she shrugged off his hand and said, *I can't.*

The next morning, she took the train to a clinic in Sunset Park and told her primary care physician that it felt as if she had wool in her lungs. While she described her symptoms, he kept glancing at his watch. In a way, this comforted her. If the situation were dire, she imagined, he would be a better audience. So she was relieved when he simply told her to go home and get some sleep. But a week later, she felt worse. As if every valuable organ in her chest were distended with dark city air. She logged into her health insurance portal—a poorly designed bit of JavaScript for patients insured through her Artists Union—and sent messages to her physician about the state of her health that did not receive a response. Richard kept in touch. As she expected, her response had not deterred him. It had encouraged him. *I'll find you,* he wrote. *It would be nothing to find your address. Maybe this is why your work has gotten so tepid? Maybe you feel a little too safe?*

She couldn't pretend that some of this didn't hurt her feelings. Comments about her cunt, about how her head might look on a stick—whatever. But the comments about her work, she carried them around with her all day. Although he was not alone. This particular critical response was familiar—that her level of self-exhibition corresponded inversely with her level of safety. *Who is this for?* her mother asked, and within the question was an accusation: that her work could not be for black people, for black women—creatures so powerless that to invite further subjugation was redundant, perverse. Myriam stammered when she tried to explain herself. She did not feel powerless. She felt searingly present in the world, and sometimes she wanted to be reduced.

When she didn't respond to his message, Richard sent a photo of a scimitar, then a Glock. She tried to report him. She put on her least threatening clothes and went to the precinct on Lafayette with a handful of printed emails, but as he hadn't actually done anything, there was nothing the authorities could do. After two days they sent an email to say that the ticket was closed, and she bought three cameras and mounted one in each room.

A few days later, she met with a pulmonologist. She sat in the waiting room for forty-five minutes after her appointment was supposed to start, and then a nurse ushered her inside and weighed her in a room with an overflowing garbage can. When the pulmonologist came, he did not make eye contact. He mispronounced her name and prescribed an antihistamine. The copay was two hundred dollars, the deductible a distant, four-figure number that she could not hope to touch, the Artists Union's HMO a collection of inscrutable fine print that covered only routine checkups and visits to in-network gynecologists who said things like *Very pretty* about her transvaginal ultrasounds.

She took the pills and wrote a few emails to her mother that she didn't send. *I had a good childhood. You didn't do anything wrong*, one email began, before she filed it away in her drafts. When the pills didn't help, she found a nebulizer on eBay and hooked herself to the machine twice a day each week. *This is what I'm going to do to you*, Richard wrote after sending a link to an upsetting pornography. *Okay*, Myriam wrote back, lank from an hour on the nebulizer, the mask still strapped to her face and sputtering mist.

Of course, this only made him angrier. In her unfortunate tenure as a heterosexual woman she had learned that men, more than anything, did not like to be surprised. They did not like there to be any place inside you they could not touch. They were allowed to be certain of things, and they expected to be certain of you. Even her ex-husband, a performance artist whose oeuvre involved significant self-mutilation, had ideas about how she should conduct herself once they were married. When they were dating, he was happy to do joint projects in which they lived under surveillance in a room made entirely of Kanekalon hair. Happy to take turns spanking each other over clips of Bill Cosby's "pound cake" speech. But when they married, he felt differently. *Your body is a temple*, he said three days before he nailed his scrotum to the floor of the Guggenheim.

While she was out and about, Richard sent another message: *I can see you. I'm behind you.* She asked him what she was wearing and he said, *a blue dress*, which was right, and then *sandals*, which was wrong. She kept two knives in her purse. She didn't walk down ill-lit streets or ride in train cars that were insufficiently populated. If she had a husband, there would at least have been someone there to know if she didn't come home. When she got up in the morning and felt her body working against her lungs, she knew she was an easy mark. She looked around her apartment and took in the entirety of what it cost to breathe sparingly. To preserve energy, there were tradeoffs, things that were left undone. The garbage, copious and cooking in the sun. The weapons fashioned from household items. The sink and shower, slippery with bacteria. Bed shirts and underwear, heavy with sweat from the exertion of breathing consciously. She took the cameras down, looked at the footage and could not believe the person she saw. She made a copy of the footage and sent it to her manager, and in a few days her manager wrote, *Is there any more?*

And there were bills. The insurance company called once a week and then twice a day. She changed her voicemail to say that she was opening a show in Beijing and not answering her American phone. She dreamt it was true: low-lit, narcotic dreams in which she walked an adult panther through a Chinese tobacco factory and people flocked into the gallery and filled the air with Mandarin. In these dreams she could breathe again.

She used to live for the summers in New York. The stinky, shimmering avenues and everyone getting cooked underground. The body resisting a solid white arm of sun. Now it was hell. There were too many people and not enough air, and her chest burned no matter how carefully she drew breath. Now she drank barium as another specialist monitored a live X-ray of her throat. *Everything looks fine*, he said, and for two days all her meals tasted alkaline. For the next procedure, an endoscopy she spread over two credit cards, they lowered a camera into her esophagus and found nothing. She did not have an escort, and when she tried to hail a cab, three went by before one stopped.

No news did not feel like good news, and the longer there were no answers the more she was sure the answers were bad. It was not insignificant for her to believe so totally in a thing she could not see. Because she was a woman, she had been taught to distrust herself, and there was no certainty she held that had not been vetted for the cute, indelible madness of female error. To be able to insist fervently that something was wrong meant that all alternatives had been thoroughly explored. It meant defying the more natural inclination to defer and allow herself to be seen as crazy, and so she needed to be right. She had seen the news stories about richer, more powerful black women. Dark, luminous women who always kept their faces partly out of view, who were emblems of what you could have when the long game was cautiously and brutally played. Even these women were sent home with aspirin as their brains were hemorrhaging.

She sent an email to her primary care physician and attached an article about respiratory illness and city smog. *I have done everything I'm supposed to do*, she wrote; *please, help*. It wasn't just that she couldn't breathe; it was that she still had to go about life. The errands, the electric bills, the sexually violent found poetry of loitering men. It was odd to be sick, to have the sensation her lungs were full of blood, and still have to be wary of men. It was odd to feel as if she was dying and still have to field comments about her breasts. She went out to buy mucus thinners, and a man trailed her from Seventh Avenue to Dekalb. When she stopped to confront him, a group of men looked on and laughed. As she climbed the stairs to her apartment, another message came. *I'm going to pay you a visit soon*, Richard wrote, and outside, the man with the trumpet was still playing "Hot Cross Buns."

For two days, she didn't sleep. She cleaned the apartment, took out weeks' worth of recycling, and pulled hair from all the drains, and then she wrote her own obituary and addressed it to the biggest critic of her work, a prominent blogger who could not be pleased. She tried to make a case for some of the pieces he'd deemed irresponsible, but as she wrote, she wondered if he'd been right. Giving private dances to patrons for a nickel a pop had not been about anything other than being oversexed and twenty-six. Letting patrons choose between giving her a rose and holding an unloaded gun to her head had been, despite her cynicism, a severe miscalculation. The critic claimed to be among one of the faceless men who chose the .22, and in his review he wrote that there was nothing radical, nothing avant-garde about a black woman's proximity to death.

She thought about this when she went for a full body X-ray. She put on the lead apron, and a nurse warned her that the quarters would be tight. When she was inside, the radiologist noticed she hadn't had a bowel movement in a while. He joked that he could see an entire cherry tomato in her large intestine, and she pretended to laugh. The imaging took forty minutes, and she fell asleep. The technician shook her awake, and then the doctor took her into a room to tell her that nothing had been found. When she began to cry, he touched her shoulder and said, *Yes, it is a huge relief.*

For an hour, the city was entirely without sound. Everything was a labor—the stairs, the turnstile, the MetroCard machine which wouldn't take any coins. It was the most humid day of the year, and not even the city was indifferent to the heat. Across Brooklyn wires were melting and lights were going out. There were fires and stroke victims and women wilting under parasols. She walked through the city and paid attention to everyone, and when she got home she began to adjust the cameras.

One camera by the door, another in the bedroom. A bowl of apples with their bruises facing out, an open window, a book cracked along its spine. She put on the nicest dress she owned. Sheer blue chiffon studded with discreet zirconiums. Four years earlier, she'd worn it on the night of her debut. It had never been washed, and now it was two sizes too big. The insurance company called while she cinched the bust with safety pins. They left a voice-mail with the information for a debt collection agency. She called her mother while she was doing her hair. *I don't have any more ideas*, she said when it went to the machine, and then she sent Richard her address. She wasn't unafraid. As she knew it would, the city had opened to her the very moment she was leaving it, given her a sense of optimism that did not comport with the project ahead, and yet there was something else. The excitement that always preceded a new project, the composure, the freaky certainty about how the pieces fit together. A feeling that came from the chest and became a thing as inevitable as breath, an insatiable resolve to live beyond the body that she had tried again and again to turn into art—which she would try to do now, one more time.

Nominated by The Yale Review

SLEEPERS

by ARTHUR SZE

from STARLIGHT BEHIND DAYLIGHT *(St. Brigid Press)*

A black-chinned hummingbird lands
on a metal wire and rests for five seconds;
for five seconds, a pianist lowers his head
and rests his hands on the keys;

a man bathes where irrigation water
forms a pool before it drains into the river;
a mechanic untwists a plug, and engine oil
drains into a bucket; for five seconds,

I smell peppermint through an open window,
recall where a wild leaf grazed your skin;
here touch comes before sight; holding you,
I recall, across a canal, the sounds of men

laying cuttlefish on ice at first light;
before first light, physical contact,
our hearts beating, patter of female rain
on the roof; as the hummingbird

whirrs out of sight, the gears of a clock
mesh at varying speeds; we hear
a series of ostinato notes and are not tied
to our bodies' weight on earth.

Nominated by David Baker, Jim Moore, David St. John

GUTTED

by CATHRYN KLUSMEIER

from AGNI

When the salmon aren't biting—which is a lot of the time—Eric and I sit with blood caked on our faces and talk about neon squid lures and diesel engine mechanics and my father's unraveling brain. As we wait—and even when the fishing is good, we do a lot of waiting—we talk about wind speeds and water temperatures. We talk about gaff hooks and hydraulic gurdies. We wax poetic about properly sharpened filet knives and salted herring threaded on barbed treble hooks. Every morning from May through September we rise at first light to discuss the state of the tides, the swells, the current. We talk about how much sleep we haven't gotten, how much food we have left. We discuss very seriously the right angle to place the knife so it glides down the salmon's belly just so. We never talk about how bad the other person smells.

When the salmon aren't biting, we spend a lot of time speculating as to why we haven't found them yet. We talk about who we know who did find them and we convince ourselves there is no way they've caught that many—that guy definitely inflated *that* score. When they aren't biting, we try and make ourselves feel better by guessing how much we've already caught this trip. We convert that guess into dollar signs and we nearly always overshoot.

Living and working every day, often sixteen hours at a time, on a two-person, thirty-seven-foot commercial salmon fishing boat in Southeast Alaska is like this. It's work that lasts all day, every day, seven days a week, for five months straight. For over six years now, I've had salmon guts woven into the fibers of my clothes and silver scales tucked under

273

the recesses of my fingernails. My captain, Eric, and I rise unreasonably early, sometimes at two in the morning. We drink thick, murky coffee from a French press forever splattered with blood, and we channel our conversations into the things we can't control. We talk a lot about prices—dock prices, market prices, prices for gillnet chums versus troll-caught versus seine. We whine a lot. On a clear day Eric will point to a bare mountain peak in the distance and say, "There should be an ice field there."

Unlike commercial seine fishermen, who use much larger boats and even larger circular nets to catch salmon by the thousands, I work on a troll boat in the Gulf of Alaska. We use hooks and lines to catch our fish. Each salmon we land is brought onboard one at a time and always by hand. Generally considered one of the most environmentally sound methods of catching salmon, trolling is the type of fishing that leads to those Hand-Caught Wild Alaskan stickers you see on expensive filets in the store. On any given day in the summer, around four a.m. on mornings full of hazy mist and vapor, you can find me on the back deck of our boat, shifting my weight from one foot to the other for stability as I lean over the worn stern railing, hauling thousands of pounds of salmon onboard with my two hands and a long metal hook.

Technically, all this business makes me a fisherman. But of course, I am not a man. Years into this work, when I try to answer the "What do you do for a living?" question, the word *fisherman* wears on me. It's like sandpaper on my tongue. "I am a fisherwoman," I'll start to say, but I almost always stop, cringing halfway through those two extra letters. These days I tell people I commercial fish for a living, and that usually satisfies their curiosities. Sends them off into elaborate visions of *Deadliest Catch* or some other predictably rugged Alaskan television show they've got lodged in the recesses of their minds. What I should tell them is that I kill fish for a living, because that's much more accurate, though far, far less romantic.

"I am a fish-killer," is really what I should say. Catching is the first part, yes. But if I'm being honest, and I'm trying to be honest here, killing is the whole reason we're out there.

✻ ✻ ✻

The night they told my mother to pick my father up from the hospital at one in the morning because he punched a nurse in the face, because he was too young and too strong, they said, because even though we were paying them exorbitant sums of money, far more money than we

274

had, they told my mother that they did not want him. They told her he was violent. They gave him pills that drugged him so much he couldn't stand up straight, so she had to drag him to the car in the middle of the night. They did not tell her they were sorry. They did not give us our money back.

The next morning, my mother called the last doctor on the list, and he told her that there was a bed in his hospital, that my father was welcome there, but that his hospital was far away. So we drove my father there, hours across the state. We drove past old and dilapidated cotton plains, past slow-moving channels cast with long, lean shadows from overhanging cliffs of corroded limestone. We drove him past oversized oaks dropping their precious acorns into the tumult of streams only to be washed away downriver to a place beyond the empty lines of dark, warm dirt that punctuate scattered fields of corn, now soybeans, now rice. We drove and we drove, past chicken slaughterhouses and cows. Big, fat females grazing, then ruminating, then grazing again on rhizomatous blades and phosphorus meal.

He slept the whole time. He slept as we passed a billboard that said *Diversity is a code word for white genocide.* Then we rounded a bend and there were flags in the periphery, all kinds of them: big, jumbo, sky-high, waving flags, decal flags taking up the entirety of car windows, flags as license plate borders, as T-shirts, as gray hoodies. Red, white, blue but in the wrong order, X's down the center. Stars. And still, he slept. His head was resting on the window. The lines of his forehead were smeared across the glass. *Does he dream now? Can he dream now?* were things I remember thinking.

We dropped him off at a cream brick building with air conditioning units going full blast and few windows. We had to be buzzed through multiple sets of double doors in order to reach his room. My mother led him into the hospital with one arm linked through his, and I put my hand above his head to shield his eyes from the sun. I remember the floor because it was blue. I remember the ceiling because it was low. But mostly I remember that after we took him to the nurses and fixed his hair for the second time and gave him three hugs each and rearranged his belongings, we had to turn around and leave him. I remember the way his face pressed up against the porthole window, how he placed his hand in the center and my mother placed hers on the other side. Their hands looked like they were touching, but they were not.

❀　❀　❀

275

I'm a good fishkiller. It's almost mechanical now, this day-in, day-out, all-summer-long cycle of hauling fish from the murky depths and gutting them. I rarely have to think about the physical act of harvesting a fish anymore. I can clean any salmon in twenty seconds. I can do it with my eyes closed. I can remove their intestines and pump the blood from their veins and scrape the kidneys from their backbone with a long metal spoon even when the winds are blowing forty knots, even when the waves send sprays over the rail and into my eyes. I can do it on the days when I can't feel my fingers anymore, they're so achy, so frigid, so clammy.

Still, six years into this work, there are things that I now know, memories I've accumulated, a knowledge I have stored up inside me that I'm not sure I'd say out loud in certain company. For instance: I have now seen nearly all the ways a fish can die. I have seen scores of big, fat fish who die with a long *thunk*. I've seen countless small, bloody ones who fight and rebound and ricochet like boomerangs. I've had fish slap me across the face right before they die. I've taken tail shots to the stomach, to my breast. I've had them bite me and then die mid-bite.

I'm always seeing hooks in places I wish I hadn't. Hooks through gills, hooks sliced through soft underbellies so the fish bleed out and die slowly. Hooks through the eyes: I'm constantly scraping off the remains of eyeballs that have been skewered like kebabs onto the bend of our hooks. They're surprisingly difficult to remove, much hardier and substantial than you'd imagine. I've pulled up fish that were so close to spawning that when I grabbed their bodies to place them into the cleaning trough, their creamy milt exploded from their bellies and sprayed all over: the runny innards of a great popped pimple launched at my open mouth.

I've seen fish I thought were long gone—fish whose hearts and eggs I've already stripped away and tossed into the sea—appear to come back to life. Sometimes, and it can be twenty minutes after I've gutted it, I'll toss a fish into our giant slush tank and it will hit the ice and start moving again. It'll start *swimming*. Furiously swimming. Long after they've died, their giant caudal fin will hit the cold water and start to pulse back and forth, plunging deeper and deeper into the ice. Sometimes I'll be standing with my knife in the cockpit—the hollowed-out space in the stern of the boat where we land and clean our catch—preparing to toss another one onto the pile when the lid on the hold will start shaking, pulsing up and down, drumming as a dead fish tries to swim to the bottom of the tank.

To be clear, these fish are dead. Still, the minute they hit that ice water they start to move again. At my most sentimental, my mind wants to add some meaning to this, like somehow their bodies *know* they're not supposed to be up here above the water, like somehow, their silver scales can sense home long after their minds have given out. Other times I'm too tired. This is usually on the days when we rise at two a.m., when our tanks are full to the brim with fish, when I have stared at all the wind and rain that I have any desire to be a part of. On those days, all I want is for the fish to go quietly into the tank. They never do, of course. And the more I kill fish, the less inclined I am to accept that there is some firm line separating the dead from the living. The more I kill fish, the blurrier this whole business gets.

❊   ❊   ❊

The morning his tears woke me up, everything smelled like mothballs. It was seven a.m., three days before Christmas. My brothers and I were sleeping on a pallet of stale quilts we'd found in my grandmother's closet, a makeshift mattress between us and the wooden floor. The three of us had been lying there, side by side, every night for a week and a half. That morning, I woke up to a series of tiny water droplets splashing onto my cheeks. When I opened my eyes I saw where the leak was coming from. They were tears falling off a face—my father's face—onto my own. He was close—too close. He was so close his features were blurry; the bridge of his nose was hovering just inches above my own, and I could just vaguely distinguish those tears running down the bumpy slope of his once broken, now crooked, nose. He was kneeling over me on all fours, knees sinking into the quilts, leaning his weight into his hands on either side of my torso. He was heaving.

"I'm a terrible person," my father said.

"I'm such a terrible person."

"I've been such an awful person," he said, as the tears kept streaming.

"I've been such a terrible person."

"I've failed you."

"I've failed you."

"I'm so sorry."

"I've failed you."

"Please forgive me. I've failed you all," he said, shaking, still leaning over me, his eyes wet and red and puffy. His nose was so stopped-up that the snotty, oversaturated paper towel wasn't cutting it anymore. He wiped green slime all over his nose, his cheeks. *I should get him a kleenex*, I remember thinking.

Instead I just sat up and offered him a hug. I led him back to his bed whispering things I had told him so many times before. That nothing was his fault. That he had failed no one, that he was good, that he was deeply good, that he would always be good, that there was nothing for him to worry about.

On Christmas morning, I found him lying in the dark on the couch-bed in the fetal position with a thin sheet pulled over his head. When I walked into the room, he curled his knees up closer to his chest. He had tucked the old sheet over his face, over his eyes, over his mouth, creating a cocoon like a child would, like a baby might do. He shook his head over and over again as I tried to wake him.

"Dad," I said.

"Dad, don't you want to come out and sit with all of us together on Christmas?"

"Dad, I'm only back for a few days and I'd love to see you."

"Dad."

"Dad."

✻   ✻   ✻

There's one morning in particular that I keep coming back to. It was just past dawn early during my first season; Eric and I had been catching kings steady for hours. I was standing alone in the cockpit. A thin layer of salt had already dried in the corners of my eyelids. Every time I blinked, it was like having tiny crumpled-up pieces of tissue paper stuck to my face. And when I looked down at my feet, as I routinely do to check the water levels in the cockpit for flooding, I saw something I had never seen before. Something that made me drop my cleaning knife so it landed just beyond my big toe.

On the floor of the cockpit, arranged in a semicircle at my feet, were hearts: eight severed salmon hearts, to be precise. Even now, I don't know how they got there. Somehow, I suppose, I had failed to toss all eight of those hearts overboard that morning and they'd found a home on the cockpit floor. But that wasn't what surprised me. What surprised me was that they were still *pulsing*. Every single one of those hearts. They were moving, each one encapsulated in its own tiny, individual red pool at my feet. Without thinking much about it, I reached down with gloved hands and picked them up—one after the other after the other—

and placed them in a line on the wooden deck rail overlooking the sea. Each heart was only about the size of a small clementine, each one the picture of vulnerability sitting there on the railing, continuing to contract as if its body were still whole. Perhaps it was curiosity that caused me to place them on the rail like that. All I know is that I stood there for many long minutes—three, four, six—before the last of the hearts stopped and went still.

❊   ❊   ❊

"He does love to dance," said Claire, a woman dressed in a purple cardigan who sat at the head of the long table. It was a week after we'd dropped my father off at the brick hospital. "We had music the other day and he was dancing up and down the hallways, playing air guitar with his hands."

"But he's having trouble with green," said Chad, the man sitting next to Claire. "He's doing okay with yellow. Not green," he said, staring at my mother, "but yellow is good."

"Everyone obviously really likes him here," Claire said. "He likes to play. He likes to go outside, to bounce balls on the concrete. And chocolate. He just loves those York peppermint patties—but he can't open them, is the problem. Sometimes he just holds them in his hand and waits for us to open them."

"One day we noticed that everyone was losing their eyeglasses, everyone in the building," Chad said. "It was just the darndest thing. Nobody could figure out what was happening. We had to do this whole search and sure enough, we found them. We found them all. He had a bunch of them in his pockets. The rest were just sitting in his room."

"He's losing function rapidly now, you know," said Claire. "Having a hard time feeding himself. Definitely can't cook. Yesterday we found him drinking the shampoo, and we had to take away his razor because he tried to brush his teeth with it."

"But he's good with yellow, like we said. Green, not so much. We play Uno and it just doesn't make sense to him. But, you know, he's a beautiful person. You can just tell he is. A really beautiful person."

"We're going to have to plan for the end soon," interjected the doctor, in an untidy suit sitting to the left of Chad. "We know the end of this story; we know what's going to happen. He looks healthy, he looks barely fifty, I know. But we have to facilitate a good ending to his story. There are ways to make things easier for him. For you, too. It's all about our choices now, how we facilitate his end."

It's a hollow sound, the dull *conk* that makes the wild eyes of a thrashing Chinook go soft. It's not a tap, it's a conk. And this distinction is important. A good hollow swinging conk to the temple with a gaff hook quells a salmon in the water. It kills her immediately. Too much force, one loud *thwack*, and you've lost her. You've knocked her off the line.

If I do it right, a conk is the sound I hear just before puncturing the gill plate, before hauling that mammoth chunk of flesh and muscle onboard. It's the sound I aim for, leaning over the worn railing, one arm cocked overhead as my hips stabilize against the ocean swell, striking not at the heart, but the brain. It's a sound that signifies death, absolutely, one less salmon returning to spawn upstream. The conk is important, but it took me years to understand why Eric kept harping on it. Why he kept yelling over the drone of the engine, "Don't tap it, conk it! Listen! Don't tap it! CONK."

Because it's not really for us, that sound. Sure, a good conk is the most efficient way to kill a fish. If a salmon dies in the water, you're less likely to lose it to a struggle at the boat. It's quick, you can move on to other lines with other fish. But most importantly, the fish dies immediately. They exit this world before ever leaving the water.

The worst is when you don't swing hard enough. That's when the tapping starts. Taps usually come in sets of three. With each tap comes more pain for her, a messier landing for you. The taps happen when you fail to conk, when instead you send one horrible ricocheting blow after another after another—*tap tap tap*. With each tap she's angry and she's flailing and now there you are, angry and flailing with her. The force of the inevitable missed blow against the sea sends salt water splashing all over and now you're flustered and throwing swings you know won't work, but all you can hear are taps now and in this world tapping is the sound of desperation and desperation sends you to places you never meant the two of you to go. It was supposed to be clean. It was supposed to be easy. It was supposed to be many things, but you're long past that now.

These fish are wild. Other than the few moments of voluntary jumps out of the water, most of them have no idea what it's like to suddenly exit the ocean, let alone to see some giant dressed in neon-orange rain gear that's got them hooked by a metal barb. Sometimes, when the intended conk is more like a tap and they're more stunned than dead and I've already hauled them onto our back deck, I realize how odd it must be for them to leave the watery suspension, to feel their weight for the first time. These fish have traveled thousands of miles. They've leapt up waterfalls, dodged sea lions, descended to ocean depths where, for the most part, we don't dare go. Yet with one hook they're here, flopping around on the deck. They're clumsy and chaotic now, not adapted to a world without water. Astronauts, I hear, train for years to adjust to feeling their weightlessness in space, and here I am, forcing that sudden knowledge on the fish. I grab the gaff hook and swing, trying to take that weight away as fast as I can. It's knowledge I never meant to give them. Pain they don't deserve. I dread the taps, now more than ever.

❖ ❖ ❖

I was fourteen the first time my father asked me to kill him. He was forty-eight. "Should the worst happen, I need you to have someone take me out and shoot me. Please, make sure I don't stay alive. It's too hard on you. If something happens to me, don't keep me alive," he said to me. "I'm asking you. Please." We were taking a walk down the street on a Southern summer evening that was bright and hot and gummy. There were fireflies flickering in the periphery. When I didn't respond, he cupped his hands on my shoulders so we were squarely facing each other. He was searching for some nonverbal agreement behind the immediate anger he knew was coming, the flash of fury I threw at him for bringing this up at all. He held onto my shoulders and waited. He was patient. Then he said it again. "Don't let them keep me alive. Don't let me burden you."

Three years after that day in the street, things started merging in my father's mind. People, places, objects. He couldn't figure out how to *name* things. Everything was so misplaced in his head that he kept asking me over and over: "When is the blood ready?" and then pointed to the oven, where we were baking bread. For years he would just stand there, staring at something he was struggling with, like it was going to come to him if we just gave him time. Like he was figuring out some elaborate math equation. Like he could see something we couldn't. Like he was on the edge of something really really important and if we would all just *trust him* and give him the time and patience, he could come back. He could surprise us. He might just return.

And he did surprise us. He had good days every once in a while. It was Thanksgiving and I was far from home, eating roast turkey off a paper plate, when my phone rang and his photo covered the screen. I just sat there and looked at it. Not only did my father usually not have any idea where his phone was, but for years we'd been under the impression

281

that he had no idea how to dial a number. His phone was a big brick that sat in his coat pocket and never seemed to be useful in the moments when we lost him, which had started happening more and more frequently.

"Cathryn," he said to me when I answered. "Happy Thanksgiving my wonderful daughter. Where are you? What can I do for you my daughter? How is your car running? When are you coming home? What can I do for you? When are you coming home? What can I do for you? What can I do for you? When can I see you again? I love you. I love you. I love you."

He talked for about two minutes, asking a bunch of questions, not really waiting for the answer. His voice sounded so with it for a moment. He sounded like he was almost there, but then it started to unravel. Then those serial questions became a repeating script. He was asking the questions that he always used to ask, using phrases that I'd rationalized were just the hard wiring of his brain. On good days, what was left of his language became distilled into phrases he'd been using all my life. The questions were still there, but there wasn't any cognition, no meaning behind them. *What can I do for you my wonderful daughter? How can I help you? What can I do for you my wonderful daughter? How can I help you?*

Sometimes he would step out the door without our knowing. On those days, my mother, brothers, and I would set out and start covering land. We would walk in a grid until we found him, sometimes sitting in the bleachers at the baseball fields two miles away where I used to play T-ball, or at a park where we used to swing every spring. Sometimes he would go to places like these, places rich with meaning from the past. Other times he was in a ditch on the side of the road, or in some barren woods, just standing there, waiting.

And then more years passed and we lost our house and the medical bills were a shadow we never did get out from under, and by the time we finally got the whispered early-onset Alzheimer's diagnosis it didn't matter anymore. We had to start making decisions for him. End-of-life care, they call it. And nobody knew what he wanted, and he certainly couldn't tell us, but I did. I knew. He'd told me exactly what he wanted. He asked me to kill him again two more times after that first day in the street—once when I was sixteen, another a year later. He wanted it to be easy. He wanted it to be fast. He wanted it simple and clean. It was none of those things, of course. I'm not sure it ever is.

❀ ❀ ❀

The bow started creaking at seven a.m. the morning I caught her. I was sitting in my bunk pretending to sleep. The old plywood above my head was warping under the weight of her pull. Just the sound of her was more than enough to spring me from the bunk, to make me reach for my gloves hanging above the stove, enough to make me jump into the cockpit without my rain gear because I was afraid of losing her. I leaned over the railing to unclip the line I suspected she was on, but I couldn't see her yet. She didn't pull. There was hardly any tension in the line. It was as if she wanted me to think she was smaller than she was, or that she had gotten off. It's not a bad strategy. I've seen Eric unclip a line he thought had a big fish on it, pull on the line for a couple seconds, see that there was no counter-pull from the fish, and then hang his head, thinking it had gone. Spit the hook. At the last second, though, that fish gave one final pull and the clip and line went flying out of Eric's hand into the sea.

I wasn't about to do that with her. After a few moments, I finally felt a slight tension, yet still she stayed under, all but invisible to me save for the clear monofilament that tethered us to each other. Slowly, I started reaching one hand over the other, hand over fist, pulling the hook toward me, coaxing her in. Often, usually with smaller fish, salmon will launch themselves high into the air, waving in an arc, announcing their presence, their displeasure at a barb poking through their lip. They fight, they dart back and forth, they splash, they protest, they holler in the only way they can, though of course the only sounds they make are the slaps of their bodies against the water.

Not her, though. There was no splashing or jumping. She stayed well under as long as she could. With each fist of line I grasped, she started to pull, but not too hard. Finally, she was close enough to the boat that I was beginning to see her, like a rising submarine from the depths. The trick with landing king salmon is to keep their head under the water until the absolute right moment. You wait, coaxing it to stay below, patient until the bridge of its head breaches the surface just long enough for the back of the wooden gaff hook to strike.

She was around forty pounds—the biggest I had seen in years. A third of my body weight. She was the lone bright spot amid a season of missing fish and commercial disaster. She was going to make me a chunk of money, which I badly needed. Truth is, I was devastated to see her.

The line never went slack, the hook never unhooked. She never jumped into the air; she never fought. She was just barely hooked. The flap of skin holding that long metal hook in her mouth was dangerously thin. Too hard a swing and she was gone. She started to surface at an angle; her right eye was wide open. I saw the gold flecks around the black pupil of her eye even before her head broke the water. She rolled over onto one side like she wanted to see who had pulled her from the depths. This happens sometimes—not often, but sometimes. Usually it's when you've waited too long to swing and they turn onto their side and the soft target right behind their head goes slightly out of reach. That's when they get a good look at you.

There are so many places that her eye could have landed. So many other places to look. So much to pay attention to above the water in this new world. A seagull waiting overhead for scraps of guts, the shape of the gaff hook, the giant, loud boat tugging along, the sea lions closing in now, coming to snatch her off the line if I didn't do it myself soon. Her head broke the water, and her metallic eye found mine. I don't know what it was that held our gaze. We weren't two enemies meeting, not friends either. It was just what it was. I was going to kill her, and she knew it. She was going to die, and I knew it, whether I killed her or she died in a stream after spawning a few weeks later. I was tethered to that line just as much as she was. And for a moment, neither of us did anything. She didn't drag, she didn't pull. I stood with my gaff hook, towering above her, hoping desperately for a *conk*. She never broke the gaze as I swung toward her head. She just stared at me, with a look that will never need translation.

Are you sure? she said.

Are you sure?

Nominated by agni

CONTENDER

by TRACI BRIMHALL

from PLOUGHSHARES

It's alright to overdress for the riot. Your rage is stunning.
It's alright to pursue the wrong pleasures and the right suffering.
Here's my permission. Take it. It's alright to replace a siren

with a bell. Let the emergency make some music. It's alright
that the meter reader broke your sunflower in half. You knew
better than to plant it where you did. Sometimes it's alright

if you call your waiter honey when you order sweet tea. It's alright
if you fall out of love with being alive, but try again tomorrow
with French pop songs and fresh croissants, wear all your gold

to church, and try—really try—to believe anything but a
    stethoscope
can hear your heart's urgency. It's alright that your mother died.
So will your father. And your son. But hopefully not before you.

It's alright to lie naked in the rain and refuse to go inside even
when the moon tries to make your cold thighs shine. It's okay
to lick the ice cream cake from your fingers. Do it. Now. In front

of everyone. And if what falls on the children lining up their cars
for the soapbox derby is not snow but ash, that's alright. Celebrate
the mutable body. And if you write notes to friends and senators

in primary colors, that's fine. It's even okay to begrudge the
    stubborn
pears in the wooden bowl. You're right, you know. They're waiting
to yellow until you turn away. It's alright that in the economy

of forgiveness you keep coming up one daffodil short. It's alright
if you ask your heart to grow the size of Secretariat's—not because
you want to outrun other horses or because your legs are classic,

but because you, too, want to be buried whole after someone
examines the insensible engine you left behind—iamb of the
beloved's name no longer metronoming the valves—and places

that slick fist in a stainless tray for weighing and shouts Sweet
Jesus before describing its ungodly heft with superlatives, your
heart the most tireless, wildest, wiliest, thirstiest heat on record.

Nominated by Ploughshares, Dan Albergotti, Catherine Pierce

MOTHER WON'T BUY POLYPROPYLENE

by PATRICIA CLEARY MILLER

from CAN YOU SMELL THE RAIN (BkMk Press)

Mother was invited skiing.
I tell her about polypropylene.
She calls it polygamy-ethylene-acetylene.
I give her a fuzzy blue ear band,
loan her my black hood.
She complains, *I'll look like a terrorist.*
I send her out for a parka.
You can't ski in mink, I explain.
What would Catherine Deneuve wear? she wonders.
She insists the geese in my down coat are dead.
She comes back with a yellow cashmere sweater.
On sale it cost about the same as polyethylene, she reasons.
Those Tibetan goats are still alive, she argues.
I send her out for jerseys and long johns.
She comes back with a gold jacket.
I'm old enough for gold lamé.
I ask, *Where will you wear it?*
She resolves, *It brightens up my apartment.*
I might ask some people over.
I can wear it to the movies.

Nominated by BkMk Press

SUFFER ME TO PASS

by DEBRA GWARTNEY

from VIRGINIA QUARTERLY REVIEW

> *Oh, savage Beauty, suffer me to pass,*
> *That am a timid woman, on her way*
> *From one house to another!*
> —*Edna St. Vincent Millay, "Assault"*

It was only a beer bottle I found in the middle of the trail, but it pinged an impulse in me to go. Get back to the car, give up our Saturday hike. I didn't tell Cheryl, who stood by while I picked up the bottle and knocked off the dust. She's known me for thirty years, since our kids were babies, and mostly she endures my jumpy nervousness. But a single empty beer bottle in the big, wide open of Oregon on a sunny June day—it was silly, even for me, to get worked up over such a thing.

Except I'd never before found trash here, not even a cigarette butt, and since the trailhead is a quick ten-minute drive from our house on the McKenzie River, I came often. I'd heard about prowling mountain lions—one had recently snatched a dog right off its leash—I almost stepped in a steaming pile of bear scat one time, and you have to watch for poison oak where you squat to pee, but all of those were tolerable as long as I could rely on encountering few people, and certainly not their beer bottles, on this six-mile loop of towering Douglas fir and cedar trees, the nearby river crashing down its channel.

I was shoving the bottle in my pack when the light shifted, or I did, and suddenly a cache of garbage appeared in front of us, chip bags and burrito wrappers, a hillock of beer bottles tangled in Oregon grape and salal. Also: a whiff of human excrement on the breeze. Cheryl said what I was thinking, *What the hell?* and that's when we heard a woman

288

scream. My knees buckled a little. I said it was probably local kids who'd partied here overnight, goofing around on the riverbank before they hauled their hangovers home, but then the woman screamed again. It was a real scream. I ducked into the trees, as if it were possible to hide from the staccato of panic in the air. My hands were shaking when I pulled out my phone. There'd be no service, but I figured I should check for bars anyway. I'd told my husband we were off to hike, but I hadn't mentioned where, so no one could easily find us, and for that and other reasons darting in my head like bats, we had to go back. Right now.

But Cheryl kept moving ahead. I didn't want to follow her and I can't say why I did, really, but together we came upon a man and a woman atop a slope. The woman saw us and said please. That one word. *Please, please.* The man had his left arm clamped across her chest and in his right hand he held a hatchet. The shiny blade was poised at her neck, which poked out of her filthy T-shirt like a cherry-red thumb.

I whispered to Cheryl, "Run." We could be back at my car in a half-hour if we hurried like we'd never hurried before, with me at the wheel, doors locked, Cheryl calling the sheriff. Wouldn't people with uniforms and guns and squawky radios be better equipped to deal with this? But my friend acted as if she hadn't heard me and she started talking to the woman on the hill in a voice I could hardly make sense of. Oddly calm, the cadence of a mother to a worried child, the singsong of someone slipping a hand under a wounded rabbit, as if we were a hundred miles from any hatchet-wielding man.

If I'd been asked back at the trailhead whether I was willing to help a woman in distress, I'd have said yes, yes emphatically, absolutely. Cheryl would have said the same and look how naturally it came to her. But the truth is, I had to pin myself down on the path that day like a wriggling moth. I remember it actually hurt to keep my feet on the ground, a pain behind my eyes, a pinch under the flat blades of my shoulders. The man with the hatchet was all taut muscle and bulging rage, and he was intent on doing harm—I could see it in his face and in the way he enclosed the young woman like a cape. She stayed motionless in his grasp except for the slight pop of her lips. Please. Her arms were pummeled raw, her face bruised, her hair in a snarl as if she'd been jerked around by it. Cheryl kept coaxing the girl—and she was a girl, younger than our daughters, maybe twenty years old—to wrench herself free of him, to get to us so we could help her. But help her how? We'd hiked in a good three miles, a couple of grandmothers with weak ankles (Cheryl) and limited stamina (me). We could shout until kingdom come; no one was going to hear, no one was going to sweep in to slam this man to the ground while we made our escape.

I hadn't been this afraid for a long time. Cheryl was afraid too, of course, and in the weeks and months ahead, we'd call each other to go over every detail and shake out our mutual terror like chunky salt in our palms, but in the moment my friend held herself together in a way I could not. She sent out soothing phrases and kept her eyes trained only on the woman, as if the man couldn't hear her, mustn't hear her, as if he were irrelevant to this discourse, and that's what worried me most. What if he was the type of man who hated being ignored? What if Cheryl's dismissal of him was the thing that would propel him to slice open the woman's throat like a grape? And then, because we had flipped the switch, he would be compelled to turn his weapon on us.

I didn't think of my father's younger sister when I was out in the woods that day, but she drifted into my thoughts not long after. I remembered late nights when she pounded on the front door of our house, her husband roaring down our street in his car. I slipped out of bed to watch from around the corner, my mother unfolding a cold washcloth for my aunt to press against her bloody teeth, my father setting a glass of whiskey on the table where she could reach it. He lowered himself next to his sister with a huff of impatience while my aunt bawled out that she had done nothing, that her husband was terrible, that he was mean to her, cruel, that he was drunk and half crazy. I was a kid, but I heard it in her voice: She didn't believe a word she was saying. She folded her body like a half-cracked nut while every signal ebbing from her was that she was the one to blame for her troubles. She'd talked back, she'd flirted with another man, she'd disappointed him in some undefined way. That's what I heard in her inflection, her tone of desperation: her fault that her husband had slammed his fist into her mouth.

When I got back into bed that night, and other nights, it wasn't a call to arms brewing in me but instead a cautionary tale. I'm sorry for that now. Sorry I had no way to imagine being a girl who could stand up against such business. A girl who'd light her own lamp and keep it lit, no matter what. What was I then, nine or ten years old? I pulled my blankets around my aunt's troubles, a nugget of trouble passed from her to me that I would carry into my own future. Like the BBs I'd watched my brother pour into the chamber of his gun, hard pellets of instruction for self-preservation got planted in me, into muscle and viscera and the synapses of my brain. Whatever it took, I was never to infuriate the man.

On a Saturday when I was around thirteen, my youngest sister reached over to change the channel on our television. Our father had football on, as he did every Saturday during the fall unless he was hunting or out of town on business or upstairs fighting with our mother. Football was his retreat, his release, and he expected to be left to it without the hubbub of children. He scooted to the edge of his chair, leaning toward the screen—maybe he thought he could get close enough for the players to hear his excoriation. *Stupid son of a bitch. Useless piece of shit.* The quarterback pumped the ball over his head, about to save the day, and the noise of the crowd rose up and up again, a roar, a resounding gong of sound as the ball was released into sparkling blue air. At this moment, my sister reached toward the knob, aiming for cartoons or a nature show, and my father punched her in the nose.

My brother, my two sisters, and the oldest one, me—none of us considered our father's propensity to hit as a big deal. Dads hit, and you could count on ours for a kick in the rear if you were moving too slow, for a clamp on the shoulder if you smart-mouthed him. Well, the others could count on it. Not me. I figured out how to give him a wide berth. When a particular rumble got going in our father—and I can't say now if I smelled it on his breath or heard a click of his rib cage, a grind of his teeth—I hurried into the garage. I sidled behind my bedroom door. I made a nest for myself behind the sofa and corkscrewed into blankets until he'd cooled down and my brother and sisters hobbled to their rooms. Not that I could always get away. Some days I was trapped in a room with our father when he blew. Those times, I'd disappear. I was good at it. A pillar of stone, an empty shell. Dig a hole, hop in. Roll into a ball. Stay there until the all clear. Take no notice of what's around you. React to nothing.

The blow delivered to my sister on that football Saturday in the family room was a wallop. Swift and exponentially more forceful than others I remember. There'd been no warning before he let loose—or my usually keen antennae had failed me—so this hit was a shock, a surprise that sucked every last bit of moisture from my mouth. It startled him as well, I think. Our father probably mistook the kid in front of him for the 250-pound tackle he'd been yelling at, except it was a skinny eight-year-old on the floor howling, blood smeared on her face, worming into her stark white hair.

I don't remember what happened after she fell—a fog, a confusion, memory in fragments. He probably muttered, *Go get your mother* before he returned to his game. If I rose off the couch to help my sister—and

I have to believe I did at least that—I swung wide around my father, tiptoeing across the rug so he might not detect my presence, pleading with her in my smallest voice to *shut up, shut up* so as not to rile him any more.

Our elderly great-aunt was also there. Aunt Bertha, well into her eighties, was the reason I was in the family room, which I would normally avoid on a football Saturday. I'd been told to settle her in a comfortable seat and keep her company until dinner. Like other tiny women, she resembled a bird, with a pretty but pinched face and reedy bones. Arms like wings that she'd forgotten how to use decades earlier. Those arms stayed glued to her sides when my father struck my sister and as that sister went flying. Not a sound from the old aunt, not a tremble of a cheek nor an eyebrow. This most ancient of our relatives didn't storm away in disgust, she didn't shout at her nephew for what he'd done; she didn't call to the other women in the kitchen to *get in here now*.

And neither did I.

How long does one hold a memory like that? By that day in the Oregon woods, a man with a hatchet shuddering before me, I'd rolled into my sixties, living on the river with my husband, children launched, my two-hundredth pot of soup on the stove. I figured the past had shed from me like old skin, cracked like a beetle's outgrown carapace. Didn't I deserve such a measure of peace? It seems not. Because here it was again, that same old hardwired reaction as if it had been lying in wait, a BB pellet worked to my surface and demanding I remain focused on appeasing the man.

As Cheryl continued her rescue of the girl, I stood stock-still, certain that my friend was about to seal our fate, all three of us dead on this path before we could make sense of the hot blood on our foreheads. But then, to my astonishment, the man lowered his hatchet. He let the woman go. She jumped apart from him, scrambling down the hill and raising enough dust to coat her already dusty legs, dislodging scree that tumbled ahead of her feet as if this were a race. She ran to Cheryl, who looped her arm around the young woman and said, "We are going to get you out of here."

With the girl tucked in between us, Cheryl and I hustled out of the forest. I kept close to the other two, hurrying over craggy roots and fallen branches, along a winding trail, while the man followed us with a creepy military precision. Twenty feet back, I'd say. No more and no less. I kept track of his presence with every step. The woman wailed as we moved ahead, her constant sound a mosquito whine in my ear. I was desperate to hush her, as I had my sister all those years ago. I was ready to clamp my hand across this stranger's mouth, to shake her until she stopped sobbing, until she stopped jabbering the story of his trouble and hers. How he'd refused to cash his last Army check. How he'd stopped taking his pills. How the US government, the military, the VA, were not to be trusted. Just after dawn that morning, his hands wrapped around her neck, he'd announced he was going to kill her. He threw her camp stove, her sleeping bag, her backpack into the river. He tossed her to the ground and sat on her until she couldn't breathe.

The man behind us, listening in, held the hatchet at his side. It ticked against his leg like a metronome, like a pendulum, in tick-and-tock rhythm with his steps, and as I heard every rustle and bump of his axe I suddenly became indescribably weary. My legs, so tired, my neck and back, my prickled hair. The two women next to me were tired too, panting, groaning; anyone hearing this story so very tired of rushing down the path while a weapon arcs in the clean, hot air, its blade sharp enough to cleave bone, and ready to land on any one of our heads.

And then we saw the trailhead sign. We spotted it at the same moment, the first silver glints of my car winking through the copse of trees. The three of us without a word picked up the pace, jogging now. The man behind us ran too, but I couldn't worry about him anymore. We were close to getting out; we might wrest free of him if we could propel our bodies a few more steps. I pitched my head, my arms, in the direction of the parking lot, yanking the girl along with me.

How do I explain the note of disappointment that cropped up in me as I opened the car door? Small as a raindrop pulsing on a windowsill. I ignored it as we climbed in and locked the doors, as I started the engine and jammed the gear into reverse, but I've had nearly two years since leaving the woods to turn over that unexpected flicker of emotion. Maybe it's this: I'd missed what might be my last chance. My final opportunity to defend a little sister in the way she deserved to be defended. I missed the opportunity to purge language stored in me for nearly half a century, clanking like a boiling pot of eggs. The words remain in place still, festering.

Cheryl and I drove back to my house in the early hours of the evening, through the rosy light of late June that bounced off the river like music. She got in her car to return to town, to her own bed, her own solace, while I poured a slug of wine and told my husband I wanted to be alone. I sat on our deck and watched the river current, mergansers drifting in a hole, ospreys preening in the Douglas firs, trout leaping from the surface of the water like ignited wire. Dusk fell and the last Saturday raft drifted by, full of teenagers squealing out their joy.

The girl we'd found in the woods was gone, transported by ambulance to the hospital in town, where she'd be bandaged up and given drugs to help her sleep. I figured that when she was released the following day, she'd begin a search for her husband, as he'd be searching for her. They'd be back together in a blink, returned to whatever they had with each other but this time without her camp stove and sleeping bag, without her backpack that held the poems she'd written about him, the ones she told the paramedic she'd planned to sell to magazines so they could buy food and cigarettes. She was without her last forty dollars of cash in the world, which she'd squirreled into a pocket of that pack in case she ever needed to get away fast. All that belonged to the river now.

A deputy had met us at the firehouse where we'd been instructed to take the girl. He asked us a series of rote questions about our encounter in the woods until Cheryl and I disagreed on the color of the man's shirt. I said it was white, that it beamed like a flashlight. She remembered it as black. He slapped his notebook shut and clicked his pen. "You had phones, didn't you?" he said. "You could have taken a picture of him."

And like that, it was done. There'd be no investigation, no search, no apprehension of a man with a hatchet. It was simply another violent Saturday in rural America. Though it wasn't simple for me. I sat on the deck, curious how to continue on. I wondered if I was to thank the man and the woman for reanimating a past I'd believed was finished but most definitely was not, or if I should hate them for the same. Behind me was the house I'd lived in for over twenty years, which neither of my sisters has visited. That's how it's been with us—they turn to each other for succor, for advice, for friendship, while I have spent decades lauding myself for being the only one to leave our father's house unscathed. As if I could forget, even for a moment, how the others took my share of the blows.

That has turned out to be the most difficult part to live with.

One of our mother's favorite stories is about our elderly Aunt Bertha's final words—how at ninety-two years old, moments before she died, she raised her head from the pillow to call out, "The angels are here to get me." Too bad I didn't know earlier about her ability to conjure angels. I could have used some creatures of heaven on an autumn day when I was thirteen, peeling my sister off the floor, hushing her, hushing her and hurrying her away. Angels to light on me. I was still young and unformed. I could still shape myself into anyone. The angels could have helped me realize that, one angel on each side, lifting me up, filling me with resolve. Murmuring in their feather voices that if I didn't act soon, become someone who could speak, who could act, the memories I was loading up one after another would live in me like a long-scorched road. Like a bombed-out road. Like a bomb.

Nominated by Virginia Quarterly Review

CEREMONY

by MARGARET ROSS

from THE YALE REVIEW

I lean against the island
in the white loft of an engineer.
He tells me he spent ten years learning
how not to get angry. People without
anger are more developed.

Aren't you angry at what's happening in the world?

I mean angry at the people I know.

I try to argue in a tone that doesn't
make him feel superior. I touch
his junk mail, sunglasses on the counter.
The same remote that summons fire
from a recess by the sofa
lowers gray blinds.

We go upstairs so I can beg him
not to fuck me while he fucks me like
we like. The tv shines an aerial shot
of terraced rice fields
pricked with blue dots which are
hats of people harvesting. The fields
fade into houses by a harbor which
becomes a desert, glacier, skyline
turning into fields again.

Then we come back into our names
and I watch that other person
tip his face back, drinking from a metal bottle.
The elegant lines of his arm. He moves
with an unembarrassed clumsiness

related to grace. He doesn't close
the bathroom door when shitting.
He says he can if I'm inhibited
but he isn't. He loved someone
with a disease and held her hands
while she cried on the toilet.

Now he loves the city we live in,
its offerings. For $20 we see
a 30-minute opera rehearsal. Singers
wearing street clothes push two chairs together
for a bed one singer dies in. The plot is revenge
says the director, before the singing starts.
Even if we speak Italian, we won't
understand, so altered is the language
by the voice. At the restaurant

afterward, the waiters have to wear
fake traditional Thai costumes and their hair
scraped up the same way. One walks
between the tables in a shoulder yoke
suspending appetizers. Many people

think people are getting smarter, freer. For $50
you can buy a ceremony starter kit to center
your self to purify your day. Something
to burn, something to say, something
to mark space. I can spread a cloth.
I can lay a rope around myself.

Nominated by Lydia Conklin

THE KALESHION

by JERALD WALKER

from CREATIVE NONFICTION

Kaleshion isn't a word in the dictionary. It's a word on your barber's wall, handwritten beneath a photo of a bald head. There are other photos up there with made-up words to identify other haircuts, but your father never selects those, because they require hair. Male preschoolers should not have hair, your father believes; that's a crime to which he'll no more be party than to genocide. Your friends' fathers feel similarly, so your friends are bald too. But as they turn seven or eight and certainly by nine, their fathers let them try different styles, while yours keeps making you get a kaleshion until you are ten. What's the deal with that? You don't know. All you know is he relaxes his stance in the nick of time, because it's 1974 and the Afro is king. You grow yours the size of a basketball and swear on your grandmother's grave that you'll never get a kaleshion again.

But it's never a good idea to swear on your grandmother's grave. One summer day, when you are twenty-six and have just moved to a new neighborhood, you try out the barbershop near your apartment. It's 1990, and the Afro long ago gave way to the Jheri curl, which gave way to flattops, which you are not particularly fond of, so now you wear your hair an inch long all around. As you sit in the chair, you tell the barber you'd like a trim. Close your eyes. Relax. Nod off after a while but be startled awake when the clippers graze your upper lip. Ask the barber, "What are you doing?" When he says, "Tightening up your mustache," you respond, "Don't touch my mustache." But, he says, "It's too late." Then he says, "I'll just finish this up," as you wonder, *What's this guy's deal?* His deal is he's incompetent, though you don't know to what extent because the mirror is behind you. When he spins the chair around, you are surprised to discover the mirror is actually a window, through which you see another man in another barber's chair staring at you. And yet, somehow, the barber standing behind that man's chair is also standing behind yours, which means the window isn't a window and the man is you. It's amazing the difference a kaleshion can make.

"So," the barber asks, "what do you think?" and you consider punching him but instead refuse to pay. He orders you to leave and bans you from returning, which is a misuse of the word *ban*. He can't ban you from doing something you'd never do. That'd be the same as banning you from eating frog legs or skydiving or from still wearing a Jheri curl like the guy at work you are about to dethrone as the office laughingstock, though maybe, it occurs to you as you walk home, you can mitigate this fate by shaving off your new pencil mustache. With this thought in mind, you start to jog, though it's sweltering outside and you haven't jogged in a while.

You cut through an alley to shorten the distance, but even with that you arrive on the back porch of your third-floor apartment breathless and sweaty—much like, one could imagine, a drug addict about to commit a burglary.

Your girlfriend imagines this. You've left your keys on the kitchen table, so you knock on the window for her to let you in. You shout her name, then realize she can't hear you because she's in the front room, where the phone is, calling the police. Don't panic; all you'll have to do is tell them about the incompetent barber. Take out your driver's license to illustrate that your new face is also your old face. If at least one of the officers is black he'll see the resemblance. There is a high likelihood, however, that—like your girlfriend—both officers will be white, which means weapons could come into play, so you need to either convince your girlfriend you are her boyfriend, or run. Lift your driver's license to the window. Press it against the glass. Watch your girlfriend squint at your photo, then at you, and then back at your photo. Beg her to let you in. A voice in your head orders you to get the hell out of there just as something in hers clicks; one hand cups her mouth, the other releases the curtain. The deadbolt and your fate turn.

Moments later, while shaving off your mustache, you vow never to set foot in another barbershop. This doesn't improve your mood, so you try another approach too. You start to feel better during your third cocktail at your favorite bar—good enough, even, to tell the bartender what happened. He doesn't believe you. Lift your baseball cap. When he bursts into laughter you can't help but join him. It *is* funny, after all. Repeat the part about seeing the stranger through the window and laugh some more. And when the bartender, who knows you're an aspiring writer, says this would make a good story, smile and say you definitely intend to write it someday.

You write a lot of other stories first, though, which earns you publications, a faculty position, your first book contract, and, after many years, an invitation to read your work at a prestigious literary conference. According to the invitation, there are some notable writers scheduled to participate, one of whom is quite famous. This is a big deal. This is huge! It could mark your arrival as a serious man of letters, and it's too bad, in a way, that your girlfriend isn't around to see it. She was supportive of your early efforts, even serving as your copy editor, an arrangement you'd projected far into a future where you'd discuss comma splices together in your old age, though perhaps you should have taken her attempt to have you arrested as a bad omen: you broke up a few months later. A lot has changed in fifteen years. You learned to copy edit, for example. You moved to a new city. You got married, had a son, moved to a different city, and had another son. One thing that hasn't changed, though, is your self-imposed barbershop ban.

Who knows, maybe one day you'll lift it after growing tired of the split ends and generally scraggly appearance that results from cutting your own hair. And you'll probably have to start taking your sons to a barbershop when they realize that their hair, which you've cut since they were babies, doesn't have to look like this either. But at ages six and eight they're still too young to pay attention to such things, and you're still wary of barbers, so every couple of weeks you break out the clippers.

You all three get the same style, a conservative cut that speaks of sophistication and a desire not to scare white people. You call it *The Obama*. To achieve it, simply use the #1 clipper guard on the top and the #1/2 for the sides and back. Sometimes you tease your sons by saying you can't find the clipper guards so they'll have to get kaleshions, and when they jump from the chair and run, you chase them around the house, all of you laughing wildly. It's a good time.

The day before the literary conference begins, you get out the clippers and give your sons their Obamas. And then it's your turn. You start on the crown of your head and work your way forward, as you always do, and then you scream because the #1 guard has tumbled before your face and landed in the sink, followed by a clump of hair. Lean toward the mirror to stare at the long strip of pale scalp. Whisper, "Please God, no, please," but God cannot help you. Nor can your wife, who runs to the bathroom and, much like your girlfriend all those years ago, is staring at you with a hand cupping her mouth. Your sons burst into the room. They want to know what the screaming is about. Your wife, speaking into her palm, says, "Daddy's giving himself a kaleshion."

The boys want to see. Reluctantly, you bend toward them. They erupt in laughter. You shoo them away. Try to convince yourself it's not as bad as you think, but you can see from the way your wife is looking at you that it is. She lowers her hand and asks, "What happened?"

That's simple: your grandmother, on whose grave you swore all those years ago, reached down from the heavens to flick off the clipper guard. But don't say this. Say you're not sure. You are sure, however, of what must be done. Ask your wife for the shoe polish.

"You can't," she responds, "wear shoe polish on your head."

"Why not?"

"Because that's insane."

"You have a better idea?"

"Yes. Shave the rest of your head."

Look horrified and say, "Are you *crazy*?"

"You have to," she insists.

Remind her that the important literary conference is tomorrow.

"Exactly," she responds, and a stalemate is reached.

Twenty-four hours later, you arrive at the important literary conference. As you enter the auditorium, a writer you know strikes up a conversation, thereby establishing the expectation that you will sit together, which is fine, as long as he doesn't go to the first row, which of course he does. Thanks to the stadium-style seating, everyone will have a clear view of the top of your head. But it will not be a view of shoe polish, because your wife convinced you not to use it on the grounds it would be difficult to remove. The same effect, she explained, could be achieved with mascara. You don't know much about mascara, having never worn it before, though you are pretty certain that under certain conditions, such as high humidity, it runs. The auditorium feels like a rain forest. You're already sweating. You're already imagining your rectangle of scalp being slowly revealed. You can all but hear the snorts and giggles.

You have to stop obsessing. Distract yourself by perusing the conference's brochure. The first scheduled reader is the famous writer. You saw him when you entered the auditorium, sitting dead center of the room with a few of his books on the desk before him, colorful Post-its sticking out from the pages, and a chill went down your spine. Everyone is eager to hear him, no doubt, but you allow yourself to believe he's eager to hear you too. Why not? Maybe it's true. Maybe he's as much an admirer of your work as you are of his. You're not famous by a long stretch, but you are, you've noticed, last on the schedule, a position, like first, often reserved for a writer of a certain ability, with a certain gravitas.

Gravitas indeed! The famous writer brings down the house and leaves the podium to thundering applause. The next reader is outstanding too. As is the next. Everyone is quite good, although, admittedly, it's difficult to pay close attention while imagining mascara working its way down your head.

Finally, you're introduced. Go to the podium. Look around the room, really for the first time, and take in the size of the crowd. It's enormous! Of the hundred or so seats, only a few are empty, one of which, you note, is the famous writer's. His books are gone too. As indignation bubbles up from some dark place inside you, you wonder what this guy's deal is, though the real question, you've begun to suspect, is what's the deal with you. For a split second you are back in the barber's chair staring into a mirror at a man you don't recognize, a man who's at an important literary conference with mascara on his head, hoping to impress a famous writer who has ducked out of the room, and not seeing the humor in the situation. It's amazing the difference an ego can make.

You look away from the famous writer's chair. Greet the audience. Announce that, before you begin, you'd like to take a brief moment, if you could, to talk about your hair. Raise your hands to the heavens. Smile. Now swear, as your beloved grandmother is your witness, that the story you are about to tell is true.

Nominated by Jennifer Lunden

PLUTO BE ORBIT UNCOMMON

by QUINTIN COLLINS

from SIDEREAL MAGAZINE

i be dead   been dead   been dying   been
   death
god i   been a body bounce round the sun been a body
celestial   outside earth atmosphere   the scientist say
at most been asteroid   say i ain't been a body
worth measure   say i got ocean beneath my skin
say my brain is full of ice   say i be cold   say i be dead
say i be dead to neptune   but water say life   on mars
so why i be dead   to NASA and them
school books   been where i be abnormal   say my
   axis sits
sideways   seasons a mess   say i always got skin dark
skin light too   say i got wondering poles   ain't no true
north atop my head   ain't no man make me wear words
for earth   i   be   orbit   uncommon   i
be   chaos   been had an orbit
upset ordinances   i be on your science magazine
methane ice glossy   halo crater scars   but i still be dead
still disposable been body   been celestial
body   be body   so who gon tell me   i be
   nothin
but rock   who gon deny   i dominate my neighborhood

Nominated by Sidereal Magazine

ELENIN

fiction by STEPHEN MORTLAND

from NOON

The air frigid near the leaking window hardened my bones and they clicked into place, tightening against one another, shrinking me. The little waitress reminded me of my mother insofar as she held her own wrist when she spoke to me. She held her wrist as if to still a tremor or to preempt my taking hold of it.

She had a voice like a toy siren that wound up and grew louder as she spoke, shrill and almost funny. "And they're saying we might pass through," she said. "Not the comet itself, but debris from its tail."

The television was bolted into an upper corner of the wall. The big rock magnified, green and grainy, moved slowly across the black-and-white tweed sky. She and I watched the terrible thing together, though neither of us could comprehend the other's capacity for pain.

Straws thrown like kindling into the front pocket of her apron pointed at my throat. Her hair, caught beneath the strap around her neck, was raised up, frayed and brittle, at her shoulder.

"How long are you in town, then?" she asked me.

"I'm waiting on someone."

A bunch of fruit flies rose against the window. They hovered beneath the overhead light, glittering like spectral particles of dust with a strange tendency to hesitate. A drumming eruption of metal spilled from the kitchen behind us.

"Do you think I could use the phone here?"

"Sure, doll," she said, watching the comet again.

"Hello?" I said.

"Yes?"

"Can I see you? I'm at the diner," I said.

"It's three in the morning," he said.

The sun rose pale and any person hearing the cicadas screaming could only conclude that the world was folding in on itself. Cottonwood trees stood black and flat, as the invisible sun spooled the night through their shattered, shadowed frames. Huddled bovines waded through the field adjacent to the small house, brushing aside yellow buds. Their thick, snouted faces made halos of the fog. Tails pitched and waned, caressing flanks, disrupting the haze of gnats seeking shelter in their short hair.

I was at his home with flowers. Daisies, chrysanthemums, lilacs wrapped in paper. A concealed plastic bladder kept them colored.

"I need you to understand." He held my shoulders. "Look at me—tell me you understand."

"I understand," I told him. "I understand you."

He always looked nervous, the way he blinked and the wetness never drying on his lips. He'd misaligned the buttons on his shirt so that the hem on one side lay long and stranded. I remembered the first time and how bad he'd felt then. The way he'd shrunk from me and how reticent he had been to accept anything like grace.

"I told you already," he said. "And it's September now. I don't know what more you want me to do."

The sun crossed over the tops of the trees. The sky turned sepia. Bright swimming amoebas cluttered my vision. The mud was swallowing us so that our shoes made suctioned cries when either of us shifted. After the last time, he'd seemed uncomfortable again, like the first time but with greater pity. Then he'd stopped calling, and it could only have been because I'd been away. But what did he see now? Nothing about me looked sick.

"Have you heard about the comet?" I asked him. "They're saying it might pass through us. I can't remember the name of it, but it sounded like something else. Like something harmless, benign."

"Again," he said, "I'm sorry. But you need to go."

He looked back over his shoulder and let his hand slide down my arm, cupping my elbow in his palm and giving it a small conciliatory squeeze. The whole of the place continued its collapse and the cows and the trees pitched against purple-tailed vines of wisteria. It all folded in and laid its hands on me and seized me.

❊   ❊   ❊

305

I orbited the house. Fog in the tall grass hugged the contours of the horizon. A window looked in on the dining room. I stopped to watch the four of them dusked in new light, sitting at the table. He kept looking, pretending not to see me. Eventually she took the children, ushering them out of the frame.

When she returned, she sat so that her face was toward me. I searched her and could not imagine she hated me. I tried to see myself in her body, but I hadn't any access.

She looked nothing like me. Her face was like a moon—all cheeks. The slender bridge of her nose divided her perfectly. Her eyes were inexpressive, deep-set plum inkwells.

It's a shame to be a stranger to someone you want to love, never to conform to their likeness or they to yours.

Occasionally she looked away from me to the chair where he was sitting.

The comet continued sluggishly across the sky. Uninterrupted, it would blot out the sun, rain acid on the earth. It would call water to rise and drown us here in the fields.

But thou, O Lord, how long?

Nominated by Noon

TRANS IS AGAINST NOSTALGIA

by TAYLOR JOHNSON

from INHERITANCE (Alice James Books)

Every day I build the little boat,
my body boat, hold for the unique one,
the formless soul, the blue fire
that coaxes my being into being.

Yes, there was music in the woods, and
I was in love with the trees, and a beautiful man
grew my heartbeat in his hands, and there
was my mother's regret that I slept with.

To live there is pointless. I'm building the boat, the
same way I'd build a new love—
looking ahead at the terrain. And the water
is rising, and the generous ones are moving on.

O New Day, I get to build the boat!
I tell myself to live again.
Somehow I made it out of being 15
and wanting to jump off the roof

of my attic room. Somehow I survived
my loneliness and throwing up in a jail cell.
O New Day, I've broken my own heart. The boat is
still here, is fortified in my brokeness.

I've picked up the hammer every day
and forgiven myself. There is a new
language I'm learning by speaking it.
I'm a blind cartographer, I know the way

fearing the distance. O New Day,
there isn't a part of you I don't love
to fear. I'm holding hands with
the poet speaking of light, saying *I made it up*

I made it up.

Nominated by Alice James Books

FINLAND

by RON RIEKKI

from BOOMERLITMAG

I'm writing this on an ice cube, well, to be more accurate,
an icicle octagon, a wintery stop sign, the one near my home
in northern Michigan, where we moved because it was most

like Kuusamo, because we like places where there aren't many
people, but a lot of snow. It's difficult to write on an ice cube,
but no tougher than heating your home with wood. I remember

hauling wood, helling wood, being wood, how my childhood
was really childwood, the slaving over slivers, was my dad
and gloves, the path to the woodpile so memorized in my mind

that I see it now, daily, before bed, during bed, after bed, even
the few weeks when I moved into this apartment and didn't have
a bed. But there it is. The pile. The wood. My dad. The sun.

The moon. The empty sky. The full sky. My dad would look
up at the sun and say, "Where's its chimney?" We'd see God
hauling wood to the sun. He'd see each star as a sauna. He'd

sing the Finnish National Anthem, which began with "Our land,
our land" which really meant "Our wood, our wood," and then
the next line—"Our fatherland"—my father singing this, his

voice echoing, father, land, fatherwood, sunwood, fatherGod,
the song, the heat, the cold, how they clashed, the song caught
fire, the sun ran out of heat, winter owned our lives, the house,

everything, and we walked backwards, to avoid the wind, and
got inside, and when I think of place I think of fireplace, of how
hot my back would be, my toes frozen, my father grabbing me

by the face, saying, straight into my iris, "You're Finn! Finn!"
his hands so cold, my nose so sooty, my life so strange, night
like lightning, snow like heat, God like fury, the house so full.

Nominated by BoomLitmag

RUTHLESS

by EMILY LEE LUAN

from NEW OHIO REVIEW

My friend lowers his foot into the stony
runoff from the mountain, lets out a burst
of frantic laughter. This, I think, is a happiness.

When I don't feel pain, is it joy that pours
in? A hollow vessel glows to be filled.
無, my father taught me, is tangible—

an emptiness held. It means *nothing*, or *to not have*,
which implies there was something to be had
in the first place. It negates other characters:

無心, "without heart";
無情, "without feeling";
heartless, ruthless, pitiless.

Is the vacant heart so ruthless?

The ancient pictogram for 無 shows a person
with something dangling in each hand. Nothingness
the image of yourself with what you once had,

what you could have. And the figure is dancing,
as if to say nothingness is a feeling, maybe even
a happiness—dancing with what is gone from you.

When I ask myself *what am I missing?* I think
of how much I loved to dance, arms awash
with air, the outline of loss leaping on the wall.

Nominated by New Ohio Review

A LITTLE LIKE GOD

fiction by MOLLY McCLOSKEY

from McSWEENEY'S

In the mornings, my bed was littered with skin. It was like sleeping with a molting thing, or a being that had passed the night evolving. I thought of tails or fins abandoned in the bedclothes. After he left, I'd shake the sheets out the window and send flakes of him over the brick patio, where they were carried on the breeze into the grass quad adjacent to my house. There were students down there—there were students everywhere, flawless and blank-eyed, plumped on fructose and a feeling of entitlement to they weren't sure what—and I loved the thought of it, the runoff of last night's friction, the acid rain of middle age drifting down on them.

The first time he stayed the night, I couldn't tell what was happening. I don't mean the sex; I mean after. He slept vehemently, violently, as though he were undergoing something, electroshock or the return of buried memories. One minute his breathing sounded like a small motor, then silence, then a sudden snorting. He would kick, shudder, flip himself over suddenly and completely, as though someone had turned him with a spatula. It looked exhausting. In the midst of all that action, I slept hardly at all, and rose the next morning bleary-eyed, while he awoke rested and refreshed. Apparently, it was not exhausting.

He was a year back from Afghanistan when we met, one of those wars Americans had begun to lose track of, so that people sometimes forgot whether we were still fighting it or just advising others who were fighting, or pretending to advise them while we fought it, in secret, ourselves. He had just turned fifty, which seemed old to me for a deployment, but he'd been on the medical side of things—gathering intel on threats, everything from snakes and fungi to weaponized chemical agents—more than on the front line. Not that there was a front line, as such. Or maybe there was. What did I know about how battles were fought? I was an English professor who'd spent my entire adult life abroad. I had once worked with a colleague in England designing what she'd called a "vet-friendly curriculum," which had prompted me, for a time, to think about the mental lives of people who go to war and about what literature might owe or could offer them. But that wasn't like knowing them. It wasn't like finding flakes of one in your bed, having him flop like a fish next to you all night long.

He said that when he came home from Kabul, they'd put his unit in some anonymous hotel in a flyover state to decompress. He'd lain on his bed with the AC maxed, drinking beer after cold beer and watching the Shopping Channel, where an ad for doggy stairs showed elderly and disabled pooches ascending to luxurious beds.

"Fucking doggy steps," he said, and laughed with a strange sort of joy. "I knew I was home then."

I wasn't long home myself when we met. I'd been gone twenty-five years. I had left for graduate school, then gotten a teaching job in Dublin. I had just taken a one-year visiting gig at a university in D.C., and I was half hoping they would offer me something permanent. A ten-year relationship in Dublin had ended. Every winter had felt drearier than the last. And I'd grown tired of being foreign, tired of the performance of my foreignness, which consisted largely of trying to underplay it without seeming apologetic or too imitative of the locals.

I was given a house in Foggy Bottom for the year. It was the tail end of August when I arrived, and the city felt tropical and fetid and buttoned-up. I couldn't get a sense of it. Some mornings I walked the length of the Mall, and monuments appeared in my path as though I were living in a pop-up book. My neighborhood sat at the city's lowest elevation, where the heat hung like in a bayou and the rats were bold. One night I watched two of them fighting on the sidewalk outside a restaurant. They rolled and tumbled like cats, like cage fighters. I couldn't tear myself away. It seemed the most savage thing I'd ever seen. On our first date, I described it to him, in exaggerated detail. I was trying to impress him. I wanted him to think of me as someone who wasn't easily fazed, who would look squarely at whatever was in front of her.

We met on the internet. A photo of him in cammies dripping medicine into the mouth of a young boy in Kandahar. Another of him dancing at an embassy party, solo, with obvious abandon. One smoking a cigar. One in uniform, looking crisp as a cracker. I knew immediately it was going to go one way or the other: either I would loathe him or I would be in deep, fast. His specialty, here in the civilian world, was continuity in emergencies, which I knew must mean something very specific but which suggested, in its broader application, a person one could count on.

At dinner, after the rats, we talked about science fiction, which we both loved. About free will, and human engineering, and computer-generated pleasure—whether believing you were having a pleasurable experience was in any way distinguishable from actually having one.

He said, "What pleasurable experience are you imagining right now?"

Dear god, I thought, and rolled my eyes. We were halfway through the meal and I was teetering in a big way. On his left pinky he wore some kind of signet ring, and his hand flamed shyly with psoriasis. I felt sorry for him, and then for myself. I thought of calling it a night as soon as the plates were cleared, but something tugged at me to wait.

Over dessert I said, "Tell me something about you that I'd never think to ask."

He smiled. He liked the question. "I'll tell you something about being with me."

"Okay," I said.

"You'll always be safe, and you'll never be bored."

It had the sound of a line he'd used before, but somehow that didn't bother me. "Quite a guarantee," I said.

He leaned back in his seat and held my gaze for a long moment. "How is this going?" he asked. It was clear he meant our date, and it was also clear the question was rhetorical. He'd sensed the shift in my attitude.

"Well," I said, "I'm not bored."

He laughed. "Then we're halfway there."

The restaurant was a few blocks from where I was staying, and by the time we finished our coffees, I had decided to invite him back for a drink. When we reached the steps leading up to my front door, he cocked his head. "Is it crooked, or has one beer done me in?"

He was right. The house was on the historic register, and to save it from demolition, it had been moved from another location and reassembled, which accounted for its slightly drunken look: the door jambs were at a tilt; the upstairs floors were raked like stages.

I got two beers from the fridge. It was mid-September, unseasonably temperate, and we went out back to the brick patio, where we sat in the gentle roar of the AC units, which seemed to come, at all hours, from everywhere and nowhere.

He clinked his bottle against mine and said, "Nice place, kiddo."

It was, actually. It was the nicest place I'd ever lived. Even the great *whooshing*—it was like living next to a waterfall or a stormy sea.

I took a swallow and put my beer on the cast iron table and turned in my chair so I was facing him. He was sitting with his legs splayed and the beer bottle held loosely in two hands, resting atop his crotch like a little rocket he was about to launch. He saw me taking him in and I caught the twitch of a smile. Without looking away from me, he put the bottle on the table, slipped a hand around the back of my neck, and, with a quick tug on my hair, kissed me.

It is said that every novel educates us about its own conventions, teaching us how to read it as we go along. The same, surely, can be said of people. They teach us how to desire or love them, schooling us in themselves. Those oddities and predilections that at first seem so alien and off-putting slowly work their way into us, until one day we realize we've crossed a line without noticing.

I'm not referring to anything horrific. We agreed on virtually nothing, but he wasn't evil. Even his life in the military—which I sensed had sometimes bled into realms of intelligence shadier than snakebite serum and gas masks for the troops—seemed as concerned with protection as destruction; he'd gone to Aceh after the tsunami and Haiti post-earthquake. I mean, he had a way of eating that was somewhat savage—very fast and almost with an air of panic. As though he hadn't seen food for days, or as though he were an animal hunched over some prey, trying to get his fill before a larger beast appeared. I'm exaggerating. But it could certainly be said that he *wolfed* his food. It repelled me at first, then I grew fascinated, and finally, on occasion, aroused. That naked display of appetite. Not that he was rough around the edges; in fact, he was quite presentable. He loved Thomas Pink shirts and a good hand-stitched leather. To see him fingering ties at Brooks Brothers, you'd think he was a different kind of man entirely.

As for his skin, there was so much more to the story than the small red blotches I'd spied at dinner that first night. On his elbows and knees were patches of psoriasis that were raised and rough as coral. When I ran my hands over him, I thought of those relief maps we had in elementary school, mountain ranges like blisters on the page. But the condition, like so much about him—his nocturnal tortures, the framed photos of right-wing heroes on his wall, his shadowy past in various trouble spots—came to seem normal. He said to me once, of a certain West African change of government (smiling slightly as he said it, half to get a rise out of me and half because the memory actually did stir in him a warm glow), "It was a good coup." I grew used to it all, and with a speed that surprised me, as though I had only ever known such skin, such men, such true believers.

My students amazed me with their complicated traumas and their hungry innocence. One had a sister who'd overdosed on a drug I had never even heard of, and another's father had run off with his sixth-grade teacher, who was a man. At least two were in recovery from cutting. They worked these things into their assignments with an inventiveness I had to admire. They had all been born after I'd left the U.S., and I had the feeling, sitting with them, that I'd been asleep for two decades and had awoken to a changed world.

One afternoon in class, a few weeks into my affair, we were reading "The Lady with the Dog," reading it through the lens of totalitarianism. I was talking about the value of secrecy, the inviolability of the private and the unshareable. I wanted them to think about the political dimensions of the inner life, even—or especially—if its particulars were never spoken. A student raised an index finger. He said, "Okay, fine, but between two people in love, nothing should be unshareable." When it came to his own girlfriend, he wanted to know everything about her, every thought and fear, every shame and desire. He said, his eyes narrowing, that if you didn't want that, that unabridged knowledge, if what you wanted instead was to know only what was convenient or attractive, then how could you say you really loved someone?

I laughed nervously, unsettled both by his sudden declamation—he was not one of my more vocal students—and by his desire to take ownership of his girlfriend's mind. I said, "Not only can't you know her to that extent, but why would you want to?"

I waxed rhapsodic, then, on the enigma of the other, the mystery that keeps us coming back and that we want both to breach and to keep sacrosanct. I said that we weren't rejecting someone by allowing them their privacies.

I said, "We don't even know ourselves that well," and the whole class looked at me like I was deluded, or middle-aged.

I thought of my own romance, how the secret corners of his psyche were given literal boundaries by a high-level security clearance. For a moment I thought of posing the scenario to the class, without naming the protagonists, as a thought experiment. What better way to concretize the abstract, to make the metaphor explicit?

Thankfully, the impulse passed.

When I got out of class, there was a text from him. *You & me, 7pm.*

On the phone or in person, he was large, expansive, gob-smacked, as though life—for all its violence and misery—were one big hoot. But his written communiqués were terse. Their very succinctness thrilled me, as though I were taking instructions in an emergency. Oh, I was high as a kite those days.

I texted back, *Yes,* and looked around, feeling illicit. There I was, bedding a Republican, and not just any Republican but an officer, one who did a sideline with Homeland Security, who disappeared on the odd weekend to an underground bunker somewhere beyond the Beltway to monitor existential threats to America.

We met that night in Georgetown. He wolfed his beef adobo. We went to a movie in which some Navy SEALs battled some Taliban fighters and hardly anyone survived. A few times during the carnage-making, he jerked in his seat, as though he'd been shot. Afterward, he was unaccountably cheerful, while I felt peevish and queasy. "It was like watching porn," I said, and he gave me that loopy smile of his, and said, "I thought you'd never ask."

We stayed the night at my house. The following morning, after he left, I found such a sea of flakes on my bedroom floor that I had to get out the vacuum cleaner. It was strange, hoovering him up like that, as though he had actually disintegrated right there beside my bed. I imagined that one day I might bid him goodbye at the front door and go back upstairs to find an entire epidermis lying crumpled on my floor, still holding the shape of him. Later, when he called me from his office—he was looking out at the Potomac, updating an anthrax response plan—I told him what I'd been thinking. I said I liked the idea. "I could inflate it and have a blow-up doll of you."

He laughed, one of those great big laughs of his. But the image of the shed husk stayed with me. I thought of tails and fins again; I thought of different kinds of men. I wondered whether he wasn't the sort of man whose time has been, and been and been, and was finally up, and I worried about that. I looked around me at the boys in Adams Morgan, with their shopping bags and their skinny jeans, and thought: Who

318

will stay steady through our wars? Who will shepherd us through our emergencies?

I became fascinated by soldiering. I read a book about the surge in Iraq in which a young marine said that to be in a platoon on active duty was to fall in love, over and over again. Another guy said there was no sexier feeling than coming under fire. I began to envy the intimacy of men, and to pity them that, too, because they didn't know what to do with it after, with all that big, big love. And so they sat there in shambles in those bleak towns, full of grief and guilt, shocked by what they'd seen or done but also by what they hadn't seen coming: the wreckage they'd become after war.

On the surface, he was not a wreck. He was robust, punctual, direct. He had a way of arriving at my house that made even the most mundane of assignations seem urgent. He would knock—two short, sharp raps—and I would open the door and before he was even over the threshold he'd take my face in his hands and kiss me; then, all business, he would slip off his overcoat, hang it on the coat stand, and stride into my living room, where he would collapse into the armchair and unlace his brogues and fall back as though he had traversed continents to reach me and had to catch his breath. Everything with him was large, declarative, certain of itself. He entered my house with the air of someone planting a flag. To witness such conviction filled me with awe, as though I were in the company of a man incapable of concerning himself with alternatives. I imagined a mind of planes and angles, surfaces that held up under the fiercest strain. My own mind is all curlicues and shadows, the impossible staircase, the Möbius strip, everything circling, each choice containing its own negation.

One evening when he was over, I was watching the news, and a story was on about two police officers beating a guy up in Queens.

I shook my head.

"You don't approve," he said.

"Do you?"

"Of that? Probably not." But, he said, he had no problem with the cops giving a few kicks to a rapist or a kiddie fiddler.

I said, "What about the rule of law, presumed innocent and all that? What if one day you're the kiddie fiddler?"

He made a face.

"The *suspected* kiddie fiddler. You think the cops are infallible?"

"I think we're too worried about being nice," he said.

"I see," I said, then upped the stakes. "Should we torture people?"

"Not for fun," he said, "or revenge. But if it's going to save lives, it should be on the table. You can't tell me that if banging some dirtbag's head against the wall a few times would save your mother's life, you'd vote against it."

I thought for a moment. "Maybe I'd recuse myself from the vote."

He laughed. "Liberals are such hypocrites." When it came down to it, he said, to saving our own skin, we'd do exactly the things we professed such horror of. "But you don't have to make those decisions. You have the luxury of outsourcing them."

"To people like you."

"I've never tortured anyone."

"Bravo!" I said.

"And I don't want to." He ran a hand through his hair and looked at me. "Would you want me to? To save your life?"

I got up from the sofa and went to get beers from the fridge. He followed me. I popped the caps and handed him one, and he took a swallow, then said, "I'm not a bad person. Believe it or not. But you're not as saintly as you think."

"I don't think I'm a saint."

He put his bottle on the counter and took mine from my hand and set it on the counter too. "Okay," he said. "I'm sorry." Then he pulled me to him and wrapped his arms around me and whispered in my ear, with what sounded oddly like sadness, "Let's talk about something else."

His own place was an eighth-floor apartment across from the National Cathedral, and we could see from the big kitchen window the clock towers rising up out of the treetops, like a lost city emerging. We could hear the church bells, which pleased us both, though atheism was one of the few things we agreed on.

The bedroom had a smaller window that slid open to the night, and I used to imagine, lying under it, some wild urban nightmare teeming beneath us. The trill of the cicadas and the tree frogs' squawks, and all those sirens. I had never lived in a city in which signals of distress were as common as birdcall; it was as if we were in the midst of a perpetual communal crisis. I tried to tell him once how sirens used to make me feel, in the days when I lived in cities of moderate alarm. I said they reassured me because they meant someone was in control; someone was in trouble, yes, but someone else was dealing with it, and the call-and-response of distress and succor was deeply comforting to me. Here, though, the relentlessness of the sirens was overwhelming. Police cars, ambulances, security details, and the motorcades that blared and hurtled up Mass. Ave. as though the very world were ending.

He said, "I learn what to tune out." He meant he sorted all stimuli, every hour of the day, into threat and non-threat.

I said, "It's not about tuning out. It's about the emotional resonance. It's about what it does to our lizard brains."

He pointed two remotes at the television and did something complicated. We were stretched out on his king-size bed, watching end-of-days stuff, which he liked almost as much as war movies. Earthquakes. Tsunamis. Biological attacks. Toxins in the water supply. An electromagnetic pulse detonated by a nuclear weapon that would wipe out the grid. His favorite show was *Doomsday Preppers* on the National Geographic channel. He had his own bug-out bag, a stack of Spam in the cupboard, a pair of bolt cutters. There were jerry cans of water in the bathroom. I wavered between regarding it as a charming quirk and worrying about my own lack of preparedness. Something in me resisted the very ethos of it all. On TV, anyone prepping for doom looked like a Hells Angel, only angrier, and not a single one seemed possessed of a communitarian spirit. It was all about having enough guns, keeping your neighbor from stealing your freeze-dried food or your woman.

I said, "I'd rather die than live in a world populated only by those people."

"Trust me," he said, "when the time comes, you won't be saying that."

We watched an episode where millennials in the Bay Area were reduced to animals after two days without water, a story line he found particularly gratifying.

"Three square meals from chaos, kiddo."

It was as though he lived there already in his head, in the aftermath, at a level of honesty about human nature that was bracing. In cold, clear air free of delusion and sentimentality. Sometimes I thought it was our only hope, and other times it sounded like martial law waiting to happen.

Later that night, rutting on his sofa, I looked up and noticed a framed photo of him shaking hands with someone I considered a criminal, and I thought: Who am I? Have I no compass? He owned a gun, probably several, and though I'd never seen him hold one, I thought of him with his gun, and I felt the most distressing sense of safety.

I began to see everything differently. When I turned on the tap, I thought of water wars. A beach scene led to visions of rising seas. I read *Homeland Preparedness News*, which focuses to a surprising degree on pathogens and biohazards, all the more alarming for their stealth and invisibility. That the internet should survive one more day without succumbing to a super-virus astonished me, that the trains ran on time, that there was food on the shelves—all of it seemed primed to implode. How could it not? I watched drone footage of a cliff slowly collapsing on the California coast, chunks of it sliding into the ocean, the edge moving closer and closer to a line of houses. Because there was no audio—no screaming, no thunder as the earth met the sea—the scene looked both cataclysmic and mundane, as though it were happening after our extinction and therefore didn't matter. I felt a little like God watching it.

I was sharing these thoughts with him one Sunday evening as we headed out for dim sum. He had just come back from the bunker, about which he told me very little. I pictured him sitting in a swivel chair, all night long the trail of threats across a screen, picked-up chatter, infrared footage. However it all got monitored, it was out there. The only thing he'd say was "You have no idea."

When we got to the restaurant, he took note of the exits. He said, just by the way, that in an emergency I should always text, not keep trying to call, because when the network came back the texts would be delivered. "You know that, right?"

I didn't know that, though it seemed obvious once he'd said it. "I should text you."

There was the briefest beat of silence, and though his hesitation had little to do with us and everything to do with the homeland, whatever I needed to know was in that silence. It hadn't occurred to me—and this was foolish, of course—that if something happened, he wouldn't come for me. He had a higher calling.

"I'd try to contact you," he said. "But I could be anywhere."

Feeling irked, I said, "You'd like it, wouldn't you? If something happened."

He turned the page of his menu and, still scanning it, told me about all the chemical-weapons sensors in the city, all the unseen ways I was being protected. My naïveté was becoming a theme with him. Something in his tone made me feel ashamed, like when I was a child and my mother would remind me, in moments of exasperation, how hard she worked for my pleasures and my privileges, how oblivious I was.

"I've been there when something happened," he said. "It isn't a thing you can like." Then he closed his menu and dropped a hand under the table, wedged it between my thighs, and said, "The pork ribs here are amazing."

One week later, as if on cue, two small bombs exploded in DC. The Metro shut down. We were asked to stay indoors, out of the way of the police. Initially, it felt unreal. Like one of those simulations he worked on to test the system's preparedness. Was I ready? Of course I wasn't. My refrigerator was its usual unstocked self: organic condiments, a bag of triple-washed arugula, two slices of leftover flatbread. Had the water been cut, I'd have been left drinking olive oil.

The first bomb, in a garbage can at Union Station, had caused a fire; though no one had been killed, several people had been hospitalized. By the time the second one ignited, at Gallery Place, about a mile from my house, the Metro system had been emptied of people. On top of this, two men had been shot near the Convention Center, and no one seemed to know whether or not this was related to the bombs. On the news, there was a lot of talk about very little information, and much back-and-forth about whether these were amateur bad guys or the advance guard of something far more serious.

I locked my doors and emailed family and friends in other places to tell them I was safe. Then I wandered around my house, not knowing what to do with myself. We were the capital, we were the nerve center, there was a chance that something big was happening. I pressed my head against the upstairs wall beside the window and stared out at the street. A few times, squad cars rolled purposefully by. The throb of helicopters was constant. I heard sirens coming from various directions.

I made tea and tried to read a novel, as though it were a normal evening, which only made me more jittery. Shouldn't I be keeping my eye on the ball? Doing my citizen part? I gave up on the novel and scoured the internet, then turned on CNN again, which made me feel less isolated, in a way the internet did not, but all of it was unsettling. The city was right outside my door and yet suddenly it was a place I couldn't wander into; it was as though it no longer existed in any concrete sense but only as a broadcast simulacrum. A journalist so flawlessly good-looking he was disconcerting to behold reported from a deserted street lined with cop cars, on the periphery of the city. I couldn't understand why the media was there—surely the bombers could see what I saw? But maybe that was the point; maybe it was a ruse cooked up by the cops, and the real stakeout was taking place in another neighborhood entirely. The scene, I now noticed, had a hyper-real quality to it. There were a few trees behind the journalist and their leaves shivered dramatically in the wind, like props in a children's play. The journalist's face was a strange hue, and because of the unusual circumstances and the need for quiet, he was standing too close to the camera, as though in an amateur YouTube video. A man in a police uniform materialized in a headlight and then vanished again in the dark. I marveled at my mind's ability to turn a straightforward city street into something mildly hallucinogenic. Oh, I didn't think, *really*, that the airwaves or the internet had been taken over and that these feeds had been concocted to distract me while a military coup unfolded or everyone of a certain kind or color was rounded up, but wasn't my very skepticism about the possibility of such a scheme a necessary condition for its enactment?

They were looking for two young men. As soon as they put a number on them and posted those furry images, I glanced around me in a new way. No longer were they incorporeal, an *idea* of violence; now they were bodies moving about the city. I went around and checked the door locks.

The archetypal fears were queueing up.

And still I didn't hear from him.

Around midnight I went up to bed. I lay there stricken, less with fear now than with longing. I wanted him with me, rather desperately. I had been glib about our affair, I had regarded him as a curio, and yet alongside that attitude—of which I felt ashamed—I had watched this other thing form, independently of whatever I might will or reason: attachment. I thought of him out there in the city, or in a bunker, or in some office, in a tank rolling through the streets—I had no idea of the role he was playing. I had texted him an hour ago. Even then, I'd thought: Don't be needy.

On the afternoon of the second day, one guy was arrested in Baltimore; by evening, the other had been found in his sister's house in Hyattsville, hiding in the boiler room. Their faces were all over the internet. They had the sleepy, tousled look of teenagers. No one had said yet to what, if anything, they were connected. The shooting, it seemed, had been just another shooting.

Two days after normal life resumed, he texted me. *That wasn't a test,* he wrote. And then a squinch-faced emoji that managed to convey two things: he knew I knew it wasn't a test, and he was stressed-out and tired. *Want to see me?*

That Friday night, he came over to my house. He didn't arrive with the usual flourish; he didn't *exclaim* himself. There was instead an intensity about him, something peremptory. He pushed me up against the wall in the foyer and kissed me hard, and I wrapped my leg high around his thigh and pressed into him for all I was worth. We stayed like that for a minute, grinding into each other, until he took me by the hips and backed me into the living room, where we fucked on the sofa, the curtains wide open behind us.

Afterward, I had to stop myself from weeping. There was some kind of need in me, something I wanted and that I knew I was never going to get from him. I don't mean his heart, or his devotion. What I needed was so much bigger and more complicated than that, and I didn't even know if it existed anymore.

With what felt strangely like sorrow, as though all that heat and ravenousness had occurred under a cloud of a bereavement, we reassembled ourselves in silence. Once we were dressed, he gave me a wan half smile and said with a lightness he clearly didn't feel, "Are we hungry, kiddo?"

Dinner was an already-roasted chicken, and while I made a complicated couscous dish—the elaborateness of it suddenly embarrassed me, as though I'd overdressed for some occasion—he loitered in the kitchen, watching me, his mind somewhere else entirely.

While we ate, we talked about what had happened, or at least aspects of it. He didn't tell me where he'd been during those two days, or what he'd been doing. He wouldn't say what he knew about the two young men. He told me about a woman in Southeast who'd started firing out her back window at what turned out to be a cat.

He said, "Any excuse to lose it."

I didn't answer. I thought every reaction could seem laughable in hindsight. Finally, I said, "When people don't know what's happening, they get scared."

"People are better off not knowing."

"Why?" I said.

"Most people don't actually want to know. They say they do, but they don't. What they really want is to feel safe without having to think about what's keeping them safe."

"What's keeping me safe?" I said.

He looked at me and cocked his head. Without smiling, he said, "Do you feel safe?"

I shrugged. "Relatively speaking, I suppose I do."

"Good," he said. "Then live your life."

Around eleven he said he needed sleep. I didn't ask him to stay the night, partly because I didn't think he would, but also because I didn't believe whatever it was I was feeling: there was something ersatz about my longing for him. It felt skin-deep, even as it tormented me. While he finished the beer he was drinking, I watched him intently, without pretending I wasn't. He didn't squirm, or even say, *What?* He just looked right back at me. I had never seen him more defiantly himself than at that moment. I had never liked him less, or understood more clearly the divide between us. We both knew, in our own way, the world we were living in, and we knew, too, that if the time came—I mean, if something truly horrific befell us—he would be part of an apparatus that swept aside the concerns of people like me in order to preserve a structural order, and that once that was accomplished, my world, if I was still around to see it, would look very different indeed.

Before he left, we said we'd get together the following weekend. But when we spoke a few days later, it was clear something had shifted. I couldn't say why for him, but for me it came down to the fact that I had begun to dislike myself for wanting him, and to blame him for that. We agreed that we would take a breather, which I think we both knew was a euphemism for calling it quits. When we hung up, I felt foolish and liberated and very alone.

In a novel, I read: "We have all kinds of ways to talk about life and creation. But when guys like me go and kill, everyone's happy we do it and no one wants to talk about it." The character who's speaking is a Vietnamese man who's spent the war killing Vietcong. Every Sunday, before the priest talks, he says, a warrior should get up and tell people who he's killed on their behalf. He says listening is the least people can do.

When I read that, I thought of him. I wanted to phone him up and read it to him, to ask what he made of the idea, of people being forced to hear about the killing done in their names. I remembered a morning he strode out the door in his shined brogues and crisp button-down and said in a tone of sardonic affection, "I'm off to protect an ungrateful nation." I remembered him, one evening, pausing on the corner of R Street and Florida Avenue. He took a deep breath and looked around him as though he were standing on a mountaintop, and said, "I love this country. *Pathologically.*" It was in response to some comment of mine; we'd been having the sort of quarrel that had become a feature of our date nights, endless variations on the question of what forms caring about your country could take, and of the relationship between what was moral and what was legal and who got to decide that. Our own relationship was becoming one long, running argument, the particulars of which are mostly lost to me now. That line I won't forget, though. You'd think there might've been menace in it, a whiff of patriotism about to run amok. But what I heard in his tone was something sensual. I saw the gleam of the erotic in his eyes. He had done things that could only be hinted at—things, he would remind me, that safeguarded my freedom to stand in judgment of him; things I had no doubt would appall me. And yet—does it sound strange?—I envied him. I looked at that love of his and it seemed a comic-book kind of love, all bold-faced caps and a belief in superheroes. But I couldn't deny it: it was a love that moved me.

I didn't get the job I wanted, but I got another job, and I stayed. I think I decided to stay during those hours I'd spent locked in my house. Something in me fell for the city then. Something in it felt human, and mine. I had drifted fretfully through the rooms of my house, imagining people all over the city moving about their own homes, imagining it all in great detail: what they were cooking, what they said to one another, whether they were afraid. Back then, there was no one here I was close to, apart from him, and so I had no hierarchy of concern or attentiveness; every unseen person in the city had the same claim on my curiosity, and my fellowship. Never had I felt so isolated and yet so deeply a part of something.

Now I have a small apartment. From the roof of my building, where I sometimes go at dusk, I can see the curved concrete flank of the Hilton, the one where Reagan was shot. The city, unfurling low-rise before me, feels oddly muted, as though it's been reduced to a smoking ruin. I like to watch the planes floating into view as they descend toward National, looking, in the deadness, like they're ferrying supplies to somewhere cut-off and in trouble.

I had a fantasy once: to be with him in some malarial war zone, making sweat-slicked love inside a mosquito net while death pressed in all around us. I wanted him to call me from unexpected places; I wanted a mental map with colored pins in it. But he never called me from anywhere surprising, just his sixth-floor office with the big window overlooking the Potomac.

To be honest, the best times of our affair were moments we weren't even together. It was the aftermath I liked, that odd repose that followed an encounter, as though I had survived something perilous and demanding. Weekday mornings I'd leave him at his bus stop, then take the 31 home, down Wisconsin to the city's low-lying neighborhood, where I lived, journeys far sweeter in my memory than the crude dawn couplings that preceded them. There was something intensely pleasurable, and also melancholic, about being on the bus at that hour with all the commuters, the smell of him still on me, the morning fugginess of the crowd, the vehicle's slow, spasmodic lurch. Being delivered back to humanity like that, after the dire isolation of sex. I have heard of people who claim to feel connected to all of creation when in the act, but I'm not one of them. I feel like the last person left alive, or someone flung to the far reaches of the galaxy. But then I'd board the bus and I *would* feel it, everything rushing to meet me, each one of us teeming with worlds. I felt enveloped, in the throes of an indiscriminate love, as though I had traveled a great distance and seen many things and was home now, and earth, I can tell you, had never looked so good.

Nominated by McSweeney's

ON AGATE BEACH

by HOLLY SINGLEHURST

from IAMB

A blue whale has fallen belly up
on the sand, and crowds of people
stand round with wet hair, hushed
voices, in their jewel bright shorts,

and the first woman I loved split
herself open from wrist to elbow and bled
out in the bath, up over its lip, slipped
under the heavy wooden door,

and the floor beneath my feet is tiny stones,
and bones, and broken glass worn by water,
and a whale's heart is as big as a car
and far more magical.

Nominated by Iamb

LETTER FROM BROOKLYN

by D. NURKSE

from THE MANHATTAN REVIEW

All my life I feared death. Passionately, dutifully, sardonically, silently. But when it came, nothing changed.

I still brush my teeth, worried the cinnamon dental floss will snag in a back molar. A nose hair protrudes. I can feel it between my thumb and forefinger but I can't see it, no matter how I angle my face to the mirror. I dress in the clothes on top of the hamper. My shoes pinch.

I walk the dog on Eastern Parkway in the lightest of snows. If anything, I'm more present, focused on the leash, alert to yank him back from the things he loves in the gutter—a bloody tampon, the yellow intricate intestine that must have been a squirrel once.

My neighbor Dolmatov is doling out peanuts to a flock of sparrows. They swoop in from nowhere, ignoring the dog's outraged stare. The ones in front gobble—*me! Me!* The ones in back puff themselves up, flaunting the faint oil-slick iridescence of their wings. Their polls glisten with a sheen of sleet. Dolmatov rolls each kernel in his fingers and chooses the recipient: *you* and *you*. With his free hand he cracks the shells. His ample belly props him against his walker.

"Snowy enough for you?" he asks. Like all neighbors, he knows nothing of death.

On the next block they are converting a padlocked factory into condos, working on Sunday in bitter cold. High silhouettes in flimsy parkas race across scaffolding, shouting jokes in Nahuatl or Bengali.

The child on his skateboard whizzes past me, close as he knows—*there is no distance! Distance is mine!* It takes all my strength to rein the dog in.

Always when I was alive "life was elsewhere," in a notebook washed blank in the laundromat, in a glance returned from the tinted window of a passing SUV. Perhaps death is also elsewhere?

The little Haredi girl wants to pet the dog—furtively, conscious of breaking a law—and the dog strains forward, fascinated. Fascinated! Is that the only change? That and the swiftness of the clouds, passing from Jersey to the Verrazano in a heartbeat?

At night here are the tenements of my childhood. A single lit window reigns, making the city so vast, so empty. The face that shines there, always in profile—is that my father?

All my life I waited for you, passionately, bitterly, in silence, counting the breaths.

Nominated by The Manhattan Review

MARK ON THE CROSS

fiction by MARIA BLACK

from THE SUN

When I was a junior in college, I spent the week before Christmas with my aunt Sallie in New Jersey. Sallie has a cabin by a lake right off Route 34. She calls it a lake, but it's a weed-choked pond put in to sell property. Sacagawea Shores. They brought in sand for the beach, so now there's a roped-off swimming area and a raft and a lifeguard. The "cabins" have sheetrock and wall-to-wall carpet and granite countertops and jacuzzis. On the outside, the logs are painted brown—a community rule—and each cabin has a dock on the pond, but only paddleboats are allowed. Sacagawea Shores. A place to pretend around, like a ouija board. Migrating geese land there, which is something, I guess. They take their small consolations, which was what I was supposed to be doing. Mom's idea. Go to New Jersey, she said. Fall out of love.

Sallie is not my real aunt. She and my mom are friends from college. Sallie doesn't have kids, so she spends Christmas with Mom and me. She makes her boeuf noel and decorates it with little plastic political figures. Last year, 2014, it was Barack and Michelle, Hillary and Bill. On Christmas Eve we were to drive up to Pine Plains, New York, where Mom and I lived. I'm an only child, so it's always just "us girls," as Sallie says. Sallie, the pretend aunt in the pretend cabin on the pretend lake.

She's a tall woman, Sallie. Big boned with a bright, snaggletoothed grin and great, ruined feet. She has her shih tzu, Lulu, and her job and her podcasts and her outrage. On our first night she fixed us gimlets and gnocchi with broccoli rabe and garlic. I'd never been with Aunt Sallie without my mother. Normally in a crisis I would be with Dani, my best

332

friend, but after what had happened, I wasn't sure I'd ever speak to her again.

Sallie shared things with me I didn't want to know: That she sleeps with a mask on her face for sleep apnea. That she has a skin tag on her labia that she's never done anything about. She beset me with stories I'd heard a million times, of her and Mom's college years at Macalester. She was trying to break the ice, working up to consoling me about Cav, so I let her. She had come from work and was wearing square-toed brown pumps with a buckle, as in some distant decade. Sheer hosiery. I'd only ever seen her in jeans. I wanted her to change clothes, be the Aunt Sallie I was used to, but she didn't. I drank my first gimlet on the stool in her kitchen, watching her cook. I asked if she dated. It was love she was supposed to be helping me with, after all. She threw a hand in the air and said, "Oh, golly, honey, I wouldn't know what to do with a man. I'd scare him off in two seconds." So, no, she didn't date anymore. I was already depressed, but this admission, and the shoes, and Sacagawea Shores, and the paddleboats, and how crowded the rooms were in her "cabin" (and that she really called it a cabin)—all of that made it worse. Aunt Sallie was bright and intelligent, and she had found no other way to live. Though my mother was different in important ways, I couldn't help thinking that she hadn't either.

On my first full day in New Jersey, I woke early and listened as Aunt Sallie got ready for work. I didn't get up, just kept dozing, balled beneath shih tzu-scented goose down. Outside the window, electric icicles hung from the eaves. I thought of Cav, who was at his parents' house in Stockbridge, maybe waking up with Robin Nash.

Aunt Sallie left, and outside the guest-room door, Lulu the shih tzu panted and ticked her nails on the kitchen tiles. At last I got up, pulled on my flannel pajama bottoms, pushed my feet into my broken clogs, and put on my coat. I let Lulu out and stepped outside, too, to light a joint and contemplate the window box full of fake greenery, the salt-stained flagstones, the mildewed porch furniture, the dock, the sky, which looked like a huge slab of chicken fat. I was wandering around the backyard when I heard someone bang on the front door. I hurried inside in time to see a UPS truck pulling out of the drive. A large rectangular box on the stoop cried out to me in big red letters: REFRIGERATE! Sallie had told me it might arrive, the pig delivery from her brother. He was, Sallie had explained, a foodie who had, in an enthusiastic rush of late-life reforms, divorced his wife, married his male lover, and converted to Judaism without quite considering what that would mean for his dining habits, pork being a passion of his. As a compromise, he started sending a gigantic cut of pork to Sallie every Christmas and then harassing her with a phone call every other day, suggesting how she should cook it.

It was much larger than I'd expected. I staggered back into the house with it, but how was I supposed to refrigerate something wider than the refrigerator? I slung it onto the counter and read the tag. It was from Niashe Farms. Twisp, Washington. I fed Lulu and changed her water, fished the joint out of the plastic greenery, put the pork on the back patio, and went out to the dock. It had never seemed entirely there to me, Aunt Sallie's dock. If a thing isn't used, isn't put to its intended purpose, can it be said to fully exist? Doesn't it disappear a little? Was that what was happening, bit by bit, to Aunt Sallie, and to my mother? It would happen to me, too, wouldn't it? Had it already started? I sat down and stared into the "lake," trying not to panic, telling myself I could make my life original, that I didn't have to settle, that I had a future, even without Cav. But it was hard to believe, sitting in that place that the powers that be had so intentionally fucked over, as they did regularly all over the globe.

I stretched out, closed my eyes, imagined disappearing. Not telling anyone, just taking off. I pictured Sallie's red and swollen face as she answered my mother's hysterical questions over the phone; the crackle of a police scanner in the cruiser in the driveway; the announcement at school; the huddle of girls in my dorm. Meanwhile I would head west, cut my hair, dress like someone else, take up running. Read nonfiction for a change, learn about something real. Lichens. Halibut. It didn't matter what. OK, I thought, I'd call Mom from the road.

The thing is, Dani *knew* Cav and I were trying to work things out, and still she set him up with Robin Nash. My best friend set up the guy she knew I loved with another girl, who he was now dating. If she could do that, what did being a best friend even mean?

Sallie's closet had a metallic, oily odor, of pennies and sweat and Elizabeth Arden face cream, which my mother also used. I put on my jeans and a red-and-blue-checked rayon blouse of Sallie's—the ugliest thing I could find—and snapped the leash on Lulu. I would walk to Starbucks for coffee. In Sallie's blouse I thought I could already feel her essence seeping into me. See how easy it is to disappear, I thought.

I was on Route 34 next to the undeveloped parcel of land Sallie referred to as "the woods on the way to town." I'd never seen them from outside a car. Close up they were a tangle of vines and brush and layered leaves in a dun-gray shade of fear and defeat, speckled here and there with bright bits of styrofoam and foil wrappers and plastic grocery-store bags caught on stubble. No one who matters is meant to view what's viewable from the shoulder of Route 34. Trees and scrub chewed to nubs by starving deer, and beyond the trees the hapless, snaking trickle Sallie likes to call "the river." As I walked, the state of my heart was all mixed up with the state of that landscape. I had intense, melodramatic thoughts. I imagined dropping to my knees, saying prayers. I didn't, of course. I waited while Lulu the shih tzu dribbled a little yellow dal-like shit onto a discarded Doritos bag, and I kept walking. Up ahead I saw a point of interest. A white cross, nailed to a tree.

When I got to it, I saw the tree had a gash in it, and on the cross was taped a cellophane-wrapped photograph of a teenager, MARK HOHN, a handwritten sign said. DEC. 19, 2013. 17 YRS. Here's what struck me like a bus. It happened to *be* Dec. 19. He'd died exactly two years earlier. I sat on the ground before the cross and told myself to pay attention, that this was no coincidence. Next to me, Lulu sniffed an ancient Vitamin-water bottle. Cars whizzed by. I could barely see the boy's face through the battered cellophane, but I could make out dark hair, bright teeth, obviously radiant health.

He died here, I thought. His spirit rose from here. If there are spirits, his rose from this very spot and found its way past this metastasis of a town, past Denims & Daisies; past Let's Make Art; past the windowless Beijing Palace with its peeling gold columns encircled in Christmas lights; past Knead a Bagel. Mark Hohn's soul would have had to thread its way through all of it, and through other obstacles that laced the invisible regions, if invisible regions even existed, which they didn't. I scooted closer, to keep him company. I thought of Cav and me, as we'd been for two and a half years at school: The time we both fell asleep on Pembroke Quad and woke in the morning just in time for class. My birthday when he brought a cupcake to me in my Victorian Novels class, set it on my desk, lit the candle, and walked out.

A deer tick made its way across the boy's blurry face. I got it to crawl onto my finger, and I ground it to a smudge, then used Aunt Sallie's house key to carefully extract Mark Hohn's photograph from its cellophane wrapping. Why, I'm not sure, except that we seemed to be partners in something now, and I didn't want to leave him there alone like that. I put the photograph between the pages of Dante's *Divine Comedy*, which was in my bag. I was supposed to be reading it for Italian class.

At Starbucks I tied Lulu's leash to a bench, went in, and studied the holiday menu. "Our new Holiday Spice Flat White combines Christmas Blend Espresso Roast with velvety-steamed whole milk infused with cinnamon, ginger, and cloves. All together in perfect harmony. Happy holidays." The Starbucks *Hawaiian Holiday Blend* CD was on display. When I looked out the front window, I saw a teenage girl petting Lulu. She hiked up her jeans so her butt crack wouldn't show, but she was fat, and it showed anyway. A tiny girl was with her. The tiny one was as tiny as the big girl was big.

"Holiday spice flat white," I told the guy with the mohawk fade behind the counter. "Grande." If I disappeared, I could go west, I thought, use the money in my savings. I'd get a job, rent a room, begin research for a novel. It would be good, and if it wasn't good, at least it would be mine.

The tiny girl had on big white hairy boots like ski bunnies wear, and an oversized maroon sweatshirt. White-blond hair gathered on top of her head the way Aunt Sallie had arranged Lulu's. She sat on the bench facing Starbucks, sipping a huge coffee, one leg thrown over the other and pumping hard. She was talking nonstop to the fat girl, whose hair was dyed black and braided into two stubby pigtails. She would not let Lulu alone, the big girl. She lowered herself onto the sidewalk and pulled Lulu onto her lap. Through all this, the tiny one kept talking, leg pumping. Around fifteen or sixteen years old, the both of them. They did not look at each other. The one on the ground seemed to ignore the torrent of words, her head bowed over the dog. All I could think of was how cold that sidewalk must have felt on her ass.

I thought about going outside, but I liked where I was. Someone had scratched "Sorrow is a white fire" into the table where I sat in the back, and those words, like Mark Hohn's picture, seemed to have been delivered especially to me. I wrote them on the title page of the *Divine Comedy*. A crowd, perhaps from a nearby office, entered the Starbucks then, and for some time my view of the girls outside was blocked. When I could see again, they were gone. It took a few seconds for me to realize that Lulu was gone, too.

I burst out of my chair, ran outside, and saw them a block down, the big girl walking fast with Lulu tucked under her arm like a ham, the leash skipping over the concrete behind her, and the little one in the giant Wookie boots walking fast alongside.

"Hey!" I called.

They kept going.

"Hey! That's my dog!"

They stopped and turned around, which I did not expect.

"What the fuck?" I said when I caught up. I wrenched Lulu out of the fat girl's arms. She seemed weirdly unperturbed and settled her gaze on a point somewhere past my left shoulder. I turned to look, but there was nothing there.

"What are you even doing?" I demanded, but the girl wouldn't look at me. She lifted a shoulder and let it fall.

"Jesus. Chill," the little one said. "We thought the dog had been left. We, like, waited and waited."

"So that's why you took off *at a run*? Please. Get your own dog if you want a dog."

The big girl gave me a weary look.

"Yeah, well," the little one said, "maybe you shouldn't keep your dog tied to a bench in the middle of winter while you hang out in a warm Starbucks sipping your coffee. Your poor dog was shaking like a leaf. We kept her warm. You should be *thanking* us."

I hesitated. "I wasn't gone that long."

"Don't tell us how long you were gone," snapped the little one. "We were out in the cold taking care of her. We know how long it was. And you don't even live around here."

"What? I do *too* live here," I said. Lied.

"No you don't."

"Well, I used to," I said. Also a lie. "I left this shithole as soon as I could."

It seemed the right moment to walk away, and I did.

Back at Starbucks, I tied Lulu to the bench again and saw that my coffee had been tossed. I got back in line to ask for a replacement, but instead of the guy with the mohawk, I got the manager. CHUCK, his nametag read. TEAM LEADER. I explained that someone had stolen my shih tzu, that I'd had to bolt, and in the meantime one of his employees had tossed my coffee. "I'd appreciate a replacement," I said.

He eyed me suspiciously. "What's a shih tzu?"

What's a Chuck? I wanted to say. *What's a team leader?*

But I'm too polite. "A dog," I said.

"Where is it?"

"There." I pointed outside, and there was the fat girl, holding Lulu again.

"Who stole it?" he asked.

"She did."

"Who?"

"That girl," I said impatiently. I turned and left without the coffee, but on the way out, as payback maybe, or to prove myself badass enough for the life I wanted, I lifted a small red-and-green Starbucks juniper-scented holiday candle.

"Are you serious?" I asked the girl outside.

She shrugged. "Are you really from here?"

"No."

"Where are you from?"

"Twisp," I said.

"What?"

"Twisp, Washington." I could have said Pine Plains, but I liked the idea of a place that was far away, and I wanted to test it out. She handed over Lulu and lit a cigarette. I took off back toward Sacagawea Shores, and for some reason the big girl walked with me. We didn't say anything. When she finished the cigarette, she stepped on the butt and left it on the sidewalk. I'm my mother's daughter. I pick up cigarette butts, recycle, and don't smoke—or shoplift, for that matter—but the old markers seemed flimsy and flyaway, and I felt up for grabs in a way that was new to me.

I told the girl my name and asked hers. Myra, she said. She asked if she could carry Lulu. "Sure," I said, and she cradled her as before.

She asked if I was in college, and I said I was. She asked my major, which I said was English literature.

We passed a deli called Angie's, a print shop called Color Connections, a walk-in, do-it-yourself pet grooming place.

"You're in high school, right?" I said. "What year?"

"Tenth."

I winced. "That's shit. I'm sorry."

She shrugged.

"You planning on college?" This was the kind of thing grown-ups used to ask me all the time, and now here I was asking it myself.

She gave a weak laugh. "No."

I waited.

"I hate this town, too," Myra said at last.

I kicked at a yellow bottle cap that didn't budge. "Right. It's like . . . I don't know, falsely reassuring or something."

I felt her look at me.

"Or maybe not reassuring," I said. "Maybe just *false*. Like a facsimile."

"Facsimile." Myra gazed about as if to measure her town against this new word.

We were walking along the sidewalk toward Mark's cross, but it was still far away.

"Did you ever know Mark Hohn?" I asked. "He died in a car crash up the road two years ago."

She knew quite a bit about Mark Hohn. Everybody knew, she said. She told me how, the day he died, everyone had gathered at the tree. They'd brought candles, flowers, photographs, and stories. Two grief counselors were stationed in the gymnasium. The memorial service had been standing room only. Myra said she'd been in eighth grade at the time. "The other guy in the car was fine," she said. "He didn't even get a scratch. Well, a few scratches, but he was fine. He was driving drunk, but he's not the one who died." "Mark's the one who died," I said unnecessarily. I pulled him out of Dante's circles of hell and showed him to Myra.

She stopped walking, and her expression sharpened. "You took him off the cross."

I thought this was an odd way of putting it.

"Why?" She was looking hard at me. "You shouldn't have." Her nose had gone white. I thought she might hit me.

"He was getting ruined," I said, though that's not why I had taken him.

"He isn't yours."

"I'm sorry," I said.

She was still holding Lulu, and now she held her more tightly.

"He's ours," she said and paused, clearly about to say something more. "You stole him."

That was rich, I thought, coming from a dog thief.

"It's a picture," I said. "And I was going to put it back." I studied Mark's face. "OK, I wasn't. But I will."

For a moment I imagined us breaking into a fight, each trying to take back what we felt was ours—me, Lulu; Myra, the photograph, though neither of these things belonged to either one of us. I began to walk again, and to my surprise, she kept walking with me. When we reached the tree, I wedged the photograph back beneath the cellophane.

"There," I said.

"Yeah, but you ripped the cellophane," Myra said. "Now the picture will be ruined." She turned and looked at the cars passing on Route 34. She was upset and probably didn't want to be seen standing there with some anonymous girl who was now sitting cross-legged on the ground.

"It's the second anniversary of his death," I said, and I pointed to the date on the cross.

"It's not the nineteenth," Myra said.

"Yeah it is."

She pulled out her phone and checked. It was.

"Sit," I said. I patted the ground. I didn't want her to leave, but she did. She handed Lulu to me and walked back the way we'd come.

I sat there a long time. I had grown confused. Maybe it was Myra's accusation. This dead kid Mark had been cheated, robbed of everything precious, like I had, though in a smaller way. I don't know. I had thought I might get some traction if he and I joined forces, something to push off of, but I'd made the mistake of sharing him, and now that was slipping away, and maybe he was just a scrap of paper taped to a cross, nailed to a tree. My candle, even if I had stolen it, was nothing next to all the other candles that had been lit for him at the right and proper time by people who'd known and loved him.

I was about to leave when I saw Myra coming from the direction of town, a plastic grocery sack around one wrist.

"You know my cousin Gina? She's going to college," she said when she reached me. She motioned behind her. "That ' girl with me."

A little joy bomb was going off inside my chest, I was so happy to see her again, so happy she hadn't left for good. "That ridiculously tiny kid?" I said. "What's the deal with those boots she wears?"

Myra laughed. "My mom says they make her look like a beer-truck horse. A Clydesdale."

"Yeah, or maybe a beer-truck Chihuahua. Though, I swear to God, she'll make a killer lawyer someday."

She was holding an empty paper cup, folding it this way and that, pressing it between her big fingers.

"What's in the bag?"

"Tape," she said.

I took the candle from my pocket and nestled it into the dirt as Myra taped up the cellophane. She was not angry or unfriendly, just determined—the same quietly unapologetic girl who'd stolen Lulu.

I asked to borrow her lighter, and I lit the candle. I told her about Cav, how I was the one who had left him. How he'd been in love with me, but I'd wanted to date other people. How he was my first real boyfriend, and I didn't want to feel like I was missing out on someone better. I put him through hell. I just . . . He loved me, and I thought he always would. I was staring at the flame. "Stupid," I murmured. "Stupid, stupid, stupid."

"It's all right," Myra said.

I heard the story later from friends. Cav and Dani had been at a party on campus, and Cav had asked Dani to introduce him to Robin Nash, a friend of hers, and Dani had said, "Sure, you two would be great together." And she did. So now it's Cav and Robin.

Myra wanted two things—the "two impossibles," she called them. One, to get out of her dad's house, and, two, to go to college. I stared into the pale flame and asked questions and listened to her answers. Lulu climbed into my lap and went to sleep. I took a pen from my bag and wrote my number on Myra's arm, and she wrote hers on mine. We both jumped when a car drove by, honking. It was Aunt Sallie, heading home for lunch, window down and waving wildly. Good Aunt Sallie, who knew to keep driving so that Myra and I could sit there on Route 34 in front of Mark's cross, keeping him company on the second anniversary of his death.

Nominated by The Sun, Becky Hagenston

SEVEN FLOWERS

by TRIIN PAJA

from GRAIN

I.
there is a small, luminous stone within the body, when you die, only
the stone remains, though we will never find it.

2.
petals fall from a damson tree over larger things, the rhubarb
leaves, the field's insect-thinned coat.
the hair of grief is spreading over my shoulders.

I place flowers over your eyes.

do you see a world that is not flower?

3.
if you begin to die in a forest, you may hear the heartbeat of deer.

4.
the living swallow light and the grieving swallow water.

now you are debacle and sirocco, so I will begin to collect the
fragments of your voice from the shores you walked.

5.

I hear you in the ocean noise, in discoloured shells and sheets of
    salt. a sound is calcified light, your hands, a lighthouse in my
    head.

night, the blinded crow, lands on the branch of me. the
    groundwater of insomnia expands, sheets of salt are where our
    unborn children sleep, our unborn cities.

6.

mostly, one finds aluminum cans in a river but once, a man found
    an entire Gallic ship in the Seine.
one may find hair in a bog, a whole body, thousands of years old.
    something of you can still be collected, someone will braid your
    hair of samite, someone will recognize your mouth as thyme, as
    the sleep of lemon blossoms, someone will hold your hand on a
    devastated bridge.

7.

today the hands of light became heartless, like hands that stitch up
    the mouths of snakes.

there is a language only those with their tongues cut out may utter,
    each dawn, I hear their singing.
each dawn, it becomes your voice.

light, the fruit that rots and blackens between my body and yours.

Nominated by Grain

MUSLIM WITH DOG

by THREA ALMONTASER

from AMERICAN POETRY REVIEW

bring home baby pitbull in a Nike shoebox,
her mother left tied to a post in the Bronx
after the owner sold her kids. The puppy hops

on hind legs when happy, pees in a pot of yucca,
licks the hollow in my throat when sleeping
on my chest. Muslims believe a dog's saliva

is nagasah, dirty impurity. Dread runs forward
as a dripping line of slobber slugged at their bodies.
I don't soap myself seven times after her tender

kiss. I want to muzzle Muslims. I've seen them
scrub hands raw when a pug sniffs it, weave
through speeding cars just to bypass a poodle

like it can spit hellfire. A dog won't attack
the owner who abuses it. We learned helplessness
by shocking dogs. It goes: a terrier was charged

with protecting a baby. The couple found it
with a mouthful of blood. The husband cried,
grabbed a rock and beat the canine to death.

Their baby inside, unharmed, beside a snake
chewed to shreds. There is a Golden Retriever
being trained to chase kids at the border.

There's another cuddled up by a fireplace,
head on someone's knee as they're stroked.
Both work hard in their purpose. Neither wants

to crouch alone in a parking lot, quivering
against whatever wind was rising. My grandfather
never had his dimple cleaned with blind devotion.

Never had one bare its fangs, ready to die
for him at the hands of a white man shouting,
Leave your plague of filth back in the desert.

Can't recall the time a starving collie carefully
carried its first kill, gave all it had to his feet.
Consider the prostitute who passed a mutt

panting near a well. Who took off her shoe,
tied it to her scarf, drew up water for it, and God
forgave her. Him? He'll hear the phone ring

and won't pick up. There is Yemen on the other end.
Six dogs and a village crier. Sunlight twizzling
the mountains. Divine messages in sand. The rabid dogs

are hungry, roaming for a man's remains, a chunk
of a child's thigh as they play. Savagery in Khormaksar
looks like the same fur that roams our block,

in this borough that never rests, where we are
unfurled, the city glinting blindly off our bodies.
Something on the street brushes my grandfather

like a wet nose and he thinks the dogs are back,
occupying our hood, asking, *Where are your papers?*
In his dreams, the dogs are treeing him onto the roof

of his store. Each bark jitters the ceiling light,
their eyes on him like a raid, claws raking the glass.
No angels will enter our house he tells me,

lifts the pitbull from sagging skin, tosses her
into tall blades of grass, her whine a low nothing.
In another land, he would hear a dog's growl

and think, *comrade.* To him, never was a noise
less lonely it sounded like his big brother
pouring sea-water over his head between waves.

But he won't let himself remember it. I'll have
the ashes of my animal buried with me. I'll push
my face deep into the folds of its sweaty neck.

Put so much of myself where he's still too afraid to reach.

Nominated by Jessica Roeder

BAIKAL

fiction by **LINDSAY STARCK**

from NEW ENGLAND REVIEW

WHAT WAS SHE THINKING?

That depends. When she stepped onto the tarmac in Irkutsk, the sky
crisp and glittering, she was wondering why it had taken her so long to
come to Siberia. But earlier, when she boarded the stale plane in Bei-
jing, she was trying not to think about the world's first marathoner. (You
know: the one who died.) And when her husband dropped her at the
airport curb in Minneapolis, she was wondering if he'd miss her.

WOULD HE?

He certainly would. They've been married eighteen years. Besides:
Lately he's been missing her even when she's standing right in front of
him. Last Sunday, after she'd returned from a fifteen-mile run, she'd
been flipping pancakes on the stovetop while he scrolled through head-
lines on his phone at the counter across from her. There were no more
than three feet between them. But when he glanced up and saw a bead
of sweat slide past her ear to her chin, her face rosy from the heat of
the gas flame, he'd been struck simultaneously by the urge to wipe it
away and by the fear that if he tried, he wouldn't be able to reach her.

WHAT DOES THAT MEAN?

He can't say, exactly. He knows it sounds strange. How absurd it is to
long for a person who is right in front of you! But then he remembered

that a colleague had described feeling something like this when she awoke in the night and leaned over the bassinet to gaze at her newborn child. "He was there, but he wasn't," she'd tried to explain when she returned to the English department from maternity leave. "I could see him growing up, changing." She'd set down her tea and picked up a book. "It's weird, I know. But he disappeared as I was watching."

WHAT DOES THAT MEAN?

He can't say, exactly. He doesn't have a child. All he knows is that he has been missing his wife for months. So when she finally vanished between the sliding glass doors of the airport terminal, his fingers grew cold around the steering wheel and he leaped out of the car and almost (almost!) dashed after her. He wanted to crush the warm weight of her to his chest; he wanted to tug her body back into his orbit and to resume his place in hers. But then the traffic control man began striding toward him with a menacing orange stick, and so he crawled into the Toyota and pulled away from the curb and turned the wheels toward home. With every tick of the odometer, the invisible thread between them tightened and stretched and grew closer to snapping.

DID SHE FEEL IT, TOO?

Yes, she did. She does. The ice is violet in this light, perilous and beautiful, and with every step she takes across it, she senses her distance from her husband growing. As she runs, struggling to find her rhythm, she hears the gas bubbling from the bottom of the lake and striking the snow-dusted surface right beneath her slipping feet. At the halfway point she stops for water in a heated tent and sees one runner being treated for the frostbite on his nose. She lifts a hand to touch the tape she wrapped over hers. Another runner, a young man in his mid-twenties, is pale and trembling and asking one of the volunteers, over and over again, what he is doing here. That's when the pressure in her ribcage grows so fierce that she doubles over. She remembers walking into the airport and easing herself down into a row of vinyl chairs beneath the windows. She remembers watching the Toyota roll out of sight. She remembers bending her head to steady her splintered breathing, her battering heart. What the hell was she trying to prove? At that moment, there was still time. So why didn't she pick up her luggage and go back home?

348

WHERE IS HOME?

Home is a drafty Victorian tilting on red clay bluffs over Lake Superior. The Toyota is parked now on the steep slope of the driveway, its wheels turned in and the emergency brake activated. The curtains are gauzy and the walls are painted indigo, and in the summer the wind whips off the lake and through the windows and the house feels like a moving, breathing thing. Days like that are almost enough to make a person forget about the rotting beams and the crumbling basement with its packed dirt floor that is, quite frankly, terrifying. Anything could be under there. More often than not, it is she who braves the spiders to reach the rattling washing machine. She's always been more courageous than he. More useful. She can fix a flat tire in under eight minutes. She knows how to build campfires with kindling and flint. There is no reason for him to be worried about her. Right? There is no reason to be worried.

IS HE WORRIED?

Of course he's worried. Only a crazy person wouldn't be worried. The official marathon website boasts the race as one of the most extreme in the world. Twenty-six miles across the earth's deepest, coldest freshwater lake. The ice shivering underfoot as hidden hot springs bubble and thunder beneath the surface. The clefts and gaps on the course; the unexpected splits. The snow that can storm down from the Eastern Sayan Mountains without warning, spinning around the runners, slipping beneath their soles, powdering their face masks and obstructing their vision. Sometimes the conditions plummet so quickly that the race is canceled after it's already started, and the runners have to be tracked down and rounded up in heated tents. He'd researched the marathon for months, the computer screen glowing in his darkened office while his wife dreamed in their oversized bed at the other end of the hallway, and so he knows that two years ago, a strapping young runner from New Zealand collapsed and died only a mile from the finish line. No cause or explanation. His heart simply stopped. "That's Lake Baikal," the bearded Siberian organizer had told news cameras with a shrug. Sunlight slanted off the snow behind him, and the wolf fur that ringed the hood of his parka framed his face in spiky shadows. "What can we say? She is tough, she is cold. She does not show mercy."

"SHE"?

Yes, he noticed that, too. It's not uncommon for the locals to refer to the lake as a living being. Some of the runners, he'd read, embrace the shamanistic element by kissing the ice at the starting line or talking to it between increasingly ragged breaths as the miles lurch by and their loneliness swells with their feet. It's bleak out there, beneath the flat granite sky. Glacial, silent. This isn't the New York City Marathon, it's not Boston or Paris or Tokyo, where spectators throng the streets with handmade signs and applaud from the balconies of high-rise apartment buildings. On Lake Baikal, if you want to hear people cheer you on, you've got to imagine them. You've got to conjure up your own illusions, look for mirages in the crystal fog of your own breath.

WHAT KINDS OF MIRAGES?

It depends on the runner. Take his wife, for instance: as she continues to drift across the ice, step by ginger step, she dreams of her husband waiting for her at the finish line. A mug of cocoa in his plush down mittens; an apology on his cracked dry lips. To her surprise, she dreams of children waiting, too: trotting on the crusty snow in tiny boots and parkas, waving smudged drawings of the famous Baikal seals.

WHAT CHILDREN?

Their children. The ones they didn't have.

WHY DIDN'T THEY?

Oh, the usual reasons. Money, work. He figured they'd eventually get around to it. Then his parents died. He had that thing with April. In retaliation, she had that thing with Max. And before they knew it, well—he was arranging the tea lights around the living room for her fiftieth birthday party, and the house was filling up with friends bearing books wrapped in tissue paper, and there were trays of catered cheese puffs and rock songs pulsing through the speakers, but there wasn't a child in sight. He stood in the doorway to the kitchen, watching her slice limes with hands that struck him suddenly, shockingly, as bony and weathered, her hair twisted up into a braid more silver than brown. His heart

350

cracked open with a longing so fierce that he almost didn't recognize it as his. They had waited too long, he realized. The window had closed.

WHO ARE APRIL AND MAX?

April and Max are not the point. He doesn't want to think about them right now. Right now, he only wants the phone to ring. The world outside the kitchen windows is wrapped in the black velvet coat of early morning; the moonlight is spindly and gray, and in the distance he can hear the roiling waves of Superior crashing against ice that lines the shore like a high lace collar. He is squinting at his watch, which he has set to Irkutsk Standard Time. So he knows that currently, on Lake Baikal, it's four in the afternoon. She'd promised him that she would call as soon as she'd crossed the finish line. The cut-off time for the marathon is six hours. If she hasn't reached the end by now, something has happened. A twisted ankle, maybe; or a spontaneous snowstorm that has blown the runners off their course. Or maybe she's gone crazy out there, alone on the ice for hours.

IS THAT A POSSIBILITY?

Let's just say that it wouldn't be the first time that a fatal combination of sun and ice has confused and beguiled a fragile human in the cold. Plenty of Arctic and Antarctic explorers have perished in pursuit of such a *fata morgana*. Some locals believe, moreover, that the lake possesses spirits. Powers. On Shamanka Rock, priests used to remove curses. Legend has it that travelers who try to reach Ryty Cape usually die mysterious deaths, and those who succeed in setting foot on the point claim to see creatures from other worlds.

DOES SHE BELIEVE THIS?

No, she doesn't. She's a scientist. When she sees the spray of silver bubbles frozen beneath the surface of the lake, she recognizes them not as the breath of some slumbering sea dragon, but as methane gas. Pure and simple. Similarly, the silent turquoise guardians ringing the edge of the far shore at dawn are not monsters or spirits, but ice-encrusted pine trees. And the spindly white trails in the ice, the lines that crosshatch its cold black surface, might look like treasure maps or blueprints

351

to a secret world below, but the truth is that they don't signify anything and they can't lead a person anywhere. They're cracks. Only cracks. She knew that there would be cracks; she knew that the ice would shift and hiss below her. (Still: She didn't expect the rumbling of the lake to grow louder as she stumbled across the course. And yet: Isn't it?)

DOES HE BELIEVE THIS?

He isn't certain. He's a poet, after all. He teaches his students that black marks on a white page can be transformed into something ineffable, transcendent. He believes that meaning is made, not discovered. Myths and legends have origins. Sources.

IS SHE A POET, TOO?

No. Generally she doesn't have the patience for it. But he used to read it to her when she was suffering from migraines. He'd carry her up to bed like a bride (or a child) and he'd lay a cool hand on her forehead and she'd close her eyes and listen to the staccato of his voice and the whisper of pages turning. Sometimes, as she tilted over the towering precipice of sleep, her temple throbbing and her skin burning, she'd think she heard something between the lines: something the poet was reaching for but couldn't find the words to say. The poem behind the poem. When she woke, she always forgot to ask her husband if this was what he meant by the *ineffable*. The *transcendent*. Something you move toward but never quite reach. Something like the finish line of this very race, in fact, which she could see from the starting point but which has not grown any closer over however many hours—three? five?—she's been out here. It's simply hovered in the distance—teasing her, flirting with her. Sunshine flags strung on twin poles, rippling over dark blue ice.

IS SHE GOING CRAZY?

Probably not. The bearded Siberian organizer had described this phenomenon the night before the race, while the runners were shoveling forkfuls of lukewarm rigatoni into stomachs taut with anxiety. She was sitting between a runner from Estonia and one from Hong Kong. She'd see them again at the starting line in the morning, hopping on their toes to keep warm, marveling over the indigo cast of the ice. At dinner the windows steamed from the heat of their bodies, and she tugged at the collar of her cable-knit sweater in a futile attempt to cool herself down. What's strange is that you can see the finish line from the moment you begin, the organizer had said. But no matter how many steps you take, it never seems to grow closer.

WHAT ELSE DID THE ORGANIZER SAY?

Since it was the fiftieth anniversary of the marathon, he talked about its history. He thanked everyone for coming all this way. And then he made what was supposed to be a surprise announcement: this year would be the final year. These runners were the last runners who would ever race across Lake Baikal. After this, the marathon would be indefinitely suspended.

WAS SHE SURPRISED?

No, she wasn't. But the others were. She listened to their musical exclamations with an expression as cold and clear as the ice that was shifting outside on the surface of the lake. She knew the ice was withdrawing. She knew that the waters were warming, the diatoms vanishing, the algae invading. She knew that holding the race even now, one more time, was risky. Bold. She guessed that there could already be patches of ice, indistinguishable from the rest, that couldn't bear a human's weight. And so she wasn't surprised, either, when the bearded organizer admitted that some city officials had argued that no one should be racing this year at all. He handed out an extra set of smudged release forms to be signed.

WAS SHE FRIGHTENED?

On the contrary: She felt invigorated. In the anxious clamor that followed the organizer's announcement, it was she who stood up and pushed back her chair and assured her fellow runners that they would be fine.

HOW HAD SHE KNOWN?

That was their question exactly. The answer: It's her job to know.

HER JOB IS LAKE BAIKAL?

No, her job is Lake Superior. When classes are in session, she rises early and catches the number seven bus over to the state university campus in Duluth. In the morning she gives lectures; in the afternoon, she's on the shore or in the lab. By dusk, she's sitting in a pool of yellow lamplight at the dining table, analyzing data and writing up results that she has never tried to publish. Her husband makes dinner. Cauliflower soup. Ratatouille. Spaghetti with clams. It used to be that when he saw the crescent-shaped wrinkle where her forehead meets her nose, he strode over and bent down and dropped a kiss in her hair. He would have liked for her to tell him why she was worried, but she didn't volunteer it, and he knew better than to ask.

WOULD HE HAVE UNDERSTOOD HER FEARS IF SHE'D EXPLAINED THEM?

Maybe. But then again, their work is so different. While she arranges zooplankton onto slides or collects samples from the rocky shores of Lake Superior, he gives elegant lectures to classrooms packed with English majors. For two decades, he was famous for his passion for the material. Then came April, and now he is famous for that.

WHO IS APRIL?

Listen: He was grieving. Aren't people allowed to make bad decisions when they're grieving? For months after the funerals, he dreamed of black roads slick with ice. Hairpin turns, bends between trees. He woke shivering in his own sweat, his wife resting a warm hand on his chest in an attempt to calm his careening heart. He waited for her to ask him what he was dreaming, what he was feeling.

WHY DIDN'T SHE?

Maybe she thought that she already knew.

HAD SHE LOST BOTH HER PARENTS, TOO?

No, but she's lost plenty of other things. Her childhood best friend to cancer, for instance; her coastal hometown to the rise of the Atlantic.

Moreover, couldn't she argue—although she hasn't—that she is losing her parents a little bit every day? To Alzheimer's. To heart disease. To old age. With every single minute that passes, they—and she, too, she knows; she isn't exempt from the spinning of the globe—are diminishing. Cell by aging cell. Wrinkle by wrinkle. Every hour, they are less than what they were.

DOES SHE OFTEN THINK ABOUT HER AGE?

More and more. She can remember the first time she thought about it: when she hit her thirties and realized that her hangovers lingered for days. In college, she had been able to close down the bars, stumble back to the dorms, and then rise at dawn to lace up her sneakers and jog through the silent streets. She used to feel the alcohol rolling away from her skin as the morning fog rolled off the silver surface of the lake.

AND NOW?

As she's grown older, she's found that nothing rolls away quickly. Not hangovers, not sprained ankles, not the occasional aches in her hips or her knees. Not the image of April's bare legs wrapped around her husband's waist. She'd been worried about him after the funeral, so she'd stopped by his office with a coffee and entered without knocking. She'd dropped the coffee on the hard blue carpet—it is not true that she hurled it at the two of them, though that's the rumor that seeped into both of their departments—and part of her still feels ashamed that someone from maintenance had to be called to come clean up her mess.

HER MESS?

His mess. Theirs. Because of course, after that, there was Max.

WHO IS—

It's not important. Why dwell on the details of their mutual betrayal? He sought solace in someone else's arms; a little later, so did she. This is neither interesting nor new. It's simply what happens to a marriage when it feels as though the world is ending.

IS THE WORLD ENDING?

Yes and no. The seas are rising, the bees are dying. Etcetera, etcetera. We've all read the reports written by scientists like her. (Although we haven't read hers.) On the other hand, the world's been ending since the day that it began. In different moments of crisis, other generations worried that the world was ending. Whatever happens, she intends to be prepared. That's why she taught herself to make a fire with flint and kindling. And that's why, after she taught herself, she taught her husband. Because that's what marriage means. When she walked into that office and discovered that her world was ending, her first instinct was to save herself. Her second instinct was to save him.

DID THEY TALK ABOUT IT?

Here's what they did. They went out to a tiny Italian place on the north side of town, where they considered each other over bread rolls and butter flowers. He apologized first; she apologized second. She laid her hand on the tablecloth, and he reached out and squeezed it. Together, they decided to move forward. She didn't ask him why he'd done it. He didn't ask her what she'd been thinking. Questions of motivation, psychology, and desire were left untouched on the tablecloth beside the breadbasket.

AND THEN WHAT HAPPENED?

Oh, you know. Life. The number seven bus. The essays to grade, the lab reports to complete, the groceries to purchase. They fell back into their rhythm. They were gentle with each other, cautious, as if they were carrying Fabergé eggs on spoons across a rocky beach. He left notes for her in unexpected places; she brought him wave-worn pebbles from the lakeshore. One day passed. Then another.

UNTIL?

The week before her fiftieth birthday party, she went to hear a guest speaker at a department function, a scientist from Irkutsk who'd been offered free dinner in exchange for his insights about Superior's sister lake, Baikal. He spoke about the similarities between the two bodies of

356

water. Calcium deficiency, mining industries, water clarity, photic zone depths. Warming temperatures, loss of species. Nothing new there. And then he said, almost as an aside, that by next year the marathon might have to be suspended.

THE MARATHON?

Her question exactly. That night, while her husband dreamed in their oversized bed at the other end of the hallway, she called his computer to life and clicked through search results that sent her imagination reeling. The description of the distant runners as tiny black birds drifting across an ice-white sky; the image of frozen rubble bubbling cold and hard from cracks in the surface. Over and over again she read clauses that painted the angling blue shadows cast by mountains. The thick, soft quilt of gray clouds. She lingered on photographs that captured scenes as otherworldly, as unlikely, as a peacock with its wings outstretched, skimming over the foamy waves of Lake Superior. She leaned back in her husband's chair, her mind fluttering on moth wings toward the light of his computer screen, and an idea began to emerge in the dark like the haunting mass of an approaching iceberg.

DID SHE TELL HER HUSBAND?

Not yet, no. She waited a week. She waited until the night of her fiftieth birthday party, when he crawled into bed beside her after loading the dishwasher with highball glasses and scrubbing frosting from the counter. She didn't know what he'd been thinking earlier that evening as he'd watched her slicing limes. And so she didn't understand why, when she wondered aloud if she might be too old to attempt it, he didn't immediately reply: "No. You're not too old at all."

IF HE DIDN'T SAY THAT, WHAT DID HE SAY?

Nothing.

WHY NOT?

Maybe he was grasping for words in the dark. Maybe he just couldn't reach them.

DID HE KNOW THAT HE WAS BEING TESTED?

He knows that she takes her Earl Grey with cream and cinnamon. He knows that her ankle cracks with almost every step because in high school she played hockey on a broken foot and the bone never healed correctly. He knows that she can identify birds by their shadows. And so he also knows that when she said that she felt old, he was supposed to correct her.

WHY DIDN'T HE?

He was angry about the children.

WHAT CHILDREN?

Their children. The ones they didn't have. And so he didn't correct her. And now he is certain, as he stares through his dark kitchen at the lump of the landline on the wall, willing the phone to ring over the sound of black waves thudding against the cold shore, that this is why she went.

IS THAT WHY SHE WENT?

She's trying not to ask herself that question. She's trying to focus on the movement of her legs and the placement of her feet. She's trying not to think about her husband, or her house. She's trying not to think about how much time has passed, or about the sound of the ice growing louder beneath her shoes. She'd read that once you start the race, you shouldn't look at who's in front of you and who's behind. That's why she is pretending that she's not the last one on the course. She's fixed her gaze on the ice that's five yards ahead of her so that she won't see the volunteers waving frantic flags in her direction. She won't see the tourists with their mittens over the black circles of their mouths. Her heart is in her ears and the wind is picking up, and so she can ignore the voices that are calling out to her.

IS SHE FRIGHTENED?

Of this lake? This race? No. She's prepared. As a girl, she used to speed skate around lakes. The frigid wind chapping her cheeks, her lips. Her limbs tingling, thrilling as she soared beneath black, leafless branches.

Since none of the ten thousand lakes in the state freeze long enough anymore, she trained for the marathon at the indoor rink where Olympic skaters used to race. It was airy, empty, clean, cold. Haunted by the ghost of a sport that no longer exists.

WHAT IS SHE FEELING?

The groaning of the ice. The sudden change in temperature. She was serious when she told the runners that they would be fine, but she didn't tell them what she meant by *fine.* She did not describe what she already feels for this sister lake of Superior: that familiar, intoxicating combination of longing, guilt, and dread. She could not have explained to them, just as she could never explain to her husband, how her passion for the lake consumes her, how her fear for it laps like hard, cold waves against her heart, how she has always known in her bones that the love she possesses is as finite as phosphorous or coal and that she would not have been able to drill down in her soul to find the reserves she needed to love a child. She is not a poet, after all. She doesn't have the words.

WHAT DOES SHE HAVE?

She has her husband, five thousand five hundred and twenty miles away, yanking the heavy receiver from its ancient cradle to place an emergency call to Siberia because it has been seven hours and she's still on the course.

She has her body, half a century old and hurtling across a body of water that is tens of millions of years older than that. She has her thudding heart, her pumping arms, the blood in her ears that sounds a lot like open water.

She has words bubbling up like hot springs in her chest: all the things they haven't told each other. Suddenly, out here beneath a slate-gray sky with the sting of the wind in her eyes, she has no idea why they've both kept silent.

AND SO?

And so if she is picking up her pace, if she is breaking into a headlong sprint, it isn't because she senses the ice that is falling away behind her. It isn't because of the wake she is leaving, the cobalt water shimmering like a contrail, the lake opening wider with every thundering step.

IS SHE TRYING TO OUTRACE HER FATE?

She's trying to catch up to it.

IS IT TOO LATE?

That depends. How fast can she run?

IS IT TOO LATE?

That depends. Too late for what?

Nominated by Nancy K. Geyer, G. C. Waldrep, New England Review

DEDICATED

by KATHY FAGAN

from PLEIADES

The way I remember it,
I caught beauty
Like a flu,

Via handshake or high five
Or a thank-you-
For-your-service

Between the guys at the V.A.
The one who lurched
Toward me, touching

Me, saying:
You like poetry,
More vision than question.

The one who said,
Overhearing me correct
My Korean conflict-era dad:

Go easy, you won't have him
Long. Or the one
Who said: You watch

Him like a hawk;
Just let him go.
In the molecular

Biology lab, each tank
Full of impossibly
Small fish bears

A sign that says: You are responsible
For your own deads.
Plural. Sure.

The older I get, the more
I am reminded of song
Dedications on the radio.

I called Cousin Brucie
To send out "I've Got You,
Babe" to my parents

On their wedding anniversary.
When he played them
"Gypsies, Tramps, and Thieves,"

Bob and Mary Anne
Were understandably confused,
But appreciative nonetheless.

I myself have
Had three partners
In my lifetime,

And what I still love best about
Two of them
Is how I never had to explain

That joke. There was all that
Time listening
To radio or TV,

TV turned internet.
I wish I could
Dedicate those spent hours

Now to my mom,
So she could come back awhile.
She wouldn't have to know

She was dead,
Like we didn't know then
How much time was passing.

I would play
With her hair like I used to,
And tell her stories until

She began to doze off
Like she used to,
Waking only to say:

I didn't ever know you
Loved me, Kath. You never
Wanted affection from us, Kath.

Just like she used to.
The wrong song, somehow
The right song, playing on and on,

Like a perfect virus.

Nominated by Pleiades

AFTERMATH

by HOLLY IGLESIAS

from HOLE IN THE HEAD REVIEW

Someone in Indiana peels a hard-boiled egg for a Starbucks protein box. Someone in Oregon holds the pose—downward dog—for a few seconds more than yesterday. Someone in Tennessee waits for the bus, a canteen clipped to her backpack. Someone in Maryland decides to buy the shoes anyway. Someone in Arizona reads the poem a second time, backwards. Someone in Ohio locks the car, the child inside still crying. Someone in Maine slips a wooden canoe into the lake and paddles toward a cloudbank. Someone in the Upper Peninsula sits in a pew with a rosary balled up in her fist. Someone in the Gulf loses sight of land. Someone upstate lies down in the orchard, apple blossoms for clouds. Someone in the next town forgets his homework and his milk money. Someone upriver watches the winter melt erode the bank. Someone in the plane sees her childhood home in a new light. Someone in the closet raps against the door, the other hand warming the handle. Someone in the building throws her children to the floor, then throws herself upon them. Someone in heaven tries to go back. To help her.

Nominated by Maureen Stanton, Hole In The Head Review

OPEN HOUSE

by JEREMIAH MOSS

from N+1

The mothers are coming up the stairs. Holding the hands of their adult children. Daughters, mostly, and one hesitant son. Asking questions like, "Is the neighborhood safe?" The real estate agent, in his starched white shirt and slick hair, replies, "The East Village used to have quite a reputation fifteen, twenty years ago, but now it's totally safe." Or did he say totally *tame*? As in domesticated, subjugated, a wild horse broken. I am listening from inside my apartment, ear pressed to the gap where door doesn't quite meet jamb, looking through the peephole, trying to see who my new neighbors might be, knowing they'll be the same as all the rest. Young and funded, they belong to a certain type: utterly unblemished, physically fit, exceptionally well dressed, as bland as skim milk and unsalted saltine crackers. "I work on Wall Street," I hear one of them call to the real-estate agent. "Awesome!" the agent replies.

They didn't used to be here.

I came in the early 1990s because it made sense for me to be here. I was a young, queer, transsexual poet, and where else would a young, queer, transsexual poet go but to the East Village? Back then the neighborhood still throbbed with its hundred years of counterculture, a dissident history going back to the early anarchists and feminists, up through the bohemians and Beats, the hippies and punks, the poets, queers, and transsexuals too. I had a pair of combat boots and an elite liberal arts education, thanks to a full ride of grants and work-study programs, but not much money. I hail from generations of peasants, washerwomen, and bricklayers, orphans raised by nuns, 12-year-old factory workers, icemen who sang opera while they slung frozen bricks, soldiers, hucksters, and bookmakers, thick-legged Italians and paper skinned Irish Catholics, most of whom didn't get to high school and not one of whom saw the inside of a college classroom. I had ambition but didn't yet understand entitlement. I was in the process of becoming something else, believed in the mythical bootstraps of meritocracy, but I also knew what I was. I took a job cleaning other people's apartments, got fired when a woman made the outrageous claim that I'd used a sponge to stick hair to her bathroom ceiling, and then took another job that involved running errands and getting yelled at, two things I knew well how to do. The East Village was full of people who were bruised like I was bruised, people who weren't quite pulled together but were trying to make something interesting with their lives. I belonged here. In this neighborhood. In this crumbling tenement.

Since my longtime landlord sold the eight-unit building to a mysterious corporate entity a few years ago, there's been a revolving door in the apartment next to mine and the one below. The turnover happens every summer. So far, maybe because young men are known to be destructive, the new owners have only admitted young women, with one exception. By design, none of them stays for more than a year. The East Village is just a way station, empty of significance. My young friends who are queers and artists have never set foot in this neighborhood. It's irrelevant to them. When I tell them I live here, they look confused. Why would you want to live *there*? The East Village is nowhere.

Before each batch arrives, after their parents have approved and co-signed, teams of hired hands sweep in to prepare the Insta-partments. First come the cleaners, sending up the chlorine tang of bleach, followed by the movers with their tidy plastic totes, followed (at least once) by professional furnishers who arrange and assemble flat-packed tables and shelves, big-screen TVs, kitchen knives gleaming in wooden blocks, sets of salt and pepper mills pre-filled with peppercorns and luminous chunks of pink salt mined from distant tendrils of the Himalayan foothills. The new people are completists. If they don't have professional furnishers, they order entire apartments through the mail in their first week: sofa, dining set, closet-organizing systems. Nothing left undone.

Most of my old neighbors predate me, have been in the building for decades. We are the "stabies," which sounds like *scabies*, and that's how I imagine the new people see us, like parasites that will contaminate them if they get too close. There's the man who plays classical piano and the one with the limp who calls me "baby." There's the architect and the couple who run a coffee shop. Two of my neighbors have died since the new owners took over, both while in the middle of eviction proceedings. The woman with the cats, the one who loved the Beatles, had cancer. I gave her referrals to support groups and witnessed her slow fade, dwindling as she climbed the stairs. After she went, I watched men take her whole apartment and load it into a truck. I stood struck by the particular sadness of a mattress, stained by the body, by years of sleep and dreams, love and worry, and I wondered, as all old New Yorkers must: Will that be my mattress one day? Who among us doesn't imagine the lonely New York death, our bodies discovered only because they begin to smell and trouble the neighbors? (Added bonus if your corpse is nibbled by your own beloved cats.) I once smelled that odor, in a flophouse hotel off Times Square when I went to visit a resident. He took me to the door of the deceased, marked with yellow caution tape, and the smell was like sour cheese jelly smeared in the air, a physical, biting thing that lingered in my nostrils for weeks. Will that be my smell one day?

Somehow, I doubt the new people worry about dying that sort of death. They know they won't be trapped here. They have other places they can go. But if they don't worry like New Yorkers worry, can they dream like New Yorkers dream? While they sleep, do the walls of their apartments miraculously open into extra rooms for them the way they do for us, or do the new people have all the space they need and so they are free to dream of other wishful things? Hashtag abundance. Hashtag gratitude.

After she died and her furniture was removed, my neighbor's apartment was quickly gutted and renovated, the rent jacked from hundreds to thousands, decontrolled. The man next to her died a year later. He was born on the block and never lived anywhere else. A hoarder who once infested us with bedbugs, he was also a kind person and a talented whistler. He would walk up the stairs, slowly, while whistling classic songs. Rodgers and Hart. Irving Berlin. The Gershwins. Tunes that would stay in my head all day. "We'll have Manhattan, the Bronx, and Staten Island too." When he went, I watched the paramedics pump his heart and lift him onto a stretcher, his eyes open but empty, not seeing the hallway he'd whistled through for decades. When the police officer asked me his name, I could only come up with his first. It bothered me that I could not remember the last name of this man who'd greeted me nearly every day for twenty-five years, talked to me about the weather, told me to "be careful" each time I went out. How could his last name be gone from my mind? Later, I understood it was because of the mailboxes. Our last names used to be printed on the slots for each mailbox, handwritten and enduring, never changing because no one ever left. I saw them every day, a reminder of the people I lived among. My people. But the new owners covered them over, replacing names with numbers, wiping us from each other's memory.

The new people come with names that chime together like beads on a string. Taylor, Ashley, Kayla, Hayley, Madison (that one guy so far—he hailed from Wisconsin, hopefully not the state capital). I know their names because they get everything delivered. The packages pile up in the small entryway where there never used to be packages. The old people shop nearby, or else we don't shop much at all. Now I am always tripping over boxes. Sometimes, I confess, in my hostility, I kick the boxes. Amazon, Amazon, Amazon. Sephora. Vineyard Vines with the smiling, pink, preppy whale. Kick, kick, kick.

I read the new people's names on the package labels and then I google them, sifting through Instagram and YouTube, spying on trips to Bali and brunch. This sounds creepy, and it probably is, but instead of some Dostoevskian fiend (though my former psychoanalyst used to delight in telling me, "You're like Raskolnikov, skulking through the streets"), I feel more like Gladys Kravitz, the nosy neighbor played by Alice Pearce on the 1960s sitcom *Bewitched*. As a kid, I watched *Bewitched* in reruns, on sick days and latchkey afternoons in my conservative, working-class hick town in Massachusetts, the state most steeped in the blood of witch trials. In the show, Samantha, a glossy blond witch, marries Darrin, a mortal man, and vows to live a normal, middle-class, suburban life. "All I want is the normal life of a normal housewife," she insists to the husband who tries to control her. But she can't stop using her supernatural powers, and this leads to all sorts of trouble. Gladys spends her days peeking through the curtains, horrified by the irregular behavior of her neighbors. I should be festooned in hair curlers, dressed in a terry bathrobe with a fistful of Kleenex stashed up the sleeve, just in case I begin to sneeze. Or weep.

Poor Gladys suffered from a Cassandra complex. She knew something strange and dark was going on next door, but no one believed her. "The Cassandra woman," writes the Jungian analyst Laurie Layton Schapira, "may blurt out what she sees, perhaps with the unconscious hope that others might be able to make some sense of it. But to them her words sound meaningless, disconnected and blown out of all proportion." I know how she feels. Powerless, hysterical, every blurt full of certainty undercut by doubt.

A new york apartment used to be a place that took time to coalesce. It formed around your body as you also evolved, mirrored by the changing geometries of your rooms as they gradually absorbed the world. I furnished the place, piece by piece, from the bounty of the streets. A modern chair from the trash on 23rd Street, carried home atop my head. A lamp in the shape of a leopard stalking its prey, bought for 50 cents from a homeless woman on Third Avenue. Jack and Jackie Kennedy salt and pepper shakers from the Broadway and Grand flea market in SoHo. I still have these scavenged objects. "An apartment in New York City tells many truths," writes the East Villager Sarah Schulman in *Rat Bohemia*. "It shows where you really stand, relationally. It shows when you came, how much you had, and what kind of people you knew."

During this most recent Open House, two of the women following in the cologne-clogged wake of the real estate agent look like they could be lesbians. Against my better judgment, I feel hopeful. They wear short hair and short-sleeved gingham shirts. Maybe they're artists. Maybe this time the new people will be my people. They'll stay. We'll become friends, allies against the landlord, lenders of proverbial cups of sugar. I play this game on the street: Won't You Be My Neighbor? That young woman in glasses and lumpy wool skirt, foraging for books at the Strand's dollar carts, won't she be my neighbor? Or the earnest-looking, boyish (maybe nonbinary) person on the steps of Union Square Park, with their black eyeliner and pink socks. Or the woman in the Angela Davis Afro, breathing in the herbs at Flower Power, waving their scents with her hands like a conductor before an orchestra. Or the young man sitting on a bench in Washington Square Park, reading Knausgaard, *My Struggle: Book 4*, in a sweatshirt that reads, WE ARE THE THINGS WE HAVE LOST.

When I worked in offices, before I became a psychoanalyst, I was a petty thief. In my twenties, underpaid and unappreciated by my corporate bosses, I seized scraps of power by stealing pens and pencils, yellow bricks of Post-its, spiral notebooks, and, once, a good Swingline stapler.

I did it because I felt angry and oppressed. Now I'm a middle-class, middle-aged, self-employed professional feeling angry and oppressed by the corporate system that has transformed my neighborhood and my building, but there is nothing to take. So I steal into the lives of my new neighbors, the ones invited and nurtured by this system. I look through the peephole and gaze into Instagram. I feel invaded by them, so I invade back the only way I can.

The Great Invasion began sometime in the late 1990s but didn't really take shape until after September 11. That's when the new people found the East Village. The new people, the emphatically normal, come from someplace else, the Midwest, the South, but that's not what makes them invaders. Many of us come from someplace else. I come from someplace else. Move anywhere and you're potentially interloping. So what is it? How can I talk about the new people and their superpower of invasion? I'm forever grappling with this question, reducing, stereotyping, and then struggling not to be reductive. What I keep coming back to is their apparent belief that their way of living belongs everywhere, that it should trickle down the ladder of power and fill every lower space, scouring and purifying as it goes. Spaces of queerness. Spaces of color. Spaces of marginalization. Spaces of *This is our little scrap of somewhere, can't you just let us have it, oh you who have everywhere?* With good reason, colonization and Manifest Destiny are the enduring metaphors of gentrification.

The longtime East Village performance artist Penny Arcade said, "The ten most popular kids from every high school in the world are now living in New York! Those are the people that most of us who moved to New York came here to get away from." But it's now a coast-to-coast problem. The queer Seattle-based artist John Criscitello had a similar response to the invasion of the city's Capitol Hill gayborhood by what he calls "bros and woo girls." He bombed the neighborhood with wheat paste posters that read, WE CAME HERE TO GET AWAY FROM YOU. This age of gentrification has been described as the reversal of white flight, the big return, the Great Inversion. The urbanist Neil Smith declared post-fiscal-crisis New York the revanchist city, a vengeful take-back that expressed "a race/class/gender terror felt by middle- and ruling-class whites."

I confess, in adolescence, I wanted to be a smooth and golden, well-off WASP. I didn't want to be Italian, Irish, Catholic, all the things I thought would hold me back. I got rid of my regional working-class accent, took up field hockey, made pilgrimages to L.L. Bean, and got a pair of Bass camp mocs, but couldn't figure out how to tie the laces in a barrel or tassel knot. Any blue-blooded Anglo-Saxon could see I was faking it. But they didn't see me; I saw them. Each morning, on my way to Catholic school, I would pass their leafy boarding school, gaze upon their abundance, and feel my lack. In a recent study about airplane travel and inequality, researchers discovered that when coach passengers have to pass through first class to get to their seats in the back, they are twice as likely to succumb to outbursts of "air rage." Seeing what you don't have makes people feel worse.

To attract new people, the owners installed a doorbell system linked to smartphones. Though not my smartphone, because I don't have one, so I can't always buzz people in. The doorbell has a camera and takes pictures of everyone who comes to visit and sends this data to the owners. They installed cameras in the hallways, too, trained on our apartment doors. My old neighbors and I stand on the street, outside the net of surveillance, and debate whether or not we're really being watched or if the cameras are dummies, duping us into good behavior. The panopticon effect in action. One day, workers from the management company were talking in the hall. I pressed my ear to the door and heard one of them say, "Every night, I have a few beers, I jerk off, and then I watch the security tapes." In that order. I want to give the finger to the wide-eyed camera standing guard outside my door, but I don't because there's a man somewhere, beery and satisfied, watching. The cameras have invaded my thoughts. I have never vandalized the hallways of my building and never would, but since the cameras came, I think about how much I would like to, but can't because they're watching, so I stop myself from thinking about vandalizing the hallways, and then I feel oppressed and controlled. The cameras created a thought in my mind and then censored that thought. Sometimes it's hard to know, in the presence of the cameras, which thoughts belong to me and which ones belong to them.

One of the reasons I google the new people is that they don't speak to us and googling is the only way to learn what they're about. When I say hello, they often don't respond. They look at the floor or down at their phones and keep walking. Sometimes they startle and freeze, avoiding eye contact, like I'm a ghost materialized in empty space. They act like it's just them living here. Them and their Amazon packages. They FaceTime in the halls, slow-walking and shouting into screens.

"My mink coat costs way more than your Canada Goose!" I heard one of them say. Their friends come in like herds of pack animals. Thirsty boys keyed up for pregaming cocktails knock on my door by mistake and then, finding it funny when I answer, rattle my doorknob every time they go by. For weeks, the doorknob rattle followed by feral, frat boy laughter. Expulsive, uncontained, the new people overspill. They slam their doors, making the flimsy building shake. They set off the fire alarms because they don't know how to make toast without burning it. They send the smells of their perfumes and shampoos slithering through the gaps around my door, invading my apartment with fruity green apple and peppery vanilla caramel.

Why do they want to be here? I'm trying to write a novel at my kitchen table as the Open House, with all its traffic, floods the hallways. Disturbed by the noise of the real estate agent leading mothers and their adult children up and down the stairs, I keep jumping to the peephole. Surely, I think as I watch them go by, the mothers will see the neglect and disrepair of this building and refuse to sign the lease. For the same $4,500 a month, the new people could live in one of the new buildings in the neighborhood, the ones with doormen and wine tastings, rooftop barbecues and beer pong games, complimentary continental breakfasts, hallways scoured and sanitized. Surely, I think, these clean, suburban, antiseptic people won't want to live here. On the unswept floors of the hallways, at this exact moment, there sits: one upside-down and almost dead water bug, its legs slowly paddling the air; a wad of intimate paper tissue smeared with something brown that might be chocolate but strongly resembles human feces; a bloody Band-Aid turned gauze-side up; and a greasy, festering sliver of bacon. Surely, I think, these items will serve as protective totems, frightening gargoyles and hunky punks, like the severed head of Medusa, to scare the new people away. But nothing scares the new people. Medusa herself could appear in my hallway to shake her snakes in their faces and they would walk right past, immune and untouched. Looking down at their phones. Obliviousness is a talent they have cultivated well.

I first saw it in the mid-2000s, in the old Meatpacking District, when the new people came to party. I watched them walk over sidewalks slippery-thick with animal fat, sliding in their Louboutins past buckets of offal haloed in clouds of buzzing flies. In the stink of death, strong enough to trigger the gag reflex, they made their merry way. It did not repel them because they did not see it. I watched them pose for photos in the reek of bovine rot, like none of it was there. Filtered out. This powerful ability to ignore signs of danger and sickness enables them to go anywhere, secure in the belief that nothing bad can touch them.

Take sidewalk sitting, for example: around the year 2008, I started to notice people sitting on sidewalks. Not homeless people, not punk kids, not hippies or crusties, but average, well-dressed, middle-class, affluent (almost always white) people, sitting in the New York soup of chewed gum, vomit, dog piss, and shit. The recurrence of this weird trend compelled me to photograph them, and I now possess a collection of young men and women sitting on the sidewalk, often on the curb, with their legs stretched in the gutter, in the traffic, eating their lunch or looking through shopping bags, drinking iced coffee, scrolling on their phones. What would Susan Sontag say about my odd habit? "There is an aggression implicit in every use of the camera," she noted. "To photograph people is to violate them, by seeing them as they never see themselves, by having knowledge of them they can never have." She called it "soft murder." I admit to feeling aggressive when I take these photos, maybe even softly murderous, putting myself in a position of power over people against whom I feel otherwise powerless. Shooting them gives me a false sense of control over the uncontrollable. But I am also gathering evidence, proof that this strange behavior came into existence, a mysterious by-product of 21st-century gentrification. Others have started photographing the sidewalk sitters, too. The East Village novelist Arthur Nersesian puts them on his Facebook page. In one photo, a young woman typing on a MacBook sits cross-legged in a short summer dress that does not fold under her, does not protect her underpants from the pestilence of Avenue A. I want to give her a blanket and a tetanus shot.

While the real estate agent is hosting the Open House, in between clients, he sits on the stairs in the hallway, looking at his phone, drifting back and forth past my door, where I watch through the peephole (I have become, unhappily, a Gladys Kravitzian peephole obsessive). He is dressed in pressed trousers and a blindingly white, starched shirt, and yet he sits. Where the water bugs go to die with slivers of bacon and bloody Band-Aids. Where I have never, in twenty-five years, seen a single human being sit. He sits for a long while. I can't write while he's out there. I can hear him breathing, clearing his throat, shifting his weight from cheek to cheek while he scrolls the phone, as if Siri herself has commanded him.

I consider buying a doormat that reads GET OFF MY LAWN, an open admission of the caricature I am rapidly becoming, but it's too much. Even for me.

I go for drinks with another writer friend and we argue about the new East Villagers. I tell her they're boring and don't belong here and she tells me I can't know that, not really, not without talking to them. Maybe they're fascinating people. This reminds me of an op-ed I once read in the *Times*. Ada Calhoun, author of *St. Marks Is Dead* (in which she concludes that it's not), writes, "Who deserves to be here? Who is the interloper and who the interloped-upon? Who can say which drunk NYU student stumbling down St. Marks Place will wind up writing the next classic novel or making the next great album? It's hubris to think you can tell by looking at them." What if Calhoun and my friend are right? What if I'm being judgy about the next Patti Smith, the next Frank O'Hara? Or some kid who's simply the next me?

When the new people walk up and down the stairs, they shout, so you can't help but hear everything they say. One of them shouts, "My father was, like, how do you live without an elevator? Or a doorman?" The other sees the bright side, explaining that walk-up tenement life provides "a good workout for your legs and butt!" They shout about the salads they just had at Sweetgreen. I have never been to Sweetgreen, a chain that refuses to take cash—though they were recently forced to accept it when Philadelphia and New Jersey banned cashless stores, which discriminate against the poor, the elderly, the "underbanked." A Sweetgreen outlet took the place of one of my favorite diners, the University Restaurant on University Place, where I once heard a cranky old couple argue about their cat and her mercurial affections:

> WOMAN: (*sorting vitamins on the table*) There's something wrong with Sunny. She doesn't sleep with me anymore.
>
> MAN: No, she sleeps with me.
>
> WOMAN: (*in a panic*) Does she? Seriously, tell me, where does she sleep? Tell me the truth so I know!
>
> MAN: Yeah, she sleeps with me. I'm cheating on you with the cat.
>
> WOMAN: Oh, be quiet and help me with these vitamins.

It went on from there, so much more colorful than anything I've heard from the new East Villagers.

While I don't buy the GET OFF MY LAWN doormat, I do have one made to say, WELCOME TO NEW YORK: NOW GO HOME, the once popular slogan of the 1980s city. I don't, however, have the heart to place it out in the hall, so I drop it in front of my kitchen sink, where the only person it urges to leave is me.

After the open house, the newest girls move in. They are not the potentially lesbian artists in the short haircuts and gingham shirts. They look like all the new people who've come before them, glossy and glowing, dressed in white, hard to tell apart in different shades of blond, floating by with identical Maison Goyard tote bags on their shoulders and white AirPods in their ears. I google them. One is a teenage heiress. The other is a lifestyle vlogger with an Instagram page full of beige, taupe, and the palest dusty blush of millennial pink. There are no photos of my dreary hallway. It's all the Hamptons and Nantucket, bottles of honey-infused hair oil and glasses of rosé held against a background of blue ocean and white sailboats. Here she is on the French Riviera. Here she is in Venice. Here she is in Starbucks. Here she is eating avocado toast. Here she is in a video about everything she bought at Whole Foods. (I dip a toe down the Whole Foods/Trader Joe's "haul" video rabbit hole and watch another vlogger, who looks uncannily like my neighbor, unpack groceries. She says, "I feel like I'm blending into the walls." An existential dread? She explains, "I wear white a lot and also my home is white.") My newest neighbor, also wearing white on white, similarly unpacks: cacao nibs, pre-shredded sweet potato ribbons, gluten-free pasta, cauliflower gnocchi, which she mispronounces "know-key."

So far, these newest new neighbors are quieter than the last bunch, and for that I am grateful. I haven't had to knock on their door once. They seem inoffensive enough and are probably nice people. Still, on their Instagrams and YouTubes and blogs, I find no evidence that they are writing the next classic novel or the next great album.

When I take out the trash, I find a perfectly good mirror left lying in a heap. It looks new, but my newest new neighbors bought an extra-new mirror and tossed this one out, even though it has nothing wrong with it. It even looks recently windexed. After considering it for myself, I take it from the trash area behind the building and drag it to the sidewalk, where I prop it against the bricks. This is what we do with old, good things we don't want. We leave them to the street, to the scavengers and collectors. We give back because we have taken. Later, when I go out for groceries, the mirror is gone and I feel gratified. There's a pleasure in finding one's offerings have been accepted. It makes you feel like the city is functioning the way it should and you are a small part of keeping that ecosystem alive.

The new people are always forgetting things. They leave their apartments, slamming the doors. They pause in front of my peephole, adjusting their AirPods. I am Gladys Kravitz holding her breath, trying not to sneeze. They look so lost. They stare at their screens awhile and then drift down the stairs. They might reach the bottom before they turn abruptly and come trudging back for whatever they forgot. Umbrella. Wallet. Whatever objects people tend to forget. They slam the door again, go in and out, slam it again, and then stare and drift, down and down, again. Sometimes this routine happens two or three times in a row. More forgetting. The minds of the new people are elsewhere. They don't know where they are or what they have.

From the beginning of urban life, the city has existed as a zone of freedom, beyond the enforced conformity of small towns and suburbs. It is both a physical and a psychic space, one in which there is always room for risk, danger, and creative chaos. But that psychic space is getting smaller as the suburbanization of the city continues to compress its unruly contours. In the past, American outsiders, all those non-normals, came to the city to become New Yorkers. Today, the new people want the city to become like them. As Sarah Schulman puts it in *The Gentrification of the Mind*, the new crowd comes to homogenize, bringing "the values of the gated community and a willingness to trade freedom for security." They also bring a different psyche to the city, and it is one of absence, detachment, and unrecognition.

As a psychoanalyst, I help people to think, and I am hyperattuned to variations in the psychic field, but anyone paying attention can feel a person's psyche in close proximity. You can feel if it runs sluggish or quick, shallow or deep, elegant or jumbled. On the sidewalks and subways, you know which people to avoid simply from their fizz in the air. What I feel from many of the new people, the ones working so hard to be normal, is the absence of mind. When I picture it, I see a tightly compressed knot, a forced blank, surrounded by a buzzy cloud of agitation and distraction. This is, of course, highly subjective and impossible to measure, so you'll just have to trust me when I say: They aren't really here. And that absence, that rapidly replicating zombie effect, makes the city a lonelier place than it used to be.

I miss the New York mind.

My *bewitched* analogy does not hold up. Or does it? In the show, Samantha is the alien in the closet and Gladys is the regulatory gaze trying to root her out. Am I the hunter or the hunted? While I am watching the new people, my new landlords are watching me. They wait for me to slip up. They want me out. I am less valuable than the new people. I am disposable. As a queer, trans person, this is not an unfamiliar feeling.

In 1992, Elizabeth Montgomery revealed to the LGBTQ magazine the *Advocate* that *Bewitched* knowingly portrayed a queer closet allegory. The show, she said, "was about people not being allowed to be what they really are"; it was "about repression in general and all the frustration and trouble it can cause." Trouble like witch hunts. Did you know that in 2005 Viacom donated a nine-foot bronze statue of a broomstick-riding Samantha to the town of Salem, Massachusetts? Residents protested the obvious advertisement, calling it an insult to the memory of those persecuted and murdered in 1692, but the statue still stands, midcentury American normal, reforged and reanimated by end-stage capitalism, covering for colonial violence. You can see the statue on Instagram, repeating and repeating.

I check in again with my newest neighbor's latest vlog, curious to see what life is like on the other side of the wall. Here she is drinking a matcha latte. Here she is in a beige dress. Here she is giving a tour of her gleaming apartment behind my kitchen with its broken stove and leaky sink. I lean in, looking for books, paintings, some sign of a creative and uncontrolled urban life, of conflict and imperfection, but there are none. Everything in the apartment is new and white. The couch is white. The pillows are white. The curtains are white. The bed, sheets, and blankets are white. The desk is white. The dining table and chairs are white. The rug is white. The new mirror, the one that replaced the old white mirror I found in the trash, has a blond wood frame that looks almost white. My neighbor loves the blond wood because, she says, "Everything's white, so I needed, like, some texture."

My heart drops. She's not a bad person, you can tell; she just doesn't know what texture is. Maybe she's afraid of texture. I once knew a woman who ate only white food. She did this because she'd experienced a horrible trauma and didn't want anything going inside her body that didn't signify purity and cleanliness. Maybe my neighbor had a horrible trauma. Maybe the enforced conformity of America is the trauma, complex and repressed, and all that whiteness is there to keep her clean and safe, to hold her together so she doesn't fly apart. Maybe the new people hope that living here, in this building and this neighborhood, will give them some texture, but not too much.

When I complain to my friends about the changed neighborhood, they get exasperated and ask, "So why don't you move?" "Move to Brooklyn," they usually add, as if that borough could be a balm for all my troubles. When they say this, I feel dyspeptic and misunderstood. Don't they get it? This is my home, and I won't let it be taken from me. I will not move. There are financial realities, of course, my fear of an unstabilized rent, that endless insecurity, and my desire to be in Manhattan, where I am walking distance from pretty much everywhere I want to go. But there is also the matter of my disposition. I am rooted and intractable. Raised by pushy people, I developed a highly resistant personality. And the more I feel pushed, the more I dig in. That psychoanalyst who used to call me Raskolnikov? She also liked to say I resembled Bartleby. "I would prefer not to," she'd say. "That's your motto." I was a difficult patient. You know the game adults play with groups of children, *Let's see who can sit still and be quiet the longest?* I always won.

The new landlords offer me money to give up my apartment so they can replace me with new people. It's not enough. Giving up this apartment would mean giving up my New York. I know I'm probably holding on to some idea that no longer exists, a romantic notion sprung from Rodgers and Hart lyrics, Frank O'Hara poems, and all that J. D. Salinger—I wanted to be some version of Zooey Glass, soaking in a clawfoot tub, smoking and reading in an urban bathroom full of books instead of my mother's *People* magazines—but I can't help it. The thing is embedded in me. The longing.

There are these lines in Ocean Vuong's novel *On Earth We're Briefly Gorgeous* where he says: "Maybe we look into mirrors not merely to seek beauty, regardless how illusive, but to make sure, despite the facts, that we are still here. That the hunted body we move in has not yet been annihilated, scraped out. To see yourself still *yourself* is a refuge men who have not been denied cannot know." Those of us who occupy hunted bodies look into the mirrors of other hunted bodies to confirm that we exist. We look into those mirrors to find ourselves reflected in another mind. The East Village, and much of the city, used to be filled with such bodies and minds. Hunted back home, they fled to the city and provided a mutual antidote to the annihilation that comes with being out of step and undesired. To watch those people vanish and be replaced by people who shine like glass, who cut through the sidewalks like knives but reflect nothing back, has been another scraping out. Am I still here? I don't know anyone here anymore.

This is not entirely true. Sometimes, sitting in the park, I run into Christine and Rosella out walking their dog. They complain about their new neighbors, identical to mine, and this complaint binds us together, so we laugh and it all feels less awful. (Christine confesses that she, too, googles the new people from the names on their Amazon packages, and I feel less like a creep.) They tell me about a movie they're making and I tell them about my novel, and it's OK again. Last night I heard someone call my name and it was Steve from my old poetry group, standing outside the movie theater in a popcorn-butter cloud, hugging me hello. Whenever I go past Gem Spa on St. Marks, Parul waves me over to insist I have a free egg cream. There's Zarina from the laundromat, telling me about her annual trip home to India in muddy monsoon season. At my local supermarket, because I buy food for the homeless man who sits outside, the manager, who also feeds the man, opens a register just for me. She waves me over and I leave the line, feeling seen and loved, spreading my groceries on the conveyor belt, not a single pasta product bastardized from a head of cauliflower.

So why would I leave this place? I am good at sitting still and waiting. I will outwait the new people. Surely, I tell myself, the bubble will burst, the tide will shift, and they will move on, the way they always do, after they've suctioned up all of what they came to eat. But I know they won't leave. They are forever replenishing themselves, like the teeth in a shark's mouth; one vacates and another steps forward to take its place. If I survive the hunt, I will be a leftover in the glittering ruins of that future world, the old neighbor whistling on the stairs, taking his time, a ghost stuttering under the electronic eyes, barely seen, but still here. Holding the memory for as long as I can. We are, after all, the things we have lost. +

Nominated by Dominica Phetteplace, N+1

THE CRYING ROOM

fiction by LUCAS SOUTHWORTH

from COPPER NICKEL

The vents exhaled the whole way, constant and raw. The shoulder slid past. The sheared edges of what had once been fields of corn. Light from the bus's windows bent into the dark. Fall was becoming winter, the blue tinge of it cautious and slow against the glass, like a patient trying his side for the first time after surgery.

I pictured my son in the aisle seat, a book on his lap, his phone plugged into the outlet, earbuds buried in his ears. He was fourteen, still. A fascinating and beguiling age. A boy, and yet capable, capable.

I pretended to hear the music, just the seams of whatever it was he listened to.

I opened a hand to him on the armrest.

I'm your mother, I said. Tell me what you need to tell me.

But even in my imagination, my son flashed anger. He pulled his legs to his chest, his socks on the seat, his chin resting on top of his knees. He sat there until he was gone again, only a scattering of crumbs from some other passenger on the vinyl. I wanted to brush them off. I couldn't bring myself to do it. Not even with a tissue or the backs of my gloves.

Five hours of dark road became six. I kept checking my watch, though I had no real reason, no real place to be. The air circled through everyone's lungs twice, three times, four. I thought, No one can take a ride like this without a little despair. I thought, How can I continue? How do any of us continue?

The bus finally wandered into the city and stopped in a lurch and flurry of breaks. The riders all stood as if choreographed. Most filed off and into the passenger seats of idling pickups and sedans. The rest dissipated sleepily down subway steps.

I watched taillights disappear. I felt the pavement stretching, stretching.

In a diner a few blocks away, the waitress gave me a newspaper for free. It was past midnight, she said, and the man would come around again soon. He'd block the door with another bundle as he always did.

She eyed me. You're a woman alone, she said.

I'm a doctor, I told her. I know the corners of the night.

She laughed and brought my eggs while I scanned the classifieds.

They don't really put much in the paper anymore, she said.

The crying rooms, I asked, what are they?

Only heard of them, she said.

I read the ad again and picked up my fork. The eggs were perfect. Yolk filled the entire plate as soon as I cut in.

I called the number the next morning. I met the owners in the afternoon.

The man pointed me toward an armchair near the window, in the sun. He took the other, and the woman steered a rolling chair from behind a front desk that looked like it should be at a hotel or spa. On the coffee table between us sat a stack of magazines, straight and untouched. Ferns softened the lobby's edges. I noticed brass, so dull, and off-white walls, maybe even almost gray. Three paintings hung, large and framed. Sailboats upon the open sea.

From what I understood, I told them, I was perfect for the place. I'd worked nights before. I liked it. I wasn't too young or old, too talkative or quiet. I wasn't easily rattled or taken in. I had no interest in family or being liked or making friends.

The owners didn't bring up that I was overqualified. They just conferred with each other for a minute. Then they listed the rules.

Pretend you don't recognize anyone, they said, even customers that come in often. Wear sunglasses to hide your eyes. Keep your hands out of sight as much as possible. Ask three simple questions. How long would you like your room? What is your preferred method of payment? Can you see the elevator, down the hall to the left?

I spent the rest of the afternoon walking. I followed the water a while. I watched the city's glow transition from day into night. At ten, I was back, ringing the doorbell, waving to the woman through the glass. She buzzed me in and showed me everything I needed to know. She introduced me to the guard in case anyone stayed over their time. She reminded me a custodian came around two.

Did you forget your sunglasses? she asked.

No, I said, I've got them.

She left me there and customers trickled in. They all waited patiently, quietly, as I fumbled with credit cards and selected keys. One woman asked if I was new, and I didn't even nod. How long would you like your room? I answered. What's your preferred method of payment?

I got the hang of it quickly, and a month passed in routine before I realized I had no idea what the crying rooms looked like, no idea what was going on above my head. I stood and sat down. I stood and sat down again. When the guard passed through the lobby, I asked if he'd watch the desk while I used the restroom. He dropped happily into my chair. I went down the hall.

On the third floor, I slipped a key I'd brought into its lock. I opened one of the doors.

I'd expected padding for some reason. I'd expected straitjackets and no furniture. What I saw was a simple family room. Twelve feet by twelve feet, a well-worn couch and a rocking chair with an afghan folded over the back. A rug covered much of the floor. Two side tables had coasters. A coatrack stood empty as if guarding something. On top of a sideboard slumped an antique radio.

I smelled lilac, chemical from an air freshener.

Okay, I said out loud. I turned to leave, but stopped. I heard crying, faint at first, then louder the more I became aware of it. I crept to one side of the room and then the other. I stood in the middle and craned my neck. I lowered myself to the rug, pressed an ear against it.

The crying seeped through two neighboring walls and the ceiling. It filled the air and mixed. I fell back on the couch like I'd been shoved. I took my sunglasses off and closed my eyes. I held my breath and listened, listened.

Some crying sounds like laughing at first. Some sounds exactly like it should. Some is wet, a blubber, and some dry as a dry throat. Some crying bursts in waves, like thunderstorms on a distant planet. And sometimes it stops, just stops, suddenly, a gasping, a choking and a gasping, before it starts up again. Some crying is jagged, like a comb. Some rises and falls like symphonies, like civilizations. Some sends jitters into the arms and hands and fingernails until they're scratching at the wall, at the floor, scraping and scraping the skin. There is heavy crying, light. There are notes in staccato, in moans. Some carry whimpers. Some shrieks and howls. Some full and upright screams. There is the crying that comes from the depths. Hundreds of thousands of years in the making. Crying that comes from among the echoes of coyotes and caves. And there is crying punctuated by words. Why and Why and Why, and O God and O God and O God.

The night it happened, I told my husband and son I'd be home for dinner. As usual, I pulled into the driveway hours late.

I'd expected every window to be blazing. My husband moving from room to room. My son finishing his homework. Two or three TVs on with nobody watching. But at nine thirty, the house was dark. I got out of the car thinking they'd gone to the movies, though they rarely did that. Inside, I smelled no evidence of cooking, so I assumed they'd eaten out, though they didn't do that much either. And when the dog didn't shuffle to greet me, I thought maybe they'd taken her for a walk.

I left all the lights off until I got to the kitchen.

There weren't any dirty dishes in the sink. No books or notebooks open on the table. No abandoned pencils on the floor. I wasn't concerned, not yet. I was happy to have the house to myself for a minute after all those extra hours of complications and surgery.

I thought, One of my son's friends must have had a birthday party. Or maybe my son had remembered something he needed for class and they'd rushed out to get it.

At ten thirty, I texted my husband as I ate a bowl of cereal. I called twice, three times, four. The silence began to wrap. Quieter than usual. Quieter even than when I sometimes woke in late morning, my husband already at work, my son at school.

I thought, Wherever they are, it must be crowded. Wherever they are, they must not be able to hear.

At eleven, I decided this was their attempt to punish me. I grinned at that. I laughed my own angry laugh.

I began turning on every light in the house. The dining room and living room. The theater my husband and son had set up for video games and movies. In the basement, I flipped every switch. On the second floor, I lit the hallway, the chandelier. I turned on lights in our bedroom, in my office and my husband's. Even the lamps we never used. Even the ones with bulbs covered in dust.

At my son's door, I shivered. I'd promised never to go in without his permission, but I turned the handle anyway. I switched on his light.

There were rules meant for the protection of the place. Rules meant for the protection of those who came in. Customers were not allowed to share rooms. Not even couples or family members or friends. No children under twelve. Before people went up, they put their phones in a Ziploc bag and gave the bag to me and I kept them locked up until they came down again.

I sat behind the desk for a second month, like a knight behind his shield and armor. I learned to speak from the top of my throat, each word growing softer as it traveled along the palate toward my teeth. I was used to slack faces at the hospital. Dull eyes. Lids that, when open, might as well be shut. I knew blue lips. I knew fingers not quite willing to touch. I knew distances that came on, the dementias of shock.

But here, pain expanded and swelled with all the qualities of a haunt. I joked to myself that time lurched at the crying rooms only when I turned my back or only when I didn't see it crawling underneath the furniture.

I imagined my son in the lobby. Darkness folding outside the glass behind him. The sidewalk streetlamp yellow. Winter limping. I pictured the dog, curled. My husband sometimes filling the other armchair, his feet without shoes, his feet up on the coffee table.

I studied the customers through my glasses, admiring the way they had to make their grief public in front of me before taking it back into private again. One woman introduced herself every time, always asked my name. She booked her room in eight-hour blocks and sometimes twenty-four, and she ate at the restaurant across the street, framed by the window, peering out.

I don't mind letting you know, she said one night. I've got all the money I can spend and nothing to spend it on and no real will.

I don't mind letting you know, she said on another. Sadness is very close to nothing. It is so much like nothing at all.

She always wore sweaters that were too big. Sweaters that covered her much too much. It took all her energy to smile, so she rarely did.

I'll tell you, she said, what I come to cry about. If you want to know.

I do, I said before I could stop myself, but I don't, but I shouldn't.

That's about right, she said. That's about right, isn't it?

I took her phone and gave her a key. As soon as the night guard came around, I asked if he'd watch the desk.

I was in the habit of going up to the rooms almost every night now, and I'd even started arranging customers around one I'd keep open for myself in the middle. My heart beat faster on the stairs, my lungs almost burning. And inside, it was like listening to an orchestra warming up. The instruments unaware of the others until every once in a while they locked into place. Harmony like magic. Magic like someone yawning in a crowd and everyone else yawning too, one by one, in strings.

I let out the breath I'd been holding. I checked my eyes for wetness of my own.

Some crying is just a tear down the cheek. Some a churning, a far-off emptiness, a stare. Some is like vomiting, a purge. Some is weightless, a body flipping, a body flailing, a body falling toward rocks. There is the crying of babies and children. Of desperation and need. There is the crying of confession, of salvation, of guilt. There is crying that takes the place of the unimaginable, the uncomfortable, the inconceivable. The crying that follows death into its darkness and pitch. Some is so clearly the crying of loss. Some is so clearly the crying of those who have lost. Tears blur the words of an unfinished letter. Tears lead like a path into sleep. Tears, unmoored from gravity, flow upward and outward in dreams. Some crying cannot be clamped or caged. With some, the chest warps and strains, the mind seals, plugs. Strength disappears, arms and legs. The stomach tries to stop it. Then the throat Then the muscles of the chin hold like a dam, fighting until they can't, fighting until they have to give way.

In my son's room that night, only his shoes and my husband's, side by side. In the center of the carpet. The police saw no evidence of a struggle or anything to indicate my family had packed and left. Nobody came forward to say they'd seen them. Nobody called demanding ransom.

Bodies streamed into the hospital as they always did. Bodies in all manner of shape and damage. I imagined my husband and son in the place of each. Bloodless, on the floor, the dog between them, it's four legs kinked and splayed. I imagined myself poking a finger into their wounds to test the depth. And my finger kept going. Deeper, deeper. Like I'd dropped a pebble into a well and was waiting for the splash and would never hear it.

I hired a private detective. I spent months searching on my own. I lost myself in the Internet and read and read. I believed in aliens for a time. In multiverses. In ghost ships and gods and airplanes vanishing in the sky.

I blamed my son. I had to. I thought, It must be his doing.

Premonitions dissolved. Suspicions led nowhere. I woke, heart racing in the empty house and empty bed. My thoughts splintered, and I grabbed at them, yanked them back. A pain began between my ribs, the pinpoint of stress spreading outward.

One of the boy's teachers told me he was the quietest student she'd ever had. He paid attention, but he hadn't said a thing all year. She didn't know what his voice sounded like. Couldn't even guess.

He was quiet at home, I said, but not like that.

It was hard not to see a shell he built around himself, she said. And in that shell, it was hard not to see a threat.

He was a teenager, I said. He was supposed to be angry.

The other kids liked him, the teacher said. I got that impression. I liked him too.

She told me they'd started sending my son to a therapist. Three periods a week. She was meant to help those who fell behind or those who had trouble grasping language or those who needed work to strengthen the right muscles. My husband had okayed it but hadn't said anything to me. My son hadn't either.

At my husband's firm, the other partners agreed he'd been a fantastic lawyer. They could tell he was a fantastic father, too, all those photos framed on his desk. The private detective found my husband had had three emotional affairs. But he hadn't seen any of the women in years, hadn't emailed, or spoken to them.

I'd always thought of myself as not easily rattled, but I finally had to admit I'd been shaken.

Had they deserved it? I asked. Had I? Could I have saved them? Can I still?

When the answers all seemed to be no, all seemed to be staying that way, I took a leave from work. I asked a neighbor to check the house once a week. I locked the door and left and wasn't sure if I'd ever come back.

The city had restaurants on every block, thousands of them. The one across the street was the type where candles flickered over white tablecloths. They'd pasted Chinese letters above the door. Hung photographs of gondolas and cathedrals, temples and the Taj Mahal.

There was no rule against eating there, and I began to go before my shifts. I often saw the woman alone at her table near the window. And one night, when we arrived at the same time, she asked if I wanted to join her. She asked again the next night, her voice unsure, rehearsed. The night after that, she sent a waiter.

I finally gave in. At her table, I told her that sometimes I didn't even order anything.

I'm not hungry either, she said. I only ever feel like I should eat.

I wasn't wearing my sunglasses and we made eye contact. In the candlelight, I could see her gathering her courage.

I just work there, I said. I'm not some kind of priest.

The waiter hovered and the woman spoke to him in a language I couldn't quite identify.

I might have ordered too much, she said. You can take whatever's left.

We stared out the window. People hustled by with their collars pulled up to cover their faces and necks and chins. The snow couldn't stop them. Couldn't slow the city down.

You said you wanted to hear, the woman asked. Do you still?

She smiled, pained. My daughter, she said. My daughter died, and I can't get over it. Everyone gave up on me. Everyone else has left.

Was she sick? I asked.

The woman shook her head. It was my fault, she said. It might have been.

We looked out the window again until the food came, and then we ate almost everything, passing dishes back and forth.

I checked the time and put my glasses on. I have to go, I said.

The woman crossed the street a half-hour later. How long would you like your room? I asked. What's your preferred method of payment?

An hour, she said. Only an hour tonight.

I swiped her card and gave her a key and marked the time. I took her phone. I locked it up.

The hour dragged as usual. Stretched like that moment between death and announcing the time of death. Tubes all lifeless. Wires. The monitor startled and humming.

When the woman didn't come back, I assumed she'd fallen asleep. I pressed the button for the bell in her room, rang it twice, three times, four. I was supposed to call the night guard, give him the number, and he was supposed to knock and check. Instead, I pocketed two keys and waited for him to come around. I asked him to watch the desk.

Someone had painted the metal bannister in the stairwell the same color as the cinderblock walls. The paint had bubbled and warted like skin. I forgot and touched it every time. I pulled my hand away every time.

On the fifth floor, I let myself into the room next to the woman's. I heard crying under my feet and to my left, but nothing on the right. I left the room and stepped back into the hallway. I went to her door. I cupped my hands against it. I shivered at the silence. I slid the key into the lock.

Inside, I saw an empty couch and chair. The yellow of the woman's coat hanging from the coatrack in the corner. I thought, She must be in someone else's room. Then I thought, She's gone too. She's disappeared.

I felt a push against the door. The woman behind it. Her laugh a true laugh, a real one.

I was standing against the wall, she said. Listening to you ring. Trying to get myself to leave.

She studied me.

Sit down a minute, she said.

She closed the door and locked it and led me to the couch. I took my sunglasses off and we sat there, side by side.

Do you ever imagine your daughter in here? I asked.

Yes, the woman said, of course.

Does she ever speak? Does she ever tell you where she is?

The woman didn't answer, and the two of us studied the wall like we might suddenly see beyond it. A customer wept in another room. One howled. One said, Why me, Why not me.

We should have made this impossible by now, I said. None of this should be possible anymore.

The woman touched her fingers to my back. Light, so light. I put my head on her shoulder.

Some crying turns like a hurricane, some falls in a patter, some hovers as mist. Some crying stalks the house in silence, pretending not to notice. Some lays dormant, ticking, a bomb. Some dismantles the horizon.

There is crying that can only come in new cities. There is crying of anger, of unhappiness, of remorse. Some crying is like being behind a curtain or being behind a world behind a curtain. Some ferries like a vessel or a ship, at the mercy of weather and wind. Some is fragile, on the edge, threatening to break until it does, a stone through glass, a sheet of ice on the sidewalk. There is crying of tragedy, of shame. There are snivels and yowls and caterwauls. And some crying sutures. Some stitches, some staples and binds. Some replaces, transplants, transforms. And some crying is the best way to get to blood, the best way to get to what lingers. Some is like seeing, almost. Some like understanding, almost. And some is like accepting, almost, what can't be, what won't be, what isn't and what is.

Nominated by Copper Nickel

THE DESCRIPTION I CARRY IN MY WALLET IN CASE EVE GOES MISSING AND I GO MUTE

by BOB HICOK

from CONDUIT

Too peaceful to chew ice, too big for her bed
in the dream of her doll house,
too soft for a career in sandpaper,
too angry with her mother to curtsy
to the Champs Élysées, too kind
to tell the sky it can be a real bastard,
too wet to be the out-of-body-experience
of rain, too expansive to be the thread
to anyone's needle, too tired to fold napkins
into swans, swans into ballerinas, ballerinas
into eating disorders, too shy to be a forest fire,
too introverted to be an orchid, too sad
about her grandmother's death
to trim a single branch from a single tree,
even a dead branch, even a branch that has fallen,
that has evolved to a stick, too honest
to be the best friend of a mirage,
too gentle to play the tambourine,
to make it as the Executive Producer of "Star Search,"
to go out for drinks with a hostile takeover,

too sad about her grandmother's death
to die herself in case the dead
aren't allowed to miss the dead, too much like air
not to be breath, too green
not to be spring, too mortal
to be one of the floating women of Chagall
and too mortal not to be the appetite
of his colors for the sun, too elsewhere
when she is gone, too gone when I blink,
too much of a garden for me to carry
in my not enough pockets, hands, mouths

Nominated by David Hernandez, Jane Hirshfield, Fred Leebron, Conduit

THE VERY GREAT ABYSS

fiction by PAM DURBAN

from THE CINCINNATI REVIEW

Her name is Miranda, and she's an Engler on her father's side, raised to be proud of the good her family did during a troubled time. To this day, at every family gathering, an ancient Engler is helped to their feet to tell the story of the weeks, months, years after the Battle of Gettysburg, and what always interested her about those stories was how new details kept being added, as though the stories hadn't ended yet. She and her brother Curtis had sat side by side among the relatives, listening hard, reviewing the details together later.

The story was about how the Engler men were too old to fight for the Union, but the family did their part. On July 1, 1863, the day the battle began, they fled to Carlisle, and when they returned on July 5, two days after it ended, they burned half a dozen dead horses in the yard. For days, as rain poured through the broken roof of the barn, they tended the wounded and dying there. They went out onto the battlefield and buried the dead, making no distinction, as some of their neighbors did, between the Union soldiers who deserved a decent burial and the traitors who could be left to rot where they fell, with only a thin covering of dirt and leaves kicked over them. An historical marker on the road in front of the Engler farm marked their place as a field hospital.

She'd been around real and make-believe soldiers all her life (her brother, her father, his father, and his), and that's how she knew that the man Jesse had brought to her door for his three o'clock appointment was dressed as a private in the Confederate army. His gray kepi sat straight on his head; his uniform was creased, like he'd just unfolded it, and a pair of new leather brogans stuck out from underneath the too-short pants. He took off his cap when she opened her door, an act of misplaced chivalry that almost made her laugh until she noticed his high-and-tight haircut. A Marine, she thought, and she saw the close clipped back of her brother's head disappear into the door of the bus the morning he left for Afghanistan. She looked at the floor to shake that sight, then went back to sizing up this soldier. A first-time reenactor, she guessed, but not a hard-core, like the men who swarmed over the battlefield every summer, obsessed with getting every nineteenth-century shoe and button right, except for their deaths, which were only temporary. He was spooked like a new one, too: fresh from their battlefield deaths, they came here to prove they were still alive.

Behind her soldier-boy, in the sour yellow light cast by the hallway wall sconces, Jesse checked the giant white wristwatch on her skinny arm. *Let's get this show on the road*, she signaled with her thin penciled eyebrows.

Last January Miranda had graduated from massage school in Pittsburgh. She knew Swedish massage and deep tissue and reflexology and Japanese shiatsu and acupressure. At school they'd called her a natural, said she had good hands, intuitive hands that felt the places where the body armors itself against the pain of walking through this world. She was the one the teachers called on in acupressure class. "Come show us the location of the Sea of Tranquility and the correct pressure to apply there," they said. "Come locate the Very Great Abyss." And every time, she'd go straight to the tiny point on wrist, hand, foot, eyebrow that set the life-force flowing again.

In March she'd rented this room, knowing what this place was, still believing she could do here just the work she'd been trained to do. Now it was September: the leaves on the oaks in Soldiers' National Cemetery were turning, the reenactment armies had left for their winter camps, and the show she was supposed to get on the road was the show you imagine as soon as you hear the name Gettysburg Massage. An old stone house where a wounded Union general had died during the battle, now reincarnated as a place where four local women, each for her own reasons, did old business. And if from time to time one of the women claimed to feel the edge of her mattress sag as though someone were sitting on it, they joked that it had to be the general. After all, this was the most haunted place in the country. Brochures in the lobby of every motel listed haunted restaurants, haunted houses, ghost tours of this hallowed, haunted ground. Why not a horny ghost from the last century? Some things, they joked among themselves, never change. Miranda joked along with them, and it *was* funny, though sometimes when she was alone in her apartment, away from the stone house and the person she was there, she allowed herself to imagine the general as just another wandering soul trying to outrun his sorrow.

Her room had two long narrow windows set high up in one wall so that the view was all sky, and she knew all its moods: bright with sun, gray with rain, pale and shining after. The wood floors in her room snapped and creaked; on cold days a steady blue flame burned behind the grate of the gas space heater in one corner. How had she gotten from Pittsburgh to here? That was the question she asked herself when she was alone in her room, and every morning as she ran on the battlefield roads, she worked it through again. She'd started running the day after Curtis left for Afghanistan, and she still hadn't missed a day. At first she ran because it kept her close to Curtis, who was a runner too, and to her father, who'd been a battlefield guide, and to this place and why it mattered. She ran along Seminary Ridge and past the Virginia monument—R. E. Lee and Traveler up there against the sky, keeping watch over the scene of the final disaster. She crossed the Emmitsburg Road and ran through the Wheatfield, the Peach Orchard, past Devil's Den and through the Valley of Death at the foot of Little Round Top. Great carnage happened here on the second day of the battle, their father told her and Curtis every time he took them there, but when night fell, so many men went out with lanterns to search for their fallen friends the valley was lit up bright as day.

Every day, her run ended in Soldiers' National Cemetery, where Lincoln had resolved that these dead had not died in vain. It was easy to share that resolve in that green, quiet place, to walk among the graves that widened out in semicircular rows from the tall soldiers' monument near the place where Lincoln spoke, and to keep the faith that there was some order and purpose to their deaths.

But in May Curtis died in Afghanistan, blown up, along with three of his men, by a suicide bomber in the Afghan army unit they were training, and shipped home in a sealed coffin, and it was like a hole got punched in the bottom of things and the meaning all drained out. She and her mother clung to each other while two Marines came up the walk and into the house and conveyed to them the commandant's deep regret. "My brother?" she said, but the tiny sound that came out of her mouth was more like a kitten's mew than a human voice. Her strength returned later as she held her mother back from trying to open the coffin, then put her on a plane to Hawaii with her sister the week after they buried him.

That same week she folded up the massage table her mother had given her for graduation and slid it into the closet in her room in the stone house, and she let Jesse bring in a new mattress and a set of purple satin sheets, because after Curtis died, it didn't matter what she did. You'd be surprised, she might have said if anyone had asked her, how you can adapt to almost anything once you find the right distance from it, the way she did every day, watching herself on the bed with the men, saying the things she said, laughing, moving her body as though she meant it. She hoped that her mother stayed in Hawaii and lived among strangers who'd never tell her what her daughter was doing, which would break her heart again. This, she thought, is how you live in vain.

Most of her clients were Confederate officers who swaggered into the room in tall shiny boots and red sashes, so she was surprised to see a private at the door, but his rank didn't matter, nothing about him mattered except that he'd paid Jesse and Jesse had brought him to her. He had a fallen-angel face and dark restless eyes that looked at her, the ceiling, floor and window, the closet door, the hall behind him, back to her again. She thought he'd been here before, he looked so familiar, and then she knew why. Curtis had watched everything that way when he was home between his second tour of duty in Iraq and the beginning of his third, in Afghanistan.

"This is Lacey," Jesse said.

"Afternoon, Private," she said, and she curtsied, which was ridiculous, and she knew it was ridiculous. She was about as far from the nineteenth century as you can get. No woman of that time ever chopped off her hair and bleached it white or wore a tiny diamond in her nose. They didn't go in for red bikinis back then either, or purple satin robes or black patent stiletto heels. What next, the women who worked there asked each other, hoop skirts? But Jesse said "Curtsy, girls," so they curtsied, which made no sense, and that was fine because nothing she did there made sense, and that was the point. So she curtsied, and most of the men got a kick out of pretending that in spite of the bikini and the heels, they were living in the nineteenth century. Her job was to help the two of them pretend as long as they could. To erase herself, become unreal, someone she no longer recognized, a citizen of a world so strange and foreign and so distant it could not be the same world where Curtis had died.

"Come on in, soldier," she said, and he winced. Jesse stepped in behind him and handed her the ticket, *Full Service* scrawled across it, which meant he'd come for sex, and they'd get there, but they had to pretend they weren't doing it until they were. *It*, doing *it*, because *it* was what *it* was, nothing more.

After Jesse closed the door, Miranda watched him scan the mattress, the pink scarf she'd draped over the lampshade to soften the light, the two white wicker chairs with the fringed shawls thrown over the backs facing each other across a wicker table, the things she'd brought here when she'd had other plans for this room. "Are you looking for something?" she asked, and he shook his head. She'd had those kind, too, the ones who wouldn't look her in the eye or speak, which was better, in a way: each of them alone in their own world, making no attempt to cross the silence between them.

"Have a seat," she said, and he eased himself down onto the edge of one chair, set his gray kepi on the wicker table between them. You can always tell a Marine, she thought. Sitting, walking, standing, they're ready for anything. She sat in the other chair and crossed her legs, let her robe fall open. "What regiment are you in?" she asked—most of them liked to tell that story—but he spread his arms and looked down at the uniform like he couldn't believe he was wearing it, like this was some kind of dream they were dreaming together. *You're right*, she wanted to say. *It is.*

"Could we dispense with the bullshit?" he said. He was jiggling his knee, eyes darting everywhere, definitely one of the spooked ones.

"You're the one in uniform, darling," she said. "But, sure, whatever. Why don't you take off your jacket, let me get my hands on you?" Some of the other women talked for as long as they could get away with, but she believed in giving good value for the money. There was dignity in doing something well, even pretending.

He unbuttoned the jacket, slipped it off, and handed it to her. Underneath he wore a white T-shirt, also creased and new. A lot of men showed up sweaty and smelly, but he was clean, and there was something touching about that. She went around behind his chair and touched the back of his neck, where the muscles spread out like tree roots into the shoulders. Tight as bridge cables; she'd figured as much. He flinched when she touched him and she wanted to say *I get it*. When someone touches you after you haven't been touched in a while, it's a shock. It brings you back to where you might not want to be because of what's waiting for you there. Best to stand back, watch yourself live, move, pretend to feel, to care.

By the time they were done with the bath and back in the room, she was barefoot and the robe was gone. He'd shucked his trousers, and he was holding a towel around his waist and breathing hard from the soaping and rubbing and stroking that went on during the bath. His eyes had stopped roaming, though, and now they watched her every move, sharp as hornets.

There was always a moment after she brought a full-service customer back from the bath when she wanted to kill the lights, pull the shades, take them down into the shadowlands, but Jesse said no. Darkness might spoil the illusion that they weren't about to do what he'd paid for. So she slid the dimmer switch down as low as she thought she could get away with. "Why don't you lie down and get comfortable? That's what I'm going to do," she said, and she knelt beside him on the mattress, slipped the straps of her top off her shoulders, and reached around to unhook the back.

"You don't mind, do you?" She looked up at him as she unhooked her top because it was time to make that move. "I work better this way," she said, moving her shoulders the way she always moved her shoulders at this moment. She took two steps back from herself like she'd been doing every day since the soldiers came up the walk and told them about Curtis. Two steps, three, four. She watched herself move, heard herself talk and pretend to care whether he minded that she'd taken off her top. Watched herself being someone else. If she could just get far enough away, it wouldn't matter that Curtis was gone or that she was doing this.

"Okay by me," he said, and he lay on his back with his arms behind his head, watching her breasts.

She squeezed some oil onto her hands (unscented to leave no trace for another man or woman to find) and slid them down his legs, knelt at his feet, kneaded and stroked, worked her knuckles into the dip just under the ball of the foot. The Bubbling Spring it's called in reflexology, The Root of Life, the wellspring of the life-force. He grunted like men do when something pleases them.

She glided her hands up the backs of his calves and around to the front of his thighs. She straddled his thighs and worked her hands up the front of the thick quad muscles and under the edge of the towel. "Any particular area you'd like me to focus on?" she asked, and she loosened his towel, opened and eased it out from under him, became an onlooker again, that strange, submerged, departed feeling. Then they went on from there.

Next day he was back, out of uniform this time, but with the same sweet, spooked face, the dark high-and-tight, those restless eyes. Jesse discouraged repeat full-service customers; she claimed a sixth sense for the vice squad or violent weirdos, so none of the women had regulars, other than a few carefully vetted men from York and that lawyer from Chambersburg who thought he was far enough from home no one would recognize him. But it looked like Jesse had made an exception, because she beamed as she handed over the slip—another full-service session.

The second day was like the first: down to the bath and back to the room and down onto the mattress, where he lay with his arms behind his head, looking so serious she had to say something. "Smile, sweetness," she said. "We're here to have fun." That was a lie, and she saw that he knew it too, because he winced and looked away from her as though he were embarrassed for both of them.

There was a puckered scar on the underside of his arm, a small purple drawstring pouch of flesh. She knew a bullet wound when she saw one, and she also knew not to ask about it. Curtis was shot through the calf during his first tour in Iraq, but he wouldn't talk about it, and when this soldier saw her looking, he said, "Work around it," no sweetness in his face then. She unhooked her top, asked if he minded, moved her shoulders, said, "Any particular area you'd like me to focus on?"

"I'd like to touch you," he said. "Please." Usually when this moment came, most men got flirtatious or gross, or they just grabbed, so his directness made her wary and hopeful and confused.

"What's your name?" she asked, and she moved off him long enough to strip off the bottom of her bikini and push it onto the floor.

"Travis," he said. "You?"

"Lacey," she said, smiling down at him.

"Come on," he said. "Nobody's actually named Lacey."

"You got me," she said. "It's Miranda," she said. "But you never heard it from me." And she rolled the condom on, straddled and rode him, and where they went felt good, but not so good that it meant anything or she lost track of the minutes left in his full-service hour.

"You're a vet, right?" she said afterward, hooking her top.

And that was a mistake and she knew it as soon as she said it because it made him wary, just like Curtis used to get. Ask him a question, any question, about his service, and *you* became the enemy; he wasn't going to tell you anything. "Marine Corps reconnaissance," Travis said. He stomped his feet down into his boots. "Afghanistan."

The word made her heart surge in fear. "My brother was there," she said. "His third tour. The first two were in Iraq."

He stopped lacing his boots, looked at the floor. "Where is he now?" he asked.

"He's dead," she said. "He died. In May. A suicide bomber." Other words rushed up behind those, and she put her hands over her mouth to hold them back, but it was too late. She'd told him Curtis was dead; it was out in the world now; it couldn't be called back.

Travis's face got really still. He swallowed hard and tied his shoes. "I'm sorry."

"I know," she said. "The Marine Corps already expressed its deep regret."

He slapped his knees and stood up, nodded, that quick, tight Marine nod. *Affirmative*, she expected him to say. He couldn't wait to get out of there.

She was sure he wouldn't be back, but next day there he was, and Jesse was so pleased, she practically wiggled like a puppy. *Got us a live one here*, Miranda could almost hear her say. He'd paid for another full-service session, and when the door closed, she said, "You again," as though she couldn't care less, which was about half-true.

He stood with his back against the door. "We're done with that other business," he said. "I want an actual massage. No fooling around. A real one."

"What makes you think I can do that?" she said. Easy, he said. He'd seen her folded massage table in the closet when she'd opened it to hang up her robe before their last session. Of course he had. He'd been in reconnaissance, and those men notice everything, Curtis had said. He'd talked about their skills all the time. Travis's eyes were steadier now, sad and warm and brown. And could she believe, he said, that it had taken him this long to work up the courage to ask for this?

"Nice try but not really," she said, teasing him a little, surprising herself.

"Okay," he said. "You got me. I liked the sex."

"Sit down," she said, and she knew she was trembling. *Me too*, she couldn't say. She stood behind his chair, smoothed the tight muscles in his shoulders. She'd forgotten how much you can learn about a person from studying the nape of their neck. It's where you see how they must have looked as a child, standing on tiptoe, craning to look through the window or over the fence, at a life they couldn't wait to get out into, one they trusted was going to be good. All those hopes stayed in a person's neck, and what became of them stayed there, too, the hurt and the sadness and the armor they'd put on to protect them from hurt and sadness.

She'd felt that armor in the bodies of the Union and Confederate re-enactors who came here straight from the battlefield and lay on her mattress afterward and talked about how we should bomb the fuck out of Iraq and Afghanistan and take out Iran and Syria while we were at it. They practice a seventh-century religion over there, the men said, so let's help them get back where they belong. Her father used to talk like that, only it was the Stone Age we should have bombed the North Vietnamese back into. Curtis said the same about the Iraqis after his second tour, the one that changed him. "The only way to win is to kill them all, and since we're not going to do that, we're not going to win," he'd said, in a perfectly reasonable, flat voice, as if just stating a logical conclusion.

She didn't want to put her hands on Travis's body in any way that made him real, but she did, and he was. "Well, look," she said as she smoothed his shoulder muscles. "How long are you here for?"

"I'm heading back to Arizona tomorrow," he said, eyes closed.

"You've come a long way," she said.

Then a struggle ensued, she felt it under her hands. "I came here for my buddy," he said.

"Did you promise him or something?" *Please say yes*, she thought.

She'd had those kind before, wished he could be predictable, familiar.

"No," he said. "Let's get this show on the road."

They were both embarrassed then. She opened the closet door, slipped on a robe over the absurd bikini, kicked the stilettos off her feet. She slid the massage table out and set it up and flared a sheet over it. She hadn't forgotten how to flare a sheet, let it float and settle. How to smooth it and cover it with another sheet and a light blanket and invite him to undress as much as he felt comfortable with and crawl underneath. She turned away while he undressed. Modesty had come back into their dealings with one another, as it should, she remembered, when you're dealing intimately with another's body. She heard zippers, dropped shoes, the rustle of the sheet as he got up onto the table, and then she stepped up next to the table and tucked the sheet around his legs.

She brought her hands up under the back of his head, cradled his skull and felt the tightness along the occipital ridge. *Where does it hurt?* she wanted to ask him, but she knew that his answer would scare them both. *Everywhere*, he might have said. She lowered his head to the table, brushed her fingers across his forehead, smoothing the deep lines there. She laced her fingers through his, pressed her thumbs on his open palms, pressed the fleshy web between thumb and forefinger. She found the acupressure points at the top of his chest and she leaned in hard; she remembered how this might be done. She moved around the table, around his body, pressed her fingers, palms, elbows into the stuck places where the body locks up to avoid the pain of walking through this world. Lesser Surge, Little Miracle, Small Ocean, Royal Spirit, she worked them all, and when she looked up, the hour was almost over, so she moved to the Very Great Abyss, which is a very small spot on the palm side of the wrist below the thumb. She pushed into it on one of his hands, then the other; she had not forgotten.

She glanced at him again and saw tears leaking from the corners of his closed eyes, running down the sides of his face, but he didn't turn his head or lift his free hand to wipe them away.

"What was your friend's name?" she asked, and she kept her hand on the pressure point. She leaned into it, and he groaned, and she remembered the groan the old people talked about, the one that people heard for days after the battle. It came from everywhere and nowhere, they said, as if the sky, the light, the ground itself were groaning. There was nowhere to go away from that sound. Inside your own house, with the windows shut tight, the doors latched and bolted, you still heard it.

"William," he said.

"My brother's name was Curtis," she said, and then, as though she'd called him and he'd come, she saw Curtis at her graduation in Pittsburgh in January. Curtis in his full dress uniform—blue tunic, white pants, shiny black belt and shoes, white hat—walking down the street without an overcoat, walking into the knife edge of the wind, the icy, swirling snow. And she'd grabbed his arm, said, Curtis, it's twenty degrees out here, don't you need a coat? But he'd said no. A coat was not part of the full dress uniform, he said, and he would wear it properly, to honor her. That cold day in Pittsburgh she'd held her brother for a long time; she'd never loved him more.

"You loved your friend," she said, and Travis nodded.

He kept his eyes closed, as if talking in his sleep. "I just wanted to get close to a place he cared about," he said. "He was from Alabama, and one of his people fought here in a regiment that attacked Little Round Top. He could tell you every move they made. He was a southerner, and that was a big deal for him. I spent the first morning at Little Round Top, walking over the ground where his people fought. For him. Then I came here, and you were good to me."

She put her hand over his mouth. "I do not understand devotion," she said.

He reached up and took it away and held it. "Yes, you do," he said. "You do." And he lay there with tears running out of the corners of his eyes and down his cheeks, and neither of them moved to wipe them away.

And then his hour was up. She pulled the sheet up under his chin, smoothed his forehead with her thumbs. She left the room so he could dress, and went into the little bathroom in the hall. She leaned her head against the cool tile wall and let herself down into that cold Pittsburgh day. She felt how much she'd loved her brother, and how that love had turned to grief, as though grief had slipped in disguised as love, and she didn't recognize it until it was too late to hide or run, so she let it come over her, and when she was done, she wiped her face with both hands and went back to her room.

Travis was standing beside one of the wicker chairs. "I'm going to stop working here soon," she said, but then she had to sit down. It was as if, since Curtis died, she'd been walking with her head down through the whipping Pittsburgh snow, and now she'd looked up and seen a future beyond this room.

"That's good," he said. "Because you've got some serious chops." He touched her shoulder. "Out," he said, like Curtis used to say when he ended a call from Afghanistan; then he was gone.

Now the day is ending, and she goes, as she's gone at the end of every day since her mother left for Hawaii, back to the Engler farm where she somehow still belongs. Every day her routine has been the same. Park in the yard behind the house, walk up the lane to the mailbox and sort the mail on the slow walk back to the house under the darkening sky, so that she can put off as long as possible the moment when she looks up and sees the banner with the gold star on a white background bordered in red, hanging in the window of the mudroom off the back of the house. But tonight she doesn't look away, and at the top of the steps that lead to the mudroom door, she stops. She doesn't want to go into the silent house tonight or see the framed medals from four wars and the folded flags in their wooden cases that hang on the dark bead-board walls of the living room, or the folded flag from Curtis's coffin on the coffee table where her mother had been persuaded to leave it when it was time to go to the airport.

Tonight she feels plain and newly arrived from a distant place. She wants to sit on the mudroom steps under Curtis's star, in sight of the barn where her family once did what they could about suffering, and watch the moon rise over the far ridge. It's September now, the Wine-sap apples ripening in the small orchard behind the barn. She wishes Curtis were here with her to feel the season change. She wants it so badly it almost seems that the wanting could bring him back, so she lets herself believe that for a minute, and then she comes back to what she knows. Curtis is dead. The scale is forever tipped that spilled him into darkness. Even so, she's free to imagine him sitting here beside her. She imagines that she would tell him about Travis and how she felt his love for his friend mix with his grief, and then she felt her own. Felt, feels, will feel forever, because there's nowhere to run where sorrow can't find you, Curtis, she would tell him; you might as well try and run out from under the sky.

She sits while the sky darkens and the moon rises and three scrawny barn cats weave around her feet, waiting to be fed. She thinks of Travis on the road to Arizona and how she'd like to tell him that when she said she'd soon be leaving the stone house where she'd tried in vain to forget what she'd lost, she'd meant now, tonight. She'd like him to know that she's glad to picture the two of them, setting off under the same sky.

Nominated by The Cincinnati Review

403

BLACK BOX

by SANDRA LIM

from SMARTISH PACE

We were in a small, grim café.

She sipped pure black droplets
from a tiny cup.

Make him come back, she said,
her voice like something brought up intact
from the cold center of a lake.

It was the kind of story I like, and I wanted
to get it right, for later:

The hot morning in the café,
feeling encroached on by a cloud
of dusty ferns and creepers

and the low earth of duty.

I can't read a book
all the way through, she said,
and most days I'm only unhappy.

My heart is always with the lovers.

Nominated by Maureen Stanton

A TALE OF TWO TROLLS

fiction by MARCUS SPIEGEL

from SANTA MONICA REVIEW

Here come the frogs. The hooded clerics of the meme. Long have they uploaded their darkness to the virtual realm. It falls on them now to bring their crypto-anarchy to the world.

Yuri and Winch are zipping their way through the tower-shaded streets, just another rain-rinsed car in the traffic gauntlet. "We're making fine time," Yuri says, cracking a window to dispel some of the fermented cabbage odor Winch carries on his clothes. "Keep speeding when you can. Quick, cut this guy off."

Winch grinds the pedal and makes a lane change to the left. "Too many normies leaving their slave posts for the day," he says. "It's like Warcraft level three out here. You'd need a flamethrower to clear a path."

Yuri is snickering as he consults his reflection in the flip down mirror only to find his fear confirmed: for the third consecutive time he's neglected to shave the right hemisphere of his face. Even if he's merely sprouted some whiskers there, the omission is disheartening.

"Do we have any stims?" Winch asks.

"My ADD meds? Left them back at the Bunker."

The Bunker is their cute name for the basement apartment they rent, the two friends and collaborators sleeping in twin bunk beds, both of them on top, like gods floating on clouds. They reserve the bottoms for storage—it's easier to keep a laundry bag on a spare mattress than to go to the trouble of folding up clothes and tucking them away in a dresser. Lately, they've abandoned the drudgery of laundry altogether, preferring to wear the same uniform without fail. It's these kinds of rituals that proliferate order in the world. And order is what's missing. Order über alles.

"From now on I'm not depending on you and your stupid doctor," says Winch. "I don't see what purpose there is in putting myself through this anymore."

"Yes, right, such a crucifixion."

Winch transmits his irritation to the cars in his vicinity, honking, even cutting off a Volkswagen, which theoretically ought to be an ally. "I've got one of those evil headaches again."

"Hang in there. We can snort some guarana powder in the university parking lot."

"I want real stims, damnit. I've already had caffeine."

"Maybe you're forgetting that the guarana vine is the most caffeinated substance known to exist?"

"I don't like it," says Winch.

"Try to be more stoical. This movement is bigger than your subjective needs, *mein Kind*. Besides, we need to save that medication for when we go live."

✽   ✽   ✽

Since the world is increasingly the battleground of propaganda, practical wisdom seems to require that everyone become her own Leni Riefenstahl. It's either that or become somebody else's dupe.

Yuri and Winch, for their part, have taken measures to adapt to the new counterpunching regime. Their most significant attempt at persuasion is the YouTube show and podcast *Tadpole Island*. They've recorded six episodes thus far, most of which feature their only other friend in the flesh, Olaf Norquist, the self-styled black magician and alt-right political commentator. But they have yet to offer up their golden ball to strangers perusing the net.

Tadpole Island is hosted by Yuri's alter-ego, Zepé—basically Yuri in a frog suit, speaking in an invented accent that Norquist has described as a cross between Jamaican, Aussie, and Martian. The frog character, of course, is modeled on Pepe, crude demiurge of the meme, though somehow Yuri's Zepé suit calls to mind Kermit or Super Mario similarly clad. Either way, Zepé is destined to be a mammoth success.

As Zepé, Yuri would interview controversial pundits and thinkers whom the normies would be all too quick to label crackpots and cranks. Not that they were about to be cowed by such slander, but as the show garnered prestige, Yuri and Winch would replace their obscure guests with right-wing-leaning celebrities, all two of them, before moving on from there to their more glamorous political rivals. They would lure stars onto the show only for Zepé to vanquish them with his scary reservoir of arguments and facts.

Who says they didn't have a brutal purpose in mind?

*　*　*

As soon as the gaps in the traffic begin to stretch out, Winch zigs and zags in full beast mode, like he's racing a Batmobile down the Autobahn. He wails something unintelligible. One of the reasons Yuri lets Winch drive his Honda Accord is that driving has proven to be one of the most responsive treatments for soothing Winch's hyperactivity. Yet it doesn't seem to be having the desired effect today. Winch is especially vulnerable to a flare-up after slugging back an extra large Mountain Dew slushie in five minutes flat, no regard for the brain freeze.

Complicating matters further is the fact that Winch, like Yuri, is an *incel*—an involuntary celibate. Monks and fakirs of ancient times have long understood that celibacy is the most potent form of Red Bull on the market. Although Yuri and Winch haven't chosen their lot, they're nevertheless profiting from the alchemy, particularly now that they've made a pact to quit beating off to the sleek goddesses of porn. No fapping for these two. They shook on it with gobs of spit on their hands. No matter the degree or the intensity of their sexual appetites, they hold their breath, they take shivering showers, they do whatever they must to resist.

"How about turning up that Shadilay?" Winch says. He can listen to the Kekistani anthem once an hour and still not tire of its mellow funkiness.

"Enough of your silly frog beats," says Yuri, scrolling on his Droid. "It's time for more crushing themes. Black metal is what we want."

Winch dries the glassy film of sweat from his forehead with the sleeve of his shirt. His hair is chestnut, though lightened by a heavy snow of dandruff that flakes onto his clothes whenever he brushes a hand through it, as he often does, his bangs being just long enough to turret his eyes. Eyes that are not blue, by the way, but a burnished copper color, like pennies gilded by the sun.

As for Yuri's eyes, they're pretty freaky these days. He's one of those who have converted myopia into an advantage: ever since his Amazon order came in the mail, some weeks ago, he's been in the habit of wearing contact lenses in the mode of a predatory cat. Always been a cat person. He alternates between Bengal tiger and jaguar mainly, throwing in mongoose once in a while to keep things from becoming rote.

407

Today is a Jaguar Friday. Yuri's irises blaze yellow and are shaped like crescent moons.

Winch charges through a red light on Yonge Street, inciting a tide of honking hate. "Fuck you too," he says to no one in particular. All that rage though is soon in the rearview as they cruise along through the pastoral scenes of the University of Toronto campus. The rain has stopped, or at least thinned to a patter, but there's still something Sturm und Drang in the weather. Typhoon winds snapping at the trees.

On the stereo the hammer clank of guitars and synthesizers pulses through the car with a supersonic ferocity. The screeching voice that comes in after the intro doesn't sound anthropomorphic in the least, let alone like the voice of a Swede.

Winch has a way of doing a modified mosh while he drives. "You think we could red-pill that goof?"

"Professor Badendorf? He seems pretty committed to staying a cuck."

*　*　*

Seven years back, Yuri took a course with Professor Badendorf in German. Never mind that the professor's hair—or what he had left of it—was fluffy and staticky and that stooping near the chalkboard in his cardigan he looked like a scarecrow that had failed to keep away the crows, Badendorf had some genuine charisma to draw on. He was a fountain of anecdotes; his jokes were rich in schadenfreude; his memory was as vast and quick as an algorithm. It was impossible not to be impressed with Badendorf's rabbinical learning when it came to Goethe and Schiller.

Unfortunately, Yuri was prevented from completing his course with Badendorf because of illness. Who knew whooping cough could be so crippling? Even more tragic was that, since it was too late to withdraw without academic penalty, he was forced to metabolize an F. To have appealed to the records department he would have to have obtained a doctor's letter, but, feverish and dizzy, it would have been unthinkable to rise from bed and denude himself of his blankets and pyjamas long enough to dress in his shabby winter coat and face the burning winds while he waited for the bus.

Naturally, once he got well, he expected Badendorf to spearhead his vindication. Surely, it would have cost the professor very little to have championed Yuri's cause. And yet, astonishingly, in spite of being cozily ensconced at the university—a tenured prof with a cascade of publications to his credit—Badendorf could not be coaxed into assisting

Yuri's attempts to have the injustice overturned. Yuri even visited the professor every day for a time in order to ask what he might do to heal the damage until the professor said he would not speak to him about it anymore. The old master had given out the last of his instructions. It didn't seem to matter if his former student perished from the elements now that he was out of the professor's sight.

Badendorf, of course, didn't exactly score points for heroism in the way he handled Yuri's struggle, but that's quite in the past. Chalk it all up to youthful sorrow. It's because of a new list of sins that Badendorf must now atone.

Which sins basically come down to the professor's politics of malice. Several months ago, Badendorf was on a CBC news show when he prophesized that far-right political groups would soon be sneaking up in Canada. A general decency in the Canadian character may not be enough to thwart the onslaught once it achieved a certain allure.

If this remark wasn't sufficiently perverse, he followed it with an even more vigorous masochism, writing a series of op-eds that were published in fake news outlets all across the bleeding lands of the West. Don't be taken in by the newfangled rhetoric, the grim professor advised. The same bitter specter is about to spit fire once again.

Badendorf's intellect had surely eroded over the years since Yuri's course with him. His political fears seemed like the ravings of a geriatric mind. Still, he had delivered a swift kick to Yuri and Winch's movement and he deserved to be challenged.

It's high time Badendorf became a special guest on *Tadpole Island*.

* * *

"Are we double sure this is his sedan?" Winch looking ahead to the baby blue car.

Yuri flicks a dark smile in the direction of his compatriot. "Don't you remember the combination of I, P, and G in his license plate? Unscramble those letters, Winch?"

"Uh, gip?"

"Keep at it. Pattern recognition is a mark of intelligence. If you don't start leveling up soon, you're sure to be replaced by AI."

At that moment the *Pitchfork into Shit* album they're listening to ends with its much-celebrated soundbites of detonating missiles while the lead vocalist holds his killing howl for a duration that borders on supernatural. Afterwards, the silence that descends quickly becomes claustrophobic. Yuri copes—he can still read print media in snatches—

but Winch is soon approaching a low-level panic. His eyes take on a desperate quality, like a dog's in a thunderstorm.

"Well, should we give episode six of *Tadpole* another listen?" Yuri wonders out loud.

"Put it on," Winch turning quickly, spraying Yuri with dandruff, "only screw the intro. I want to hear the part where Norquist debunks the so-called debunkers of Pizzagate, proving that Podesta was as big a perv as Wiener."

"Glad to hear you're cultivating your mind, Winchester," Yuri says, though secretly he's hurt that Winch doesn't want to listen to Zepé's opening monologue, clearly the highlight of the show. In any case, it doesn't take long before he's feeling restless. "I'm going to wander around campus to see if I can track down Badendorf," he says, sliding out into the chilled evening air. "You stay here. You may have to perform the kidnapping yourself."

❖   ❖   ❖

Yuri ambles up the dark lawn of the campus, taking meditative puffs from his vape. His exhalations materialize as a wispy genie, thinly visible and redolent of mango before fading away. He carries a briefcase to help him pass as a student—and, well, it's a convenient place to stash the taser he will need should he become involved in a contretemps with the professor. Sure, some people die from being stunned with a taser, but Yuri's learned to live with the burden of all his cumulative risks.

Ducking beneath a contorted maple tree in the quad, he takes one last suck of the mango-flavored tobacco from his electronic device before climbing the staircase to the old castle of Brennan Hall. He threads through the snaky interior, passing small libraries of rare books for specialists. Various humanities departments unfurl before him. He can't help but notice there is something dingy and slapdash about Germanic Studies. The lighting is bad, the floor overrun with a garish orange carpet.

He knocks on Badendorf's door, calling out the professor's name, "Helmut, oh Helmut." The professor though—let's give our Mephisto his due—is too clever to be taken in by the tender bait.

Outside the office is a little slot filled with graded papers and Yuri amuses himself by skimming the student drivel. In the margins of the pages he recognizes Badendorf's distinctive script—the lean sexiness of his j's and h's, the round cheeriness of his o's, the lit menorah of his capital w. The arguments are so weak in logic they smack of conspiracy theories. But as he reads on his mirth mutates to rage.

He digs up a pen from a pocket of his briefcase and proceeds to shade out one of Badendorf's flattering appraisals. Doing his best to mimic the professor's fancy graffiti, he writes above it: "Total confusion! This paper is a marvel of idiocy! You should be whipped for writing such trash!"

* * *

Winch has often noticed a strange effect after he's snorted a lot of guarana powder: he begins to crave gaming in the worst kind of way. Not just any kind of gaming either—retro gaming. He wants to drop back into the primitive cosmos of the original *Zelda* or *Castlevania*. RPGs in their infancy. He wants his avatar to explore medieval towns and hamlets, calling on smiths and potion brewers to guide him along on his chivalrous path.

Above all, he wants to heat up a Pillsbury Toaster Strudel and play *Metroid*. The feeling he gets from *Metroid* is indescribable—it's almost mystical. He saves *Metroid* for when he's in a very special mood.

The way he prepares the strudel is not trivial either. It has to be smeared with icing to the point where you'd almost think it overdone, that it's going to be way too gooey and sweet. But that's where you want to be when it comes to the icing, that's the—haha—sweet spot. The upshot is that Winch's icing preferences place him in a double bind. He can limit himself to a single icing packet per strudel—a situation that is far from ideal—or he can choose to glaze his strudels with the amount of icing that matches his desires, in which case his taste buds reach a transcendent plane but then he's left with half a box of dry strudels that end up going to waste.

His phone vibrates in his jeans pocket so close to his dick it makes him hard. "So," says Winch. "You got that cuck by the collar?"

"I can't find him," Yuri says. "He was supposed to be done his lectures by now, and he's not in his office. We might have to modify our approach."

"Yuri? After we kidnap Badendorf and get him set up in his cage could I maybe game for a while? I'm really jonesing to draw the curtains, turn on the toaster oven, and curl up in front of the—"

"Winch. Focus, okay?"

"—for three solid hours of *Metroid*."

"This is bigger than gaming, alright?"

Winch always gets nervous whenever Yuri says anything is bigger than gaming because he's already been traumatized by a mother who routinely

411

punished him by restricting his gaming rights, even going so far as to confiscate his controller for entire weekends, which, of course, is especially cruel—that being the time when he'd be needing it most.

"Did you hear me, Winch? This might be the most crucial thing you hear in your life. Sehr wichtig, you read me?"

"Go on."

"I want you to put on the frog suit."

Well, when Winch hears this he just about flips out, hopping up and down on the seat like he's being electrocuted. "But that suit is sacred. You're the only one who can wear it, Yuri. There's no way I can even pretend to be Zepé."

"Just get in the suit."

Winch can hardly breathe he feels so honored.

❊   ❊   ❊

Yuri and Winch had long ago decided that it was not enough to launch *Tadpole Island* on the Light Web. They had to employ a double strategy; they would simultaneously infiltrate and transgress.

To this second end they would have to kidnap the venerable professor of Germanic Studies. They would intimidate him with death threats—and other nightmare suggestions—before drugging him and trapping him inside a burlap sack.

Once Badendorf was loaded into the Honda's trunk, they would drive to the Bunker and transfer him into what they were calling his "cage"— which actually looked more like an igloo made out of cardboard boxes that they'd spent much of the night constructing.

The days would creep along for Badendorf. He would have little to hope for apart from his two meals of frozen corn nibblets served to him in a doggie bowl.

At some point during the professor's imprisonment they would haul him from his cage and force him to do the show. Badendorf and Zepé would have a dialogue. Zepé would quash him with his superior intellect. Zepé and Winch would then subject him to some light torture on camera, afterwards returning him to his cage.

Those Dark Web episodes of *Tadpole* would be legendary in no time. Zepé would be elevated to a great figure in the theater of cruelty, on par with De Sade. Oh, they could taste their numbers growing already. In a matter of days, or even hours, their subscriber list would bloom.

Nothing clickbaits like suffering.

Yuri/Zepé would soon be christened as the highest minister of the alt-right. Perhaps even its darling and prince. He would soon have an ensemble of subordinates working under him, coordinating his appointments and interviews with the media, leaving him free to calculate his next set of moves in the war of memetics.

❋   ❋   ❋

The hunt for Badendorf is very much on. Having glimpsed on a poster that a celebrity academic is giving a talk at an auditorium in another building, Yuri decides to attend in hopes of spotting the apostate professor pontificating to the crowd. If Badendorf doesn't have a chair on the panel he's sure to be injecting himself into the discussion with those typical verbose rants disguised as questions. Pompous fool that he is.

But by the time Yuri makes his way to the auditorium it's nothing more than a deserted banquet. A few nasally-voiced stragglers lurk about, chitchatting, nibbling black grapes, cubes of marbled cheese. Yuri scrutinizes every cardigan. No sign of the professor.

Yuri's ready to about-face—he's already chafing with remorse for ordering Winch to don the frog suit—when he notices a smile and a fluttering hand. Has to assume the gesture is not meant for him. When was the last time he stirred any stranger to spontaneous joy?

That's no stranger though—it's Hannah from European Mythology. Yuri sat beside her, three rows behind the blackboard, at a little kidney-shaped desk carved up with obscenities. They used to meet in the cafeteria to talk Ovid over cinnamon buns. Hannah always dressed in flagrantly wanton colors. She had a predilection for silky fabrics; she was perpetually rereading Virginia Woolf's *The Waves*.

Today Hannah is modeling an updo, swirling honey brown hair constrained at intervals with silvery clips. Her clothes—dark jeans, knitted sweater, a scarf coiled about her throat—are in a more downbeat register than in the past, though her smile is in the puckish range, somewhat tentative and confined to one side of her mouth. No makeup either. Won't get any argument from Yuri there. He resents the chicanery of lipstick and mascara.

"Yuri, what are you doing here? You recognize me, I hope?"

"Of course, Hannah." Yuri scans the room. How does he know he's not being manipulated? Badendorf deploying a saucy girl to distract him. "I suppose you haven't changed very much. Maybe you dress a little differently, more like a—" he swallows hard to avoid saying *normie*, "adult, I guess. Like one of those *Sex in the City* chicks."

Hannah laughs, showing her methodical, straight teeth. In their undergrad days those teeth were bound in purple braces. All that oral conditioning has turned her smile into an orthodontist ad. "Well, you look different too," she says. "What kind of hairstyle is that? And those combat boots you're wearing. I'd say you look a bit more like a punk if it wasn't for those contacts. Bright yellow eyes look good on you, actually."

Should he tell her that they glow at night? You can discern him from a distance, a fit mate in the jungle. Sexual selection requires eyes that leap past one's inherited genes into the transhuman domain. Well, Yuri doesn't mind being ahead of the curve, Übermensch already, Winch still needs to catch up.

Yuri is suddenly conscious of being an incel. His virginity weighs on him like an armor he's forced to wear. He is rigid inside it, barely animate. Proving dangerous to talk to Hannah—it's always been dangerous. They'd gone on a couple of dates together and it had all been so hopelessly romcom. When he kissed her on a terrace—champagne, stars out, a balmy windless night—she told him she didn't see him like that, for her he would always remain a friend. In a script they would have been one-third of the way to a boy-gets-girl denouement. Yuri would still have had plenty of scenes left to establish himself as the ideal arrangement of rugged pirate and domesticated eunuch. Gradually, though, he saw that their romance would not play out like Hollywood. He had not been cast as Hannah's male counterpart but instead as a victim in a low-budget horror film. His death would be unforgettable, harrowing to the extreme. He had not figured out if he would be stabbed, strangled, or thrown into a pool of lava, but he knew that it would be an exquisite end.

"Not a punk," he says. "It's just that I get to wear whatever I want. Being that I'm self-employed."

"You're not a programmer, are you?"

"No, I host a show."

"Like . . . for television?"

Yuri can't stop himself from sneering. "I would have to be pretty stupid to chain myself to the carcass of that dying elephant. Television is deader than God. My show will be for the internet. I'm about to release the first episode in a couple of weeks."

Hannah takes a small step back as if she wants to see him anew. "You seem very much the same, only somehow edgier. Maybe even angrier? Am I allowed to say that?"

"I'm not the censorship police," Yuri says, casting a sour look at the celery stalks and raw cauliflower trees arrayed on the table beside him. With the token exception of lettuce, which he could tolerate in sandwiches, anything plucked out of the soil, pigmented by lycopenes and beta-carotenes, brings on a form of nausea that reminds him of the spins. And yet he must struggle against his sense of loathing because he suddenly feels lightheaded to the point where it's even conceivable that he could faint. He picks up a round slice of cucumber—a relatively inoffensive vegetable all things considering—and dunks it into a parsley-dusted dip. Then he stands there wincing for a few seconds before he commits to the necessary evil. "You can judge me as you like," he says, risking the bite. "Anyway, I'm sure you've already bought into the rumors you've no doubt heard."

Hannah adjusts the strap of her leather handbag so that it's slung across the opposite arm. Like an arrow quiver, Yuri thinks. She'd make a hot Amazonian shit-kicker. Or would she be more at home in an enchanted land of horse-riding mages and elves?

"I'm not sure I've heard much of anything about you," Hannah says. "It seemed to me that at some point you disappeared."

"I was sick. I'd rather not go into it."

Hannah nods. "Well, I'd give your show a listen."

Yuri feels a tide of tension ray through the core of his being. Should he tempt himself with the possibility? That Hannah is the one who has been foretold? The heroine who, with a kiss, could break the spell of his inceldom?

Yuri, captive on a fire-wreathed altar, cries out to his saviour. Free me from these shackles! His cheeks flush to a rosé, lurid with expectation.

"You'd adore the show," he says. "Yes, I could really see you getting into it."

"What's it called?"

"*Tadpole Island*," Yuri says gravely. "Think *Dick Cavett* without the commercials."

        ✧   ✧   ✧

Camouflaged in the green quad, Winch squats froggishly some meters behind Badendorf's sedan. For comfort he strokes the handle of his samurai sword in its holster. It was his idea to add a symbol of war to Zepé's costume. Only two weeks ago, when he and Yuri came to the university to make notes on the professor's arrival and exit times, they had seen a racoon clawing scraps out of a garbage can, and Winch had pursued it with a stick until it fled up a tree. If Winch could only find it again today—or at the very least a gopher or squirrel—he would be pleased to test out his swordplay on a living thing.

Sometimes at the Bunker, when Yuri is still knocked out on dream tablets in the dawn, Winch would undertake some martial drills with the sword, lunging and thrusting in vintage Jedi style. He's developed some scary abilities, to be sure. Yoda would have been impressed with all that his disciple has perfected.

Winch secured the samurai sword on eBay six months ago for fifteen hundred American, squandering pretty much all the savings he'd built up from years of working at a call center, gathering statistics. Not that he regrets the purchase. How many people can say they own a collector's item, worthy of a museum, from seventeenth-century Japan?

The fact that a student has already called him a Ninja Turtle has not hurt his pride. Between a turtle and a frog there is a gaping chasm. But it was pointless to correct him. Winch knows who he is.

Freeing his sword from the leather sheath, Winch observes a phenomenon he has often wondered at: the blade is so sharp he can see a soft halo rising off it. The shine seems to extend beyond its physical limit. He's already tested the sword on pomelos, pineapple, watermelon. He's applied it to the limbs of saplings. It only remains to see how it stands up in battle.

❁   ❁   ❁

In ten minutes, Yuri has managed to consume more vegetables than he has in the previous ten months. He is desperate for anything to cool his appetites, and the wedges of Gouda and Camembert seem oceans away. He dare not leave Hannah's side.

Leaning closer to her, he immerses himself in her intimate vanilla scent—the fragrant wraith of some hair product or conditioner she used. The more they talk, the more he fancies himself Tristan to her Isolde. What does it matter that somewhere at the periphery of his consciousness the problem of Badendorf still plagues him? He could simply slough it off the way one sloughs off the dawning awareness that one is dreaming so as to cherish an erotic dream. Why should he pass beyond the pleasure principle? Rarely has his Id felt so alive.

Yuri can't help but sniff wolfishly in Hannah's direction. "Since you're so interested, why don't we have dinner? Afterwards, I could show you around my studio. I might even let you hear an episode we have in the works. The editing is nearly complete. Are you familiar with the black magician, Olaf Norquist?"

"I can't say I am." Hannah sips her pale wine, her attention landing upon her own open-toed shoes. "I really wouldn't have predicted this for you, Yuri. I might've guessed you'd become an academic like me."

So that's what she was doing on campus. He's become so fixated on wooing her that he can't even finesse the small talk. Don't come after me now, Superego. Can Yuri be blamed if he despised anything that would delay his and Hannah's progress to the nearest bed? How is he supposed to play the part of a gentleman when his sole function is to propagate his DNA? He can actually feel the spermatozoa inside him— surging, replicating—as if his body is no more than an extension of his genitals, a one hundred and seventy pound testicular mass.

"I wouldn't become an academic if they offered me a truckload of money," he says. "Not if they begged me. My internet show is sure to go viral in an instant. You're meeting me, Hannah, in the last moments before the explosion of my fame."

☼   ☼   ☼

Winch, more komodo dragon than frogman Zepé, crouch walks through the castle's shadow only to spring up from the darkness and draw his fearful blade. Lifting the cowl from where it droops over his eyes, he makes out a lanky bald man with an anorak jacket tossed over one shoulder and a red leather briefcase swaying at his hip. Although roughly the same height as Badendorf it doesn't seem to be the man himself but a sort of decoy or impostor. Perhaps Badendorf has arranged for his colleague to pick him up in a nearby parking lot. The lookalike could easily be Badendorf's chauffeur.

Winch watches him halt on the path. "State your business," he calls out.

"What is it you're holding there?" The man says, squinting through the fog. "What are you—nuts? I suggest you clear out of here immediately."

"I can't allow you to pass this way. Going any further is your death."

☼   ☼   ☼

Yuri reaches for a trunk of broccoli and flings it into his crocodilian mouth. "What do you say, Hannah? Will it be dinner and a tour of the studio?" He chews, grinning a gap-toothed grin, his gums lubed in vegetal slime. "We can call this the appetizer course and jump straight to the entrees."

417

Hannah crosses her arms, making a very faint humming sound. With her long lean neck and her soft sweet features, she could have made a model Madonna to a painter. Her tinkling bracelets produce a tiny music like the ringing of the celestial spheres. Yuri's chieftain posture has been thawed. His body has become an ashram at the center of which stands a lingam devoted to Hannah.

She touches his hand, merely grazes it, but it's almost enough. He must clench up, fight off the urge to release. Oh, don't touch me again. The slightest mingling of flesh on flesh would make him sing out and shudder, heaving like a Niagara of exuberant, teeming life.

"I don't think that will be possible," Hannah says. "I have plans already. But it was good to see you."

"Cancel! Cancel your plans! How often do we run into each other? These kinds of synchronicities might never recur."

"Yuri," she reproaches him, backing away, some of her charm already withheld. "No, I can't. I'm seeing someone. And, besides, don't be silly."

Yuri staggers. His face is hot. "What did I do to deserve this legacy of rejection? Am I really so foul to the feminine eye?"

"Stop this, Yuri."

"You're only a C minus yourself, yet you act as if you've never looked on a rodent so repulsive."

"I'm leaving."

Yuri contemplates the remnants of the veggie platter as Hannah makes her escape. Will you accept defeat again? Everything that's on offer, just stand back and let it pass, right? No.

He rushes through the auditorium, knocking over a couple of empty wine glasses in his violence. He finds Hannah in a stairwell. "I have a right to ask," he says, breathing heavy, not exactly in the best cardiovascular form. "Tell me the reason you have to deny me."

"Go away, Yuri!"

"Is it the way I look at you? Is it something about my body that I'm not aware of? Is it this mole that looks like a weird zit on my cheek?"

"Leave me alone."

"Is it my teeth? Is it my breath? Is it my hair?"

"Get away!"

"Do my armpits stink? Is it because of the dirt underneath my—"

Yuri, too intent on Hannah, trips down the final three stairs, and, while he recovers his balance in time to keep from being upended entirely—with one hand he steadies himself on the rails—by then Hannah has already run through the doors into the quad. He follows her outside but can't figure out which way she went. He stands still, trying to detect movement through the trees. His eyes might be yellow and feline, but they can't pierce the dark. The wind is making the conifers dance with a strange artificial life.

"That's the last time I'll be made into a fool because of lust," Yuri soliloquizes. "You did this to me, Professor. I could have had status! You robbed me of that."

He reaches inside his briefcase for his taser gun and presses its cold tip to his chest. "I suppose I'll remain a virgin forever then. An angry virgin. Deadly to the touch."

And with that he fades off—screaming, shrieking—into a sleep.

❅   ❅   ❅

Belly in the grass, Winch is hiding in a sort of leafy trench. He lies there watching as the Badendorf double returns to the spot of their confrontation, this time accompanied by a security guard, a young heavyset man with a crew cut whose pants are freighted down with tools.

The men converse in the insect-swirling glow of the castle's lamps. Winch clutches his sword. He could ambush these normies if necessary—even if he was partly blinded by the cowl. He could slaughter eyeless if he had to. Kek would marshal him to his prey.

Having slain so many normies and cucks in his Doom-inspired dreams, he feels initiated for the task. These people have no interiority anyway, as Yuri often says. Cattle on the conveyor. They're all AI-controlled, small-fry villains, who once annihilated will leave behind a stream of jewels in their wake.

Lord Kek would decide.

O Kek. Lead us not into cuckoldry. But deliver us from the shills. For thine is the memetic kingdom, and the shitposting, and the winning, forever and ever.

He slithers further into the shadows, before rising up in the dirt, where he remains, watching, squatting on his hams.

They might even contain life points or magic icons. Those indispensable magic icons. You'd never know until you destroyed them what kind of gifts their deaths would yield.

Ravening, shadow-haunted, a joke to the world but a hero to the trolls, Winch marches into the lamplight like a knight.

Nominated by Santa Monica Review

419

A SMALL BLIP ON AN ETERNAL TIMELINE

fiction by IFEOMA SESIANA AMOBI

from NARRATIVE

Emeka and I built our kingdom in a slanted row house on a patch of green grass in Highland Park, Pittsburgh, PA. Our floors creaked, our toilet growled, our heater hiccupped and often went out for the night, but it was our kingdom. Ours. Our little hideaway where time stopped for us, stretching into forever at our whim. It was where I could paint pomegranates and daffodils and portraits of an eager eyed girl without feeling like I was wasting my life away. It was where Emeka could beat his *igba* to the Afrobeats of Fela Kuti and dream.

It infuriated me the way he hunched over his desk into the early morning hours, squeezing his head with sweaty palms. Huffing through the names of pathogenic organisms and their virulence factors for med school, chasing a fantasy that wasn't even his: shadows of a dead throne in a dusty village in a land far, far away that his father, its long-lost king, wanted to bring back to life. Lurking in these shadows were tales my mother used to whisper in my ear. Of war and corruption. Aunts, uncles, and cousins who took weekly Sunday-Sunday medicine so they wouldn't drop dead from disease. *There was a time when you took this pill, nne.* Of chosen people whose divine purpose was to journey into the heart of the other world to save home. My family came to America when I was one, and in my tiny luggage bag my mother stuffed dreams too large for me to carry. I would pull Emeka away from his desk and into bed when the taste of bitter became too much for me to bear. Our arms and legs would entwine like thirsty vines, and heat from the blood rushing through our veins thrilled us. After making love, we cupped our hands to each other's lips and whispered our deepest fears into them. With a flourish of our fingers, we released them into the universe.

It was a cool night in April, five years after I left my mother, two years after I met Emeka, and nine months after I moved in, his wandering concubine of twenty-three, when he grabbed my waist at 2:00 a.m.—my heavy eyes wandering in the dark—and told me that he did not want to be with anyone else. "You will paint and I will play the *igba* forever."

I went cold. Then hot. Real hot. An aching fire devoured me. I turned to him and cooled. He looked at me with eyes so large, so gentle. So forgiving. A week earlier in a drunken rage, I threatened to leave him. Smashed a wineglass on his drums. Tore down the Christmas lights strung on the walls. I split the skin on his bicep as he fought to hold me in the house, shushing me so that I wouldn't alert the Ghanaian grad students on the other side of our left wall or the Indian med school couple on our right. Ha! How uncouth of me! How selfish I have been! I did not deserve him. I knew this. I'd had enough of being subjected to phone calls from the potential wives his parents were arranging for their hallowed son.

"When will you tell your parents about me? About you?" I whispered.

He wove his fingers through mine. I caressed the raised flesh of his wrist where he had just gotten his first tattoo. Earlier, we'd been running back from a U2 concert, smashed and happy like the rest of the folks who attended, me leading him by the hand, weaving our way through bodies still screaming, still dancing. The rumble of the ground underneath our feet lifting us. He was singing "I Still Haven't Found What I'm Looking For" at the top of his lungs in his beautiful, rugged Igbo accent, botching the words, when he suddenly pulled me into a tattoo parlor we were passing. While waiting for the artist, Emeka's light dimmed when he spoke of home. He went on about President Buhari's lies, how he was only out for himself. "He turns a blind eye to corruption to guard his cushioned seat while the Naira grows thinner. One dollar to three hundred fifty-nine Naira. Unemployment—" I grabbed him by the face and told him life only comes to a person once. "Don't we have a responsibility in this unforgiving world to find our happiness before we die?" He took a long, deep breath. When the tattoo artist was ready, Emeka pointed to the tattoo on the back of my wrist, of a tiny phoenix with wings of fire, and asked the artist to copy it. Later that night, Emeka roared, "This is me! This is me!" I held his palms, caressing the calloused skin that came from planting and carrying yams on his

421

grandfather's farm in Ogidi before he left for America at the age of fifteen to pursue his father's dreams.

Hanging above us on the ceiling was a painting Emeka helped me make of two yellow daffodils reaching for the heavens. We stared up at it. I squeezed his fingers tight. So tight I felt I was bursting.

"Do you like it here?" I asked.

He nestled his bristly, hot cheek in the nook of my neck.

"In America? Of course, my sweet."

"I mean with *me*, dummy."

He chuckled. "You know I do. So much. So, so much."

He placed his other hand over his head.

His most prized prospect was someone named Amaka. A law student from the University of Pittsburgh, where he went to school. I made him show me her Facebook page. There were pictures of her all dolled up in custom-made halter tops and form-fitting skirts of the finest Nigerian prints. She was runner-up for Miss Nigeria. Started an African Coalition for the Humanity of Lives. She came from the same ancestral village as Emeka in Ogidi. Members of his family knew members of hers. She called him last week to meet in person for lattes at Tazza D'Oro (our favorite spot). He agreed. After the call, I took his phone and hurled it out the window into the bushes.

I tried to pull my hand away from his. He tightened his grip.

"Do you think I like what I am doing to you? To me? I hate it. If I had my way, I would leave school-o. I would. I would live my life playing music. I am not as brave as you, Soma. I am learning. *Abeg*, give me a little more time. I will tell them," he said, his face pressing into my neck.

The toilet growled.

"I've given you two years."

"Help me, *biko*."

"I *am* helping you."

"Apply for one grant. One. One fellowship. Get your GED and go to a visual arts college. Show my parents that what you are doing can move and shake, then we have some leverage."

He had said this a week ago, and I had told him to never say it again.

I felt the heat in my body rise to a boil as a familiar sense of doom came over me.

I yanked my hand away from his and sat up.

He sat up.

"Isn't this what you've always wanted?" he said. "To do the extraordinary? How can you do it if you sit around this house, painting for an imaginary audience?"

"Are you a figment of my imagination?"

He sighed.

"Are you?" I repeated. I grabbed his face and squeezed his skin like it was putty. I squeezed harder. He pried my hands off, gritting his teeth in what I knew was anger. In the dirt-stained window I caught my reflection, dark as night, all sharp, angular lines jutting out into the world, scattered and dangerous.

"Prove your mother wrong," he said.

According to my mother, I was never right with the world. She had let it out when I was nine in a fit of hysteria after finding me at the fridge tasting sips of my father's beer. I had been born an *ogbanje* child, she'd yelled. A child who dies young and returns again to torment her parents only to be called back to the spirit world. She had lost her first child in the womb, so she had a native doctor do a rite on me before leaving for America, one tiny vertical slash on my right cheek to keep me in their world, her new beginning, her new hope. I never got the grades she wanted, never felt anything like a god watching over me. I didn't understand why I was born where I was born to the mother who birthed me. "You are on a path to misfortune," she cried the night I left her. "What woman lives a good life playing with crayons and opening her legs to men?"

"What am I doing?" I whispered, shutting my eyes. I took in a slow, deep burn of breath.

I opened them and saw Emeka smiling at me. His fingers grazed the spikes of my hair.

I cooled.

"Somadina the great," he whispered. "When will you let the world see what I see?"

"You're being a hypocrite," I whispered.

A spark vanished from his eyes.

"Tell me, Emeka the great, how will you chase your dreams with me if you're stuck at that desk or in the library with your nose sniffing those silly books? You are not so innocent."

He nodded slowly, cautiously. "I will chase my dreams with you."

"You are not so innocent."

A vein running down the left side of his forehead began to pulse. I cupped it in my hand.

I imagined him in the future sitting on a newly made golden throne as the *Igwe* of Ogidi. Daily items on his agenda: fix the potholed roads, renovate the compounds, mend civil disputes, modernize their health facilities, pour his heart and soul into their happiness while that vein in his forehead bulged like mad. His father, a village doctor turned big-city doctor, wanted a new Ogidi. A new Nigeria, really, and believed only the best of the best were worthy of being on the front lines, which included Emeka's wife. His parents lived in Texas, but their leash on their son was short and tight.

He squeezed his head with both hands and screamed. I screamed. The walls around us shook. He kissed me hard and climbed out of bed. I crawled to its edge. His pants were like silk the way they clung to the contour of his thighs. All tight muscle, rippled and lean. He was different from my other boyfriends, the good-for-nothings my mother despised. Emeka was smart. He came from a good family. He was going places. We were going places. We met at an art festival on the great lawn of Point State Park under a blazing sun. He wasn't too hard to miss with his salmon-colored shorts and multicolored dashiki top. It was my over-size Bob Marley shirt that got him talking. He told me that the boy in him had dreams of being a musician. He said that the boy was still chasing him. That the boy wanted to go on tours like the rock star Fela. The great Fela, the freedom warrior who waged his own war against the system. The great Fela, who once said he had death in his pouch. He could not die.

Emeka took a seat behind his *igba* splattered with wine and beat a hard and rapid and painfully soft tune on the animal hide. "What am I doing-o?" he whispered, his eyes looking to a far-off place inside himself. He landed them finally on me. "Come," he said. I came. And danced, gyrating my hips and stomping my feet, trying to forget my worries. Trying to keep my mind on our little haven that I vowed would never slip from my grasp.

On Sunday, the following day, I was off from work at Bruegger's Bagels. I swept every room and corner of our house waiting for Emeka's return. I scrubbed the rust around the drain in the porcelain tub until it shone bright, my nails cracked and knuckles bleeding. I flipped through Internet catalogs of home decor, envisioning an upscale kingdom for real adults. Couples with children who had careers of instant value. I saw all the glass tables, islands in the kitchens, glossy state-of-the-art appliances and realized that it didn't matter where I was as long as Emeka was there. Our small wooden kitchen table carried our meals okay, held us just fine too; so what if we had to light a match to get the stove to work. I just spent hours cooking the tastiest fucking pot of *egusi* soup, which he taught me how to make on that stove. Baked an apple pie too. His favorite. Emeka loved our house. He loved it.

I sat at the window staring at the clouds drifting by, the sun blazing then slowly burning out to a rusty orange. When our Indian neighbors wearing their matching navy-blue scrubs walked to their car laughing, carrying their heavy book bags on their shoulders, I snapped the curtain shut. I peeked out through a tiny crack. The girl always looked so happy. Like something far beyond our reach had been taking care of her and would continue to keep her in this world happy. Like all the potentially rotten things about a person's nature had been sucked back by the universe, never to fill her up. I wondered where she was going with her med school degree. Where was she going with her long, shiny black hair and light-brown skin? The soft, confident lilt of her Bengali? The graceful pride in her walk whenever she wore her sari? How many phone calls did she eagerly make to family in her home far away? I wondered what kind of tales of India her mother told her where she played the starring role of Perfection.

When I saw two Ghanaian boys carrying book bags march across our lawn to the bus stop, I began to paint the final touches of my sea of daffodils to keep my mind from running into the woods. That's what I was known to do, run into the woods.

Nine years before, when I was fourteen, my mother found me wandering the street in the middle of the night like a stray animal. A week earlier, I had broken my virginity with a skater with sideswiped golden-brown hair who smoked blunts and drew lusciously cool versions of me in anime after he saw my tulips à la Van Gogh's *Irises* from art class hanging in the hall. He passed a note to me that read, "You are going places." A dam in me broke, and I floated on the upswell. He called my character Princess of the Night Sky. In social studies one day, when the teacher skipped Africa, he blurted out, "Why?" The teacher said that Africa wasn't relevant to what we needed to know to be upstanding citizens of America. Golden boy glanced at me. I looked down at my dark hands, at the bitten-down nails I'd been picking raw for as long as I could remember. I felt somewhat grateful to have heard his voice. We hung out at Pamela's Diner. He taught me how to skate. He gabbed about his family in Michigan, Ohio, California. Asked about the tiny scar on my cheek. There were always gaps of silence he wanted me to fill. I was grateful he never pushed. God, I remember feeling so lucky, basking in his presence. An erasure had finally come to wipe out my past. I gave myself up in the back of his brother's BMW. He was kind. Timid. We giggled a lot. He told me I tasted sweet. Afterward, we avoided each other. Entirely. I dreamed of being his girl, but I didn't think he was that type of boy. A week later, I told my mother about it because I didn't know what to do with the guilt that was chewing my insides raw. I knelt down at her feet, and after the words spilled out of my mouth, I found myself on the floor, a searing burn on my cheek.

This thirst. My hunger. Is it just how I came into this world? Or did it seize me when I was a little girl alone in my room, wilting in the loveless silence that came after words no child should ever hear were thrown between mother and father in their bedroom. *This marriage was a mistake. Everything about it, a godforsaken mistake!* Me, reaching my hand out to the stars, not knowing exactly what I was searching for. Just wanting. Desperately. The day before I ran away for good, my mother and I screamed things that we most definitely believed of each other. I was a sorry excuse for a Nigerian daughter. A selfish slut. *There are loved ones, you know, who are suffering while you are entertaining yourself with idiotic things. What good are you? Look at how your spirit is bumping around a dark place!* I hurled a book at her. Told her she was a no-good African mom who couldn't keep a family. Her home was not a safe place for me. It was a filthy place. It stank of incompetence. As I hid behind an oak tree shaking, I saw her drive by calling my name, wailing like a wounded animal.

I tiptoed away from my painting of daffodils and into the kitchen, the floor creaking softly under my feet. The nutty smell of cooked *egusi* sitting confidently in the air. I lifted the lid and proudly took a whiff. I paced around our kitchen, my eyes fixed on my phone. Emeka was at the library. He had texted me six times asking me things I liked to hear: how were my daffodils coming along, don't forget to add more light to the landscape; was there anything I wanted him to pick up; what was for dinner, it'd better be his favorite-o.

I marched back into the family room and took a seat in front of my flowers. I gritted my teeth as I added more texture to the sky with quick, circular brushstrokes across the page to make swirls of royal blue. I studied the picture. *Not right.* I added two birds in flight. *Not right.* I added light cascading from a source outside the canvas. My yellow daffodils took on a lighter tint. I took a few steps back and stared at my work until my eyes lost focus. *Something isn't right!* I could see my mother standing there with her hand pressed against her chest, her tongue clicking in utter disappointment. *An artist's life is not the life you want to live, nne.* I grabbed the painting and dumped it in the corner of the room. It fell with a thump. Streaks of paint smeared on the cracked wooden floor. I paced back and forth. Who was this Amaka to intrude on my life? I went to the bathroom and washed my face. I applied foundation to conceal the lack of sleep under my eyes, the mark on my cheek. I applied red to make what I kissed him with pop. I took a selfie in three-quarter pose, puckering my lips and widening my eyes, which was something I never did. Emeka was into the natural look, so I thought. I texted him the photo with this message: *Egusi soup is ready. The best you'll ever eat. Take a break from studying tonight. Let's go to heaven.* He texted back immediately that he was thinking of me. I relaxed.

When he walked through the door that evening, I was standing there waiting. He wrapped his arms around me. His eyes were bloodshot. His back was bent over slightly from the weight of his books. His shoulders were tense. His breath reeked of roasted coffee beans. How many shots of espresso that day? I held him until the cadence of our breathing matched. I gave him gentle rubs up and down and across his back. He relaxed.

He reached into his pocket, pulled out a piece of paper, and found my hand. It was a flyer from a lounge called Speakeasy calling for musical acts for after-dinner hours. In his eyes I saw resolve.

"Show me your painting?" he asked.

I pulled the mess from the corner. He sat down, sinking into our threadbare sofa, and propped it on his lap. I caught a glimpse of the bird on his wrist. He rested his eyes on the painting for what felt like forever.

"Fine. So fine," he finally said, snapping out of his trance.

"Do you think?" I said, my voice shaking.

"Of course, baby."

I shook my head and pointed like a madwoman to different spots on the canvas. "Look. Look at how the light isn't hitting the flowers quite right here. That petal. There. It's awkward. You don't see that? The lines are too crooked. The daffodils, they need more magic. They need more pop."

"They are popping. They are popping."

He placed it on the easel. My sea of daffodils. It wasn't a Njideka Akunyili multimedia piece or Chinwe Uwatse's *Impossible Dreams.* I did not paint pictures of Nigerian landscapes. I did not delve into cultural or social themes. The first time Emeka saw my work, he squinched his face and asked in a scholarly tone what it meant. What kind of commentary was I making as an African woman drawing fruits and flowers? I had a teacher once, in a continuing ed studio workshop, who asked me the same thing. He told me that I would have a hard time competing with African artists who were making bold statements as a result of living in a state of existential urgency. He did not realize that my flowers were also coming from existential urgency. I asked him why my paintings had to mean something. Why they couldn't just make me feel something. Something indescribable. Why couldn't they just open a door for anyone to walk through and experience an existence that's greater than they will ever be but also in this strange and relieving way, a part of them. An alternate reality that is ours. Isn't this what we all want? To find that magical place in the midst of our tiny, broken-up lives? The teacher gave me a B. It took Emeka time to warm up to my flowers and fruits. As he began to appreciate them, I realized that all along what I truly wanted was someone special to see what was special about me.

Emeka ate his soup ravenously. He broke big pieces off the mound of *fufu* on his plate, sculpted them into balls, dipped them into the soup, and swallowed them whole. It was as if America were a hunting ground and he had just come home starving, wounded, and shaken from chasing a wild, shadowy beast. I wanted to tell him to slow down, relax. We were home now. I put on Pachelbel's Canon in D, another piece of me he has grown to love. When the soft, sweet sound of the piano began to skip lightly into the room, he stretched his long legs out underneath the table. Our toes touched.

"My food good?"

He nodded enthusiastically like a child licking his favorite ice cream. "Yes, Ma. You will make a great wife to a blessed Nigerian man one day," he said, laughing. *"Dalu."*

"You're welcome." I took tiny bites of my *fufu* and soup. I never enjoyed it when I was with my mother. I was more of a spaghetti and meatballs, steak and potatoes kind of gal, but I was learning.

I eyed him. He still looked jittery. Too jittery. I wondered how his whole day went. What all he had carried into our house. I cleared my throat. "Are *you* taken, Nigerian man?"

He stopped chewing his food and curled his lips to the side. "Not at the moment."

"There's no one but me in your line of vision?"

He looked up at me. His eyes grew wide. They were drowning in what looked like heartache. "Nope."

"You know what I mean?" I asked, raising my voice slightly.

"Hear my plan," he finally said. "I've decided that I will have coffee with her again, out of respect."

I pushed my bowl of *fufu* away.

"Hear me, please," he said. "Out of respect. I will tell her then that it won't work."

"When? When will you have coffee with her?"

"Next week sometime."

"Have you scheduled a time?"

"Soma, please."

"Tell me."

He broke off another piece of *fufu* with a snap of his wrist.

"What have you been hiding from me?"

He put his ball of *fufu* down slowly.

"On Tuesday. I will see her on Tuesday."

I felt faint. "This Tuesday? In two days?"

"Yes."

"And you weren't going to tell me?"

"Look at how you are reacting."

I got up with my bowl and plate and dropped them on the counter. Soup splattered everywhere. I pressed my palms against my forehead to stop the room from spinning. I turned around to face him.

"What else are you keeping from me?" I clenched my teeth to hold back tears. "Did you meet with her for coffee today too?"

He pushed his plates away from himself. "Be reasonable."

"You sound like your father. Like father, like son."

"Selfish. This is what you are that you can't understand. You are free, Soma. You can dance around and do what you like. I've had a whole village relying on me since I came to this country. Do you want to know what this is like? For once, stop thinking about yourself."

"Your father has the stupid little throne. It's his. Stop letting his bloated dreams drag you into a mess you can't fix. Let him go back to Nigeria and save them his fucking self."

He bit his lower lip. "Tell me one family member you keep in touch with. One."

My heart tensed. "That has nothing to do with anything."

"You are talking about people's lives."

"What about yours?"

"Their pain is greater."

"You're wasting your life, Emeka."

"Don't say that."

"The boy is chasing you. It's like a death. It will kill you."

"Stop saying this."

"*You're* the one making this a problem."

He pointed a firm finger at me. "Bring more to the table than Amaka does and there won't be a problem."

My breath left me.

"I'm sorry," he whispered. "Please forgive me."

I walked out of the kitchen. He didn't come after me.

When I entered our bedroom and heard a loud bang from the kitchen like a foot striking the table, something inside me snapped. Who was he fighting? Me or Amaka? I emptied his book bag and scanned every single thing that fell out of it. His notebooks. Planners. Crumpled receipts and flyers. I went into his desk drawer. Flipped through his checkbook. Sticky pads full of sketches of two birds in flight. Grabbed his phone. Stopped myself. My heart beat so hard I could feel it pounding in my ears. I kept going. I scrolled through his text messages. Nothing. I took a slow, deep breath. I exited his text messages, pressed the phone icon, and went to his call history. My heart stopped. I saw a list of phone calls between him and Amaka other than the two I knew about. Five other phone calls to be exact. One was this evening. It had lasted for thirty minutes. He had called her.

I walked back into the kitchen through a heavy, watery haze. He looked up at me. His own eyes carrying water.

"I'm worth more than this," I said, barely in a whisper. "I am." I dumped the phone on the table.

He looked at it. His eyes fixed on the screen. He dropped his head in his hands, shaking it as he asked himself over and over again what to do. "I am lost. I am lost."

It took every bit of power I had to turn away and walk. Heavy, frantic footsteps rushed up to me. The floor creaked loud under us. With my back still turned, I lifted my hand up at him. He stopped. I kept moving.

I wasn't sure how I found my way back to the bedroom. Time must have skipped forward. I begged it to keep skipping for me. *Carry me away from this moment and to a place that is safe.* I crawled into bed and buried myself deep underneath the covers, thinking about my future. A wave of dread ripped its way up from the pit of my stomach to my chest. I shut my eyes waiting for time.

* * *

After running through every decision I had made in my life that got me to this point—falling for guys who didn't give a damn, leaving school, leaving my mom—I rolled to my side, exhausted. Static from the scratchy comforter made sparks like fireflies fluttering around me. Emeka crawled into bed and under the blanket. We both lay there, silently, in a dark cocoon for what felt like eternity. Eventually he nudged me with his elbow. I didn't turn around. He nudged me again. I needed to turn. I needed to. So I turned. He flashed a boyish grin and tickled me in the stomach. I didn't laugh at first. He looked different now, like something alien and unsettling had taken over the body I knew. Maybe this distance was for the best. Yes, for the best. I choked out laughter. I choked it out because I needed to laugh. We escaped that night to a place Emeka liked to call *ani eze eluigwe nke uwa.* Heaven on earth. Heaven was in an old rickety house with Christmas lights strung up all over the place and paintings of fruit hanging on its walls. It growled and hiccupped and creaked, but we didn't mind. In heaven, he unzipped himself for me and I for him.

He told me for the first time that he had recently developed chronic pain in his belly. He pointed to it with a tight fist. I kissed every single inch of his stomach hoping for a return to what I knew. I told him about the new pain I felt in the center of my heart. I pointed to it with a loose, tired fist. He rested his lips on my center and grazed it tenderly. I opened my mouth to let in air.

We then cupped our hands. He whispered into mine and I into his:

"I am afraid of my life, Soma."

"Change it."

"I have too many loved ones suffering that I cannot let down."

"Are you going to let *me* down?"

Silence.

"*Abeg*, give me more time to figure this out."

Silence.

"I'm afraid of my life, Emeka."

"Why?"

"It's full of dead ends. I'm afraid of what the next one might be."

"You are not going anywhere."

"I think that's the problem."

Emeka fidgeted. A firefly showed itself and disappeared.

"Do you believe in destiny, Emeka?"

"Yes."

"If I hadn't lived out my life the way I felt I needed to, moment by moment, we might not have met each other. In the grand scheme of things, as ugly as life gets sometimes, I haven't made any mistakes. Am I wrong? Am I making a mistake?"

He closed his eyes.

"What are you thinking?"

He shook his head.

"Please tell me."

Silence.

"I'm applying for grants, Emeka. A lot of them. My work is going to be in the Carnegie, the Guggenheim, MOMA, all those places. I'm going to travel the world, Emeka. My art will lift people to higher places. My husband will be proud of me. So, so proud. He'll be an artist too. He's going to be brave. Not a coward. Both of us will live exciting lives being happy doing what we love."

His eyes had grown wide as if he were a plant drinking in my every word. "I remember the Andy Warhol Museum you took me to," he said. "The floating silver pillows. For those moments that we were there, playing, I felt weightless. I could see myself beating the drum. I saw crowds in front of me jumping up and down, dancing, clapping their hands like they were flying. I saw you in the crowd, your eyes focused on me. Proud. I dream every day for heaven to exist here, where we are, and no matter where we go, it will follow us."

"It does. It will. Just make a move. Claim your life."

"In our hearts, it exists forever. Not in the world. At least not right now. Family means too much for me to leave it completely. You know this is what I would have to do?"

Coward, I thought.

"I love you. You know this? My love for you will never end."

"Prove it," I snapped.

"I do not want to make mistakes either."

At four in the morning, I gently pulled his arm off my waist, grabbed my computer, and crept across our creaking floor, past a silly photo that hung on the wall of the two of us with our tongues sticking out, making googly eyes at each other. In our kitchen I scoured the Internet for grants for Pittsburgh artists. The requirements involved so much. Quality of work, evidence of formal or informal training, history of exhibitions, critical reviews, letters of recommendation from professionals. Under each grant on my list, I wrote, "**THE BEST OF SOMA IS YET**

TO COME!" I shut down my computer and went for the black-eyed beans in the pantry rather than the usual eggs, pancake mix, or Lucky Charms I left for Emeka, and soaked them in a bowl of water. Then I shelled them as best I could and mixed them in the blender, adding water, onions, a pinch of salt, red pepper flakes, and other spices I tried to remember my mom using. Emeka and I didn't have a deep fryer, so I fried the *akara* in a skillet. Sweat dripped from my pores as I stood at the stove dodging angry projectiles of grease and puréed beans. Out of nowhere, I felt the urge to cry. I gritted my teeth and curled my toes. The *akara* ended up one part burnt to two parts goopy. I nibbled on one and spit it out. Spit it all out and dumped everything in the trash.

At Bruegger's that day, I was training a new employee at the counter to strive for "Best in Class": smile at your customer, ask politely how they can be helped, cut their bagels down the middle as clean as possible, pick only the freshest-looking ingredients for their sandwiches. Be proud of how you've brightened their day so that your great work continues. Somewhere in the middle of smearing mayo on a bagel, I had to turn away and shut my eyes tight to keep myself from losing it.

Two years ago, before I met Emeka, the father of a childhood friend had walked into our shop and was at first pleasantly surprised to see me. When I ran away from home, I had no doubt my mom disconnected herself from the Nigerian community to keep from exposing her dirty laundry. He told me that his daughter, Ndidi, was at Georgia Tech getting her master's in computer science. His son, Chike, was a resident doctor at University of Pittsburgh Medical Center. My uncle was so eager to know what I was doing, he leaned over the counter, his dark skin, shiny, balding head, plump cheeks, and twinkling eyes making me hunger for a childhood that had escaped me. "My dear, are you a student at Carnegie Mellon holding a job to help Mama?"

When I told him, *"Mba,"* he said, frowning, "University of Pittsburgh?"

"No."

He then asked, "Where are you attending university then? What is your focus?"

When I told him that I hadn't gone to college, the light in his eyes faded, and what I saw in them was a reflection of a child who would never measure up in this world. One of their own had been left behind, still standing on the shore while the rest were kicking their legs and stroking their arms with all their might into the vast ocean of opportunity and self-realization. They believed love was easier to find there. I let him down. He would tell the whole community about me, and I would let them down.

There was an uncomfortable silence between us while I toasted his bagel. I piped up and told him that I was an artist, that I had shown my work in some galleries in Pittsburgh. That sparkle in his eyes came back a little. I rattled off the list of spaces: Boom Concepts, Most Wanted Fine Art, Fieldwork, but he didn't seem impressed. I had had a sinking feeling that I'd lost my chance to be courted by his son or someone else who was looking. I wish I had told him then that being different was okay. *I am trying.* When he paid, he said he would tell Ndidi that he saw me. Tell my mama hello. Everyone missed us. The last thing he did, I've tried my hardest to forget. He took me by my hand and told me that he loved me and that I should work very hard to better myself so that I got what I deserved in this short life.

I threw that memory away in a faraway corner of my mind, but like all memories, I carried it with me wherever I went. I snapped out of my reverie to a room full of bagels.

As I was leaving work, Emeka called. "I want to move forward," he said.

I picked at the skin around my nails.

"What does that mean?" I said.

"Museums, your gallery crawls. You will watch me play onstage. We will teach our children how to paint, drum, dance, and sing. We will laugh. There will be a lot of laughter."

Nothing more was said between us. Just a gaping silence. I wanted to ask, *Why are you playing this game with me?* He hung up.

That night I opted for homemade spaghetti and meatballs. Emeka ate his meal in his room while taking his father's call, which happened at least once a week. I sat at the kitchen table scraping my fork against my plate, listening to all the strained "yes, sahs" flying like razor-edged boomerangs out of his mouth. His father gave him updates on the order of things back home. This cousin needed money for school fees, that aunt was sick and needed money for medicine, this uncle couldn't pay rent. The village needed a new medical facility and better nurse and doctor training because one botched surgery was one too many. I wondered if anywhere in that conversation his father asked Emeka how he was feel-

434

ing. *How are* you *getting along, Son?* He gave his father an update on his studies. All As. Aced his physiology exam not too long ago. He was looking forward to finals. They laughed over going fishing for the first time when Emeka would visit Texas over the summer. Emeka didn't talk about me. I had never existed between him and his family. My toes curled. The topic of Amaka came up. Emeka agreed she was marriage potential, but he didn't know if he was ready to marry just yet. My ears perked up. He wanted to focus on his studies. Dabble in other things he would later be too busy to try. "Life is too short, Papa," he said. "Trust me. Amaka will wait." As soon as that feeling came over me, like waves ramming into my insides, I got up, stormed into the bedroom, inserted one of his Fela CDs into the stereo, and put "He Miss Road" on blast. I stormed out, slipped on my sneakers, ran out into the night.

The maple and sycamore trees rustled in the cool breeze. I walked down Highland Avenue past Tazza D'Oro, where Emeka and Amaka would meet the next day. My cross section of pomegranates in midnight blue had once graced the café walls.

I walked a long way down Highland, trying to imagine life somewhere else. No clear picture came to mind.

Still, somehow, the farther I walked, the easier it was for me to picture Emeka and Amaka living in that house in Highland Park. I imagined them sitting at the kitchen table covered in a sea of big books as they studied together, pushing each other relentlessly to be their best. He would grow to love her. I imagined them cooking our native food over intellectually stimulating discussions and glasses of wine. I saw them planning a future where they would live in a big house peacefully, have children, and accomplish other grown-up things. They would take yearly trips to Nigeria until it was time for the permanent move. She, of course, would support his father's mission to save Ogidi, and she, their princess, would be loved. I saw him telling her about a girl he once knew that was very dear to him, who took him to museums and gallery crawls and other such artsy things in his past. He will take her often to these places, and she will enjoy them. He will beat his *igba* for her, the way he beat it for me, maybe even thinking about me every once in a while, and she will dance for him.

I approached the house a few hours later in a daze and saw Emeka sitting on the steps. He was struggling to pull a weed out of a crack in the concrete. When he looked up, he jumped to his feet. "What happened? Where were you?"

"I took a walk."

"My stomach. I was sick with worry."

"It will be okay in the end," I said as I walked past him.

The next day, I called in sick. As I lay in bed, Emeka came to me. "I promise you that I will cut Amaka off today. I am tired. I need my freedom. We will conquer the world together. The two of us. Just give me a little more time. Please." He would make a nice Nigerian dinner, and we would eat it with merlot, then work through the next steps: true change.

"Am I a bad person?" I blurted.

"What? No, of course not."

He kissed me on the cheek. His lips were soft and wet. The kiss lingered there. Hope flew into my chest.

As he walked out the door, I went to the window, watching him walk away and searching for a sign that I might be making the wrong decision. His back hunched a little from his heavy book bag. *Poor thing.* I saw that the obstacle would never go away. No matter how hard he tried. I kept my eyes on him until he faded. I pulled out my two suitcases from the closet and packed. I didn't take much. Clothes, easel, palette, paints, and my art. I neatly folded the list of grants and tucked it in my purse. I left him my sea of daffodils.

When would I stop running? Running away from myself? I started to write him a note then crumpled it and threw it in the trash. It felt so final. *Make up your mind!* I pulled my phone from my pocket. Held it in my hands until I felt the weight of it. I tapped my toes until my ankles fatigued. I texted: *I'm doing what will make life easier for the both of us. I'll send you my rent. I wish you the best. Love you forever. No mistakes.* I got up and grabbed my stuff. I heard the alert of a message. I walked forward, the floor silent under me. I heard another alert. I slipped my phone into the pocket of my jeans. My phone rang. It rang and rang and rang. I wiped my eyes with my arm. At the front door I took one more look at what once was our kingdom. The cracked-up floor. The streaks of paint on it that I hoped to one day call my beautiful failure. I pictured in my mind's eye his *igba* sitting majestic in the bedroom. My sea of daffodils.

I took one long, deep breath, and walked into the sun.

Nominated by Narrative

PAROLE HEARING, CALIFORNIA INSTITUTION FOR WOMEN, CHINO CA

by JOYCE CAROL OATES

from BOULEVARD

Why am I requesting parole another time?—because I am penitent.

Because I am remorseful for the wrongs I have inflicted upon the innocent.

Because I am a changed person.

Because I have punished myself every day, every hour, and every minute of my incarceration.

Because the warden will testify on my behalf: I have been a *model prisoner.*

Because the chaplain will testify on my behalf: I have welcomed Jesus Christ into my heart.

Because I have served 51 years in prison. Because I have been rejected for parole 15 times.

Because I am 70 years old, I am no longer 19 years old.

Because I cannot remember who I was, when I was 19 years old.

Because I regret all that I was commanded to do in August 1969.

Because the person I hurt most at that terrible time was—myself.

Why am I requesting parole?—because (I believe) I have paid what is called my *debt to society.*

Because I have completed college while in prison, I have a community college degree, Chino Valley Community College.

Because I have taught generations of inmates to read and write.

Because I have assisted the arts and crafts instructors and they have praised me.

(I love the thrill of power, making lesser beings my slaves.)

Because I have goodness in my heart, that yearns to be released into the world.

Because I would *make amends*.

Because I am an example to the younger women.

Because I am the oldest woman prisoner in California, and there is shame in this.

Because the other prisoners are all younger than I am, and pity me.

Because I am not a *threat to society*.

Because I was a *battered woman*, and did not realize.

Because all that happened in 1969, happened because of that.

Because it was not fair, and is not fair.

Because the person I hurt most was—myself.

Why am I requesting parole?—Because Jesus has come into my heart, and He has forgiven me.

Because Jesus understood, it was the Devil who guided my hand to smote the innocent with evil intent.

Because the Devil whispered to us—*Do something witchy!*

Because I had no choice, I had to obey.

Because *he* would have punished me, if I did not.

Because *he* would have ceased to love me, if I did not.

Because *he* has passed away now, and left me with this (swastika) scar on my forehead.

Because seeing this scar I have borne for fifty-one years, you will judge me harshly.

Because the person *he* hurt most was—me.

Because I was abused by others.

Because I was trusting in my heart, and so I was abused by others.

Because I was abused by *him*.

Because I was weak-willed. Because I was a victim of what the therapist has called *low self-esteem*.

Because I was starving, and *he* gave me nourishment.

Because he asked of me—*Don't you know who I am?*

Because I dissolved in tears before him, at such words. Because all of my life, I had been awaiting such words.

Because the Family welcomed me, at *his* bidding.

Because soon they called me Big Patty. Because they called me Pimply Face. Because they made me crouch down, and eat from the dog's dish.

Because they laughed at me.

Because *he* did not protect me from them.

Because I gave my soul to *him*.

Because I am begging understanding and forgiveness of you, on my knees.

Because I am a good person, in my heart.

Because you can see—can't you?—I am a good person, in my heart.

Because it was easy to hypnotize me.

Because it was easy to drug me.

Because I could not say *no*.

Because very feebly I did say *no, no*—but *he* laughed at me, and made me serve him on my knees.

Because I was ravenous for love—for *touch*.

Because stabbing the victims, I was stabbing myself.

Because sinking my hands in the wounds of the victims, to mock and defile them, I was mocking and defiling myself.

Because tasting the blood that was "warm and sticky" I was tasting my own blood that spurted out onto walls, ceilings, carpets.

Because at my trial prejudiced jurors found me guilty of "seven counts of homicide" not knowing how I was but *his* instrument.

Because you who sit in judgment on me have no idea of the being I am in my innermost heart.

Because you gaze upon me with pity and contempt thinking—*Oh she is a monster! She is nothing like* me.

But I am like you. In my heart that is without pity, I am *you*.

Because it is true, certain terrible things were done by my hand, that was but *his hand*.

Because it is true, these were terrible acts and yet joyous, as *he* had ordained.

Because it is true, I showed no mercy to those who begged for their lives on their knees.

On my knees for all of my life, I did not receive mercy, and so I had no mercy to give.

Well, yes—it is true, I stabbed her sixteen times. The beautiful "movie star."

And it is true, each stab was a shriek of pure joy.

And it is true, in a frenzy I stabbed the baby in her belly, eight months five weeks old. For a mere second it crossed my mind, I could "deliver" this baby by Caesarean, for I had a razor-sharp butcher knife, and if I did this, and brought the baby to Charlie . . . But I could not think beyond the moment, I did not know if Charlie would bless me, or curse me, and I could not risk it.

For the baby too, that had no name, I showed no mercy. For no mercy had been shown me.

Because for these acts which are so terrible in your eyes, I have repented.

For these acts and others, I have repented.

Because in this prison I am a white woman.

A pearl in a sea of mud. A pearl cast before swine.

Amid the brown- and black-skinned my skin shines, it is so pure.

He entrusted us with the first battle of Helter Skelter.

He sent us on our mission, to pitch the first battle of the Race War.

He kissed my forehead. *He* told me—*You are beautiful.*

Because I had not known this!—in my soul I believed that I was ugly.

Because at school, in all the schools I had gone to—there were jeering eyes, cruel laughter.

Because when I was not yet twelve years old already dark hairs grew thick and coarse on my head, and beneath my arms, and at the pit of my belly. In that place between my legs that was sin to touch. On my legs that were muscled like a boy's, and on my forearms. Wiry hairs on my naked breasts, ticklish at the nipples.

Yet of my body Charlie declared—*You are beautiful.*

Except: blood like sludge oozed between my thighs. A nasty smell lifted from me.

Go away, you disgust me, Charlie said.

Because you are saying—*The poor girl!*—*she was abused, hypnotized.*

Because you are saying—*She wasn't herself.*

Because none of that was true. Because love is a kind of hypnosis but it was one I chose.

Because Charlie favored the pretty ones, even so.

Because I hated them. Because I had always hated them—beautiful women and girls.

Because it is not fair, that some that are sluts are beautiful like Sharon Tate and some are ugly like me.

Because when we were done with her she was not so beautiful.

Because I would not do it again!—I promise.

Because I stuck a fork in a man's belly, and laughed at how it dangled from the flab of his belly, but I can scarcely remember.

Because I have been washed clean of these sins, through the grace of Jesus.

Because I am a Christian woman, my savior dwells in my heart.

Because I was not evil but weak.

Because I was a "criminal" in the eyes of the law but a "victim" in the eyes of God.

Because the swastika scar between my eyes calls your eye to it, in judgment. Because you think—*She is disfigured! She bears the sign of satan, she must not ever be paroled.*

Because the scar is faded now. Because if you did not know what it was, you would not recognize it.

Because I was a *battered woman*—a therapist has told me.

Because my case should be reopened. Because my incarceration should be ended. Because I have *served my time.*

Because sin has faded in my memory.

Because where there was the Devil, there is now Love.

Because in the blood of the dying I wrote on the walls of the fancy house—DEATH TO PIGS HEALTER SKELTER

Because it was not to be, that I would have a baby—so it was fitting, *she* could not have her baby.

Such a big belly! Big white drum-belly! Screaming, like they say a stuck pig screams, and squeals, and tries to crawl away—so you must straddle it, knees gripping her slippery naked back, to wreak the greatest vengeance.

Because she was so beautiful, the sun shone out of her face.

Because she was so beautiful, she did not deserve to live.

All of them, strangers to us—they did not deserve to live.

Do it gruesome—Charlie commanded.

Because that was the address he'd given us on a winding canyon road in the night—*Leave no one alive there.*

Because we did not question. (Why would *we* question?)

Because rage is justice, if you are the meek.

Because it is said—*Blessed are the meek, they shall inherit the earth.*

Because when flames burst inside you, you know that you are redeemed.

Because it is time for my parole, Jesus is commanding you—*Turn my minion loose!*

Because you are fools who think you see a putty-skinned plain old woman in prison clothes humbling herself before you, harmless old bag with a collapsed face and collapsed breasts to her waist—you have not the eyes to see who I am, as with his laser eyes Charlie saw at once—*You are beautiful.*

Because Charlie perceived in me within a minute of seeing me, I might be a sword of God.

Because I might a scourge of the enemy.

Because I had wanted to be a nun but the nuns rejected me.

Because you will all pay, that the nuns rejected *me.*

Because if you release me, I have more justice to seek.

Because you hold the keys to the prison but one day you will suffer as we suffer, in the flaming pits of Hell.

Because you are trying to find a way to comprehend me. So you can pity me. So you can be superior to me. *She was brainwashed,. She was not responsible. She was fed hallucinogens—LSD. She was weak-minded, under the spell of the madman.*

Because you are mistaken. Because you have no idea what is in my heart.

Because beside Charlie who was our beautiful Christ, you are vermin. *He* would grind you beneath his feet.

Because we made her famous—"Sharon Tate."

Because the slut would be forgotten by now if we had not made her famous.

Because I dipped my hands in her hot pulsing blood. Shoved my hands into her big belly. *Eviscerate*—Charlie commanded.

Because you see?—I am meeting your eyes, I am not looking away.

Because I am not servile to the Board of Parole, like others who appear meekly before you.

Because I am a woman of dignity. Because prison has not broken my spirit, that is suffused with Charlie's love.

Because I can see, you are filled with loathing of me. As I am filled with loathing of you.

Because even in death her eyes were the color of burnt sugar, her skin was flawless and so smooth . . . I thought that I would tell Charlie—*I will go back and skin her! Should I go back and skin her!*

Because I was sure that Charlie would laugh and say—*Yes! Go back and skin the slut and return to me wearing her skin, then I will love you above all the others because you are more beautiful than all of them.*

Because this did not happen, and yet it is more real to me than many things that have happened.

As Charlie is more real to me, than any of you.

Because we would tear out your throats with our teeth, if we could.

Because it is ended now—my (last) parole hearing.

Because I leave you with my curse—DEATH TO PIGS.

Nominated by Boulevard

BECAUSE

by GRACE SCHULMAN

from THE MARBLE BED *(Turtle Point Press)*

Because, in a wounded universe, the tufts
of grass still glisten, the first daffodil
shoots up through ice-melt, and a red-tailed hawk

perches on a cathedral spire; and because
children toss a fire-red ball in the yard
where a schoolhouse facade was scarred by vandals,

and joggers still circle a dry reservoir;
because a rainbow flaunts its painted ribbons
and slips them somewhere underneath the earth;

because in a smoky bar the trombone blares
louder than street sirens, because those
who can no longer speak of pain are singing;

and when on this wide meadow in the park
a full moon still outshines the city lights,
and on returning home, below the North Star,

I see new bricks-and-glass where the Towers fell;
and I remember my love's calloused hand
soften in my hand while crab-apple blossoms

showered our laps, and a yellow rose
opened with its satellites of orange buds,
because I cannot lose the injured world

without losing the world, I'll have to praise it.

Nominated by Marianne Boruch, Joan Murray

LAKEWOOD

by CHARLES BAXTER

from THE GEORGIA REVIEW

For Edward Hirsch

Because the nearby parks
were crowded with escapees
from all the shelters—condos, apartments,
rented rooms—and because
the virus from which we fled
had arrived wherever we
were going before we managed
to get there on our own, I found
myself in Lakewood Cemetery
on a snapshot early summer day,
seeing a "Welcome, walkers!" sign
out front, a sunny, cheerful city
boneyard glorious with apple
blossoms, aggressive birdsong, odor
of mown grass, and twisting indecisive
roads where you could lose
your intended way and where any
body was, yes, quite welcome no matter
in what direction it might transport
itself, so I could be lost-and-found at
once near the marble mausoleums,
the heroic flowery cenotaphs, hooray
for all the dead—and thus, before setting
out in no particular direction, I checked
my iPhone for mileage, put on
sunblock, breathed in, laced my running
shoes, and headed over there.

How cheerful all these cemetery slabs
in picnic weather, the Minnesota sun
shaded by that oak, this elm, a leafy frame
around that marble grieving woman
quite consumed in drapery
halfway up a sobersided Greek Revival
pedestal whose height runs out before
it successfully can penetrate the sky's iconic,
brilliant blue sent to us from somewhere
godlike as a gift, and there, in that glade
the marker for the author of *Mister Roberts*,
big Broadway hit, Thomas Heggen, who
didn't know, poor guy, how the hell
he ever wrote it, before drowning, drunk,
dispirited, more irony, in the bathtub,
and now white-throated sparrows set
up a four-note racket near the big majestic
marker for Hubert Humphrey, vice
president and friend to labor, but I'm just
passing by, a visitor, and so I wave to Hubert
and to Tom because in the pleasant warmth
of day I'm sweating now, grave-etiquette
demanding that I do not run but walk
thoughtfully and with reverence past
that cannon memorial for the G.A.R.,
commemorating those old—well,
they're not old, not now—vets whom
my stepfather as a boy once saw parading,
upright ancient men proud to have saved
the Union and freed the slaves; in his own
old age, he said: *they limped, had beards,
and gave off a funny smell* to him, back then,
a little boy still knee-high, in spectacles
gazing at their torn blue uniforms.

Walking now, I refuse the sadness
invited by heraldic marble names of
Jones, Walter, Shevlin, Tuttle, Wells,
etc., some of whom I know, or knew,
and having passed two miles,

lightheaded, I discover quite by accident
this funereal stone girl with wings,
somehow dove and angel both, though
not especially poetic or rhetorical,
not like Rilke's angel—terrible to look upon,
a fiery carrier of Being, raw and alive
with the uncompromised and inhuman
love to penetrate down through the flesh
into the soul's unguarded heart, quivering
with its own shy appetite for dissolution
into that greater being whose power
can kill like childbirth while speaking
German—no, *this* angel playing hide-and-seek
is a harmless, local, domesticated thing,
more like a hired governess, the curate's
daughter, plain as day, unmarried,
somehow polite: *Here's a bench,*
take a breather, don't worry, I won't bite,
please, I'm your contemporary, slow
down and sit, she says, and so I do, under
shades whispering in the shallow branches
overhead, protecting me from sun.

How calm it all seems, and how detached.
Not like the other part of town
I just came from: both festive and funereal
where the pavement's painted with the names
of men and women, and flowers both fresh
and wilted pile up in memory of the man
who died there, neck kneeled upon,
and where, one hour ago, I saw a woman,
head shaved, punk, wearing black, also
kneeling, this time in prayer, while one
block away a band was playing, people
dancing, handwritten signs everywhere
in joy and grief commemorating
the man who died, who is still here,
here, here, living, the motto beneath
his picture, "I can breathe now," a recognition
and refusal of his death, and who am I

but a watcher at this wake, a mere old
anonymous white guy, hands clasped
in front of me, and, surprised by sorrow,
I break out into tears, overcome like everyone,
and still weeping, I walk away
and am stopped by a kindly woman
offering to spray my hands with sanitizer.
Say his name: George Floyd. American.

Thinking of his face, and now tiring
and still shook up, in Lakewood, I walk
past all the Baxters underground,
and now at last I'm really lost in this gigantic,
landscaped, cultivated, tended, sublime
locale where redundant adjectives
pile up, and I can't help hearing
that music from two miles away,
or the memory thud of dirt that dropped
from a shovel onto the casket of my
friend's son, years ago—every death
is yesterday and unerased. Sky blue air,
still nearby, the life as well. Clouds drift
aloft. Birds sing. Whereupon I cannot walk
and even though I refuse the cemetery,
and would like to refuse all death and all forgetting,
nonetheless I still join
all the sleepers and the anonymous forgotten
here, bless them all, forgive them,
and forgive me too. I'm on my knees and don't
know how I got here, can't remember how
I dropped down with my hands together
at my forehead. And now I rise and look
around and head back to my parked
car, and where I came from.

Nominated by Michael Collier, Edward Hirsch, Andrea Hollander, Maura Stanton
The Georgia Review

THE GOD PHONE

by LEORA SMITH

from LONGREADS

THE GOD PHONE

In between the fabric folds of towering red and white tents, a small, gray push-button phone sat on a dusty cushion, shaking with a high-pitched ring.

Outside, the air throbbed with music. Deep bass notes crisscrossed the landscape, merged with the voices and footsteps of Burning Man's tens of thousands of attendees, and flooded the desert with sound.

But inside, there was only the phone, its ring echoing off the tent walls.

"Hello?" I answered.

"Hi," said the voice on the other end. "Is this god?"

❈   ❈   ❈

A well-worn phone booth stood off a busy thoroughfare in Black Rock City, the temporary metropolis that Burning Man's participants build together every year in Nevada's Black Rock Desert. During frequent dust storms, a sign above it reading TALK TO GOD beamed through the thick, whitewashed air like a desert marquee.

Below the booth a buried phone line ran about 100 feet to a secret location. There, it connected to the God Phone. Anyone who found it got to play god.

When I discovered the God Phone in 2017, the first few calls I fielded were silly, easy. Callers asked me, "What should I do tonight?" Or, "What's god's favorite thing out here?" Over and over they expressed

450

glee at my gender. "I knew god was a woman," people said, or sometimes, "I'd hoped you were."

But about 30 minutes in, a man called, and a hesitation in his voice drew me in so closely that I felt like we were meeting in an ethereal space deep inside the phone cord.

"There's something I want to do," he said, "and I want you to tell me if I should or not." The otherworldly room we inhabited shrunk around me. "What's the thing?" I asked, already knowing he wouldn't tell me. "I've tried it in the past," he said, "and it didn't work. But this weekend I might try it again."

I can't say why I thought the man might harm himself. But in the moment I felt that threat as solidly as the receiver in my hand. And I wish I'd been motivated otherwise, but all I wanted to do was drop it and run.

I asked if the thing would make him happy, and he said he thought it would. "You should do the things that make you happy," I told him, my tongue pushing out the words while the knots in my stomach tightened, trying to rope them back in. He whispered a thank you and hung up.

A few nights later, during Burning Man's culminating event—the burning of a giant effigy called The Man—a man died by suicide. Before he died, he was sitting just 20 feet away from me.

In a crowd that big, I know it's unlikely he was the same person who called. But for two years I haven't been able to shake the thought from my head.

*　*　*

Almost a year after my night on the God Phone, the legal services organization where I worked held a training on recognizing when clients are thinking of suicide and making space for conversations about it.

Our teacher was Karen Grant-Simba, a trainer with the suicide prevention organization LivingWorks and a former case manager at a hospital's mental health department. She wore her hair in thick locs and spoke in a voice so soft I felt I could crawl right up and fall asleep inside it.

Karen's training focused on "invitations," the hints people drop that they are struggling. An invitation might be something a person said, the way they looked, or just a feeling you got in your gut around them. She described the fear we feel acknowledging these invitations. The way our voices catch in our throats. The way our better instincts bubble up like heartburn and how we push them down, back, and anywhere but out.

451

When someone seems like they are hurting, Karen encouraged us, take a risk and tell them you noticed. Then, she had us practice. She told us to turn to a partner and say these words out loud: "Are you thinking of suicide?" The question quickly filled the room; it pinged between partners and off the walls and my mind traveled on it, back to the man in the phone booth.

"Are you thinking of suicide?" I imagined asking, curled up by the God Phone. "Are you thinking of suicide?" I thought, and I walked to the phone booth to see him face-to-face. "Are you thinking of suicide?" I asked as I led him back to the God Phone so we could sit and talk through it. "Are you thinking of suicide?" I said and we shared a long conversation that ended in a hug.

The words began slipping off my tongue, easier and easier each time. I wished someone had painted them on the phone, had given me a warning that I might need them.

✿   ✿   ✿

A common refrain at Burning Man is "safety third." Every year, artwork at the event is physically dangerous.

Dance Dance Immolation, a famed installation set up a few times between 2005 and 2013 by the artist collective Interpretive Arson, had participants play a game inspired by Dance Dance Revolution in fire proximity suits that protected against flames shot directly at dancers with every missed step.

In 2018, artist Dustin Weatherford stacked seven old cars, one on top of the other, in a piece called Night at the Climb-In. People scaled the structure, navigating the rickety mirrors and rusted doors to the top where they could sip drinks in a canned-ham trailer 34 feet in the air. (Officials from the Bureau of Land Management and Burning Man closed the installation to climbers a few days into the event after someone fell and got hurt.)

But the God Phone's risks felt different from Burning Man's usual danger. There was no purposeful climb to a precarious lookout, no donning of fireproof gear in preparation for something that was obviously a bad idea. What sort of responsibility did the artists have for this other kind of art, I wondered, the kind where the risks were more hidden?

I never thought I'd go back to Burning Man after my God Phone experience, and I definitely didn't think I'd go back to the phone. But in 2019, I did. I sat there for 24 hours, because I wanted to know if other conversations like mine were happening there. Was the God Phone safe? If someone got hurt, how would we know?

❋   ❋   ❋

At 10 a.m. on the day I visited the Talk to God phone booth, a line of people already stretched from it. Would-be callers formed an impromptu catalogue of Burning Man fashion: tutus, bedazzled military hats, leather fanny packs, and dusty combat boots on every foot.

I passed the queue and traced ever-widening circles searching for the gods' lair until I found it, just a few hundred paces away, kitty-corner from the booth, obscured only half-heartedly by a gauzy curtain.

Inside, 10-foot-tall black light paintings of a dragon and the Buddhist deity Quan Yin loomed over a man in a weathered white armchair, holding the receiver to his ear. By his feet, a speaker quietly projected both sides of the conversation, and onlookers gathered around it, sitting on large cushions draped in green faux fur.

The whole setup sat atop a plush black carpet patterned with geometric shapes in bright, elementary-school colors. Taken together, the space had the feeling of a 20-year-old's first grown-up living room, or the basement hangout from a grainy sitcom.

I walked in and joined the group huddled around the speaker. From there, we had a clear sightline to the phone booth, and everyone who approached it.

The calls came in quickly, with barely any break between them. Lighter questions (*What do you think about Christmas?*) and universal ones (*Why do you let natural disasters happen?*) were peppered with confessions (*I'm in love with someone but I'm married to someone else*) and personal requests (*Can you watch over my son in rehab? I'm worried this might be his last shot*).

The speaker muffled everyone's voices slightly, insulating us in the sound. We were voyeurs floating in a secret room wallpapered with worries.

A 30-something named Benji sat beside me in the huddle, his plain gray T-shirt and khaki shorts the most nonconformist outfit in a sea of eccentrics. He smiled while he talked and told me he was raised ultra orthodox Jewish just outside New York City ("Black hat, the real deal," he said), but declared himself an atheist about five years ago. Around that time, he attended Burning Man and found the God Phone.

"The conversations we have on the God Phone are very similar to the conversations I used to have with my god," Benji said. "There's just one

453

difference," he added, laughing. "The Burning Man variation of god has it so when you pick up the phone to speak, god actually responds." He said it with such positivity, but I couldn't relate. My own flawed, too-mortal response had been the very thing that made me worry about this whole experiment.

More calls came: *Can you tell me why my mom left? What is my purpose here? Why do children get sick?*

The next time it rang, the man in the god chair looked at me. "You're god," he said, holding out the receiver. I shook my head, no.

✿   ✿   ✿

The Talk to God phone booth first appeared at Burning Man in 2003, the brainchild of a group of artists from Ojai, California, who camped together under the banner OBOP, short for "Ojai Bureau of Pleasure." While many installations only make the difficult trek to the Nevada desert once, the booth has been there, in different iterations, every year since.

OBOP member Michael Shevchuk remembered four muses merging in his brain to form the concept: Burning Man's 2003 art theme "Beyond Belief"; a line from a U2 song ("God has got his phone off the hook, babe, would he even pick up if he could?"); an exchange between a fictionalized Andy Warhol and Jim Morrison in the film *The Doors* ("Somebody gave me this telephone. . . . And she said that I could talk to God with it, but I don't have anything to say"); and an old telephone booth that Shevchuk walked past daily in his neighbor's yard.

When campmates and artists Steven Jeffre and Scott Siedman heard the idea, they rushed to make it real. Within days they found an abandoned booth already missing its phone by a highway, and mined it for parts: hinges, handles, a ceiling unit that housed its lights, and the shelf where the phone rested. Using these parts and some plywood, they built a slightly enlarged replica of a classic Ma Bell booth, and the first Talk to God phone was born.

In the vast expanse of Burning Man, a small phone booth could get lost, but instead it made a mark. Over 16 years, thousands of people have interacted with the installation, placing a call or answering one. Reddit and Facebook threads overflow with accounts of phone calls that left an impact.

In early 2018, the Smithsonian's Renwick Gallery hosted an exhibit of Burning Man art. That year, Smithsonian curator Nora Atkinson gave a TED Talk, positioning Burning Man as a new art movement, one where a piece's value is determined by the emotional connection it creates between people. As she spoke, a picture of the Talk to God phone booth appeared over her left shoulder, an example of an iconic piece in a bizarro pantheon.

In 2007, OBOP disbanded and, in a ceremony common at Burning Man when a piece of art has run its course, some camp members decided to burn the phone booth. When word spread of its destruction, a community swooped in to ensure its return and continued presence. A member of a neighboring camp scavenged a new booth in a Seattle junkyard. A retired phone enthusiast in Boston recreated its technical parts, boxed them up, and mailed them to California.

Since then, two people—Jaye Hersh and Miles Eastman—have each brought the booth in different years. They call themselves its shepherds. I talked to both Jaye and Miles, and to Scott who helped build the first booth, about my unnerving God Phone experience before going back this year, and none were surprised.

"I've heard so many stories of people having those kinds of conversations," Miles told me.

"Does that worry you?" I asked. On the contrary, he said, "I think that you stumbled on the purpose and the beauty of the piece."

His answer worried me.

* * *

This year, a clipboard holding a bright orange piece of paper rested by the God Phone. BE KIND! the page read in big, rounded purple letters across the top.

Jaye—who goes by "Yay" at Burning Man—was shepherding the phone booth. On the first day I met her she wore flowers in her hair and electric blue lipstick that somehow stayed perfectly applied for the entire week of dry, lip-cracking desert heat.

As a shepherd, she had two rules. The first: Encourage "a kinder, gentler god." The second: God always answers. Her campmates took shifts, acting as standby gods in the lair when the chair sat empty. On two nights, nobody signed up for the 4 a.m.–6 a.m. shift, so Jaye slept by the phone.

Her instructions provided a kind of lightness. When the questions got hard, kindness was easy. Sitting with experienced gods, newer gods got support and even a bit of a script. Many gods mimicked Jaye's signature "I love you" signoff, though I couldn't always tell if they meant it, or if they just liked hearing it back. Either way, I was unreasonably moved listening to adult men exchange unabashed, tender "I love you"s at the end of their calls.

It was a very different God Phone from the one I found two years prior.

From the God Phone's first day at Burning Man, members of OBOP disagreed on how to run it. Scott's approach was "get out of the way and trust people." He said he was chasing honesty and intimacy between strangers. For him, those moments of feeling stuck, unscripted, or unsettled but forced to engage—those were the whole point.

Miles, who shepherded the booth the year I first found the phone, shared Scott's ethos: no instructions, no supervising gods. They described their hands-off approach as an act of faith. "I trust in the love and compassion of our fellow human beings to show up for each other," Miles said. "It's worth the risk," he added, "to allow that natural sort of serendipity."

I understood that, as an artist, Miles celebrated the varied, sometimes difficult experiences people had on the phone. But as someone who lived one, I didn't.

❖   ❖   ❖

By 2 p.m. on my day at the God Phone, there was still a line at the phone booth. By 3 p.m. the gods had answered nearly 30 calls.

God, can you watch over my house in Florida? I just heard about the hurricane and I didn't close the shutters.

Can you check on my brother in New York? He's depressed and I'm worried about him.

Can you send a message to my mom and dad? One of them has been there a while, but the other is a newer arrival.

Do people who die by suicide get into heaven?

Do you know who stole my bike?

Some of the calls felt serendipitous in their timing: One caller talked about a partner leaving her and connected to a god who'd just finalized a divorce. A caller struggling in an open relationship talked to a god who had just opened up her marriage. And a person in need of a bike tire somehow reached a god who had a spare that was just the right size.

Around 3 p.m., Courtney, a woman in big rhinestone sunglasses and exuding a mama bear energy, sat beside me. She seemed like someone who, if she passed a broken-down car on the side of the road, would

456

both stop to fix it and feed the driver home-baked muffins while they waited. Laughter danced at the edges of her words, a warm South Carolina accent curling them like a mischievous smile.

As we listened together, Courtney told me about the town where she grew up, how she learned about Burning Man online, and that the God Phone's camp adopted her when she sought advice about the event on an online forum. "I don't have much family," she said, and arriving in the camp felt like coming home.

After eyeing the phone for a few calls, she decided to take one.

Hello, this is god.

I'm freaking out a little, the caller jumped right in. *How do I let go of trying to control everything?*

I'm god, she said, laughing. *I get it.*

I need to know I'm gonna be OK, he said.

Yeah. You're wonderful, and I love you unconditionally and you can do anything you want to do.

The caller burst out in relieved laughter.

I love this, he said, with a new energy in his voice. *Thank you so much.*

The call hardly lasted two minutes. But as I watched that man walk out of the booth in the distance, I saw him transformed. Something lifted just by speaking his worries out loud.

So many people shared God Phone stories with me in the months leading up to Burning Man. *You're writing about the Talk to God booth?* they'd say excitedly. *I just have to tell you the most amazing thing that happened there.*

More often than not, the conversations they described were short. To me, they often sounded almost inconsequential. But I learned that this simple opportunity to pause, to share a hurt, to hear someone acknowledge it stuck with people for years.

As the afternoon went on, more calls came in. Most weren't about thoughts of self-harm or big life decisions. For the most part, they were the kind of everyday sadnesses we carry around quietly all the time.

Sometimes, I followed the callers to learn more about them. Nearly every one shooed away their friends before we talked about their experiences, not wanting to share the topic of their calls. "I don't want to be a burden on them," one woman told me.

Talking with them I realized how many people, like me, had run away from hard conversations. How we did it on purpose, and sometimes without realizing. How people who needed to talk waited for invitations to spit out the hard stuff, and how good it felt when they did.

In between calls, Courtney asked why I was writing about the God Phone, and for the first time that week, I told someone the whole story.

When I finished, she said, "You did the best you could that day." And I almost believed her.

* * *

Before heading to Burning Man this year I had lunch with Karen, my teacher from the suicide training, to ask her thoughts on the booth. Was it safe to have untrained people fielding calls? Did she agree with Miles that it was worth the risk?

"There is power in just being able to verbalize how you are feeling," Karen said, explaining that talking about thoughts of suicide was better than keeping them in. "People live their lives with thoughts of suicide in the background," she told me. "The more we can normalize the experience the better we'll be for it."

Listening to Karen, I realized what she was saying wasn't just true about thoughts of suicide, but about all kinds of sad thoughts. Still, her answer surprised me. The phone felt so risky—for the callers *and* the gods.

I reached out to Dan Reidenberg, the executive director of the advocacy group Suicide Awareness Voices of Education (SAVE), for a second opinion.

Shortly before the premiere of the Netflix series *13 Reasons Why,* the streaming giant reached out to "Dr. Dan" for advice on a scene that depicted a teenager dying by suicide. When Netflix released the scene, to widespread criticism, SAVE partnered with another nonprofit to release a guide to help parents and teachers discuss the series with young people watching it, and to help prevent a possible copycat effect—that vulnerable people watching the scene might try to harm themselves. I imagined he'd given a lot of thought to art that engaged with issues of self-harm.

"I've talked to people who used that phone," he said, shocking me. And he echoed everything Karen said.

"Obviously," he explained, "it would be best if the people hearing these things were trained." But faced with the option of having the phone booth as is, or not having it, he said he'd pick having it. "It doesn't take any training to be a good person," he added. "You just have to be compassionate, caring, empathetic, and willing to listen."

Dr. Dan did have a word of caution. "You have to hope," he said, "that whoever is answering isn't going to support someone toward self-harm." I'd planned on asking him about my conversation, but shame sank it like concrete in my throat. I managed to push it out and ask Karen directly.

"That was not a bad conversation," Karen assured me. "A bad conversation is saying, 'Just do it.' A bad conversation is hanging up the phone and walking away." Then, she added something that hit me hard: "Sometimes the fear that people have is that once they become aware of something that serious, there is an expectation to do something they are not skilled to do. But, she added, "We don't need to be able to fix things for people."

I thought back to the course I took with her. The way I imagined saying the right words and inviting the caller to the God Phone, imagined us talking, imagined us hugging and walking away. The way I wished I could have fixed the ache I thought I heard.

I realized that of all the people who talked to me about their God Phone experience, not one of them said god actually solved their problem. Most didn't even remember exactly what the person who answered the phone said.

What stuck with them was that someone answered at all, that they had a space to say, "I'm in the middle of the biggest party in the world, and something inside me hurts."

❊ ❊ ❊

In the early evening, two women approached the phone booth. One, in a neon-orange mesh bodysuit, lifted the phone and posed while the other snapped a photograph.

In the gods' lair, the phone rang.

This is god, Courtney said. *How may I help you?*

The woman in the bodysuit, unaware the phone actually connected, startled at the sound of Courtney's voice.

Is this god? She turned around, moving as far into the booth as she could. *Do you answer prayers?* Then she whispered, *Can you help my boyfriend to be faithful?*

I watched the conversation and I thought, it's really not very hard to ask someone if they are struggling with something. On just a moment's notice, almost anyone could tell you that they are.

❊ ❊ ❊

It's easy to be cynical about Burning Man. At its worst, the event is capitalist escapism. A party where the wealthy run away from, and disdain, the most toxic elements of a system that, for 356 days of the year, many of them sustain, advance, and profit from.

But sitting at the God Phone reminded me that, at its best, Burning Man is an immersive art project. One based on values of communalism, kindness, and generosity.

Many of the people I met at the God Phone had attended Burning Man three, four, even 15 times. Some of them were wealthy, but many weren't. I learned that a lot of people first went to Burning Man for the parties, but almost no one went back just because of them.

People went back because it was a place where they felt they could be their fullest selves, which meant wearing a tutu, taking on a new name, or just telling a stranger that sometimes they found themselves on a dance floor and all they wanted to do was cry. Then trusting that someone would say, "You're wonderful, and I love you unconditionally."

✦   ✦   ✦

Just after 11 p.m. I stepped away from the phone for a nap and to change into warmer clothes. As I stood up, a new god plonked himself in the chair. When I got back at 3 a.m., he was still there, nodding off between calls.

I sat down by the speaker, untangling myself from a long string of lights woven through my shoelaces to keep me visible at night. When I was settled, the tired man in the chair handed me the phone. "You're god," he said, standing up before I could decline. When the phone rang and I answered it, the receiver weighed heavily in my hand.

God, what do you know about shame?

The man calling wore a gray steampunk jacket and large goggles to protect against the dust. He explained how hard he'd worked to get to Burning Man, but once he arrived, he just felt lonely. Then he felt ashamed for being lonely. *A lot of people feel that way,* I told him. *They all call me.*

He laughed, then got quiet. I thought of Karen's advice, and instead of pulling back, I stepped in further. *Do you want to come sit with me?* I asked. He said he'd think about it, then ended the call. Twenty minutes later he called back, and I guided him to the God Phone.

Over the next few hours we sat together. We talked a bit, but not very much, and we listened to the calls come in. By morning I was still carrying shame inside me, and I think he was too. Neither of us had fixed anything, but it was cozy at the God Phone, and I was grateful for the company.

*   *   *

In the early hours of the morning, the sky lit up, its pastel colors form-
ing a rainbow. A woman stopped in to take a few calls and explained it
was her nightly ritual before going to sleep. Later, a man wearing a cap-
tain's jacket and a top hat joined us. He said he was part of the original
camp that brought the Talk to God phone booth, and he'd been taking
calls at sunrise for years.

They were just two of a handful of people I met who, once they found
the phone, visited it again and again.

When I got home, I reached out to Benji to ask why he returned so
often. "It's therapeutic," he told me. "It reminds you that we are all
struggling with things, we are all insecure, and we're all lonely." He
added, "It's not nice to know that other people are suffering, but it's
comforting to know that not everyone is having the best time all day
long. . . . It feels not alone."

*   *   *

Unexpectedly, 24 hours at the Talk to God phone booth reminded me
of my first year of law school, when I felt so sad and overwhelmed that
I sought out counseling for the first time.

In the counselor's office at the school, she asked my field of study and
I told her. She responded, *Oh, I'm seeing all of your classmates.* Before
she said that, I'd thought I was the only one struggling. But afterward,
a warm feeling washed over me. It was the same one that Benji described
at the God Phone, and the same one that Karen tried to foster in her
courses: normalcy.

I still wish the God Phone had some referrals or instructions for really
hard moments, but my time there won me over to Karen and Dr. Dan's
perspective: Given the choice of having the phone as is, or not having it
at all, I'd pick having it every time.

Because the God Phone bathed everyone—callers and gods—in that
feeling of normalcy. In a place where, most of the time, everyone and
everything was striving to be extraordinary, it provided an oasis of or-
dinary. And people gravitated to it. At every hour of the day they gath-
ered around speakers, they lined up, they came back again and again
just to feel it.

Surely, that was worth the risk.

*   *   *

461

At the end of the week, after most people had packed up and gone home, Jaye's partner John walked out to the phone booth to disassemble it. Jaye always left it standing to the last possible minute, tearing down all the tents and rolling up the wall hangings until the booth and the God Phone lay out in the dust alone, just in case someone needed to make a call.

Finally, when everything else was done, John unplugged the God Phone. Then, they dug up the phone line, carefully refilling the trench where it lay, erasing the mark it left in the sand. They hauled the heavy booth to their pickup truck and lay it upside down for the drive home. Plonked there, legs in the air, the booth didn't look like much, just a blue metal box with some stickers on it.

"We took it out there having no idea what would happen with it," Jaye remembered about the booth's first year at Burning Man. But people gravitated to it immediately. "It was clear that people needed that," she said, "and we could give that to them."

Jaye wrapped the God Phone's dangling cord around it, tucked it carefully into the dusty nightstand, and packed it away for next year.

Nominated by Longreads

SPECIAL MENTION

(The editors also wish to mention the following important works published by small presses last year. Listings are in no particular order.)

FICTION

Jackson Bliss—The Geography of Desire (Juked)

Becky Hagenston—Witnesses (Ninth Letter)

Jamel Brinkley—Comfort (Ploughshares)

K.L. Browne—Harmony (Pembroke Magazine)

Kim Chinquee—Mick and Dick (Noon)

Steven Millhauser—Summer of Ladders (Zoetrope)

Melinda Moustakis—At The Salty Dawg Saloon We Break Our Own Hearts (American Short Fiction)

Mala Gaonkar—The New Maid (Catamaran)

Jinwoo Chong—The Lesser Light of Dying Stars (Salamander)

Jenzo Duque—The Rest of Us (One Story)

Alanna Schubach—Next Door (Juked)

Askold Melnyczuk—Nom de Guerre (Missouri Review)

Joanna Hershon—The Queen of Bark and Darkness (Yale Review)

Gothataone Moeng—Small Wonders (One Story)

L.L. Babb—Where Have You Been All Your Life? (Cleaver)

Neshat Khan—Gifted (Mississippi Review)

Brock Clarke—The Big Book of Useless Saturdays (Sewanee Review)

Sara Pritchard—Two Studies In Entropy (New Letters)

Jenn Alandy Trahan—The Freak Winds Up Again (One Story)

Brandon Hobson—Yonder Shines The Big Red Moon (Conjunctions)

Michael X Wang—Further News of Defeat (*Further News of Defeat*, Autumn House)

Lina Meruane—Wir die Deutschen (Brick)
Chris Eagle—Situation Cards (Agni)
Ander Monson—This Time With Feeling—(Harvard Review)
Katherine Vas—The Treasure Hunt of August Dias (The Common)
Kelly Link—The White Road (The Musician of Bremen)
    (A Public Space)
Clare Beams—Milk (Conjunctions)
Jiaming Tang—Where Flowers Bloom But Have No Scent (Agni)
Michelle Herman—The Darling (Ploughshares)
Mai Nardone—The Tum-Boon Brigade (McSweeney's)
Kiik Araki-Kawaguchi—akira-hirata (Grand)
Rachel Hall—Those Girls (New England Review)
Yalitza Ferreras—You Must Be This Tall (Kenyon Review)
Molly Patterson—And The Rivers and The Caves, And The Moon
    And the Earth (Shenandoah)
Jason Ockert—Golden Vulture (Granta)
Diane Williams—Nick Should Be Fun To Be With (Lake Effect)
Zoe Dutka—The Witch (Shenandoah)
Christine Sneed—Direct Sunlight (Boulevard)
Jacob Frommer—May You Be Comforted (Broadkill Review)
Rita Chang-Eppig—The Miracle Girl (Virginia Quarterly Review)
Jack Driscoll—The New World Merging (River Styx)
Ted Thompson—The Electric Slide (American Short Fiction)
Haley Crigger—Not In Any Trouble (Colorado Review)
Scott Nadelson—In Black And White (*One of Us*, BkMk Press)
Lulu Miller—Animal Planet (Orion)
Robert Tindall—Henrietta (Noon)
Perry Lopez—The Hurricane Opportunity (Southampton Review)
Jonathan Escoffery—Odd Jobs (Zyzzyva)
Yxta Maya Murray—No Good Word (Conjunctions)
K-Ming Chang—The Chorus of Dead Cousins (McSweeney's)
Sydney Rende—Lopsided (Michigan Quarterly Review)
Amber Burke—Bed (Quarterly West)
Aisha Ginwalla—White Guavas (New Letters)
Louise Marburg—Love Is Not Enough (Hudson Review)
Stuart Nadler—Fania (Bennington Review)
Michael Byers—Nobody's Dead (Story)
Joseph Hurka—War (Woven Tale Press)
Katherine Vondy—Birds of New Mexico (Iowa Review)
Richard Stim—Closer To Heaven (Reed)

Jake Bartman—Night Swim (Ninth Letter)
Amaworo Wilson—Nazaré (A Public Space)
Cary Holladay—Blackbeards Head (Hudson Review)
Laura Schmitt—Snow Mountain (New England Review)
Cara Blue Adams—The Birdcage (Story)
Enyeribe Ibegwam—Tomorrow Harbors The Unknown
    (Southampton Review)

NONFICTION

Sestinamerica: Poetic Form In The Age of Trump—Bruce Snider
    (West Branch)
Paul Crenshaw—Cold Cola Wars (Ninth Letter)
K. Robert Schaeffer—Tarkovsky by Count Light (Gettysburg Review)
Vicki Madden—Heart Problems (A Public Space)
Eileen Vorbach Collins—Two Tablespoons of Tim (Reed)
Rose Skelton—Little Starts (Ecotone)
Kristen Dorsey—Semper Fi (Chautauqua)
Latoya Faulk—In Search of A Homeplace (The Common)
Christopher Kempf—Local Color (Narrative)
Anne McGrath—Leaving Helen (Columbia Journal)
Natalie Vestin—Optical Illusions of the Lower Atmosphere (Pleiades)
John Griswold—Fragments From An Imagined Apocalypse
    (Common Reader)
Camellia Freeman—A Thing Happens (River Teeth)
Tang Danhong—Chairman Mao Is Dead (Manoa)
Megan Doney—The Wolf and the Dog (Creative Nonfiction)
Melissa Febos—Les Calanques (The Sun)
Nicolas Medina Mora—An American Education (N+l)
Jennifer Haigh—1988 (Sewanee Review)
Elizabeth M. Dalton—Burying Molly (Fourth Genre)
Stephanie Anderson—What The Prairie Dog Knows (TriQuarterly)
Morgan Talty—The Citizenship Question: We The People
    (Georgia Review)
Anna Badkhen—The Pandemic, Our Common Story (Granta)
Louise A. Blum—How It Ends (The Sun)
Meredith Hall—We Are Built To Forget (Paris Review)
Maureen McCoy—Ghost Girl At The Polka Dot Cleaners
    (Antioch Review)
Katherine Scott Nelson—Dinner and A Fight (Ninth Letter)

Victoria Blanco—Border Funeral (Kenyon Review)
Jennifer Tseng—Most of My Dream Fathers Are Women (Ecotone)
David Searcy—Yellowbelly (Oxford American)
William Pierce—The Peculiarities of Literary Meaning (Agni)
Garrett Hongo—On My Therapist, Late In Life (Georgia Review)
Susan Jackson Rodgers—If They Ask What Are you Working on?
    (River Teeth)
Daniel Uncapher—100 Dollars (The Sun)
Francisco Cantu—Murmurs On The Plain (Virginia Quarterly)
Major Jackson—Surroundings More Congenial (Orion)
Mark Doty—You Are Here, You Are Not A Ghost (Paris Review)
Jennifer Genest—The Mills (Colorado Review)
B. Domino—Champagne Room (Iowa Review)
Destiny O. Birdsong—Build Back A Body (Ecotone)

POETRY

Matthew Olzmann—Field Guide for Identifying Winged Creatures
    (Leon Literary Review)
Ashley M. Jones—For the Men Who Made Sure I Knew They Did
    Not Love Me (Cherry Tree)
Danielle De Tiberus—The Artist Signs Her Masterpiece, Immodestly
    (Poem-A-Day)
L. Renee—Fish Fry (Sheila-Na-Gig)
Thomas Q. Morin—A Pile of Fish (Poem-A-Day)
Anne Haven McDonnell—The Swimmers (Terrain)
Shane Seely—Our First Mistake (Gettysburg Review)
Claire Wahmanholm—Glacier One (Beloit)
Linda Gregerson—If The Cure For Aids (Yale Review)
Danusha Lameris—The Grass (Bonfire Opera, Pitt Poetry Series)
Tim Seibles—Simple Song Blues Villanelle (Poetry)
Tommye Blount—'Dahmer Mostly Took Home Black Men (Gertrude)
T.J. Clark—Class (Threepenny Review)
Clarinda Harriss—Black Widow (Smartish Pace)
Jessica Hincapie—Coping Mechanism (Radar Poetry)
Kathryn Levy—They (VoxPopuli)
Jennifer Santos—Madriaga Obscuring (Bamboo Ridge)
Jessica Pierce—I Propose Worshiping the Mud Dauber
    (New Ohio Review)
Q.M.—Look at This Young Foreigner (The Roadrunner Review)

David Roderick—Cicadas (New England Review)
Jamie Wendt—Uprooting a Tree (The Good Life Review)
Knute Skinner—The Mouth Of The Heart (The Hong Kong Review)
Jennifer Perrine—Dog (Again, Airlie Press)
Oscar Garcia Sierra—Cocoa Puffs and MDMA (New Poetry
  in Translation)
Brian Clifton—The Complicated Thing (Broadsided Press)
Ulalume Gonzalez de Leon—Inventario/Inventory
  (Sixteen Rivers Press)
Derrick Austin—In The Decadence of Silence (Adroit Journal)
Threa Almontaser—I Crack An Egg (Split Lip)
Glenn Ingersoll—Personal Testimony (Spillway).
Madeline Barnes—Forty Black Ships (Trio House)
Kary Wayson—Untitled Poem (for a Feeling) (The Volta)
Sherine Gilmour—Hunger (Third Coast)
Jeanne Marie Beaumont—Origin Story (Manhattan Review)
William Olsen—Lament For The Hummingbird Drones
  (Michigan Quarterly Review)
David Wojahn—Written on The Anniversary of My Teacher's Death
  (Michigan Quarterly Review)
Brendan Constantine—What's Not To Love (Poetry)
Tanya Larkin—My Nature (Pangyrus)
Stephen Kuusisto—Horse Dream Man, Helsinki 1980 (Tiger Bark)
Mark Halliday—Toodlers (The Florida Review)
Joe Wilkins—The Sorrowful Mysteries (Southern Review)

PRESSES FEATURED IN THE PUSHCART PRIZE EDITIONS SINCE 1976

A-Minor
About Place Journal
Abstract Magazine TV
The Account
Adroit Journal
Agni
Ahsahta Press
Ailanthus Press
Alaska Quarterly Review
Alcheringa/Ethnopoetics
Alice James Books
Ambergris
Amelia
American Circus
American Journal of Poetry
American Letters and Commentary
American Literature
American PEN
American Poetry Review
American Scholar
American Short Fiction
The American Voice
Amicus Journal
Amnesty International
Anaesthesia Review
Anhinga Press
Another Chicago Magazine

Antaeus
Antietam Review
Antioch Review
Apalachee Quarterly
Aphra
Aralia Press
The Ark
Arkansas Review
Arroyo
Art and Understanding
Arts and Letters
Artword Quarterly
Ascensius Press
Ascent
Ashland Poetry Press
Aspen Leaves
Aspen Poetry Anthology
Assaracus
Assembling
Atlanta Review
Autonomedia
Avocet Press
The Awl
The Baffler
Bakunin
Bare Life
Bat City Review

Bamboo Ridge
Barlenmir House
Barnwood Press
Barrow Street
Bellevue Literary Review
The Bellingham Review
Bellowing Ark
Beloit Poetry Journal
Bennington Review
Bettering America Poetry
Bilingual Review
Birmingham Poetry Review
Black American Literature Forum
Blackbird
Black Renaissance Noire
Black Rooster
Black Scholar
Black Sparrow
Black Warrior Review
Blackwells Press
The Believer
Bloom
Bloomsbury Review
Bloomsday Lit
Blue Cloud Quarterly
Blueline
Blue Unicorn
Blue Wind Press
Bluefish
BOA Editions
Bomb
Bookslinger Editions
Boomer Litmag
Boston Review
Boulevard
Boxspring
Brevity
Briar Cliff Review
Brick
Bridge
Bridges
Brown Journal of Arts
Burning Deck Press
Butcher's Dog

Cafe Review
Caliban
California Quarterly
Callaloo
Calliope
Calliopea Press
Calyx
The Canary
Canto
Capra Press
Carcanet Editions
Caribbean Writer
Carolina Quarterly
Catapult
Cave Wall
Cedar Rock
Center
Chariton Review
Charnel House
Chattahoochee Review
Chautauqua Literary Journal
Chelsea
Chicago Quarterly Review
Chouteau Review
Chowder Review
Cimarron Review
Cincinnati Review
Cincinnati Poetry Review
City Lights Books
Cleveland State Univ. Poetry Ctr.
Clover
Clown War
Codex Journal
CoEvolution Quarterly
Cold Mountain Press
The Collagist
Colorado Review
Columbia: A Magazine of Poetry and Prose
Columbia Poetry Review
The Common
Conduit
Confluence Press
Confrontation
Conjunctions

Connecticut Review
Constellations
Copper Canyon Press
Copper Nickel
Cosmic Information Agency
Countermeasures
Counterpoint
Court Green
Crab Orchard Review
Crawl Out Your Window
Crazyhorse
Creative Nonfiction
Crescent Review
Cross Cultural Communications
Cross Currents
Crosstown Books
Crowd
Cue
Cumberland Poetry Review
Curbstone Press
Cutbank
Cypher Books
Dacotah Territory
Daedalus
Dalkey Archive Press
Decatur House
December
Denver Quarterly
Desperation Press
Dogwood
Domestic Crude
Doubletake
Dragon Gate Inc.
Dreamworks
Dryad Press
Duck Down Press
Dunes Review
Durak
East River Anthology
Eastern Washington University Press
Ecotone
Egress
El Malpensante
Electric Literature

Eleven Eleven
Ellis Press
Emergence
Empty Bowl
Ep;phany
Epoch
Ergol
Evansville Review
Exquisite Corpse
Faultline
Fence
Fiction
Fiction Collective
Fiction International
Field
Fifth Wednesday Journal
Fine Madness
Firebrand Books
Firelands Art Review
First Intensity
5 A.M.
Five Fingers Review
Five Points Press
Fjords Review
Florida Review
Foglifter
Forklift
The Formalist
Foundry
Four Way Books
Fourth Genre
Fourth River
Frontiers: A Journal of Women Studies
Fugue
Gallimaufry
Genre
The Georgia Review
Gettysburg Review
Ghost Dance
Gibbs-Smith
Glimmer Train
Goddard Journal
David Godine, Publisher
Gordon Square

Graham House Press

Grain

Grand Street

Granta

Graywolf Press

Great River Review

Green Mountains Review

Greenfield Review

Greensboro Review

Guardian Press

Gulf Coast

Hanging Loose

Harbour Publishing

Hard Pressed

Harvard Advocate

Harvard Review

Hawaii Pacific Review

Hayden's Ferry Review

Hermitage Press

Heyday

Hills

Hobart

Hole in the Head

Hollyridge Press

Holmgangers Press

Holy Cow!

Home Planet News

Hopkins Review

Hudson Review

Hunger Mountain

Hungry Mind Review

Hysterical Rag

Iamb

Ibbetson Street Press

Icarus

Icon

Idaho Review

Iguana Press

Image

In Character

Indiana Review

Indiana Writes

Indianapolis Review

Intermedia

Intro

Invisible City

Inwood Press

Iowa Review

Ironwood

I-70 Review

Jam To-day

J Journal

The Journal

Jubilat

The Kanchenjunga Press

Kansas Quarterly

Kayak

Kelsey Street Press

Kenyon Review

Kestrel

Kweli Journal

Lake Effect

Lana Turner

Latitudes Press

Laughing Waters Press

Laurel Poetry Collective

Laurel Review

L'Epervier Press

Liberation

Ligeia

Linquis

Literal Latté

Literary Imagination

The Literary Review

The Little Magazine

Little Patuxent Review

Little Star

Living Hand Press

Living Poets Press

Logbridge-Rhodes

Longreads

Louisville Review

Love's Executive Order

Lowlands Review

LSU Press

Lucille

Lynx House Press

Lyric

The MacGuffin
Magic Circle Press
Malahat Review
Manhattan Review
Manoa
Manroot
Many Mountains Moving
Marlboro Review
Massachusetts Review
McSweeney's
Meridian
Mho & Mho Works
Micah Publications
Michigan Quarterly
Mid-American Review
Milkweed Editions
Milkweed Quarterly
The Minnesota Review
Mississippi Review
Mississippi Valley Review
Missouri Review
Montana Gothic
Montana Review
Montemora
Moon Pie Press
Moon Pony Press
Mount Voices
Mr. Cogito Press
MSS
Mudfish
Mulch Press
Muzzle Magazine
n + 1
Nada Press
Narrative
National Poetry Review
Nebraska Poets Calendar
Nebraska Review
Nepantla
Nerve Cowboy
New America
New American Review
New American Writing
The New Criterion

New Delta Review
New Directions
New England Review
New England Review and Bread Loaf
    Quarterly
New Issues
New Letters
New Madrid
New Ohio Review
New Orleans Review
New South Books
New Verse News
New Virginia Review
New York Quarterly
New York University Press
Nimrod
9×9 Industries
Ninth Letter
Noon
North American Review
North Atlantic Books
North Dakota Quarterly
North Point Press
Northeastern University Press
Northern Lights
Northwest Review
Notre Dame Review
O. ARS
O. Blk
Obsidian
Obsidian II
Ocho
Oconee Review
October
Ohio Review
Old Crow Review
Ontario Review
Open City
Open Places
Orca Press
Orchises Press
Oregon Humanities
Orion
Other Voices

Oxford American
Oxford Press
Oyez Press
Oyster Boy Review
Painted Bride Quarterly
Painted Hills Review
Palette
Palo Alto Review
Paper Darts
Paris Press
Paris Review
Parkett
Parnassus: Poetry in Review
Partisan Review
Passages North
Paterson Literary Review
Pebble Lake Review
Penca Books
Pentagram
Penumbra Press
Pequod
Persea: An International Review
Perugia Press
Per Contra
Pilot Light
The Pinch
Pipedream Press
Pirene's Fountain
Pitcairn Press
Pitt Magazine
Pleasure Boat Studio
Pleiades
Ploughshares
Plume
Poem-A-Day
Poems & Plays
Poet and Critic
Poet Lore
Poetry
Poetry Atlanta Press
Poetry East
Poetry International
Poetry Ireland Review
Poetry Northwest

Poetry Now
The Point
Post Road
Prairie Schooner
Prelude
Prescott Street Press
Press
Prime Number
Prism
Promise of Learnings
Provincetown Arts
A Public Space
Puerto Del Sol
Purple Passion Press
Quademi Di Yip
Quarry West
The Quarterly
Quarterly West
Quiddity
Radio Silence
Rainbow Press
Raritan: A Quarterly Review
Rattle
Red Cedar Review
Red Clay Books
Red Dust Press
Red Earth Press
Red Hen Press
Reed
Release Press
Republic of Letters
Review of Contemporary Fiction
Revista Chicano-Riqueña
Rhetoric Review
Rhino
Rivendell
River Styx
River Teeth
Rowan Tree Press
Ruminate
Runes
Russian *Samizdat*
Salamander
Salmagundi

San Marcos Press
Santa Monica Review
Sarabande Books
Saturnalia
Sea Pen Press and Paper Mill
Seal Press
Seamark Press
Seattle Review
Second Coming Press
Semiotext(e)
Seneca Review
Seven Days
The Seventies Press
Sewanee Review
The Shade Journal
Shankpainter
Shantih
Shearsman
Sheep Meadow Press
Shenandoah
A Shout In the Street
Sibyl-Child Press
Side Show
Sidereal
Sixth Finch
Slipstream
Small Moon
Smartish Pace
The Smith
Snake Nation Review
Solo
Solo 2
Some
The Sonora Review
Southeast Review
Southern Indiana Review
Southern Poetry Review
Southern Review
Southampton Review
Southwest Review
Speakeasy
Spectrum
Spillway
Spork

The Spirit That Moves Us
St. Andrews Press
St. Brigid Press
Stillhouse Press
Storm Cellar
Story
Story Quarterly
Streetfare Journal
Stuart Wright, Publisher
Subtropics
Sugar House Review
Sulfur
Summerset Review
The Sun
Sun & Moon Press
Sun Press
Sunstone
Sweet
Sycamore Review
Tab
Tamagawa
Tar River Poetry
Teal Press
Telephone Books
Telescope
Temblor
The Temple
Tendril
Terrain
Terminus
Terrapin Books
Texas Slough
Think
Third Coast
13th Moon
THIS
This Broken Shore
Thorp Springs Press
Three Rivers Press
Threepenny Review
Thrush
Thunder City Press
Thunder's Mouth Press
Tia Chucha Press

Tiger Bark Press
Tikkun
Tin House
Tipton Review
Tombouctou Books
Toothpaste Press
Transatlantic Review
Treelight
Triplopia
TriQuarterly
Truck Press
True Story
Tule Review
Tupelo Review
Turnrow
Tusculum Review
Two Sylvias
Twyckenham Notes
Undine
Unicorn Press
University of Chicago Press
University of Georgia Press
University of Illinois Press
University of Iowa Press
University of Massachusetts Press
University of North Texas Press
University of Pittsburgh Press
University of Wisconsin Press
University Press of New England
Unmuzzled Ox
Unspeakable Visions of the Individual
Vagabond
Vallum
Verse
Verse Wisconsin
Vignette
Virginia Quarterly Review

Volt
The Volta
Wampeter Press
War, Literature & The Arts
Washington Square Review
Washington Writer's Workshop
Water-Stone
Water Table
Wave Books
Waxwing
West Branch
Western Humanities Review
Westigan Review
White Pine Press
Wickwire Press
Wigleaf
Willow Springs
Wilmore City
Witness
Word Beat Press
Word Press
Wordsmith
World Literature Today
WordTemple Press
Wormwood Review
Writers' Forum
Xanadu
Yale Review
Yardbird Reader
Yarrow
Y-Bird
Yes Yes Books
Zeitgeist Press
Zoetrope: All-Story
Zone 3
ZYZZYVA

THE PUSHCART PRIZE FELLOWSHIPS

The Pushcart Prize Fellowships Inc., a 501 (c) (3) nonprofit corporation, is the endowment for The Pushcart Prize. "Members" donated up to $249 each. "Sponsors" gave between $250 and $999. "Benefactors" donated from $1000 to $4,999. "Patrons" donated $5,000 and more. We are very grateful for these donations. Gifts of any amount are welcome. For information write to the Fellowships at PO Box 380, Wainscott, NY 11975.

FOUNDING PATRONS

The Katherine Anne Porter Literary Trust
Michael and Elizabeth R. Rea

PATRONS

Anonymous
Margaret Ajemian Ahnert
Daniel L. Dolgin & Loraine F. Gardner
James Patterson Foundation
Neltje
Charline Spektor
Ellen M. Violett

BENEFACTORS

Anonymous
Russell Allen
Hilaria & Alec Baldwin
David Caldwell
Ted Conklin
Bernard F. Conners
Catherine and C. Bryan Daniels
Maureen Mahon Egen
Dallas Ernst
Cedering Fox
H.E. Francis
Mary Ann Goodman & Bruno Quinson Foundation

Bill & Genie Henderson
Bob Henderson
Marina & Stephen E. Kaufman
Wally & Christine Lamb
Dorothy Lichtenstein
Joyce Carol Oates
Warren & Barbara Phillips
Stacey Richter
Glyn Vincent
Kirby E. Williams
Margaret V. B. Wurtele

SUSTAINING MEMBERS

Anonymous
Agni
Jim Barnes
Ellen Bass
Wendell Berry
Rosellen Brown
Phil Carter
David Caldwell
Lucinda Clark
Suzanne Cleary
Martha Collins
Linda Coleman
Ted Colm
Lisa Couturier
Dan Dolgin & Loraine Gardner
Jack Driscoll
Maureen Mahon Egen
Alice Friman
Ben & Sharon Fountain
Robert Giron
Alex Henderson
Bob Henderson
Jane Hirshfield
Helen Houghton
Christian Jara
Diane Johnson
Don and Renee Kaplan
John Kistner
Peter Krass
Edmund Keeley

Ron Koertge
Paul Kurzeja
Wally & Christine Lamb
Linda Lancione
Sandra Leong
Maria Matthiessen
Alice Mattison
Rick Moody
Joan Murray
Neltje
Joyce Carol Oates
Dan Orozco
Pam Painter
Barbara & Warren Phillips
Horatio Potter
Elizabeth R. Rea
Stacey Richter
Schaffner Family Fdn.
Jody Stewart
Sybil Steinberg
John Tepper-Marlin
Elaine Terranova
Universal Table
Upstreet
Glyn Vincent
Rosanna Warren
Michael Waters
Diane Williams
Kirby E. Williams
1–70 Review

SPONSORS

Altman / Kazickas Fdn.
Jacob Appel
Jean M. Auel
Jim Barnes
Charles Baxter
Joe David Bellamy
Laura & Pinckney Benedict
Wendell Berry
Laure-Anne Bosselaar
Kate Braverman
Barbara Bristol
Kurt Brown
Richard Burgin
Alan Catlin
Mary Casey
Siv Cedering
Dan Chaon
James Charlton
Andrei Codrescu
Linda Coleman

Ted Colm
Stephen Corey
Tracy Crow
Dana Literary Society
Carol de Gramont
Nelson DeMille
E. L. Doctorow
Penny Dunning
Karl Elder
Donald Finkel
Ben and Sharon Fountain
Alan and Karen Furst
John Gill
Robert Giron
Beth Gutcheon
Doris Grumbach & Sybil Pike
Gwen Head
The Healing Muse
Robin Hemley
Bob Hicok

Jane Hirshfield
Helen & Frank Houghton
Joseph Hurka
Christian Jara
Diane Johnson
Janklow & Nesbit Asso.
Edmund Keeley
Thomas E. Kennedy
Sydney Lea
Stephen Lesser
Gerald Locklin
Thomas Lux
Markowitz, Fenelon and Bank
Elizabeth McKenzie
McSweeney's
Rick Moody
John Mullen

Joan Murray
Barbara and Warren Phillips
Hilda Raz
Stacey Richter
Schaffner Family Foundation
Sharasheff—Johnson Fund
Cindy Sherman
Joyce Carol Smith
May Carlton Swope
Glyn Vincent
Julia Wendell
Philip White
Diane Williams
Kirby E. Williams
Eleanor Wilner
David Wittman
Richard Wyatt & Irene Eilers

MEMBERS

Anonymous (3)
Stephen Adams
Betty Adcock
Agni
Carolyn Alessio
Dick Allen
Henry H. Allen
John Allman
Lisa Alvarez
Jan Lee Ande
Dr. Russell Anderson
Ralph Angel
Antietam Review
Susan Antolin
Ruth Appelhof
Philip and Marjorie Appleman
Linda Aschbrenner
Renee Ashley
Ausable Press
David Baker
Catherine Barnett
Dorothy Barresi
Barlow Street Press
Jill Bart
Ellen Bass
Judith Baumel
Ann Beattie
Madison Smartt Bell
Beloit Poetry Journal
Pinckney Benedict
Karen Bender
Andre Bernard
Christopher Bernard
Wendell Berry
Linda Bierds

Stacy Bierlein
Big Fiction
Bitter Oleander Press
Mark Blaeuer
John Blondel
Blue Light Press
Carol Bly
BOA Editions
Deborah Bogen
Bomb
Susan Bono
Brain Child
Anthony Brandt
James Breeden
Rosellen Brown
Jane Brox
Andrea Hollander Budy
E. S. Bumas
Richard Burgin
Skylar H. Burris
David Caligiuri
Kathy Callaway
Bonnie Jo Campbell
Janine Canan
Henry Carlile
Carrick Publishing
Fran Castan
Mary Casey
Chelsea Associates
Marianne Cherry
Phillis M. Choyke
Lucinda Clark
Suzanne Cleary
Linda Coleman
Martha Collins

Ted Conklin
Joan Connor
J. Cooper
John Copenhaver
Dan Corrie
Pam Cothey
Lisa Couturier
Tricia Currans-Sheehan
Jim Daniels
Daniel & Daniel
Jerry Danielson
Ed David
Josephine David
Thadious Davis
Michael Denison
Maija Devine
Sharon Dilworth
Edward DiMaio
Kent Dixon
A.C. Dorset
Jack Driscoll
Wendy Druce
Penny Dunning
John Duncklee
Nancy Ebert
Elaine Edelman
Renee Edison & Don Kaplan
Nancy Edwards
Ekphrasis Press
M.D. Elevitch
Elizabeth Ellen
Entrekin Foundation
Failbetter.com
Irvin Faust
Elliot Figman
Tom Filer
Carol and Laueme Firth
Finishing Line Press
Susan Firer
Nick Flynn
Starkey Flythe Jr.
Peter Fogo
Linda Foster
Fourth Genre
Alice Friman
John Fulton
Fugue
Alice Fulton
Alan Furst
Eugene Garber
Frank X. Gaspar
A Gathering of the Tribes
Reginald Gibbons
Emily Fox Gordon
Philip Graham

Eamon Grennan
Myma Goodman
Ginko Tree Press
Jessica Graustain
Lee Meitzen Grue
Habit of Rainy Nights
Rachel Hadas
Susan Hahn
Meredith Hall
Harp Strings
Jeffrey Harrison
Clarinda Harriss
Lois Marie Harrod
Healing Muse
Tim Hedges
Michele Helm
Alex Henderson
Lily Henderson
Daniel Henry
Neva Herington
Lou Hertz
Stephen Herz
William Heyen
Bob Hicok
R. C. Hildebrandt
Kathleen Hill
Lee Hinton
Jane Hirshfield
Hippocampus Magazin
Edward Hoagland
Daniel Hoffman
Doug Holder
Richard Holinger
Rochelle L. Holt
Richard M. Huber
Brigid Hughes
Lynne Hugo
Karla Huston
1–70 Review
Iliya's Honey
Susan Indigo
Mark Irwin
Beverly A. Jackson
Richard Jackson
Christian Jara
David Jauss
Marilyn Johnston
Alice Jones
Journal of New Jersey Poets
Robert Kalich
Sophia Kartsonis
Julia Kasdorf
Miriam Polli Katsikis
Meg Kearney
Celine Keating

Brigit Kelly
John Kistner
Judith Kitchen
Ron Koertge
Stephen Kopel
Peter Krass
David Kresh
Maxine Kumin
Valerie Laken
Babs Lakey
Linda Lancione
Maxine Landis
Lane Larson
Dorianne Laux & Joseph Millar
Sydney Lea
Stephen Lesser
Donald Lev
Dana Levin
Live Mag!
Gerald Locklin
Rachel Loden
Radomir Luza, Jr.
William Lychack
Annette Lynch
Elzabeth MacKieman
Elizabeth Macklin
Leah Maines
Mark Manalang
Norma Marder
Jack Marshall
Michael Martone
Tara L. Masih
Dan Masterson
Peter Matthiessen
Maria Matthiessen
Alice Mattison
Tracy Mayor
Robert McBrearty
Jane McCafferty
Rebecca McClanahan
Bob McCrane
Jo McDougall
Sandy McIntosh
James McKean
Roberta Mendel
Didi Menendez
Barbara Milton
Alexander Mindt
Mississippi Review
Nancy Mitchell
Martin Mitchell
Roger Mitchell
Jewell Mogan
Patricia Monaghan
Jim Moore

James Morse
William Mulvihill
Nami Mun
Joan Murray
Carol Muske-Dukes
Edward Mycue
Deirdre Neilen
W. Dale Nelson
New Michigan Press
Jean Nordhaus
Celeste Ng
Christiana Norcross
Ontario Review Foundation
Daniel Orozco
Other Voices
Paris Review
Alan Michael Parker
Ellen Parker
Veronica Patterson
David Pearce, M.D.
Robert Phillips
Donald Platt
Plain View Press
Valerie Polichar
Pool
Horatio Potter
Jeffrey & Priscilla Potter
C.E. Poverman
Marcia Preston
Eric Puchner
Osiris
Tony Quagliano
Quill & Parchment
Barbara Quinn
Randy Rader
Juliana Rew
Belle Randall
Martha Rhodes
Nancy Richard
Stacey Richter
James Reiss
Katrina Roberts
Judith R. Robinson
Jessica Roeder
Martin Rosner
Kay Ryan
Sy Safransky
Brian Salchert
James Salter
Sherod Santos
Ellen Sargent
R.A. Sasaki
Valerie Sayers
Maxine Scates
Alice Schell

Dennis & Loretta Schmitz
Grace Schulman
Helen Schulman
Philip Schultz
Shenandoah
Peggy Shinner
Lydia Ship
Vivian Shipley
Joan Silver
Skyline
John E. Smeleer
Raymond J. Smith
Joyce Carol Smith
Philip St. Clair
Lorraine Standish
Maureen Stanton
Michael Steinberg
Sybil Steinberg
Jody Stewart
Barbara Stone
Storyteller Magazine
Bill & Pat Strachan
Raymond Strom
Julie Suk
Summerset Review
Sun Publishing
Sweet Annie Press
Katherine Taylor
Pamela Taylor
Elaine Terranova
Susan Terris
Marcelle Thiebaux
Robert Thomas
Andrew Tonkovich
Pauls Toutonghi
Juanita Torrence-Thompson
William Trowbridge
Martin Tucker
Umbrella Factory Press
Under The Sun

Universal Table
Upstreet
Jeannette Valentine
Victoria Valentine
Christine Van Winkle
Hans Vandebovenkamp
Elizabeth Veach
Tino Villanueva
Maryfrances Wagner
William & Jeanne Wagner
BJ Ward
Susan O. Warner
Rosanna Warren
Margareta Waterman
Michael Waters
Stuart Watson
Sandi Weinberg
Andrew Wainstein
Dr. Henny Wenkart
Jason Wesco
West Meadow Press
Susan Wheeler
When Women Waken
Dara Wier
Ellen Wilbur
Galen Williams
Diane Williams
Marie Sheppard Williams
Eleanor Wilner
Irene Wilson
Steven Wingate
Sandra Wisenberg
Wings Press
Robert Witt
David Wittman
Margot Wizansky
Matt Yurdana
Christina Zawadiwsky
Sander Zulauf
ZYZZYVA

CONTRIBUTING SMALL PRESSES FOR PUSHCART PRIZE XLVI

(These presses made or received nominations for this edition.)

AbstractMagazineTV.com, 124 E. Johnson St., Norman, OK 73069

ABV Publishing, 213 Canterbury Dr., State College, PA 16803

Abyss & Apex, 116 Tennyson Dr., Lexington, SC 29073

Academy of American Poets, 75 Maiden Lane, #901, New York, NY 10038

Accents Publishing, PO Box 910456, Lexington, KY 40591-0456

The Account 257 15th St., PH2, Brooklyn, NY 11215

Acre Books, University of Cincinnati, English, 248 McMicken Hall Cincinnati, OH 45221

Active Muse, 3080 St. Rose Pkwy, Apt 1133, Henderson, NV 89052

Adanna Literary Journal, P.O. Box 547, Manasquan, NJ 08736

The Adroit Journal, LaBerge, 1223 Westover Rd., Stamford, CT 06902

Aeon Media, Level 5/100 Flinders Street, Melbourne VIC 3000 Australia

After Happy Hour, Simms, 599 Blessing St., Pittsburgh, PA 15213

After the Art Journal, Randon Billings Noble, 3000 Connecticut Ave. NW #233, Washington, DC 20008

Agni Magazine, Boston Univ., 236 Bay State Rd., Boston, MA 02215

Agorist Writers Workshop, Mickel, 2305 130th St. W, Rosemount, MN 55068

Airlie Press, PO Box 68441, Portland, OR 97268

Air/Light Press, 2026 N. Bronson Ave., Los Angeles, CA 90068-3505

Alaska Quarterly, ESH 208, 3211 Providence Dr., Anchorage, AK 99508

Alaska Women Speak, PO Box 90475, Anchorage, AK 99509

Alba, Ravenna Press, PO Box 1166, Edmonds, WA 98020

Albuquerque The Magazine, ABQ, 1550 Mercantile Ave. NE, Top Floor Albuquerque, NM 87107

Algonquin Books, PO Box 2225, Chapel Hill, NC 27515-2225

Alice James Books, 114 Prescott St., Farmington, ME 04938-6801

Alien Buddha Press, 335 Draymont Dr., Spartanburg, SC 29303

Al-khemia Poetica, Lecrivain, 6028 Comey Ave., Los Angeles, CA 90034

Alternative Field Notes, 135 N. Avenue 50, Los Angeles, CA 90042

Always Crashing, 1401 N. St. Clair, #3A, Pittsburgh, PA 15206

American Journal of Poetry, 14969 Chateau Village Dr., Chesterfield, MO 63017

American Poetry Journal, 2347 Hollywood Dr., Pittsburgh, PA 15235

American Poetry Review, 1906 Rittenhouse Sq., Philadelphia, PA 19103

American Short Fiction, 109 West Johanna St., Austin, TX 78704

The Amistad, Seifert, Howard Univ., 2441 6th St. NW, #248, Washington, DC 20059

Ananke Press, 178 Columbus Ave., #230137, New York, NY 10023

And Other Poems, 51 Avenue Rd, Trowbridge, Wiltshire, BA14 0AQ, UK

Another Chicago Magazine, 1301 W. Byron St., Chicago, IL 60613

Antioch Review, One Morgan Place, Yellow Springs, OH 45387

aperture, 548 W. 28th St., 4th floor, New York, NY 10001

Apogee Press, 2308 Sixth St., Berkeley, CA 94710

Appalachia Journal, Woodside, 41 Bridge St., Deep River, CT 06417

Appalachian Heritage, Berea College, CPO 2166, Berea, KY 40404

Apple Valley Review, 88 South 3rd St., #336, San José, CA 95113

Aquarius Press, PO Box 23096, Detroit MI 48223-0096

Arachne Press, 100 Grierson Rd., London SE23 1NX, UK

The Ardent Writer Press, 1014 Stone Dr., Brownsboro, AL 35741

Arizona Authors, 1119 E. LeMarche Ave., Phoenix, AZ 85022

Arkana, Thompson Hall 324, 201 Donaghey Ave., Conway, AR 72035

Arkansas International, UAR, Kimpel Hall 333, Fayetteville, AR 72701

Armstrong Literary Journal, Queens Hall 330A, 65-30 Kissena Blvd., Flushing, NY 11367

Arrowsmith Press, 11 Chestnut St., Medford, MA 02155

Arroyo Seco Press, 6081 Cerritos Avenue, Long Beach, CA 90805

Art Night Books, Vasquez, 218 S. Walbridge Ave., Madison, WI 53714

Arts & Letters, CBX 89, Georgia College, Milledgeville, GA 31061

Ashland Poetry Press, 401 College Ave., Ashland, OH 44805

Asian American Writers Workshop, 110-112 W. 27th St., Ste. 600, New York, NY 10001-3808

ASPECT, Virginia Tech, 202 MW Hall, #0192, Blacksburg, VA 24061

Aster(ix), Cruz, 81 Cabrini Blvd., #22, New York, NY 10033

Atticus Review, 1201 N 3rd St., #308, Philadelphia, PA 19122

Aubade Publishing, Puckett, 19938 Alexandras Grove Dr., Ashburn, VA 20147-3113

Aurora Poetry, 1918 S. Harvard Blvd., #10, Los Angeles, CA 90018

Autumn House Press, 5530 Penn Ave., Pittsburgh, PA 15206

Awst Press, PO Box 49163, Austin, TX 78765

Baltimore Review, 6514 Maplewood Rd., Baltimore, MD 21212

Bamboo Ridge Press, PO Box 61781, Honolulu, HI 96839-1781

Barcelona Review, Jill Adams, Editor, TBR, Barcelonareview.com

Bare Life Review, PO Box 352, Lagunitas, CA 94938

Barren Magazine, 10755 Chancellor St., Portage, MI 49002

Basset Hound Press, 1116 N. Carlos St., Wichita, KS 67203

Bat City Review, 2507 Givens Ave., Austin, TX 78722

Bear Review, 4211 Holmes St., Kansas City, MO 64110

Believer, UNLV, MS 455085, 4505 S. Maryland Pkwy, Las Vegas, NV 89154

Beliveau Books, 295 Willow St., #104, Stratford, ON N5A 3B8, Canada

Bellevue Literary Review, 221 E. 29th St., New York, NY 10016

Beloit Fiction Journal, Box 11,700 College St., Beloit, WI 53511

Beloit Poetry Journal, PO Box 1450, Windham, ME 04062

Beltway Poetry Quarterly, 1630 Park Rd. NW, #305, Washington, DC 20010

Bending Genres, Vaughan, 7735 North River Rd, River Hills, WI 53217

Bennington Review, Turner, 461 Lorimer St., #2F, Brooklyn, NY 11206

Berkeley Fiction Review, 1308 Burnett St., Apt B, Berkeley, CA 94702

Better Than Starbucks, 146 Lake Constance, West Palm Beach, FL 33411

BHC Press, 885 Penniman #5505, Plymouth, MI 48170

Big Other, 1840 W. 3rd St., Brooklyn, NY 11223

Big Windows, 2012 Marra Dr., Ann Arbor, MI 48103-6186

bioStories, 225 Log Yard Ct, Bigfork, MT 59911

Birmingham Poetry Review, English, UAB, Birmingham, AL 35294-0110

The Bitchin' Kitsch, 1635 Cook St., #214, Denver, CO 80206

Bitter Southerner, PO Box 1611, Athens, GA 30603

BkMk Press, UMKC, 5101 Rockhill Rd., Kansas City, MO 64110-2446

Black Earth Institute, P.O. Box 424, Black Earth, WI 53515

Black Hare Press, Ste. 600, Unit 2, 134-136 Pascoe Vale Rd., Moonee Ponds,
    Vic 3039, Australia

Black Mountain Press, PO Box 9907, Asheville, NC 28815

Black Rose Writing, Rothe, 2481 CR 4516, Hondo, TX 78861

Black Warrior, Univ. of Alabama, Box 870244, Tuscaloosa, AL 35487

Blackbird, VCU, English, PO Box 843082, Richmond, VA 23284-3082

Blank Spaces, 282906 Normanby/Bentinck Townline, Durham ON N0G
    1R0, Canada

Blanket Sea Magazine, 516 ½ N. Ainsworth Ave., Tacoma, WA 98403

Blink-Ink, P.O. Box 5, North Branford, CT 06471

Blood Orange Review, W.S.U., English, Box 645020, Pullman, WA 99164-5020

Bloodroot Literary, Mosteirin, 71 Baker Hill Rd., Lyme, NH 03768

Bloomsbury Review, 1245 E. Colfax Ave., #304, Denver, CO 80218-2238

Bloomsday Literary, 1039 Orchard Hill St., Houston, TX 77077

Blue Light Press, PO Box 150300, San Rafael, CA 94915

Blue Mountain Review, Southern Collective Experience, 55 Brer Rabbit Trail, Jasper, GA 30143

Blue Nib, Ecklands, Carnhill, Loughshinny, Skerries, Co. Dublin. K34WR02, IRELAND

Blue Unicorn, 13 Jefferson Ave., San Rafael, CA 94903

Bluegrass Writers Studio, EKU, Mattox 101, 521 Lancaster Ave., Richmond, KY 40475

Bodega Magazine, 451 Court St., #3R, Brooklyn, NY 11231

Bomb, 80 Hanson Place, Ste. 703, Brooklyn, NY 11217

Boomer Lit, 4509 Beard Ave So., Minneapolis, MN 55410

Booth, 4600 Sunset Ave., Indianapolis, IN 46208

Borda Books, 19 E. Islay St., Santa Barbara, CA 93101

Border Crossing, 650 W. Easterday Ave., Sault Ste. Marie, MI 49783

Borderlands: Texas Poetry Review, P.O. Box 33096, Austin, TX 78764

Bottom Dog Press, PO Box 425, Huron, OH 44839

Boulevard, 3829 Hartford St., Saint Louis, MO 63116-4807

Box Turtle Press, Hoffman, 184 Franklin St., New York, NY 10013

Brain Mill Press, 1051 Kellogg St., Green Bay, WI 54303-2968

Brevity, c/o Moore, 265 E State St., Athens, OH 45701

Briar Cliff Review, 3303 Rebecca St., Sioux City, IA 51104-2100

Brick, c/o Lasorda, 36 Head St., Oakville, ON L6K 1L5, Canada

Brick Road Poetry Press, 341 Lee Rd. 553, Phenix City, AL 36867

Brilliant Flash Fiction, 4201 Corbett Dr., #343, Fort Collins, CO 80525

Brittle Paper Magazine, A. Edoro, English, 600 N. Park St., Madison, WI 53706

Broadkill Review, PO Box 63, Milton, DE 19968

Broadsided, PO Box 24, Provincetown, MA 02657

Broadstone Books, 418 Ann St., Frankfort, KY 40601-1929

Brooklyn Poets, 544 South Ave., Beacon, NY 12508

Brooklyn Rail, 253 36th Street, 3rd Fl., Ste. C304, Brooklyn, NY 11232

Brooklyn Sunday Stories, c/o T. Carroll, 201 Java St., #2, Brooklyn, NY 11222

BSC Publishing Group, 210 N. Broadway, #1136, New Philadelphia, OH 44663

Burial Day Books, Pelayo, 4417 W. Montana, Chicago, IL 60639

Burningwood Literary Journal, PO Box 6215, Kokomo, IN 46904-6215

Caesura, Poetry Center of San José, 1650 Senter Rd., San José, CA 95112

Café Irreal, PO Box 87031, Tucson, AZ 85754

Cagibi, 801 Avenue C, #4C, Brooklyn, NY 11218

Canary, 5 Del Mar Court, Orinda, CA 94563

Capsule Stories, PO Box 11762, Clayton, MO 63015

Carve Magazine, PO Box 701510, Dallas, TX 75370

Casa Express Editions, c/o Jobin, E.S.J., 107 rue de Tolbiac, Paris 75013, France

Catamaran, 1050 River St., #118, Santa Cruz, CA 95060

Catapult 1140 Broadway, Ste. 704, New York, NY 10001

Cave Wall Press, PO Box 29546, Greensboro, NC 27429-9546

Central Avenue Publishing, 396-5148 Ladner Trunk Rd., Delta BC V4K 5B6, Canada

Červená Barva Press, PO Box 440357, W. Somerville, MA 02144

Chaffin Journal, Mattox 103, 521 Lancaster Ave., Richmond, KY 40475

Chattahoochee Review, GSU, English, 33 Gilmer St. SE, Atlanta, GA 30303

Chautauqua, UNC-W, Creative Writing, 601 S. College Rd., Wilmington, NC 28403

Cheap Pop, Russell, 801 O St., #260, Lincoln, NE 68508

Cherry Tree, 300 Washington Ave., Washington College, Chestertown, MD 21620

Chestnut Review, 213 N. Tioga St., #6751, Ithaca, NY 14850

Chicago Academic Press, 5923 N. Artesian Ave., Chicago, IL 60659

Chicago Quarterly, S. Haider, 517 Sherman Ave., Evanston, IL 60202

Chillfiltr Review, PO Box 460, Ashland, OR 97520

Chiron Review, 522 E. South Ave., St. John, KS 67576-2212

Cholla Needles, 6732 Conejo Ave., Joshua Tree, CA 92252

Chronicles of Now, T. Cabot, 178 Altamont Ave., Tarrytown, NY 10591

Cimarron Review, English, 205 Morrill, OSU, Stillwater, OK 74078

Cincinnati Review, English, PO Box 210069, Cincinnati, OH 45221-0069

Circling Rivers, 7532 Rockfalls Dr., Richmond, VA 23225-1043

Cirque Press, 3157 Bettle's Bay Loop, Anchorage, AK 99515

Cleaver Magazine, PO Box 4337, Philadelphia, PA 19118

Clockhouse, Beardsley, 27 Norcross Lndg, W. Chesterfield, NH 03466

Cloudbank, PO Box 610, Corvallis, OR 97339-0610

Coal City, English Dept., University of Kansas, Lawrence, KS 66045

Coal Hill Review, 5530 Penn Ave., Pittsburgh, PA 15206

Coastal Shelf, 8841 Mission Greens Rd., #3, Santee, CA 92071

Collateral Journal, 8026 152nd Street Ct. E., Puyallup, WA 98375

Colorado Review, CSU, English, Fort Collins, CO 80523-9105

Columbia Poetry Review, 600 So. Michigan Ave., Chicago, IL 60605

Columbia Journal, Columbia Univ. School of the Arts, 415 Dodge Hall New York, NY 10027

Columbia Review, 415 Dodge Hall, Columbia U., New York, NY 10027

The Common, Everett, 166 North St., Northampton, MA 01060-2303

The Common Reader, Washington & Lee, CB 1098, 1 Brookings Dr., St. Louis, MO 63130-4899

Complete Sentence, J. Thayer, 59 Lorene Ave., Athens, OH 45701

Conduit, 788 Osceola Ave, St. Paul, MN 55105

Conjunctions, Bard College, Annandale, NY 12504-5000

Connecticut River Review, 9 Edmund Pl, West Hartford, CT 06119

Consequence, PO Box 323, Cohasset, MA 02025-0323

Constellations, 127 Lake View Ave., Cambridge, MA 02138-3366

Contemporary Haibun Online, Youmans, POB 1424, North Falmouth, MA 02556

Contra Viento, S. McCoy, 85 Governor St. #6, Providence, RI, 02906

Contrary Journal, S. Beers, 615 NW 6th St., Pendleton, OR 97801

Copper Nickel, Wayne Miller, UC-D, English - CB 175, PO Box 173364, Denver, CO 80217

Cornell University Press, Sage House, 512 East State Street Ithaca, NY 14850

Cortland Review, Van Prooyen, 118 Inslee, San Antonio, TX 78209

Cosmonauts Avenue, Montreal, Canada

Counterclock Journal, Feng, 26055 Newbridge Dr., Los Altos Hills, CA 94022

Crab Creek Review, 15327 SE 45th St., Bellevue, WA 98006

Crannóg Magazine, 6 San Antonio Park, Salthill, Galway, Ireland

Crazyhorse, College of Charleston, 66 George St., Charleston, SC 29424

Cream City Review, UW-M, PO Box 413, Milwaukee, WI 53201

Creative Nonfiction, 607 College Ave., Pittsburgh, PA 15232

Crisis Chronicle, 3431 George Ave., Parma, OH 44134

Crone Girls Press, 2305 Mirror Lake Dr., Fayetteville, NC 28303

Crosswinds, 10 Algonquin Dr., Middletown, RI 02842

CSU Poetry Center, 2219 Lamberton Rd., Cleveland Heights, OH 44118-2811

Cultural Weekly, 3330 S. Peck Ave., #14, San Pedro, CA 90731

Cutthroat, A Journal of the Arts, 5401 N. Cresta Loma Dr., Tucson, AZ 85704

Daily Drunk, 318 E. 78th St., Apt 20, New York, NY 10075

Dash, Cal State Fullerton, English, PO Box 6848, Fullerton, CA 92834

december, P.O. Box 16130, St. Louis, MO 63105

Décor Maine, PO Box 17799, Portland, ME 04112

Deep Wild, 500 Kennedy Dr., #15, Rangely, CO 81648

Defunkt Magazine, 12710 Corning Dr., Houston, TX 77089

Delmarva Review, PO Box 544, St. Michaels, MD 21663

Delta Poetry Review, 523 Guthrie Rd., Sterlington, LA 71280

Departure Mirror Quarterly, PO Box 6372, Lancaster, CA 93539-6372

Dew Drop, V. Able, 2417 Laura Lane, Mountain View, CA 94043

Diagram, New Michigan Press, PO Box 210067, ML 424, University of Arizona, Tucson, AZ 85721

Dillydoun Review, PO Box 1208, Hanceville, AL 35077-1208

Diode Editions, PO Box 5585, Richmond, VA 23220

The DMQ Review, 16393 Bonnie Lane, Los Gatos, CA 95032

DNA EZINE, PO Box 746, Columbia, CA 95310

Doire Press, Aille, Inverin, County Galway, Ireland

Dope Fiend Daily, 301 Regency Dr., Deer Park, TX 77536

Dos Madres Press, 10590 Fallis Rd., Loveland, OH 45140-1934

DreamForge Magazine, 2615 Detroit St., Grapeville, PA 15634

Dreich, Hybrid Press, Fife, Scotland, KY11 4BN, UK

The Drift, magazine of Culture and Politics, editors(at)thedrift.com

Drifting Sands, R. Grahn, 1121 Church St., Apt 305, Evanston, IL 60201-5939

Driftwood Press, 14737 Montoro Dr., Austin, TX 78728

Drunk Monkeys, 252 N Cordova St., Burbank, CA 91505

Dryland, 4437 Radium Dr., Los Angeles, CA 90032

DSTL Arts, c/o Pichardo, 3529 Fletcher Dr., Los Angeles, CA 90065

Eastern Iowa Review, 6332 33rd Avenue Dr., Shellsburg, IA 52332

ecotone, UNCW, 601 S. College Rd., Wilmington, NC 28403-5938

Eden Stories Press, 469 Monroe St. N, Alderson, WV 24910

805 Lit+Art, 1301 1st Ave. W., Bradenton, FL 34205

Ekphrastic Review, 602-49 St. Clair Ave West, Toronto, ON M4V 1K6, Canada

Elder Mountain, Missouri State, 128 Garfield, West Plains, MO 65775

Electric Literature, Ste. 26,147 Prince St., Brooklyn, NY 11201

Ember Chasm Review, 4336 E. Milky Way, Gilbert, AZ 85295

Emerge Literary Journal, PO Box 815, Washingtonville, NY 10992

Emergence Magazine, PO Box 1164, Inverness, CA 94937

Empty Bowl Press, Daley, 14172 Madrona Dr., Anacortes, WA 98221

The Emrys Journal, PO Box 8813, Greenville, SC 29604

Entropy, janice(at)entropy mag.org

Epiphany, 71 Bedford St., New York, NY 10014

Epoch, 251 Goldwin Smith Hall, Cornell University, Ithaca NY 14853

Equinox, 1409 Chase St., Eugene, OR 97402

Escape Into Life, Kirk, 108 Gladys Dr., Normal, IL 61761

Essay Daily, A. Monson, ML 445, PO Box 210067, 1423 E University, Tucson,
    AZ 85721.

Evening Street, 2881 Wright St., Sacramento, CA 95821

Event, PO Box 2503, New Westminster, BC, V3L 5B2, Canada

EX/POST, 1054 Wild Dunes Way, Johns Creek, GA 30097

Exile, 144483 Southgate Rd. #14, Holstein ON N0G 2A0, Canada

Exit 7 Journal, 4810 Alben Barkley Dr., Paducah, KY 42001

Exit 13, PO Box 423, Fanwood, NJ 07023

Exposition Review, 380 Talbot Ave., #205, Pacifica, CA 94044-2658

Eye to the Telescope, Science Fiction & Fantasy Poetry Assoc., PO Box 1563,
    Alameda CA 94501

The Fabulist Magazine, 1377 5th Ave., San Francisco, CA 94122

failbetter, 2022 Grove Ave., Richmond, VA 23220

Fairy Tale Review, English, Univ. of Arizona, Tucson, AZ 85721

Fatal Flaw, 61 East 3rd St., Apt 21, New York, NY 10003

Fathom Books, Box 1689, Provincetown, MA 02657

Fern Literary Magazine, 9533 Caraway Dr., Boise, ID 83704

Fiction International, SDSU, English, 5500 Campanile Dr. San Diego, CA 92182-6020

Fiction on the Web, 12 Leigham Vale, London SW2 3JH, UK

Fictive Dream, Black, #1803,1 Cassar Sq., York Rd., London SE7 7GT, UK

Fiddlehead, Box 4400, Univ. New Brunswick, Fredericton NB E3B 5A3, Canada

Final Thursday, 815 State St., Cedar Falls, IA 50613

Fine Print Press, PO Box 49102, Austin, TX 78765

Finishing Line Press, Leah Maines, POB 1626, Georgetown, KY 40324

Five Points, Georgia State University, Box 3999, Atlanta, GA 30302

Fjords Review, 2347 Hollywood Drive, Pittsburgh, PA 15235

Flapper Press, 10061 Riverside Dr., #115, Toluca Lake, CA 91602

Flash Back Fiction, Jendrzejewski, 2 Pearce Close, Cambridge, CB3 9LY, UK

Flash Fiction Magazine, 3448 Colonial Ave., Los Angeles, CA 90066

Flash Fiction Online, Yeatts, 110 Canter Ln, Pinehurst, NC 28374

Flash Flood, Jendrzejewski, 2 Pearce Close, Cambridge CB3 9LY UK

Fleas on the Dog, 3-527 Victoria St. S., Kitchener, ON N2M 3A8, Canada

Fledging Rag, 1838 Edenwald Lane, Lancaster, PA 17601

FlowerSong Press, 1218 N. 15th St., McAllen, TX 78501

Flying Ketchup Press, 11608 N. Charlotte St., Kansas City, MO 64155

Flying South 2020,546 Birch Creek Rd., McLeansville, NC 27301

Flypaper Lit, J. David, 9919 Biddulph Rd., Brooklyn, OH 44144

Foglifter, 214 Grand Ave., #40, Oakland, CA 94610

Folio, Amer. Univ., Battelle Tompkins 237, Washington, DC 20016-8047

Foothill Poetry Journal, 425 N. Cambridge Ave., Claremont, CA 91711

Fordham University Press, 45 Columbus Ave., New York, NY 10023

Forge, 4018 Bayview Ave., San Mateo, CA 94403-4310

Four Way Books, 11 Jay St., 4th Floor, New York, NY 10013

Four Way Review, 1217 Odyssey Dr., Durham, NC 27713

Fourth Genre, 434 Farm Lane, Rm. 235, MSU, East Lansing, MI 48824

Fractured Lit, Dean, 518 Nancy St., Warsaw, TX 46580

Frayed Edge Press, Parlew Dist, 4722 Larchwood Ave., Philadelphia, PA 19143

Free State Review, 3222 Rocking Horse Lane, Aiken, SC 29801

FreeFall Magazine, 250 Maunsell Close NE, Calgary, AB T2E 7C2, Canada

Frontier Poetry, PO Box 700, Joshua Tree, CA 92252

Fugue, 875 Perimeter Dr., MS 1102, Moscow, ID 83844-1102

Full Crescent Press, PO Box 541591, Columbus, OH 43234

Future Cycle Press, 283 Frederick Drive, Athens, GA 30607

Galleywinter Poetry, 2778 Elizabeth Pl., Lebanon, OR 97355

Galway Review, 75 Portacarron, Ballymoneen Rd., Knocknacarra, Galway H91 T1XF, Ireland

Gemini Magazine, PO Box 1485, Onset, MA 02558

Georgia Review, University of Georgia, Athens, GA 30602-9009

Gertrude Press, 605 Brentwood St., Austin, TX 78752

Gettysburg Review, Gettysburg College, Box 2446, Gettysburg, PA 17325

Ghost Parachute, Pribble, 1062 Azalea Lane, Winter Park, FL 32789

Gigantic Sequins, 4610 Skyline Dr., Anniston, AL 36206

Gimmick Press, 598 Ann St., Plymouth, MI 48170

Gival Press, PO Box 3812, Arlington, VA 22203

Glass Lyre Press, PO Box 2693, Glenview, IL 60025

Glass Poetry Press, 1667 Crestwood, Toledo, OH 43612

Glassworks, 260 Victoria St., Glassboro, NJ 08028

Gleam: Journal of the Cadralor, 1305 E. Garfield St., Laramie, WY 82070

Glimpse, Box 51, Clinton, NY 13323

Gnashing Teeth, PO Box 143, Rockport, TX 78381-0143

Gold Man Review, 4626 Nantucket Dr., Redding, CA 96001

Golden Antelope Press, 715 E. McPherson, Kirksville, MO 63501

Golden Foothills Press, 1438 Atchison St., Pasadena, CA 91104

Golden Streetcar, 1086 Campanile, Newport Beach, CA 92660

Goodnight, Sweet Prince, N. Greer, 1331 Gilman St, Berkeley, CA 94706

Gordon Square Review, 10429 Baltic Rd., Cleveland, OH 44102

Grain Magazine, PO Box 3986, Regina, SK S4P 3R9, Canada

Grand Journal, 75 Main St # 426, Narrowsburg, NY 12764

Granta, 12 Addison Ave., Holland Park, London W11 4QR, UK

The Gravity of the Thing, 17028 SE Rhone St., Portland, OR 97236

Grayson Books, PO Box 270549, West Hartford, CT 06127

great weather for MEDIA, 515 Broadway, #2B, New York, NY 10012

Green Linden Press, 208 Broad St South, Grinnell, IA 50112

Green Mountains Review, Johnson State College, 337 College Hill, Johnson, VT 05656

Green Silk, 228 Main St., Woodstock, VA 22664

Greensboro Review, 3302 MHRA Bldg., UNC, Greensboro, NC 27402-6170

Guernica, Lambert 157 Columbus Ave., c/o The Yard, New York, NY 10023

Guesthouse, Huffman, 219 N. Linn St., #210, Iowa City, IA 52245

Gulf Coast Journal, University of Houston, Houston, TX 77204-3013

Gunpowder Press, 1336 Camino Manadero, Santa Barbara, CA 93111

Gyroscope Review, 1 Declaration Lane, Gillette, WY 82716

Half Mystic Press, 2746 Frist Centre, Princeton Univ., Princeton, NJ 08544

Halfway Down the Stairs, Roberts, 6425 164th St., Chippewa Falls, WI 54729

Hamby Stern Publishing, PO Box 39124, Washington, DC 20016-9124

Hand Type Press, P.O. Box 3941, Minneapolis, MN 55403-0941

Harpur Palate, English, B.U., PO Box 6000, Binghamton, NY 13902

The Harvard Advocate, 22 South St., Cambridge, MA 02138

Harvard Review, Lamont Library, Harvard Univ., Cambridge, MA 02138

Hawaii Pacific Review, 3121 Pualei Cir. #39, Honolulu, HI 96815

Hayden's Ferry Review, ASU, P.O. Box 875002, Tempe, AZ 85287

Here, ECSU, English Dept., 83 Windham St., Willimantic, CN 06226

Hermine Annual, PO Box 70505, 2938 Dundas St. W, Toronto, ON M6P 4E7, Canada

HerStry, 2520 N. Pierce St., #4, Milwaukee, WI 53212

High Desert Journal, 110 65th Ave. NW, Havre, MT 59501

High Shelf Press, 2425 NE Saratoga St., Portland, OR 97211

Highland Park Poetry, 376 Park Ave., Highland Park, IL 60035

Hippocampus Magazine, 210 W. Grant St., #108, Lancaster, PA 17603

Hobart, 2228 Glencoe Hills Dr., Ann Arbor, MI 48108

The Hollins Critic, Hollins University, Box 9538, Roanoke, VA 24020

Holy Cow Press, PO Box 3170, Mount Royal Station, Duluth, MN 55803

Homology Lit, c/o Slone, PO Box 127, Skykomish, WA 98288

Honey Press, 802 Aster Blvd., Rockville, MD 20850

Hong Kong Review, 2306 Prosper Commercial Building, 9 Yin Chong St., Kowloon, Hong Kong

Hoot Review, 4534 Osage Ave., C-102, Philadelphia, PA, 19143

The Hopper, 4935 Twin Lakes Rd., #36, Boulder, CO 80301

Hotel Amerika, Columbia College, Creative Writing, 600 S. Michigan Ave., Chicago, IL 60605

House of Zolo's Journal of Speculative Literature, N. Andersen, 1362 Bathurst Street, 2nd Fl., Toronto, ON M5R 3H7, Canada

How We Are, English, Univ. of St. Thomas, 1221 Summit Ave., Saint Paul, MN 55015

Hoxie Gorge Review, SUNY, English, PO Box 2000, Cortland, NY 13045

Hub City Press, 186 West Main St., Spartanburg, SC 29306

The Hudson Review, 33 West 67th St., New York, NY 10023

Hunger Mountain, Vermont College of Fine Arts, 36 College St., Montpelier, VT 05602

Hypertext c/o Rice, 1821 W. Melrose St., Chicago, IL 60657

Hypocrite Reader, 121 Cottonwood Court, Doylestown, PA 18901

iamb, 57 Thorpe Gardens, Alton, Hampshire GU34 2BQ, UK

Ibbetson Street Press, 25 School Street, Somerville, MA 02143

Ice Box, UAF, English, PO Box 755720, Fairbanks, AK 99775

Ice Cube Press, 1180 Hauer Dr., North Liberty, IA 52317

Icefloe Press, 30 Kensington Place, Toronto, ON M5T2K4, Canada

IHRAF Publishes Literary Journal, tom@ihraf.org, New York, NY

Illuminations, English Dept, 66 George St., Charleston, SC 29424-0001

Image, 3307 Third Avenue West, Seattle, WA 98119

Impossible Archetype, M. Ward, 21 Maxwell Street, Dublin 8, D08 R2H7, Ireland

Indiana Review, English, Ballantine 554, 1020 E. Kirkwood Ave, Bloomington, IN 47405

Indiana Writers Center, 1125 E. Brookside Ave., Ste. B-25, Indianapolis, IN 46202

Indianapolis Review, 5906 W. 25th St., Apt. B, Speedway, IN 46224

Intima Journal, 36 N. Moore St., #4W, New York, NY 10013

Into the Void, 382 Skeena St., Vancouver, BC V5K 0E5, Canada

Inverted Syntax, PO Box 2044, Longmont CO 80502

Iowa Poetry Association, Baszczynski, 16096 320th Way, Earlham, IA 50072

The Iowa Review, Nugent, 1037 E. Washington St., Iowa City, IA 52280

IPB Books, c/o Schwartz, 47-46 40th St., #3E, Sunnyside, NY 11104

Iris G. Press, 1838 Edenwald Lane, Lancaster, PA 17601

Iron City Magazine, PO Box 370, Tempe, AZ 85280

Iron Horse, Patterson, 9003 Memphis Dr., Lubbock, TX 79423

Isele Magazine, 530 Elm Street, Box 82, Vermillion, SD 57069

Italian American Journal, Terrone, 35-56 77th St., #31, Jackson Heights, NY 11372

J Journal, 524 West 59th St., 7th Fl, New York, NY 10019

Jabberwock Review, MSU, Drawer E, Mississippi State, MS 39762

Jacar Press, 6617 Deerview Trail, Durham, NC 27712

James Dickey Review, Etowah Valley Writers MFA Program, Reinhardt University, 7300 Reinhardt Circle, Waleska, GA 30183

Jersey Devil Press, 1826 Avon Rd. SW, Roanoke, VA 24015

jmww, 2306 Altisma Way, #214, Carlsbad, CA 92009

Johannesburg Review of Books, 2367 Camino Capitan, #1, Santa Fe, NM 87505

The Journal, OSU - English, 164 Annie & John Glenn Ave., Columbus, OH 43210

Joyland Magazine, M. King, 49 Eugenia Ave., Johns Island, SC 29455

Jubilat, South College, Univ. of Massachusetts, Amherst, MA 01003

Juked, 108 New Mark Esplanade, Rockville, MD 20850

JuxtaProse, 4430 Aster St., Springfield, OR 97478

Kattywompus Press, Losak, 50 Monterey Ave., Teaneck, NJ 07666

Kelsay Books, 502 S. 1040 E, #A119, American Fork, UT 84003

Kenyon Review, Finn House, 102 W. Wiggin St., Gambier, OH 43022

Kissing Dynamite, C. Taylor, POB 662, Scotch Plains, NJ 07076

Kitty Wang's, Mambo Academy, PO Box 5, North Branford, CT 06471

Knights Library Magazine, 7460 Drew Circle, #9, Westland, MI 48185

Knot, 721 East 8th Ave., Springfield, CO 81073

Kurt Vonnegut Museum & Library, 543 Indiana Ave., Indianapolis, IN 46202
Kustom Imprints, 1661 N. Glassell St., Orange, CA 92867
Kweli Journal, POB 693, New York, NY 10021

La Vague, 7809 Estancia St., Carlsbad, CA 92009
Labello Press, McMenamy, Blacklion, County Cavan, Ireland
LaHave Review, 5294 Highway 332, Middle LaHave, NS B46 3L9, Canada
Lake Effect, Humanities, 4951 College Drive, Erie, PA 16563-1501
Lamar University Literary Press, Maes 20, PO Box 10023, Beaumont, TX 77710
Lamplit Underground, 1301 West Anderson Hwy, #102-2, Austin, TX 78757
Last Stanza Poetry Journal, 634 N. A St., Elwood, IN 46036
Laurel Review, NWMSU, 800 University Dr., Marysville, MO 64468
Lavender Review, P.O. Box 275, Eagle Rock, MO 65641-0275
Leaping Clear, 214 Calcita Dr., Santa Cruz, CA 95060
Leavings Literary Magazine, 5501 45th Ave., #532, Hyattsville, MD 20781
Leon Literary Review, 2 Saint Paul St., #404, Brookline, MA 02446
Levine Querido Press, Alexandra, 34 Newark St., Hoboken, NJ 07030
Library Partners Press, 330 ZSR Library, Wake Forest University, Winston-Salem, NC 27109
Ligeia Magazine, Wagner, 7802 Chevalier Ct., Severn, MD 21144
Light 1515 Highland Ave., Rochester, NY 14618
Lily Poetry Review, E. Cleary, 223 Winter Street Whitman, MA 02382
Limberlost Press, 17 Canyon Trail, Boise, ID 83716
Limpwrist, 520 NE 28th St., #708, Wilton Manors, FL 33305
Lips, P.O. Box 616, Florham Park, NJ 07932
Liquid Imagination, 7800 Loma Del Norte Rd. NE, Albuquerque, NM 87109
Literarti Magazine, Aegeristrasse 112, 6300 ZUG, Switzerland
The Literary Hatchet, 345 Charlotte White Rd., West Port, MA 02790
Literary Hub, 154 West 14th St., Floor 12, New York, NY 10011
Literary Mama, 24 Helen's Way, Ithaca, NY 14850
Literary Matters, 9205 Chenoak Ct, Parkville, MD 21234
Literary Review, Fairleigh Dickinson, M-GH2-01,285 Madison Ave., Madison, NJ 07940
Literary Veganism, Tague, 562 76th St., Brooklyn, NY 11209
LitMag, c/o Berley, 23 Ferris Lane, Bedford, NY 10506
Live Encounters Poetry, S. Kaul, A1-A2 Sunset Town House, Jalan Pura Merta Sari III, Abian Base, Kuta, Bali 80361, Indonesia
Live Mag!, P.O, Box 1215, Cooper Station, New York, NY 10276
Livingston Press, Stn 22, Univ. West Alabama, Livingston, AL 35470
Loch Raven Review, 1306 Providence Rd., Towson, MD 21286
long con magazine, 76 Main Ave., Halifax, NS, B3M 1A6, Canada
Longleaf Review, 107-261 Vaughan Rd., Toronto, ON M6C 2N2, Canada

Longreads, 189 Smith Ave., Kingston, NY 12401

Longship Press, 1122 4th St., San Rafael, CA 94901

Los Angeles Review of Books, 6671 Sunset Blvd., #1521, Los Angeles, CA 90028

Lost Balloon, 1402 Highland Ave., Berwyn, IL 60402

Louisville Review Corp, 436 St. James Court, Louisville, KY 40208

Louisiana State University Press, S. Anselmo, 228 Johnston Hall, Baton Rouge, LA 70803

Loving Healing Press, 5145 Pontiac Trail, Ann Arbor, MI 48105-9238

Lowestoft Chronicle, 1925 Massachusetts Ave, #8, Cambridge, MA 02140

The MacGuffin, 18600 Haggerty Rd., Livonia, MI 48152

MacQueen's Quinterly, PO Box 365, Wade, NC 28395

Madville Publishing, PO Box 358, Lake Dallas, TX 75065

Main Street Rag Publishing, POB 690100, Charlotte, NC 28227-7001

Maine Arts Journal, Mayers, 538 Townhouse Rd., Whitefield, ME 04353

Maine Review, 1000 River Rd., Dresden, ME 04342

Manhattan Review, 440 Riverside Dr., #38, New York, NY 10027

Mānoa, UH-M, English, 1733 Donaghho Rd., #626, Honolulu, HI 96822

Mantle Poetry, c/o Jackson, 4422 Milgate St., Pittsburgh, PA 15224

Manzano Mountain Review, 1804 Ridgecrest Cir. SE, Albuquerque, NM 87108

The Margins, Asian American Writers, 110-112 W. 27th St., Ste. 600, New York, NY 10001-3808

Mason Jar Press, I. Anderson, 3708 Hickory Ave, Baltimore, MD 21211

Master's Review, 70 SW Century Drive, Ste., 100442, Bend, OR 97702

matchbook, 333 Harvard St., #5, Cambridge, MA 02139

McSweeney's, PO Box 410987, San Francisco, CA 94141

Meadowlark, PO Box 333, Emporia, KS 66801

Meal Media, 1901 5th St., NE, Minneapolis, MN 55418

Mercer University Press, 1501 Mercer University Dr., Macon, GA 31207

Meridian, U. of VA, PO Box 400145, Charlottesville, VA 22904-4145

Michigan Quarterly Review, 0576 Rackham Bldg., 915 E. Washington St., Ann Arbor, MI 48109

Middle Creek Publishing, 9167 Mountain Park Rd., Beulah, CO 81023

The Midnight Oil, 1255 Alpine Way, Provo, UT 84606

Midway Journal, 216 Banks St., #2, Cambridge, MA 02138

Midwest Quarterly, PSU, 44 Grubbs, 1701 South Broadway, Pittsburg, KS 66762

Midwest Review, UW-M, c/o Chambers, 5125 Pepin Pl., Madison, WI 53705

Milk Candy Review, Ulrich, 3145 Grelck Ln, Billings, MT 59105

Minerva Rising Press, 11707 Glen Wessex Court, Tampa, FL 33626

Minola Review, 669-A Crawford St., Toronto, ON M6G 3K1, Canada

Mississippi Review, USM, 118 College Dr., #5037, Hattiesburg, MS 39406

Missouri Review, 357 McReynolds Hall, UMO, Columbia MO 65211

Mizna, 2446 University Ave. W., #115, Saint Paul, MN 55114

Mobius, Journal of Social Change, 149 Talmadge, Madison, WI 53704

MockingHeart Review, 2783 Iowa St., #2, Baton Rouge, LA 70802

Modern Language Studies, Susquehanna Univ., English, 514 University Ave., Selinsgrove, PA 17870-1164

Mom Egg Review, POB 9037, Bardonia, NY 10954

Monkeybicycle, 1921 New Garden Rd., #J-105, Greensboro, NC 27410

Moon City, English, MSU, 901 So National Ave., Springfield, MO 65897

Moon Park Review, PO Box 87, Dundee, NY 14837

Moon Pie Press, 16 Walton St., Westbrook, ME 04092

Moonpath Press, PO Box 445, Tillamook, OR 97141-0445

Mountain State Press, PO Box 1281, Scott Depot, WV 25560

Mud Fish, c/o Hoffman, 184 Franklin St., New York, NY 10013

Mud Season, Pentaleri/Savage, 330 Dan Sargent Rd., Bristol, VT 05443

Muddy River Poetry Review, 15 Eliot St., Chestnut Hill, MA 02467

Muse-Pie Press, 73 Pennington Ave., Passaic, NJ 07055

N+l, PO Box 26428, Cadman Plaza Stn., Brooklyn, NY 11202

Narrative, 2443 Fillmore St., #214, San Francisco, CA 94115

Narrative Northeast, 32 Valleyview Rd., Verona, NJ 07044

Nashville Review, Vanderbilt U. English, 331 Benson Hall, Nashville, TN 37235

Natural Bridge, English, UMSL, 1 University Blvd., St. Louis, MO 63121

Naugatuck River Review, 45 Highland Ave., #2, Westfield, MA 01085

Nelle, 4725 Overwood Circle, Birmingham, AL 35222

Neologism Poetry Journal, Fields, 8 Prospect Ave., Fl 1, Greenfield, MA 01301

Neon Books, 15/2 Gordon St., Edinburgh, EH6 8NW, UK

New American Writing, 369 Molino Ave., Mill Valley, CA 94941

New England Review, Middlebury College, Middlebury, VT 05753

New Flash Fiction, Brown, 19798 90th St., Morning Sun, IA 52640

New Letters, 5101 Rockhill Rd., Kansas City, MO 64110

New Ohio Review, Ohio University, 201 Ellis Hall, Athens, OH 45701

New Pop Lit, 2074 17th St., Wyandotte, MI 48192

New Southern Fugitives, 416 Point View Crt., Wilmington, NC 28411

The New Territory Magazine, Foster, 2002 6th Ave., Canyon, TX 79015

New Verse News, Greenlot Sambandha M-32, Mengwi-Badung, Munggu, Bali 80351, Indonesia

New York Quarterly, PO Box 470, Beacon, NY 12508

Newfound Journal, 6428 Alamo Ave., St. Louis, MO 63105

Night Ballet Press, Borsenik, 123 Glendale Ct, Elyria, OH 44035

Night Picnic Press, PO Box 3819, New York, NY 10163-3819

Nightboat Books, 310 Nassau Ave., Unit 205, Brooklyn, NY 11222-3813

Ninth Letter, English Dept, 608 S. Wright St., Urbana, IL 61801

No Contact Mag, 629 W. 115th St., #1-A, New York, NY 10025

Noon, 1392 Madison Ave., PMB 298, New York, NY 10029

The Normal School, English, CSU-F, Fresno, CA 93740

North Carolina Literary Review, ECU Mailstop 555 English, Greenville, NC 27858-4353

North Dakota Quarterly, Univ. Nebraska Press, 1111 Lincoln Mall, Lincoln, NE 68588-0630

Northampton House Press, 7018 Wildflower Lane, Franktown, VA 23354-2504

Northern Virginia Review, NVCC, English, 7900 Westpark Drive, Ste., A550, McLean, VA 22102

Northwest Review, Nelson, 1137 SE Lexington St., Portland, OR 97202

Northwestern University Press, 629 Noyes St., Evanston, IL 60208-4170

Novel Slices, 136 Muriel St., Ithaca, NY 14850

Nowhere Magazine, 3876 E. Whitney Lane, Phoenix, AZ 85032-5272

Ocotillo Review, Burnett, 1801 E. 51st Street, #365-246, Austin, TX 78723

October Hill Magazine, 342 East Marina Pointe Dr., East Rockaway, NY 11518

The Offing, PO Box 220020, Brooklyn, NY 11211

Okay Donkey, 3756 Bagley Ave., #206, Los Angeles, CA 90034

On the Sea Wall, R. Slate, PO Box 179, Chilmark, MA 02535

One Art, Danowsky, 219 Sugartown Rd., Wayne, PA 19087

One Story, 232 3rd St., #A108, Brooklyn, NY 11215

Orbis, 17 Greenhow Ave., West Kirby, Wirral, CH48 5EL, UK

Orca, 6516 112th Street Ct., Gig Harbor, WA 98332

Orchards Poetry Journal, 502 S 1040 E, #A119, American Fork, UT 84003

Oregon Humanities, 921 SW Washington St., Ste. 150, Portland, OR 97205

Origami Poems Project, 1948 Shore View Dr., Indialantic, FL 32903

Orion, 1 Short St., Ste. 3, Northampton, MA 01060

Osiris, 106 Meadow Lane, Greenfield, MA 01301

Oversound, 1202 Woodrow St., Columbia, SC 29205

Oxford American, PO Box 3235, Little Rock, AR 72203-3235

Oyster River Pages, 1 Greenwood Ave., Glen Burnie, MO 21061

P. R. A. Publishing, PO Box 211701, Martinez, GA 30917

Palette Poetry, 818 SW 3rd Ave., #221-5911, Portland, OR 97204

Paloma Press, 110 28th Ave., San Mateo, CA 94403

Pangyrus Lit Mag, Bargar, 11 Howland St., Provincetown, MA 02657

Pank, 2347 Hollywood Dr., Pittsburgh, PA 15235

Paper Djinn Press, Klimek, 1232 Greenfield Pl., #103, O'Fallon, IL 62269

The Paris Review, 544 West 27th St., 3rd FL, New York, NY 10001

Parks and Points, 707 Beverley Rd., #2K, Brooklyn, NY 11218

Parlor Press, 3015 Brackenberry Dr., Anderson, SC 29621

Pasque Petals, PO Box 294, Kyle, SD 57752

Passage, N. Price, 1426 N Riverfront Blvd, Dallas TX 75207

Passages North, English, NMU, 1401 Presque Isle Ave., Marquette, MI 49855-5363

Peach Magazine, 138 Harvard Pl., #2, Syracuse, NY 13210

Peauxdunque Review, 4609 Page Dr., Metairie, LA 70003

Pelekinesis, 112 N. Harvard Ave., #65, Claremont CA 91711

Pembroke Magazine, P.O. Box 1510, Pembroke, NC 28372-1510

PEN America, PEN American Center, PEN Writing Awards for Prisoners, 588 Broadway, Ste. 303, New York, NY 10012

Peripheries, Harvard Divinity School, 42 Francis Ave., Cambridge, MA 02138

Persea Books, 90 Broad St., Ste. 2100, New York, NY 10004

Perugia Press, PO Box 60364, Florence, MA 01062

Philadelphia Stories, Rodriguez, 10 Sycamore Ct., Media, PA 19063

Phoebe, GMU, MSN 2C5,4400 University Place, Fairfax, VA 22030

Pigeonholes, 5823 16 Avenue, Delta, BC V4L 1G8, Canada

Pilot Editions, Publication Studio Hudson, 108 Jefferson St., Ste. 2, Troy, NY 12180

The Pinch, English, UM, 467 Patterson Hall, Memphis, TN 38152

Pine Row Press, 107 W. Orchard Rd., Ft Mitchell, KY 41011

Pink Plastic House, PO Box 1491, Pensacola, FL 32591

Pinwheel, S. Brook Corfman, 1453 W. Winona St., Chicago, IL 60640

Pinyon, 23847 V66 Trail, Montrose, CO 81403-8558

Pithead Chapel, 110 Montgomery St., #403, Syracuse, NY 13202

Placeholder, Millard, 37 Quebec Rd., Norwich, Norfolk, NR1 4HZ, UK

Places Journal, 2875 21st St., #15, San Francisco, CA 94110

Pleasure Boat Studio, 3710 SW Barton St., Seattle, WA 98126-3844

Pleiades, UCM, English, Warrensburg, MO 64093-5214

Ploughshares, Emerson College, 120 Boylston St., Boston, MA 02116

Plume, 740 17th Avenue N, Saint Petersburg, FL 33704

Poem-A-Day, Alex Dimitrov, Academy of American Poets, 75 Maiden Lane, Ste. 901, New York, NY 10038

Poet Lore, 4508 Walsh St., Bethesda, MD 20815

Poetic Justice, 2585 SE Lyman Circle, Port Saint Lucie, FL 34952

Poetry Box, 3300 NW 185th Ave., #382, Portland, OR 97229

Poetry Center San José, 1650 Senter Rd., San José, CA 95112

Poetry Daily, MS 3E4, 4400 University Drive, Fairfax, VA 22030

Poetry Magazine, 61 West Superior St., Chicago, IL 60654

Poetry Northwest, ECC, 2000 Tower St., Everett, WA 98201-1390

Poetry Salzburg Review, English Dept., Univ. of Salzburg, Unipark Nonntal, Erzabt-Klotz-Str. 1, A-5020 Salzburg, Austria

Poetry Society of America, 15 Gramercy Park, New York, NY 10003

Poetry South, 1100 College St., MUW-1634, Columbus, MS 39701

Poets Wear Prada, 533 Bloomfield St., 2nd floor, Hoboken, NJ 07030

The Point, 2 N. LaSalle St., Ste. 2300, Chicago, IL 60602
Pole to Pole Publishing, Harmon, 5312 Brandy Dr., Mt Airy, MD 21771
Ponder Review, 1100 College St., MUW-1634, Columbus, MS 39701
Portland Review, PSU-English, PO Box 751, Portland, OR 97207-0751
Posit, 245 Sullivan St. #8-A, New York, NY 10012
Post Road, 140 Commonwealth Ave., Chestnut Hill, MA 02467
Potomac Review, 51 Mannakee St., MT/212, Rockville, MD 20850
Prairie Journal Trust, 28 Crowfoot Terr. NW, PO Box 68073, Calgary, AB, T3G 3N8, Canada
Prairie Schooner, PO Box 880334, Univ. of Nebraska, Lincoln, NE 68588
Press 53, 560 N. Trade St., Ste. 103, Winston-Salem, NC 27101
Pretty Owl Poetry, 460 Melwood Ave., #208, Pittsburgh, PA 15213
Prism International, 1202-888 Homer St., Vancouver, BC V6B 0H7, Canada
Prism Review, Univ. of La Verne, 1950 Third St., La Verne, CA 91750
Proem, Sias Univ., US office, 150 S. Los Robles Ave., Ste. 930, Pasadena, CA 91101
Prospectus, Hamby Stern, PO Box 39124, Washington, DC 20016-9124
Provincetown Arts, 650 Commercial St., Provincetown, MA 02657
Psaltery & Lyre, 4917 E. Oregon St., Bellingham, WA 98226
A Public Space, PO Box B, New York, NY 10159
Puerto Del Sol, NMSU, PO Box 30001, MSC 3E, Las Cruces, NM 88003
Pulp Literature Press, 21955 16th Ave., Langley, BC, V2Z 1K5, Canada
Puna Press, PO Box 7790, Ocean Beach, CA 92107
Punctuate, English, 600 South Michigan Ave., Chicago, IL 60605
Purple Vall Stories, 707 Leahy, Apt 322, Redwood City, CA 94061

Qu Magazine, Queens Univ., 1900 Selwyn Ave., Charlotte, NC 28274
Quarterly West Univ. of Utah, English/LNCO 3500,255 S. Central Campus Dr., Salt Lake City, UT 84112-9109
Quiet Lightning, 256 40th Street Way, Oakland, CA 94611
Quill and Parchment, 4567 W. Cedar Lake Rd., Greenbush, MI 48738

Rabid Oak, 8916 Duncanson Dr., Bakersfield, CA 93311
Racket Journal, 1536 Alabama St., San Francisco, CA 94110
Ragged Sky Press, 270 Griggs Dr., Princeton, NJ 08540
Raleigh Review, Box 6725, Raleigh, NC 27628
Rain Taxi, PO Box 3840, Minneapolis, MN 55403
Random Sample Review, 853 Harritt Dr. NW, #101, Salem, OR 97304
Raritan, Rutgers, 31 Mine St., New Brunswick, NJ 08901
Rat's Ass Review, 309 Chimney Ridge, Perkinsville, VT 05151
Rattle, 12411 Ventura Blvd., Studio City, CA 91604
Raven Chronicles, 15528 12th Ave. NE, Shoreline, WA 98155
The Raw Art Review, 8320 Main St., Ellicott City, MD 21043

Read Furiously, 555 Grand Ave., #77078, West Trenton, NJ 08628
Red Fez, 3811 Northeast Third Court, #G-208, Renton, WA 98056
Red Light Lit Press, 557 8th Ave., San Francisco, CA 94118
Red Wheelbarrow, Weisner, 225 Waugh Ave., Santa Cruz, CA 95065
Redactions, 182 Nantucket Dr., Apt U, Clarksville, TN 37040
Reed Magazine, SJSU, English, 1 Washington Sq., San Jose, CA 95192-0090
Reflex Press, Borrowdale, 16 Glyme Close, Abingdon, UK
Relief, D. Bowman Jr., Taylor Univ. 236 W. Reade Ave, Upland, IN 46989
Rescue Press, 2219 Lamberton Rd., Cleveland Heights, OH 44118-2811
Reuts Publications, 13811 NE 65th St., Vancouver, WA 98682
Rhino, PO Box 591, Evanston, IL 60204
River Glass Books, 349 Clairmonte Ave., Syracuse, NY 13207
River Mouth, 2023 E. Sims Way, #364, Port Townsend, WA 98368
River Styx, 3301 Washington Ave., Ste. 2C, Saint Louis, MO 63103
River Teeth, English, BSU, 2000 W. University Ave., Muncie, IN 47306
Roadrunner, Fordham, 4383 Oakwood Pl., Riverside, CA 92506
Rockford Review, PO Box 858, Rockford, IL 61105
Room, PO Box 46160, Stn. D, Vancouver, BC V6J 5G5, Canada
Rootstock, 27 Main St., Ste. 6, Montpelier, VT 05602-2929
Ruminate, 2723 SE 115th Ave., Portland, OR 97266
The Rumpus, PO Box 295, Middlesex. NJ 08846
Running Wild Press, 2101 Oak St., Los Angeles, CA 90007
The Rupture, 2206 W. Broadway Ave., Spokane, WA 99201
Rust + Moth, 4470 S. Lemay Ave., #1108, Fort Collins, CO 80525
Rusty Truck Press, PO Box 451, Theodosia, MO 65761
Rutgers University Press, 106 Somerset St., 3rd Fl, New Brunswick, NJ 08901
Rye Whiskey Review, 301 Regency Dr., Deer Park, TX 77536

Sagging Meniscus Press, 115 Claremont Ave., Montclair, NJ 07042
Salamander, Suffolk U., English, 8 Ashburton Pl., Boston, MA 02108
San Antonio Review, Pate, 603 Hammack Dr., #A, Austin, TX 78752
San Diego Poetry Annual, Klam, 4712 Leathers St., San Diego, CA 92117
San Pedro River Review, 5403 Sunnyview St., Torrance, CA 90505
Sandpiper, Sandpipermag.com
Santa Fe Literary Review, 6401 Richards Ave., Santa Fe, NM 87508
Santa Monica Review, 1900 Pico Blvd., Santa Monica, CA 90405
Sarabande Books, 822 E. Market St., Louisville, KY 40206
Saturnalia Books, 105 Woodside Rd., Ardmore, PA 19003
Scarlet Leaf Review, 320-176 The Esplanade, Toronto M5A 4H2, Canada
Schuylkill Valley Journal, Danowsky, 219 Sugartown Rd., #J-304, Wayne, PA 19087
Sci-Fi Lampoon, Treiber, 18624 Orlando Rd., Fort Myers, FL 33967
Scores, 31/5 Arden St., Edinburgh EH9 1BS, United Kingdom

Scoundrel Time, 6106 Harvard Ave., #396, Glen Echo, MD 20812

Scurfpea Publishing, c/o Snethen, PO Box 294, Kyle, SD 57752

The Selkie, 191 Christopher Columbus Dr., #1R, Jersey City, NJ 07302

Sentient Publications, PO Box 1851, Boulder, CO 80306

Sequoyah Cherokee River Journal, 6143 River Hills Circle, Southside, AL 35907

Serving House Books, 28 W. 3rd St., #2237, South Orange, NJ 07079

Seven Kitchens Press, 2547 Losantiville Ave., Cincinnati, OH 45237

Sewanee Review, 735 University Ave., Sewanee, TN 37383

Shabda Press, 3343 E. Del Mar Blvd., Pasadena, CA 91107

Shade Mountain Press, PO Box 11393, Albany, NY 12211

Shark Reef, Reese, 66 Country Rd. Lopez Island, WA 98261

Shawnte Orion, 15552 N 156th Ln, Surprise, AZ 85374

Sheila-Na-Gig, 203 Meadowlark Rd., Russell, KY 41169

Sibling Rivalry Press, PO Box 26147, Little Rock, AR 72221

Sidereal Magazine, 11305 Clifton Blvd., #2, Cleveland, OH 44102

Sideshow Media Group, 8033 Sunset Blvd., #164, Los Angeles, CA 90046

Silver Blade, 9841 Hickory Lane, Saint John, IN 46373

Silver Star, 2201 N Lakewood Blvd., #D1887, Long Beach, CA 90815-2552

Silverfish Review, PO Box 3541, Eugene, OR 97403

Sinister Wisdom, 2333 McIntosh Rd., Dover, FL 33527-5980

Sink, sinkreview.org

Sinking City, 15020 SW 75th Ct, Miami, FL 33158

Sixteen Rivers Press, PO Box 640663, San Francisco, CA 94164-0663

Sixth Finch, 95 Carolina Ave., #2, Jamaica Plain, MA 02130

Sky Island Journal, 1434 Sherwin Ave., Eau Claire, WI 54701

SLAB Magazine, Slippery Rock Univ., English, 317-L, SWC, Slippery Rock, PA 16057

Slag Glass City, Borich, 1021W. Bryn Mawr, #2A, Chicago, IL 60660

Slapering Hol, 300 Riverside Dr., Sleepy Hollow, NY 10591

Sleet Magazine, 1846 Bohland Ave., St. Paul, MN 55116-1906

Slice Literary, 7 Charles St., Newburyport, MA 01950

Slipstream, Box 2071, Niagara Falls, NY 14301

Smart Set, 3301 Arch St., Philadelphia, PA 19104

Smartish Pace, 2221 Lake Ave., Baltimore, MD 21213

Smokelong Quarterly, c/o C. Allen, Ulrich-von-Hutten, Str. 8, 81739 Munich, Germany

So It Goes, Kurt Vonnegut Museum & Library, 543 Indiana Ave., Indianapolis, IN 46202

So to Speak, MSN 2C5,4400 University Dr., Fairfax, VA 22030

Social Justice Anthologies, 812 13th St., Mc Kees Rocks, PA 15136

Solstice, 47 Bosson St., Revere, MA 02151

South Dakota Review, English, USD, 414 Clark St., Vermillion, SD 57069

The Southampton Review, 239 Montauk Hwy., Southampton, NY 11968

Southeast Review, English, FSU, Williams Bldg. 205, Tallahassee, FL 32306

Southern Humanities Review, 9088 Haley Center, Auburn Univ., Auburn, AL 36849-5202

Southern Indiana Review, USI, Orr Center #2009,8600 University Blvd., Evansville, IN 47712

The Southern Review, LSU, 338 Johnston Hall, Baton Rouge, LA 70803

Southwest Review, PO Box 750374, Dallas, TX 75275-0374

Spillway, 1296 Placid Ave., Ventura, CA 93004

Split Lip Magazine, 409 E. Cherry St., Walla Walla, WA 99362

Split Rock Review, 30330 Engoe Rd., Washburn, WI 54891-5855

Split This Rock, 1301 Connecticut Ave. NW, #600, Washington, DC 20036

Spoon River Poetry, ISU, Campus Box 4241, Normal, IL 61790-4241

Spork Press, 2011 E. 12th St., Tucson, AZ 85719

Square Wheel Press, 2520 County Rd. 855, McKinney, TX 75071

St. Brigid Press, 9619 Critzers Shop Rd., Afton, VA 22920

Stairwell Books, 161 Lowther St., York, YO31 7LZ, UK

Star 82 Review, PO Box 8106, Berkeley, CA 94707

Statorec, 510 E. 7th, Brooklyn, NY 11218

Still, 89 W. Chestnut St., Williamsburg, KY 40769

Stillhouse Press, 4400 University Dr., #3E4, Fairfax, VA 22030

Stinging Fly, PO Box 6016, Dublin 1, Ireland

Stone of Madness Press, Braley, 37 Cornhill St., Annapolis, MD 21401

Stone Soup, 126 Otis St., Santa Cruz, CA 95050

Stonecoast Review, DeGroat, 13 Barker St., Jay, ME 04239

Storm Cellar, c/o Goodney, 601 E. Washington St., #4, Greencastle, IN 46135

Story, 312 E. Kelso Rd., Columbus, OH 43202

Storybrink, Sean, 61 Harris Ave., Albany, NY 12208

storySouth, UNC Greensboro, 3143 MHRA Bldg, Greensboro, NC 27402-6170

Stranger's Guide, PO Box 15007, Austin, TX 78761

Streetlight Magazine, 56 Pine Hill Lane, Norwood, VA 24581

Subterranean Press, PO Box 190106, Burton, MI 48519

Subtropics, PO Box 112075, 408 Turlington Hall, Univ. of Florida, Gainesville, FL 32611-2075

Sugar House Review, PO Box 13, Cedar City, UT 84721

The Summerset Review, 25 Summerset Dr., Smithtown, NY 11787

The Sun, 107 North Roberson St., Chapel Hill, NC 27516

Sunbeams, 756 N 100th Ave., Hart, MI 49420

Sundial, Murphy, 5932 Valley Forge Dr., Coopersburg, PA 18036

Sunlight Press, 3924 E Quail Ave., Phoenix, AZ 85050

Surveyor Books, PO Box 600548, Dallas, TX 75360-0548

Sweet: Lir, 83 Carolyn Lane, Delaware, OH 43015

Sweet Tree Review, 423 E. North St., Bellingham, WA 98225

SWWIM Every Day, 301 NE 86th St., El Portal, FL 33138

Tahoma Literary Review, PO Box 924, Mercer Island, WA 98040

Tailwinds Press Enterprises, 401 Commons Park S., Unit 673, Stamford, CT 06902

tall-lighthouse, 104 Woodyates Rd., London SE12 9JL, UK

Tar River Poetry, ECU, MS 159, Greenville, NC 27858-4353

Tell-Tale Chapbooks, 18 Davis Ave., Walpole, MA 02081

Terminus, 686 Cherry St., NW, Atlanta, 6A 30332

Terrain.org, P.O. Box 41484, Tucson, AZ 85717

Terrapin Books, 4 Midvale Ave., West Caldwell, NJ 07006

Territory, 3414 Meadowbrook Blvd., Cleveland Heights, OH 44118

Terror House, 30 N. Gould St., Ste. N, Sheridan, WY 82801

Texas Observer, PO Box 6421, Austin, TX 78762

Texas Review Press, Box 2146, Huntsville, TX 77341-2146

That Painted Horse, 9535 N. Pottawatomie Rd., Harrah, OK 73045

Thimble, 18 Larry Dr., Duncanville, TX 75137

Third Coast WMU, English, 1903 W. Michigan Ave., Kalamazoo, MI 49008-5331

Third Point Press, 12 N. Linden St., Manheim, PA 17545

Third Thing, 902 Olympia Ave. NE, Olympia, WA 98506

34 Orchard Lit Journal, 249 Great Plain Rd., Danbury, CT 06811

32 Poems, English Dept, 60 South Lincoln St., Washington, PA 15301

This Broken Shore, 15 Sandspring Dr., Eatontown, NJ 07724

Thorn Literary Magazine, Ste. 352, 100-2 Toronto St., Toronto ON M5C 2B5, Canada

3: A Taos Press, P.O. Box 370627, Denver, CO 80237

3 AM Magazine, A. Gallix, 2 Avenue Amilcar Cabral, La Plaine 93210 Saint-Denis, France

3 Elements Review, 198 Valley View Rd., Manchester, CT 06040

Three Mile Harbor Press, PO Box 1, Stuyvesant, NY 12173

Three Rooms Press, 243 Bleecker St., #3, New York, NY 10014

Threepenny Review, PO Box 9131, Berkeley, CA 94709

Thrush Poetry Journal, 889 Lower Mountain Dr., Effort PA 18330

the tide rises, the tide falls, 234 S. Westgate Ave., Los Angeles, CA 90049

Tiferet Journal, Kenny, 207 Coriell Ave., Fanwood, NJ 07023

Tiger Bark Press, 202 Mildorf St., Rochester, NY 14609-6619

Tikkun Magazine, 2342 Shattuck Ave., Ste. 1200, Berkeley, CA 94704

Tinderbox Poetry Journal, 114 SE H St., #201, Bentonville, AR 72712

Tiny Boar, Water Street, Port Townsend, WA 98368

Tipton Poetry Journal, 642 Jackson St., Brownsburg, IN 46112

TL;DR Press, 11420 E 26th Ave., Aurora, CO 80010

Tolsun Books, PO Box 24, Flagstaff, AZ 86002

Treveccan, English, 333 Murfreesboro Rd., Nashville, TN 37210-2877

TriQuarterly, English, University Hall 215, 1897 Sheridan Rd., Evanston, IL 60208

Trnsfr Books, 57 Holland Ave NE, Grand Rapids, MI 49503

True Blue Press, 1302 Prosperity Ct., Williamsburg, VA 23188

TulipTree Review, PO Box 723, Canon City, CO 81215

Tupelo Quarterly, Tupelo Press, PO Box 1767, North Adams, MA 01247

Twin Bill, 3778 Burkoff Dr., Troy, MI 48084

Two Sylvias Press, PO Box 1524, Kingston, WA 98346

Twyckenham Notes, 14223 Worthington Dr., Granger, IN 46530

Tyche Books, PO Box 45028 Brentwood Rd., Calgary, AB T2L 1Y4, Canada

Typehouse Magazine, Gryphin, PO Box 68721, Portland, OR 97268

U. S. 1 Poets' Cooperative, PO Box 127, Kingston, NJ 08528-0127

Umbrella Factory, Winters, 209 McConnell Court, Lyons, CO 80540

Uncollected Press, 8320 Main St., Ellicott City, MD 21043

Under Review, CWP-Hamline Univ., MS A1730,1536 Hewitt Ave., St. Paul, MN 55104

Under the Gum Tree, 3768 4th Ave., Sacramento, CA 95817

Under the Sun, 2121 Hidden Cove Rd., Cookeville, TN 38506

underblong, Chen, 105 Crescent St., #1A, Waltham, MA 02453

Undertow, PO Box 490, 9860 Niagara Falls Blvd., Niagara Falls, NY 14304

Undomesticated Magazine, 123 So. Adams St., Hinsdale, IL 60521

University of Iowa Press, 119 W. Park Rd., 100 Kuhl House, Iowa City, IA 52242

University of Tampa Press, 401 W. Kennedy Blvd., Tampa, FL 33606

University Press of Kentucky, 663 South Limestone St., Lexington, KY 40508-4008

upstreet PO Box 105, Richmond, MA 01254-0105

Vagabond, 4342 Elenda St., Culver City, CA 90230

Valley Voices, MVSU 7242, 14000 Hwy 82 W., Itta Bena, MS 38941

Vallum, 5038 Sherbrooke St. W., PO Box 20377 CP Vendome, Montreal, QC H4A 1T0, Canada

Vegetarian Alcoholic Press, 642 S. 2nd St., Milwaukee WI 53204-1616

Veliz Books, PO Box 961273, El Paso, TX 79996

A Velvet Giant 951 Carroll St., #3A, Brooklyn, NY 11225

Verdad Magazine, verdadsubmissions(at)gmail.com

Vext Gomez, 1000 Chestnut St., #14-A, San Francisco, CA 94109

Village Sun, Anderson, 301 E. 38th St., Apt 15B, New York, NY 10016

Vinal Publishing, 193 Delaware Ave., Buffalo, NY 14202-2102

Virginia Quarterly Review, 5 Boar's Head Lane, PO Box 400223, Charlottesville, VA 22904-4223

Volume, Gilmore, 55 Clifton Pl., #1, Brooklyn, NY 11238

The Volta, J. Wilkinson, 3715 38th Ave. So., Seattle, WA 98144

Voyage LA Journal, c/o Henry, 110 N. Orlando Ave., Ste. 13, Maitland, FL 32751

Waccamaw Journal, CCU, PO Box 261954, Conway, SC 29528-6054

Wandering Aengus, 1459 North Beach, Box 334, Eastsound, WA 98245

Wards Lit Mag, 3212 E. Hillery Dr., Phoenix, AZ 85032

Washington Square Review, 30 Saint Marks Pl, #2A, New York, NY 10003

Water~Stone Review, MS A1730,1536 Hewitt Ave., St. Paul, MN 55104

Waters Edge Press, 615 South Pier Dr., Sheboygan, WI 53081

Waterwheel Review, Smith, 52 Grey Rocks Rd., Wilton, CT 06857

Wave Books, 1938 Fairview Avenue E., Ste. 201, Seattle, WA 98102

Waxwing, 32 Patterson St. Barre, VT 05641

West Branch, Stadler Center, 1 Dent Dr., Lewisburg, PA 17837

The West Review, 5500 Sampson St. #8306, Houston, TX 77004

West Trestle Review, 220 Sierra Way, Auburn, CA 95603

Whale Road Review, 3900 Lomaland Dr., San Diego, CA 92106

Whistling Shade, 1495 Midway Pkwy, St. Paul, MN 55108

The Whitefish Review, 708 Lupfer Ave., Whitefish, MT 59937

Wigleaf, Univ. of Missouri, 114 Tate Hall, Columbia, MO 65211

The Wild Word, Zimmermannstrasse 6,12163 Berlin, Germany

Willow Springs, 668 N. Riverpoint Blvd., #259, Spokane, WA 99202

Willows Wept Review, 2300 S. Gaines St., Little Rock, AR 72206

The Windsor Review, 401 Sunset Ave., Windsor, ON N9B 3P4, Canada

Winnow, 131 Green Meadow Court, Washington, PA 15301

Wipf & Stock Publishers, 199 W. 8th Ave., Ste. 3, Eugene, OR 97401-2960

Wising Up Press, PO Box 2122, Decatur, GA 30031-2122

Witness, Black Mountain Inst., PO Box 455085, Las Vegas, NV 89154

Witty Partition, 136 Muriel St., Ithaca, NY 14850

WMG Publishing, PO Box 269, Lincoln City, OR 97367

Woodhall Press, 81 Old Saugatuck Rd., Norwalk, CT 06855

The Worcester Review, PO Box 804, Worcester, MA 01613

Wordpeace Journal, 45 Highland Ave., #2, Westfield, MA 01085

Wordrunner eChapbooks, PO Box 613, Petaluma, CA 94953-0613

World Literature Today, 630 Parrington Oval, #110, Norman, OK 73019-4033

World Stage Press, Community Literature Initiative, Los Angeles, CA

World Weaver Press, PO Box 21924, Albuquerque, NM 87154

Woven Tale Press, PO Box 2533, Setauket, NY 11733

Wrath-Bearing Tree, 8550 Cirrus Ct, Colorado Springs, CO 80920

Write Launch, PO Box 2612, Lancaster, PA 17608

Yale Review, PO Box 208243, New Haven, CT 06520-8243
Yellow Arrow Publishing, PO Box 12119, Baltimore, MD 21281
Yalobusha Review, Graduate Writing, Univ. of Mississippi, MS 38677
Yes Yes Books, 1614 NE Alberta St., Portland, OR 97211
Yossarian Universal News, PO Box 236, Millbrae, CA 94030
Your Impossible Voice, 4972 Fairview Rd., Columbus, OH 43231

Zephyr Press, 400 Bason Dr., Las Cruces, NM 88005
Zoetrope: All Story, 916 Kearny St., San Francisco, CA 94133
Zone 3 Press, APSU Box 4565, Clarksville, TN 37044
ZYZZYVA, 57 Post St., Ste. 604, San Francisco, CA 94104

CONTRIBUTORS' NOTES

SENAA AHMAD is working on her first short story collection. She lives in Toronto.

THREA ALMONTASER is the author of *The Wild Fox of Yemen,* winner of the Walt Whitman Award.

IFEOMA SESIANA AMOBI was born in Nigeria and is a recent graduate of the Iowa Writers Workshop.

JABARI ASIM directs the MFA program at Emerson College. He's the author of seven books for adults and ten books for children.

CHARLES BAXTER's most recent novel is *The Sun Collective* (2020). He first appeared here in PPVII and many times since.

MARIA BLACK lives in Florence, Massachusetts. Her work has appeared in *Harvard Review, Gulf Coast, Indiana Review* and *The Seattle Review.*

TRACI BRIMHALL teaches at Kansas State University. She is the author of *Saudade* (Copper Canyon 2017) and other books.

REBECCA CADENHEAD lives in Dobbs Ferry, New York. She writes for the *Harvard Crimson* and other publications.

CHEN CHEN's second book of poetry, *Your Emergency Contact Has Experienced An Emergency* is forthcoming from BOA Editions. He teaches at Brandeis University.

OLIVIA CLARE's novel *Here Lies* is forthcoming from Grove Atlantic. She lives in Hattiesburg, Mississippi.

QUINTIN COLLINS is the author of *Dandelion Speaks of Survival* (Cherry Castle Publishing).

PATRICK DACEY is the author of the story collection *We've Already Gone This Far* and the novel *The Outer Cape.*

PAM DURBAN is the author of two short story collections and three novels. She won a Whiting Writers Award and a Lillian Smith Award for Fiction.

KATHY FAGAN's *Bad Hobby* is due soon from Milkweed. She directs the MFA program at Ohio State University.

B.H. FAIRCHILD is the author of eight books of poetry from W.W. Norton Co. His honors include an NEA Fellowship and a Bobbitt Prize for Poetry from The Library of Congress.

SETH FRIED lives in Austin, Texas. He is the author most recently of *The Municipalists* (Penguin Books, 2019).

ROSS GAY won a National Book Critics Circle Award. He is the author of *The Book of Delights*, a collection of essays.

LOUISE GLÜCK won the 2020 Nobel Prize for Literature. She lives and teaches in Cambridge, Massachusetts.

DEBRA GWARTNEY is the author of two memoirs—*Live Through This* and *I Am A Stranger Here Myself*. She lives in Oregon.

DEVON HALLIDAY is a literary agent at Transatlantic Agency. She lives in Athens, Ohio.

RED HAWK is an earth name given by our "Mother Earth". He lives in Monticello, Arkansas.

DENNIS HELD lives in Vinegar Flats, Spokane, Washington. He is the author of two poetry collections and numerous essays.

JENNIFER BOWEN HICKS lives in St. Paul, Minnesota with her two sons and a dog. Her work has appeared in *Orion* and *Kenyon Review*.

BOB HICOK's ninth poetry collection, *Hold*, was published by Copper Canyon. He won the Bobbitt Prize from The Library of Congress.

RICHARD HOFFMAN is the author of seven books of memoirs, stories and poems. He edits *Solstice*.

HOLLY IGLESIAS is the author of three poetry collections. *Theories of Flight* is her current project, a memoir in prose fragments.

TAYLOR JOHNSON is from Washington, D.C. and is the author of *Inheritance* (Alice James Books).

ILYA KAMINSKY holds the Borne Chair in Poetry at Georgia Institute of Technology. This is his second Pushcart Prize.

MICHAEL KARDOS teaches at Mississippi State University. His most recent book is *Bluff*.

CATHRYN KLUSMEIER lives in Sitka, Alaska. Her essays have won prizes from *Crazy Horse* and MIT Media Lab.

JENNIFER L. KNOX's fifth book of poems *Crushing It* is just out from Copper Canyon. She lives in Nevada, Iowa.

DORIANNE LAUX was elected a Chancellor of the American Academy of Poets in 2020. Her most recent poetry collection is *Only As the Day Is Long* (W.W. Norton Co.)

RAVEN LEILANI'S work has been published in *Granta*, *The Yale Review* and *The Cut*. Her first novel is *Luster*.

SANDRA LIM was born in Seoul, Korea. She is the author of three poetry collections most recently *The Curious Thing* (W.W. Norton Co. 2021).

KARIN LIN-GREENBERG's novel *You Are Here* is out soon from Counterpoint. She lives in Halfmoon, New York.

EMILY LEE LUAN is the author of *I Watch the Boughs*. She lives in Brooklyn, New York.

KURT LUCHS' *Falling In the Direction of Up* was recently issued by Sagging Meniscus Press. He lives in Portage, Michigan.

LARA MARKSTEIN lives in New Zealand. Her work has appeared in *Glimmer Train*, *Agni* and elsewhere.

MCKENNA MARSDEN's short stories have appeared in *New England Review* and *Pithead Chapel*.

MOLLY MCCLOSKEY latest novel, *Strain*, was published by Scribner. She lives in Washington, D.C.

PATRICIA CLEARY MILLER's most recent poetry collection is *You Can Smell the Rain*. She lives in Kansas City, Missouri.

DANTIEL W. MONIZ received the Alice Hoffman Prize for Fiction. Her *Milk Blood Heat* is an Indie Next pick.

STEPHEN MORTLAND teaches at Washington University's MFA program. His work has appeared in *Noon* and *New York Tyrant*.

JEREMIAH MOSS is the author of *Feral City*, due soon from W.W. Norton Co.

CAROL MUSKE-DUKES is the author of nine books of poems, four novels and two essay collections. She teaches at the University of Southern California.

D. NURKSE's most recent collection is *Love In the Last Days*. He lives in Arlington, Virginia.

JOYCE CAROL OATES is a Founding Editor of the Pushcart Prize. She and her late husband, Ray Smith, published *The Ontario Review* for many years.

DANIEL OROZCO is the author of *Orientation and Other Stories*. He teaches at the University of Idaho.

TRIIN PAJA lives in rural Estonia and is the author of two prize winning collections in Estonia.

DOMINICA PHETTEPLACE is a math tutor who writes fiction and poetry. She lives in San Francisco.

CARL PHILLIPS teaches at Washington University, St. Louis. His most recent book is *Pale Colors In A Tall Field*.

LIA PURPURA is author of nine collections of essays, poems and translations. She is Writer In Residence at the University of Maryland.

RON RIEKKI is the author of three books from Loyola University. He lives in Florida.

MARGARET ROSS is the author of *Timeshare*. She teaches at the University of Chicago.

GRACE SCHULMAN won the 2016 Frost Medal for Distinguished Lifetime Achievement in American Poetry.

HOLLY SINGLEHURST lives and works in Cambridge, England. She was commended in the National Poetry Competition, 2016.

TOM SLEIGH is a former poetry editor of this series and is the author of several collections. He lives in Brooklyn, New York.

LEORA SMITH writes for The Atlantic, Salon and Propublica

LUCAS SOUTHWORTH's *Everyone Has A Gun* won the AWP Grace Paley Prize. He teaches at Loyola University.

MARCUS SPIEGEL lives in Toronto and is at work on a novel and a collection of essays.

LINDSAY STARCK's first novel *Noah's Wife* was published by G.P. Putnums in 2016. She writes and teaches in Minneapolis.

ARTHUR SZE's latest collection, *The Glass Constellation*, is just out from Copper Canyon.

JERALD WALKER is the author of *How To Make A Slave and Other Essays*, a 2020 finalist for the National Book Award. He teaches at Emerson College.

KEVIN WILSON's *Nothing To See Here* is published by Ecco. He teaches at the University of the South.

XIAO XIAO lives in Beijing. She won the Wen Yiduo Poetry Prize in 2019.

INDEX

The following is a listing in alphabetical order by author's last name of works reprinted in the *Pushcart Prize* editions since 1976.

516

519

521

528

529

530

541

545

551

FROM THE PUSHCART PRIZE ARCHIVES:

"A distinguished annual literary event."
   Anne Tyler, reviewing Pushcart Prize III in The New York Times Book Review, 1978